The Translator

SANDRA SMITH is the translator of Albert Camus' *The Stranger* and Irène Némirovsky's *Suite Française*, which won the French American Foundation and Florence Gould Foundation Translation Prize and the PEN/Book-of-the-Month-Club Translation Prize.

The Editor

ROBERT LETHBRIDGE is Emeritus Honorary Professor of nineteenth-century French Literature at Cambridge University and Professor Emeritus of French Language and Literature at the University of London. He was formerly Master of Fitzwilliam College, Cambridge. He is the author of *Maupassant: 'Pierre et Jean'* and has edited *Pierre et Jean* and *Bel-Ami* for Oxford University Press's World Classics series. The majority of his publications have been devoted to the work of Émile Zola and the relationship between literature and the visual arts in late nineteenth-century France.

NORTON CRITICAL EDITIONS
European Realism & Reform

For a complete list of Norton Critical Editions, visit
wwnorton.com/nortoncriticals

A NORTON CRITICAL EDITION

GUY DE MAUPASSANT'S
SELECTED WORKS

A NEW TRANSLATION

CONTEXTS

CRITICISM

Translated by

SANDRA SMITH

Edited by

ROBERT LETHBRIDGE
CAMBRIDGE UNIVERSITY

W · W · NORTON & COMPANY · *New York* · *London*

W. W. Norton & Company has been independent since its founding in 1923, when William Warder Norton and Mary D. Herter Norton first published lectures delivered at the People's Institute, the adult education division of New York City's Cooper Union. The firm soon expanded its program beyond the Institute, publishing books by celebrated academics from America and abroad. By midcentury, the two major pillars of Norton's publishing program—trade books and college texts—were firmly established. In the 1950s, the Norton family transferred control of the company to its employees, and today—with a staff of four hundred and a comparable number of trade, college, and professional titles published each year—W. W. Norton & Company stands as the largest and oldest publishing house owned wholly by its employees.

Library of Congress Cataloging-in-Publication Data

Names: Maupassant, Guy de, 1850–1893, author. | Smith, Sandra, 1949– translator. |
    Lethbridge, Robert, editor.
Title: Guy de Maupassant's selected works: a new translation, contexts, criticism /
    Translated by Sandra Smith, Cambridge University; Edited by Robert Lethbridge,
    The University of London.
Description: New York: W. W. Norton & Company, 2016. | Series: Norton critical edition |
    Includes bibliographical references and chronology.
Identifiers: LCCN 2016018262 | **ISBN 9780393923278** (pbk.)
Subjects: LCSH: Maupassant, Guy de, 1850–1893—Criticism and interpretation.
Classification: LCC PQ2349 .A2 2016 | DDC 843/.8—dc23 LC record available at
https://lccn.loc.gov/2016018262

W. W. Norton & Company, Inc., 500 Fifth Avenue, New York, NY 10110-0017
    wwnorton.com

W. W. Norton & Company Ltd., Castle House, 15 Carlisle Street, London W1D 3BS

1 2 3 4 5 6 7 8 9 0

*This book is dedicated
to the leading Maupassant scholars
of this generation:
Gérard Delaisement,
Louis Forestier, and
Marlo Johnston*

Contents

Contents

Criticism

Introduction

It has been persuasively argued that "the nineteenth century is the golden age of short fiction in France."[1] What is equally certain is that Guy de Maupassant enjoys a reputation as one of the finest short story writers of his generation. And it is not by chance that, for over more than a hundred years, his tales have so often been translated into English. Indeed, the short story as a genre has always been popular with an Anglo-Saxon reading public, and Maupassant's influence on American practitioners has been the subject of a full-length academic study.[2] That is not to forget that he also wrote six novels, the success of which can be judged by the fact that their sales figures, during his lifetime, were second only to those of Émile Zola (1840–1902), whose twenty-volume *Rougon-Macquart* series (1871–93) underpinned his recognized status as the greatest European writer of the period. Maupassant's own productivity was astonishing: he began by writing poetry; he composed three travel books and two plays; he provided prefaces to the work of colleagues and friends; he published well over 200 articles in the press. But it was as a teller of tales, following the acclaimed reception of *Boule de suif* in 1880, that Maupassant really made his mark on the literary scene: he wrote over 300 short stories; at the height of his creative powers he was producing sixty a year, provoking some of his more envious fellow writers to claim maliciously that this required no more effort than shaking a fully laden apple tree. The tales vary in length, but the usual format of something between 2,500 and 3,000 words was specifically designed for the newspapers that assured him an income and a vast readership. Many appeared in the conservative *Le Gaulois* which, in the 1880s, had a daily circulation of 15,000. Maupassant strategically placed others (sometimes under a pseudonym), of a less dignified temper, in the *Gil Blas*, which was selling some 30,000 copies each day. His so-called *contes d'hiver* (winter tales), complete with falling snow, were published in winter, appealing to the fireside reader. Commercially astute, he often subsequently reprinted

---

1. Peter Cogman, *Narration in Nineteenth-Century French Short Fiction* (Durham: Durham University Press, 2002), p. 1.
2. Richard Fusco, *Maupassant and the American Short Story* (University Park: Pennsylvania University Press, 1994).

nearly all of his stories elsewhere, with minimal revision and as many as half a dozen times, as well as collecting approximately related texts in volume form, in due course supplemented by illustrated or luxury versions with the same title. Those selected for this Norton Critical Edition offer a range of themes, contexts, techniques, registers, and moods, all of which allow the modern reader to analyze his craftsmanship and gain an insight into Maupassant's vision of human experience.

Maupassant was born on August 5, 1850. His life has been subject to unbridled speculative imaginings, starting with the apparent mysteries surrounding his imprecise birth certificate, which led early biographers to conclude that it served to conceal a shameful family secret. Marlo Johnston's recent and encyclopaedic *Guy de Maupassant*[3] lays to rest all the myths and errors which have inevitably tainted studies of his writing. What is certain is that he was born and brought up on the Normandy coast; his frequent returns there even after he moved to Paris in 1869 testify to Maupassant's passion for the place that forms the setting of so many of his texts. For the best part of a decade he was forced to earn a living by working as a civil servant, the tediousness of which he bitterly evokes in his newspaper articles and in the suffocating routine endured by fictional characters based on his own lowly employment in the Ministry of the Navy and the Colonies and in the Ministry of Education. With a robust and athletic physique, one of his great pleasures was to leave the French capital and spend days and nights boating on the Seine, west of Paris, at those picturesque spots memorialized by the Impressionists. That aspect of his life is equally evident in a number of the tales in this Norton Critical Edition. Maupassant was also, it must be said, extraordinarily and unapologetically promiscuous. Whole books have been pruriently devoted to his serial or simultaneous love affairs, passing fancies, one-night stands, and sexual proclivities, taken to extremes in a deliberately scandalous exhibitionism for which there are numerous reliable, and often complicitous, witnesses. It can be debated whether or not this obsessive behavior can be traced back to his excessive adoration of his mother, Laure de Poittevin, or to the nefarious example of her womanizing and feckless husband, Gustave de Maupassant, from whom she parted ten years after the writer's birth. But Maupassant's views of women, love, and marriage are clearly inseparable from an intimate narrative peopled by mistresses and prostitutes. So too, in the most literal way, is his death. And, there again, Maupassant has provoked

---

3. *Guy de Maupassant* (Paris: Fayard, 2012); this definitive biography has to date been published only in French.

attention of a non-literary kind: serious medical treatises have
detailed the appalling progression of the tertiary stage of the syphilis he had initially contracted in 1875, leading to his physical disintegration, insanity, and terrible end on July 6, 1893, at the age of
just forty-two.

There is one less dramatic chapter of Maupassant's biography
which explains not so much the themes and settings of his writing
as his artistic preferences and techniques, notably the crucial role
played by Gustave Flaubert (1821–1880) in the shaping of his aesthetic. Laure de Poittevin had been a childhood friend of Flaubert,
to whom she commended her son when Maupassant went off to
school in Rouen. The contact had been renewed through its city
librarian, the distinguished poet Louis Bouilhet (1821–1869), closely
associated with Flaubert. Both men encouraged Maupassant's
early literary efforts, but Bouilhet's premature demise meant that it
was to Flaubert that Maupassant submitted his drafts for correction and comment throughout the 1870s. Such was the quasi-filial
relationship between Flaubert and the aspiring young writer that
one of the baseless dimensions of the speculation occasioned by
Maupassant's birth was that he was in fact his son! Flaubert's sudden death, on May 8, 1880,[4] was a blow that engendered not just an
immense personal sadness but a series of essays, over the years, in
which Maupassant explicitly acknowledged his debt to the author of
Madame Bovary (1857). In the preface to *Pierre et Jean*,[5] his 1888,
novel, he recalls his affection for Bouilhet but mainly evokes his
seven-year apprenticeship under Flaubert, whose seminal influence
ranges from the imperatives of verisimilitude to the importance of
observed and differentiating descriptive detail.

The brevity of the short story, some twenty times shorter than a
novel, imposes in this respect various constraints. Character and
situation have to be evoked in a single telling detail rather than elaborated across a multi-stranded plot, with a cast of secondary figures, and developments tracking the passing of the years. Maupassant
does sometimes provide a coda, which gives to a story a retrospective finality freighted with nostalgia or irony. But the story itself,
even if introduced as having taken place in the past, is located in
the immediacy of its presentation. It often amounts to no more than
an anecdote, an apparently insignificant meeting, outing, social
occasion, or fortuitous intersection, on a train or on a street, of individual men and women. The structure of experience chronicled in
the stories is underlined by precisely those ironic twists which

---

4. Maupassant's reaction to Flaubert's death is included in the Contexts section, p. 287.
5. An excerpt from this important essay, written in September 1887, is included in the
Contexts section, pp. 245–53.

transform the apparently slight into the potentially disturbing. That the anecdotal is often constructed from the *accidental* (as, literally, in *On Horseback*) underlines the extent to which Maupassant's career as a journalist has to be taken into account in any approach to the singularity of his fiction. As is still the case today, the so-called *faits divers* filled the margins of contemporary papers and periodicals with snippets of barely newsworthy items, second-hand reports culled from the press, almost incredible events or bits of information hardly worthy of the gossip column. Maupassant was perfectly aware of their ephemerality: in *Boule de suif*, newspapers are used as a make-shift tablecloth and the very words "*faits divers*" (here translated as *News in Brief*) are left imprinted on the creamy surface of the wedge of Gruyère cheese that had been wrapped in them. Maupassant often constructs his tales from such trifles, but endows them with a significance which is moral, social, or universal. And it is integral to their impact that he employs a variety of devices to draw the reader into the text, suspending disbelief while paradoxically still aware of *listening* to a narrative, the truth of which is uncertain. That needs to be stressed. Unlike the novel as a genre, the short story retains an *oral* quality, its telling not that of a disembodied authorial voice but rather of a narrator regularly foregrounded, in Maupassant's case, by a double framing of teller and, thereby, embedded tale.

Maupassant found in Flaubert, however, a likeminded approach to life rather than simply a mentor whose critical severity honed his craftsmanship. This is evident in the letter he wrote to Caroline Commanville in May 1880, in the immediate aftermath of Flaubert's death.[6] He refers there to the latter's pessimistic vision of human experience and the absurdity of the ways in which men and women struggle in vain to defy the fatalities over which they have no control. Such a vision is a contemporary one, shared by writers such as Zola who translated its philosophical and scientific assumptions into the theoretical principles of Naturalism, militantly substituted for an outdated Romanticism as the dominant aesthetic mode of the second half of the nineteenth century. While giving *Boule de suif* his warm approval, Flaubert's habitual contempt for labels and dogma explains the reservations with which he reproached Maupassant for publicly aligning himself with this particular literary school by inserting it within *Les Soirées de Médan* (1880), the collective volume whose title alludes to Zola's country house at Médan, outside Paris, where colleagues and acolytes got together. Posterity has qualified such an alignment, notably in analyses of the more nuanced personalities in Maupassant's later novels and of the mental states in tales of the supernatural, works which move away from a purely

6. Part of this letter is to be found in the Contexts section, p. 287.

physiological conception of behavior. But, in this increasingly secular age, he does share with both Flaubert and French Naturalism an emphasis on the material determinants of time and place, and the fatalities of bodily disintegration and mortality.

His early critics, both in France and abroad, target this general tendency (to explain behavior solely in relation to instincts and appetites) as much as Maupassant's texts, at odds as it was with their own beliefs, assumptions, and aesthetic priorities.[7] A professed admirer like Henry James, for example, regretted that Maupassant's characters seemed devoid of an inner life, let alone psychological complexity, and was frankly appalled by the author's depiction of sexual motivation and activity. There are a number of stories in Maupassant's work as a whole that border on the licentious: leaving aside walk-on parts, at least twenty-five have a prostitute as a protagonist; most notoriously, *La Maison Tellier* (1881) is the name of, and set in, a house of ill repute—however anodyne it may seem to us, with its commerce as un-erotic as any other business transaction; beyond the brothel, couplings take place in private dining rooms and train compartments, taken to lubricious absurdity in the excursion to the banks of the Seine, in *Mouche* (1890), spiced by the eponymous good-time girl who grants her favors to all five members of the boating party, each in turn (and leaving each of them with the vague feeling of having been cuckolded by a friend); they fill the narrative space in the shape of prologues, interludes, and dénouements, or form the stuff of digressions in after-dinner conversations over a cigar. There are catalogues of desire: uncontrolled to the point of attempted rape (*Ce Cochon de Morin*, 1882); catalyzed by the sight of an unmade bed (*La Patronne*, 1884); reignited by a wife's vicarious enjoyment of an inventory of her husband's premarital conquests (*Imprudence*, 1885); there are both adulterous liaisons and lesbian "vice" (*La Femme de Paul*, 1881), as well as brutal wedding nights and chillingly dispassionate seductions. In *L'Inconnue* (1885), the respectable stranger of the title consents to be clumsily undressed, on a Sunday morning no less, by a predatory male a year after a mere two-minute interchange on a Parisian boulevard. There is incest in ignorance as a father picks up a waitress in the Latin Quarter only to discover, at the point of rewarding her for her services, that she is his long-lost daughter (*L'Ermite*, 1886). No wonder that Henry James was shocked by what he called Maupassant's "exaggerated" emphasis on the "sexual sense . . . which we scarcely mention in English fiction!"[8] Although such a carnal

---

7. See the excerpts from such commentary, including that of Henry James, in the Criticism section.
8. *Partial Portraits* (Westport, CT: Greenwood Publishers, 1970), p. 253.

emphasis is not proportionately represented in this Norton Critical Edition, it is contextually illuminating. In *Mademoiselle Fifi*, for example, the Prussian officer is overcome by a "vicious desire to ravage" Rachel, and the concupiscence of soldiers eying the spoils of victory is shared elsewhere by travellers ogling a female fellow passenger and by men out for a walk or an afternoon row on the river. It has to be said that, by today's standards, Maupassant's stories of consummated lust, such as in *Boule de suif* or *A Day in the Country*, are positively discreet, if arguably more suggestive by leaving the reader, respectively, to fill in the gaps of a night at the inn and decode the joyous shrieks emanating from a forest glade.

That reminds us that there is a subtle link between worldview and fictional devices. In *L'Art de Rompre* (The Art of Breaking Off), in *Le Gaulois* of January 31, 1881, Maupassant cynically reflects on how best to bring to an end a sexual relationship which has run its course. Elsewhere, he notes that optimal desire coincides with unfulfilled anticipation rather than satisfaction.[9] A number of modern critics have explored the analogies offered by the manipulation of the reader of Maupassant's stories, carefully seduced and strung along, and unprepared for a sudden ending.[1] Gaps and textual silences, an authorial refusal to explain or confirm, can all be justified by the economy of the short story as a genre. In the process, the reader's desire to know the truth of the matter, or where a tale will end, is left intact. Only with the closure so skilfully arranged by Maupassant does a retrospective purview, or a rereading of suppressed meanings, identify the enigmatic signposts initially hidden from plain sight.

Maupassant's worldview, his pessimism, nevertheless remains one that not merely his contemporary opponents found problematic. For his stories are grounded in inanity and delusion, hopeless idealism, regret and shattered dreams, selfishness and self-interest, inhuman violence and the finality of death, love's labors lost, the meaninglessness of existence and the absence of redemption, either quotidian or spiritual. The backdrop of nature serves to put into sharper relief the insignificance of human dramas. Maupassant's winter landscapes, veiled by curtains of snow, are a privileged space in which to render a world losing outline and definition, a reality

---

9. In the preface to René Maizeroi's *Celles qui osent* (1883), included in the Contexts section, pp. 278–80, Maupassant writes that passion "should be limited to the period of anticipation. Once desire has been satisfied and the unknown explored, love loses its principal value."
1. This is elaborated in Charles J. Stivale, *The Art of Rupture: Narrative Desire and Duplicity in the Tales of Guy de Maupassant* (Ann Arbor: U of Michigan P, 1994); see also Angela Moger, "Narrative Structures in Maupassant: Frames of Desire" (*PMLA* 100 (1985): 315–27); excerpts from this study, largely devoted to *The Journey*, are included in the Criticism section, pp. 328–41.

without substance, and its tonalities are as pale as his own stylistic
effects negate grandiloquence. He clearly delights in demystification, the highlighting of venality, the puncturing of hypocrisy and
the unmasking of what lies below the surface of social respectability
and convention. His sense of humor is seldom generous, characterized as it is by what seems like derision at the expense of human
folly. But such a summary of Maupassant's vision is inadequate.
Modern criticism of his writing has left behind a Jamesian stance of
moral condemnation, rigorously focusing instead on formal structures and thematic patterning to tease out better the ambiguities of
Maupassant's positioning. A case in point is what appears to be, at
first sight, a misogyny no less offensive for it being prevalent at the
time—if nonetheless thereby historically interesting in its own
right. But that sits somewhat uneasily with Maupassant's sympathetic treatment of women exploited for social or sexual purposes,
imprisoned in the servitude of marriage as much as that of the
brothel.[2] And that would be to ignore his assertion of the independence in mind and body of women, so often married *off* but still able
to liberate themselves from prejudice and protocol. It would therefore be a mistake for the female reader to feel totally excluded from
those unbuttoned exchanges between masculine friends which
often set a story in motion. From the ribald to the hallucinatory,
Maupassant's telling explores a range of emotions at some distance
from an unequivocal despair. More generally, an absolute nihilism
or cynicism would preclude the simple virtues Maupassant ascribes
to the Norman peasantry or the courage of those who refuse to surrender their integrity to financial temptation or be cowed by the
dictates of convention or the atrocities of war. And the discerning
reader will find in his tales both cruelty *and* compassion, the kind
of ironic wisdom and sense of perspective he attributed to Flaubert
and which, as he said, made life "bearable."

Tales of French Life

If *The Necklace* is one of the most frequently anthologized of Maupassant's stories, it is also emblematic. Its setting is the milieu of
petty civil servants, to which he often returns in organizing an opposition between social worlds: of class, values and prosperity. What
is common across the social spectrum is the fact that money is more
important than provenance, facilitating the outward show necessary
to disguise humble origins or secondary status. If Madame Loisel's
borrowing of the jewelry speaks of pretension (as well as rehearsing

2. The best and most extended study, in this respect, is Mary Donaldson-Evans, *A Woman's
Revenge. The Chronology of Dispossession in Maupassant's Fiction* (Lexington, KY:
French Forum, 1986).

the clichés of women's predilection for pretty things and bored housewives dreaming of a more glamorous existence), her and her husband's sacrificing the rest of their lives to make good its loss counters the irony at their expense by asserting a fundamental honesty not vitiated by their precarious financial circumstances. Or, at least, that is what it *seems* like. More ambiguously, such a virtue may be no more than keeping up appearances, which was precisely where the story began. In terms of narrative structure, *The Necklace* sustains a rigorous concentration on the item in question, using it to tell us all we need to know about character and situation. And the text's surprise ending, modifying the entire story in retrospect, is exemplary of Maupassant's fashioning of the reader's response, caught between sympathy and derision. Edward Sullivan has rightly dismissed the legend that *all* Maupassant's stories rely for their effect on the "trick-ending."[3] But *The Necklace* does illustrate a carefully built textual momentum, leading us to turn the pages in anticipation of a dénouement which can only be guessed, whether bathetic or genuinely miserable. Such a momentum is often sustained by a fictional journey, the destination of which is not obvious. As Artine Mortimer has written of the writer's technique more generally, "our guesses may range from the salacious to the frivolous,"[4] for the possible *unreliability* of the narrator is consistent with Maupassant's own awareness of the play-acting of human behavior and the duplicity of social spectacle and stage.

The social implications of *The Necklace* lie in Maupassant's focus on layers of French society below the ostentatious luxury associated with the Third Republic. If this text is, in every sense, about *appearances*, the theme is a recurrent one, and at several levels. *The Umbrella* repeats, in ludicrous and penny-pinching mode, Madame Loisel's concern about how one is seen in a capitalist society that transforms the most utilitarian of instruments into an object of value. *On Horseback*'s evocation of the gilded carriages returning down the Champs-Élysées contrasts, of course, with the constraints on Hector de Gribelin's monotonous domestic life; but the catastrophic consequences of his vanity, galloping a horse down the same avenue, prompt further reflection, not least on social ambition: his own, but also that of the victim of his accident remorselessly suing him for compensation. From both his newspaper articles on topical issues and his tales of French life, it is not difficult to conclude that Maupassant's view of contemporary society is unmistakably conservative: he is deeply uncomfortable with democratic

---

3. *Maupassant: The Short Stories* (London: Arnold, 1962), p. 19; Sullivan's study remains the most lucid introduction to Maupassant's tales.
4. "Secrets of literature, resistance to meaning," in K. Grossman, ed., *Confrontations: Politics and Aesthetics in Nineteenth-Century France* (Amsterdam: Rodopi, 2001), p. 59.

principles and the erosion of class boundaries; his contempt for the
politicians of his time is unbounded, whether in their domestic, colonial or educational policies (as in *The Question of Latin*); his dis-
respect for pompous officials of state or unworthy men of the cloth
gives to *The Protector* a satirical intensity aimed at nepotism and
corruption. Whether in his letters at the time or in the press, Maupassant can barely contain an eviscerating rage.[5] For behind self-
importantly closed doors and the corridors of power, he constantly
reveals servility and gross ineptitude.

It is never, however, quite that simple. Behind the caricatural
priest in *The Baptism* lies a private suffering, which cuts across the
polemics of anti-clericalism: his attitude toward his peasant flock
replicates the reader's virtually anthropological distance; but the tenderness awakened by the baby has been described as the "displacement of his frustrated sexual needs,"[6] with the shifting perspective
of the narrator ensuring the instability of our sympathies. The banal-
ities of *The Journey* and *Adieu* gradually allow us sight of passion
unspent or estranged. And, far from the sophistication of right-bank
Paris,[7] there is another France, that of Maupassant's Normandy:
with its impoverished families, as in *My Uncle Jules*, destined to be
disappointed; as is Mademoiselle Pearl, in Rôuy-le-Tors, the artificial
annual rituals of Epiphany stripped away to the reality that she was
never to be a married "Queen," even for a day. *In the Countryside*
brings two social worlds into cruel juxtaposition: on the one hand,
that of the peasantry, living in hovels overrun by badly nourished
children; on the other, the aristocratic visitor to their humble cottages, dispensing cake and candy as a prelude to negotiating the
purchase of a child. For the urban reader, Maupassant unravels the
myths of rustic charms for which the beautiful background is a
deceptive topography, enriching his dialogues with the dialect and
incorrect grammar of a world apart.

A Day in the Country operates between these two worlds. In *Mademoiselle Pearl*, we are told that the Chantals live in Paris as if it were
a provincial town. Conversely, the Dufours plan a day out in keeping
with Parisian weekend pleasures, which turns out to be a narrative

---

5. It is significant that, in his letter about politics to Flaubert of December 10, 1877
(included in the Contexts section, pp. 255–56), Maupassant has recourse to visceral bodily
metaphors.
6. R. A. York, "Le Baptême: a Reading," *Journal of the Modern Language Association of
Northern Ireland* 13 (1984): 18.
7. Maupassant's Parisian focus is as self-limiting as the Chantals, in *Mademoiselle Pearl*,
who live near the Observatory, on the Right Bank, and for whom "the entire section
of Paris located on the other side of the Seine makes up a new part of the city, an area
inhabited by strange, noisy, barely respectable people who throw their money out the
window, spending their days indulging their extravagances and their nights at parties." It is also worth noting that Maupassant's social geography excludes the urban
proletariat.

journey ribald in conception and design. With her ample forms
shaking like a jelly, Madame Dufour, being pushed on her swing,
is a spectacle of the derision also aimed at her husband's lack of
virility as he gets her going "but with very great difficulty." In this
supposedly rural interlude prompting Parisian sentimentality, the
forest glade is transformed into a *cabinet particulier*,[8] the notorious
location of refined urban seductions. The story of a romantic idyll
stripped of romance is organized in such ironic contrasts: between
city and countryside, the beauty of Nature and the basest of instincts,
adventure and routine, sensual hunger and culinary appetites (developed, at much greater length, in *Boule de suif*), a glimpse of emotional intensity and a "fat calf muscle," escape and circularity,
ecstasy and disillusionment, marriage and adultery, sporting men
and sedentary visitors. The two athletic young oarsmen eying mother
and daughter cynically plot which *petite bourgeoise* they intend to
have, one of them making the "sacrifice" to go off with the less
attractive of the two. It is as predictable as the signalling of the two
skiffs lying side by side, compared to "slender young women." While
the contrastingly "enormous" Madame Dufour displays a post-coital
nonchalance, Henriette and her afternoon lover, on returning from
"their grassy bed," are initially overcome with mutual disgust. But
the tale's playful tone is restored, back in the city and again in the
woods a year later, in an epilogue in which both the now-married
Henriette and her mother suggest to Henri, recalling their "day in
the country," that a boring marriage might be the context of a nos-
talgic *au revoir*. At one level, the story is utterly banal. What enriches
it are its variations of mood and theme: a comedy of manners leaving us *between* amused complicity and dramatic irony as spectators
(like the watching kids) of an inconsequential episode with potentially more general implications. Maupassant's tales of French life
are clearly located in the social fabric of his age, but limited neither
to a specifically nineteenth-century context nor to France.

Tales of War

Contemporary readers of Maupassant's tales of war would have
needed no reminding of their context. For they are all inspired by
the Franco-Prussian War of 1870–71, a conflict now largely forgotten but which remains one of the most important events in French
and European history. Indeed it can be argued that, ever since the
catastrophic defeat suffered at the hands of the Germans in 1870–71,

8. Translated here as "my private hideaway," the original French *cabinet particulier* was a
   private dining-room provided by fashionable restaurants for discreet amorous meetings,
   furnished with a couch or divan for relaxation after the waiters had withdrawn at the
   end of the candle-lit meal!

France's national identity and foreign policies have been inseparable from the perception of the threat across the Rhine. Two world wars (and, as a consequence, the dynamic of Franco-German relations in the second half of the twentieth century) can be traced back through a causal pattern which originates in the Franco-Prussian War. As a direct result of it, by the Treaty of Frankfurt in May 1871, France lost its eastern provinces of Alsace and Lorraine, an amputation only avenged by the terms of the Treaty of Versailles (1919) which, in turn, provided Hitler with the opportunity to reverse them.

For most modern readers, Maupassant's references to the battles, military commanders, and politics of the Franco-Prussian War do need some elucidation. While there is no room here to explain in full its complex origins, the apparently unlikely *casus belli* was the Spanish throne, vacant since 1868. In supporting the candidature of King William of Prussia's obscure relative Prince Leopold of Hohenzollern, Chancellor Otto von Bismarck (1815–1898) had found the perfect pretext to draw France into a war necessary to drive the southern German states into a powerful union with Prussia. It is not surprising that Maupassant's fictional officer in *A Duel* vaunts his herculean ambition. Consternation in France, at the prospect of having to guard its Iberian frontier too, escalated into an ultimatum to the Prussian government to withdraw the Hohenzollern candidacy. In the ensuing diplomatic maneuvering, during the first two weeks of July 1870, France played into Bismarck's hands. Relying on its alliance with Italy and Austria, and supremely confident of crushing the pretensions of an incipient German Empire, France declared war on Prussia on July 19. Maupassant's generation of writers would often recall, and ironically evoke, the jingoistic rejoicing in Paris at the news, with crowds sweeping down the boulevards, brandishing torches, and crying "To Berlin! To Berlin!" The background to Maupassant's tales of war is the doomed French resistance to the Prussian invasion and its humiliating aftermath.

This invasion was masterminded by Field Marshal von Moltke whom Maupassant would later depict, in an anti-militarism diatribe, as "one of the supreme practitioners of the art" of killing people.[9] Maupassant and the other contributors to *Les Soirées de Médan* had considered giving it the alternative title of *L'Invasion comique*, comic, from a French point of view, only in the sense of everything going tragicomically wrong. *Boule de suif* itself is best understood as one episode in a *sequence* of events each represented by one of the six

---

9. In Maupassant's article in *Le Gaulois* of April 10, 1881, included in the Contexts section, pp. 261–63.

texts in the collective volume.[1] The invasion was spearheaded by
three brilliantly led German armies: General Karl von Steinmetz's
across the Moselle; that of the King's nephew, Prince Frederick
Charles, from the Palatinate (the region north of Alsace on the left
bank of the Rhine) heading towards Metz; and Crown Prince Frederick's from the upper Rhine towards Strasbourg. A French army
advanced into the Saar and won a minor victory at Saarbrücken. But
then the German "avalanche"—to use a contemporary metaphor—
began. On August 4, the force under General Abel Douay was
defeated at Wissenbourg. Two days later, at Frœschwiller, Marshal
MacMahon was routed (with his 35,000 men outnumbered by
140,000 Prussians) and forced to evacuate Alsace-Lorraine, as the
Crown Prince surrounded Strasbourg and moved toward Nancy. The
indecisive Marshal Bazaine was soon shut up in Metz. His army's
final destruction was only a matter of time. Between August 14
and 18 (in the battles of Borny, Rezonville-Gravelotte and Saint-
Privat), his attempts to break out were repulsed, and the Germans
advanced on Châlons-sur-Marne. When MacMahon tried to relieve
Bazaine at Metz, he found the road closed and was decisively
defeated at the battle of Sedan on September 1. His army, with
Emperor Napoleon III himself, capitulated the following day. Mac-
Mahon would be another of the prominent figures of the Franco-
Prussian War subsequently the object of Maupassant's contempt.[2]

When the news of the defeat reached Paris, on September 4, the
end of the Second Empire was formally voted by the legislature, with
responsibility for the war transferred to Léon Gambetta's government of National Defence. But, after Sedan, the German armies
swept on. Bazaine surrended at Metz on October 27, with 6,000 officers and 173,000 men. As Maupassant reminds us in the opening
sentences of a number of his tales of war, Paris was besieged and its
population reduced to virtual starvation before its capitulation on
January 28, 1871. Before that, on January 18, and in the very same
Hall of Mirrors, at Versailles, where revenge would only be exacted
half a century later, France was subjected to the humiliating spectacle of William (with his new title of *Kaiser*) being proclaimed as

---

1. Only Zola's *L'Attaque du Moulin*, heading the volume but previously published in 1877,
   described fighting as such; *Sac au dos*, by J.-K. Huysmans (1848–1907) tracks two
   soldiers suffering from dysentery; *L'Affaire du Grand 7*, by Léon Hennique (1850–1935)
   relates the massacre of the inmates of a brothel by a mutinous garrison; *La Saignée*, by
   Henri Céard (1854–1921), is set during the siege of Paris; *Après la bataille*, by Paul Alexis
   (1847–1901) centers on a meeting between a soldier and a young woman with a coffin
   containing the remains of her husband killed in the war; as its title (After the Battle)
   suggests, this story forms an epilogue both to Maupassant's account of the French
   retreat and to the volume as a whole.
2. In his letter to Flaubert of December 10, 1877, included in the Contexts section,
   pp. 255–56, Maupassant scathingly refers to MacMahon as "the Archduke of Sedan."

Emperor of Germany, thus bringing Bismarck's grand strategy to a successful conclusion.

For the French, however, there was worse to follow. Faith in the government's ability to prosecute the war had been progressively undermined throughout the winter by a virtually unbroken sequence of military reverses, most acutely felt in Paris by the abortive attempts to break through the German encirclement of the city. Having undergone the fruitless suffering of four months' siege, the disaffected population felt itself betrayed by the government's negotiation of an armistice and the ensuing national elections which returned a conservative-leaning (and largely provincial) majority pledged to end the War at any price. This included the further humiliation of the entry of German troops into the capital within the devastating peace terms accepted by the National Assembly, meeting in Bordeaux, on March 1. Paris refused to accept that authority. The National Guard there then played a crucial role in events, and it is worth noting Maupassant's fleeting allusions, in tales like *Two Friends* and *The Adventure of Walter Schnaffs*, to its uniformed members (such as Monsieur Dubuis, to take another example, in *A Duel*). For the National Guard, which the Germans had failed to disarm by the armistice of January 28, appointed a central committee and seized the cannon belonging to the regular army on March 18. The subsequent election of the Commune, both to run the city and as an alternative government, effectively marked the beginning of a civil war. This war continued through the spring, with Paris besieged for a second time, now by French forces under the orders of Adolphe Thiers's officially recognized government, which had moved to Versailles. Only between May 21 and 28 (known as *la semaine sanglante*, the "Bloody Week") did these forces succeed in taking back control of the city, and then at a terrible cost. On both sides there were calculated atrocities and an almost unimaginable barbarity. The Versailles troops worked their way through the barricades in indiscriminate slaughter compounded by mass executions often carried out with unspeakable cruelty. Summary court martials and deportations would continue into the months and years ahead, the last of them in 1875, with a general amnesty declared only in 1880. That was the very year Maupassant published *Boule de suif* within *Les Soirées de Médan*, further evidence that, even at this distance, the Franco-Prussian War continued to haunt the national psyche. It remained topical, a source of patriotic introspection and political lamentation. The Commune itself was simply its traumatic epilogue. It is estimated that at least 25,000 French died at the hands of their countrymen during that one week in May 1871, more than in any single battle against the Prussians. As the Communards retreated, they set fire to the city. Paris was in ruins. The Third Republic had been born in what Victor Hugo called *L'Année terrible*.

Maupassant's personal experience of that "Terrible Year" was somewhat more prosaic. By virtue of his age, he had been due to be called up for the standard five years of compulsory military service in July 1871. As a result of the national emergency, this service was brought forward to August 1870 so that, after training at Vincennes, he was attached to the Supply Corps of the Second Army Division based in Rouen. While his educational attainments had ensured that he avoided the obvious risks posed to front-line infantry, the fact that he was to carry out his mainly bureaucratic duties far from Paris also meant that he escaped being trapped in the besieged capital. But the eventual military decision, on December 4, to withdraw from Rouen and declare it an open city, judged to be impossible to defend against a three-pronged Prussian advance, did involve Maupassant being part of the northern retreat across Normandy toward the coast, thereby potentially placing him more directly in the line of fire. But as he wrote to this father in January 1871:[3]

> I wasn't at risk of being taken prisoner by the Prussians—we retreated as they advanced on Rouen—as I remained at the very rear of our troops in order to be able to take messages from HQ to the general, and then spent a night walking some 35 miles on foot—a few Prussian cavalry came after us but not for long. At Pont-Audemer every house was filled with soldiers and I had to sleep in a cellar without a blanket so as not to have [to] stay outside in the freezing cold (minus 10° C.).

And although he therefore did not see action, he did see with his own eyes the pitiable remnants of armies retreating towards Le Havre: men straggling across the barren countryside, increasingly dying on their feet as ferocious winter weather set in from December 7 onward. The opening of *Boule de suif* exactly replicates the "wreckage" Maupassant had seen: gloom, exhaustion, dejection, listless and bedraggled soldiers "hunched over under the weight of their rifles," the indiscipline of troops so dehumanized as to scare their own officers.

Maupassant would buy himself out of military service in July 1871 and return to civilian life. But this particular experience left its mark, notably in an unchanging assessment of the ludicrous incompetence of the French army and a sympathy for the suffering of ordinary men and women caught up in the vicissitudes of armed conflict. These feelings were exacerbated by the fact that, in the 1880s, French politics was infected by a rash of *revanchard* enthusiasm, in other words, repeated calls to avenge the humiliation of the

---

3. At http://maupassant.free.fr/corresp1.html; translated by Robert Lethbridge.

Franco-Prussian War. Maupassant's articles in the press, particularly in 1881, warn against this hysteria which he viewed as exemplary of instincts triumphing over reason. His anti-militarism is extended to more recent campaigns in North Africa and Indochina.[4] A tale such as *The Adventure of Walter Schnaffs*, with a hapless Prussian equally the victim of the senselessness of war, testifies to an authorial concern over and beyond nationality. But Maupassant himself, it can be argued, was not totally immune to the *revanchard* discourse of the period: the Prussians in *Two Friends* or *La Mère Sauvage* are clearly depicted as guilty of the war crimes which were the stuff of the popular imagination; in *Père Milon*, they are merciless; in *Boule de suif* and *Mademoiselle Fifi*, they are brutal and rapacious; in all the stories, they are caricaturally drawn, with Germanic stiffness, arrogance, and dismal attempts at jollity; and Maupassant parodies their incorrect French grammar and heavy accents.[5]

There are also contradictions in his conception of war itself. In his most important article devoted to the subject, published in *Le Gaulois* on April 10, 1881, Maupassant takes issue with the view that war is one of the inescapable laws of nature. Yet, and going beyond a quasi-Darwinian rehearsal of the survival of the fitter Prussians at the expense of the weaker French (often cited in contemporary explanations of France's defeat),[6] Maupassant consistently demonstrates in his stories that war is another of those impersonal forces over which men and women have no control. Only *Lieutenant Laré's Marriage*, dating from 1878 and the very first of his tales of war, has a happy (Hollywood) ending; but even here this is a result of chance rather than an unlikely expression of optimism on Maupassant's part; and it is revealing that, when he came to republish the story with less concern to please his readers, each successive version is progressively darker: in the 1882 version, the young girl does not marry the officer; in the next, in 1884, any reference to her subsequent destiny is totally eliminated. As well as representing a new-found confidence in his unconcern for reader sensitivity, these textual modifications indicate a hardening of Maupassant's conception of war,[7] characterized as the most uncompromising of fatalities, leaving in its wake the destruction of lives, families, homes, and all semblance of honor and human dignity. Every one of the tales subsequent to *Lieutenant Laré's Marriage* is about the victims of man's inhumanity to man.

---

4. On military campaigns in Tunisia, see Maupassant's article in *Le Gaulois* of April 10, 1881, included in the Contexts section, pp. 261–63; on the Gulf of Tonkin episode, see *Mademoiselle Pearl*.
5. The translator of the stories in this Norton Critical Edition, Sandra Smith, has tried to replicate these mispronunciations by transcribing a Germanic accent into the English.
6. This is explored in Laurence A Gregario, *Maupassant's Fiction and the Darwinian View of Life* (New York: Peter Lang, 2005).
7. This is analyzed in detail in Rachel Killick's essay, included in the Criticism section.

In responding to Flaubert's concern that *Les Soirées de Médan* might be viewed as incompatible with patriotic sentiments, Maupassant stresses that the underlying motivation of the contributors to the volume was to strip war of its glory. The black humor at the expense of the battlefield tourists of *A Duel* is also one with readers in its sights. *The Adventure of Walter Schnaffs* may be farcical, but its metaphorical infrastructure reduces human beings to animals. In *Boule de suif*, the opening pages offer a stark military reality inseparable from the brilliant satirical story which follows. For although much of the text seems to be a more general and devastatingly comic exposition of self-serving hypocrisy, the degraded values of the officer who imposes himself on Maupassant's heroine are at one with those of the Prussians who kill innocent fishermen (in *Two Friends*), fathers and sons (*Père Milon; La Mère Sauvage*), and women who have lost their minds (*The Madwoman*). The French engage in equal savagery: the officer known as "Mademoiselle Fifi" is stabbed in the throat; Prussian cavalry are found with the sadistic delight of "their stomachs cut open" (*Père Milon*); the well-named Madame Sauvage burns enemy soldiers alive; troops trapped in a cellar are flooded into terrified surrender (*The Prisoners*). All moral sense dissipates in the facility and fascination of slaughter and suffering.

At the same time, however, Maupassant seems to afford his compatriots a measure of courage denied to the enemy. The two friends of the story with that title are heroic in spite of themselves, at least in comparison to the merciless Prussians. In *A Duel*, *Père Milon*, and *La Mère Sauvage*, unusually brave individuals sacrifice their lives in gestures of resistance and revenge. And the recurring figure of the prostitute, for whom Maupassant retains an innate sympathy in both life and art, displays a particular kind of integrity, in a corporeal sacrifice heightened by the paradox of her profession. In *Le Lit 29* (1884), she knowingly contaminates her Prussian clients with syphilis. The story almost certainly has as real-life origins as the plots of *Mademoiselle Fifi* and *Boule de suif*.[8] In the first of these, Rachel's refusal to service the victorious Prussians elevates all the prostitutes in the brothel above the servitude to, and for which, they are condemned; and if the heroine of *Boule de suif* finally submits, she retains a dignity forfeited by the malignant hypocrisy of fellow travelers who themselves force her to surrender. The metaphors are chosen with care: a sinister conspiracy "to force this human citadel to crumble and yield," "a plan of attack . . . as if they were in a fortress under siege," resistance, assault, and capitulation. The unfolding of *Boule de suif* is also a symbolic narrative.

---

8. Details can be found in the two studies by Richard Bolster listed in the Tales of War section of the Selected Bibliography.

For Maupassant, and indeed his generation, the Franco-Prussian War was an open sore and a niggling point of reference. Even in a story like *Adieu*, apparently far removed from it, the anecdote is situated "about twelve years ago, shortly after the war." This Norton Critical Edition contains only a selection of the war stories threaded through Maupassant's writing. *L'Angélus*, his unfinished novel of the early 1890s, returns once again to the historical context of *Boule de suif*: its opening pages evoke in some detail, two decades later, the entry of Prussian troops into Rouen on December 6, 1870 and the attempts by the better-off inhabitants of Rouen to flee to Le Havre. But it is also true that, for the modern reader, the specificity of the Franco-Prussian War is overlaid by more generalized conclusions. Maupassant's achievement, in his tales of war, lies in his refusal to simplify. The responses of mortally threatened human beings range from fear to denial, and from cowardice to the ruthlessness of survival. And the process of demystification reveals more than butchery and barbarity in an endless cycle of revenge, or that, in the greater scheme of things and set against the terrifying forces unleashed by war, individual acts of heroism change nothing. *Père Milon* closes not with a meditation on bravery but on those left behind. The different registers of the texts, however, open up dimensions beyond the abject pointlessness of such personal suffering. War also engenders the laughable, the derisory counterpoint to the morbid and the tragic. In *Two Friends*, the characters meet their deaths in circumstances which are absurd. *The Prisoners* is essentially a story of stupidity characteristic of Maupassant's sense of humor. The feminized Prussian of *Mademoiselle Fifi* takes it into the territory of parody. Walter Schnaffs is a fool. At the end of *Boule de suif*, moralizing pathos is undercut by an image of steaming dung in the sparkling sunlight, as life and the journey go on. These modulations of focus and mood suggest the extent to which writing itself affords that sense of perspective which Maupassant learned from Flaubert.

Tales of the Supernatural

While his tales of war are clearly linked to Maupassant's personal experience of the events of 1870–71, his stories staging the supernatural have a far more debatable relation to his biography. His contemporaries were all too ready to assume, in the light of his slide into insanity, that Maupassant's exploration of hallucinatory mental states was inseparable from his own deteriorating medical condition. Rather like today's sensationalist media, newspaper editors were keen to exploit what was certainly a hypothetical link between public and private. When *The Apparition* (1884) was reprinted in 1891, by which time Maupassant's condition was common knowledge, it was prefaced by speculation about his health. When *Le Horla* (1887) was republished in January 1892, in the year before his death, it was presented in *L'Écho de Paris* as a virtually autobiographical account of scopic delusion, with journalists citing fragments of the text to explain the latest clinical bulletins issued by Maupassant's doctors. Such wisdom of hindsight, however, needs to be considerably qualified.

In fact, Maupassant's interest in the supernatural long predates his own mental disintegration. Even some of his earliest poems bear witness to this, notably "Fear" and "Terror," both initially published in 1875. In the same year, *La Main d'écorché* (The Flayed Hand) is his first tale in which the macabre takes on a life of its own. The stories selected for this Norton Critical Edition were written between 1876 and 1890. But it was only toward the end of that period that Maupassant's symptoms indicated, over and above migraines, hair loss, and stomach pains, a diseased brain. The problems with his eyesight, in particular, did lead to hallucinatory episodes. But that was not the case at the time he was composing *Le Horla*, for example. On the other hand, the fate of his younger brother, Hervé, furnished Maupassant with an example worryingly close to premonition. Hervé, afflicted by what was called the "general paralysis"—almost certainly as a result of his own syphilis—was showing such signs of related mental instability, including paroxysms of violent rage, from 1887 onward that Maupassant had him committed to an asylum near Paris for a month and then, when it was clear that he was raving mad, to another, near Lyons, where he died on November 13, 1889, at the age of thirty-three. To spare his over-sensitive mother, Maupassant had taken responsibility for all the medical arrangements since his brother's diagnosis, had visited him frequently in his frightening decline and was at his bedside at his death. He was thus very close to a horrific presage of the destiny he so rightly feared. And even though the then-current theories of *hereditary* syphilis have no foundation, it was in the very year of his brother's gruesome end that Maupassant had finally understood from his doctors the terminal mechanics of his own disease.

While such distressing factors may have lent a personal edge to Maupassant's longstanding interest in aberrant mental and pathological states, the latter has a wider context. For the majority of his tales of the supernatural coincide with more general developments, in the France of the period, in the field of psychiatry. One of these was the pseudoscientific belief, popularized by Franz Anton Mesmer's theory of "animal magnetism," which posited a natural transfer of energy between animate and inanimate objects. A more credible advocate of therapeutic hypnotism was Dr. Jean-Martin Charcot, with a global reputation for his early work on neurology and hysteria.

Both are mentioned in *Le Horla*. Charcot gave lectures and demon-strations at the Salpêtrière Hospital in Paris, some of which Mau-passant attended. He also consulted Charcot in 1886 (who seems to have recommended merely hot showers!), as he did Dr. Emile Blanche, another specialist in mental illness, in whose famous clinic he would in due course die. His brother's illness, as well as his mother's precarious health, had put him in touch with prominent members of the medical establishment, and he was as familiar with various theories as he was unconvinced that any of them could pro-vide a cure. But, beyond this direct contact with contemporary med-icine, the far-reaching implications of this new-found contemporary focus on the vicissitudes of the mind lie in its radical questioning of a purely physiological conception of behavior. This is reflected in an essay which Maupassant wrote back in 1883, entitled "The Fantas-tic,"[9] in which he expresses his ironic regret that modern science claimed to offer a rational explanation of all phenomena. It is clearly his own view that there remain layers of mystery which are compel-ling in their own right. And it is here that he invokes the illustrious examples of Hoffman and Edgar Allan Poe in a literary tradition offering fresh challenges to the modern writer.

Maupassant's tales of the supernatural are indebted to that tradi-tion. In his 1883 essay, he singles out his predecessors' talent for leaving the reader unsure of the status of a narrative of this kind: is it the rambling of a delusional personality? Or is it an experience of the invisible that is the privilege of a mind freed from the constraints of consciousness? And that is exactly Maupassant's technique, one of the distinguishing features of these texts being the ambig-uous verisimilitude of supernatural experience subject to the reintroduction of explanatory reasoning. *On the Water*, dating from 1876, starts off by evoking an utterly ordinary setting on the Seine, prior to the disintegration of the organizing categories of the ratio-nal world, notably those of time and space. *Lost at Sea* is, in effect, a ghost story, in which the reincarnation of a sailor in the guise of a parrot is both impossible but no less troubling in the reappearance of a lost voice. In *Fear*, the terrifying anecdote is framed by seafar-ing reminiscences. *The Apparition* places a question mark over whether the narrator has been subject to "just a hallucination, a trick of the senses," with its conclusion providing no confirmation one way or the other. The judge at the end of *The Hand*, reminds his audience of trembling ladies that "I did warn you that you wouldn't like my explanation." *Who Can Know?* is an emblematic story in this respect, its enigmas accommodated in its very title. And

9. Published in *Le Gaulois* on October 7, 1883, a long excerpt of which is included in the Contexts section, pp. 284–85.

who can deny the very real emotions of a nightmare? Many of these tales are about disorientation, the losing of bearings, in the darkness or the flowing depths of a river. Struggling to determine whether a story is real or fantastic, readers prevented by external evidence from applying purely psychological interpretation to it, also lose their footing, thereby reduplicating the hesitations of a narrator caught between the explicable and the inexplicable. In the process, between these two interpretative registers, Maupassant powerfully conveys what has been called the "floating frontier" between illusion and reality.[1] Each of these tales invokes the bizarre or the horrific, given dramatic credibility by fear and solitude. They intimate the presence of a disembodied other self, watching the protagonist in the mirror of his mind.

It has been argued that both their themes and techniques represent, on Maupassant's part, an apprenticeship leading to the acknowledged masterpiece of *Le Horla*,[2] to which *A Nightmare* and *Who Can Know?* are a coda in a minor key. As in *Lost at Sea*, it centers on an invisible but obsessive presence. In *Le Horla*, the double and dispossession are made flesh, in an immediacy reinforced by the entries in a diary. Using the first-person perspective encourages the reader's identification with an insane but paradoxically convincing logic. Alternating between concrete notations (such as the ships on the river) and hallucinatory visions, and between self-directed scepticism and the invocation of Charcot and Mesmer's explanations, Maupassant organizes, with almost clinical exactitude, the story's progression in terms of a fever. Its crises and abatements, conveyed in the present tense, serve to displace the reader's response, once again locked in the tension between a feverish loss of control and a retrospective tranquility which is never definitive. It is partly for this reason that, starting with its neologistic title, *Le Horla* has continued to exercise some of the finest critical minds—without achieving consensus. Responses have ranged from seeing it as a precursor of Surrealism to offering insights into schizophrenia. It is also a text that allows us to further contrast and compare Maupassant's various techniques as a writer. In his tales of French life and his tales of war, he generally adopts an objective point of view, conveying with authority the world outside the text. In his tales of the supernatural, that authority seems to dissolve within the subjectivity of its expression. What these different kinds of texts nevertheless share is the evidence that writing itself, whether in overcoming existential despair or exploring the incomprehensible, serves to articulate and clarify a vision of the world and the self.

1. Morris D. Hampton, "Variations on a Theme: Five Tales of Horror by Maupassant," *Studies in Short Fiction* 17.4 (1980): 479.
2. Notably by Allan H. Pasco, in his "The Evolution of Maupassant's Supernatural Stories," *Symposium* 21 (1969): 150–59, included in the Criticism section.

GUY DE MAUPASSANT'S
SELECTED WORKS

Tales of French Life

The Necklace[†]

She was one of those pretty, charming young women born into a working-class family, as if by some error of fate. She had no dowry, no hopes, no way of ever becoming famous, understood, loved or married to a rich, distinguished man; she agreed to be married off to a low-ranking clerk in the Ministry of Public Education.

She dressed simply as she couldn't afford any jewelry, and she was unhappy, feeling she had lowered herself; for women belong to neither a cast nor a race: their beauty, grace and charm are their heritage and family background. Their innate sensitivity, instinct for elegance and adaptable minds are their only hierarchy, and these qualities can transform an ordinary young woman into the equal of any high society lady.

She suffered continually, feeling she had been born to enjoy every possible delicacy and all sorts of luxury. She suffered from the shabbiness of her home, the cheapness of the walls, the worn-out armchairs, the ugly upholstery. All of these things—things that any other woman of her class would not have even noticed—tortured her and infuriated her. The sight of the young Breton girl who did the housework in her humble home aroused in her a sense of despairing regret and lost hope. She dreamed of silent antechambers hung with Oriental tapestries, lit by high, bronze candelabra, and two tall valets in breeches who fell asleep in wide armchairs, drowsy from the heavy heat of the stove. She dreamed of great reception rooms decorated in antique silk, expensive furniture displaying priceless curios, and intimate, charming sitting rooms filled with the lingering scent of perfume, perfect for long conversations in the late afternoon with her closest friends, famous, sought-after men whose attention was envied and desired by every woman.

When she sat down to supper at their round table with its tablecloth that hadn't been changed in three days, opposite her husband

† First published in *Le Gaulois* on February 17, 1884, before being included in *Contes du jour et de la nuit* (1885).

3

who opened the tureen and said, absolutely delighted, "Ah! Beef stew! I can't think of anything better than that . . . ," she would be dreaming of elegant dinners, sparkling silverware, tapestries on the walls with ancient figures and extraordinary birds in a fairy-tale forest. She would dream of exquisite dishes served on wonderful china, of compliments whispered to her that she would return with the smile of a sphinx while savoring the delicate pink flesh of a trout or the wings of a grouse.

She had no expensive dresses, no jewelry, nothing. And those were the only things she liked; she felt she had been born for such things. She would have so desired to be attractive, envied, seductive and elegant.

She had one wealthy friend, a former school friend from the convent; but she didn't want to visit her any more because she suffered so much when she had to go home. And she would cry for days at a time, from sadness, regret, despair and distress.

One day, her husband came home holding a large envelope and looking triumphant.

"Here," he said, "this is for you."

She eagerly tore open the envelope and took out an engraved invitation:

"The Minister of Public Education and Madame Georges Ramponneau request the pleasure of the company of Monsieur and Madame Loisel at the Ministry on the evening of Monday, January 18."

Instead of being delighted, as her husband had hoped, she angrily threw the invitation down on the table.

"And what do you expect me to do with that?"

"But, my dear, I thought you'd be happy. You never go out and this is an opportunity, and a fine one, at that! It was incredibly difficult to get the invitation. Everyone wants one; it's very sought after and they don't give out many to the clerks. Everyone important will be there."

She looked at him, annoyed and impatient, and asked:

"And what am I supposed to wear to go to something like that?"

He hadn't thought of that.

"What about the dress you wear to go to the theater?" he stammered. "I think it looks very nice . . ."

He fell silent, stunned when he realized his wife was crying. Two large tears flowed slowly down her face, from the corners of her eyes to the corners of her mouth.

"What's wrong?" he muttered. "What's wrong?"

Through an intense effort, she had gotten control of herself; she wiped her damp cheeks and calmly replied:

"Nothing. It's just that I have nothing to wear and so I can't go to the ball. Give your invitation to a colleague whose wife has fancier clothes than me."

He felt sorry for her.

"Come now, Mathilde," he said, "how much would a suitable outfit cost, something you might wear again for other occasions, something very nice but simple?"

She thought for a few seconds, working out the figures in her mind and thinking of how much she could ask for without getting a horrified response and immediate refusal from her thrifty clerk.

She hesitated, then finally replied:

"I'm not exactly sure, but I think I could manage with four hundred francs."

He had gone a little pale, for he had put aside exactly that amount to buy a rifle and treat himself to some hunting parties on Sundays the following summer, in the Nanterre region, with a few friends who were going down there to shoot larks.

"Fine," he said, nonetheless, "I'll give you four hundred francs. But make sure you get a beautiful dress."

The day of the ball was approaching and Madame Loisel seemed sad, anxious, nervous. But she had her dress.

"What's wrong?" her husband asked one evening. "You've been acting very strangely for three days now."

"I'm upset because I have no jewelry," she replied. "Not a single thing to wear. I'll look as poor as anything. I would almost rather not go to the reception."

"You can wear some fresh flowers," he replied. "That's very chic at this time of year. For ten francs you can have two or three magnificent roses."

She was not convinced.

"No . . . there's nothing more humiliating than looking poor in the company of wealthy women."

"You're so silly!" he husband exclaimed. "Go and see your friend Madame Forestier and ask her to lend you some jewelry. You're close enough to her to do that."

She cried out in joy.

"That's true. It hadn't even occurred to me."

The next day, she went to her friend's house and explained why she was so upset.

Madame Forestier went over to her armoire, took out a large jewelry box, brought it over, opened it and said to Madame Loisel:

"Take anything you like, my dear."

First she looked at some bracelets, then a string of pearls, then a Venetian cross, beautifully crafted with gold and gemstones. She tried on the necklaces in front of the mirror, hesitated, unable to bring herself to take them off and give them back.

"Do you have anything else?" she kept asking.

"Of course. Keep looking. I don't know what kind of thing you like."

Suddenly, she found a superb diamond necklace in a black satin box. And her heart began to beat faster with unbridled desire. Her hands shook as she held it. She put it around her neck, over her high-collared dress, and stood entranced by her image in the mirror.

"Could you lend me this," she finally asked, hesitantly, full of anguish. "Just this?"

"Certainly; of course."

She threw her arms around her friend's neck, gave her a big kiss, then ran off with her treasure.

The day of the ball came. Madame Loisel was a great success. She was prettier than anyone else, elegant, gracious, smiling and mad with joy. All the men were watching her, asking her name, trying to get introduced. All the attachés from the Ministry wanted to waltz with her. The Minister himself noticed her.

She danced as if exhilarated, carried away, intoxicated with pleasure, lost in a dream, in the triumph of her beauty, the glory of her success, in a sort of cloud of happiness created by all the compliments, all the admiration, all the desire she aroused, created by the complete and utter victory that felt so sweet to a woman's heart.

She left about four o'clock in the morning. Her husband had been sleeping in an empty little sitting room with three other men whose wives were having a wonderful time.

He threw the coat over her shoulders he had brought with him for going home, an inexpensive coat she wore every day, whose shabbiness clashed with the elegance of her ball gown. She felt this and wanted to rush away so she wouldn't be noticed by the other women who were wrapping themselves up in expensive furs.

Loisel stopped her:

"Wait here. You'll catch cold outside. I'll go and get us a carriage."

But she refused to listen to him and quickly rushed down the stairs. When they were in the street, there were no carriages, so they tried to find one, calling out after any driver they saw going by in the distance.

They walked down toward the Seine, shivering and feeling hopeless. On the quayside, they finally found one of those old cabs you only see in Paris after dark, as if they were too ashamed of their scruffiness to be seen during the day.

It took them back to their door on the Rue des Martyrs, and they sadly went upstairs to their apartment. To her, it was all over. And all he could think about was that he had to be back at the Ministry at ten o'clock.

She took her coat off in front of the mirror, so she could see herself in all her glory one last time. Suddenly, she let out a cry. The diamond necklace was no longer there!

"What's wrong?" her husband asked; he was already half undressed.

She turned toward him, terrified:

"I . . . I . . . I've lost Madame Forestier's necklace."

He stood up, panic-stricken:

"What! . . . But how! . . . That's impossible!"

And they looked in the folds of her dress, in her coat, in the pockets, everywhere. They couldn't find it.

"Are you sure you still had it when we left the ball?" he asked.

"Yes. I remember touching it in the lobby of the Ministry."

"But if you'd lost it in the street, we would have heard it fall on the ground. It must be in the cab."

"Yes, probably. Did you get its number?"

"No. Did you see what it was?"

"No."

They stared at each other, devastated. Then Loisel got dressed.

"I'll go back to where we started and retrace our steps to see if I can find it," he said.

Then he left. She sat there in her evening gown, without the strength to go to bed, collapsed in a chair, depressed, with no fire lit, her mind a blank.

Her husband came back at about seven o'clock. He hadn't found it.

He went to the police station, to the newspapers to offer a reward, then to the cab companies, everywhere, in fact, where there was even a glimmer of hope.

She waited all day long, in the same state of fear in the face of this horrible disaster.

Loisel came back that evening; his face was gaunt and pale; he had found out nothing.

"You must write to your friend," he said, "and say you broke the clasp of the necklace and that you're getting it fixed. That will buy us some time."

She wrote as he suggested.

By the end of the week, they had lost all hope.

And Loisel, who had aged by five years, said:

"We must find out how we can replace the necklace."

The next day, they went to the jewelry shop whose name was inside the case. The jeweler looked through his books:

"I did not sell this necklace, Madame; I must have only sold the case."

So they went from one jeweler to another, looking for a necklace that was just like the one they had lost, trying to remember it in detail, both of them in a terrible state, miserable and distressed.

In a boutique near the Palais-Royal, they found a diamond necklace that was exactly what they were looking for. It cost forty thousand francs. They could have it for thirty-six thousand.

They asked the jeweler not to sell it for three days. And they made it a condition that he would take it back, for thirty-four thousand francs, if they found the one they'd lost before the end of February.

Loisel had eighteen thousand francs that his father had left him. He would have to borrow the rest.

And borrow he did, asking a thousand francs from one person, five hundred from another, five louis[1] here, three louis there. He signed for loans, accepted ruinous conditions, dealt with moneylenders and every kind of loan shark. He committed himself for the rest of his life, risked signing for loans without even knowing whether he could pay them back. And terrified by the suffering to come, by the horrible poverty he was about to face, by the prospect of all the physical deprivation and moral torment he was going to suffer, he went to the jeweler's, put thirty-six thousand francs on the counter, and bought the new necklace.

When Madame Loisel brought the necklace back to Madame Forestier, she said coldly:

"You should have returned it sooner; I might have needed it."

She didn't open the case, as her friend had feared she might. What if she had noticed the substitution, what would she have thought? What would she have said? Wouldn't she have thought Madame Loisel was a thief?

Madame Loisel came to know the horrible life of the poor. She accepted her fate at once, however, and bravely. That terrible debt must be paid. And she would pay. They let their maid go; they moved; they rented an attic.

She did all the heavy housework and the disgusting chores in the kitchen. She washed the dishes, breaking her pink nails scouring greasy pots and the bottoms of saucepans. She washed the dirty linen, the shirts and the dishcloths, and dried them on a clothesline; she carried the garbage down to the street every morning and brought back the water, stopping at every floor, out of breath. And

1. A gold coin worth about 20 francs.

dressed like a working-class woman, carrying a basket, she went to the fruit stall, the grocer's, the butcher's, bargaining, being sworn at, trying to hold on to every single penny of what little money she had.

Every month, they had to pay off certain debts, renew others, ask for more time.

Her husband worked evenings, doing a merchant's accounts, and late at night, he often made handwritten copies of documents for five cents a page.

And this life lasted ten years.

By the end of ten years, they had paid everything off, everything, at outrageous repayment rates and with compound interest.

Madame Loisel looked old now. She had become like every other poor woman: heavy, hard and harsh. With unkempt hair, ragged clothes and raw hands, she talked in a loud voice while throwing buckets of water on the floor to wash it. But sometimes, when her husband was at the office, she would sit beside the window and think of that wonderful evening so long ago, of the ball where she had been so beautiful and so popular.

What would have happened if she hadn't lost that necklace? Who knows? Who can know? How strange and unpredictable life is! How little it takes to make us or break us!

One Sunday, she went for a walk along the Champs-Elysées, to relax after working so hard all week; she suddenly noticed a woman who was taking a child for a walk. It was Madame Forestier, still young, still beautiful, still attractive.

Madame Loisel was filled with emotion. Should she speak to her? Yes, of course. And now that she had paid, she would tell her everything. Why not?

She went over to her.

"Hello, Jeanne."

The other woman did not recognize her, and was surprised to be spoken to in such a familiar way by this working-class woman.

"But . . . Madame! . . . I don't . . . You must be mistaken," she stammered.

"No. It's me, Mathilde Loisel."

Her friend let out a cry.

"Oh! . . . my poor Mathilde, but you've changed so much!"

"Yes, I've had a very hard life since I saw you last; and I've been very poor and miserable . . . and all because of you!"

"Because of me! But how?"

"Do you remember that diamond necklace you lent me to go to the ball at the Ministry?"

"Yes. What about it?"

"Well, I lost it."

"What! But you gave it back to me."

"I gave you back a necklace that was exactly like it. And it's taken us ten years to pay it off. You know that wasn't easy for us, for we had nothing . . . It's finally over, and I'm really glad."

Madame Forestier had stopped.

"Are you saying that you bought a diamond necklace to replace mine?"

"Yes. So you never noticed! They were virtually identical."

And she smiled with proud, naïve joy.

Madame Forestier, deeply moved, took her hands.

"Oh, my poor Mathilde! But my necklace was a fake. It was worth no more than five hundred francs!"

My Uncle Jules[†]

A poor old man with a white beard asked us for some money. My friend, Joseph Davranche, gave him one hundred sous.[1] I was surprised.

"This poor old beggar reminds me of a story I'll tell you," he said. "I'm haunted by the memory of it. This is what happened."

My family was originally from Le Havre[2]; we weren't rich. We got by, that's all you could say. My father had a job; he came home late from the office and didn't earn much. I had two sisters.

My mother suffered a lot because they were always worried about money, and she said many bitter things to her husband—thinly disguised, sly reproaches. The poor man would then make a gesture that truly distressed me. He would wipe his forehead with his open hand as if wiping away sweat that wasn't there. I could feel his helpless pain. We spent as little as possible on everything; we never accepted an invitation to dinner because we couldn't return it; we bought food at reduced prices, the leftover stock from the shops. My sisters made their own dresses and had long discussions about the price of a piece of braid that cost fifteen centimes a yard. Our normal meals consisted of greasy soup and beef cooked in many different ways. Apparently, this is a healthy and comforting kind of food; I would have preferred something else.

[†] First published in *Le Gaulois* on August 7, 1883, and then, a few days later, in *Le Voleur* (August 16, 1883); reprinted in the collection *Miss Harriet* (1884). The text there was dedicated to Jean-Achille Bénouville (1815–1891), a landscape painter who may have been a contemporary of Maupassant's father at the École des Beaux-Arts.

1. One *sou* was equal to 5 *centimes*; there were 100 *centimes* to a franc, so he gave the beggar 5 francs.

2. Major transatlantic port, at the mouth of the Seine.

Whenever I lost a button or tore my pants, there was a terrible argument.

But every Sunday, we all got dressed up in our best clothes and went for a walk along the pier. My father, in a frock coat, a large hat and gloves, offered his arm to my mother, who was decked out like a ship on a special holiday. My sisters, always the first ones ready, waited anxiously until it was time to go; but at the last moment, someone always discovered a stain my father forgot to remove on his coat, and it had to be quickly removed with a rag soaked in benzine.

My father waited in his shirtsleeves, still wearing his big hat, until the task was done, while my mother rushed to finish the job, having adjusted the glasses she wore for close work and taken off her gloves so she didn't get them dirty.

We set out with great ceremony. My sisters walked in front, arm-in-arm. They were of marriageable age, and my parents showed them off around the town. I walked to the left of my mother, and my father to her right. And I can still remember the ostentatious demeanor of my poor parents during these Sunday walks, their serious faces, their stern appearance. They walked solemnly, standing tall, their legs straight, as if their attitude bespoke a matter of extreme importance.

And every Sunday, when they saw the great ships returning from unknown, foreign lands, my father invariably said the very same words:

"Ah! What a surprise it would be if Uncle Jules were on that ship!"

My Uncle Jules was my father's brother, and after being the black sheep of the family, he became their only hope. I had heard him talked about ever since I was a child, and the thought of him had become so familiar to me that I believed that if I saw him, I would recognize him instantly. I knew all the details of his existence right up until the day he left for America, even though everyone spoke about that earlier part of his life in whispers.

He had, so it seemed, behaved very badly, that is to say, he frittered away some money, which is the greatest of all crimes in a poor family. In rich families, if a man who has money spends it on having a good time, he is "being silly." They just smile and say he likes to live it up. In needy families, a boy who forces his parents to make a dent in their savings is a good-for-nothing, a rascal, a scoundrel!

And this difference is fair, even if the behavior is the same, for it is only the consequences of an action that determine its seriousness.

In brief, Uncle Jules had reduced the inheritance my father had been counting on, after having spent every single penny of his own.

He had been sent to America, as was done in those days, on a merchant ship going from Le Havre to New York.

Once he arrived, my Uncle Jules set himself up as some sort of salesman, and he soon wrote to say he was earning a bit of money and that he hoped to make up for the wrong he had done to my father. That letter had a great impact on the family. Jules, whom they said was not worth a damn, suddenly became an honest man, a sensitive young man, a true Davranche, with as much integrity as any Davranche.

Moreover, one of the captains told us he had rented a large shop and was making a lot of money.

A second letter, two years later, read: "My dear Philippe, I am writing so that you don't worry about my heath, which is good. Business is going well. I am leaving tomorrow for a long trip to South America. You may not hear from me for several years. Don't worry if I don't write to you. I will return to Le Havre once I have made my fortune. I hope that it will not take too long, and that we will one day be happy living together again. . . ."

That letter became the family's Gospel. Any excuse to read it, to show it to everyone.

And, in fact, it had been ten years since we'd heard from Uncle Jules; but my father's hopes grew with each passing day; and my mother often said:

"When that kind Jules comes back, our situation will be different. Now there's someone who knew how to make his way!"

And every Sunday, as he watched the large black steamers approaching from the distance, belching out streams of smoke into the sky, my father would always say the exact same thing:

"Ah! What a surprise it would be if Uncle Jules were on that ship!"[3]

And we almost expected to see him waving a handkerchief, shouting:

"Ahoy there! Philippe."

They had fabricated a thousand plans around this guaranteed return; we were even going to use our uncle's money to buy a little house in the country, near Ingouville.[4] I believe that my father might have actually started negotiations about it.

My eldest sister was then twenty-eight; the other was twenty-six. They couldn't find husbands, which was very sad to everyone in the family.

A suitor finally asked to marry the younger one. He wasn't rich but he had a job and was an honorable man. I've always believed that

3. An allusion, also caught in the title, to the *Oncle d'Amérique* legend, based on the widely held assumption that all emigrants to North and South America (some 30,000 annually at this time) would make a fortune and return to share it with their impoverished relatives; the ironic topicality of Maupassant's story is enhanced by the 1883 recession in the United States which reduced even further the small number of those fulfilling this illusory scenario.
4. Village, some seventeen miles inland from Fécamp in Normandy.

showing him. Uncle Jules' letter one evening was what ended his hesitations and convinced the young man to make the decision.

His proposal was eagerly accepted, and it was agreed that after the wedding, the whole family would go on a little trip together to Jersey.[5]

Jersey is the ideal vacation spot for poor people. It isn't far; you cross the sea on a steamship and you're in a foreign country, as this little island belongs to the English. So a Frenchman only has to spend two hours on a boat to treat himself to the experience of a neighboring race of people and to study the customs, quite deplorable actually, of this island under the protection of the British flag, as ordinary people would describe it.

This trip to Jersey became the focus of all our attention, the only thing we looked forward to, our perpetual dream.

We finally set off. I can picture it as if it were yesterday: the steamer heating up at the Granville[6] dock; my father, amazed, supervising the loading of our three bags; my anxious mother taking the arm of my unmarried sister, who seemed lost after the departure of the other one, like a chick who's the only one left in the brood; and behind us the newlyweds, who always kept well back, which made me turn my head around quite often.

The steamer whistled. Here we were, on board, and the ship left the pier, sailing along a sea as flat as a green marble table. We watched the coastline disappear into the distance, as happy and proud as anyone who does not travel often.

My father held in his stomach under his frock coat, which, that very morning, had carefully had all its stains removed, and he gave off the odor of benzine as on the days we went for our outings, which always made me think of Sundays.

Suddenly, he noticed two elegant ladies being offered some oysters by two gentlemen. An old sailor in tattered clothes opened each shell with a quick flick of a knife and handed them to the gentlemen, who in turn passed them to the ladies. The ladies ate them in a very refined way, holding the shell with a delicate handkerchief and bringing their lips forward so as not to stain their dresses. Then they drank the water with a quick little movement and threw the shell into the sea.

My father, without a doubt, was enthralled by this sophisticated act of eating oysters on a moving ship. He found it respectable, refined, superior, and he walked over to my mother and sisters and asked:

---

5. The largest of the Channel Islands, British Crown dependencies off the French coast.
6. Port to the south of the Cotentin peninsula, one of the embarkation points for travel to Jersey.

"Would you like me to get you some oysters?"

My mother hesitated, because of the expense; but my two sisters accepted at once. "I'm afraid I'll get an upset stomach," my mother said, sounding annoyed. "Just get some for the children, but not too many, you'll make them sick."

Then she turned toward me and added:

"As for Joseph, there's no need; boys shouldn't be spoiled."

And so I stayed with my mother, finding this disparity unfair. I watched my father ostentatiously lead his two daughters and his son-in-law toward the old sailor in tattered clothes.

The two ladies had just left, and my father told my sisters how to eat the oysters without spilling the water; he even wanted to show them how it was done and took hold of an oyster. Trying to imitate the ladies, he immediately spilled the liquid all over his coat, and I could hear my mother murmur:

"Can't he stop being so childish."

Suddenly, my father seemed upset; he took a few steps back, stared at his family huddled around the sailor shelling the oysters, then quickly came over to us. He looked very pale, with a peculiar expression in his eyes.

"It's extraordinary," he said quietly to my mother, "extraordinary how much that man opening the oysters looks like Jules."

"Which Jules?" my mother asked, shocked.

"Well . . . my brother . . . ," my father continued. "If I didn't know he was well set up in America, I'd really think it was him."

"You're mad!" my mother muttered, aghast. "Since you know it can't be him, why say such a stupid thing?"

But my father was insistent:

"You go and look at him, Clarisse; I'd rather you judge with your own eyes."

She stood up and went over to join her daughters. I also looked at the man. He was old, dirty, full of wrinkles and never looked up from his task.

My mother came back. I could see she was shaking.

"I think it *is* him," she said very quickly. "Go and try to get some information from the Captain. But make sure you're careful; we don't want that scoundrel to end up our problem now!"

My father walked away, and I followed him. I felt strangely moved.

The Captain was a tall, thin gentleman with long sideburns who walked up and down the gangway looking important, as if he were in charge of the mail ship to the Indies.[7]

7. The mail route to India was set up in 1839 and lasted for a century; it first went overland through Europe to the southern Italian port of Brindisi and, as the longest and fastest transit in the world, was a source of fascination to Maupassant's contemporaries.

My father approached him with great formality, asking him questions about his profession, accompanied by many compliments.

"What is Jersey known for? Its products? Its population? Customs? What kind of soil?" etc. etc.

You would have thought they were talking about the United States at the very least.

Then they talked about the ship we were on, the *Express*,[8] then he finally got to the crew.

"You have someone here who shells the oysters," my father finally said, at last, sounding anxious. "Do you know anything about the old man?"

The captain, who was getting irritated by this conversation, replied dryly:

"He's an old French tramp I found in America last year, and I brought him home. It seems he has relatives in Le Havre, but he doesn't want to go back to them because he owes them money. His name is Jules. Jules Darmanche or Darvanche, something like that. Apparently, he was rich for a while over there, but you can see what he's reduced to now."

My father turned white.

"Ah! Ah! I see . . . , very good . . . ," he managed, looking distraught. "I'm not surprised . . . Thank you very much, Captain."

And he left, while the sailor watched him walk away in surprise.

He went over to my mother looking so upset that she said:

"Sit down; everyone will notice that something's wrong."

He fell onto the bench.

"It's him," he stammered, "it's really him!"

Then he asked: "What are we going to do?"

"We have to keep the children away from him," she replied quickly. "Since Joseph knows everything, he can go and get them. We must be particularly careful that our son-in-law suspects nothing."

My father looked completely dismayed. "What a catastrophe!" he murmured.

"I've always thought that thief would come to nothing and end up a burden on us!" my mother continued, suddenly furious. "As if you'd expect anything else from a Davranche!"

And my father wiped his forehead with his open hand as he always did when his wife criticized him.

"Give Joseph some money right now, so he can go and pay for the oysters. All we need is to be recognized by that beggar. Just imagine what people on the ship would think. Let's get over to the other end of the ship and make sure that man doesn't come near us!"

8. Maupassant renames the steamship, called the *Victoria*, run by the London and South-West railway company, for its best-known quality—namely its ability to make the 55-mile crossing to Jersey in about two hours.

She stood up, and they walked away after giving me a hundred-sous coin.

My sisters were surprised, as they were waiting for my father. I said that Mama had felt a little seasick.

"How much do we owe you, Monsieur?" I asked the man shelling the oysters. What I wanted to say was "Uncle."

"Two francs and fifty centimes," he replied.

I handed him the hundred sous and he gave me my change.

I looked at his hand, the poor, wrinkled hand of a sailor, and I looked at his face, an old, unhappy face, sad, overworked, and I said to myself:

"That's my uncle, Papa's brother, my uncle!"

I gave him ten sous as a tip. He thanked me:

"God bless you, young man!"

He sounded like a poor man accepting charity. I thought he must have been a beggar over in America!

My sisters stared at me, astounded by my generosity.

When I gave the two francs back to my father, my mother was surprised and asked:

"They bought three francs worth? . . . That isn't possible."

"I gave him ten sous as a tip," I said in a firm voice.

My mother started and looked me straight in the eyes:

"You're mad! Giving that person, that scoundrel ten sous!"

She stopped herself after my father gave her a look, gesturing toward their son-in-law.

Then no one said any more.

In front of us, on the horizon, a purplish shape seemed to emerge from the sea. It was Jersey.

As we were approaching the dock, I felt an intense urge in my heart to see my Uncle Jules one more time, to go over to him, to say something consoling, something kind.

But no one was eating oysters any more, so he had disappeared, undoubtedly down into the squalid hold where this poor wretch lived.

And we returned home on the Saint-Malo[9] boat, so we wouldn't run into him again. My mother was worried sick.

I never saw my father's brother again!

And that is why you will sometimes see me give one hundred sous to beggars.

9. Port opposite Granville, on the other side of the Bay of Saint-Michel.

The Protector[†]

He never would have dreamed of coming so far! The son of a bailiff in the provinces, Jean Marin, like so many others, had come to study law in the Latin Quarter. In the various cafés where he'd become a regular customer, he made friends with several loud-mouthed students who went on and on about politics while drinking beer. He became smitten with them and obstinately followed them from café to café, even paying for their drinks when he had any money.

He then became a lawyer and took on cases that he lost. Now one morning, he read in the papers that one of his former friends from the Latin Quarter had just been appointed a Député.[1]

He became his faithful dog again, the friend who does the unpleasant chores, gets things going, the person you send for when you need him without doing any favors in return. Then, because of some incident in Parliament, the Député became a Minister; six months later, Jean Marin was appointed a Conseiller d'État.[2]

At first, he was so full of pride that he nearly went crazy. He would walk down the streets so everyone could see him, as if they could guess how important he was just by looking at him. He found a way to say who he was to the shopkeepers whose stores he frequented, the newspaper salesman, even the carriage drivers, managing to bring it up for the slightest reason:

"I'm a Conseiller d'État, you know . . ."

Then, quite naturally, because of his innate dignity, out of professional necessity, given his duty as an influential and generous man, he felt an imperious need to become a protector, a patron.

He offered his support to everyone, whenever the occasion presented itself, and with boundless generosity.

Whenever he met anyone he knew while walking along on the boulevards, he would go up to them, looking delighted, shake hands, ask how they were, then, without waiting for them to question him, he would say:

"I'm a Conseiller d'État you know, and completely at your service. If I can help you in any way, please do not hesitate to ask. In my position, one has great influence."

[†] First published, under the pseudonym "Maufrigneuse," in the *Gil Blas* on February 5, 1884; subsequently reprinted in the collective volume *Toine* (1886).
1. The approximate equivalent of a congressman in the French Parliament.
2. A senior member of the Council of State, the highest administrative body overseeing government legislation and also acting as a tribunal in cases of conflict between branches of the civil service.

Then he would go into the café with the friend he'd just run into and ask for a pen, some ink and a piece of paper—"Just one, waiter, it's to write a letter of recommendation."

And he wrote ten, twenty, fifty letters of recommendation a day. He wrote them at the Café Américain, Bignon's, Tortoni's, the Maison Dorée, the Café Riche, the Helder, the Café Anglais, the Napolitain,[3] everywhere, absolutely everywhere. He wrote them to all the government officials, from the Justices of the Peace right up to the Ministers. And he was happy, utterly happy.

One morning when he was leaving his house to go to the Council Chambers, it began to rain. He thought about taking a cab, but decided against it, and started walking down the street.

The rain was coming down in torrents, flooding the sidewalks and the streets. Monsieur Marin had to take shelter in a doorway. An old priest was already there, an old priest with white hair. Before he became a Conseiller d'État, Monsieur Marin did not like the clergy at all. Now he treated them with respect, ever since a cardinal had politely consulted him on a complicated matter. The rain continued to pour down, forcing the two men further inside, to take shelter in front of the concierge's lodge and avoid getting splashed. Monsieur Marin, who was always itching to talk to show off, said:

"This is horrible weather, Father."

The old priest nodded:

"Oh! Yes, Monsieur, it's very unpleasant when you only have a few days in Paris."

"Ah! Have you come from the provinces?"

"Yes, Monsieur. I'm just passing through."

"It really is very unpleasant to have it rain when you only have a few days in the capital. We officials who live here all year round, we think nothing of it."

The priest didn't reply. He looked at the street; the rain seemed to have eased up a bit. Then, suddenly making a decision, he lifted up his cassock to step over the streams of water, the way women raise their skirts.

Seeing he was about to leave, Monsieur Marin cried out:

"You'll get drenched, Father. Stay a few minutes; it will stop."

The priest hesitated, waited, then said:

"It's just that I'm in a rush. I have an urgent meeting."

Monsieur Marin felt sorry for him.

"But you'll get absolutely drenched. May I ask where you're going?"

---

3. Maupassant lists the most fashionable Parisian cafés of the period, situated on what were known as the *grands boulevards*, the Boulevard des Capucines and the Boulevard des Italiens, radiating from the Place de l'Opéra.

The priest seemed to hesitate, then replied:

"I'm going in the direction of the Palais-Royal."[4]

"In that case, if you will allow it, Father, let me share my umbrella with you. I'm going to the Council Chambers. I'm a Conseiller d'État, you know."

The old priest raised his head and looked at the man beside him.

"Thank you, Monsieur," he said. "With pleasure."

So Monsieur Marin took his arm and they started walking. He directed him, watched over him, gave him advice.

"Be careful of that stream, Father. And be especially careful of the carriage wheels; they can sometimes cover you in mud from head to foot. Watch out for the umbrellas of the people passing by; there's nothing more dangerous for the eyes than the tips of them. The women are particularly insufferable; they pay no attention to where they're going and always jab you in the face with their parasols or umbrellas. And they never have any consideration for anyone else. You'd think they owned the city. They take over the streets and the sidewalks. I think they've been very badly brought up, I do."

And Monsieur Marin started to laugh.

The priest didn't reply. He kept walking, slightly bent over, stepping over the puddles with care so he wouldn't get his boots or cassock muddy.

"So you've come to Paris for a little break, have you?" Monsieur Marin asked.

"No," the priest replied, "I've come on business."

"Ah! Is it anything important? Would you mind if I asked what it's about? If I can help you in any way, I am at your disposition."

The priest appeared embarrassed.

"Oh! It's just a small personal matter. A little problem with . . . with my Bishop. You wouldn't find it interesting. It's a . . . a Church matter . . . an . . . ecclesiastical issue."

Monsieur Marin pressed him.

"But that's exactly the kind of thing that the Council deals with. So do let me help."

"Yes, I'm going to the Council Chambers too, Monsieur. You really are very, very kind. I have to see Monsieur Lerepère and Monsieur Savon and Monsieur Petitpas[5] as well, perhaps."

Monsieur Marin, stopped in his tracks.

"But they're my friends, Father, my best friends, excellent colleagues, delightful men. I'll give you a letter of recommendation for all three of them, a very good one at that. You can count on me."

---

4. The magnificent building housing the Conseil d'État can be seen, still today, at the entrance to the Palais Royal, built in 1629, with its garden enclosed by arcades.

5. Maupassant's choice of names is indicative of his sense of humor; they translate as, respectively, "reference-point," "soap," and "tiptoeing."

The priest thanked him, apologized profusely, and stammered endless words of thanks.

Monsieur Marin was delighted.

"Ah, you can boast of having some very good luck, Father. You'll see, you'll see; thanks to me, your matter will go like clockwork."

They reached the Council Chambers. Monsieur Marin took the priest up to his office, offered him a chair in front of the fire, then sat down at his desk and started to write:

"My dear colleague,

Allow me to recommend to you most highly a venerable and particularly worthy and deserving priest, Father . . ."

He stopped:

"What is your name, please?"

"Father Ceinture."[6]

Monsieur Marin continued writing:

". . . Father Ceinture, who requires your services regarding a little matter that he will explain to you. I am pleased to have this opportunity, my dear colleague . . ."

And he ended with the customary compliments.

When he'd finished writing the three letters, he handed them to his protégé, who left after endless declarations of gratitude.

Monsieur Marin did his work, went home, spent a quiet day, slept peacefully, woke up in a good mood and had the newspapers brought to him.

The first one he opened was very left wing. This is what he read:

OUR CLERGY AND OUR GOVERNMENT OFFICIALS

We could never finish listing the damaging acts of the clergy. A certain priest, Father Ceinture, convicted of conspiracy against the present government, accused of such disgraceful acts that we cannot even mention them, suspected, moreover, of being a former Jesuit who has become a simple priest, suspended by a Bishop for reasons confirmed to be unmentionable, and summoned to Paris to give an explanation of his conduct, has found an ardent defender in one Marin, a Conseiller d'État, who was not afraid to provide this ecclesiastical criminal with the most glowing letters of recommendation to his colleagues, all the Republican officials.

We would call the Minister's attention to the unspeakable attitude of this Conseiller d'État . . .

---

6. French for "belt," suggesting the priest's caricatural girth.

Monsieur Marin leaped up, got dressed and rushed to see his colleague, Petitpas.

"Well really; you must have been mad to recommend that old conspirator to me!" he said.

Monsieur Marin was beside himself.

"But no . . . you see . . . I was deceived," he stammered. "He looked like such an honest man. He played me . . . he played me shamefully! Please, convict him; give him a harsh sentence, a very harsh sentence. I'll write a letter. Tell me who I should write to about convicting him. I'll go and see the Public Prosecutor and the Archbishop of Paris, yes, the Archbishop . . ."

And he rushed over to Monsieur Petitpas's desk, sat down and started writing:

"Monseigneur, it is my honor to bring to Your Grace's attention the fact that I have recently been the victim of the intrigues and lies of a certain Father Ceinture, who took advantage of my trusting natures.

"Misled by the statements of this clergyman, I was . . ." etc., etc.

Then he signed the letter, sealed it, and turned to his colleague.

"You see, my dear friend, let this be a lesson to you," he said. "Never give a letter of recommendation to anyone."

The Journey[†]

I

Once they left Cannes,[1] the train compartment was full; everyone was chatting; they all knew each other. When they passed Tarascon, someone said: "This is where people get murdered."[2] And they started talking about the mysterious, elusive killer who had been giving himself the occasional treat for the past two years by murdering a passenger on a train. Everyone made assumptions, offered an opinion; the women shuddered and looked out at the pitch-black night, frightened they might suddenly see a man's face appear at the compartment door. And they began telling terrifying stories of horrible

† First published in *Le Gaulois* on May 10, 1883; reprinted in *Miss Harriet* (1884). The text in this collection was dedicated to Gustave Toudouze (1847–1904), novelist, art and drama critic, and a lifelong friend of Maupassant.

1. Already, in the second half of the nineteenth century, a fashionable resort on the French Riviera, its climate propitious for convalescence; elsewhere Maupassant ironically describes it as "the California of pharmacists."

2. Rumor based on fact: a number of murders on trains took place in 1882–83, in the Tarascon area, just south of Avignon. The town survives for literary posterity in Alphonse Daudet's famous novel of 1872, *Tartarin de Tarascon*. Maupassant's reference to its sinister reputation is at odds with Daudet's affectionally comic and sentimental evocation of its Provençal inhabitants.

events, of coming face to face with madmen on an express train, of hours spent sitting opposite a suspicious person.

Each of the men knew a story that made him look like a hero; each of them had intimidated, beaten to the ground and strangled some evildoer in amazing circumstances, with exemplary coolness and daring. A doctor, who spent every winter in the Midi,[3] also wanted to tell a story:

"I've never had the chance to test my courage in such situations," he said, "but I knew a woman, one of my patients who is now dead, who had the most extraordinary thing in the world happen to her, and it was also the most mysterious and the saddest imaginable.

"She was Russian, the Countess Marie Baranova,[4] a very great lady and exquisitely beautiful. You know how very stunning Russian women are, at least, how stunning they seem to us with their delicate noses, fine mouths, close-set eyes—eyes of an indefinable color, a grayish-blue—and their detached gracefulness that seems almost harsh! They have something wicked and seductive about them, haughty yet sweet, tender but severe, altogether charming to a Frenchman. Perhaps, in the end, it is only the differences between our cultures and natures that make me see so many things in her."

For several years, her doctor had tried to convince her go to the South of France, as she was in danger of dying from a chest condition. But she stubbornly refused to leave St. Petersburg. Finally, last autumn, thinking there was nothing more he could do for her, the doctor warned her husband, who immediately ordered his wife to leave for Menton.[5]

She took the train and was alone in a compartment; her servants were in a different one. She sat next to the window, rather sad, watching the countryside and villages go by, feeling very isolated, very abandoned in this life, with no children, virtually no family, a husband whose love for her had died, and who forced her to leave for the other end of the world without going with her, just as he would send a sick valet to the hospital.

At every station, her servant Ivan went to see if his mistress needed anything. He was an old man who had been with the family for many years; he was blindly devoted to her, prepared to carry out any order she gave him.

---

3. Familiar term for the South of France.
4. The original French is "Baranow," the name of a lady who did indeed exist. Maupassant may have heard of her through the beautiful and enchanting Russian expatriates he knew such as the Comtesse Potocka and Marie Barshkitseff, or the character may be a composite portrait based on his intimate acquaintance of these women.
5. The last French city before the Italian border; like Cannes a popular destination for those seeking the sun and warmth to restore them to health.

Night fell; the train raced along at top speed. She couldn't sleep; she was excessively upset. Suddenly, the thought occurred to her to count the money her husband had given her just as she was leaving: French gold coins. She opened her small bag and poured all the shining money out onto her lap.

But a cold rush of air suddenly whipped across her face. Surprised, she looked up. The door to her compartment had just opened. The Countess Marie, flustered, quickly threw a shawl over the money spread out across her dress and waited. A few seconds passed, then a man appeared wearing a tuxedo but no hat: he was panting; he was injured. He closed the door, sat down, looked over at his neighbor with a gleam in his eyes, then wrapped his bleeding hand up in a handkerchief.

The young woman thought she would faint from fear. This man had surely seen her counting her gold coins and he had come to rob her and kill her.

He never stopped staring at her, out of breath, his face contorted, no doubt ready to pounce on her.

"Madame," he suddenly said, "don't be afraid!"

She said nothing, unable to open her mouth, listening to her pounding heart and the buzzing in her ears.

"I am not a criminal, Madame," he continued.

Still she said nothing, but she made a sudden movement and as her knees came closer together, her money started to fall onto the carpet like water flowing down a drainpipe.

The man, surprised, looked at the stream of coins and immediately bent down to pick them up.

Terrified, she stood up, spilling her entire fortune onto the ground, and ran toward the carriage door to hurry out onto the platform. But he understood what she intended to do, rushed forward, grabbed her, put his arms around her and forced her to sit down. Holding her by her wrists, he said: "Hear me out, Madame, I am not a criminal, and I will prove it by picking up all of your money and giving it back to you. But I am doomed, condemned to death, if you do not help me cross the border. I can't tell you anything else. We're going to pass the Russian border in an hour and twenty minutes. If you refuse to help me, I am lost, even though, Madame, I have never killed anyone, never robbed anyone, never done anything that could be considered dishonorable. I swear this to you. I can't tell you anything else."

He got down on his knees and collected all the gold coins that had fallen underneath the seats, even finding the money that had rolled furthest away into the corners. Then, when the little leather bag was full once more, he gave it to his neighbor without saying another word, and went to sit down on the other side of the compartment.

Neither of them moved. She sat motionless, said nothing, weak with terror but calming down little by little. The man remained absolutely still; he sat very tall, staring straight ahead; he was extremely pale, as pale as a corpse. Every now and again, she glanced quickly toward him, then very quickly away. He was about thirty years old, very handsome, and looked like a true gentleman.

The train sped through the darkness, its heartrending cries tearing through the night, sometimes slowing down, then rushing ahead at great speed. Then, suddenly, it whistled several times and stopped completely.

Ivan came to the door to see if she needed anything.

The Countess Marie, her voice trembling, looked at her strange companion one last time, then spoke to her servant brusquely: "Ivan, you're to go back home to the Count; I don't need you any more."

Taken aback, the man looked very surprised.

"But . . . Barine . . ."[6] he muttered.

"No," she continued, "you won't be going with me; I've changed my mind. Here, take this money to pay for your return journey. Now give me your hat and coat."

The old servant was frightened but took off his hat and coat, obeying without a word, as always, accustomed to the sudden desires and unpredictable whims of his masters. Then he left, tears in his eyes.

The train started to move again, speeding toward the border.

Then the Countess Marie said to her neighbor:

"These things are for you, Monsieur, you are Ivan, my servant. I have only one condition: you must never speak to me, never say a single word to me, not to thank me, not for any reason whatsoever."

The stranger bowed without saying a word.

Soon they stopped again and official inspectors in uniform got on the train. The Countess handed them her papers.

"That is my servant, Ivan," she said, pointing to the man sitting opposite, at the other end of the compartment. "Here is his passport."

The train set off again.

All night long, they were alone together, and said not a single word.

When it was morning, they stopped at a German station and the stranger got up to go out onto the platform.

"Forgive me for breaking my promise, Madame," he said, standing at the doorway, "but I have deprived you of your servant and it is only fair that I replace him. Do you need anything?"

"Go and get my maid," she replied coldly.

6. Alternate Russian title for Countess.

He went to get her. Then disappeared.

When she went to get some refreshments, she saw him watching her from a distance. They arrived at Menton.

II

The doctor fell silent for a moment, then continued:

"One day, when I was seeing clients in my office, a tall young man came in.

"'Doctor,' he said, 'I have come to ask you for news of the Countess Marie. Even though she does not know me at all, I am a friend of her husband.'"

"'She is dying. She will not return to Russia.'

"And this man suddenly began to sob, then stood up and staggered out as if he were drunk.

"That very evening, I told the Countess that a stranger had come to ask me about her health. She seemed moved and told me the story I have just told you.

"'This man whom I do not know at all,' she added, 'is like my shadow, following me everywhere; I see him every time I go out. He looks at me so strangely, but he has never spoken to me.'

"She thought for a moment, then continued:

"'In fact, I would bet that he is outside my window right now.'

"She got up from her chaise longue, went over to the window, pulled back the curtain and pointed to the very man who had come to see me; he was sitting on a bench along the promenade, his eyes raised upward toward the villa. He saw us, stood up and walked away without once turning to look back.

"And so, I was witness to a sad and surprising thing: the silent love between these two people who did not know each other at all.

"He loved her, yes, he did, and with the devotion of a wild animal she had rescued, grateful and loyal until death. Every day, he came to see me and asked: 'How is she?', understanding I had guessed everything. And he cried horribly when he saw her grow weaker and paler each day.

"'I have only spoken to this remarkable man once,' she told me, 'yet I feel as if I've known him for twenty years.'

"Whenever they met, she returned his greeting with a charming, serious smile. I felt she was happy—she was so alone and knew she was dying—I felt she was happy to be loved this way, with respect and loyalty, so extremely romantically, with such unlimited devotion. And yet she was faithful to her dignified determination and so obstinately refused to allow him to visit her, to know his name, to speak to him. 'No, no,' she would say, 'that would ruin our unusual friendship. We must remain strangers.'

"As for him, he too was surely a kind of Don Quixote,[7] for he did absolutely nothing to try to get closer to her. He wished to keep the absurd promise he had made on the train to never speak to her, right until the bitter end.

"During the long hours of her illness, she often got up from her chaise longue and opened the curtain to see if he was there, opposite her window. And when she had seen him, sitting motionless on the bench, she would go back to bed with a smile on her face.

"She died one morning, at about ten o'clock. As I was leaving her villa, he came over to me, his face distraught; he already knew.

"'I would like to see her for a moment, with you present,' he said.

"I led him by the arm back into the house.

"When he reached the dead woman's bedside, he took her hand and held it to his lips in an endless kiss, then ran out like a madman."

The doctor fell silent for a moment before continuing:

"And there you have, I am certain, the most unusual story of a train journey that I know. I must say that men are very strange when they are madly in love."

One of the women murmured softly:

"Those two people were not as mad as you might think . . . They were . . . they were . . ."

But she couldn't say any more; she was crying too much. We changed the conversation to calm her down, so we never knew what she wanted to say.

Mademoiselle Pearl[†]

I

What a strange idea I had, truly, to choose Mademoiselle Pearl as Queen that evening.

Every year, I go to my old friend Chantal's house on January 6, to celebrate.[1] My father, who was his closest friend, used to take me there when I was a child. I continued the tradition, and will certainly continue it for the rest of my life, as long as there is still a Chantal in this world.

---

7. Picaresque hero of Miguel de Cervantes' *Don Quixote* (1605–16), whose essential nobility underpins this comparison.

† First published in *Le Figaro littéraire* on January 16, 1886; reprinted in *La Petite Roque* later the same year. It was conceived as one of Maupassant's "contes d'hiver" (winter tales), by virtue of its date of publication and its subject.

1. The tradition in France is to celebrate Epiphany (January 6) by eating a special cake called the *Galette des Rois*, the cake of kings. A little charm is hidden inside it and whoever gets it is considered to have good luck; the "King" then chooses a "Queen," or vice versa.

The Chantals, moreover, have a very unusual lifestyle: they live in Paris as if they were living in Grasse, Yvetot or Pont-à-Mousson.[2]

They own a house set in a little garden near the Paris Observatory. They live there as if they were in the provinces. They know nothing about Paris, the real Paris, they have no idea what it's really like. They are far away, so very far away! Sometimes, however, they go on a journey, a long journey. Madame Chantal goes out on a "shopping spree," as it's called in the family. This is how the shopping spree works:

Mademoiselle Pearl, who holds the keys to the kitchen cabinets (for the linen closets are overseen by the lady of the house herself), Mademoiselle Pearl alerts Madame Chantal to the fact that they are nearly out of sugar, that there are no more canned goods, that there is hardly anything left at the bottom of the coffee bag.

Thus forewarned and able to prevent a full-scale famine, Madame Chantal inspects what remains, writing everything down in a notebook. Then, after adding many numbers, she begins some long calculations followed by lengthy discussions with Mademoiselle Pearl. They do, however, end up agreeing on the quantities of everything they will need for three months: sugar, rice, prunes, coffee, jam, cans of peas, beans, lobster, salt and smoked fish, etc., etc.

After that, they decide on the day they will go shopping; they set out, in a horse-drawn carriage, a carriage with a roof rack, and go to a sizable shop owned by a grocer who lives on the other side of the bridges, in the new part of the city.

Madame Chantal and Mademoiselle Pearl go on this journey together, in secret, and come back at suppertime, exhausted but still excited, having being jolted about in the carriage, whose roof is piled high with packages and bags, as if someone were moving to a new house.

To the Chantals, the entire section of Paris located on the other side of the Seine makes up the new part of the city, an area inhabited by strange, noisy, barely respectable people who throw their money out the window, spending their days indulging in extravagances and their nights at parties. From time to time, however, the family takes their young ladies to the theater, to the Opéra-Comique or the Comédie française,[3] as long as the newspaper Monsieur Chantal reads recommends the play.

The young women are now nineteen and seventeen years old; they are both beautiful girls, tall and cheerful, very well brought up—too

2. Places that are all considered provincial: Grasse is inland from Cannes in the South of France; Yvetot is a small town in Normandy; Pont-à-Mousson is in eastern France, near Nancy.
3. Today the Opéra-Comique is called the Théâtre National de l'Opéra-Comique; both this theater and the Comédie française are known for putting on serious operas and literary works.

well brought up—so well brought up that they go unnoticed, as if they were two pretty dolls. Never would it occur to me to pay attention to them, or to court the Chantals' daughters; they are so unsullied that you barely dare speak to them. You're almost afraid to say hello to them in case it is deemed inappropriate.

As for their father, he is a charming man, highly educated, very open, very cordial, but someone who loves peace, calm, tranquility above all else; he has greatly contributed to mummifying his family in order to live as he wishes: in stagnant immobility. He reads a lot, enjoys chatting and is easily moved. The absence of contact with others, of mixing with people and dealing with conflict has given him a very sensitive, delicate skin, a moral skin. The slightest thing sets him off, upsets him and causes him anguish.

The Chantals do have relationships with others, though, but very limited relationships, chosen with care from within their area. They also exchange visits with relatives who live far away two or three times a year.

I always have dinner at their house on August 15 and January 6.

I consider this my duty, just as taking Communion at Easter is obligatory for Catholics.

On August 15, a few friends are invited, but on January 6, I'm the only stranger.

II

And so, this year, like every other year, I went to have dinner at the Chantals' house to celebrate Epiphany.

According to the custom, I embraced Monsieur Chantal, Madame Chantal and Mademoiselle Pearl, and gave a long bow to Mademoiselle Louise and Mademoiselle Pauline. They asked me a thousand things about what was happening in town, politics, what people thought about the Tonkin Affair[4] and our representatives. Madame Chantal, a heavy woman whose every idea gives me the impression of being squared off like a freestone, has the habit of ending every political discussion by saying: "All that is a bad omen for the future." Why have I always imagined that Madame Chantal's thoughts are square? I have no idea; but everything she says takes that shape in my mind: a square, a large square with four equal angles. There are other people whose ideas always seem round to me, and moving as fast as a hoop. As soon as one of those people start saying something about any subject, it starts rolling, it takes off, coming through

---

4. Region now within Vietnam; the assassination of the French colonial governor in 1883 led to troops being sent to Hanoi to reassert the French protectorate threatened by China. Until this was resolved in 1885, the ongoing conflict was a source of intense political debate.

in ten, twenty, fifty round ideas, big ones and little ones that I can picture running one after the other, as far as the eye can see. Other people have pointed ideas . . . But none of that really matters.

We sat down to dinner as always, and the meal ended without anyone saying a thing worth remembering.

When it was time for dessert, they brought in the Galette des Rois. Now, every year, Monsieur Chantal was King. Whether that was due to endless good luck or a family tradition, I have no idea, but he inevitably got the charm in his piece of cake and named Madame Chantal as Queen. And so I was astonished to feel something very hard in a mouthful of my pastry that nearly broke my tooth. I carefully removed the object from my mouth and saw a small, porcelain doll, no bigger than a bean.

I was so surprised that I cried out: "Ah!" Everyone looked at me and Chantal clapped his hands and shouted: "It's Gaston. It's Gaston. Long live the King! Long live the King!"

Everyone continued the chant: "Long live the King!" And I turned completely red, the way people often blush, for no reason, in rather silly situations. I sat there with my eyes lowered, holding this little piece of china between two fingers, forcing myself to laugh, not knowing what to do or say, when Chantal added: "Now you must choose a Queen."

I was utterly dismayed. In the space of a second a thousand thoughts, a thousand assumptions flashed through my mind. Did they want me to choose one of the Chantal daughters? Was it a way to make me say which one I preferred? Was it a soft, gentle, subtle push by their parents toward a possible marriage? The idea of marriage lurks incessantly around every home with grown-up daughters and takes all sorts of shapes, forms, disguises. A horrid fear of compromising myself rushed through me, as well as a feeling of extreme shyness in the face of the obstinately correct and expressionless demeanor of both Mademoiselle Louise and Mademoiselle Pauline. To choose one of them over the other seemed as difficult as choosing between two drops of water; and the fear of getting myself involved in a situation that would lead me into marriage in spite of myself, little by little, by means that were as discrete, subtle and serene as this insignificant royalty, also troubled me horribly.

But suddenly, I had a flash of inspiration, and I handed the symbolic doll to Mademoiselle Pearl. Everyone was surprised at first, then they undoubtedly understood my sensitivity and discretion, for they all clapped loudly, shouting: "Long live the Queen! Long live the Queen!"

As for her, the poor spinster, she had gone completely to pieces; she was shaking and alarmed. "No . . . no . . . ," she stammered, "no . . . not me . . . please . . . not me . . . please . . ."

Then, for the first time in my life, I looked at Mademoiselle Pearl, and wondered who she really was.

I was used to seeing her in this house, the way you see the old armchairs upholstered in tapestry that you've been sitting on since you were a child without ever thinking about them. One day, you don't know why, perhaps because a ray of sunlight has fallen onto the chair, you suddenly say to yourself: "This piece of furniture is really odd, you know." And you realize that the wood was carved by an artist, and that the fabric is remarkable. I had never really given any thought to Mademoiselle Pearl.

She was part of the Chantal family, that's all there was to it; but how? What was her role? She was a tall, thin woman who did her best to go unnoticed, but who was not insignificant. She was treated amicably, better than a housekeeper, but not as well as a relative. I suddenly became aware, just then, of a great number of nuances I had been unaware of up until now! Madame Chantal called her "Pearl." The daughters "Mademoiselle Pearl," and Chantal only ever called her "Mademoiselle," to be more respectful, perhaps.

I began watching her—How old was she? Forty? Yes, forty—She wasn't old, this woman, she made herself look old. I was suddenly struck by having noticed that. The way she did her hair, dressed and wore jewelry was ridiculous, yet, in spite of everything, she had such simple, natural, inner grace, grace that was hidden, and carefully, that she was in no way ridiculous. What an odd creature she was! How was it that I had never really looked at her closely? She wore her hair in a truly grotesque style, with little old-fashioned ringlets that were completely farcical; and beneath this hairstyle befitting the Virgin Mary was her wide, calm forehead, cut across by two deep wrinkles, two wrinkles of long-suffering sadness, then blue eyes, soft and wide, so timid, so fearful, so humble, beautiful eyes that had remained innocent, full of childlike surprise, the feelings of a young girl and the sadness she had known, all these things showed in her tender eyes but without detracting from them.

Her whole face was delicate and discreet, one of those faces that had lost its light without ever having been burned out, or faded due to weariness or the intense emotions of life.

What a lovely mouth! And such pretty teeth! You would have thought she didn't dare smile!

And suddenly, I started comparing her to Madame Chantal. Mademoiselle Pearl was certainly more attractive, a hundred times better, more refined, more dignified, prouder.

I was stunned by what I was seeing. They poured the champagne. I stretched my glass out toward the Queen, toasting her good health with a well-phrased compliment. I noticed that she looked as if she wanted to hide her face in her napkin; then, as she brought her lips to her glass and sipped some of the sparkling wine, everyone cried out: "The Queen is drinking! The Queen is drinking!" She turned bright red, and nearly choked. They all laughed; but I could tell that everyone in that household loved her a great deal.

III

As soon as dinner was over, Chantal led me away. It was time for his cigar, a sacred moment. When he was alone, he went out into the street to smoke it; when he had a dinner guest, they went into the billiard room and had a game as they smoked. That evening, they had even lit a fire in the billiard room, because it was Epiphany; and my old friend picked up his cue, a very slim cue that he chalked with great care.

"Your turn, my boy," he said.

He still spoke to me as if I were a young boy, even though I was twenty-five, because he had known me ever since I was child.

So I started the game. I struck a few balls, missed a few others. But as the thought of Mademoiselle Pearl was still present in my mind, I suddenly asked:

"Tell me, Monsieur Chantal, is Mademoiselle Pearl related to you?"

He stopped playing, very surprised, then looked at me.

"What? You don't know? You don't know about Mademoiselle Pearl?"

"No, I don't."

"Your father never told you?"

"No."

"Well, well, that's very strange! Ah! Now that's very strange indeed! Oh! But it's quite a story!"

He stopped for a moment, then continued:

"And if you only knew how odd it is that you should ask me about it today, on Epiphany!"

"Why?"

Ah! Why! Listen. It's been forty-one years, forty-one years to the day, January 6. We were living in Roüy-le-Tors[5] then, on the ramparts; but I have to explain what the house was like, so you'll understand. Roüy was built on a slope, or rather on a knoll that overlooks a vast plain. We had a house there with a beautiful hanging garden, supported by the old battlement walls. And so the house was in the city, on the street, while the garden overlooked the plain. There was also a door at the end of a secret passageway cut through the thick stone

---

5. A town invented by Maupassant.

wall—the kind you read about in novels—that led from the garden to the countryside. There was a road in front of this door, and the door had a heavy bell, for the farmers brought their provisions that way to avoid a long detour.

You can picture the place, right? Well, that year on January 6, it had been snowing for a week. It felt like the world was coming to an end. When we went over to the ramparts to look at the plain, the immense white landscape chilled our souls: it was totally white, frozen and as shiny as gloss. It made you wonder if the good Lord had wrapped up the earth to store it away in the attic of old worlds. I can assure you it was a very sad sight.

We were with our whole family then, and there were many of us, a great many of us: my father, my mother, my aunt and uncle, my two brothers and my four cousins, all girls; they were very pretty; I married the youngest. Out of everyone who was there, only three of us are left: my wife, myself and my sister-in-law, who lives in Marseille. Good Lord, how a family dwindles away! It makes me shudder just to think of it! I'm now fifty-six, so I was fifteen then.

So we were going to celebrate Epiphany and we were very cheerful, very cheerful! Everyone was in the reception room waiting to be called for dinner when my eldest brother, Jacques, started to say: "There's a dog that's been howling on the plain for the last ten minutes; he must be lost, the poor little thing."

He had barely finished his sentence when the bell from the garden chimed. It sounded like one of those great church bells that make you think of the dead. It made everyone shudder. My father called the servant and told him to go and see who it was. We all waited in absolute silence; we were thinking about the snow completely blanketing the ground. When the man came back, he said he had seen nothing. The dog was still howling, continuously, and from the very same spot.

We sat down to dinner; but we were all rather upset, especially the children.

Everything was fine until we got to the meat course; then the bell started ringing again, three times in a row, three loud, long tolls that we could feel vibrating to the tips of our fingers; it took our breath clean away. We sat there, looking at each other, forks suspended in midair, straining to hear and gripped by a kind of supernatural fear.

My mother finally spoke: "It's surprising that someone has waited so long before coming back; don't go alone, Baptiste; one of these gentlemen will go with you."

My Uncle François stood up. He was a kind of Hercules, very proud of his strength and afraid of nothing in the world. "Take a shotgun," my father said, "we don't know what we might find."

But my uncle just took a cane and immediately went out with the servant.

The rest of us sat there, trembling with terror and anguish, without eating, without speaking. My father tried to reassure us: "You'll see," he said, "it will just be some beggar or some passerby who got lost in the snow. After ringing the bell the first time, and seeing that no one answered right away, he probably tried to find his own way; but when he couldn't manage it, he came back to our house."

It felt like my uncle had been gone for an hour. He finally returned, furious and swearing: "Nothing, for goodness sake, someone playing a joke! Nothing but that damned dog howling, a hundred yards from the walls. If I'd taken a shotgun with me, I'd have killed him to shut him up."

We went back to our meal, but everyone was still nervous; we sensed that it wasn't over, that something was going to happen, that the bell would ring again, and very soon.

And it did ring, just as we were cutting the Galette des Rois. All the men stood up at the same time. My Uncle François, who had drunk some champagne, announced that he was going to kill IT, in such a rage that my mother and my aunt rushed over to stop him. My father, while remaining very calm, and slightly disabled (he was limping after falling off a horse and breaking his leg), said that he too wanted to know what was happening and that he would go. My brothers, aged eighteen and twenty, ran to get their shotguns; and since no one was paying any attention to me, I grabbed a small hunting rifle and headed out along with the expedition.

We left at once. My father and uncle walked in front, with Baptiste, who carried a lantern. My brothers, Jacques and Paul, came next, and I was at the back, despite my mother's pleas; she stood at the doorstep with my sister and cousins.

It had started snowing again an hour before, and the trees were weighed down with it. The firs bent beneath this heavy, pale covering, like white pyramids, or enormous sugar loafs. And through the grayish curtain of tightly packed, dainty snowflakes, you could barely make out the slimmer bushes, very pale in the darkness. The snow fell so thick and fast that you could barely see ten feet ahead of you. But the lantern shed a strong light in front of us. When we started to go down the winding staircase dug out of the wall, I was truly afraid. I felt as if someone was walking behind me, someone who would grab me by the shoulders and carry me away; and I wanted to turn back; but as I would have had to cross the entire garden, I didn't dare.

I heard someone opening the door onto the plain; then my uncle started to swear: "For goodness sake, that dog's started up again!

If I see even his shadow, I won't miss my chance this time, that stupid b . . ."

Seeing the plain felt sinister, or rather sensing the plain in front of us, for we couldn't see it; all we could see was an endless veil of snow, above, below, in front, to the right, to the left, everywhere.

"Well, now that dog's started howling again," my uncle said. "I'll show him what a good shot I am. That will be something, at least."

But my father, who was a good man, said: "It would be better to go and find him; that poor animal must be howling out of hunger. He's howling for help, the poor, wretched thing; he's crying out like a man in distress. Come on, let's go."

And we set off through the curtain of thick, endless, falling snow, through the frothy mist that filled the night and the sky, and whirled, floated, fell and chilled your body as it melted, freezing you as if you were burning, with a sudden, sharp stinging on your skin, every time the little white snowflakes touched you.

We were up to our knees in this limp, cold slush, and we had to raise our knees very high to walk through it. The dog's howls became louder and clearer the further we went. "There he is!" my uncle shouted. We stopped to watch him, the way you must when you come across an enemy in the dark.

I couldn't see a thing, so I joined the others and then I spotted him; that dog was terrifying and mysterious to see; he was large and black, a sheepdog, with long shaggy hair and the head of a wolf; he was standing on all fours, at the very end of the light cast by the lantern onto the snow. He stood dead still. He had stopped howling. He was watching us.

"That's odd," my uncle said, "he's not coming toward us and he's not moving away. I'd really like to shoot him dead."

"No," my father said, decisively. "We should get hold of him."

Then my brother Jacques added: "But he's not alone. There's something near him."

There was, in fact, something behind him, something gray, impossible to make out. We continued walking toward him with great care.

When he saw us coming nearer, he sat down. He didn't seem unfriendly. He seemed more satisfied to have succeeded in attracting someone's attention.

My father walked straight over to him and petted him. The dog licked his hands; then we realized that he was tied to the wheel of a small cart, a kind of miniature carriage entirely covered in three or four woolen blankets. They carefully removed the covers, and when Baptiste held the lantern over the cart that looked like a little house on wheels, we saw a baby who was fast asleep.

We were so stunned that we couldn't say a word. My father was the first to recover, and since he had a warm heart and a rather noble soul, he reached out and placed his hand on the roof of the carriage, say-ing, "Poor abandoned child! You will become one of the family!" And he ordered my brother Jacques to wheel our discovery out in front.

My father, thinking out loud, continued: "Some love child whose poor mother came to ring at my door on this night of Epiphany, in memory of the Son of God."

He stopped again, and shouted four times, with all his might, through the night, into the four corners of the, heavens: "We have taken her in!" Then, placing his hand on his brother's shoulder, he whispered: "Just think, François, what would have happened if you had shot the dog? . . ."

My uncle did not reply but he made a large sign of the cross, there in the darkness, for he was religious man, despite his blustering.

We had untied the dog and he was following us.

Ah! Our return to the house was so very moving. At first, it was quite difficult to get the little carriage up the stairs in the ramparts; we managed it, though, and pushed it into the entrance hall.

Mama was so funny, happy but aghast! And my four little cousins—the youngest was six years old—looked like four hens around a nest. We finally took the child out of the carriage; she was still asleep. The little girl was about six weeks old. And inside her swaddling clothes, we found ten thousand francs in gold, yes, ten thousand francs! And Papa invested the money so she would have a dowry. So she wasn't the daughter of poor people . . . perhaps the child of some nobleman and a middle-class woman from the town . . . or even . . . we imagined a thousand things but never really knew a thing . . . never knew anything . . . never . . . No one even recognized the dog. No one in the area knew him. In any case, the man or woman who rang the bell three times at our house must have known my parents well to have chosen them that way.

So that is how Mademoiselle Pearl became part of the Chantal household when she was only six weeks old.

However, she was only named Mademoiselle Pearl later on. At first, she was baptized Marie Simonne Claire, and Claire was meant to be her last name.

I can assure you that we were a funny sight as we went back into the dining room with this tiny little thing; she had woken up and was looking all around her at the people and the lights, her blue eyes all misty and gazing vacantly into space.

We sat back down at the table and cut up the cake. I was the King; and I took Mademoiselle Pearl as my Queen, as you did, just before. But that day, she understood nothing of the honor being bestowed upon her.

And so the child was adopted and brought up as part of the family. The years passed; she grew up. She was kind, sweet and obedient.

Everyone loved her and would have spoiled her terribly if my mother had not prevented it.

My mother was a woman who believed in order and hierarchy. She agreed to treat little Claire like her own children, but she insisted on a clear distance between us, and the distinction was firmly established.

Moreover, as soon as the child was old enough to understand, my mother made her aware of her background, and very gently, even tenderly, instilled in the little girl's mind that to the Chantals, she was an adopted child, taken in and welcomed by the family, but in the end, a stranger.

Claire understood the situation with remarkable intelligence and surprising intuition and she understood how to occupy and maintain the place she had been given with so much tact, grace and kindness that she touched my father to the point of tears.

Even my mother was so moved by the passionate gratitude and somewhat fearful devotion of this adorable, loving creature that she started calling her "My daughter." Sometimes, when the little girl had done something good, or sensitive, my mother would raise her glasses onto her forehead, which always indicated she was touched, and say: "But she's a pearl, this child is a real pearl!"—That name stuck with the little Claire, who, to us, became and will always be Mademoiselle Pearl.

IV

Monsieur Chantal fell silent. He was sitting on the billiard table, his legs swinging, holding a billiard ball in his left hand while fiddling with a cloth in his right hand; it was the one used to erase the score from the slate board that we called the "chalk cloth." Blushing somewhat, his voice quieter, he was talking for himself now, lost in thought, moving slowly through memories of things past and former events now awakened in his mind, the way you stroll through the old family gardens where you were brought up—where every tree, every path, every plant, the pointy holly, the laurels that smell so good, the yews whose thick, red berries can be crushed between your fingers—with every step you take, all these things bring back a brief moment from your past life, one of those little, insignificant but delightful moments that form the very foundation of existence.

As for me, I stood opposite him, my back against the wall, my hands holding my billiard cue.

After a moment, he started speaking again: "Goodness, she was so pretty at eighteen . . . and graceful . . . and perfect . . . ah! Such a pretty . . . pretty . . . pretty . . . and good . . . and decent . . . and charming young woman! . . . And her eyes . . . blue . . . and clear . . . bright . . . eyes like I'd never seen before, or since . . . never!"

He fell silent again.

"Why did she never marry?" I asked.

He reacted, but not to me: he reacted to the word "marry":

"Why? Why? She didn't want to . . . didn't want to. And yet, she had thirty thousand francs as a dowry, and she was asked several times . . . but she didn't want to! She seemed sad back then. It was the time when I married my cousin, little Charlotte, my wife, to whom I'd been engaged for six years."

I looked over at Monsieur Chantal and felt as if I had seen into his soul, as if I had suddenly entered into one of those obscure, cruel tragedies of honest hearts, moral, irreproachable hearts, one of those secret tragedies that had been left buried, that no one had ever known about, not even the silent, resigned victims who carried those tragedies within them.

Then, bold curiosity suddenly pushed me to ask:

"You're the one who should have married Mademoiselle Pearl, aren't you, Monsieur Chantal?"

He shuddered, looked at me and replied:

"Me? Marry who?"

"Mademoiselle Pearl."

"Why are you saying that?"

"Because you loved her more than your cousin."

He looked at me with a strange expression, his eyes wide with apprehension.

"Me . . . loved her? . . . What?" he stammered. "Who told you that? . . ."

"It's obvious, for goodness sake . . . and it's even because of her that you put off marrying your cousin for so long, your cousin who waited for you for six years."

He dropped the billiard ball he had been holding in his left hand, grabbed the chalk cloth in both hands and, covering his face with it, he started sobbing. He cried in a distressing, ridiculous way, tears pouring out of his eyes, nose and mouth all at the same time, the way a sponge releases water when you squeeze it. And he coughed, spluttered, blew his nose with the chalk cloth, wiped his eyes and sneezed, tears pouring down every wrinkle on his face, making the kind of gurgling sound you make when you gargle.

I was alarmed, ashamed, and wanted to run away; I had no idea what to say or do or suggest.

Then, suddenly, Madame Chantal's voice called up the staircase:

"Will you soon be finished smoking?"

I opened the door and called out: "Yes, Madame, we're just coming down."

Then I rushed over to her husband and grabbed him by the shoulders: "Monsieur Chantal, my dear friend, listen to me. Your wife is

calling you, pull yourself together, and quickly, we have to go downstairs; pull yourself together."

"Yes . . . yes . . ." he stammered, "I'm coming . . . the poor
woman! . . . I'm coming . . . Tell her I'm coming."

And he began carefully wiping his face with the cloth that had been
used to clean off the marks on the slate board for two or three years,
so he looked partly white and partly red, his forehead, nose, cheeks
and chin dotted with chalk, his eyes swollen and still full of tears.

I grabbed his hands and led him into his bedroom. "Please forgive me," I whispered. "I really hope you will forgive me for having
caused you such pain, Monsieur Chantal . . . but . . . I didn't
know . . . you . . . you do understand . . . ?"

He squeezed my hand. "Yes . . . yes . . . some moments are
difficult . . ."

Then he dipped his face into his washbowl. When he raised his
head, he still didn't look any more presentable; but I had a clever
idea. Since he was worried when he saw himself in the mirror, I said:
"All you have to do is say that you got a bit of dust in your eye, then
you can cry in front of everyone as much as you like."

So he did, in fact, go downstairs, dabbing his eyes with his handkerchief. Everyone was concerned; they all wanted to look in his eye
for the bit of dust that no one could find, and everyone told stories
of similar cases when it had been necessary to go and get a doctor.

As for me, I had gone over to Mademoiselle Pearl and was looking at her, tormented by intense curiosity, curiosity that became
unbearable. She must have really been pretty, with her soft eyes, so
big, so calm, so wide that she looked as if she never closed them,
unlike everyone else. Her outfit was a little ridiculous, truly something an old maid would wear; it detracted from her but without
making her look awkward.

It seemed that I could see her thoughts; the way I had just seen
into Monsieur Chantal's soul, and I could completely understand her
devoted, simple, humble life. But I had the urge to say something, an
irresistible urge to question her, to know if she too had loved him, if
she too had suffered the way he had from the same intense, secret,
enduring anguish that no one sees, no one knows about, no one
guesses, but which escapes at night, in the loneliness of a dark bedroom. I looked at her, I could see her heart beating beneath the chif-
fon wrap over the top of her dress, and I wondered whether she
with her sweet, honest face had moaned every night into her thick,
damp pillow, sobbing, her body shaking with intense frustration.

So I spoke to her very quietly, the way children shatter a gem to see
what there is inside: "If you could have seen the way Monsieur Chantal was weeping just a while ago, you would have felt sorry for him."

She shuddered: "What do you mean, he was crying?"

"Oh! Yes, he was!"

"But why?"

She seemed very moved.

"Because of you," I replied.

"Because of me?"

"Yes. He was telling me how much he loved you in the past, and how hard it was to marry his wife instead of you . . ."

Her pale face seemed to fall. Her calm, wide eyes suddenly closed, so quickly that it seemed as if they would never open again. She slipped off her chair onto the floor and collapsed, slowly, very slowly, like a scarf falling to the ground.

"Help! Help!" I shouted. "Mademoiselle Pearl has fainted."

Madame Chantal and her daughters rushed over, and while they were getting some water, a towel and some vinegar, I grabbed my hat and ran out.

I was practically leaping away, my heart pounding, my mind full of remorse and regrets. Yet sometimes, I was happy; I felt as if I had done something admirable and necessary.

"Was I wrong?" I wondered. "Was I right?" They both carried that weight in their hearts the way some people carry fragments of a bullet in a wound that has healed. Would they not be happier now? It was too late for their torture to begin again but early enough for them to remember it lovingly.

And perhaps one day next spring, touched by a moonbeam shedding its light through the branches onto the grass at their feet, they will hold each other and clasp each other's hands and remember all their repressed, cruel suffering. And perhaps, as well, that brief embrace will send a quiver of joy through their veins, a kind of joy they will have never before experienced, rejuvenating in a moment their dead hearts through the power of the rapid, divine sensation of the intoxication, the madness that gives two people in love more happiness in that brief moment of pleasure than other people may experience throughout their entire lives!

The Umbrella[†]

Madame Oreille[1] was thrifty. She knew how to count her pennies and possessed an arsenal of strict principles on how to make money.

[†] First published in Le Gaulois on February 10, 1884, and subsequently collected later that year in Les Sœurs Rondoli. The text there was dedicated to Camille Oudinot (1860–1929), the novelist and playwright, and reputedly the close friend to whom Maupassant confided the vicissitudes of his private life.

1. Maupassant gives his characters a deliberately silly surname, possibly playing on the expression "to give somebody an earful" and the French "nous échauffer les oreilles," meaning "to irritate," which is what husband and wife certainly do.

Her maid had great difficulty indeed in keeping anything for herself out of the shopping money. And Monsieur Oreille only got his allowance with extreme difficulty. They were comfortably off, however, and had no children; but Madame Oreille found it really painful to spend even the slightest amount of money.[2] She felt as if her heart would break; and every time she had to spend a large sum of money, even if it was completely unavoidable, she slept very badly indeed the following night.

"You really must be more generous," her husband constantly said to his wife. "We never spend what we earn."

"You never know what could happen," she would reply. "It's better to have too much rather than too little."

She was a small woman of about forty; she had a wrinkled face, was energetic, very neat and often irritable.

Her husband constantly complained about the hardships she forced him to endure. Some of these things had become particularly unpleasant, as they wounded his pride.

He was the head clerk at the Ministry of War, a post he kept solely to obey his wife, so he could increase the income they never spent.

For two years, he had been going to the office with the same patched-up umbrella that was the butt of jokes amongst his colleagues. Tired of their jeers, he finally demanded that Madame Oreille buy him a new umbrella. She bought one that was on sale at one of the larger department stores for eight and a half francs. When the other employees saw he had one of those umbrellas that were a dime a dozen all over town, they started making jokes again, and Monsieur Oreille suffered horribly. The umbrella was cheap. In three months, he couldn't use it any more, and everyone in the Ministry joined in the laughter. They even made up a song about it that you could hear from morning till night everywhere in the enormous building.

Oreille, exasperated, ordered his wife to get him a new umbrella covered in good silk that cost twenty francs, and to bring him the receipt as proof.

She bought one for eighteen francs and gave it to her husband.

"This should last you five years, at least," she said, her face bright red with irritation.

Monsieur Oreille, triumphant, was a big hit at the office.

One evening, when he got home from work, his wife looked anxiously at the umbrella and said:

"You shouldn't leave it closed; the elastic band will cut the silk. You have to be careful with it; I won't be buying you another one in a hurry."

2. The original French here is *pièces blanches*, the small change, or "silver," including 0.20, 0.50, 1, 2 and 5 franc coins.

She took the umbrella, unfastened it and shook it out. Then she stood dead still, stunned. There was a round hole, as large as a penny, in the middle. It had been burned by a cigar!

"What's that?" she stammered.

"What's wrong? What do you mean?" her husband replied calmly, without looking at it.

She was choking with rage now, barely able to speak:

"You . . . you . . . you burned . . . your . . . your . . . umbrella. But you . . . you . . . you must be mad! You want to bankrupt us!"

He turned around and felt the color drain from his face:

"What do you mean?"

"I mean you burned a hole in your umbrella. Look!"

She rushed at him as if she were going to hit him, then thrust the little circular hole under his nose.

He stood there, distraught, looking at the hole.

"What . . . what . . . what is that?" he stammered. "I have no idea! I didn't do anything, I swear to you, I didn't do anything. How should I know what happened to the umbrella?"

She was shouting now:

"I bet you were fooling around with it in your office, doing tricks and opening it to show it off."

"I only opened it once," he replied, "to show everyone how beautiful it was. That's all. I swear."

But she was shaking with fury, and she started one of those fights between married couples that, to a peaceful man, make the home more dangerous than being caught in the crossfire on a battlefield.

She mended it with a piece of silk cut from the old umbrella, which was a different color; and the next morning, Monsieur Oreille left, looking sheepish, with the patched-up umbrella. He put it away in the closet and tried not to think about it, the way you try to forget some bad memory.

The moment he walked through the door that evening, his wife grabbed the umbrella, opened it to examine it and stood dumbfounded when she saw it: it was a disaster, irreparable. It was covered in tiny holes, which were obviously little burns, as if someone had emptied the ashes from a lit pipe onto it. It was ruined, beyond repair.

She stared at it without saying a word, too indignant to utter a single sound. He too looked at the damage and stood dumbfounded, terrified, filled with dismay.

Then they looked at each other. Then he lowered his eyes. Then she threw the damaged umbrella in his face. Then she shouted—she had recovered her voice—filled with rage:

"Ah! You bastard! You did this on purpose, you bastard! I'll make you pay for this! You can forget about ever getting another umbrella . . ."

And the fight started all over again. After she had ranted and raved for an hour, he was finally able to explain. He swore he knew nothing about it, that it could only be the work of some malicious person or a petty act of revenge.

He was saved when the doorbell rang. It was a friend who had come to have dinner with them.

Madame Oreille told him all about it. As for buying a new umbrella, out of the question, her husband would have to do without.

The friend argued logically:

"Well, Madame, then he'll ruin his clothes, which surely cost more than an umbrella."

The little woman, still furious, replied:

"Well, he can take one from the kitchen, then; I'm not paying for another silk umbrella."

The very idea appalled Monsieur Oreille.

"Fine, then I'll resign from my job. I will! I'm not going to the Ministry with a shabby umbrella."

"Have the silk replaced on this one," their friend suggested. "That shouldn't cost very much."

"That would cost at least eight francs!" Madame Oreille stammered, exasperated. "Eight francs plus the eighteen we paid, that makes twenty-six francs! Twenty-six francs for an umbrella, why that's madness! It's insane!"

The friend, who was a middle-class man without much money, had an idea:

"Why not get your insurance company to pay for it? They pay for anything that gets burned, as long as it happens in the house."

The little woman immediately calmed down at this thought; then, after thinking for a minute, she turned to her husband:

"Tomorrow, before going to the Ministry, go to the Maternelle Insurance Company and show them what happened to your umbrella and demand they pay for it."

Monsieur Oreille recoiled.

"Never in my life would I do such a thing! It's eighteen francs down the drain, that's all. It won't kill us."

He went to work the next day with a walking stick. Fortunately, it was a nice day.

Alone in the house, Madame Oreille could not get over losing those eighteen francs. She had put the umbrella on the dining room table and walked back and forth, up and down, unable to make up her mind.

She couldn't stop thinking about the insurance company, but she could never stand up to the scornful looks of the gentlemen who would deal with her, for she was shy with strangers, blushing for the slightest reason, embarrassed whenever she had to talk to anyone she didn't know.

But losing those eighteen francs tormented her as if she had been physically wounded. She didn't want to think about it any more, yet the idea of how much she had lost kept hammering at her painfully. What should she do? Hours passed; she couldn't make up her mind. Then, suddenly, like all cowards who are stubborn, she made her decision.

"I'll go, and we'll just see!"

But first she had to make sure that the damage to the umbrella was complete, and the reason for it obvious enough to make her case. She took a match from the mantelpiece and burned a hole as big as her hand inside the umbrella. Then she carefully rolled up what remained of the silk, put the elastic around it, got her hat and shawl and walked quickly toward the insurance company's offices on the Rue de Rivoli.

But the closer she got, the slower she walked. What would she say? What would *they* say?

She looked at the numbers on the houses. There were still twenty-eight buildings to go. Good! She would have time to think. She walked slower and slower. Suddenly she shuddered. There was the door: it had a large plate with the words "Maternelle Fire Insurance Company"[3] engraved in gold. Already! She waited a moment—nervous, anxious, ashamed—walked away, came back, walked away again, then came back again.

"I really must go in," she told herself. "It's now or never."

But as she entered the building, she could feel her heart beating faster.

She went inside; it was an enormous room with counters all around. Each window had a little opening where only a man's head could be seen; their bodies were hidden.

A man walked by, carrying some documents. She stopped. "Excuse me, Monsieur," she asked shyly, "can you tell me where to go to make a claim for something that has been accidentally burned?"

He replied in a booming voice:

"Second floor, door on the left. Claims Department."

The word frightened her even more; she wanted to run away, say nothing, sacrifice her eighteen francs. But when she thought about the money, she felt a little more courageous again, and she went upstairs, stopping at every step to catch her breath.

When she got to the second floor, she saw the door and knocked.

"Come in!" someone shouted out.

---

3. Almost certainly a Maupassant variant on the real *Paternelle* insurance company.

She went inside and saw a large room where three stern men, all wearing military medals, were standing and talking.

"How can we help you, Madame?" one of them asked.

She could barely speak.

"I've come . . . I've come . . . to . . . to make a claim," she stammered.

He very politely pointed to a chair.

"Please take a seat, I'll be with you in just a moment."

And, turning back to the two other men, he picked up their conversation.

"The company, gentlemen, considers our obligation in your matter to come to no more than four hundred thousand francs. We cannot accept your claim for the additional hundred thousand francs you wish us to pay. Moreover, the appraisal . . ."

One of the others cut in:

"That will do, Monsieur, the courts will decide. This meeting is over." And they left after many courteous exchanges.

Oh! if she had dared leave with them, she would have; she would have run away, given up! But how could she? The gentleman came back, and bowed.

"And how can I help you, Madame?" he asked.

"I've come about . . . about this," she said with difficulty.

The manager looked down at the object she held out to him in bemused surprise.

Her hands trembling, she was trying to undo the elastic band. After several attempts, she finally managed it and quickly opened the tattered remains of the umbrella.

"It looks in very bad condition," he said sympathetically.

"It cost me twenty francs," she said, haltingly.

He was astonished: "Really! As much as that?"

"Yes, it was superb. I wanted you to see the state it's in now."

"Of course; I do see. But I really don't understand how it concerns me."

Anxiety ran through her. Perhaps this company didn't pay for small items.

"But . . . it's all burned . . . ," she said.

The gentleman couldn't deny it.

"Yes, I can see that," he replied.

She stood there, dumbstruck, not knowing what else to say; then, suddenly realizing what she had forgotten to mention, she quickly said:

"My name is Madame Oreille; we have insurance with the company; and I have come to be reimbursed for this damage."

And fearing an outright refusal, she quickly added:

"I'm only asking to have the silk replaced."

"But . . . Madame . . ." the manager said, looking uncomfortable, "we do not sell umbrellas. We cannot take responsibility for these kinds of repairs."

The little woman felt her self-assurance return. She had to fight. And fight she would! She wasn't afraid any more.

"I'm only asking you to pay for the repair, "she said. "I can arrange to have it done myself."

The manager seemed embarrassed.

"Really, Madame, it is a very small claim! We are never asked to offer compensation for such minor accidents. You must understand that we cannot reimburse people for handkerchiefs, gloves, brooms, slippers, all types of small items that are liable to get burned every day."

She blushed, feeling her anger rise.

"But, Monsieur, last December, one of our chimneys caught fire and caused at least five hundred francs worth of damages. Monsieur Oreille made no claim then, so it is only fair that you pay for my umbrella now."

The manager guessed she was lying.

"You must admit, Madame," he said, smiling, "it is very surprising that Monsieur Oreille would make no claim for damages amounting to five hundred francs but would now ask for five or six francs to repair an umbrella."

She was not in the least intimidated.

"Excuse me, Monsieur," she replied, "but the five hundred francs came out of Monsieur Oreille's money, while this eighteen francs is coming out of Madame Oreille's money, which is a very different matter."

He could see he had no chance of getting rid of her and that he would only be wasting his whole day.

"Would you be so kind as to tell me how the damage was done?" he asked, resigned.

She could sense victory, and began telling her story:

"This is what happened, Monsieur: I have a kind of bronze stand in our entrance hall where we put walking sticks and umbrellas. Well, the other day, I put my umbrella in it when I got home. There is a shelf where I keep my candlesticks and matches just above it, you see. I reached up to get four matches. I struck one, but it wouldn't light. So I tried another, which did light, but then went right out. The same thing happened with the third."

The manager cut in to make a joke.

"So they were government matches?"[4]

4. Since January 18, 1875, matches had been a government monopoly, but public dissatisfaction with their quality led to clandestine manufacturing in France and illegal imports, notably from Sweden.

She didn't understand.

"I suppose so, probably. Anyway, the fourth match worked and I lit my candle; then I went up to my room to go to bed. But a quarter of an hour later, I thought I smelled something burning. I'm always afraid there might be a fire. Oh! If we ever have a fire it will not be my fault! I'm a nervous wreck since the fire I told you about. So I get up, go out, look around, sniffing everywhere, like a hunting dog, and finally I see that my umbrella is on fire. A match had probably fallen into it. You can see the state it's in . . ."

The manager had made up his mind.

"How much do you think it will cost to repair the damage?" he asked.

She didn't know what to say; she was afraid to ask for a specific amount.

"You should get it repaired," she replied, wishing to appear accommodating. "I'll leave it in your hands."

He refused: "No, Madame, I could not do that. Just tell me how much you wish to claim."

"Well . . . I think . . . that . . . Monsieur, I don't want to take advantage of you, you know . . . So why don't I take my umbrella to a professional who will re-cover it in good, hard wearing silk, and I will bring you the bill. Would that be all right with you, Monsieur?"

"Absolutely, Madame, agreed. Here is a note for the cashier, who will reimburse you for whatever it costs."

He gave Madame Oreille a piece of paper; she quickly took it, got up and went out, thanking him, anxious to get away in case he changed his mind.

She walked cheerfully down the street now, looking for a fashionable umbrella maker. When she found a boutique that looked expensive, she went inside.

"I'd like the silk on this umbrella replaced; use very good silk," she said, confidently. "The very best you have. Money is no object."

On Horseback[†]

The poor couple struggled to get by on the husband's meager salary. Two children had been born since they were married, and after that, their initial financial problems had turned into one of those humiliating kinds of poverty, hidden and shameful, the poverty of a noble family still hoping to maintain its place in society.

[†] First published in *Le Gaulois* on January 14, 1883; subsequently reprinted in the second edition of *Mademoiselle Fifi* the same year. The text translated here is in the 1893 edition of this collection, the last revised by Maupassant before his death.

Hector de Gribelin had been educated in his father's manor house in the provinces by an elderly priest. They were not rich, but they managed to get by and keep up appearances.

Then, when he was twenty, they looked for a position for him, and he entered the Ministry of the Navy as a clerk, earning fifteen hundred francs a year.[1] He ran aground on this reef as anyone would who hadn't been prepared for life's harsh struggles from an early age, anyone who looks at life through a cloud, who is at a loss and doesn't know how to defend himself, people in whom unique aptitudes, specific abilities, a keen desire to fight have not been developed from childhood, anyone who never held a tool or a weapon in his hand.

His first three years in the office were horrible.

He had met a few family acquaintances again, elderly, old-fashioned people who were also poor but who lived in upper-class neighborhoods, on the gloomy streets of the Faubourg Saint-Germain;[2] and he made a group of friends.

Strangers to modern life, modest and proud, these poor aristocrats lived in the upper stories of quiet houses. From the top to the bottom of these buildings, the tenants had titles; but money was just as scarce on the ground floor as on the sixth.

Their eternal prejudices, obsession with status, fear of losing their rank, haunted these families that were once so accomplished but had been ruined by lazy men.

In this social circle, Hector de Gribelin met a young girl as noble and as poor as he was, and married her.

They had two children in four years.

For the next four years, the family was plagued by poverty; their only entertainment was walking down the Champs-Élysées on Sundays and going to the theater once or twice in the winter, thanks to complimentary tickets given to them by a colleague.

But it happened that around springtime, Hector de Gribelin's employer offered him some extra work, and he received a one-off bonus of three hundred francs.

When he brought the money home, he said to his wife:

"My dear Henriette, we must treat ourselves to something, a day out for the children, for example."

And after a long discussion they decided to have a day out and lunch in the country.

1. Exactly Maupassant's salary during his own employment at the Ministry of the Navy (see Introduction, p. xii), though the similarities between author and character end there.
2. Prosperous area near the Place de la Concorde and the Champs-Élysées.

"Well," exclaimed Hector, "just the once won't hurt; we'll rent a carriage for you, the children and the maid, and I'll hire a horse from the riding school. It will do me good."

And for the entire week, all they talked about was the day out they were planning.

Every evening when he got back from the work, Hector picked up his oldest son, sat him astride on his leg and bounced him up and down as hard as he could, saying:

"That's how Daddy will ride his horse when we go to the country next Sunday."

And all day long, the little boy straddled chairs, dragging them around the room, shouting:

"It's Daddy on horsey."

Even the maid looked at Monsieur in awe, thinking of him riding alongside the carriage on horseback; and at every meal she listened to him talk about riding, telling stories of his former adventures, when he lived with his father. Oh! He'd been to a good school, and once his legs were around a horse, he feared nothing, nothing at all!

"If they gave me an animal that's a bit difficult, I'd be really happy," he said over and over again to his wife while rubbing his hands together. "You'll see how good I am; and we can come back along the Champs-Élysées, if you like, just when everyone is coming back from the Bois de Boulogne.[3] We'll look so impressive that I hope we run into someone from the Ministry. That's all it would take to gain the respect of my employers."

The day came, and both the carriage and the horse arrived at their house at the same time. Hector went down immediately to examine his mount. He'd had straps sewn onto the bottom of his pants and was waving a riding crop that he'd bought the day before.

He lifted each of the horse's legs and felt them one after the other, patted the animal's neck, flank and hocks, felt the small of his back, opened his mouth, examined his teeth and said how old he was. And while the whole family was coming downstairs, he gave a little lecture on the theory and sport of riding in general, and this horse in particular, declaring him an excellent one.

When they were all settled in the carriage, he checked the straps on the saddle. Then, raising himself up in the stirrup, he got onto

---

3. Fashionable park on the western outskirts of Paris, the return from which—down the Champs-Élysées from the Arc de Triomphe to the Place de la Concorde—figures as a classic set piece in many nineteenth-century French novels. Maupassant captures here many of its iconic details, from the "endless black ribbons" of anonymized pedestrians to the sight of carriages and harnesses sparkling in the late-afternoon sun. This may also pay discreet homage to Flaubert (see Introduction, pp. xiii–xiv) whose *retour du Bois* in chapter 4 of *L'Éducation sentimentale* (1869) can be precisely compared to Maupassant's abbreviated description.

the horse, who started rearing under his weight and nearly threw off his cavalier.

Hector was alarmed and tried to calm him down:

"There, there, that's a good horse, you're a very good horse!"

Then, when the horse had calmed down and the rider had steadied his nerves, Hector asked:

"Ready to go?"

"Yes," they all replied together.

"Let's go!" he ordered.

And the cavalcade set off.

Everyone was watching him. He trotted in the English style, exaggerating the rise and fall. Just as he had touched the saddle, he would bounce up again, as if he were launching himself into space. He often looked as if he might crash down onto the horse's mane; and he stared straight ahead of him, his face tense and his cheeks pale.

His wife held one of the children on her lap, and the maid the other one.

"Look at Papa!" they said over and over again. "Look at Papa!"

And the two children, overexcited by the movement of the carriage, their utter joy and the fresh air, screamed and screamed. The horse, frightened by the noise, started to gallop, and as Hector was trying to control him, his hat fell off and rolled onto the ground. The coach driver had to get off the carriage to pick it up, and after he'd handed it to Hector, he called out to his wife from a distance:

"Don't let the children shout like that; the horse might bolt!"

They had the lunch they'd brought with them on the grass in the Vésinet woods.[4]

Even though the carriage driver was taking care of the three horses, Hector continually got up to see if his own needed anything; he patted him on the neck, and fed him bread, cakes and sugar.

"He's a fine trotter," he said. "He even shook me up a little at first; but you saw that I got control pretty quickly. He knows who's in charge now and won't rear any more."

They came back along the Champs-Élysées, as they'd decided to do.

That enormous boulevard was swarming with carriages. And on the sidewalks, so many people were walking along that they looked like two endless black ribbons unwinding from the Arc de Triomphe to the Place de la Concorde. Sunlight flooded down on everyone, reflecting off the polished horse-drawn carriages, the steel of the harnesses and the handles of the carriage doors and making them sparkle.

4. At the time Vésinet was a picturesque village in the curve of the Seine, west of Paris.

The mad hustle and bustle combined with an intense feeling of joie de vivre seemed to excite this crowd of people, carriages and animals. And in the distance, the Obelisk[5] rose in a golden mist.

As soon as Hector's horse had passed the Arc de Triomphe, he suddenly recovered his fieriness and started trotting fast through the rows of carriage wheels, toward his stable, in spite of all his rider's efforts to calm him down.

The carriage was far away now, a long way behind them; and when the horse reached the Palais de l'Industrie,[6] he saw an empty road, so he turned to the right and started to gallop.

An old woman wearing an apron was calmly crossing the street. She happened to be just in Hector's way; he was heading at her at top speed. Unable to control his horse, he shouted as loudly as he could:

"Hey! Look out! Watch out!"

Perhaps she was deaf, for she continued calmly on her way until she was hit by the horse, who was coming at her as fast as a train. She landed ten feet away, her dress flying up around her, after hitting her head and rolling on the ground three times.

Voices shouted:

"Stop him!"

Hector, terrified, grabbed the horse's mane and shouted:

"Help!"

One terrible jolt launched him over his horse's ears and into the arms of a policeman who had just come toward him.

In seconds, an angry, gesticulating, noisy crowd had surrounded him. One gentleman in particular seemed exasperated; he was an elderly man with a full white moustache, wearing a large round medal.

"Good Lord," he said over and over again, "if you're that clumsy, you should stay at home. You shouldn't come out and kill people in the street when you don't know how to handle a horse."

Then four men appeared, carrying the old woman. She looked almost dead, with her yellowish complexion and her hat askew, covered in dust.

"Take this woman to the pharmacy," the elderly man ordered, "and we'll go to the police station."

Hector set off, between the two men. A third policeman led his horse. A crowd followed; and suddenly, the carriage arrived. His wife leapt out, the maid was beside herself, the children were whining.

5. Standing in the very center of the Place de la Concorde since 1836, the Obelisk of the Temple of Luxor had been given to France by the then-ruler of Egypt.
6. Towards the bottom of the Champs-Élysées, on the right-hand side, opposite today's Grand Palais on what was then the Avenue Alexandre III (since 1966, the Avenue Winston Churchill), and into which the fictional Hector turns his horse. The Palais de l'Industrie was built in 1853 for the Universal Exhibition of 1855. Until it was replaced by the current Petit Palais in 1900, it was used for exhibitions, notably the annual *Salon* of painting.

Hector explained that he would be home soon and that he'd knocked a woman down, but it was nothing to worry about. So his terrified family left.

At the police station, his explanation was brief. He gave his name, Hector de Gribelin, employee at the Ministry of the Navy. And they waited for news of the injured woman. A policeman who'd been sent to find out how she was came back. She had regained consciousness but had terrible pains inside, she said. She was a housekeeper, sixty-five years old, named Madame Simon.

As soon as he learned she wasn't dead, Hector was filled with hope once more; he promised to pay her medical bills. Then he rushed over to the pharmacy.

A crowd of people stood in front of the door; the good woman sat slumped in a chair, moaning, her hands motionless, a dazed expression on her face. Two doctors were still examining her. Nothing was broken but they were concerned there might be some internal injuries.

"Are you in a lot of pain?" Hector asked her.

"Oh! Yes."

"Where does it hurt?"

"It's like I got a fire inside me."

A doctor walked over to him:

"Are you the gentleman responsible for the accident?"

"Yes, Monsieur."

"This woman must be sent to a nursing home; I know one where they can take care of her for six francs a day. Would you like me to arrange it?"

Hector was delighted, thanked him, and went home feeling relieved.

His wife was waiting for him, in tears.

"It's nothing," he said to calm her down. "Madame Simon is already feeling better; she'll be fully recovered in three days; I sent her to a nursing home; it's nothing to worry about."

Nothing to worry about!

The next day, after leaving the office, he went to ask how Madame Simon was doing. He found her eating a bowl of thick soup and looking contented. "So how are you?" he asked.

"Oh! my poor Monsieur," she replied, "nothing's changed. I feel real worn out. It ain't any better."

The doctor said they'd have to wait and see, in case there was some complication.

He waited three days, then went back. The old woman looked very well; her eyes were bright; but as soon as she saw him, she started moaning. "I can't seem to move, my poor Monsieur; I just can't. It's gonna be like this till the end of my days."

A shudder ran through Hector, right down to his bones. He asked to see the doctor. "What can I say, Monsieur," the doctor said. "I just don't know. She screams every time we try to stand her up. We can't even move her chair without her letting out heartrending screams. I have to believe what she tells me, Monsieur; I can't see what's going on inside her. Until I've seen her walking, I don't have the right to conclude she's lying."

The old lady was listening, a sly look in her eyes. A week passed; then two weeks, then a month.

Madame Simon never got out of her chair. She ate from morning till night, got fat, chatted cheerfully with the other patients, seemed to have grown accustomed to remaining motionless as if it were the well-deserved rest she had earned after fifty years of going up and down the stairs, turning over mattresses, carrying coal from floor or floor, sweeping and cleaning.

A distraught Hector went to see her every day, and every day he found her calm and peaceful.

"I can't seem to move, my poor Monsieur; I just can't," she said every time.

And every evening, Madame Gribelin, worried sick, would ask: "So how is Madame Simon?"

And he would always reply in abject despair: "Nothing's changed, absolutely nothing!"

They had to let their maid go: they couldn't afford to pay her any more. They made other economies as well; his entire bonus was used up.

Then Hector got four specialists to see the old woman. She let them examine her, test her, feel her injuries, as she maliciously watched them.

"We have to get her to walk," one of them said.

"I can't, doctor," she cried, "I just can't!"

So they all got hold of her, lifted her up and dragged her along a few steps; but she got free of them and collapsed onto the floor, making such horrific noises that they put her back into her armchair with infinite care.

They discreetly expressed their opinion but concluded there was nothing to be done.

And when Hector brought the news to his wife, she fell into a chair, muttering:

"We'd be better off taking care of her here; it would be less expensive."

He started:

"Here? In our house? Really?"

Resigned to her fate now, tears in her eyes, she replied:

"What can we do, dear. It's not my fault!"

The Baptism[†]

All of the men stood in front of the farmhouse door dressed in their Sunday finery. The May sun shed its bright light onto the apple trees in bloom, as round and sweet-smelling as immense white and pink bouquets. They formed a canopy of flowers that covered the entire courtyard. All around them, the trees continually shed a flurry of delicate petals that swayed and floated as they fell onto the tall grass where dandelions shone like flames and poppies like drops of blood.

A sow was dozing beside the dunghill; her teats were swollen and her stomach enormous; a group of little piglets swarmed around her, their tails coiled up like a rope.

Suddenly, beyond the trees on the farms, a church bell tolled in the distance. Its steely sound rose through the joyful sky with a faint, faraway call. Swallows swooped like rows of arrows through the blue skies surrounded by tall, rigid beech trees. Every now and then, the rank odor from the stables mixed with the sweet, gentle scent of apple trees.

One of the men standing in front of the door turned toward the house and shouted:

"Come on, Mélina, come on, it's ringin' now!"

He was about thirty years old. He was tall, a farmer, but not yet deformed or bent over through long hours spent working in the fields. An old man, his father, as gnarled as the trunk of an oak tree, with bulbous wrists and bowlegs, said:

"Women, you know, they ain't never ready."

The old man's other two sons started to laugh, and one of them, turning toward his older brother who had called first said:

"Go find 'em, Polyte. Or they won't be ready before noon."

So the young man went into his house.

A group of ducks had stopped near the farmers and started quacking and flapping their wings; then they slowly waddled off toward the pond.

Then a stout woman came out of the door carrying a two-month-old baby. The white strings of her tall bonnet hung down her back,

---

[†] First published in *Le Gaulois* on January 14, 1884, and subsequently reprinted the same year in *Miss Harriet*. The text there was publicly dedicated to the Impressionist landscape painter Antoine Guillemet (1843–1918), who depicted scenes from Maupassant's much-loved Normandy coast and countryside. In a review of the 1886 *Salon*, Maupassant classed Guillemet among "les maîtres incontestés" (unrivalled masters) of contemporary painting, an admiration not unrelated to the fact that he was also the writer's friend and boating companion. With its play of light on the trees and its splashes of red, white, and gold, the opening paragraph of the tale is properly pictorial in its notations, thereby reinforcing the link between writer and dedicatee.

falling over a red shawl, as bright as fire, and the babe, wrapped up all in white, rested against the wet nurse's bulging stomach.

Then his mother, a tall, strong woman, came outside on her husband's arm; she was barely eighteen, young and cheerful. Then the two grandmothers followed, as wrinkled as old apples, their backs obviously deformed, damaged over time by difficult, painstaking work. One of them was a widow; she took the grandfather's arm; he had waited in front of the door, and they walked at the head of the party, behind the child and the midwife. And the rest of the family followed behind. The youngest ones carried paper bags full of sugared almonds.[1]

The little church bell rang continuously, calling to the frail little baby with all its might. The young children climbed back up from the ditches; people came out to their gates; farm girls stood between two pails of milk they had put down on the ground to watch the Christening party go by.

And the wet nurse, triumphant, carried her living burden, avoiding the puddles of water in the hollow paths between the embankments lined with trees. And the old people walked ceremoniously, tottering along because of their age, and feeling their pain; and the young men wanted to dance and watched the girls who looked back as they passed by; and the mother and father walked solemnly, looking more serious, following this child who one day, in the future, would take their place in life and carry on their name here, the name of Dentu, known throughout the county.

They came out onto the flat open country and walked toward the fields since it was shorter than following the winding road.

They could see the church now with its pointed steeple. There was an opening just below the slate roof; and something was moving inside, quickly swaying from side to side behind the narrow window. It was the church bell, still ringing, calling for the newborn baby to come inside the good Lord's house for the first time.

A dog had started following them. They threw him some candy and he leapt around all the people.

The church door was open. Father Dentu, the priest, a tall young man with red hair, thin but strong, was waiting in front of the altar. He was the baby's uncle, one of the father's brothers. And following the rites of the Church, he baptized his nephew Prosper-César, who started to cry when he tasted the salty water.

Once the ceremony was over, the family waited at the church door while the priest took off his surplice; then they all headed back. They

---

1. Colored pale pink, pale blue, or white, these *dragées* (as they are termed in the original French) are still offered in little presentation cornets at weddings, christenings, and first communions.

walked quickly now, for they were thinking about the meal. All the little kids from the area followed, and every time they were thrown a handful of candy, there was a wild rush, pushing and shoving, and hair-pulling; and even the dog charged into the fray to get at the sweets, though they pulled his tail, his ears and his paws; but he was more determined than the children.

The wet nurse walked alongside the priest; she was rather tired and said:

"Tell me, Father, if you don't mind, do you think you could carry your nephew a bit to give me a break. I've got a pain or something in my stomach."

He took the child; the baby's white Christening robe made a large, bright mark against the priest's black cassock, and he kissed the boy, embarrassed by this light bundle, not knowing how to hold him, where to put him. Everyone started to laugh.

"Tell me, Father," one of the grandmothers called from behind, "don't it make you sad that you won't ever have one of those?"

The priest did not reply. He took great strides as he walked, staring at the little baby with his blue eyes and feeling the urge to kiss his chubby cheeks. He could restrain himself no longer and raising the child toward his face, gave him a long kiss.

"Hey, Father," his father shouted. "If you want one, all you have to do is say the word."

And they started teasing him, the way countryfolk do.

As soon as they sat down to eat, the unbridled cheerfulness of these country people burst out like a storm. The two other brothers were also going to get married; their fiancées were there; they had just come to the meal; and the guests continually made remarks that alluded to all the future generations promised by these unions.

They used rude words, very dirty words that made the blushing young women giggle and the young men double up. They banged the table with their fists, roaring with laughter. Neither the father nor the grandfather hesitated, and made risqué remarks. The mother smiled; the old women also took part in the fun, shouting out bawdy remarks.

The priest was used to this kind of coarse behavior from the countryfolk; he sat calmly beside the wet nurse, wiggling his finger in his nephew's mouth to make him laugh. He seemed surprised by the sight of this child, as if he'd never seen one before. He studied him with thoughtful attention, pensive seriousness and a feeling of affection for this fragile little person who was his brother's son, a feeling that was awakened within him, the kind of affection that was strange to him, unique, intense and somewhat sad.

He heard nothing, saw nothing: he was watching the child. He wanted to hold him in his lap again, for he could still feel, against his chest and in his heart, the sweet sensation of having just carried him back from the church. He was moved by this embryo of a man as if confronted with an ineffable mystery he had never thought about, a noble and holy mystery, the incarnation of a new soul, the great mystery of life renewed, of love awakened, of a race continuing, of humanity moving ever forward.

The wet nurse was eating, her face red, eyes shining, irritated by the little one who kept her away from the table.

"Give him to me," the priest said. "I'm not hungry."

And he held the child once more. Then everything around him disappeared, vanished; and he sat there, staring at the baby's pink, chubby face; and little by little, the warmth of that little body flowed through his blanket and the cassock and into the priest's legs, like a very soft, very chaste, very gentle caress, a wonderful caress that brought tears to his eyes.

The noise the guests made grew louder and louder, frightening. Upset by the din, the child began to cry.

Someone shouted out:

"Hey, Father, give him some of yer milk."

Everyone laughed so loud that the room shook. But the mother stood up; she took her son and carried him into the next room. She came back a few minutes later and said he was sleeping peacefully in his cradle.

So the meal continued. Every now and then, some men and women went outside into the courtyard, then came back and sat down at the table. Meat, vegetables, cider and wine filled their mouths, made their stomachs swell, lit up their eyes and made them feel intensely happy.

It was nightfall by the time they had their coffee. The priest had disappeared a long time before, but no one was surprised he'd gone.

The young mother got up to go and see if her little one was still asleep. It was dark now. She felt her way into the bedroom and stretched her arms out in front of her so she wouldn't bump into any of the furniture. But a strange noise made her stop in her tracks; she ran out, terrified, sure she had heard someone moving in the room. Very pale and trembling, she went back to where everyone was eating and told them what she'd heard. All the men jumped up, slightly drunk and threatening; the baby's father rushed ahead, carrying a lamp.

The priest was on his knees beside the cradle, sobbing, his head on the pillow next to the child.

In the Countryside[†]

The two cottages stood side by side, at the foot of a hill, not far from a small seaside town. The two farmers worked hard on the barren land to provide for their children. Each family had four little ones. The whole gang of kids gathered to play outside their front doors from morning till night. The two eldest boys were six, and the two youngest about fifteen months old; the weddings and then the births had happened almost simultaneously in both households.

When they were all together in a heap, the two mothers could barely tell whose children were whose; and the fathers were at a complete loss. The eight names went round and round in their heads, constantly getting confused; and when they wanted to call one of them, the men often had to try three times before getting the right name.

The first of the two cottages, as you came up from the seaside town of Rolleport,[1] belonged to the Tuvaches, who had three girls and a boy; the other hovel belonged to the Vallins, who had one girl and three boys.

They all got by with great difficulty on soup, potatoes and fresh air. At seven in the morning, then at noon, then at six o'clock in the evening, the housewives got their kids together to feed them, just as gooseherds round up their birds. The children were seated, according to age, around the wooden table, polished by fifty years of use. The youngest kid's mouth barely came up to the top. They got a bowl full of soggy bread mixed with the water they'd used to cook the potatoes, half a cabbage and three onions; and the whole row of them ate until they were full. The mother fed the youngest one herself.

A small piece of meat in the stew on Sunday was considered a feast; and on those days, the father took longer over the meal, saying over and over again: "I'd love to have this every day."

One August afternoon, a small carriage suddenly stopped in front of the cottages, and a young woman, who was driving the horses herself, said to the man sitting next to her:

"Oh! Look at all those children, Henri! See how lovely they are, so many of them rolling around together in the dirt like that!"

---

† First published in *Le Gaulois* on October 31, 1882. It was reprinted in *Le Voleur* on October 11, 1883, with the title *L'Enfant vendu* (The Sold Child), before being included in *Contes de la bécasse* (1883). In the latter, the version of the text translated here was dedicated to Octave Mirbeau (1848–1917), a lifelong friend of Maupassant, a fellow journalist and later an accomplished novelist, best known for his *Journal d'une femme de chambre* (1900).

1. An invented name, but derived onomastically from Normandy coastal villages near Le Havre and Fécamp such as *Rolle*ville and *Y*port.

The man did not answer: he was used to such adoring remarks, remarks that were painful and almost a reproach to him.

"I must give them a hug!" the young woman said. "Oh, how I would love to have one of them, that one there, that tiny little boy!"

She jumped down from the carriage and ran over to the children, picked up one of the two youngest, the Tuvache boy, and lifting him up in her arms, gave him lots of big kisses on his dirty cheeks, on his curly blond hair caked with dirt, and on his little hands, which he waved about trying to escape her unwanted affection.

Then she got back into the carriage and they galloped away. But she came back the next week, sat down on the ground with them, took the little kid in her arms, stuffed him with cake and gave candy to all the others; and she played with them as if she were a young girl, while her husband waited patiently in the little carriage.

She came back again; got to know the parents, and appeared every day, her pockets full of treats and money.

Her name was Madame Henri d'Hubières.

One morning, as soon as they got there, her husband got out of the carriage with her, and without stopping to talk to the kids, who knew her very well by now, she went into the farmer's cottage.

They were chopping wood for the fire so they could make the soup. They stood up, completely surprised, offered the couple a seat and waited.

Then the woman, in a broken, trembling voice, started to speak:

"My dear people, I have come to see you because I would love . . . I would love to take . . . your . . . your little boy home with me . . ."

Astonished and confused, they said nothing.

She took a deep breath and continued: "We have no children, my husband and I. We are alone . . . We would keep him . . . Would you agree to that?"

The woman began to understand.

"You wanna take our Charlot?" she asked. "Huh, no, no for sure!"

Then Monsieur d'Hubières spoke up:

"My wife hasn't explained herself very well. We would like to adopt him, but he would come back to see you. If everything turns out well, as it should, he will be our heir. If we happen to have children, he will share everything equally with them. But if he does not respond well in our care, we will give him the sum of twenty thousand francs when he comes of age, which will be immediately deposited in his name through a lawyer. And since we also wish to be considerate of you, we will pay you an allowance of one hundred francs a month, for life. Do you understand?"

The woman had stood up, furious.

"You want me to sell you our Charlot? Ah! No, that ain't the kinda thing you ask a mother! Ah! No! That would be horrible!"

The man said nothing, thinking and looking serious; but he showed he agreed with his wife by continually nodding his head.

Madame d'Hubières was distraught and began to cry; turning to her husband, sobbing, sounding like a child used to having her own way, she stammered:

"They won't do it, Henri, they won't do it."

So he tried one last time: "But, my dear friends, think of the child's future, of his happiness, of . . ."

The farmer's wife, exasperated, cut in:

"We got it, we understand, there ain't nothing to think about . . . Now get outa here, and don't let me see you round here again, or else. Like it's okay to take away a kid like that!"

Then, as she was leaving, Madame d'Hubières remembered that there were two very young children, and she asked, through her tears, with the tenacity of a willful, spoiled woman who never wants to wait for anything:

"Is the other little one yours too?"

"No, he's our neighbors' kid," Tuvache replied. "You can go 'n see them if you want."

And he went back inside his house, where they could hear his wife shouting with indignation.

The Vallins were sitting around the table, slowly eating; on a plate between them were two slices of bread spread with a tiny amount of butter.

Monsieur d'Hubières began making them offers, but more cleverly, with more innuendos, choosing his words with great care.

The two countryfolk shook their heads, a sign of refusal, but when they learned they would get a hundred francs a month, they looked at each other, glanced over at each other, very shaken up.

They said nothing for a long time, tormented, hesitant.

"What do you think, husband?" the woman finally asked.

"I say it ain't such a bad thing," he said, sounding serious.

Then Madame d'Hubières, trembling with anguish, talked to them about their child's future, his happiness, and all the money he could give them later in life.

"This allowance of twelve hundred francs," the farmer asked, "you'll swear to it in front of a lawyer?"

"But of course," replied Monsieur d'Hubières. "We can do it tomorrow."

The woman thought for a moment.

"A hundred francs a month ain't enough for us to give up the kid," she said. "He'd be workin' in a few years; we'd need a hundred and twenty."

Madame d'Hubières, who was impatiently stamping her feet, agreed at once; and since she wanted to take the child away with her then and there, she gave them a hundred francs extra, as a gift, while her husband wrote down the details. The village mayor and a neighbor were immediately called over to act as obliging witnesses.

And the young woman, radiant, carried off the howling kid, the way you come away with some priceless curio you've always longed for in a boutique.

Standing outside their door, the Tuvaches watched in silence as the child was taken away; they looked serious, regretting perhaps their own refusal.

Nothing more was ever heard of little Jean Vallin. His parents went to the lawyer's office every month to collect their hundred and twenty francs. They had fallen out with their neighbors because Tuvache's wife continually tormented them with insults, saying over and over again in every household how it was unnatural to sell your child, how it was horrible, disgusting, corrupt.

And sometimes she would hold her Charlot in her arms, showing off, shouting to him, as if he could understand:

"I didn't sell you, not me! I didn't sell you, me little one! I ain't rich, but I don't sell my children!"

And this went on every day for years and years; every day, crass allusions were shouted outside the front door so they would be heard inside the neighbor's house. Tuvache's wife ended up believing she was better than anyone else in the entire area because she hadn't sold Charlot. And everyone who talked about her said:

"I know it sure was tempting, but all the same, she did what a good mother would."

Everyone used her as an example; and Charlot, who was nearly eighteen and had been brought up with that idea, which he heard continually, believed he was better than his friends, because his parents hadn't sold him.

Thanks to the allowance, the Vallins had a rather comfortable life, which was the cause of the relentless fury of the Tuvaches, who were still very poor.

Their oldest son left to go into the army; the second oldest boy died; Charlot alone was left to work with his old father to provide for his mother and two younger sisters.

He had just turned twenty-one when, one morning, an elegant carriage stopped in front of the two cottages. A young man, wearing a gold watch chain, got down, then offered his hand to help an elderly woman with white hair.

"That one, my child, the second house," the woman said to him.

And he went into the Vallins' house as if he was going home.

His old mother was washing her aprons; his father, disabled now, was dozing near the hearth. Both of them looked up.

"Hello, Papa; hello, Mama!" the young man said.

They both stood up, frightened. The farmer's wife was so stunned that she dropped her soap into the water.

"Is it you, my boy?" she stammered. "Is it really you?"

He took her in his arms, hugged and kissed her, saying over and over again: "Hello, Mama." Meanwhile, the old man was trembling all over. "So you're come back, Jean," he said in the calm tone of voice he never lost, as if he had just seen him a month ago.

After they had got acquainted again, his parents wanted to take their son out right away, to show him off all over the neighborhood. They took him to see the mayor, the deputy mayor, the priest and the schoolteacher.

Charlot stood outside the front door of his cottage and watched him go by.

That evening, during supper, he said to his elderly parents:

"You must've been real stupid to let 'em take the Vallins' boy."

"I wouldn't've sold my child," his mother stubbornly replied.

His father said nothing.

"Ain't it a shame, being sacrificed like that," his son added.

Then Tuvache got angry:

"You ain't gonna blame us for keeping you now, are you?" he said.

"Yeah, I do blame you, 'cause you're such fools," the young man said cruelly. "Parents like you two make your kids' life a misery. I should get outa here, that's what you deserve."

The old woman was crying into her plate. She groaned while swallowing the spoonfuls of soup, spilling half of them:

"And you kill yourself to bring up kids!"

"I wish I hadn't been born instead of bein' what I am," her son said harshly. "When I saw him, that other one, my heart near stopped. I says to myself, 'See what I could've been now!'"

He stood up.

"Listen, I can tell I'd be better off not stayin' here, 'cause I'd be throwin' it up to you from morning till night, and I'd make your life a misery. I won't never forgive you for it, you know!"

The two old people said nothing, distraught and in tears.

"No, that would be too much," he continued. "I'd sooner look for a place to live my life somewhere else."

He opened the door. They heard the sound of voices. The Vallins were celebrating their child's return.

Then Charlot stamped his foot on the ground and turned toward his parents, shouting:

"Peasants!"

And he disappeared into the night.

Adieu[†][1]

The two friends were just finishing dinner. From the café window, they could see the wide avenue, crowded with people. They felt the gentle breeze that wafts through Paris on warm summer evenings and makes passersby look up, giving everyone the urge to leave, to go somewhere far, far away, where there are trees, creating dreams of moonlit rivers, glowworms and nightingales.

One of the two men, Henri Simon, gave a deep sigh:

"Ah! I'm getting old. It's sad. On evenings like this in the past, I felt a fire in my blood. Now, I only feel regret. Life goes by so quickly!"

He was already somewhat heavy, about forty-five years old and very bald.

His friend, Pierre Carnier, was slightly older, but thinner and more dynamic.

"Well, as for me, I have hardly noticed growing old. I've always been cheerful, strong and energetic, you know. Now, because we look at ourselves in the mirror every day, we don't notice how we age, for it happens slowly, steadily, and it changes our faces so gradually that the transformation is barely obvious. That's the only reason we don't die of sadness after only two or three years of time's devastating effects. It's because we don't notice them. To really see them, we'd have to not look at ourselves in a mirror for six months—Oh! Wouldn't that be a shock?

"And as for women, I do feel sorry for the poor things! All their happiness, their power, their lives depend on their beauty, which only lasts ten years.

"As for me, I grew older without noticing it; I thought I was almost an adolescent, even when I was almost fifty. I didn't feel frail in any way, so I lived my life, happy and peaceful.

"I realized I was aging in a simple and terrible way, and it overwhelmed me for nearly six months . . . then I accepted my fate.

"I had often fallen in love, as all men do, but one time in particular stands out."

I met her at the seaside in Étretat,[2] about twelve years ago, shortly after the war.[3] Nothing is nicer than the beach there in the early

---

† First published, under the pseudonym "Maufrigneuse," in the *Gil Blas* on March 18, 1884, before being included in *Contes du jour et de la nuit* (1885).

1. The French make a distinction between *Adieu*—"farewell," which has a sense of finality, and *au revoir*—"goodbye," or "until we see each other again."

2. Maupassant spent most summers at this small Normandy seaside town, though that does not imply that the anecdote is based on his own recollections.

3. This reference to the Franco-Prussian War of 1870–71 thus dates the story at approximately the time it was written, in 1884.

morning, when people go out for a swim. It's small, in the shape of
a horseshoe, framed by high white cliffs that are full of unusual
holes called the "Portes."[4] One enormous stretch of stone extends a
giantlike leg into the ocean; the one on the other side is low and
circular. A crowd of women gather on the narrow strip of this pebbly beach, transforming it into a dazzling garden of bright clothing,
set against the high rocks. The sun beats down on the shores, on
the multicolored parasols, on the bluish-green sea; and everything
is cheerful, charming, a delight to the eyes. You sit down right at
the water's edge and you watch the women swim. They come down,
wrapped in thick flannel bathrobes; then they take them off with
a lovely gesture when they reach the frothy top of the low waves;
and they walk into the water, taking quick little steps, stopping from
time to time to gasp and shiver a little when they feel the lovely,
cool water.

Very few can pass the test of the water. It is there that they are
judged, from head to foot. When they come out of the water, their
defects are particularly revealed, although seawater tightens flabby
skin wonderfully.

The first time I saw this young woman coming out of the water, I
was thrilled, infatuated. She passed the test well, very well indeed.
And then, there are some bewitching faces that suddenly strike you
and take hold of you. You sense you have found the woman you were
born to love. I felt that feeling and that shock.

I found a way to be introduced, and was soon more in love than
ever before. She devastated my heart. It's a frightening yet wonderful thing to be under a woman's spell.

It is almost torture, but at the same time, endless joy. Her look,
her smile, her hair fluttering in the wind, even the tiniest lines on
her face, the slightest movement of her features, delighted me, overwhelmed me, drove me wild. Everything about her enthralled me,
her gestures, her bearing, even the clothes she wore, which seemed
to cast a spell on me. I melted at the sight of her hat with its veil on
some piece of furniture, her gloves thrown onto a chair. The way
she dressed seemed unique. Nobody had hats like hers.

She was married, but her husband only came to join her every
Saturday and left again on Monday. He didn't matter to me. I
wasn't jealous of him at all, I don't know why; never in all my life
did anyone seem less important or warrant my concern less than
this man.

But her! I loved her so much! She was so beautiful, graceful and
young! She was youth, elegance, brightness itself! Never before had

---

4. These striking arches of the eroded cliffs are captured in the famous paintings of Étretat
by Gustave Courbet and Claude Monet.

I realized what pretty, refined, delicate creatures women are, full of charm and grace. Never before had I appreciated the seductive beauty of a curve of a cheek, the movement of a lip, the circular folds of an ear, the shape of the silly feature called the nose.

It lasted for three months, then I left for America, my heart crushed, in despair. But the thought of her stayed with me, persistent, dominant. Even at such a distance, she possessed me, just as she had owned me when I was near her. Years passed. I could not forget her. Her bewitching face remained in my heart and mind. And my love for her never died. But it was a peaceful feeling now, like the treasured memory of the most beautiful and enchanting moment in my life.

Twelve years are so little in the life of a man! You don't feel them slipping away. The years go by, one after the other, steadily but quickly, slowly yet pressing, each one long yet over so soon! And they add up so fast, leaving so few traces behind, disappearing so completely, that when you try to look back at the years gone by, you can no longer recapture them, and you can't understand how you got to be old.

I really felt that only a few months had passed since that wonderful time on the pebbly beach of Étretat.

Last spring, I was on my way to have dinner with some friends who live in Maisons-Laffitte.[5]

Just as the train was leaving, a stout lady with four little girls climbed onto the train and into my carriage. I barely noticed the mother hen; she was very big, very round and wore a hat with ribbons that framed a face like a full moon.

She was breathing heavily, out of breath from having walked so quickly. The children started chattering. I opened my newspaper and began to read.

We had just passed Asnières[6] when my neighbor suddenly asked: "Excuse me, but are you Monsieur Garnier?"

"Yes, I am, Madame."

Then she started to laugh, the happy laugh of a good woman, yet tinged with sadness.

"You don't recognize me, do you?"

I hesitated. I thought I'd seen her face somewhere before, but where? And when?

"Yes . . . and no . . . ," I replied. "I certainly know you, but I can't remember your name."

She blushed a little.

---

5. In the département of Seine-et-Oise, near St. Germain-en-Laye, ten miles west of Paris.
6. Village on the Seine, now within the western suburbs of Paris.

"Madame Julie Lefèvre."

Never had I been so shocked. In a split second, it seemed as if my life had ended! I felt as if a veil had been ripped from my eyes and I was about to witness terrifying, distressing things.

It was her! Could that fat, ordinary woman really be her? And she'd produced those four girls since I'd last seen her. And those four children astounded me as much as their mother did. She'd given birth to them; they were already big girls; they were an important part of her life. She, however, no longer counted, she, that miracle of coquettish, elegant grace. I felt it was only yesterday that I'd seen her, and this is how she looked now! Was it possible? An intense feeling of grief rushed through my heart, as well as a sense of revolt against nature itself, an illogical surge of indignation against nature's brutal, infamous acts of destruction.

I looked at her, aghast. Then I took her hand; tears filled my eyes. I cried over her lost youth. I cried for the woman who had died. For I no longer knew this fat lady at all.

She too was overcome with emotion.

"I've changed a lot, haven't I?" she stammered. "What can you do, everything changes. I'm a mother now, you see, nothing but a mother, a good mother. Adieu to the rest, that's all over. Oh! I thought you'd never recognize me if we ever saw each other again. You've changed as well, though; it took me a while to be sure it was really you. You've gone all gray! Imagine. It's been twelve years! Twelve years! My oldest daughter is already ten."

I looked at the child. And I recognized some of her mother's former charm in her, but not yet fully formed, a promise to be fulfilled, something yet to come. And I felt as if life moved by as swiftly as a passing train.

We were approaching Maisons-Laffitte. I kissed my former love's hand. All I'd been able to say to her were terribly trite words. I was too overwhelmed to talk.

That night, alone, at home, I looked at myself in the mirror for a long time, a very long time. And I finally managed to conjure up the man I had once been, picturing my brown moustache, my dark hair, and my youthful face. Now, I was old. Adieu!

A Day in the Country†

For five months, they had been planning a trip to have lunch in the outskirts of Paris to celebrate Madame Pétronille Dufour's Saint's Day.[1] Since they had been looking forward to the outing with great impatience, they got up very early that day.

Monsieur Dufour himself drove a horse-drawn cart he had borrowed from the milkman. It had two wheels and was very clean; it had a covered top supported by four iron poles with curtains attached. The curtains had been raised so they could see the countryside; only the one at the back fluttered in the wind, like a flag. Madame Dufour sat next to her husband, looking striking in an extraordinary cherry red silk dress. Behind them, on two chairs, sat their elderly grandmother and a young woman. You could just make out the head of a young man with blond hair who was stretched out at the back of the cart because there wasn't another seat.

After driving down the Champs-Élysées, they passed the fortifications at the Porte Maillot[2] and began looking at the countryside.

When they arrived at the Neuilly bridge;[3] Monsieur Dufour said: "Here we are in the countryside, at last!" and his wife, taking his lead, began making sentimental comments about nature.

At the Rond-Point de Courbevoie,[4] they were filled with admiration at the sight of the horizon in the distance. To the right was Argenteuil, with its tall belltower; above it were the Sannois hills and the mill at Orgemont. To the left, the Marly Aqueduct was outlined against the bright morning sky, and far away in the distance,

---

† First published, in two installments, in *La Vie moderne* on April 2 and 9, 1881. It was reprinted in *La Maison Tellier* (1881), the subsequent edition of which, ten years later, includes the version translated here. That it remains one of Maupassant's best-known texts is due to the fact that, under its original French title—*Une Partie de campagne*—it was made into a film in 1936 by Jean Renoir, the son of the Impressionist painter. Those interested in this particular cinematic adaptation, which is illuminating for the text itself, can find details in Robert Lethbridge, "Transpositions: Renoir, Zola, Maupassant," *Text(e)/Image*, edited by Margaret-Anne Hutton (Durham University Press, 1999), pp. 126–42. *Partie* plays on the sexual innuendoes of the term: it is not just an outing but also a licentious occasion; for example, *une partie carrée*, which involves the swapping of partners, as in Maupassant's tale.

1. Saint Pétronille is celebrated on May 31. She was a first-century Christian martyr, as was Cyprien, the name equally wittily chosen by Maupassant for Madame Dufour's husband. This tale of those "martyred on the altar of love" appropriately ends on the Rue des Martyrs.
2. The entrance to Paris at its western edge, and still today a metro stop at the end of the line.
3. Neuilly is now a western outer suburb of Paris. The bridge is where the present-day Avenue Charles de Gaulle crosses the Seine beyond the Bois de Boulogne.
4. Courbevoie was then an industrial zone on the far edge of the capital. The westward itinerary of the Dufour family can be traced on a modern map.

they could also see the wide avenue leading to Saint-Germain,[5] while opposite them, at the end of a series of hills, the freshly dug earth was evidence of the work being done to construct a new fort at Cormeilles.[6] Far away, very far away in the distance, beyond the plains and the villages, they could just make out the dark green forests.

The sun was starting to burn their faces; dust constantly got in their eyes, and on both sides of the road stretched the countryside, dirty and reeking, barren as far as the eye could see. It looked as if a plague had ravaged it, eaten away at the houses, for the skeletons of dilapidated, abandoned buildings and small cabins, unfinished because their owners couldn't pay the workmen, stood empty with four walls and no roof.

Every now and then, tall factory chimneys rose up from the barren earth, the only vegetation on those putrid fields where the spring breeze carried the smell of gasoline and shale, mixed with another odor that was even worse.

Finally, they crossed the Seine a second time, and the view from the bridge was wonderful. The river sparkled in the light; a mist rose up from it, filtered by the sun, and they felt a sweet sense of pleasure, a cooling mist that made them feel good as they drank in the cleaner air, air that had never been filled with black smoke from the factories or the disgusting fumes from the sewage works.

A passerby told them the name of the area: Bezons.[7]

The cart stopped and Monsieur Dufour began to read the attractive sign outside a cheap restaurant: *Restaurant Poulin,*[8] *fried fish in wine sauce, private dining rooms, orchards and swings.* Well, Madame Dufour! Will this do? What do you think?"

Then his wife read the sign: *Restaurant Poulin, fried fish in wine sauce, private dining rooms, orchards and swings.* She studied the restaurant for a long time.

It was a country inn, painted white, set by the roadside. Through the open door, you could see the shiny counter of the bar where two workmen sat in their Sunday best.

At last, Madame Dufour made a decision: "Yes," she said, "this is fine; and it also has nice views." The cart entered a huge field behind

5. These are all references to the panoramic landscape, as seen from Saint-Germain-en-Laye—which enjoys an elevated view of the surrounding countryside—and looking toward Argenteuil, on the Seine, famous for being a favorite setting for the Impressionist painters.
6. The Fort of Cormeilles-en-Parisis was constructed between 1874 and 1877 as part of a new plan for the defense of Paris.
7. Now an industrial zone, then a picturesque area just over a mile west of Argenteuil. Charles Daubigny's painting, *View of the Seine at Bezons* (ca. 1865) illustrates why it was a preferred boating stretch of the river for Maupassant and his contemporaries.
8. Well-known restaurant, playing on the name of its owner (Mr Poulain), situated by the bridge at Bezons; Maupassant often rented a room there during his weekend boating excursions.

the inn; it was planted with tall trees and was only separated from the Seine by a towpath.

They got out of the wagon. The husband jumped down first, then held out his arms to help his wife. The running board was supported by two pieces of iron; it was low down, so in order to reach her husband, Madame Dufour had to reveal the lower part of her leg, whose former slenderness had now disappeared into the rolls of fat on her thigh.

Monsieur Dufour, who was already getting frisky by being in the countryside, pinched her calf hard, then, taking her in his arms, heaved her onto the ground, as if she were some enormous package. She shook the dust from her silk dress, then looked around to see what kind of place it was.

She was a heavy woman, about thirty-six, radiant and attractive. She was squeezed so tightly into her corset that she breathed with difficulty; and the pressure of the corset forced her overabundant, jiggling bosom right up to meet her double chin.

Next, the young woman put her hand on her father's shoulder and jumped lightly down, by herself. The young man with the blond hair had got down by stepping on the wheel, and he helped Monsieur Dufour lift his grandmother out.

Then they unharnessed the horse and tied it to a tree; the cart dropped straight down, both shafts resting on the ground. The men took off their jackets, washed their hands in a bucket of water, then went to join the ladies, who were on the swings.

Mademoiselle Dufour was trying to swing standing up, but she couldn't get a good push off. She was a pretty girl of about eighteen or twenty, one of those young women who suddenly arouse intense desire when you come across them on the street, leaving you with heightened senses and a vague feeling of restlessness well into the night. Tall, with a small waist and broad hips, she had very dusky skin, very big eyes, very black hair. Her dress clearly outlined her curvaceous, firm body, accentuated even further by the way she used her hips in an effort to swing higher. She stretched her arms up to hold onto the ropes above her head, which made her bosom rise smoothly with every push she gave. Her hat was blown off by a gust of wind and hung down her back; and when the swing rose higher and higher, you could see her shapely legs up to the knee every time the swing came down again, and a puff of air from her skirt, more intoxicating than the scent of wine, blew right into the faces of the two men who were watching her and laughing.

Sitting on the other swing, Madame Dufour moaned in a continual, monotonous way: "Cyprien, come and push me; come and give me a push, Cyprien!" In the end, he went over to her, and after rolling up his sleeves, the way you do before getting down to some hard work, he got his wife swinging, but with very great difficulty.

Clutching the ropes, her legs straight out in front of her so they wouldn't touch the ground, she was enjoying the heady feeling of the swing going up and down. Her body was shaking, trembling continually like Jell-O on a plate. But as she swung higher and higher, she got very dizzy and was afraid. Every time she came down, she let out a piercing cry that made all the local kids come running; and further away, beyond the hedge in the garden, she could vaguely make out a line of naughty little faces, laughing and making silly faces.

A servant girl came out and they ordered lunch.

"Fried fish, sautéed rabbit, salad and dessert," Madame Dufour said proudly. "And bring us two quarts of beer and a bottle of Bordeaux," her husband said. "We'll have lunch on the grass," the young woman added.

The grandmother got emotional when she saw the owners' cat and ran after it for ten minutes, trying to coax it to come to her by calling it by the sweetest names. But in vain. The animal, doubtless secretly flattered by her attentions, came close to the good woman's hand, but stayed just out of reach and slowly circled the trees, rubbing itself against them, tail in the air and purring softly with pleasure.

The blond young man was wandering around when he suddenly shouted, "Look! There are some really great boats!" They all went to have a look. In a wooden shed hung two superb skiffs; they were as beautiful and finely worked as expensive furniture. They were side by side, as narrow and bright as two tall, slender young women, and they filled you with a desire to drift along the riverbanks covered in flowers on bright summer mornings and warm summer evenings, down the river where the trees dip their branches into the water, where the rushes are continually rustling, where the swift kingfishers fly off like flashes of blue lightning.

The whole family looked at them respectfully. "Oh yes, they really are nice!" Monsieur Dufour said solemnly. And he examined them as if he were an expert. He had often gone rowing when he was younger, he said; and when he had those things in his hands—he mimed pulling on the oars—the rest of the world disappeared. He had thrashed more than one Englishman in the past, at the Joinville[9] regattas; and he made a joke about the word "ladies" because the two mountings where the oars rested were called "the ladies," and he said that rowers could never go out without their "ladies." And he got very excited while he was showing off and stubbornly bet that in a boat like that he could effortlessly row eighteen miles-an-hour.

9. On the upper reaches of the Seine, east of Paris, where rowing competitions on the river between there and Nogent were still being held in the modern era.

"Lunch is ready," said the waitress, who appeared at the entrance to the boathouse; they all hurried off. But two young men had taken the best spots that Madame Dufour had chosen in her mind, and they were eating lunch there. They were surely the owners of the skiffs, for they were wearing boating clothes.

They were stretched out, almost lying on the chairs; their faces were tanned by the sun and their thin, short-sleeved white cotton shirts showed their bare arms, which looked as strong as a blacksmith's. They were two strapping young men, showing off their muscles, but whose every movement displayed an elasticity and gracefulness in their arms and legs that is only achieved by exercise, and is so different to the deformity that monotonous, hard work stamps on ordinary workmen.

They exchanged a quick smile when they saw the mother, then another look when they spotted the daughter. "Let's give them our spot," one of them said. "It will give us a chance to meet them." The other one immediately stood up, and holding his black and red boating cap in his hand, offered the ladies the only shady place in the garden with great chivalry. After apologizing profusely, they finally accepted, and to make the experience more befitting the countryside, they sat down on the grass, with no tables or chairs.

The two young men took their dishes and silverware a little further away and started eating again. They showed off their bare arms at every opportunity, which embarrassed the young woman a little. She even deliberately looked away, but Madame Dufour, who was rather bolder, and drawn by a woman's curiosity that might have even been desire, looked at them constantly, comparing them, with regret, no doubt, to her husband, whose naked body she found ugly.

She had rolled down onto the ground, her legs crossed in front of her, and she kept wriggling around, on the pretext that ants were crawling on her somewhere. Monsieur Dufour, in a bad mood due to the presence of the polite, friendly strangers, was trying to get into a comfortable position, but he couldn't, and the young man with the blond hair was silently stuffing himself.

"It's a really lovely day, Monsieur," the fat woman said to one of the rowers. She wanted to be friendly because they had given them their spot. "Yes, Madame," he replied. "Do you often come out to the country?"

"Oh! Just once or twice a year, to take in some fresh air. And you, Monsieur?"

"I come and sleep here every night."

"Ah! That must be very nice."

"It certainly is, Madame."

And he spoke poetically about his everyday life, so poetically that it aroused a foolish love of nature in the hearts of these middle-class people who stood all year long behind the counter of their shop, deprived of the sight of grass and thirsting for long walks in the country.

The young woman was moved and looked up at the rower. Monsieur Dufour spoke for the first time: "Now that's what I call the good life," he said. "A bit more rabbit, my dear?" he asked his wife. "No thank you, dear."

She turned toward the young men again, and pointing to their arms, asked: "Don't you ever get cold like that?"

They both began to laugh, and astounded the family with stories about the extreme exhaustion they had endured, swimming while sweating profusely and rowing in the fog at night; then they banged their chests hard to show how they sounded. "Ah! You look very strong," said the husband, who had stopped talking about the time he had thrashed more than one Englishman.

The young woman was now secretly studying them, and the blond young man had a coughing fit—his drink had gone down the wrong way—spluttering all over Madame Dufour's cherry red silk dress. She got angry and had some water brought over so she could get out the stains.

Meanwhile, it had become terribly hot. The sparkling river looked on fire, and the wine was going to their heads.

Monsieur Dufour, who gave a violent hiccough, had opened his vest and the top button of his pants, while his wife, who was suffocating, unfastened her dress one button at a time. The apprentice was happily shaking his shaggy blond hair and kept pouring himself one glass of wine after the other. The old grandmother realized she was drunk and sat up very tall and dignified. The young woman gave nothing away; only her eyes looked somewhat brighter, and her swarthy cheeks turned more rosy.

By the time they finished their coffee, they were done for. They suggested singing and each of them sang a verse, which the others applauded enthusiastically. Then they stood up, with difficulty, and while the two women, who were rather dizzy, were trying to get a breath of air, Dufour and the blond young man, who were completely drunk, started doing gymnastics. Heavy, limp, their faces bright red, they hung awkwardly from the iron rings but couldn't hoist themselves up; and their shirts were continually on the verge of flying out of their pants to flutter in the wind like flags.

Meanwhile, the two rowers had put their boats in the water and came back to politely offer to take the ladies for a ride down the river.

"Would that be all right, Monsieur Dufour?" his wife cried. "Please say yes!" He gave her a drunken look, without understanding. Then one of the rowers handed the two men fishing rods. And the hope of catching a gudgeon, a city shopkeeper's dream, made the man's

dull eyes light up; and he let the ladies do whatever they wanted
while he sat in the shade, under the bridge, his feet dangling over
the river, next to the blond young man who was asleep beside him.

One of the rowers made the sacrifice: he took the mother. "Let's
go to the little wood on the Ile aux Anglais!"[1] he shouted as he rowed
away. The other boat went more slowly. The rower was looking at
his female companion so intently that he could think of nothing else,
and a feeling had seized hold of him that left him weak.

The young woman, who was sitting in the cox's seat, relaxed,
enjoying the sweet sensation of being on the water. She felt overcome by a need not to think, a sense of tranquility in her arms and
legs, a feeling of complete luxury, as if she had been simultaneously
overcome by several forms of intoxication. She had turned bright red
and was breathing fast. The exhilaration of the wine, increased by
the torrid heat, made all the trees along the bank seem to bow to
her as she passed. A vague need for sensual pleasure and the blood
she could feel flowing in her veins rushed through her whole body,
aroused by the heat of the day; and she was also flustered by being
alone with a young man on the water, in a place that was deserted
because of the blazing heat, a young man who thought she was beautiful and whose passionate eyes seemed to kiss her skin, and whose
desire for her was as penetrating as the sun.

Their inability to speak heightened their emotion, so they looked
around at the scenery. Then he made an effort and asked her name.
"Henriette," she said. "Really!" he replied. "My name is Henri."

The sound of their voices had calmed them; they looked out at
the riverbanks. The other boat had stopped and seemed to be waiting for them. The rower shouted: "We'll meet you in the wood; we're
going to Robinson's,[2] because Madame Dufour is thirsty." Then he
leaned over his oars and took off so fast that he was soon out of sight.

Meanwhile a continual rumbling that they had vaguely heard for
some time was coming closer, fast. The river itself seemed to shudder, as if the muted sound were rising from its depths.

"What's that noise?" she asked. It was the sound of the lock closing that cut the river in two at the island. He was in the middle of
explaining it to her when they heard a bird singing from very far
away, through the noise of the waterfall. "Listen!" he said. "The
nightingales are singing during the day: that means the female birds
must be brooding."

---

1. One of the numerous small islands dotted through this part of the Seine. It is not by
chance, of course, that the name of the one singled out by Maupassant, downriver from
Bezons and otherwise known as the Île Saint-Martin, follows on from bravura at the
expense of the English.
2. A riverside inn. One authoritative scholar, Louis Forestier, has pointed out that it was
not in fact possible to go by boat from Chatou to this establishment.

A nightingale! She had never heard one before, and the idea of listening to one aroused a vision of poetic tenderness in her heart. A nightingale! The invisible witness of Juliet's meetings with her lover on the balcony; the celestial music that accompanies man's kisses, the eternal inspiration for all the languorous love stories that offer an idyllic blue sky to all the poor little tender hearts of sensitive young women!

So she was going to hear a nightingale sing.

"Don't make a sound," her companion said. "We can get off at the woods and sit down near him."

The boat seemed to glide. They could just see the trees on the island; its banks were so low that they could look deep into the thickets. They stopped. He tied up the boat. Henri helped Henriette out and they made their way through the branches of the trees. "Bend down," he said. She leaned down, and they entered a tangled web of creepers, leaves and reeds that led to a secret shelter; the young man laughed and called it "my private hideaway."

Just above their heads, perched in one of the trees that hid them from sight, the bird was still singing as loudly as he could. He trilled and warbled, then made loud, echoing sounds that filled the air before fading in the distance, floating along the river and disappearing above the plains, through the fiery silence that descended upon the countryside.

They didn't speak in case they frightened it away. They were sitting close together; slowly, Henri put his arm around the young woman's waist and gently squeezed it. She wasn't angry, but she pushed his bold hand away, and continued moving it every time he put it around her, without, however, feeling any embarrassment from his caress, as if it were something quite natural that she was pushing away just as naturally.

She was listening to the bird, enraptured. An endless longing for happiness, a sharp desire for affection rushed through her, an overwhelming desire for poetic declarations of love, and she felt her tension subsiding and her heart melting so fast that she began to cry, without knowing why. The young man was now holding her close; she no longer resisted; it didn't even occur to her.

Suddenly the nightingale stopped singing. A voice called out in the distance:

"Henriette!"

"Don't answer," he whispered. "You'll frighten the bird away."

She had no desire to reply.

They remained as they were for quite some time. Madame Dufour had sat down somewhere, for every now and then they could vaguely hear the fat woman letting out little shrieks when the other rower, no doubt, tried to fondle her.

The young woman was still crying, filled with very sweet sensations; her skin was hot and aroused in a way she had never experienced before. Henri's head rested on her shoulder; suddenly, he kissed her on the lips. She pushed him away angrily, and fell backwards, trying to avoid him. But he threw himself on top of her, covering her entire body with his. For a long time, he tried to kiss her, but she kept turning away; finally, he pressed his lips against hers. Then, overcome by intense desire, she returned his kiss, clutching him to her breast, and all her resistance crumbled, as if crushed by a very heavy weight.

Everything was still. The bird started singing again. He let out three piercing notes that sounded like a call to love, then, after a moment's silence, he continued warbling very slowly, very softly.

A gentle breeze drifted in, rustling the leaves, and deep beneath the branches, passionate sighs mingled with the nightingale's song and the soft sound of the wind in the woods.

The bird was filled with ecstasy, and his song gradually grew faster, like a fire that is lit or passion that grows stronger, a musical accompaniment to the sound of kisses beneath the tree. Then he started singing at the top of his voice, lost in frenzy. He let out long, swooning notes, great melodious tremors.

Sometimes, he rested for a while, drawing out two or three soft sounds that suddenly ended on a shrill note. At other times, he sang madly, going through all the scales, trilling, starting and stopping, like a song of wild love, followed by triumphant cries.

Then he fell silent, hearing beneath him such a deep moan that you would have thought a soul was leaving a body. The sound lasted for a time, then ended in a sob.

They were both very pale when they left their grassy bed. The blue sky looked clouded over; the burning sun had lost its glimmer to their eyes; all they felt was the solitude and the silence. They walked quickly, side by side, without speaking, without touching each other, for they seemed to have become irreconcilable enemies, as if a feeling of disgust had taken over their bodies and hatred filled their minds.

Every now and then Henriette called out: "Mama!"

They heard a lot of commotion coming from under a bush. Henri thought he saw a white petticoat quickly being pulled down over a fat calf muscle; and the enormous woman appeared, rather flustered and even redder, her eyes shining brightly and her chest heaving, standing a little too close, perhaps, to her companion. The young man must have seen something very amusing, for his face was contorted with laughter; he was doing his best to control himself, but without much success.

Madame Dufour took his arm affectionately and they headed back
to the boats. Henri, still silent, was walking ahead, alongside the
young woman; he suddenly thought he heard them give each other
a long kiss, which they tried to do quietly.

They finally got back to Bezons.

Monsieur Dufour, now sober, was waiting impatiently. The young
man with the blond hair was having something to eat before leaving the inn. The cart was harnessed in the courtyard and the grandmother had already got in; she was upset because she was afraid to
be out on the plains in the dark; the outskirts of Paris were not very
safe.

Everyone shook hands, and the Dufour family set off. "Goodbye!"
shouted the rowers. They were answered by a sigh and a tear.

Two months later, when Henri was walking along the Rue des Martyrs, he saw a sign over a door: *Dufour's Hardware Store.*

He went in.

The fat woman was even larger behind the counter. They recognized each other immediately, and after endless polite remarks, he
asked what they had been doing lately. "And Mademoiselle Henriette,
how is she?"

"Very well, thank you; she got married."

"Ah!"

He felt moved.

"But . . . who did she marry?" he asked.

"That young man who was with us, you know who I mean; he'll
be joining the business."

"Oh! I see."

He started to leave, feeling very sad, but without really knowing why.

Madame Dufour called him back.

"And how is your friend?" she asked, shyly.

"Oh, he's fine."

"Do send him our regards; and tell him to come and see us if he
happens to be in the neighborhood . . ."

She turned bright red and added: "Tell him I would be very happy
to see him again."

"Of course, I will. Well, this is goodbye then!"

"Not at all . . . see you soon, I hope."

The following year, one very hot Sunday, all the details of that
moment of love, which Henri had never forgotten, suddenly came
back to him so clearly and made him feel such desire that he went
back to their love nest in the woods all alone.

He was astonished when he went inside. She was there, sitting on the grass, looking sad, while next to her, his shirtsleeves still rolled up, the young man with the blond hair looked like some animal, fast asleep.

She turned so pale when she saw Henri that he thought she might faint. But then they began to chat quite naturally, as if nothing had ever happened between them.

But when he told her that he liked this place very much and often came on Sundays to relax, thinking about many past memories, she looked into his eyes for a long time.

"I think about it every night," she said.

Her husband yawned. "Come on, girl," he said. "I think it's time for us to get going."

The Question of Latin[†]

The question of Latin, which has been the subject of endless discussions[1] for some time now, reminds me of a story, a story from my youth.

I was finishing my studies in one of the large cities in central France, enrolled in a private school, the Robineau Institute, run by a money-grubbing principal; it was famous throughout the area for the excellent Latin courses it offered.

For ten years, the Robineau Institute had beaten the city's top lycée[2] and all the middle schools in the suburbs in all the national competitions in Latin, and its success was due to a tutor, an ordinary tutor—or so they said—named Monsieur Piquedent,[3] or rather Old Man Piquedent.

He was one of those middle-aged men whose age is impossible to guess but whose life story you understand the minute you see them. He'd started as a tutor in some educational establishment or other when he was twenty, so he could continue his own studies, to get his college degree, then even a doctorate. But he'd become so caught up in that miserable world that he'd remained a simple tutor

---

† First published in *Le Gaulois* on September 2, 1886; reprinted in the posthumous collection *Le Colporteur* (1900).

1. Raoul Frary's *La Question du Latin* (1885), the title of which is picked up in Maupassant's own (and note that his narrator is addressed as "Monsieur Raoul" [p. 81], had provoked an intensifying polemical debate in the aftermath of Jules Ferry's educational reforms of the 1880s. These had downgraded the traditional importance of Greek and Latin within the secondary school curriculum. As a former pupil of the Jesuits and a competent Latinist himself (displayed in the text's quotations), Maupassant believed in the civilizing value of the classics, though only in the case of boys from well-to-do families.

2. Senior school for fifteen-to-eighteen-year-olds aspiring to go on to higher education by passing their "baccalaureate" (p. 83).

3. The name translates loosely as "Mr. Toothache."

all his life. Yet he'd never lost his love for Latin, and it plagued him like an unhealthy passion. He continued reading the poets, prose writers and historians, interpreting them, examining them closely, writing critiques of them with the kind of perseverance that bordered on obsession.

One day, he got the idea of making all his students speak to him only in Latin and he persisted in that resolution until they were able to hold an entire conversation with him as if they were speaking their native language.

He listened to them the way a maestro rehearses the musicians in an orchestra, continually banging his ruler on the edge of his desk:

"Monsieur Lefrère, Monsieur Lefrère, you're making a grammatical mistake! Can you really not remember the rule . . . ?

"Monsieur Plantel, your sentence structure is completely French and in no way Latin. You must understand the spirit of a language. Listen, listen to me. . . ."

And this is why the students at the Robineau Institute won all the prizes at the end of the school year, all the prizes for writing, translating and speaking in Latin.

The following year, the owner of the school, a little man as cunning as a monkey—he even resembled one with his grotesque, fixed grin—the owner had printed on his brochures and advertisements, and painted on the school's main entrance:

> Specialists in Latin. Five First Prizes won in all Five Classes of the Lycée. Two Top Prizes in the National Competition of all the Lycées and Middle Schools of France.

For ten years, the Robineau Institute triumphed in the same way. Now my father, enticed by such success, sent me as a day student to this Robineau, which we called Robinetto or Robinettino, and had me take extra private lessons with Old Man Piquedent, at five francs an hour, out of which the tutor got two francs and the owner three. I was eighteen years old and in my final year.

These lessons took place in a little room that looked out onto the street. It happened that instead of making me speak Latin, as he did in class, Old Man Piquedent told me all about his problems in French. With no family, no friends, the poor man took a liking to me, and poured his heart out.

It had been ten or fifteen years since he'd spoken to anyone alone.

"I am like an oak tree in the wilderness." he said, *"Sicut quercus in solitudine."*

The other tutors repelled him; he knew no one in the city because he had no free time to form relationships.

"Not even at night, my boy, and that's the hardest for me. I dream of having a room with my own furniture, my books, all the little knick-knacks that belong to me and that no one else could touch.

"And I have nothing, nothing but my pants and frock coat, nothing, not even my own pillow and mattress! I don't have four walls where I can shut myself away, except when I come here to give you your lessons. Can you understand that, can you, a man who spends his entire life without ever having the right or the time to shut himself away, all alone, anywhere, to think, to reflect, to work, to dream? My dear boy, a key, a key to a door that you can lock, that's happiness, that and that alone would be true happiness!

"I'm here at the school during the day, in the classroom with all the little rascals running around, and at night, in the dormitory with the same rascals, who snore. And I sleep in a bed in the same room, at the bottom of two rows of those naughty boys who I have to watch over. I can never be alone, never! If I go out, the street is crowded with people, and when I'm tired of walking, I go into a café and that too is also full of people smoking and playing billiards. I'm telling you, it's hell."

"Why didn't you do something else, Monsieur Piquedent?" I asked.

"What could I have done, my dear boy?" he cried. "I'm not a shoemaker, or a carpenter, or a hat maker or a baker or a hairdresser. All I know is Latin, that's all, and I don't even have any degrees that would allow me to make any real money from it. If I had my doctorate, I'd make one hundred francs for the twenty cents I get now; and I'd most likely not do as good a job because my title would be enough to maintain my reputation."

Sometimes he said:

"The only peaceful moments I have in life are the times I spend with you. But don't worry; you won't lose out. I'll make up for it by having you speak twice as much as the others during lessons."

One day, I decided to be bold and offered him a cigarette. At first, he stared at me in astonishment, then he glanced over at the door:

"But what if someone came in, my boy?"

"Well then, let's smoke over by the window," I said.

And we went and leaned over the window that looked out over the street, hiding the thin, hand-rolled cigarettes in our cupped hands.

Opposite us was a laundry: four women wearing flowing white blouses pressed the clothes that were laid out in front of them with a hot, heavy iron that gave off steam.

Suddenly, another young woman, a fifth, came outside, carrying a basket on her arm that was so heavy she bent under its weight; she started giving the clients their shirts, handkerchiefs and sheets. She stopped at the door, as if she were already tired, then she looked up, smiled when she saw us smoking, and with her free hand, blew us a kiss—the mischievous kiss of a carefree working girl; then she walked slowly away, dragging her feet.

She was about twenty, petite, rather thin, pale, pretty with a girlish expression, smiling eyes and messy blond hair.

Old Man Piquedent was moved.

"What a terrible job for a woman!" he murmured. "Real donkey's work."

He was touched by the poverty of the working classes. His heart was full of sentimental, democratic ideas, and he spoke of the exhaustion of the poor, quoting Jean-Jacques Rousseau[4] in a voice choked with emotion.

The next day, we were leaning out of the same window when the same young woman saw us. "Hello there, schoolboys!" she said in a funny little voice, thumbing her nose at us.

I threw her a cigarette and she started to smoke it right away. Then the four other laundresses rushed out to the door, stretching out their hands, so they could each have one as well.

And every day, the friendship grew between the women workers on the sidewalk and the lazybones in the school.

Old Man Piquedent was really funny to see. He was terrified of being caught, for he could have lost his job, and he made shy, laughable gestures, an entire sign language of lovers on the stage, to which the women replied with a hail of kisses.

A perfidious idea was growing in my mind. One day, as we were going into the study room, I whispered to the old tutor:

"You won't believe this, Monsieur Piquedent, but I met the little laundress! You know who I mean, the one with the basket, and I spoke to her!"

He was quite worried by my tone of voice and asked:

"What did she say to you?"

"She told me . . . good Lord . . . she told me . . . that she thought you were really nice . . . Actually, I think . . . I think . . . that she's a little in love with you . . ."

I watched the color drain from his face. "She's making fun of me, no doubt. That kind of thing doesn't happen to a man my age."

"Why not?" I said, sounding serious. "You're very attractive!"

When I realized he was moved by my ruse, I didn't insist.

But every day, I pretended to have run into the young woman and to have talked to her about him; I was so convincing that he ended up believing me, and he started blowing passionate kisses to her.

4. With his pioneering views on child-centered education, Jean-Jacques Rousseau (1712–1778) was widely regarded, in his concern for the working classes, as a precursor of Socialism. His *Social Contract* (1762) advocates democratic principles with which Maupassant had little sympathy, mocking them here.

Then, one morning, on my way to school, I actually did run into her. I went straight up to her as if I'd known her for ten years.

"Hello, Mademoiselle, How are you?"

"Very well, Monsieur, thank you."

"Would you like a cigarette?"

"Oh! Not out in the street."

"Well, you can smoke it at home."

"In that case, thanks very much."

"Tell me, Mademoiselle, do you realize that . . ."

"What, Monsieur?"

"The old man, my teacher . . ."

"Old Man Piquedent?"

"Yes, Old Man Piquedent. So you know his name?"

"Well, really! What about him?"

"He's in love with you, that's what!"

She started laughing like a madwoman and cried: "You're joking, right?"

"No, it's no joke. He talks to me about you during our lessons. I bet he wants to marry you."

She stopped laughing. The idea of marriage makes all young women go serious. "You're joking, right?" she said again, incredulous.

"I swear it's the truth."

She picked up the basket she'd put down at her feet. "We'll see about that!" she said.

Then she walked away.

As soon as I got inside the school, I took Old Man Piquedent to one side:

"You must write to her; she's crazy about you."

So he wrote a long letter, sweet and tender, full of loving words and innuendos, metaphors and comparisons, academic ideas and compliments, a true masterpiece of ludicrous elegance. And he gave me the letter to deliver to the young woman.

She read it with the utmost seriousness, with emotion, then whispered:

"He writes so well! You can tell he's very educated! Is it true he wants to marry me?"

"Good Lord!" I replied boldly. "He's crazy about you."

"Well then, he must invite me to dinner on Sunday on the Ile des Fleurs."

I promised she would be invited.

Old Man Piquedent was very moved by everything I told him about her.

"She loves you, Monsieur Piquedent," I added, "and I think she's a decent young woman. You mustn't seduce her and then abandon her!"

"I too am a decent person, my boy," he replied firmly.

I didn't have any particular plan, I admit that. I was playing a practical joke, a schoolboy's prank, nothing more. I had guessed the old tutor's naïveté, his innocence and his weakness. I was having fun without ever wondering how it would all turn out. I was eighteen, and I'd had the reputation at school of being a sly joker for some time.

And so it was agreed that Old Man Piquedent and I would get a carriage to the dock at Queue-de-Vache[5] where we would meet Angèle, and I would take them out in my boat, for I was a rower back then. I would take them to the Ile des Fleurs, where all three of us would have dinner. I had imposed my presence on them so I could really enjoy my triumph, and the old man, accepting my offer, proved that he actually was crazy about her by risking his job that way.

When we arrived at the dock, where my boat had been tied up since morning, I noticed an enormous red parasol through the tall grass, or rather above the reeds on the riverbank; it looked like some monstrous poppy. Beneath the parasol, the little laundress was waiting for us, in her Sunday best. I was surprised; she was really very nice, despite being rather pale, and she was gracious, even though she looked rather common.

Old Man Piquedent took off his hat and bowed to her. She reached out her hand and they looked at each other, without saying a word. Then they got into my boat and I took the oars.

They sat side by side in the back of the boat.

The old man spoke first.

"Now this is lovely weather for a boat ride."

"Oh, it is!" she said softly.

She put her hand into the water, letting her fingers trail along its surface, which brought up a little trickle of clear water, like a shard of glass. It made a soft sound, a gentle lapping, all along the boat.

When we were in the restaurant, she found her voice again and ordered her meal: some fried fish, chicken and some salad; then she showed us around the island, which she knew extremely well.

She was cheerful, coquettish and even rather mocking.

Until dessert, no one brought up the subject of love. I had treated them to some champagne and Old Man Piquedent was drunk. She was a little tipsy too and called him "Monsieur Piquenez."[6]

Suddenly, he said: "Mademoiselle, Monsieur Raoul has told you how I feel."

She became as sober as a judge. "Yes, Monsieur!"

---

5. All the places mentioned in this paragraph are Maupassant's inventions in a comic vein: "Queue-de-Vache" translates as "Cow's tail;" the "Île des Fleurs" parodies a pastoral idyll.
6. Translates as "Mr. Hurts your nose."

"Do you feel the same way?"

"You never answer questions like that!"

He was choking with emotion and continued: "Well then, do you think that the day might come when you could like me?"

She smiled: "Silly thing! You're very nice."

"Well then, Mademoiselle, do you think that at some later date we could . . . ?"

She hesitated, just for a second; then she asked, her voice trembling: "Are you asking to marry me? Because I'd never any other way, you know?"

"Yes, Mademoiselle!"

"Well then, that's fine, Monsieur Piquenez!"

And that is how these two scatterbrains promised to marry each other, thanks to a naughty schoolboy. But I didn't believe it was serious; neither did they, perhaps.

She thought of something and hesitated:

"You know I have nothing, not a penny."

He stammered, for he was as drunk as Silenus:[7]

"But I've got five thousand francs saved up."

"Then we can buy a business," she cried triumphantly.

"What kind of business?"

"How would I know? We'll have to see. With five thousand francs, you can do a lot. You don't want me to come and live with you at the school, do you?"

He hadn't thought that far ahead and he became very perplexed: "Buy some kind of business?" he stammered. "That wouldn't do at all! All I know is Latin!"

She thought about it as well, going over in her mind all the professions she aspired to.

"Couldn't you be a doctor?"

"No, I haven't got the qualifications."

"A pharmacist?"

"Not that either."

She let out a cry of joy. She'd found it. "Well, then we'll buy a grocer's shop! Oh, what a stroke of luck! We'll buy a grocer's shop! Not a big one, you know; five thousand francs won't go that far."

He rebelled: "No, I can't be a grocer . . . I'm . . . I'm . . . I'm too well known . . . All I know is . . . is . . . Latin, just Latin . . ."

But she thrust a glass of champagne to his lips. He drank it and fell silent.

---

7. In Greek mythology, Silenus was tutor to Dionysis, the god of wine. As the chief Satyr, he was represented as a hairy old man with a huge paunch and always drunk.

We got back into the boat. It was dark out, very dark. I could see, however, that they had their arms around each other and kissed several times.

It was a catastrophe. Our little escapade was discovered and Old Man Piquedent was fired. And my father, furious, sent me to finish my final year at the Ribaudet boarding school.

I took my baccalaureate six weeks later. Then I went to Paris to study law. I didn't go back to my hometown for two years.

At the bend of the Rue du Serpent,[8] a shop caught my eye. The sign said *Piquedent: Exotic Products.* Then underneath, to explain to the less well educated: *Grocery.*

"*Quantum mutatus ab illo!*"[9] I cried.

And he looked up, walked away from his client and rushed toward me with outstretched arms.

"Ah! My good friend, so you're here, my good friend! What a stroke of luck! Real luck!"

A beautiful but ample woman quickly came out from behind the counter and threw her arms around me. I barely recognized her, she had grown so fat.

"So, things are going well?"

Piquedent had gone back to weighing something:

"Oh! Very well, very well, very well indeed. I had three thousand francs profit this year!"

"What about your Latin, Monsieur Piquedent?"

"Oh! Good Lord. Latin, Latin, Latin. A man can't live on Latin alone!"[1]

---

8. A Parisian street of such a name has never existed. It is a variant on the Rue de la Serpente, which denotes a curve rather than a more symbolically freighted snake.
9. "How the man has changed since then!"
1. One of the satirical targets of this tale is the recently deceased (February 16, 1885) Jules Vallès, whose radical left-wing views had been expressed in his largely autobiographical 1881 novel, *Le Bachelier.* In *Le Gaulois* on January 4, 1882, Maupassant had quoted its dedication "To those who, suckled on Greek and Latin, have died of hunger." Monsieur Piquedent's final words clearly echo this inversion of the saying "Man cannot live on bread alone."

Tales of War

Boule de Suif[†][1]

For several days in a row, the remnants of the defeated army had been passing through the city.[2] They were no longer a unified regiment, just a scattered group of soldiers. The men had long, dirty beards, uniforms in shreds, and advanced listlessly, without a flag, without a regiment. All of them looked dejected, exhausted, incapable of coming up with a single idea or plan. They simply kept marching through habit, dropping with exhaustion the moment they stopped. Some were peace-loving men who had lived a life of ease and were then called up to serve, hunched over under the weight of their rifles. Some were eager volunteers, easily frightened but full of enthusiasm, as ready to attack as to flee. And among them were a scattering of soldiers in their red breeches, the wreckage of a division that had been overwhelmingly defeated in a great battle. Gloomy artillerymen marched along with these various foot soldiers, and every now and again they were joined by the shiny helmet of some dragoon who could barely keep up with the faster pace of the ordinary soldiers.

Bands of snipers and guerrillas with heroic-sounding names—"Avengers of the Defeat," "Citizens of the Tomb," "Dealers of Death"—also passed by, looking like bandits.

Their leaders, former fabric or grain merchants, tallow or soap sellers, soldiers by chance, were appointed officers because of their wealth or the length of their moustaches; they were heavily armed, wore flannel uniforms with stripes indicating their rank, and spoke in booming voices, discussing campaign plans and bragging that they alone could support a dying France on their shoulders. Yet they

† First published in 1880, in the collective volume *Les Soirées de Médan* (see Introduction, pp. xxi–xxii).
1. While this nickname translates literally as "Ball of Soot," the colloquialism has connotations of plumpness, sustained in the story by the "appetizing" qualities of the character. Attempts to capture this in English have ranged from "Butterball" to "Dumpling"; it can be argued that none quite catches the sense of the nickname, which is why modern translations of the title and its eponymous heroine often retain the original French.
2. Rouen, the capital of Normandy. Having been defeated by the Prussians in a skirmish on 4 December 1870, and in anticipation of a force of 25,000 enemy soldiers marching toward the city, the French decided to withdraw from it without further fighting. The Prussians made their triumphal entry into Rouen on December 6.

sometimes feared their own soldiers, criminals who were often excessively brave but basically debauched looters.

People were saying that the Prussians were about to enter Rouen.

For the past two months, the National Guard had cautiously sent reconnaissance scouts into the nearby woods; they sometimes shot their own sentries and were ready for action whenever a small rabbit stirred under the brush. They had all gone back home. Their weapons, their uniforms, all their murderous gear that had formerly terrified everyone up and down the main road for miles around, all of this had mysteriously disappeared.

The last of the French soldiers had just managed to cross the Seine, making their way through Saint-Sever and Bourg-Achard to reach Pont-Audemer; and bringing up the rear, in between two orderlies, their general walked in despair, unable to do anything with this mass of stragglers, dismayed by the great debacle of a nation used to victory yet disastrously beaten despite its legendary bravery.

Then a profound sense of calm, a silent and terrifying waiting game descended on the town. Many portly middle-class men had grown soft thanks to their easy lives; they anxiously awaited the arrival of their conquerors, quaking at the thought that their roasting spits or large kitchen knives might be considered weapons.

Life seemed to have stopped; the shops were closed, the streets silent. Sometimes, one of the people who lived there would quickly walk down the road, huddling against the buildings, frightened of the silence.

The anguish of waiting made them wish the enemy would actually arrive.

On the afternoon of the day after the French troops had left, a few lancers—who seemed to have come out of nowhere—sped through the city. Then, a little later, a dark mass of bodies came down from Saint Catherine's Hill, while two other waves of invaders appeared on the roads from Darnetal and Boisguillaume. The advance guard of these three battalions arrived at the square in front of the Town Hall at exactly the same time. Then the German army poured in from every nearby street, their battalions pounding along the sidewalks with their harsh, rhythmical steps.

Orders shouted in foreign, guttural voices rose up through the houses that seemed empty and dead; but behind closed shutters, people watched out fearfully for these victorious men, masters over their town, their destinies and their lives, determined by the "rules of war."

The townspeople sat in their darkened rooms, overwhelmed with the kind of fear brought about by such cataclysmic events, huge upheavals that destroy the land, that neither wisdom nor strength can overpower. For the same feeling emerges every time the established order is overthrown, when no one feels safe any more, when everything that protected the laws of nature or of man is suddenly at the mercy of ferocious, reckless brutality. An earthquake that buries an entire population beneath their crumbling homes; a river that floods, sweeping away farmers and the dead bodies of their cattle alike, along with beams ripped from the roofs of houses; or the glorious army massacring anyone who fights back, taking the rest as prisoners, pillaging in the name of the Sword and thanking their God to the sound of cannon fire—all terrifying plagues that destroy any belief in eternal justice, any confidence we are taught to have in protection from Heaven and human rationality.

Small detachments of troops knocked at every door before disappearing inside the houses. Occupation followed the invasion. The conquered were obliged to be gracious to their conquerors.

After a while, once the initial terror had worn off, a new sense of calm returned. In many families, a Prussian officer sat down to eat with them. Sometimes he had good manners and showed pity for France out of politeness, expressed his repugnance at having participated in the war. People were grateful for such feelings; and, of course, his protection might be needed one day. By handling him properly, they would perhaps have fewer men they had to feed. And why upset someone you were completely dependent on? To behave in such a way would be more reckless than brave. And recklessness was no longer one of the faults of the good people of Rouen, as it had been during their heroic resistance in the past, which had made their city famous. In the end, people told themselves that it was quite permissible to be polite to the foreign soldiers inside their houses, as long as they did not appear friendly in public, a supremely rational idea in keeping with French manners. Outside the house, they were strangers, but inside, they happily chatted together, and the Germans stayed longer and longer each evening, to keep warm by the fire in the living room.

Little by little, the city started looking like itself again. The Frenchmen still hardly ever went out, but the Prussian soldiers milled about in the streets. Moreover, the officers of the Blue Hussars, who arrogantly dragged their great deadly weapons along the pavement, did not seem to be significantly more disdainful of the ordinary people than the French cavalry officers who had drunk in the very same cafés the year before.

And yet there was something in the air, something subtle and strange, an intolerable foreign atmosphere, like a bad smell that spreads, the stench of invasion. It filled the houses and public squares, changed how the food tasted, gave everyone the impression they were

on a journey, very far away, a journey to the land of dangerous, barbaric tribes.

The conquerors demanded money, a lot of money. The townspeople always paid; besides, they were rich. But the richer a Norman
merchant becomes, the more he suffers from having to sacrifice anything, any small part of his fortune, watching it pass into someone
else's hands.

However, six or seven miles south of the city, following the course
of the river as it flowed toward Croisset, Dieppedalle or Biessart,[3]
sailors and fishermen often hauled out the swollen corpse of some
German in uniform, beaten to death with a wooden shoe, or
stabbed, or his head bashed in by a stone, or someone who had been
pushed into the river from the top of a bridge. The sludge of the
river buried these obscure acts of vengeance, savage but justifiable,
unknown acts of heroism, silent attacks, more dangerous than
battles fought in broad daylight and without any hint of glory.

For the hatred of the Foreigner always arms a few Brave Men who
are prepared to die for an Idea.

In the end, even though the invaders had subjugated the city with
their strict discipline, they had not carried out any of the horrific
deeds they were rumored to have committed throughout their long,
triumphal march, and so the inhabitants grew bolder: the need to
trade arose again in these merchants' hearts. Some of these men had
important commercial dealings in Le Havre, which was occupied by
the French army,[4] so they wanted to try to get there by traveling overland to Dieppe[5] where they could get a boat to the port.

The German officers they had got to know used their influence
with the General in charge to get them a permit to leave.

And so, a large carriage pulled by four horses was hired for the
journey and ten people signed up to travel with the owner. They decided to leave one Tuesday morning, just before daybreak, to avoid
attracting a crowd.

For some time now, the frost had hardened the ground, and that
Monday, around three o'clock, great dark clouds descended from the
north, and it snowed steadily all that evening and continued snowing throughout the night.

---

3. These are the first riverside villages downstream from Rouen. The mention of Croisset,
   in particular, is gestural: Maupassant's readers would not need to have been reminded
   that Flaubert, his publicly acknowledged mentor, had his home there (see Introduction,
   pp. xiii–xiv).
4. Of the towns north of the Seine, only the commercial port of Le Havre resisted the Prussian attack; this explains the determination to reach it in order to be able, if necessary, to
   escape across the Channel to England.
5. What was then mainly a fishing port, Dieppe is some forty miles due north of Rouen.
   The more direct route to Le Havre would have taken the travellers through an area
   whose fate was still uncertain, whereas the Prussians had established their occupying
   forces north of the Seine.

At four-thirty in the morning, the travelers gathered in the court-yard of the Hôtel de Normandie, where they were supposed to meet the coach.

They were still very sleepy and shivered beneath their blankets. It was difficult to see in the darkness, and the way everyone was bundled up in heavy winter clothing made them all look like fat priests in their long cloaks. But two of the men recognized each other; a third one went up to them and they started chatting: "I'm bringing my wife along," one of them said. "So am I." "Me too." "We're not going to come back to Rouen," the first one said, "and if the Prussians make it to Le Havre, we're going to head for England." They were all very much alike, so they all had the same plans.

Meanwhile, the horses were not being harnessed. A little lantern carried by a stable boy appeared every now and then from a dark door-way only to disappear at once into another. The horses' hooves stamped on the ground, muted by the dung and straw, and a man's voice talking to the animals and swearing could be heard inside the building.

The faint jingle of bells meant they were fixing the harness; the soft sound soon became a clear, continuous ringing that followed the rhythm of the horse's movement, sometimes stopping, then suddenly continuing once more, accompanied by the dull thud of a horseshoe striking the ground.

The door suddenly closed. Not a sound could be heard. Everyone was freezing and had stopped talking: they simply stood there, stiff from the cold.

An endless blanket of white snow shimmered as it fell to the ground; it made it impossible to see any shapes, covering everything in a powdery layer of frost. And in the great silence of the calm city buried beneath the winter's snow, all that could be heard was the strange rustling of the falling snow, more a feeling than a sound, the mingling of invisible particles that seemed to fill the sky and cover all the world.

The man reappeared with his lantern, pulling a sad-looking horse along by a rope, who didn't seem eager to follow. He placed him beside the beam, secured the ties and walked slowly all around to make sure the harness was properly fitted, for he could only use one hand as he was carrying the lantern in the other. When he was going inside to get the next horse, he noticed all the motionless travelers, already covered in snow. "Why don't you get into the carriage?" he asked. "At least you'll be out of the snow."

They hadn't thought of that, of course, and rushed into the carriage.

The three men helped their wives inside and then got in themselves; then the other hesitant people covered in snow took their seats without exchanging a word.

Their feet sank into the straw that covered the floor.

The women had brought along little copper foot-warmers filled with some sort of chemical fuel; they lit them and spoke quietly for some time, explaining the advantages of having them, repeating things to each other that they already knew for quite some time.

Finally, six horses were harnessed to the carriage instead of four because of the weight of the load. A voice from outside asked: "Is everyone in?" A voice from inside replied: "Yes." And they set out on their way.

The carriage moved slowly, very slowly.

The wheels sank in the snow; the entire carriage groaned with a muted, creaking sound; the animals slipped, huffed and puffed, and the coachman's enormous whip snapped continuously, flicking in all directions, curling up and unfolding like some slim serpent, sharply stinging the horses' flanks which instantly tensed and made them strain to go faster.

But day was gradually breaking. The delicate snowflakes that one of the travelers, a native of Rouen, had described as a stream of cotton wool, no longer fell. A murky light filtered through heavy, dark clouds, making the countryside look even more dazzling white; sometimes they could see a row of tall trees covered in ice, sometimes a cottage with a roof laden with snow.

Inside the carriage, in the bleak light of daybreak, everyone looked at each other with curiosity.

Right at the back, in the best seats, Monsieur and Madame Loiseau, wine distributors from the Rue Grand-Pont,[6] sat opposite one another, dozing.

A former assistant to an employer who had lost everything, Loiseau had bought the business and made his fortune. He sold very bad wine at very low prices to retailers in small villages and was known amongst his friends and acquaintances as a sly devil, a true Norman, tricky and jovial.

His reputation as a rogue was so well established that one evening, at the city's administrative offices, Monsieur Tournel, a writer of fables and songs, a local legend thanks to his subtle, biting wit, had suggested to some of the ladies who seemed about to doze off that they play a game called "Loiseau the Thief."[7] The term immediately caught on and spread rapidly through the local area, then into the heart of the city, and had made everyone roar with laughter for an entire month.

6. This street, which leads from the Cathedral square to the present-day Pont Boïeldieu, was filled with the most luxurious shops in Rouen. Maupassant thereby identifies his passengers with the most prosperous and bourgeois area of the city.
7. Wordplay on his name: *L'oiseau* is a "bird" and *voler* means both "to fly" and "to steal."

In addition, Loiseau was well known for playing tricks of all kinds and telling jokes, sometimes funny and sometimes mean, and no one could ever mention him without immediately adding: "That Loiseau is just a scream!"

He was short and stocky, with a round belly and ruddy complexion beneath his long, graying moustache.

His wife was tall, sturdily built, confident, and had a high-pitched voice; she made snap decisions and was the one who organized and kept the accounts of the business, which her husband ran with great joy.

Next to them was Monsieur Carré-Lamadon,[8] a more dignified gentleman belonging to a higher social class, who was considerably wealthy and the owner of three cotton mills, an officer of the Legion of Honor[9] and a member of the Conseil général.[1] During the entire reign of the Empire,[2] he had been the leader of the benevolent opposition party, solely in order to make himself more money by recruiting others to the cause he was fighting, using what he called "polite weapons." Madame Carré-Lamadon, who was much younger than her husband, brought solace[3] to the officers from the best families who were garrisoned at Rouen.

Sitting opposite her husband, she looked adorable: very pretty, petite, curled up in her fur coat, as she glanced sadly at the terrible condition of the inside of the carriage.

The people next to her, the Count and Countess Hubert de Bréville, bore one of the most ancient and noble names in Normandy. The Count, an elderly gentleman of aristocratic appearance, attempted to emphasize, by artificial means, his natural resemblance

8. Like the others in this tale, his name is invented. But this particular character almost certainly has a real-life model: Augustin Pouyer-Quertier (1820–1891), one of Rouen's most prominent political figures who would go on to become Minister of Finance, in the government of Adolphe Thiers, having been one of the latter's chief representatives in negotiations leading to the 1871 Treaty of Frankfurt which formally completed the national humiliation of the Franco-Prussian War. He was known in Rouen as the owner of a cotton factory and president of the Chamber of Commerce, as well as being mayor of Fleury-sur-Andelle. Flaubert writes contemptuously about him in letters to Maupassant and, in 1879 (the very year *Boule de suif* is being composed), talks about developing a fictional work whose protagonist would be based on this quintessentially self-important bourgeois.

9. The highest French civil honor awarded for services to the State.

1. See *The Protector*, p. 17, note 2.

2. The Second Empire (1852–70), during which parliamentary opposition to the quasi-dictatorship of Napoleon III was nominal only, at least until 1867.

3. The original French reads "demeuraient la consolation" of the young officers; together with the detail that she is beautiful and "much younger than her husband," Maupassant subtly suggests a behavior undermining social respectability. This is later reinforced when we are told that "the pretty Madame Carré-Lamardon" experiences some ambivalence when imagining herself "being taken by force by the officer" (p. 110), and favorably compares the Prussian with other men about whom she is "an expert" (p. 109).

to Henri IV,[4] who, according to a proud family legend, had gotten one of the de Bréville ladies pregnant and so had made her husband a count and governor of the province.

A colleague of Monsieur Carré-Lamadon in the Conseil général, Count Hubert was head of the Orléanist Party[5] in the region. The story of his marriage to the daughter of an insignificant shipowner from Nantes had always remained a mystery. But as the Countess looked very aristocratic, was second to none as a hostess, said even to have been loved[6] by one of the sons of Louis-Philippe, every member of the nobility invited her to their parties; and her *salon*[7] was considered the best in the country, the only one where traditional values of gallantry were still respected, and the most difficult to be accepted into.

The de Brévilles' fortune consisted entirely of property and was worth, or so it was said, five hundred thousand francs a year.[8]

These six people sat in the back of the carriage, the place reserved for the landed gentry, confident and strong men and women, the honest members of society who were Religious and had Principles.

Through a strange coincidence, all the women were seated on the same side, and the Countess had two additional neighbors: good nuns who wore long rosary beads and whispered their *Paters* and *Aves*. One of them was old, with a face so marked and pitted by smallpox that she looked as if she had been hit by machine gun fire. The other nun was scrawny but had a rather pretty yet sickly-looking face and her chest sounded as if she had consumption, her strength sapped by the all-devouring faith that creates martyrs and eccentric visionaries.

Everyone was looking at the man and woman who sat opposite the two nuns.

4. King, initially just of Navarre but subsequently of France (1589–1610), famed for his energy and political skill, bringing an end to the Wars of Religion and establishing the authority of the monarchy across the country. But he was also notorious for his womanizing and insatiable sexual appetite, fathering at least fifteen children with a succession of wives and mistresses alike. This is the allusion here.
5. At this time, there were two sets of claimants to the French throne, abolished by the Revolution of 1789 but restored in 1814: the House of Orléans, the last representative of which (Louis-Philippe, King of France, 1830–48), had been ousted by the 1848 Revolution; and the Bourbons, otherwise known as the "Legitimists," descended from Charles X whose reign (1824–30) had been terminated by the Revolution of 1830.
6. The original French suggests that one of the four sons (surviving into adulthood) of Louis-Philippe had been her lover, rather than simply, and euphemistically, "in love" with her. Maupassant once again delights in inventing scabrous back-stories behind respectable facades and aristocratic pretensions so as to more effectively highlight the hypocrisy of these characters' condemnation of his heroine's moral turpitude. He also suggests that political allegiances have little to do with politics.
7. Ladies of the upper class held regular, exclusive, and early evening gatherings to which friends and prominent people were invited. These were called *salons* because they were held in the reception rooms of their splendid houses.
8. While it is difficult to calculate the modern equivalent, the size of such a fortune can be gauged by comparing it to a contemporary civil servant's annual salary of something like 2,000 francs.

The man was famous: Cornudet, *le démoc*,[9] who inspired fear in the hearts of respectable people. He had been dipping his red beard into the beer glasses of every republican café for the past twenty years. He and his friends had already spent the rather large fortune that had been left to him by his father, a former confectioner, and he was waiting, impatiently, for the rise of the Republic so he could finally take the place he rightly deserved after consuming so many revolutionary glasses of beer. On September 4,[1] perhaps as a result of a joke, he believed he had been appointed Prefect; but when he tried to take up his post, the office workers who had taken over the place refused to recognize his authority and he was forced to leave. Despite all of this, he was a rather likable young man, inoffensive and helpful, and he threw himself into defending Paris with unequaled passion. He had holes dug in the plains, cut down all the young trees in the neighboring forests, scattered traps along all the roads and then, satisfied with all his preparations, as soon as the enemy was getting closer, he hightailed it back to the city. He now thought he would be more useful in Le Havre, where new entrenchments were going to be needed.

The woman, one of the kind known as "courtesans," was famous for her youthful sexuality and voluptuous figure, which had earned her the nickname "Butterball."[2] Short, curvaceous, extremely chubby, with puffy fingers pressed in at the joints like rows of little sausages, she had smooth, glowing skin and an enormous bosom that bulged over her low-cut dress. She was quite delectable and extremely popular; her fresh youthfulness made her very attractive. Her face was like a red apple, a peony bud about to blossom; thick eyelashes cast a shadow over her magnificent dark eyes. She had shiny little baby teeth, and her enchanting mouth with its slender, moist lips was made to be kissed.

She also possessed, or so people said, other inestimable qualities.

As soon as she was recognized, the righteous women started whispering, and at once the words "prostitute" and "shameful hussy"

9. Short for *démocrate*, designating a militant of the Second Republic proclaimed in 1848 and informed by the principles of true democracy, an ideal for which Maupassant had no sympathy—as is self-evident from his portrait of Cornudet. The latter was based on Charles Cord'homme, who was the second husband of Louise de Maupassant, the writer's aunt. He was infamous in Rouen for his loud-mouthed opposition to the Second Empire, his subsequent participation in the revolutionary Commune of 1871 and his endless electoral campaigns advocating universal suffrage.
1. The date of Napoleon III's abdication as Emperor, when republicans thought their time had come.
2. The heroine of *Boule de suif*, is also modelled on a real person: Adrienne Legay, a Rouen prostitute who had the same nickname as Elisabeth Rousset. Details of her life, ending in suicide in 1892, can be found in the Pléiade edition of Maupassant's *Contes et nouvelles*, I, 1304–05. See also Richard Bolster, "The Patriotic Prostitutes of Maupassant: Fact or Fantasy?" *French Studies Bulletin* 51 (1994): 16–17; and (but in French only), this same scholar's "*Boule de suif*: une source documentaire?" *Revue d'histoire littéraire de la France* 84 (1984): 901–908.

were murmured so loudly that she looked up. She then gave each of her neighbors such a provocative, scathing look that a great silence immediately followed, and every one of them lowered their eyes, except for Loiseau, who was enticed and salaciously watched her every move.

But soon the conversation among the three women started up again, since the presence of this young woman suddenly made them bond as friends, almost intimate acquaintances. For they believed they had to create a pact, as it were, based on their dignity as honest wives, to stand together against this shameless hussy.

For legitimized love always takes the high moral ground in the face of its more licentious sister.

The three men, bound by an instinct for conservatism at the sight of Cornudet, began talking about money in a contemptuous way that was insulting about the poor. Count Hubert listed the damage the Prussians had done to him, the losses suffered due to the cattle he'd had stolen and the lost harvest, but with the smug confidence of a noble lord who was a millionaire ten times over who would recoup these losses within a year. Monsieur Carré-Lamadon, an experienced cotton manufacturer, had had the foresight to send six hundred thousand francs to England, a nest egg for the disastrous time he anticipated he might one day face. As for Loiseau, he had made sure he'd sold all the cheap table wine left in his cellars to the French Military Supply Corps, so the state owed him a great deal of money, which he hoped to be paid in Le Havre.

All three of them looked at each other in a friendly way. Despite their different social status, they felt themselves united in the brotherhood of money whose members could always hear the sound of gold coins jingling whenever they reached into their pockets.

The carriage was traveling so slowly that by ten o'clock in the morning, they had barely gone twelve miles. The men got out three times to walk up the hills on foot.

Everyone was starting to get anxious, for they were meant to be having lunch at Tôtes,[3] but now they feared they wouldn't even make it there by evening. They were all gazing outside in the hope of finding an inn along the road when the carriage sank in a bank of snow; it took two hours to dig it out.

They were getting hungrier and hungrier and more and more disheartened. Not a single cheap restaurant or wine shop could be found: the approach of the Prussians and the starving French troops that passed through had frightened everyone away, so they had closed all their stores.

3. Village nearly halfway between Rouen and Dieppe, and possibly another gesturing toward Flaubert who had evoked it in Part I of *Madame Bovary* (see also p. 99, note 2).

The gentlemen rushed out to see if they could find some food in the farms along the road, but they couldn't even get any bread: the wary farmers hid all their reserves out of fear of being pillaged by the soldiers who, having nothing whatsoever to eat, grabbed anything they could find by force.

At around one o'clock in the afternoon, Loiseau announced that he definitely felt a big hollow in his empty stomach. Everyone had been suffering the same way for a long time, and the desperate need to eat continued to grow, killing all conversation.

Every now and again, someone yawned; someone else did the same almost immediately, and each one of them, in turn, according to his character, sophistication and social status, either noisily opened his mouth or modestly held a hand to cover the gaping hole, their breath escaping in a kind of mist.

Butterball bent down several times, as if she were looking for something under the folds of her dress. She hesitated for a moment, looked at her companions, then calmly sat up straight again. Everyone looked pale and tense. Loiseau said he would pay a thousand francs for a hunk of ham. His wife began to make a gesture as if to protest, then stopped herself. She always found it painful to hear talk about money being wasted and could not really understand how anyone could make jokes about such a thing. "I don't feel well at all," said the Count. "How could I have not thought of bringing along some food?" Everyone reproached himself in the same way.

Cornudet, however, had a bottle of rum; he offered it around: everyone coldly refused. Only Loiseau accepted and took a few sips, thanking him when he handed back the bottle: "That's good, it really is, it warms you up and makes you forget about being hungry." The alcohol put him in a good mood and he suggested they follow the words of a sailor's song: to eat the fattest passenger. This indirect allusion to Butterball shocked the respectable people in the carriage. No one said a word; only Cornudet was smiling. The two good nuns stopped saying their rosary and sat very still, their eyes looking stubbornly down, their hands hidden inside their wide sleeves, doubtlessly offering back the suffering Heaven had sent them as a sacrifice.

At three o'clock, they found themselves in the middle of flat, open country as far as the eye could see, without a single village in sight. Butterball quickly bent down and pulled out a large basket covered in a white cloth from under her seat.

First she took out a small earthenware plate, then a small silver cup and finally an enormous dish that contained two whole chickens cut into joints preserved in aspic, and everyone could see many other wonderful things wrapped up in the basket—pâtés, fruit, sweets—enough food to last three days without having to depend on stopping at inns.

The necks of four bottles peeked out from between the packages of food. She picked up a chicken wing and began to daintily nibble at it, along with one of the rolls known in Normandy as a "Regency."

Everyone was staring at her. Then the smell of chicken filled the carriage, causing their nostrils to flare, their mouths to water and their jaws to contract in pain. The scorn the ladies felt toward this young woman grew savage: they would have liked to kill her or throw her out of the carriage into the snow, her, her silver cup, her basket and all her food.

Loiseau's eyes devoured the dish of chicken. "Well, well! I can see that Madame thought ahead more than we did. Some people always manage to think of everything." She looked up at him: "Would you like some, Monsieur? It's difficult to go without food all day." He bowed. "Well, to tell the truth, I wouldn't say no. I'm at the end of my tether. All's fair in love and war, don't you think, Madame?" And looking all around him, he added:

"At times like this, it's very lucky to find such generous people."

He spread some newspaper over his trousers so he wouldn't stain them and using the pocketknife he always carried, helped himself to a chicken thigh covered in aspic, tore a piece off with his teeth and chewed it with such obvious satisfaction that a great sigh of distress from the others filled the carriage.

Then Butterball, in a soft, humble voice, asked the nuns if they would like to share her food. They both accepted immediately, and, without looking up at her, began eating quickly, after mumbling a few words of thanks. Cornudet did not refuse his neighbor's offer, and, along with the nuns, they made a kind of table by spreading the newspaper out over their knees.

Mouths opened and closed, chewing, swallowing, greedily devouring the food. In his corner of the carriage, Loiseau was hard at work, and quietly urged his wife to follow his example. She resisted for a long time, but after her stomach contracted painfully, she gave in. Her husband, assuming his most polite manner, asked whether their "charming companion" would mind offering a little bit to Madame Loiseau.

"But of course, Monsieur," she replied with a kind smile, as she held out the dish.

There was an awkward moment when the first bottle of Bordeaux was opened: there was only one drinking cup. It was wiped clean before being passed to the next person. Only Cornudet, undoubtedly out of gallantry, drank from the same moist spot as his neighbor.

Surrounded by people who were eating, virtually choking on the wonderful smell of food, the Count and Countess de Bréville and Monsieur and Madame Carré-Lamadon suffered the hideous form of torture that has long been associated with the name of

Tantalus.[4] Suddenly, the young wife of the cotton manufacturer let out such a great sigh that everyone turned to look at her; she was as white as the snow outside; her eyes closed, her head dropped forward: she had fainted. Her husband, extremely upset, begged everyone for help. No one knew what to do until the older nun supported the sick woman's head, placed Butterball's drinking cup in between her lips and made her take a few sips of wine. The pretty young woman stirred, opened her eyes and said in a faint voice that she felt quite well again now. But to prevent her from fainting again, the nun made her drink a whole glass of wine. "She's just hungry, that's all," she said.

Butterball then blushed terribly from embarrassment. "Good Lord," she stammered, looking at the four travelers who had had nothing to eat, "if I presumed to offer these ladies and gentlemen . . ." She stopped herself, fearing their contempt. But Loiseau spoke up: "Well, in such situations we are all brothers and should help each other. Come now, ladies, don't stand on ceremony: accept her offer, for goodness sake! Are we even sure we'll find somewhere to spend the night? At the rate we're going, we won't even make it to Tôtes before noon tomorrow." They hesitated; no one wanted the responsibility of being the first to say yes. But the Count solved the problem. He turned toward the frightened, chubby girl and using his most sophisticated manner said: "We accept most gratefully, Madame."

The first step was the most difficult. Once the Rubicon was crossed,[5] they didn't hesitate to tuck in. The basket was emptying but still had much food left: there was a pâté de foie gras, a lark pie, a piece of smoked tongue, some Crassane pears,[6] a square Pont L'Evêque[7] cheese, some petits fours and a cup full of pickles and pickled onions, because Butterball, like all women, adored raw vegetables.

It was impossible to eat this young woman's food without speaking to her. And so they began to chat, reservedly at first, then, as she seemed more well mannered and better educated than they had imagined, more openly. The de Bréville and Carré-Lamadon ladies, who were very sophisticated, became quite gracious but tactful. The Countess especially displayed the kind of amiable condescension typical of an upper-class nobility that cannot be stained by contact of any kind with lesser beings, and could not have been more charming. But the stocky Madame Loiseau, who had the soul of a policeman, remained surly, speaking little and eating a great deal.

4. The mythical figure condemned by Zeus to a life of constant hunger and thirst.
5. Expression derived from Caesar's fateful decision, in defiance of orders from Rome, to cross the small river of that name separating Italy from transalpine Gaul.
6. The Crassane late-ripening winter pear is available from December to March, reputedly having a finer flavor and texture than any other variety; as well as being seasonally accurate, it is also appropriate for this story that it was first developed in France in 1849 by a nurseryman from Rouen.
7. Since the thirteenth century, Pont l'Evêque (near Lisieux, in the Calvados region of Normandy) has been famous for its cheeses.

Naturally, they talked about the war. They told terrible stories about the Prussians, gave examples of the courageous qualities of the French; and all these people who were running away, paid homage to the bravery of the others. Soon they began talking about themselves, and Butterball, with great emotion, with that warm way of speaking that young girls sometimes have to express their natural passions, explained how she had left Rouen: "At first, I thought I could stay on there," she said. "I had my house, well stocked with food, and I preferred to feed a few soldiers than to run away heavens knows where. But when I saw those Prussians, I just couldn't stand it! They made my blood boil with anger and I cried with shame all day long. Oh! If only I were a man, you'd see! I watched them from my window, the fat swine with their spiked helmets, and my maid had to grab my hands to stop me throwing furniture down at them. Then some of them came and said they would be lodging with me, so I lunged at the throat of the first one I saw. It's no more difficult to strangle them than anyone else! I would have finished him off if I hadn't been pulled away by the hair. After that, I had to go into hiding. And so, when I saw the opportunity, I left, and here I am now."

Everyone congratulated her warmly. She rose in the estimation of her companions, who had not demonstrated such courage; and as Cornudet listened to her, he smiled with the kindly, approving smile of an apostle, the same smile a priest might wear when he hears a devout person praising God, for the long-bearded democrats have the monopoly on patriotism just as priests have on religion.

When it was his turn, he spoke dogmatically, stressing his words in a way he had learned from the proclamations hung on the walls of the city every day, and he concluded with a choice morsel of oratory in which he eloquently crushed Louis-Napoleon, that "villain, Badinguet."[8]

Now Butterball got angry, for she was for Bonaparte.[9] She blushed redder than a cherry and stammered in indignation: "I would have liked to see what you would have done in his place. Oh, yes! What a mess you would have made! *You're* the ones who betrayed him! No one would have any choice but to leave France[1] if we were governed

---

8. The name of the worker who lent his clothes to Louis-Napoleon (the future President [1848–51] and self-styled Napoleon III [1852]) so he could escape from prison in 1846. The derogatory nickname was used throughout the years of his Second Empire by opponents of his 1851 *coup d'état.*

9. Louis-Napoleon was the nephew of Napoleon Bonaparte and exploited this to assert the imperial and hereditary legitimacy of his regime.

1. After his abdication, Napoleon III was initially imprisoned by the Prussians before leaving (in March 1871) for exile in England, where he died in 1873. There is therefore a slight anachronism here: although a captive at the château of Wilhelmshöne, near Cassel, at the time the story supposedly takes place, at the end of 1870, the former Emperor had not actively left France as the character's indignation suggests. But, of course, the readers of *Boule de suif* in 1880 enjoyed the benefit of hindsight.

by scoundrels like you!" Cornudet, impassive, kept smiling in a superior, disdainful way, but they could sense that insults would soon be exchanged, so the Count intervened. He managed to calm the angry young woman down, but not without difficulty, stating firmly that all sincerely held opinions should be respected. But the Countess and the manufacturer's wife, who felt the irrational hatred of all respectable people toward the Republic, along with the instinctive tenderness that women cherish for despotic, ostentatious governments, felt drawn, in spite of themselves, to this prostitute who was full of dignity and whose feelings so closely resembled their own.

The basket was empty. Ten people had easily emptied it; their only regret was that there had not been more. The conversation continued for a while, though everyone was more distant since they had finished eating.

Night was falling; it was getting darker and darker, and the cold, which everyone felt more as they were digesting their food, made Butterball shiver, in spite of her plumpness. So Madame de Bréville offered her her foot-warmer, which had been refueled several times since the morning, and she accepted at once, for her feet were freezing cold. Madame Carré-Lamadon and Madame Loiseau gave theirs to the two nuns.

The driver had lit his lanterns. They cast a bright glow over the mist that hovered above the horses' sweating rumps, and on the snow along both sides of the road that seemed to uncurl beneath the moving reflection of the lamps.

It was so dark inside the carriage that it was impossible to see anything. Then suddenly, something moved between Butterball and Cornudet, so Loiseau peered into the darkness and thought he saw the man with the long beard pull quickly away as if he had been hit, silently but hard.

Several small lights appeared on the road ahead. It was Tôtes. They had been traveling for eleven hours, fourteen if you counted the four times they had stopped to let the horses rest and eat some oats. They entered the town and stopped in front of the Hôtel du Commerce.[2]

The coach door opened! A well-known sound made all the travelers shudder: it was the harsh noise of scabbards being dragged along the ground. Then someone shouted something in German.

---

2. Maupassant's description is based on the Hôtel du Cygne at Tôtes, the very old coaching inn which, since the seventeenth century, was positioned on the mail route to Dieppe to allow horses to rest or be changed. Flaubert had stayed there while writing the pages of *Madame Bovary* devoted to Tôtes, as had Maupassant himself. The address of the refurbished Auberge du Cygne is now, appropriately, 5, Rue de Guy de Maupassant. The name given in the story, the Hôtel du Commerce, anticipates the *commercial* transaction whereby the heroine sells herself. Maupassant was familiar with nineteenth-century French slang, in which *le commerce (amoureux)* designates sexual intercourse.

Even though the carriage was standing still, no one got out, as if they expected to be massacred the moment they did. Then the driver appeared with one of the lanterns in his hand, lighting up the inside of the carriage with its two rows of frightened faces, their mouths gaping open and their eyes wide with surprise and terror.

In the bright light, they could see a German officer standing next to the driver. He was a tall young man, excessively thin and blond, stuffed into his uniform like a woman in a corset, wearing his flat, shiny cap tilted to one side, which made him look like a bellboy in some English hotel. His extremely long, straight moustache tapered off at both ends into a single strand of blond hair so thin that it seemed endless, and the weight of the moustache seemed to drag down the corners of his mouth, pulling at his cheeks and making his lips droop.

He spoke the French of the Alsace region; in a dry voice, he asked the passengers to come out of the carriage: "Vill you please to come out, ladies und gentlemen?"

The two nuns were the first to obey, with the compliance of religious women used to always being submissive. The Count and Countess were next, followed by the manufacturer and his wife, then Loiseau, who pushed his larger, better half in front of him. Once out of the carriage, Loiseau said: "Hello, Monsieur," more out of a feeling of prudence than politeness. The officer, as insolent as anyone in a position of power, looked at him without replying.

Butterball and Cornudet were the last to emerge, even though they were seated next to the door; they looked serious and dignified in the face of the enemy. The plump young woman tried to control herself and seem calm; the democrat twisted his long, reddish beard in anguish, his hand trembling. Both of them wanted to maintain their dignity, understanding that in such situations every individual represents his country; and, equally revolted by the servility of their companions, Butterball tried to look prouder than her neighbors, the respectable women, while Cornudet, feeling it was up to him to set an example, maintained an attitude of sabotage, which was his mission ever since he had decided to travel.

They went into the enormous kitchen at the inn and the German asked them to show him their travel passes authorized and signed by the General in command; these gave the names, description and profession of each traveler. He studied them carefully, comparing the people in front of him with their details.

Then he said briskly: "Es gut," and walked out.

They could breathe again. They were still hungry; supper was ordered. It would take half an hour to prepare, so while two servants started getting it ready, everyone went to see their rooms. They were all located along a long corridor; a glazed door with a ¢ ("cent") sign on it—the bathroom—was at the very end.[3]

They were about to sit down to eat when the owner of the inn appeared. He was a former horse trader, a heavy, asthmatic man who was always wheezing, coughing and clearing his throat. His father had given him the name Follenvie.[4]

"Mademoiselle Elisabeth Rousset?" he asked.

Butterball shuddered and turned around:

"Yes, that's me."

"Mademoiselle, the Prussian officer wishes to speak to you at once."

"To me?"

"Yes, if you are Mademoiselle Elisabeth Rousset."

She was flustered, thought for a second, then declared firmly:

"He may want to see me, but I'm not going to see him."

Everyone gestured all around her, talking and trying to understand why the officer had asked to see her.

"You are wrong, Madame," said the Count, going over to her. "Your refusal could cause a great deal of trouble, not just for you, but for all of us as well. You must never oppose the people who are strongest. Your agreement to this request could not be dangerous in the least: it is undoubtedly to do with some detail that's been overlooked."

Everyone agreed with him. They begged her, pressured her, lectured her and ended up convincing her, for everyone feared the complications that might result from her stubbornness.

"I will do this for your sakes," she finally said, "for you!"

The Countess took her hand:

"And we thank you for that."

She left the room. They waited for her to come back before sitting down at the table. Each of them was upset at not having been summoned instead of this impulsive, short-tempered girl and mentally prepared the platitudes they would say in case they were the next to be called.

Ten minutes later, she returned, staggering, bright red and terribly upset. "That bastard!" she stammered. "That bastard!"

Everyone pressed her to find out what had happened but she wouldn't say a word, and when the Count became insistent, she replied with great dignity: "No, it has nothing to do with any of you: I cannot tell you."

3. In certain hotels, the bathroom door used to be indicated by the number 100 because, in French, the word for hundred (*cent*) phonetically replicates "smell" (*sent*). The translation here transposes the pun using the (s)cent sign.
4. The caricatural name translates as "Mad Desire."

So everyone sat down at the table where a large soup tureen gave off the aroma of cabbage. In spite of the incident, the meal was enjoyable. The cider was good, so the Loiseaus and the nuns had some; they didn't want to spend a lot of money. The others ordered wine; Cornudet asked for a beer. He had an unusual way of opening the bottle and getting a head on the drink; he leaned the glass on its side and studied it, then raised it up beneath the light to take a good look at its color. As he drank, his long beard, which was about the same color as the drink he liked so much, seemed to tremble lovingly; his eyes squinted so he could keep his beer mug in sight, and he looked as if he were fulfilling the unique purpose for which he had been born. It was almost as if he had established in his mind an affinity between the two great passions in his life—Lager and the Revolution—and he obviously could not drink the one without thinking of the other.

Monsieur and Madame Follenvie were seated at the very end of the table. The gentleman, groaning like a broken-down train, wheezed too much to be able to speak while eating; his wife, however, talked incessantly. She shared all her impressions of when the Prussians first arrived in great detail, how they behaved, what they said, and how she loathed them—in the first place because they cost her money, but also because she had two sons in the army. She spoke mainly to the Countess, flattered at being able to have a conversation with a grand lady.

Then she lowered her voice and started talking about more delicate subjects, though her husband interrupted her from time to time: "You really should be quiet, Madame Follenvie." But she paid no attention to him.

"Yes, Madame, these Germans do nothing but eat potatoes and sausages or sausages and potatoes," she continued. "And don't think they are clean. Oh, no! With all due respect, they leave garbage everywhere. And if you could see them doing maneuvers all day long for days on end: there they all are in some field, marching forward, marching backward, turning this way, turning back. If only they could plow the fields or go back home and work on fixing the roads! But no, Madame, these soldiers do nothing worthwhile. Why should we poor people have to feed them so that they can learn how to kill us! I'm just an old woman with no education, it's true, but when I see them wearing themselves out marching about from dawn to dusk, I say to myself: 'When there are people who make so many discoveries that are helpful, why should others go to so much trouble to do harm! Really, isn't it horrible to kill people, whether they are Prussian, or English or Polish or French?' If we take revenge against someone who has done us harm, it's considered wrong and we're punished for it; but when they hunt down our boys with rifles as if they're game, that's just fine, because they award medals to whoever kills the most? You see? I'll never understand that!"

Cornudet spoke up:

"War is barbarous if you attack a peaceful neighbor, but a sacred duty if it is a matter of defending your country."

The old woman lowered her head:

"Yes, when you act in self-defense, that's another matter; but wouldn't it perhaps just be better to kill all the kings who make war to amuse themselves?"

Cornudet's eyes blazed with passion as he said:

"Bravo, Madame citizen."

Monsieur Carré-Lamadon was deep in thought. Although he was an enthusiastic admirer of famous military men, the great common sense of this countrywoman made him think of the wealth that could be brought to a country by so many idle and consequently expensive hands, by so much unproductive strength, if only they were used to work on great industrial projects that would take centuries to complete.

Loiseau stood up, went over to the innkeeper and said something to him in a low voice. The big man laughed, coughed, spluttered; his enormous belly wobbled with joy at his neighbor's jokes, and he bought six casks of Bordeaux wine from Loiseau to be delivered in the spring, after the Prussians had gone.

Everyone was completely exhausted, so as soon as supper was over, they all went to bed.

Now Loiseau, who had noticed certain things, sent his wife to bed. He then looked through the keyhole and listened by the door to try and uncover what he called "the secrets of the corridor."

After about an hour, he heard a rustling sound and quickly had a look; there was Butterball, looking rounder than ever in a blue cashmere peignoir trimmed with white lace. She was holding a candle in her hand and walking toward the bathroom at the end of the corridor. Then one of the doors at the side opened a little, and when she came back after a few moments, Cornudet, suspenders holding up his pants, followed her. They spoke to each other quietly, then stopped. Butterball seemed to be firmly refusing to allow him into her room. Unfortunately, Loiseau couldn't hear exactly what they were saying, but toward the end, he managed to catch a few words as they were speaking more loudly. Cornudet was extremely insistent.

"Really, you're being stupid. What difference should it make to you?" he said.

She looked indignant.

"No, my dear," she replied. "There are certain times when you just don't do such things, and in this place, it would be shameful."

He did not understand at all and asked her why. Then she got really upset and spoke even louder:

"Why? You really don't understand why? When there are Prussians in this inn, perhaps even in the room next door?"

He said nothing. The patriotic modesty of this harlot who refused to allow herself to be touched because the enemy was close by must have awakened his own failing dignity within his heart, for he just gave her a kiss and slipped back into his own room.

Loiseau, who was quite aroused, walked away from the keyhole, pranced around the room, tied a handkerchief around his head as a kind of sleeping cap, lifted up the sheet where the hard carcass of his wife was laying, woke her with a kiss and whispered: "Do you love me, my darling?"

The entire house fell silent. But soon a sound was heard from somewhere, perhaps the cellar or maybe the attic, the sound of someone snoring loudly, a steady, regular, muted series of snores like a kettle bubbling over. Monsieur Follenvie had fallen asleep.

They had decided to leave early in the morning, so everyone was in the kitchen by eight o'clock, but the carriage, its roof covered in snow, stood by itself in the middle of the courtyard, with no horses and no driver. They looked for the coachman in the stables, the storage houses, the sheds, all in vain. So the men decided to go out and find him, and they left. They found themselves in the town square; the church was at the far end with low houses on either side; they could see some Prussian soldiers. One of them was peeling potatoes. Another was cleaning a barbershop. Yet another, a soldier with a very long beard, was hugging a little kid who was crying, rocking him on his lap to try to calm him down; and the fat countrywomen, whose husbands were "in the army at war," gestured to their obedient conquerors to make them understand what tasks they had to do: chop the wood, ladle soup over the bread, grind the coffee; one of them was even washing his hostess's laundry, as she was so old she could hardly move.

The Count, astonished, questioned the verger who was coming out of the presbytery. The old church mouse replied: "Oh! Those men aren't so bad: they're not Prussians, apparently. They're from far away, I don't exactly know where they come from, but all of them have left a wife and children behind; they don't like war, not at all!

"I'm sure that people are crying over them back home just as we are here, and the war is causing terrible problems for them as much as for us. It's not too bad here at the moment, because they aren't doing any harm and they're working as if they were in their own homes. You see, Monsieur, the poor have to help each other . . . It's the noblemen who make war."

Cornudet, indignant at finding such amiable relations between the conquerors and the conquered, walked away, preferring to stay inside the inn. "They are trying to repopulate the place," Loiseau joked. But Monsieur Carré-Lamadon spoke seriously: "They are repairing the damage they've done." Meanwhile, the coachman was nowhere in sight. They finally found him in the village café, having a friendly chat with the officer's orderly.

"Weren't you told to harness the horses at eight o'clock?" Carré-Lamadon asked.

"Yes, but I got another order after that."

"What other order?"

"Not to harness them at all."

"Who gave you such an order?"

"The Prussian officer."

"But why?"

"I have no idea. Go and ask him. If I'm told not to harness the horses, I don't harness the horses. That's all there is to it."

"And the officer himself gave you that order?"

"No, Monsieur: it was the innkeeper who passed the message on to me."

"When was that?"

"Last night, just as I was about to go to bed."

The three men went back to the inn, very worried.

They asked for Monsieur Follenvie, but the servant replied that because of his asthma, he never got up before ten o'clock. He had expressly forbidden them to wake him earlier unless there was a fire.

They wanted to see the officer, but this was absolutely impossible, even though he was staying at the inn. Monsieur Follenvie was the only person authorized to speak to him about matters to do with civilians. And so they waited. The women went back to their rooms and kept themselves busy with this and that.

Cornudet sat down alongside the tall fireplace in the kitchen, beside a blazing fire. He had a small table and a bottle of beer brought to him, and he smoked his pipe. The pipe was appreciated by all democrats almost as much as it was by him, as if it served the country by serving Cornudet. It was a superb meerschaum pipe, admirably seasoned, as black as its owner's teeth, but sweet-smelling, curved, shiny, fitted to his hand and complementing his appearance. He sat there, very still, sometimes staring at the flames in the fireplace, sometimes at the froth that crowned his beer; and every time he took a drink, a look of satisfaction spread across his face and he would run his long thin fingers through his long greasy hair as he sucked the foam up from his moustache.

Loiseau, pretending he wanted to stretch his legs, went out to sell some wine to the local merchants. The Count and the manufacturer started talking politics. They were imagining the future of France. One of them believed in the Orléans, the other in some unknown saviour, a hero who would emerge when everyone was on the verge of despair: a du Guesclin,[5] a Joan of Arc, perhaps? Or another Napoleon I? Ah! If only the Prince Imperial Louis-Napoleon[6] wasn't so young! Cornudet listened to them, smiling like a man who can predict the future. The smell of his pipe wafted throughout the kitchen.

At ten o'clock, Monsieur Follenvie appeared. They quickly asked him all sorts of questions, but all he could do was to repeat word for word what the officer had said to him two or three times: "Monsieur Follenvie, you will forbid them to harness these travelers' carriage tomorrow. I do not want them to leave until I give the order. You understand. Now go."

So they wanted to see the officer. The Count sent in his calling card on which Monsieur Carré-Lamadon added his name and all his titles. The Prussian replied that he would allow these men to speak to him after his lunch, which meant at about one o'clock.

The ladies came downstairs and everyone had a bit of food, in spite of their anxiety. Butterball looked sick and extremely worried.

They were just finishing their coffee when the orderly came to get the two gentlemen.

Loiseau joined the two men; when they tried to get Cornudet to come along as well, to give more weight to their interview, he proudly stated that he would never have anything to do with the Germans.

He sat back down near the fireplace and ordered another beer.

The three men went upstairs and were shown into the most beautiful room in the inn, where the officer received them; he was stretched out in an armchair, his feet resting on the mantelpiece, smoking a long porcelain pipe and wrapped in a flamboyant bathrobe that he doubtless stole from some abandoned house belonging to some bourgeois with bad taste. He did not get up, did not greet them, did not even look at them. He was a magnificent example of the rudeness that comes naturally to a victorious army.

After a few moments he finally spoke:

"Vat do you vant?"

"We wish to leave, Monsieur," said the Count.

"No."

"Might I ask the reason for your refusal?"

5. Bernard du Guesclin (1320–1380), known as the Eagle of Brittany because of his valor, was a legendary figure of the Hundred Years' War.
6. The son of Napoleon III was born in 1856 and was thus only fourteen at the time of the Franco-Prussian War; he was killed fighting the Zulus, on the side of the British, in 1879, affording another level of dramatic irony for contemporary readers of *Boule de suif.*

"Because I do not vish it."

"With all due respect, Monsieur, I must point out that your general gave us permission to travel to Dieppe, and I don't believe we have done anything to deserve your orders."

"I do not vish it . . . That is all . . . You go now."

The three men bowed and left the room.

The afternoon was awful. No one understood this German's whim, and the strangest, most upsetting thoughts filled their heads. Everyone was sitting in the kitchen, talking continuously, imagining the most bizarre things. Perhaps they wanted to keep them hostage—but why?—or take them prisoner? Or maybe demand a large ransom? This idea left them panic-stricken. The richest ones were the most terrified, picturing themselves forced to hand over sacks of gold to this arrogant soldier in order to save their own lives. They wracked their brains trying to work out believable lies, how to hide their wealth so they would seem poor, very poor. Loiseau removed the chain from his watch and hid it in his pocket. As night fell, they grew more and more apprehensive. They lit the lamp and since they wouldn't be having dinner for another two hours, Madame Loiseau suggested a game of *trente et un*.[7] It would take their mind off things. Everyone agreed.

Even Cornudet politely put out his pipe and joined the game.

The Count shuffled the cards and dealt out the hands; Butterball had 31 right away and soon everyone concentrated on the game, which lessened the fears that haunted them. Cornudet noticed that Loiseau and his wife were cheating.

Just as they were about to sit down to eat, Monsieur Follenvie returned. In his hoarse voice, he said: "The Prussian officer wished me to ask Mlle Elisabeth Rousset if she had changed her mind yet."

Butterball went very pale and stood deadly still; then she suddenly turned bright red and was so overcome with fury she couldn't speak. Finally, she shouted: "Please tell that Prussian scoundrel, that filthy pig, that bastard, that I will never change my mind. Do you hear me? Never, never, never!"

The fat innkeeper went out. Then everyone swarmed around Butterball, questioning her, begging her to reveal the secret of her visit to the officer. She refused at first, but her frustration won out in the end: "What does he want? . . . What does he want? . . . He wants to sleep with me!" she cried. Everyone was so indignant that they weren't even shocked. Cornudet banged his beer mug so violently on the table that it shattered. A great outcry of protest broke out against this repulsive thug, mixed with a wave of anger; everyone

7. A card game in which the winner has to get the closest to, but not more than, thirty-one points.

was united in resistance, taking a common stand, as if the sacrifice demanded of Butterball was shared by each of them. The Count declared in disgust that those people behaved like barbarians did in the past. The women especially expressed tender and enthusiastic sympathy toward Butterball. The two nuns, who only came downstairs for meals, looked away and said nothing.

Once the initial anger had subsided, they had dinner; but they hardly spoke: they were thinking.

The ladies went to bed early; the men continued to smoke and organized a game of écarté,[8] which they invited Monsieur Follenvie to join, so they could subtly question him as to how to convince the officer to change his mind. But he concentrated on his cards, wouldn't listen to them, wouldn't answer them; he just said over and over again: "Let's play cards, gentlemen, cards!" He was so intent on the game that he forgot to spit out the phlegm from his lungs, which made his chest sometimes wheeze like a note held too long on a keyboard. His whistling lungs hit every note of the asthmatic scale, from the deep serious chords right up to the sharp screeches of young roosters trying to crow.

He even refused to go up to bed when his wife came looking for him. She was exhausted—she was an "early bird," always up at dawn—so she went upstairs alone; her husband, however, was a "night owl," always eager to stay up late with friends. "Put my eggnog in front of the fire," he shouted after her, then went back to his cards. When the others saw that they couldn't get anything out of him, they said it was time to go to bed, and everyone went to his room.

They were up fairly early the next day, feeling a vague sense of hope, an even greater desire to leave than before and great fear at having to spend another day at this horrible inn.

Alas! The horses were still in the stable; the driver was nowhere in sight. They walked round and round the coach, bored, with nothing else to do.

Lunch was depressing, and everyone seemed colder toward Butterball, for after thinking it over during the night, their opinion had changed. They now virtually held a grudge against her for not having secretly gone to the Prussian so that her companions would have a nice surprise that morning. What could be easier? Who would even have known? She could have saved face by telling the officer that she felt sorry for the others who were so upset. What difference would it make to someone like her!

But no one admitted what they were thinking, at least, not yet.

8. Another card game, similar to gin rummy, so-called from the French verb *écarter* ("to set aside") as players discard cards not suitable for their hand and replace them with others from the pack.

That afternoon, they were bored to death, so the Count suggested they take a walk on the outskirts of the village. Everyone dressed up warmly and the little group set off, except for Cornudet, who preferred to sit by the fire, and the nuns, who spent their days in church or with the priest.

The cold, which was getting worse and worse every day, bitterly stung their noses and ears; their feet became so painful that every step they took brought more suffering, and when they finally reached open ground, the fields looked so mournful and gloomy under an endless sheet of snow that they immediately turned back, their souls and hearts icy cold.

The four women walked in front, followed a little way behind by the men.

Loiseau, who understood the situation, suddenly asked if "that slut" was going to force them to spend much more time in such a place. The Count, who was always polite, said they could not demand such a painful sacrifice from any woman; it had to be her decision. Monsieur Carré-Lamadon pointed out that if the French were preparing a counterattack from Dieppe, as was rumored, there would most likely be a battle at Tôtes. This thought worried the other two men. "What if we got away on foot?" asked Loiseau. The Count shrugged his shoulders: "Do you really think we could, in this snow? With our wives? We'd be hunted down and found in ten minutes and taken back as prisoners, at the mercy of the soldiers." It was true; everyone fell silent.

The ladies talked about clothes, but a certain sense of reserve seemed to come between them.

Suddenly, the officer appeared at the end of the street. Against the snowy backdrop of the horizon, he looked like a wasp in uniform; he walked with his legs apart, with that gait unique to military men who are trying not to dirty their meticulously polished boots.

He bowed as he passed the ladies, then looked scornfully at the men, who at least enjoyed the dignity of not having tipped their hats to him, though Loiseau at first had started to.

Butterball's whole face turned red, and the three married women felt a great surge of humiliation to have run into this soldier in the company of this young woman whom he had treated so cavalierly.

And so they began talking about him, his physique, his face. Madame Carré-Lamadon, who had known many officers and considered herself an expert, remarked that he was not bad at all; she even regretted he wasn't French, for he would make a very handsome Hussar, and all the women would be mad about him.

Once back at the inn, they did not know what to do. Bitter words were exchanged over really insignificant things. The silent dinner was soon over and everyone went up to bed, hoping to sleep longer to kill the time.

The next day, they all came downstairs looking tired and frustrated. The women barely spoke to Butterball.

A church bell rang out. It was for a baptism. The chubby young woman had a child who was being raised by countryfolk in Yvetot.[9] She saw him barely once a year, and never thought about him, but the idea of the child about to be baptized filled her heart with a sudden, urgent wave of tenderness for her own son, and she was determined to go to the ceremony.

The moment she had gone, everyone looked at each other and brought their chairs closer together, for everyone felt they had to make some sort of decision. Loiseau had a brainwave: he suggested they propose that the officer should only keep Butterball and let the rest of them leave.

Monsieur Follenvie was given the task, but he returned almost immediately. The German, who knew something about human nature, had thrown him out. He intended to hold everybody there until his desire had been satisfied.

Then Madame Loiseau's vulgar character revealed itself: "We're not going to die of old age here," she shouted. "Since it's that tart's profession to sleep with men, I don't see why she has the right to refuse any one man in particular. Honestly, that thing had anyone and everyone in Rouen, even the coach drivers! Yes, Madame, the coachman from the police station! I know it's true, yes, I do, because he buys his wine from us. And now, when it's a question of getting us out of this bad situation, she gives herself airs and graces, the snotty little thing! . . . If you ask me, this officer has behaved properly. Perhaps he has done without it for a long time; and there were three others he would have no doubt preferred. But no, he'll make do with the woman anyone can have. He respects married women. Think about it: he's in charge here. All he had to say was: 'I want . . .' and he and his soldiers could have taken us by force."

The other two women shuddered. The pretty Madame Carré-Lamadon's eyes shone and she went a bit pale, as if she could feel herself being taken by force by the officer.

The men, who had been discussing the problem amongst themselves, joined the women. Loiseau, furious, wanted to hand "that wretched woman" over to the enemy by force. But the Count, having come from three generations of ambassadors and endowed with the physique of a diplomat, was more inclined to use subtler tactics: "We must persuade her," he said.

---

9. Market town on the Caux plateau, about twelve miles west of Tôtes.

And so began their conspiracy.

The women huddled together, lowered their voices and a general discussion began with each person giving her opinion. They spoke, however, in the most polite terms. The ladies in particular found the most delicate turns of phrase and the most subtly charming expressions to say the most shocking things. They were so careful about their language that an outsider wouldn't have understood a thing. But since only a thin layer of modesty veils the surface of any society woman, they really began to enjoy this naughty little adventure, actually finding it a great deal of fun, feeling they were in their element, toying with love with the kind of sensuality a gourmet chef feels when he prepares dinner for someone.

In the end, the situation seemed so funny to them that their cheerfulness returned. The Count told some rather risqué jokes, but in such a clever way that they made everyone smile. Then Loiseau added some even more explicit stories, but no one was in the least offended. And the thought so brutally expressed by his wife stood out in all their minds: "Since it's that tart's profession to sleep with men, I don't see why she has the right to refuse any one man in particular." The sweet Madame Carré-Lamadon even seemed to think that if she were in Butterball's place, she would be less inclined to refuse this officer than any other man.

The plan of attack was carefully prepared, as if they were in a fortress under siege. Each of them agreed the role they would play, the arguments they would use, the maneuvers they had to carry out. They decided their campaign, their strategies, their surprise attacks, to force this human citadel to crumble and yield to the victorious enemy.

Meanwhile, Cornudet stood apart, wanting nothing to do with this business.

Their minds were so completely concentrated that they didn't even hear Butterball come in. Then the Count softly whispered "Shush," which made everyone look up. She was there. Everyone quickly fell silent and a kind of embarrassment prevented anyone from speaking to her at first. The Countess, more skillful at the duplicity practiced in high society, asked: "Did you enjoy the baptism?"

The chubby young woman, still moved, described everything, the people, what they looked like, even the church itself. Then she said: "It feels so good to pray sometimes."

Until lunchtime, the ladies were happy to be pleasant to her, in order to encourage her trust and convince her to accept their advice.

As soon as they sat down to dinner, they began maneuvers. First came a thinly veiled conversation about self-sacrifice. They gave examples from ancient times: Judith and Holofernes,[1] then, for no apparent reason, Lucretia and Sextus,[2] and Cleopatra, who slept with all the generals who opposed her in order to turn them into her slaves. Next they told a totally unbelievable story, made up by these ignorant millionaires, which detailed how the women of Rome seduced Hannibal, in Capua,[3] along with all his lieutenants, soldiers and mercenaries. They named all the women who were victorious over their conquerors by turning their bodies into a battlefield, a means of domination, a weapon, women who conquered hideous, hateful beings through heroic caresses, sacrificing their chastity to the noble cause of vengeance and loyalty.

They even described, in veiled terms, the Englishwoman from a noble family who allowed herself to be given a horrible, contagious disease in order to infect Bonaparte;[4] but he was miraculously saved moments before their deadly tryst by a sudden moment of weakness.

And all these things were said with moderation and politeness, interspersed with moments of forced enthusiasm designed to encourage a spirit of competition.

By the end, one would almost have believed that the unique role of a woman on this earth was to endlessly sacrifice herself, to offer up her body continually to the desires of military men.

The two nuns seemed to hear nothing at all and remained lost in thought. Butterball didn't say a word.

All afternoon, she was left to think things over. But instead of calling her "Madame" as they had up until now, they simply called her "Mademoiselle," without actually knowing why, but sensing that it would lower her a notch in their esteem, and to make her understand her shameful situation.

Just as the soup was being served, Monsieur Follenvie returned, repeating the question he had asked the night before:

"The Prussian officer wished me to ask Mlle Elisabeth Rousset if she had changed her mind yet."

"No, Monsieur," Butterball replied curtly.

During dinner, the coalition weakened. Loiseau made three inappropriate remarks. Everyone was wracking their brains to find new

---

1. Escaping from the city of Béthulia being besieged by Holophernes, Judith is supposed to have seduced him before murdering the Assyrian general. Based on the deuterocanonical *Book of Judith* (13.1–10), the image of him being beheaded was popularized from the Renaissance onward.

2. Apart from adding to the salacious catalogue exemplifying the link between sex and politics, it is not obvious why Maupassant invokes the story of Lucretia's rape by Sextus Tarquinius which, according to ancient historians like Livy, led to the fall of Rome.

3. This debatable episode, propagated by Livy, would have been familiar to any French person who had undergone an education in the Humanities, necessarily involving the study of ancient history.

4. The examples become even more apocryphal, as Maupassant makes clear in the next two paragraphs commenting on the increasingly implausible direction of the conversation.

illustrations, in vain, when the Countess, perhaps without malice or forethought, perhaps simply feeling a vague need to pay homage to the Church, questioned the older of the nuns about the important facts in the lives of the saints. Now, many saints had committed acts that would be considered crimes to us, but the Church gives total absolution to any acts carried out for the glory of God or for the good of their fellow man. It was a powerful argument; the Countess took advantage of it. And so, either through tacit understanding or disguised collusion—anyone wearing an ecclesiastical habit excels in such things—or simply out of simple ignorance or sheer stupidity, the old nun provided great support to the conspiracy.

They had believed she was shy, but she showed them she was bold, talkative, passionate. This nun was not concerned by the trials and errors of casuistry; her doctrine was ironclad; her faith resolute; her conscience devoid of scruples. She found the sacrifice of Abraham a simple matter, for she would have killed her mother and father at once if she had been commanded to do so from on high; and nothing, in her opinion, could displease the Lord when the intention was admirable. The Countess, taking advantage of the holy authority of her unexpected accomplice, coaxed her on to make a salutary paraphrase of the ethical axiom: "The end justifies the means."

"And so, Sister," the Countess asked, "do you think that God would accept any means and would forgive any act if the intention is pure?"

"Who could doubt it, Madame? An act that is guilty in itself often becomes praiseworthy through the thought that inspires it."

And they continued talking in this way, determining God's will, predicting His decisions, assuming Him to be interested in things that barely truly concerned Him.

Everything said was veiled, skillful, discreet. But every word of the holy sister in her cornet headpiece weakened the indignant resistance of the courtesan.

Then the conversation took a somewhat different turn and the nun wearing the long string of rosary beads spoke about the convents in her order, about her Mother Superior, about herself and her darling little companion, Sister Saint Nicephore. They had been asked to go to the hospitals in Le Havre to nurse the hundreds of soldiers who had caught smallpox. She described these poor men, giving details of their illness. And while they were being held here on their way to Le Havre, a great number of Frenchmen might be dying who could have been saved! Nursing soldiers was her particular specialty; she had been in the Crimea, in Italy, in Austria,[5] and as she told stories about the various military campaigns she had been

5. Reference to Napoleon III's military campaigns or, as his opponents would put it, "adventurism" at the expense of French lives: in the Crimean War (with the British, 1854–56); and in Italy in the war against Austria (1859).

involved in, she suddenly revealed herself to be one of those nuns who seemed eager to follow the army from camp to camp, gathering up the wounded in the midst of battles; and she could control these great undisciplined ruffians with a single word better than any of their leaders. She was a true drum-beating nun, and her haggard face, covered in pockmarks, seemed the very incarnation of the destructive nature of war.

The effect of her words was so excellent that no one spoke when she had finished.

As soon as the meal was over, everyone rushed up to their rooms, and only came back down again late the next morning.

They had a quiet lunch. They were giving the seed sown the night before time to grow and bear fruit.

The Countess suggested they go for a walk in the afternoon; the Count offered Butterball his arm, as arranged beforehand, and walked with her a little behind the others.

He spoke to her in that familiar, paternal and slightly condescending tone that upper-class men use with young women, calling them "my dear child," talking down to her because of his social position, his indisputable respectability. He came straight to the point:

"So you prefer to keep us here, leaving us vulnerable—along with yourself—to all the violence that would surely follow a Prussian defeat rather than consent to an act of sacrifice, as you have so often in your life?"

Butterball said nothing.

He used kindness, reasoning, sentiment to try to persuade her.

He knew how to maintain his status as "the Count," while showing himself to be gallant when necessary, complimentary, even amiable. He glorified the service she would be doing them, mentioned their gratitude; then suddenly, he spoke to her in a very familiar tone: "And you know, my darling, he would be able to brag at having had the pleasure of knowing you, because he wouldn't find many pretty girls like you in his country."

Butterball said nothing and joined the others.

As soon as they got back, she went upstairs and did not come back down again. Their anxiety was extreme. What would she do? How embarrassed they would feel if she held out!

The dinner bell rang; they waited for her, in vain. Then Monsieur Follenvie came in and stated that Mlle Rousset was not feeling well and wouldn't be having dinner. Everyone listened intently. The Count went over to the innkeeper. "So it's done?" he asked quietly. "Yes." He said nothing to his companions, out of politeness; he simply nodded slightly to them. A great sigh of relief rose up at once and everyone's face lit up with joy. "Splendid!" shouted Loiseau. "The champagne's on me, if they have any in this place!" and Madame

Loiseau was very upset when the owner came back with four bottles. Everyone had suddenly become talkative and boisterous; vulgar joy filled their hearts. The Count noticed that Madame Carré-Lamadon was charming; the manufacturer paid compliments to the Countess. The conversation was lively, cheerful, witty.

Suddenly, Loiseau, looking anxious, raised his arms and shouted, "Be quiet!" Everyone fell silent, surprised and almost frightened. Then he raised his eyes toward the ceiling, strained to hear something, gestured them to be quiet, listened again and finally said: "Don't worry, it's all right," his voice sounding normal again.

At first they didn't understand, but soon they all smiled.

A quarter of an hour later, he pulled the same prank again, and repeated it often during the evening; and he pretended to question someone on the floor above, giving him advice that had double meanings drawn from his traveling salesman's sense of humor. Sometimes he looked sad and sighed: "Poor girl!" or muttered from between clenched teeth:

"Well, well! you Prussian devil!" Sometimes, just when they had forgotten all about it, he would shout, "Enough, enough!" several times, adding, as if he were talking to himself, "I hope we will see her again; I hope that contemptible man doesn't kill her!"

Even though these jokes were in the worst possible taste, everyone found them funny and no one was offended, for a feeling of indignation depends on the atmosphere, as does everything else, and the atmosphere they had gradually created was full of risqué thoughts.

During dessert, even the women made witty, funny allusions. Their eyes sparkled; they had all drunk a lot. The Count, who retained a serious demeanor even when relaxed, made a comparison that was much appreciated by everyone between their situation and the end of the icy winter at the North Pole and the joy of shipwrecked passengers who finally see a path leading south.

Loiseau, on a roll, stood up, a glass of champagne in his hand: "A toast to our freedom!" Everyone stood up and cheered. Even the two nuns, encouraged by the ladies, agreed to take a sip of the bubbly, which they had never tasted. They declared it was like sparkling lemonade, but much more subtle.

Loiseau summed up the situation.

"It's a shame there isn't a piano; we could dance a quadrille."

Cornudet hadn't said a word or made a gesture; he even looked as if he were lost in deep thought, tugging angrily at his long beard now and then, as if he were trying to make it even longer. Finally, around midnight, just as they were all about to go, Loiseau, who was staggering a little, suddenly poked Cornudet's stomach and mumbled: "You weren't much fun tonight; don't you have anything to say, man?"

Cornudet quickly raised his head and gazed at the others, one by one, a cutting, horrible look in his eyes. "I say that you have all done a vile thing!" He stood up, went over to the door, said, "Vile!" once more and walked out.

At first, this had a sobering effect. Loiseau was taken aback and said nothing; but he suddenly recovered his composure and bent over with laughter, saying over and over again: "They have no idea, they just have no idea."

No one understood, so he revealed the "secret of the corridor." Everyone became extremely cheerful. The women were laughing like idiots. The Count and Monsieur Carré-Lamadon laughed so hard they cried. They couldn't believe it.

"What! Are you sure! He wanted to . . ."

"I'm telling you that I saw it with my own eyes."

"And she refused . . ."

"Because the Prussian was in the next room."

"And you're sure?"

"I give you my word."

The Count was choking with laughter. The manufacturer clutched his stomach with both hands.

"And so you see why he didn't find tonight very funny," Loiseau continued, "not funny at all."

And all three men began to laugh again, choking, spluttering, out of breath.

Then they all parted. But Madame Loiseau, who had a spiteful nature, remarked to her husband as they were going to bed that Madame Carré-Lamadon—"the little vixen"—had forced herself to laugh all evening. "You know that when a woman is attracted by a uniform, she couldn't care less if it belongs to a Frenchman or a Prussian; it's all the same to her, I'm telling you. Good Lord, it's disgusting!"

And all night long, flutters, distant sounds, barely audible, like breathing, the light touch of bare feet and faint creaking noises filled the dark corridor. And of course, they all slept very late; slivers of light slipped beneath their doors for a very long time. Champagne has that effect; it causes restless sleep, or so it's said.

The next day, a bright winter's sun made the snow sparkle. The carriage, harnessed at last, was waiting at the door, while a flock of white pigeons with pink eyes that had a small black dot in the center, heads tucked beneath their thick feathers, walked calmly between the legs of the six horses, pecking about for food in the steaming manure.

The coachman was in his place, wrapped up in a sheepskin coat, smoking a pipe, and all the delighted passengers quickly wrapped up some food for the rest of the journey.

They were waiting for Butterball. At last she appeared.

She seemed rather upset and ashamed as she walked shyly toward her companions; all of them turned away at once, as if they hadn't seen her. The Count took his wife's arm with great dignity and led her far away from this impure contact.

The chubby young woman stopped, astonished; then, gathering all her courage, she walked over to the manufacturer's wife and humbly murmured, "Good morning, Madame." The other woman merely nodded slightly in an insolent way and looked at her with an expression of offended virtue. Everyone seemed busy and kept their distance from her, as if some disease were festering under her dress. Then they hurried toward the carriage, followed by Butterball, who, all alone, was the last to climb in; she silently sat down in the same seat she had taken during the first part of the journey.

It was as if no one saw her, no one knew her; though Madame Loiseau looked at her with indignation from a distance and remarked to her husband, loud enough to be heard: "Thank goodness I'm not sitting next to *her*."

The heavy carriage started out and continued on its way.

At first, no one spoke. Butterball didn't dare look up. She felt indignant toward all her companions, and, at the same time, humiliated to have given in; she felt dirty for having allowed the Prussian to kiss her and hold her in his arms where the others had so hypocritically forced her.

But soon the Countess turned toward Madame Carré-Lamadon and broke the silence:

"I believe you know Madame d'Etrelles?"

"Yes, she's one of my friends."

"She's such a charming woman!"

"Delightful! An exceptional person, highly educated as well, and a true artist: she sings beautifully and her drawing is sheer perfection."

The manufacturer was chatting with the Count, and in between the rattling of the windows, certain words stood out now and again: "Share—maturity date—bonus—futures."

Loiseau, who had stolen the old pack of cards from the inn, covered in grease from five years of contact with badly cleaned tables, began a game of bezique with his wife.

The nuns took hold of their long rosary beads that hung down below their waists, made the sign of the cross, and suddenly began mumbling quickly, getting faster and faster, rushing their words as if they were in a race to see who could say the most prayers; and they kissed a medallion from time to time, crossing themselves again, then went on with their rapid, continual muttering.

Cornudet sat motionless, deep in thought.

After they had been traveling for three hours, Loiseau put away the cards. "Time to eat," he said.

His wife picked up a package tied with string and took out a piece of cold veal. She cut it up properly into neat, thin slices and both of them began to eat.

"Shall we eat as well?" said the Countess. Everyone agreed, and she unwrapped the provisions prepared in advance for the two couples. In one of those long earthenware dishes with a lid decorated with a hare to show that it contains a game pie, there was a succulent pâté with white streaks of lard crisscrossing on top of the mixture of finely chopped dark meats. A large wedge of Gruyére cheese that had been wrapped in newspaper had the words *News in Brief* on its creamy surface.

The two nuns took out some sausages that smelled of garlic; and Cornudet dug into both deep pockets of his thick coat to pull out four hard-boiled eggs from one and a piece of bread from the other. He peeled the eggs, threw the shells on the straw beneath his seat and began biting into them, dropping tiny bits of yolk into his long beard; they stuck there, looking like little stars.

In the haste and confusion of the morning, Butterball had not had time to think about anything, and she watched in stifled rage and frustration as all these people ate so calmly. Her extreme anger caused her whole body to tense at first, and she started to open her mouth to shout a flood of insults at them for what they had done; but she was choked by so much exasperation that she couldn't say a single word.

No one looked at her or gave her a second thought. She felt as if she were drowning in the disdain of these virtuous villains who had first sacrificed her, then rejected her, as if she were unclean and useless. Then she thought back to her large basket full of all the delicious things they had greedily devoured, her two chickens shining in aspic, her pâtés, her pears, her four bottles of Bordeaux wine, and her fury suddenly gave way, like a rope pulled too tightly that finally snaps, and she felt herself on the verge of tears. She made a great effort to control herself, sat up taller, stifled her sobs the way children do; but her tears rose up, glistened in the corners of her eyes, and soon two heavy teardrops broke free and rolled slowly down her cheeks. Others followed more quickly, rushing down like drops of water filtering from behind a rock, falling steadily onto the rounded curve of her bosom. She continued to sit tall, staring straight ahead, her face tense and pale, hoping that no one would see her.

But the Countess noticed and warned her husband with a gesture. He shrugged his shoulders as if to say: "What can I do? It's not my fault." Madame Loiseau gave a silent laugh and whispered triumphantly: "She's crying out of shame."

The two nuns had wrapped up what was left of their sausages and gone back to their prayers.

Then Cornudet, who was digesting his eggs, stretched his long legs out under the seat opposite, leaned back, crossed his arms, smiled like a man who has just heard a good joke, and began whistling the *Marseillaise*.[6]

The faces of all his companions went dark. This song of the common people did not please them in the least. They grew anxious, irritated, and looked as if they were about to howl, the way dogs do when they hear the sound of a hurdy-gurdy.

He noticed but didn't stop. At times, he even started singing the words:

> *Amour sacré de la patrie,*
> *Conduis, soutiens, nos bras vengeurs,*
> *Liberté, liberté chérie,*
> *Combats avec tes défenseurs!*[7]

They were traveling more quickly now, for the snow was harder. And all the way to Dieppe, throughout the long, dreary hours of the journey, through the jolts of the carriage along the road, at dusk, then in the heavy darkness of the carriage, he continued, with ferocious determination, his vengeful, endless whistling, forcing his weary, frustrated listeners to follow the song from start to finish, to remember every word of every verse.

And Butterball continued to cry, and every now and then, a sob she could not hold back was heard between two lines of the song, in the darkness.

Mademoiselle Fifi[†]

The Major, the Prussian Commandant, Count von Farlsberg,[1] was finishing reading his mail; he was settled back in a large tapestry-covered armchair, his boots propped up against the elegant marble

---

6. The French national anthem was composed in 1792 by Rouget de Lisle for the French Army of the Rhine. The irony here—Cornudet's "good joke" is also Maupassant's—is that this victorious military marching song, subsequently adopted by generations of revolutionaries, is sung in the context of a terrible defeat at the hands of, precisely, those on the other side of the Rhine.

7. Drive on sacred love of country,
   Support our avenging, arms,
   Liberty, cherished liberty,
   Join the struggle with your defenders!

† First published in the *Gil Blas* on March 23, 1882, before being included in the volume of tales using this same title a few weeks later; this story came out in a second edition in 1883 and within *Contes et nouvelles* (1885), and was considerably revised yet again in 1893, the version of the text translated here.

1. All the names are invented, Maupassant taking care to give them an unmistakably Germanic ring (he had first called the Major "Rego d'Anglesse").

fireplace where his spurs, during the three months he had occupied the Château d'Uville,[2] had made two holes that got deeper with every passing day.

A cup of steaming coffee sat on a small marquetry gridiron table that was stained with liquor, burnt by cigars, scratched by the conqueror's penknife; every now and again, he would stop sharpening a pencil and carve some numbers or drawings on the beautiful piece of furniture, according to his whims.

When he had finished the letters and looked through the German newspapers his orderly had just brought him, he stood up and threw three or four enormous pieces of green wood onto the fire, for these gentlemen were gradually cutting down all the trees in the estate in order to keep warm. He walked over to the window.

The rain flooded down, the kind you typically have in Normandy, rain that looked as if it were being unleashed by some furious hand; it came down in great diagonal sheets that formed a kind of wall with slanted stripes, the driving, splashing rain that floods everything, the true downpour you get in the outskirts of Rouen, that chamberpot of France.

For a long time, the officer stared at the flooded lawns and the Andelle River[3] in the distance that was overflowing its banks. He was tapping out a German waltz on the window pane when a noise made him turn around: it was his second in command, Baron von Kelweingstein, who held the rank of Captain.

The Major was an enormous man with broad shoulders and a long beard that spread out and covered his chest like a fan; his solemn, noble bearing made him look like a peacock in uniform, a peacock who carried his tail spread out over his chin. He had blue eyes that were pale and cold, and a scar on one cheek from a sword he'd been cut with in the war with Austria.[4] And he had the reputation of being a decent man as well as a brave officer.

The Captain was a short, fat, red-faced man who looked as if he'd been poured into his tight uniform; his fiery beard was cut so short it was almost like stubble, and in a certain kind of light, his face looked as if he were covered in phosphorous. He'd lost two teeth one night at someone's wedding party—he couldn't exactly remember how—and because of this, he spat out his words and you couldn't always understand what he was saying. He had no hair at the very

---

2. While no such château existed, there is an "Urville" seven miles west of Cherbourg and another thirteen miles south of Caen.

3. The Andelle rises not far from the spa town of Forges-les-Eaux, twenty-five miles east of Rouen and flows into the Seine upstream from Pont-de-Arche. A number of Maupassant's tales of war are set in this area of Normandy, as it was from here that Prussian troops were closing in on Rouen itself.

4. Prussia had defeated Austria at the Battle of Sadowa on July 3, 1866, confirming its new-found status as a political and military power.

top of his head; the bald spot was surrounded by golden, shiny, curly hair, so that he looked like a monk.

The Major shook his hand and drank his cup of coffee in one gulp (his sixth of the morning), while listening to his subordinate's report on the various incidents that had occurred; then the two of them walked over to the window, remarking on how gloomy it looked. The Major, a calm man who had a wife back home, adjusted well to everything; but the Captain, a tenacious pleasure-seeker who frequented seedy dives, and an obsessive womanizer, was furious at having been forced into celibacy in the middle of nowhere for the past three months.

Someone tapped at the door and the Captain shouted for him to come in; one of his orderlies appeared at the door; the fact that he was there meant that lunch was ready.

In the dining room, they found three lower-ranking officers: a lieutenant, Otto von Grossling, and two second lieutenants, Fritz Scheunaubourg[5] and the Marquis Wilhem d'Eyrik, a very short dandy who was proud and brutal toward men, harsh toward the people they had beaten and as dangerous as gunpowder.

Ever since he had arrived in France, his comrades refused to call him anything but "Mademoiselle Fifi." The nickname was a result of his coquettish manner, his slim waist that looked as if he was wearing a corset, his pale face on which you could barely see any moustache growing, and the habit he had adopted of expressing his supreme disdain for people and things by constantly using the French phrase "*fi, fi donc*,"[6] which he pronounced with a slight whistle.

The dining room in the Château d'Uville was a long, majestic room; its antique crystal mirrors were cracked by bullets, and its long Flemish tapestries were cut to ribbons, falling down in places from being slashed with a sword: both evidence of how Mademoiselle Fifi amused himself when he had nothing better to do.

Three family portraits hung on the walls: a knight in his suit of armor, a cardinal and a judge; all three had long porcelain pipes sticking out of their mouths, so it looked like they were smoking. And in an antique frame whose gilding was worn with age, a noblewoman in a tightly corseted dress proudly displayed an enormous moustache added to the painting in charcoal.

The officers ate their lunch in virtual silence in this mutilated room that looked even gloomier in the rain, sadder in its vanquished appearance, the old oak parquet as grimy as the floor in a tavern.

---

5. The name "Fritz" was used in French slang for any German.
6. Translates roughly as "To hell with that!"

After the meal, when they started smoking and drinking, they began talking about their boredom, as they did every day. Bottles of cognac and liquors were passed around, and all of them, leaning back in their chairs, kept taking sips of drink, never removing the long, curved stem of the pipes whose faience bowls were gaudily painted as if to attract some Hottentot.[7]

As soon as their glasses were empty, they would refill them with a gesture of resigned weariness. But Mademoiselle Fifi constantly smashed his, so a soldier immediately brought him another.

A cloud of bitter smoke shrouded them, and they seemed to slump into a sad, drowsy state of drunkenness, the kind of gloomy intoxication of men with nothing to do.

Then the Baron suddenly sat up. He was shaken awake by a feeling of revolt. "For God's sake," he swore, "we have to think of something to do; we can't go on like this."

Lieutenant Otto and Second Lieutenant Fritz, both eminently endowed with the heavy, serious traits of the German race, each replied at the same time: "But what, Captain?"

He thought for a few seconds. "What? Well, we should organize a party," he continued, "that is, if the Commandant will allow it."

The Major took the pipe out of his mouth: "What kind of party, Captain?"

The Baron walked over to him: "I'll take care of everything, Major. I'll send Le Devoir[8] to Rouen to bring us back some women; I know where to get them. We can have dinner here; we have everything we need, and at least we'll have a good time."

Count von Farlsberg smiled and shrugged his shoulders. "You must be mad."

But all the officers had stood up, surrounding their leader: "Oh, please let the Captain arrange it, Major," they begged. "It's so depressing here."

In the end, the Major gave in. "Fine," he said; and the Baron immediately called for Le Devoir. He was an old, non-commissioned officer whom no one had ever seen smile, but he fanatically carried out all the officers' orders of the officers to the letter, whatever they were.

He stood there, impassively, taking the Baron's instructions, then left; and five minutes later, a large military wagon covered in tight canvas was hitched to four horses and galloped off in the driving rain.

The officers all suddenly felt lively; their languid bodies stood tall, their faces lit up and they started chatting.

---

7. Contemptuous reference to a nomadic tribe of South-West Africa (the present-day Namibia).
8. Ironically named by Maupassant, meaning "duty" or "obligation."

Even though it was raining as hard as ever, the Major said it didn't look so dark, and Lieutenant Otto declared with great conviction that it was going to clear up. Even Mademoiselle Fifi didn't seem to be able to sit still. He got up, sat down again. His harsh, pale eyes looked around for something to break. Suddenly, staring at the Noblewoman with the Moustache, the blond young man pulled out his revolver.

"*You* will not see it," he said, and from his chair, took aim. He fired twice, and two bullets pierced the eyes of the portrait.

Then he shouted: "Let's make a *mine!*" which is what he called his bomb![9] And the conversations suddenly stopped, as if some powerful, new amusement had taken hold of everyone.

The bomb was his invention, the way he destroyed things, his favorite pastime.

When he left the château, the rightful owner, Count Fernand d'Amoys d'Uville, didn't have time to take anything with him; the only thing he managed to hide was the silver, which he hurriedly stashed in a crevice in the wall. The dining room adjoined the large reception room, which was richly and magnificently decorated; before its owner fled, it had resembled a gallery in a museum.

Expensive paintings, drawings and watercolors hung on the walls, while the furniture, the shelves, the elegant display cabinets held hundreds of antiques: ornamental vases, statuettes, Dresden figurines, Chinese pagoda figures, old ivory pieces and Venetian glass, all these strange, precious objects filled the enormous room.

Hardly anything was left now. Not that they had been pillaged; the Major would never have allowed that, but Mademoiselle Fifi made a bomb every now and again, and, on those days, all the officers had five minutes of good fun.

The little Marquis went into the reception room to get what he needed. He came back with a really lovely *famille rose* china teapot that he filled with gunpowder. Then he carefully pushed a long piece of tinder down its spout, lit it, and rushed to put his deadly toy in the adjoining room.

Then he ran quickly out, closing the door behind him. All the Germans were standing there, waiting, smiling with childish curiosity; and as soon as the explosion shook the château, they all ran in together.

Mademoiselle Fifi got there first; he clapped his hands in delight when he saw the terra-cotta Venus[1] whose head had blown off; then they all picked up bits of porcelain, surprised and delighted by their

9. The French expression *faire une mine* can mean either "let's make a face" or "let's make a bomb."
1. As the goddess of Love, Venus is associated with the prostitute; the figurine's head being "blown off" anticipates the fate of Mademoiselle Fifi.

odd, jagged shapes and examined them again, declaring that some of the damage had been done by a previous bomb, and the Major looked with a fatherly expression at the enormous reception room destroyed by these explosions in a manner worthy of Nero[2] and strewn everywhere with fragments of fine works of art. He was the first to leave, after saying, in quite a friendly way: "It worked very well this time."

An enormous cloud of smoke in the dining room had merged with the tobacco smoke from before, so they couldn't breathe. The Commandant opened the window, and all the officers, who had come back to have another glass of cognac, walked over to it. The damp air rushed into the room, bringing with it the smell of floodwater and a kind of powdery mist that settled in their beards. They looked at the tall trees weighed down by the heavy flood, the wide valley covered in fog by the water unleashed from the low, dark clouds, and the church's belltower, in the distance, rising up like a gray spike in the driving rain. The bells had stopped ringing when they arrived. In fact, the only resistance the invaders had encountered in the region was the refusal to ring the bells. The country priest had not refused to take in or feed the Prussian soldiers, not at all; on several occasions, he had even agreed to drink a bottle of wine or beer with the enemy Commandant, who often used him as a benevolent intermediary. But there was no point in asking him to ring a single bell; he would have sooner offered to be shot. This was his own way of protesting against the invasion, by peaceful resistance, by remaining silent, the only form of resistance, he claimed, that was suitable to a priest, a man of kindness, not a bloodthirsty man; and everyone, for thirty miles around, praised the strength and heroism of Father Chantavoine, who dared proclaim the mourning of the French, who shouted it out by the stubborn silence of his church bells.

The entire village, fired up by his resistance, was prepared to support their priest to the very end, to risk anything at all, considering his tacit resistance the safeguard of their national honor. The people of the region thought that because of this, they deserved to be considered more patriotic than Belfort or Strasbourg,[3] believing they had set just as good an example, and that the name of their village would become immortalized. Apart from this one thing, however, they offered no resistance at all to the Prussian conquerors.

The Commandant and his officers laughed among themselves at such harmless bravery, and since everyone in the area was

---

2. The infamously degenerate Roman Emperor, "fiddling," as the saying has it, "while Rome burns."
3. Cities in eastern France which gallantly resisted the Prussian invasion: Strasbourg only surrendered at the end of September 1870, after being subjected to fierce bombardment for two months; Belfort's resistance lasted until February 16, 1871.

adaptable and obliging toward them, they gladly tolerated their silent patriotism.

Only the little Marquis Wilhem wanted to force them to ring the bells. He was furious about his superior's political concession to the priest, and every day he begged the Commandant to let him ring "ding-dong" once, just once, as a joke. And he made his request with the charm of a little kitten, the cajoling voice of a woman, the sweet tones of a mistress mad with desire; but the Commandant did not give in, so to console himself, Mademoiselle Fifi set off a bomb in the Château d'Uville.

The five men crowded around there for a few minutes, breathing in the damp air. Then Lieutenant Fritz gave a hoarse laugh and said: "These ladies vill definitely not have a good ride in such bad weather."

Then everyone left, as they each had to get back to their official assignments, and the Captain had a great deal to do to prepare for the dinner party.

When they met up again toward evening, they laughed at seeing how they had all spruced themselves up to look attractive, like the days on formal inspections: squeaky clean, hair slicked back, wearing cologne. The Commandant's hair looked less gray than it had in the morning; and the Captain had shaved, keeping only his moustache, which made him look as if his upper lip was on fire.

In spite of the rain, they left the window open; and every now and then, one of them went over to see if they could hear anything. At ten past six, the Baron said he heard a wagon rumbling in the distance. Everyone rushed over; and soon the large truck arrived, its four galloping horses caked in mud, panting and foaming at the mouth.

And five women came out onto the steps, five beautiful women, carefully chosen by the Captain's friend to whom *Le Devoir* had delivered the officer's calling card.

The women hadn't hesitated at all, certain of being well paid; they knew the Prussians, after all, as they'd been servicing them, and they had resigned themselves to the men as they did to all things. "That's how it is in this job," they told each other during the journey, no doubt to stifle a secret resentment in their hearts.

They all went into the dining room at once. It seemed even more dismal in its pitiful, dilapidated condition when the lights were on; and the table covered in food, on fine, silver plates they'd found in the wall where their owner had hidden them, made the scene look like a tavern where bandits would go to eat after a pillage. The Captain, absolutely delighted, grabbed hold of the women as if he knew them, complimenting them, kissing them, sniffing them, determining their worth as ladies of the night; and when the three young men wanted to take one each, he firmly refused, reserving to himself the right of handing them out fairly, according to the soldiers' rank, in order to respect the hierarchy.

So, to avoid any discussion, objection or suspicion of partiality, he lined them up in size order, then spoke to the tallest:

"Name," he said, making it sound like an order.

"Pamela," she replied in a loud voice.

"Number one, the aforementioned Pamela, assigned to the Commandant," he stated.

He immediately kissed Blondine, the second one, to indicate he was having her, then offered the chubby Amanda to Otto; Eva, the Tomato, to Second Lieutenant Fritz; and the smallest one of all, Rachel, a very young brunette with eyes as black as ink—a Jewess[4] whose snub nose was the exception to the rule attributing hooked noses to everyone of her race—Rachel was given to the youngest officer, the frail Marquis Wilhem d'Eyrik.

All of them, though, were pretty and plump, with no distinctive features, their looks and the way they held themselves very similar as a result of having sex every day and living in a brothel together.

The three youngest men immediately tried to get their women upstairs, using the pretext of offering them some soap and hairbrushes to freshen up; but the Captain wisely opposed this, stating that they were quite clean enough to sit down to dinner and that the men who wanted to go upstairs would want to change partners when they came back down, which would cause a problem for the other couples. His experience won out. They settled for many kisses, many kisses of anticipation.

Suddenly, Rachel started choking, coughing until her eyes watered, and smoke flowed out of her nostrils. The Marquis, pretending he wanted to kiss her, had blown tobacco smoke into her mouth. She didn't get angry, didn't say a word, but she stared at her owner with rage simmering deep in her dark eyes.

They sat down. Even the Commandant seemed delighted; he placed Pamela to his right, Blondine to his left, unfolded his napkin and said: "This was a charming idea of yours, Captain."

Lieutenants Otto and Fritz, as polite as if they had been in the company of socialites, intimidated the women a little; but Baron von Kelweingstein felt right at home: he beamed, made risqué remarks and looked as if he were on fire with his crop of red hair. He flattered the women in the French of the Rhine; and his gross compliments, spluttered through the hole left by his two missing teeth, covered the young women in a spray of saliva.

---

4. The fact that Rachel is a Jewess makes her bravery and patriotism all the more striking. While the reference to "hooked noses" reflects racial stereotyping, Maupassant refuses to subscribe to the increasingly virulent French anti-Semitism of the final decades of the century.

In fact, they didn't understand a word; and they did not seem to wake up until he started spitting out obscene words, crude expressions, distorted by his accent. Then all of them started laughing at the same time, laughing like mad things, falling over onto the men beside them, repeating the words the Baron had said; then he started saying them all wrong again, on purpose this time, just to hear the women say the dirty words. They gladly spewed them out, for they were drunk after the first few bottles of wine; then they got control of themselves and fell back into their usual behavior, kissing the moustaches of the men on either side of them, pinching their arms, shouting loudly, drinking from all the glasses, and singing French verses and bits of German songs they'd picked up from their daily contact with the enemy.

Soon even the men went wild, howled, smashed dishes, intoxicated by the women's flesh they could smell and touch, while impassive soldiers stood behind to serve them.

Only the Commandant showed restraint.

Mademoiselle Fifi had sat Rachel on his lap, and, getting very aroused, he would sometimes passionately kiss the little dark curls that fell onto her neck, breathing in the sweet warmth of her skin and the scent of her flesh through the slight gap between her dress and her body, and sometimes pinch her brutally through the cloth, making her scream, for he was overwhelmed by ferocious rage, a vicious desire to ravage her. He often held her with both arms, pressing down on her as if to join her body to his, placing his lips on the young Jewess's cool mouth, kissing her for so long she could hardly breathe; then, suddenly, he bit her so hard that a trickle of blood flowed down the young woman's chin onto her bodice.

She looked hard at him again, and, dabbing water on her wound, she murmured: "I'll make you pay for that." But all he did was give a merciless laugh and say: "Yes, I vill."

Dessert was being served; they poured some champagne. The Commandant stood up and in the same tone of voice he might use to drink to the health of the empress Augusta,[5] he made a toast: "To our ladies!" And a round of toasts started, toasts full of the kind of compliments paid by roughnecks and drunkards, toasts filled with obscene jokes that sounded even more brutish because of the soldiers' inability to speak the language.

5. Princess Augusta of Saxe-Weimar (1811–1890) married the future Kaiser William I of Prussia in 1829, taking the title of Empress only when her husband (formerly merely King Frederick-William) accepted the imperial crown of Germany on January 18, 1871, in the Hall of Mirrors at Versailles, thereby adding to French humiliation ten days before the signing of the Armistice bringing the Franco-Prussian War to a close (see Introduction, pp. xx–xxiv). The notion of a toast in her honor thus marks the immediate consequences of French defeat—the triumphant realization of Chancellor Otto Bismark's grand strategy of creating a unified German Empire—rather than a personal homage to the Emperor's wife.

They stood up, one after the other, trying to be witty, forcing themselves to be funny; and the women, who were so drunk they could barely stand up, with slurred speech and vacant expressions, applauded wildly at each one.

The Captain, wishing no doubt to give the orgy the appearance of gallantry, raised his glass again and said: "To our triumph over your hearts."

Then Lieutenant Otto, a kind of bear from the Black Forest, stood up, drunk as a skunk, and suddenly overwhelmed by alcoholic patriotism passionately cried: "To our triumph over the French!"

As drunk as they were, all the women fell silent, but Rachel was trembling. "I know certain Frenchmen you wouldn't dare say that to, you know," she retorted.

But the little Marquis, who still had her sitting on his lap, started to laugh, for the wine had made him very giddy. "Ha! Ha! Ha! Well, *I've* never met any. As soon as we show up, they run away!"

The young woman, furious, shouted straight at him: "You're lying, you bastard!"

For a moment, he stared at her with his pale eyes, the way he stared at the paintings he destroyed with his gun, then he started to laugh. "Ah! Yes, Let's talk about those Frenchmen, my pretty! Would we even be here at all if they were really brave!" Then, getting even more worked up, he shouted: "We are the masters here! France belongs to us!"

She jumped off his lap and fell into a chair. He stood up, raised his glass toward the center of the table and said once more: "France and the French belong to us—we own their woods, their fields and all the houses in France!"

The others, completely drunk, were suddenly overwhelmed by military enthusiasm, the enthusiasm of brutes; they grabbed their glasses while shouting: "Long live Prussia!" then emptied them in a single gulp.

The young women did not protest; they were reduced to silence and overcome with fear. Even Rachel felt helpless and could find nothing to reply.

Then the little Marquis refilled his champagne glass and balanced it on the head of the Jewess, shouting: "And all the women in France belong to us as well!"

She got up so quickly that the glass tipped over, spilling the golden wine over her black hair, as if she were being baptized, before it dropped to the floor and shattered. Her lips quivering, she glowered at the officer, who was still laughing, then stammered in a voice choked with rage: "That . . . that . . . that's not true; you won't have all the women of France, you know."

He sat down again so he could laugh more comfortably, and putting on a Parisian accent said: "Zat is very funny, very funny, so what are you doing here, my dear?"

She was so stunned that she said nothing at first, so upset that she didn't really understand him; then, once she realized what he was saying, she grew indignant and shouted vehemently: "Me! Me! I'm not a woman; I'm a whore, and that is all you Prussians deserve."

She had barely finished speaking when he slapped her hard across the face; when she saw him raise his arm again, she flew into a rage, grabbed a small silver dessert knife from the table and quickly—so quickly that no one saw what had happened at first—she stabbed him right in the neck, right in the hollow of his neck, just above his chest.

Something he was about to say stuck in his throat, and he sat there with his mouth gaping open and a horrible look in his eyes.

All the men let out a roar and leaped up in a panic, but she threw her chair at Lieutenant Otto's legs, knocking him to the ground, rushed over to the window, opening it before they got to her, and ran out into the night, where the rain was still pouring down.

In two minutes, Mademoiselle Fifi was dead. Then Fritz and Otto drew their swords and wanted to kill the women, who threw themselves at their feet and clutched their legs. The Major prevented the massacre, but not without difficulty, and had the four terrified women locked in a room with two guards at the door. Then he organized a party to hunt down the fugitive, as if he were ordering soldiers into combat, quite certain she would be caught.

Fifty men, fired up by threats, were sent running into the grounds. Two hundred others searched the woods and every house in the valley.

The table was cleared in a flash to be used as a bed on which to lay the dead man, and the four officers, now standing upright and sober, with the harsh expression of men of war carrying out their duties, remained at the windows, trying to see whatever they could in the dark.

The torrential rained continued. An endless lapping sound filled the darkness, the murmur of flowing water that rises and falls, water that drips and then splashes up again.

Suddenly, they heard a gunshot, then another, quite far away; and for the next four hours, they could hear shots fired, some close by, some in the distance, along with calls to regroup, foreign words shouted as a rallying call in guttural voices.

Everyone returned the next morning. Two soldiers had been killed and three others wounded by their own soldiers in the heat of the chase and the confusion of their search through the darkness.

Rachel had not been found.

Then the people in the area were terrorized, their houses turned upside down, the entire region searched, the countryside scoured; they looked everywhere. The Jewess seemed not to have left a single trace of where she had gone.

The General was informed and ordered that the business be hushed up, so as not to set a bad example in the army, but he severely reprimanded the Commandant, who punished his inferiors. "We didn't go to war for a good time and to have fun with prostitutes," the General had said. And the frustrated Count Farlsberg swore to avenge his country.

Since he needed a pretext to act ruthlessly, he called for the country priest and ordered him to ring the bells at the funeral of the Marquis d'Eyrik.

Much to his surprise, the priest was docile, humble, considerate. And when Mademoiselle Fifi's body left the Château d'Uville to be taken to the cemetery, carried by soldiers, followed by soldiers, surrounded by soldiers, all with loaded rifles, for the first time the church bells pealed the funeral toll, but cheerfully, at a lively pace, as if a friendly hand were caressing them.

The church bells rang again that night, and the next day, and every day; they rang as often as anyone could have wished. Sometimes, they even started ringing in the middle of the night, all by themselves, gently releasing two or three notes into the darkness, full of a strange kind of cheerfulness, awakened for some unknown reason. All the townspeople believed the belltower was bewitched, and no one except the priest and the sexton dared go near it.

All this happened because a poor young woman was living up there, alone and frightened, and those two men secretly brought her food.

She remained there until the German troops were gone. Then, one evening, the priest borrowed the baker's horse-drawn wagon and drove the woman he had been hiding to the edge of Rouen. When they got there, he gave her a peck on the cheek; she got out and quickly ran back to the brothel, whose Madame thought she was dead.

A little while later, a patriotic gentleman with no prejudices took her away from the brothel, admiring her for her good deed. Then he fell in love with her in her own right, married her and made a lady of her, as worthy as many others.

The Madwoman[†]

"You know," said Monsieur Mathieu d'Endolin, "These woodcocks remind me of a very appalling story about the war.

"You know my property on the outskirts of Cormeil.[1] I was living there when the Prussians arrived.

"I had a neighbor at the time who was mad; she had lost her mind after some terrible misfortunes. A long time ago, when she was twenty-five, her father, her husband and her newborn baby all died within the space of a month.

"Whenever death enters a household, it returns there almost immediately, as if it recognizes the door.

"The poor young woman, overwhelmed by grief, grew gravely ill, and was delirious for six weeks. Then, a kind of calm weariness followed that violent attack and she froze, hardly ate and only moved her eyes. Every time someone tried to get her to stand up, she would scream as if she were being murdered. And so they left her in her bed, only pulling her from under the sheets to wash her and turn over the mattress.

"An old maid stayed with her, making her drink something from time to time, or take a few mouthfuls of cold meat. What was going through her hopeless heart? No one ever knew, for she never spoke again. Was she thinking about the dead? Was she lost in sad daydreams about nothing in particular? Or was her vacant mind as stagnant as still waters?

"For fifteen years, she remained withdrawn and indifferent.

"War broke out; and during the early part of December, the Prussians pushed through to Cormeil.

"I remember it as if it were yesterday. It was freezing cold outside and I was stretched out in an armchair, laid up with gout, when I heard the sound of their heavy, regular marching. I could see them going by from my window.

"They filed past in an endless line, in unison as always, like puppets on a string. Then their leaders sent their men to lodge with various townspeople. I had seventeen of them. My neighbor, the madwoman, had twelve, including a major, a real roughneck, violent and surly.

"The first few days, everything went on as usual. They had told the officer who lived next door that the woman was not well; and he

† First published in *Le Gaulois* on December 5, 1882; reprinted in *Contes de la bécasse* the following year. The translation here is based on the definitive 1887 edition of the latter. In the volume, the text was dedicated to Robert de Bonnières de Wierre (1850–1905), poet, novelist, critic, and journalist; he was a prominent figure in contemporary literary circles and a lifelong friend of Maupassant.

1. There is a village named Cormeilles, not far from Pont-Audemer, about twenty-five miles west of Rouen.

barely gave it a second thought. But he soon became annoyed by this woman he never saw. He asked about her illness; they said that the woman who owned the house had not left her bed for fifteen years after a severe bout of grief. He didn't believe a word of it, no doubt, and thought that the poor madwoman would not get out of bed so she didn't have to see the Prussians, didn't have to speak to them or be near them.

"He demanded that she see him; he was taken into her room.

"'I ask you, Madame, zat you get out from bed und come down so vee can see you,' he said sharply.

"She turned her blank, vacant eyes toward him and said nothing.

"'I vill not tolerate such insolence,' he continued. 'If you do not get out from bed by yourself, I vill find a vay to make you.'

"She remained dead still, as if she hadn't even seen him.

"He became furious, taking her calm silence as a sign of utter scorn.

"'You better come down tomorrow . . . he added.

"Then he walked out.

"The next day, the old maid, panic-stricken, wanted to get her dressed, but the madwoman started to scream and fight her. The officer rushed upstairs, and the servant threw herself at his knees, crying:

'She won't, Monsieur, she won't. Please forgive her; she is so unhappy.'"

"The soldier didn't know what to do, not daring to tell his men to force her out of bed, in spite of his anger. Then suddenly, he started to laugh, and shouted out some orders in German.

"Soon after, a group of soldiers was seen carrying a mattress, the way they would carry a wounded man on a stretcher. On the mattress, still with its bedding intact, was the madwoman, ever silent, ever calm, indifferent to whatever was happening, as long as she could stay in her bed. One man followed behind, carrying a bundle of women's clothing.

"And the officer rubbed his hands together and said:

"'I vill make sure you get yourself dressed und go for a little valk.'

"Then we saw the cortège heading for the Imauville forest.[2]

"Two hours later, the soldiers returned, alone.

"No one ever saw the madwoman again. What had they done with her? Where had they taken her! No one ever knew.

"Snow fell now, all day and all night, burying the plains and the woods with a shroud of icy frost. The wolves howled, coming right up to our doors.

2. In the area between Bolbec and the Normandy coast at Fécamp, known by Maupassant since his childhood and the setting for many of his tales.

"The thought of this doomed woman haunted me; and I made several requests to the Prussian authorities to try to get some information. I nearly got myself executed.

"Spring returned. The occupying forces were leaving. My neighbor's house remained locked up; thick grass grew in the paths.

"The old maid had died during the winter. No one was concerned about what had happened any more; I was the only one who thought about it constantly.

"What had they done with that woman? Had she escaped through the woods? Had she been taken in somewhere, put into a hospital where they could learn nothing from her? Nothing happened to lessen my concerns, but gradually, time calmed my troubled heart.

"The following autumn, the woodcocks flew by in a large group; and as my gout was not very painful at the time, I hobbled into the forest. I had already killed four or five long-billed birds when I hit one that disappeared into a ditch full of branches. I had to climb down into it to retrieve my bird. I found it lying next to someone's skull.

"The memory of the madwoman hit me at once, as if I had been punched in the chest. Many others had surely died in these woods during that terrible year, yet I don't know why I was sure, completely sure, I'm telling you, that I had found the head of that poor, miserable madwoman.

"And suddenly, I understood, I could picture it all. They had left her here on her mattress, in the cold, deserted forest, and, in keeping with her obsession, she had simply let herself die beneath the thick, light blanket of snow, without moving at all.

"Then the wolves had eaten her.

"And the birds had made their nests with the stuffing from her torn bed.

"I kept that sad skull. And I prayed that our sons would never have to experience war again."

Lieutenant Laré's Marriage[†]

At the very beginning of the war,[1] Lieutenant Laré had captured two cannons from the Prussians. His general said: "Thank you, Lieutenant," and awarded him the *Croix d'honneur*.[2]

Since he was as modest as he was brave, skillful, creative, clever and resourceful, he was put in charge of a hundred men; he orga-

---

[†] First published in *La Mosaïque* on May 25, 1878, under the pseudonym "Guy de Valmont."

1. See Introduction, pp. xxv–xxvi.

2. Medal worn by those awarded the *Légion d'Honneur*, the order established by Napoleon Bonaparte in 1802.

nized a group of reconnaissance scouts who saved the army on several occasions while they were in retreat.

But the invasion flooded in from all sides, like an ocean crashing
onto the beach. Great waves of men arrived one after the other, casting marauders from their crests onto the shore. General Carrel's
brigade, separated from its division, continually had to retreat, fighting every day but suffering very few losses, thanks to the vigilance
and swiftness of Lieutenant Laré, who seemed to be everywhere at
once, foiled all the enemy traps, outwitted them, led their Uhlans[3]
on a wild goose chase and killed their scouts.

One morning, the General asked to see him.

"Lieutenant," he said, "here is a dispatch from General Lacère who
will be in grave danger if we do not come to his aid by dawn tomorrow. He is in Blainville, twenty-four miles from here. You will leave
as soon as it is dark with three hundred men whom you will position
all along the roads. I will wait two hours and then follow you. Study
the route carefully; I'm afraid we might run into an enemy division."

It had been freezing cold for a week. At two o'clock, it started
snowing; by evening, the ground was covered in it, and thick, white
swirls of snow hid even the closest objects.

At six o'clock, the detachment set off.

Two men were sent out first, alone, as scouts, about three hundred yards ahead. Then came a platoon of ten men whom the Lieutenant commanded himself. The rest of the men followed in two long
columns. Three hundred yards to each side of the small troop, to
the right and to the left, a few soldiers walked in pairs.

The snow kept falling, covering the men in white powder; it didn't
melt on their clothes, and because it was dark, they blended in with
the endless whiteness of the countryside.

Every now and again, they stopped. Then, all they could hear was
the faint rustling of falling snow, more a feeling than a sound, a distant whisper, sinister and difficult to make out. An order was passed
along, very quietly, and when the troop started walking again, it left
some men behind, ghostly, white shapes in the snow who gradually
grew fainter and finally disappeared. These living signposts had to
guide the army that followed.

The reconnaissance team slowed down. There was something
up ahead.

"Go around to the right," said the Lieutenant, "to the de Ronfé
woods. The château is over to the left."

Soon the order to "Halt!" spread. The detachment stopped and
waited for the Lieutenant; he went up to the château with only ten
other men.

3. Light cavalry often accompanying reconnaissance parties.

They advanced, crawling beneath the trees. Suddenly, they all stopped dead. A terrifying stillness hovered above them. Then, close by, a young woman's voice—clear and lyrical—floated through the silent woods:

"We're going to get lost in the snow, Father, we'll never make it to Blainville."[4]

"Don't you worry, my girl," a stronger voice replied. "I know this countryside like the back of my hand."

The Lieutenant said a few words and four men set out, as quiet as shadows.

Suddenly, a woman's piercing cry rose in the night. Two prisoners were led in: an old man and a very young woman. The Lieutenant questioned them, still speaking very softly.

"Name?"

"Pierre Bernard."

"Profession?"

"Head butler to Count de Ronfé."

"Is this your daughter?"

"Yes."

"What does she do?"

"She's a laundress at the château."

"Where are you going?"

"We're running away."

"Why?"

"Twelve Uhlans were there tonight. They shot three guards and hung the gardener; I was afraid for my daughter, you see."

"Where are you going?"

"To Blainville."

"Why?"

"Because the French army is there."

"Do you know how to get there?"

"Absolutely."

"Very well, come with us."

They returned to the rest of the troop and continued walking through the fields. The old man was silent; he walked alongside the Lieutenant. His daughter walked next to him. She suddenly stopped.

"Father," she said, "I'm so tired that I don't think I can go on much longer."

Then she sat down. She was shivering from the cold and looked as if she were about to die. Her father wanted to carry her. He was too old and too weak.

---

4. Blainville is about twelve miles east of Rouen. This identifies the action of the tale as taking place in December 1870 as one half of the Army of the Loire vainly attempted to resist the Prussian advance from the north.

"Lieutenant," he said, sobbing, "we're going to get in your way and slow you down. France comes first. Go on without us."

The officer had already given an order. A few men had left. They returned with some cut-off tree branches. In a minute, they had made a stretcher. The entire detachment had joined them.

"There is a woman here dying of the cold," said the Lieutenant. "Will anyone offer to give up his coat for her?"

Two hundred coats were offered.

"Now who wants to carry her?"

They all stretched out their arms. The young woman was wrapped up in the soldiers' warm greatcoats and gently placed on the stretcher; then four strong arms lifted her up. And like an Oriental queen carried by slaves, she was taken to the middle of the detachment. They walked more briskly now, more courageously, more cheerfully, moved by the presence of a woman, that supreme inspiration that allowed so many prodigious events to be accomplished in the long-standing tradition of France.

After an hour, they stopped again and everyone lay down in the snow. In the distance, in the middle of the field, they could see a large, dark shape. It was like some surreal monster that grew longer, like a snake, then suddenly coiled back into a mass, darted quickly forward, stopped, and continuously changed shape. Orders were whispered and circulated among the men, and every now and then they heard the sharp, short click of metal. The moving mass was fast approaching, and they could see twelve Uhlans, one behind the other, lost in the dark, galloping quickly toward them. A bright flash of light suddenly revealed two hundred men on the ground in front of them. The sound of rapid gunfire faded away into the silent, snowy night, and all twelve of them, along with their horses, fell down dead.

The French detachment waited a long time. Then they started walking again. The old man they had met served as their guide.

At long last, a distant voice cried out: "Who's there!"

Someone closer by replied with the watchword.

They waited some more; discussions took place. It had stopped snowing. A cold wind swept the clouds away, and behind them, high in the night sky, countless stars were shining. They grew fainter as the sky turned pink in the east.

A staff officer arrived to welcome the detachment. When he asked who the person was being carried on the stretcher, it moved; two small hands threw off the heavy blue greatcoats, and an adorable little face appeared. It was as rosy as dawn, with eyes as bright as the stars that had now disappeared, and a smile as bright as the rising sun.

"It's me, Monsieur," she said.

The soldiers, wild with delight, broke out into applause and carried the young woman triumphantly back to camp, where the soldiers were taking up arms. Soon after, General Carrel arrived. At nine o'clock, the Prussians attacked. They were forced to retreat at noon.

That evening, Lieutenant Laré, utterly exhausted, was sleeping on a bale of hay when the General called to see him in his tent. He was chatting with the elderly man the Lieutenant had met during the night. As soon as Lieutenant Laré came in, the General shook his hand.

"My dear Count," he said to the man, "here is the young man you were just telling me about. He's one of my best officers."

He smiled, lowered his voice and added:

"Actually, *the* best."

Then, turning toward the stunned Lieutenant, he said:

"Allow me to introduce Count de Ronfé-Quédissac."

The old man took both the Lieutenant's hands in his.

"My dear Lieutenant," he said, "you saved my daughter's life and I know of only one way to thank you . . . come and see me in a few months to let me know if . . . if you find her appealing . . ."

One year later, to the day, Captain Laré married Mademoiselle Louise-Hortense-Geneviève de Ronfé-Quédissac in the Church of Saint Thomas Aquinas.[5]

She brought him a dowry of six hundred thousand francs, and everyone said she was the prettiest bride they had seen all that year.

Two Friends[†]

Paris was besieged,[1] starving, on the verge of death.[2] There were hardly any sparrows on the rooftops and even the rats had deserted the sewers. People ate anything they could find.

---

5. Fashionable Parisian church in the Rue du Bac, a favored location for society weddings, as is underlined by the bride's impressive dowry and multiple aristocratic family names. The illustration by Edmond Morin, adjoining the text in *La Mosaïque* is entitled "A Marriage at Saint-Thomas Aquinas." This is the only one of Maupassant's war stories with a happy ending.

† First published in the *Gil Blas* on February 5, 1883, under the pseudonym "Maufrigneuse." Maupassant reprinted it at least eleven times over the next nine years. In the *Annales politiques et littéraires* of March 18, 1888, it is prefaced by this newspaper's reference to the recent death of Kaiser William I, affording the tale a renewed topicality. The version translated here is the text in the second edition of *Mademoiselle Fifi* (1893), the last revised by the author.

1. See Introduction, pp. xxii–xxiii.

2. Louis Forestier (in his Pléiade edition of *Contes et nouvelles*, I, 1512) has pointed out that the opening line of the text is a (twelve-syllable) Alexandrine, arguing that this is a deliberately coded allusion to Victor Hugo's evocation of the suffering of the French, during the winter of 1870–71, in the poet's memorable *L'Année terrible* (1872).

One bright morning in January, Monsieur Morissot was walking sadly along a street on the outskirts of the city, his hands in the trouser pockets of his uniform;[3] he was hungry. He was a watchmaker by profession and a homebody by nature. He stopped in his tracks when he suddenly ran into someone he knew. It was Monsieur Sauvage,[4] a friend he had made at the riverbank while out fishing.

Every Sunday, before the war, Morissot would set out before dawn with a bamboo fishing rod in his hand and a tin box slung over his shoulder. He would take the train to Argenteuil,[5] get out at Colombes, and then walk to the Ile Marante,[6] the place of his dreams. As soon as he arrived, he would start to fish, and he would fish all day long, until night fell.

Every Sunday, they met there. Monsieur Sauvage was a short, stout, jovial man, a notions seller from the Rue Notre-Dame-de-Lorette, and another enthusiastic fisherman. They would often spend half a day together, sitting side by side, holding their fishing rods and swinging their legs above the flowing water. And they became good friends.

On certain days, they didn't even speak. Sometimes they would chat a bit, but they got along extremely well without saying a word because they shared the exact same tastes and feelings.

In the springtime, around ten o'clock, when the morning sun cast a fine mist over the water and warmed the backs of the two keen fishermen, Monsieur Morissot would sometimes say to his companion: "Isn't it wonderful here!"

And Monsieur Sauvage would reply: "I can think of nothing better." And those simple words were enough to prove that they understood and respected each other.

In the fall, toward dusk, when the setting sun blazed on the horizon, turning the sky blood red, when the water reflected scarlet clouds from above, made the entire river crimson, burned the faces of the two friends as if they were on fire and cast a golden glow on

---

3. By implication, his National Guard uniform. The depiction of such a member of what was a reserve force, recruited to defend French towns and cities, leaves us in little doubt of the amateur and ineffectual qualities of its manning of the ramparts during the Franco-Prussian War.

4. *Sauvage* has several possible meanings in French: "naïve," "uncultured," or "someone without social graces"; or, as in the English sense, literally "savage." Maupassant ironically plays on this in the savagery of the Prussians toward the unsophisticated Monsieur Sauvage.

5. On the Seine some eight miles west of central Paris, a favourite leisure destination for inhabitants of the capital once the railway line from the Gare Saint-Lazare had made it so accessible. The area around Argenteuil and Colombes was where the front-line French forces confronted the besieging Prussians.

6. Otherwise known as the Île de Colombes, downstream from Argenteuil, this has now been incorporated into a park on the edge of the Boulevard Périférique to the west of Paris. But the reference is not merely geographical: since the eighteenth century, the Île Marante had been for Parisians a rural idyll (*marante* means "fun" or "enjoyable"), as it is for Morissot "the place of his dreams."

the russet trees that already shimmered in a wintry haze, Monsieur Sauvage would smile and look over at Monsieur Morissot and say: "What a wonderful sight!" And Morissot, entranced, would continue staring at his floater and reply: "This is so much better than the city, don't you think?"

Now, as soon as they recognized each other, they shook hands enthusiastically, both men poignantly moved at having met again under such different circumstances. Monsieur Sauvage sighed and murmured: "What terrible times we're going through!" Monsieur Morrisot groaned gloomily: "And the weather's been so awful! Today is the first nice day this year."

The sky was, indeed, a cloudless bright blue.

They started walking along together, side by side, sad and lost in thought. Monsieur Morrisot added: "And remember when we went fishing? Oh, it's so good to think back to those times!"

"When do you think we'll be able to go back there?" asked Monsieur Sauvage.

They went into a small café and drank some absinthe; then they went back outside and continued walking.

Monsieur Morrisot suddenly stopped. "How about another, what do you think?" Monsieur Sauvage agreed. "Your wish is my command." And they went into another bar.

They were extremely drunk when they came outside again, like people who have been fasting and then have a stomachful of alcohol. It was warm out. A gentle breeze tickled their faces.

Monsieur Sauvage, totally drunk now because of the warm weather, stopped walking: "What if we went?"

"Went where?"

"Went fishing."

"But where?"

"To our little island. The French outposts are near Colombes. I know Colonel Dumoulin; we can easily get through."

Monsieur Morrisot trembled with desire: "Right. I'm in." And they went their separate ways to pick up their fishing gear.

An hour later, they were walking side by side on the main road. Then they reached the house where the Colonel lived. He smiled at their request and agreed to their whim. They continued on their way, armed with their travel pass.

Soon they crossed the outposts, walked through the deserted region of Colombes and followed a little vineyard that led down to the Seine. It was about eleven o'clock in the morning.

On the other side of the river, the village of Argenteuil looked dead. The Orgemont and Sannois hills towered above the entire region. The vast plain that stretched to Nanterre was deserted, completely deserted, with nothing but bare cherry trees and gray earth.

Monsieur Sauvage pointed to the tops of the hills and whispered: "The Prussians are up there!" And the two friends stood dead still in this isolated spot, terrified.

"The Prussians!" They had never seen any, but for months now, they could sense they were there, all around Paris, destroying France, pillaging, massacring, causing everyone to starve, invisible and all-powerful. A kind of superstitious terror mingled with the hatred they felt toward these victorious foreigners.

"Hey! What if we ran into some of them?" Monsieur Morissot stammered.

Monsieur Sauvage's Parisian cockiness returned to him, in spite of everything.

"We'll offer them some fish to fry," he replied.

But they hesitated when it came to venturing into the country-side, intimidated by the silence that stretched across the horizon.

Finally, Monsieur Sauvage made a decision: "Come on, let's go! But let's be careful." And they went down into the vineyard, hunched over, crawling, using the bushes as cover, fearfully on the lookout and straining to hear any noise.

One strip of bare land remained to be crossed before they could get to the river. They started running, and as soon as they reached the riverbank, they huddled in the dry reeds.

Monsieur Morissot pressed his ear to the ground to hear if anyone was marching in the area. He heard nothing. They were alone, completely alone.

They felt reassured and began to fish.

Opposite them, the deserted Ile Marante hid them from view from the other side of the river.

The little restaurant was closed and seemed as if it has been neglected for many years.

Monsieur Sauvage caught the first fish, a gudgeon. Monsieur Morissot caught the second one, and every minute or so, they would reel in their lines with a wriggling, silvery fish attached; it was a truly miraculous catch.

They very carefully slipped the fish into a fine mesh fishing net that dripped water down onto their feet. And a wonderful sense of joy ran through them, the kind of joy that takes hold of you when you once again experience a pleasure you love, and that you have been deprived of for so long.

The delightful sun spread its warmth down their backs; they no longer listened out for anything, no longer thought about anything; the rest of the world just didn't exist: they were fishing.

But suddenly, a muffled sound that seemed to come from underground made the earth shake. A cannon had started firing again.

Monsieur Morissot looked around and, beyond the bank, to the left, he saw the high outline of Mont-Valérien,[7] there was a wispy white feather at its summit, a cloud of smoke it had just spit out.

Immediately, a second spurt of smoke shot from the top of the fortress; and a few seconds later, a new explosion roared out.

Then others followed, and every few minutes the mountain spewed its deadly breath, billowing out its milky mist that rose slowly into the calm sky, forming a cloud above the summit.

Monsieur Sauvage shrugged his shoulders. "Here they go again," he said.

Monsieur Morissot, who was anxiously watching the feather of his floater sink with every roar of the cannon, was suddenly overwhelmed with the kind of anger a peaceable man feels toward the madmen who fought like this. "How stupid do you have to be to kill each other this way!" he grumbled.

"They're worse than animals," replied Monsieur Sauvage.

And Monsieur Morissot, who had just caught a fish, said: "And to think it will always be like this as long as there are governments."

Monsieur Sauvage cut in: "The French Republic wouldn't have declared war . . ."

But Monsieur Morissot interrupted him: "With kings we have wars in other countries; with the Republic, we have wars in our own."[8]

And they calmly began a discussion, trying to untangle the great political problems of the day with the clear logic of kind, ordinary men of average intelligence, agreeing on this one point: that people would never be free. And Mont-Valérien thundered tirelessly, firing cannonballs that demolished French homes, crushed lives, destroyed people, put an end to dreams and to so many anticipated joys, to so much hope and happiness, filling the hearts of women, the hearts of daughters, the hearts of mothers, far away, in other lands, filling their hearts with endless suffering.

"That's life," said Monsieur Sauvage.

Monsieur Morissot laughed and added: "You mean, that's death."

But they shuddered in fear, sensing that someone was walking behind them, and they were right. They looked around and saw four men standing there, four big, bearded men with guns, dressed like livery servants and wearing flat caps, four men who were pointing their rifles at them.

They dropped the two lines they were holding, which slowly sank down into the river.

7. The fort of Mont-Valérien, overlooking Suresnes, on the highest hill in the Paris area, was by now the Prussian headquarters from which they could bombard the French.
8. Reference to the civil war of the Commune; see Introduction, pp. xxiii–xxiv.

In a few seconds, the two friends had been grabbed, tied up, carried off, thrown into a small boat and taken to the island.

And behind the house they had thought was deserted, they saw twenty-odd German soldiers.

A kind of hairy giant sat straddling his chair and smoking a long porcelain pipe. "Now then, gentlemen," he said in excellent French. "Have you caught a lot of fish?"

A soldier had made sure to bring the fish with them and he placed the full net at the officer's feet. The Prussian smiled.

"Well! Well! I can see that you didn't do badly at all. But that's not what I want to discuss. Listen to me and don't worry.

"As far as I am concerned, you are two spies sent to find me. I catch you and shoot you. You were pretending to be fishing in order to best hide your real plan. You fell into my hands, too bad. That's war for you.

"But since you got past the outposts, you surely have a password to get you back. Tell me the password and I'll let you live."

The two friends, pale as ghosts, stood side by side, their hands trembling slightly from anxiety. They said nothing.

The officer continued: "No one will ever know and you can go safely back home. The secret will go with you to your grave. If you refuse, you will die, and right now. Choose."

They stood dead still without saying a word.

The Prussian remained calm and pointed toward the river. "In just five minutes, you will be at the bottom of that water," he continued. "Just think about it: in five minutes! You must have families, don't you?"

Cannon fire from Mont-Valérien continued to thunder.

The two fishermen stood there in silence. The German gave orders in his own language. Then he moved his chair away so he wouldn't be too close to the prisoners, and twelve men came and stood at twenty paces from them, rifles at their sides.

"You have one minute," the officer added, "not a second more."

Suddenly, he stood up, went over to the two Frenchmen, took Monsieur Morissot by the arm and dragged him further away. "Quickly," he said very quietly, "tell me the password, all right? Your friend will never know; it will just look as if I've calmed down a bit."

Monsieur Morissot said nothing.

The Prussian then dragged Monsieur Sauvage to the side and asked him the same question.

Monsieur Sauvage said nothing.

The two friends stood side by side once more.

The officer started shouting out orders. The soldiers raised their weapons.

Then Monsieur Morissot happened to glance over at the fishing net full of gudgeon that sat on the grass a few feet away.

A ray of sunlight reflected off the heap of fish that were still moving, making them shine brightly. And a feeling of weakness swept through him. He just couldn't help himself, his eyes filled with tears.

"Goodbye, Monsieur Sauvage," he stammered.

"Goodbye, Monsieur Morissot," his friend replied.

They shook hands, trembling uncontrollably from head to foot.

"Fire!" shouted the officer.

The twelve bullets hit them all at once.

Monsieur Sauvage fell straight down, face-first. Monsieur Morissot, who was a bigger man, swayed, pivoted around and fell diagonally across his friend, his face raised to the heavens as blood gushed from his chest beneath his jacket.

The German shouted more orders.

His men scattered, came back with ropes and stones and tied them to the dead men's feet, then carried them to the riverbank.

Mont-Valérien, now shrouded in smoke, never stopped thundering.

Two soldiers took Monsieur Morissot by the head and feet; two others got hold of Monsieur Sauvage in the same way. They swung the bodies with great effort and heaved them far into the river; their bodies flew up, arched, then fell straight down into the water, the stones pulling them in feet-first.

The water splashed, bubbled up, rippled, then was calm, while tiny little waves hit the riverbanks.

A bit of blood floated on the surface.

The officer, still very calm, said quietly: "Now the fish can get even."

Then he headed back to the house.

Suddenly, he noticed the net full of gudgeon in the grass. He picked it up, examined it, smiled and shouted: "Wilhelm!"

A soldier wearing a white apron came running out. And the Prussian, throwing him the two dead men's catch, ordered:

"Throw these little fish into a frying pan for me right away, while they're still alive. They'll be delicious!"

Then he picked up his pipe and started to smoke.

Père Milon[†][1]

For a month now, the sun's scorching rays have been raining fire down onto the fields. All life is blossoming radiantly beneath this

† Published in *Le Gaulois* on May 22, 1883.
1. The French often use *Père* (Father) to describe someone older or to distinguish the person from his son; the title could thus be translated as "Old Man Milon."

torrent of fire; the land is green as far as the eye can see. The blue
sky stretches out over the horizon. From a distance, the farms scattered over the flat, open countryside of Normandy look like clusters
of small woods, surrounded as they are by circles of tall beech trees.
From close up, after you open the worm-eaten gate, you think you
have entered an enormous garden, for all the old apple trees, as
knobby as the farmers, are in bloom. Their old dark trunks, gnarled,
bent, set in rows in the courtyard, reach upward toward the sky,
showing off their dazzling canopy of pink and white blossom. The
sweet scent of their flowers mingles with the thick smells from the
open stables and the steaming dung as it ferments, pecked at by
the hens.

It is noon. The family is eating in the shade of a pear tree planted
in front of the door: the father, the mother, their four children and
five servants—two women and three men. They hardly speak. They
eat their soup, then dish out the meat stew with plenty of potatoes
and bacon.

Every now and again, one of the servants gets up and goes down
to the cellar to refill the cider jug.

The man, a tall fellow, about forty years old, is staring at a grape-
vine growing up toward the shutters over one wall of the house; it
has no fruit yet; it is as long and twisted as a snake.

"Father's vine is budding early this year," he says at last. "May be
that it'll have some fruit."

The woman turns around and looks at it as well, without saying
a word.

The vine was planted at the very spot where his father had been
shot and killed.

It happened during the 1870 war. The Prussians were occupying the
whole country. The French general Faidherbe and the Northern
army were fighting them.[2]

The Prussians had set up their headquarters at this farm. The old
farmer who owned it, Père Milon, Pierre, had accepted them and
made them as comfortable as possible.

For a month, the German vanguard had kept watch in the village.
The French soldiers held their position, about thirty-five miles away.
And yet, every night, some Uhlans disappeared.

None of the small groups of scouts, the ones that had only two or
three men sent out on patrol, ever came back.

2. After the disaster at Sedan (see Introduction, p. xxii), General Faidherbe (1818–1890)
   had been given command of the Army of the North, holding up the Prussian advance
   by its victories in battles at Pont-de-Noyelles and Bapaume in the winter of 1870–71
   and only finally defeated at Saint-Quentin on January 19, 1871.

Their dead bodies were found the next morning, in a field, or outside a courtyard or in a ditch. Even their horses were found dead along the roadside, their throats cut by a sword.

These murders seemed to be carried out by the same men, who were never found.

The whole region was terrorized. Farmers were shot if anyone simply pointed a finger at them; women were put in prison. Children were threatened to try to get information out of them. They learned nothing.

Now it happened that one morning, Père Milon was found in his stable with a gash on his face.

Two Uhlans[3] had been found dead, their stomachs cut open, about three miles from the farm. One of them still had his bloody sword in his hand. He had fought back, trying to defend himself.

A military tribunal was set up right in front of the farm, and the old man was brought out.

He was sixty-eight years old. He was short, thin, a little bent over, with large hands that looked like the claws on a crab. His drab hair was as soft and downy as a duckling's, so you could see patches of his scalp here and there. The suntanned, wrinkled skin on his neck had thick veins that ran down into his jaws and reemerged at his temples. He was known in the area as stingy and hard to do business with.

They stood him between four soldiers, in front of the kitchen table that they'd brought outside. Five officers and the Colonel sat opposite him.

The Colonel began speaking in French:

"Père Milon, ever since we have been here, we have had only praise for you. You have always been considerate and even attentive toward us. But today, a terrible accusation is hanging over you, and we must clear things up. How did you get that wound on your face?"

The farmer did not reply.

"Your silence tells us you are guilty, Père Milon," the Colonel continued. "I want you to answer me, do you understand? Do you know who killed the two Uhlans that were found this morning near the cross at the roadside?"

"Me," the old man said clearly.

The Colonel, surprised, fell silent for a moment, staring at the prisoner. Père Milon remained impassive; he looked like an old, confused farmer, his eyes lowered as if he were speaking to his priest. Only one thing gave away what he was feeling inside: he continually swallowed his saliva, with visible difficulty, as if his throat had completely closed up.

---

3. Also known as "lancers."

Père Milon's family, his son Jean, daughter-in-law and two grand-children, stood a few feet behind him, terrified and filled with dismay.

"Do you also know who killed all the scouts from our army we've been finding in the countryside every morning for a month?" the Colonel continued.

The old man replied with the same brutish passivity:

"Me."

"You are the one who killed all of them?"

"Each and every one of 'em, yes, me."

"You, just you?"

"Only me."

"Tell me how you did it."

This time, the old man seemed upset; it was clear he was uncomfortable at having to talk at length.

"Don't know, just did it, however it happened," he muttered.

"I'm warning you," the Colonel said, "that you have to tell me everything. You would be better off to resign yourself to that right now. How did it start?"

The man looked anxiously over at his family who were listening attentively behind him. He hesitated again for a moment, then suddenly, made a decision.

"I was coming back one night, must've been around ten o'clock, the day after you got here. You and your soldiers had robbed me of more than fifty écus worth of fodder and a cow and two sheep. So I says to myself: whatever they're takin' from me, fifty écus or whatever, that's what I'll take back from them. And I also had other things I was feeling that I'll tell you about. I seen one of your cavalrymen smoking his pipe near the ditch behind my barn, I went and got my scythe and come back real quiet like from behind so he didn't hear a thing. And I cut off his head in one go, just one, like it was an ear of corn, before he could even say 'Ouch!' You just look in the bottom of the pond: you'll find him in a coal sack, with a stone from the wall.

"Then I got an idea. I took all his stuff, from his hat right down to his boots, and hid 'em in the vaulted tunnel leading to the lime kiln in the Martin woods, behind the farm."

The old man fell silent. The officers, stunned, looked at each other.

The interrogation continued, and this is what they were told:

Once he had carried out this murder, the man had been obsessed by one thought: "Kill the Prussians!" He hated them with the sly, fierce hatred of a greedy farmer, and a patriotic one. He knew his mind, as he put it. He waited a few days.

He had displayed such humility, submission and compliance toward the conquerors that he was allowed to come and go as he pleased. He saw the dispatch riders leaving every evening, so he went out one night, after overhearing the name of the village where they were headed, having learned the few words of German he needed from living with the soldiers.

He left by the courtyard, slipped into the woods, reached the tunnel leading to the lime kiln, went to the very end of it where he found the dead man's clothes he'd left on the floor and put them on.

Then he started prowling through the fields, crawling on all fours, following the embankment so he wouldn't be seen, listening out for the slightest noise, as anxious as a poacher.

When he'd felt the time was right, he got closer to the road and hid behind a bush. He waited a while. Finally, around midnight, he heard the sound of a horse galloping along the solid earth on the road. He put his ear to the ground to make sure that only one horseman was coming, then got ready.

The Uhlan was galloping fast, bringing back the dispatches. He listened carefully, kept his eyes open. When he was no more than ten feet away, Pére Milon crawled out onto the road,' groaning: "Hilfe! Hilfe!—Help, help!" The horseman stopped, thinking there was a wounded German on the ground; he got off his horse, went up to him, suspecting nothing, and leaned over the stranger. The long, curved blade of a sword sliced through his middle. He fell down dead at once, without realizing what had happened, his body quivering in the final throes of death.

The Norman farmer beamed with the silent joy of an old farmer; he stood up and cut the dead man's throat, just for fun. Then he dragged the body to the ditch and threw it in.

The horse was calmly waiting for his master. Pére Milon mounted him and took off at a gallop across the flat, open country.

About an hour later, he spotted two more Uhlans riding side by side, on their way back home. He headed straight at them, again shouting: "Hilfe! Hilfe!" The Prussians, recognizing the uniform, made way for him, utterly trusting. And the old man charged through them like a cannonball, killing one with his sword, then shooting the other.

Then he slit the horses' throats, German horses! He calmly returned to the tunnel leading to the lime kiln and hid his horse at the back. He took off the uniform, put on his old, tattered clothes, went home to bed and slept until morning.

He didn't go out again for four days, waiting for the inquest that had been ordered to finish; but on the fifth day, he went out again and killed two more soldiers using the same technique. After that, he never stopped. Every night, he wandered around, prowled about wherever his fancy led him, killing Prussians wherever he found them, galloping through the empty fields in the moonlight, a lost Uhlan, on a manhunt. Once he had completed his task, leaving dead bodies lying beside the road, the old rider went back to the tunnel where he hid his horse and his uniform.

Every day around noon, he calmly took oats and water to his horse in his underground hiding place; he gave him a lot to eat, as he demanded a great deal of work from him.

The night before, however, one of the men he'd attacked had been suspicious, and had slashed the old farmer's face with his sword.

He had still managed to kill them though, both of them! He had gone back to the woods again, hidden his horse and put on his tattered clothes; but as he was coming home, he felt very weak and had dragged himself to the stable, unable to make it to the house.

He had been found there, bleeding, stretched out in the hay . . .

When he'd finished his story, he suddenly raised his head and looked proudly at the Prussian officers.

The Colonel, who was pulling at his moustache, asked: "Do you have anything else to say?"

"No, nothing, the debt is paid. I killed sixteen of 'em, not one more, not one less."

"You know that you are going to die?"

"I don't want no mercy."

"Were you ever a soldier?"

"Yes. I was in the service, in the past. And back then, you were the ones who killed my father, he was a soldier under the first Emperor.[4] And don't forget you killed my youngest son, François, last month, near Evreux.[5] You had it comin' and I give it to you. We're even."

The officers looked at each other.

"Eight for my father," the old farmer continued, "eight for my son, so we're even. I didn't go lookin' for a fight, not me! I don't even know you! I don't even know where you come from! Here you are, in my house, givin' orders like you owned the place. I got back at you through the others. And I ain't sorry."

Then, pulling his stiff old body straight, he crossed his arms, striking the pose of a humble hero.

The Prussians talked amongst themselves for a long time. One of the captains, who had also lost his son the month before, defended the high-minded villain.

Then the Colonel stood up and went over to Père Milon.

4. Napoleon I.
5. About twenty-five miles due south of Rouen.

"Listen to me old man," he said quietly, "there is perhaps a way to save your life, if you . . ."

But Père Milon was not listening; staring straight at the conquering officer, as the wind rustled through the downy hairs on his head, he grimaced terribly, tensing his thin face with the gash on it, and puffing out his chest, he spit; as hard as he could, right into the Prussian's face.

The Colonel, furious, raised his hand, and for the second time, the man spit at him, right in the face.

All the officers had stood up and were shouting orders at once.

In less than a minute, the old man, still impassive, was pushed against the wall and, smiling at Jean, his older son, his daughter-in-law and his two grandchildren; he was shot dead, as they all looked on in horror.

The Adventure of Walter Schnaffs[†]

Ever since he had entered France with the invading army, Walter Schnaffs considered himself the unhappiest of men. He was very round, walked with difficulty, was often out of breath and suffered terribly from painful feet that were very thick and very flat. Besides all this, he was a kindly, peaceful man, neither bloodthirsty nor overly generous, the father of four children he adored and married to a young blond woman whose kisses, attention and affection he missed desperately every night. He liked getting up late and going to bed early, savoring good food and drinking beer in restaurants. He also believed that everything sweet in life eventually disappears; and in his heart, he held a horrific, instinctive, and logical hatred for cannons, rifles, guns and sabers, but most especially for bayonets, as he felt incapable of maneuvering that particular weapon quickly enough to defend his fat belly.

When night fell and he was wrapped up in his coat and stretched out on the ground next to his snoring comrades, he thought for a long time about the family he'd left back home, and about the dangers he might encounter along the way. What would happen to his little ones if he were killed? Who would provide for them and bring them up? They still weren't rich, in spite of the debt he'd gotten himself into so he could give them a bit of money before he left. And so Walter Schnaffs sometimes cried.

† First published in *Le Gaulois* on April 11, 1883, before being included in the *Contes de la bécasse* later the same year. In that volume, the tale was dedicated to Robert Pinchon (1846–1925), one of Maupassant's most enduring friends since his schooldays. Dedicating it to him also speaks of a shared ribald sense of humor, Pinchon having collaborated in the writing of, as well as acting in, Maupassant's mildly obscene early play, *À la feuille de rose* (1875), set in a brothel.

At the start of the fighting, he felt his legs were so weak that he would have let himself fall to the ground if he hadn't believed that the entire army would trample his body. The sound of bullets whizzing past made his hair stand on end.

For many long months he had lived in terror and anguish.

His platoon was advancing toward Normandy; one day he and a small reconnaissance party were sent on ahead simply to explore a section of the area and then withdraw. Everything seemed calm in the countryside; nothing led them to believe they would meet with any organized resistance.

The Prussians were calmly going down a little valley cut through by deep ravines when heavy rounds of gunfire stopped them in their tracks, killing about twenty of their men; and a group of snipers suddenly rushed out from a tiny wood, running forward, bayonets on their rifles.

At first, Walter Schnaffs stood dead still, so astonished and terrified that he didn't even think of running away. Then he was seized by a mad desire to make a run for it; but he immediately realized he ran as slow as a tortoise in comparison to the thin Frenchmen who were leaping about like a herd of goats. Then he noticed there was a large ditch full of brushwood covered in dry leaves a few steps in front of him, so he jumped into it feet-first, without even stopping to wonder how deep it was, just as you might jump into a river from a bridge.

Straight and sharp as an arrow, he pierced a thick layer of vines and sharp brambles that scratched his hands and face, then fell heavily on his bottom onto a bed of stones.

He immediately looked up at the sky through the hole he'd made. This gaping hole might give him away, so he carefully crawled, on all fours, to the back of the ditch, under the roof made of linked branches, going as fast as possible, to get far away from the battlefield. Then he stopped and sat down again, crouching out of sight like a hare in the tall, dry grass.

For some time, he could still hear explosions, shouting and cries. Then the clamor of the battle died down, stopped altogether. Everything became silent and calm once more.

Suddenly, something moved next to him. He jumped in terror. It was a little bird who had scattered the dead leaves as he landed on a branch. For nearly an hour, Walter Schnaffs's heart raced and pounded wildly.

Night fell, engulfing the ravine in darkness. And the soldier began to think. What was he going to do? What would happen to him? Could he get back to his army . . . ? How? Which way? But if he went back, he would have to start living that horrible life all over again, the life of anguish, terror, exhaustion and suffering he'd led since the beginning of the war! No! He couldn't face it any more! He no longer had the strength he needed to endure the marches and face danger at every moment.

But what could he do? He couldn't hide in this ravine until the end of the hostilities. No, certainly not. If he hadn't needed to eat, this idea would not have been such a bad one; but he did need to eat, and every day.

And so he found himself all alone, in uniform, armed, on enemy territory, far from anyone who could help him. He was shaking from head to toe.

"If only I were taken prisoner!" he suddenly thought, and his heart quivered with desire, an intense, passionate desire to be captured by the French. Prisoner! He would be saved, fed, given shelter, safely away from the bullets and sabers, with nothing to possibly feel anxious about, in a well-guarded, good prison. Prisoner! How perfect!

And he immediately made his decision:

"I'm going to be taken prisoner."

He stood up, determined to carry out his plan without wasting another minute. But he stood very still, suddenly overwhelmed by dreadful thoughts and terrifying new fears.

Where should he go to be taken prisoner? How? Which way? And horrifying images, images of death, rushed through his soul.

He would be in great danger, roaming about the countryside in his pointed helmet.[1]

What if he ran into some farmers? If any farmers saw a lost Prussian, a helpless Prussian, they would kill him as if he were stray dog! They would murder him with their pitchforks, their pickaxes, their scythes, their shovels! They would reduce him to a pulp, give him a real beating, with the fierceness of frustrated losers.

What if he ran into any snipers? Snipers who were madmen, who obeyed no rules and had no discipline: as soon as they spotted him, they would shoot him just for fun, to help pass the time, for a laugh. And he could already picture himself crushed against a wall facing the butts of twelve rifles whose little round black eyes seemed to be staring at him.

What if he ran into the French army itself? The men in the front lines would take him for a scout, some bold, malicious private who had gone on a reconnaissance mission all alone, and they'd open fire on him. And he imagined the erratic blasts of gunfire from soldiers hidden in the brush, imagined himself standing in the middle of a field, then falling to the ground, riddled with holes from the bullets he could already feel penetrating his body.

---

1. The Prussians wore distinctive helmets with sharp metal spikes on top.

He sat down again, in despair. There seemed to be no way out of his situation.

It was completely dark now, silent and dark. He didn't move, shuddering at the slightest strange noise he heard in the shadows. A rabbit, thumping his bottom at the edge of a burrow, nearly made Walter Schnaffs run for his life. The hooting of the owls pierced his soul, cut through his heart with sharp, painful blows that terrified him. He squinted, trying to see in the dark; and he constantly imagined he could hear people walking close by.

After endless hours and suffering the terrors of the damned, he looked through the covering of branches and saw that day was breaking. Then he felt enormously relieved; he stretched out his arms and legs and suddenly relaxed; his heart felt calm; his eyes closed. He fell asleep.

When he woke up, the sun seemed to be more or less in the middle of the sky; it must have been noon. Not a single sound disturbed the gloomy silence of the fields; and Walter Schnaffs realized that he was extremely hungry.

He yawned, salivating at the idea of some sausages, the good sausages that soldiers eat; and his stomach hurt.

He stood up, took a few steps, felt that his legs were weak, and sat down again to think. For two or three hours more, he considered the pros and cons, changing his mind from one minute to the next, defeated, unhappy, torn between contradictory ideas.

One thought finally seemed both logical and practical to him, and that was to keep an eye out for some villager who was walking past all alone, unarmed, and without any dangerous workman's tools, to run out in front of him and put himself in his hands, making it very clear that he was surrendering.

Then he took off his helmet, as its sharp point could give him away, and taking infinite care, he poked his head outside his hiding hole.

Not a single soul was in sight. Further away, to the right, he could see the smoke rising from the rooftops of a little village, the smoke from the kitchens! Further away, to the left, he saw a wide passageway lined with trees, leading to a large château flanked by turrets.

He waited until nightfall, his hunger causing him terrible pain, seeing nothing but crows in flight, hearing nothing but the muted rumbling of his entrails.

And night descended upon him once more.

He stretched out at the back of his shelter and fell asleep: it was a feverish sleep, haunted by nightmares, the sleep of a starving man.

Dawn broke once more above his head. He started keeping watch again. But the countryside was as empty as the day before; and a new fear spread through the mind of Walter Schnaffs, the fear of starving to death! He could picture himself stretched out in the corner of his hiding place, on his back, his eyes closed. Then the animals, all sorts of small animals, went over to his corpse and started eating him, attacking him everywhere at once, sliding underneath his clothes to bite at his cold flesh. And a large black crow was pecking at his eyes with its sharp beak.

Then he nearly went mad, imagining he might faint from weakness and wouldn't be able to walk any more. And he was just about to rush toward the village, determined to brave everything, when he spotted three farmers walking through the fields, their pitchforks slung over their shoulders, and he jumped back into his hiding place.

But as soon as night fell over the plain, he slowly came out of the ditch, and started to walk toward the château he could see in the distance; bent over, frightened, his heart pounding, he preferred to go there rather than the village which seemed as terrifying to him as a lair full of tigers.

Light shone through the downstairs windows. One of them was even open; a strong smell of roasted meat wafted out, an aroma that quickly filtered through Walter Schnaffs, from his nose right down to his stomach; it made him flinch, made him pant, irresistibly attracting him, filling his heart with desperate daring.

Then, without stopping, to think, he pressed his face against the window; he was still wearing his helmet.

Eight servants were having dinner around a large table. Suddenly, one of the maids stood stock-still, stunned, eyes wide, and dropped her glass. Everyone turned to see what she was staring at!

It was the enemy!

Good Lord! The Prussians were attacking the château!

At first, there was a cry, a single cry, made up of the cries of eight different voices, a horrible cry of terror, then a chaotic jumping up, a scramble, a free-for-all, a mad rush toward the back door. Chairs fell back, men knocked women down and stepped over them. In two seconds, the room was empty, deserted, the table piled high with food. Walter Schnaffs stood looking at it through the window, stunned.

After hesitating a few minutes, he climbed over the parapet and walked over to the plates of food. His extreme hunger made him tremble like a man delirious with fever: but one terrible fear held him back, nailed him to the spot. He listened. The entire house seemed to be shaking; doors slammed shut, footsteps raced through the floor above. The anxious Prussian listened to the baffling din; then he heard some muted sounds, as if bodies were falling onto the soft ground, at the foot of the walls, bodies jumping from the first floor.

Then all the movement, all the commotion stopped, and the large château became as silent as a tomb.

Walter Schnaffs sat down in front of one of the plates that had not been broken and began to eat. He gulped down great mouthfuls, as if he were afraid he might be interrupted too soon, before having wolfed enough down. He used both hands to throw bits of food into his mouth, which was opened as wide as a trap door; and lumps of food fell into his stomach one after the other, making his throat swell as he swallowed them. Every now and again he stopped, ready to explode like a pipe about to burst. Then he took the pitcher of cider and cleared his esophagus the way you wash out a clogged pipe.

He emptied all the plates, all the dishes and all the bottles; intoxicated on food and drink, dazed, bright red, shaking from hiccups, his mind confused and his mouth greasy, he unbuttoned his uniform so he could breathe, incapable of taking a single step. His eyes closed, his mind grew sluggish; he placed his heavy head on the table, onto his crossed arms, and little by little lost all consciousness of everything around him.

The last crescent of the moon dimly lit up the horizon above the trees on the grounds of the château. It was the time of morning just before dawn when it was still cold.

Shadows slipped through the many silent thickets, and every now and then, a moonbeam struck a piece of steel, making it glow in the darkness.

The imposing, dark silhouette of the peaceful château stood tall. Only two windows on the ground floor still had their lights on.

Suddenly, a booming voice shouted:
"Forward men! Go! Charge!"

In seconds, the doors, the shutters and the windows crashed down under a wave of men who rushed forward, shattered everything, broke everything, and swarmed into the house. In seconds, fifty soldiers armed to the teeth flooded into the kitchen where Walter Schnaffs was peacefully resting; they held fifty loaded rifles to his chest, knocked him down, rolled him over, held him down and tied him up from head to toe.

He was panting with shock, too stunned to understand what was happening, beaten, hit with their rifle butts and absolutely terrified.

And suddenly, a fat soldier wearing many gold medals set his foot on the stomach of Walter Schnaffs, shouting:
"I am taking you prisoner, surrender!"

The Prussian only understood the word "prisoner," so he groaned, "Ja, ja, ja."

His conquerors hauled him up, tied him to a chair and examined with keen curiosity this prisoner who was wheezing like a whale. Several of them were so overcome with emotion and exhaustion that they had to sit down.

And Walter Schnaffs was smiling, he was smiling now, certain at last that he had been taken prisoner!

Another officer came in.

"Colonel, the enemy has fled," he said. "Several of them seem to have been wounded. We have taken control of the château."

The fat soldier wiped his forehead and shouted: "Victory!"

Then he made some notes in a small business diary that he took out of his pocket:

"After a fierce battle, the Prussians were forced to retreat, taking their dead and their wounded with them, an estimated fifty men put out of action. Several of them were taken prisoner."

"What arrangements shall I make, Colonel?" the young officer asked.

"We are going to withdraw," the Colonel replied, "to avoid a new offensive with superior troops and artillery."

And he gave the order to leave.

Two lines of soldiers formed in the dark, beneath the walls of the château, and started to move, surrounding Walter Schnaffs on all sides; he was tied up and led along by six warriors pointing guns at him.

A reconnaissance patrol was sent on ahead to scout the road. They advanced cautiously, stopping from time to time.

As day broke, they reached the subprefecture of La Roche-Oysel,[2] whose National Guard had brought home this military victory.

The eager, overexcited townspeople were there, waiting. When they saw the prisoner's helmet, they started shouting vehemently. Younger women raised their arms in the air; the old women wept; one grandfather threw his crutch at the Prussian but hit one of the guards on the nose, wounding him.

"Stand guard over the prisoner," the Colonel shouted.

They finally reached the Town Hall. The prison door was opened and Walter Schnaffs was untied and thrown inside.

Two hundred armed men stood watch around the building.

And then, in spite of the symptoms of indigestion that had been troubling him for some time, the Prussian, mad with joy, began to dance, dance frantically, raising his arms and legs in the air, dancing and shouting frenetically, until he finally dropped down, exhausted, against a wall.

He was a prisoner! He was saved!

And that is how the Château de Champignet was won back from the enemy after being occupied for only six hours.

2. Although invented, the name recalls the town of Oissel, between Rouen and Elbeuf.

Colonel Ratier,[3] a fabric salesman, who pulled off this coup as chief of the National Guard of La Roche-Oysel, was awarded a medal.

La Mère Sauvage[†][1]

I

I hadn't been back to Virelogne[2] for fifteen years. I returned in the autumn, to stay with my friend Serval and go hunting; he had finally rebuilt his château after the Prussians had destroyed it.

I loved this part of the country a great deal. It is one of those wonderful places that appeal to the eye with sensual charm. The kind of place you feel a physical love for. People like us who are seduced by the countryside remember with great affection certain streams, certain woods, certain lakes, certain hills, for we have seen them so often and they have touched us the way all joyful events do. Sometimes, our thoughts return to one part of a forest, or the edge of a riverbank, or an orchard filled with flowers, perhaps seen only once, on a happy day, but they have remained in our hearts like images of women you happened to meet in the street, one spring morning, women wearing light, transparent dresses who leave in our bodies and souls an unforgettable feeling of unrequited desire, the sensation of having briefly encountered happiness.

I loved all the countryside around Virelogne; it was dotted with little woods and brooks that ran through the ground like veins, carrying blood deep into the earth. You could fish there for trout, crayfish and eels. Such divine happiness! There were places to go swimming, and you often found wading birds in the tall grass that grew along the banks of these narrow streams.

I was walking along, as sprightly as a goat, watching my two dogs sniffing the ground ahead of me. Serval, who was about a hundred yards to my right, was stamping through a field of alfalfa. I turned past the bushes at the edge of the Saudres woods and noticed a cottage in ruins.

Suddenly, I remembered the way it looked the last time I'd seen it, in 1869: clean, covered in vines, with chickens outside the door.

---

3. Another witty name: a *ratier* is "a dog that hunts down rats."
† First published in *Le Gaulois* on March 3, 1884; reprinted later the same year in *Miss Harriet*. In that volume, the text was dedicated to Georges Pouchet (1833–1894), a medical scientist from Rouen about whom Maupassant had written admiringly and at length in an article in *Le Gaulois* on March 23, 1881. He was a close friend of Flaubert, in whose company Maupassant got to know him well enough to consult him about his own and his mother's health problems.
1. As in *Two Friends* (see above, p. 138, note 4), Maupassant plays on the various meanings of *sauvage*. To call someone *Mère* indicates she is elderly as well as a mother.
2. A place invented by Maupassant.

Is there anything sadder than a lifeless house, with its dilapidated, sinister skeleton still standing?

I also remembered that one day when I was very tired, a kind woman had given me a glass of wine in that house, and that Serval had told me the story of the people who lived there. The father, an old poacher, had been killed by the police. The son, whom I had seen in the past, was a tall, thin young man who was also known as an aggressive game hunter. People called them the Savages.

Was that their real name or a nickname?

I called out to Serval. He took long steps, like a wading bird, and came over to me.

"What happened to the people who lived over there?" I asked.

And he told me this story.

II

When war was declared,[3] the son, who was then thirty-three, enlisted, leaving his mother alone in her house. No one felt very sorry for the old woman because she had money, and everyone knew it.

And so she lived all by herself in this isolated house, at the edge of the woods. But she wasn't afraid; she came from the same stock as the men in her family; she was a tough old woman, tall and thin, who hardly ever laughed and the kind of person you didn't joke with. In fact, none of the women who worked in the fields in these parts hardly ever laughed. Only the men could laugh and joke around. The women have sad, poor hearts, because their lives are gloomy and dull. The farmers learn a bit of cheerfulness at the taverns, but their wives remain serious and always look stern. The muscles in their face never learned how to laugh.

La Mère Sauvage continued her ordinary life in her cottage, which was soon covered in snow. She went to the village once a week to buy bread and a little meat; then she returned to her hovel. Because everyone talked about wolves in the woods, she always went out with a rifle on her shoulder, her son's rusty rifle with the worn-down butt; and she was a strange sight, the tall Mère Sauvage, a little bent over, walking slowly through the snow, the gun barrel sticking out above the black hat everyone wore in those parts that fit tightly on her head and kept her white hair well covered; no one had ever seen her hair.

One day, the Prussians arrived. They were sent to lodge with the townspeople, according to their wealth and resources. The old woman, who was known to be rich, got four soldiers.

They were four big young men with pale skin, blond beards and blue eyes; they had remained fat in spite of the strain they had

3. See Introduction, p. xxi.

already endured, and they were good lads, even though occupying the country they had defeated. Alone in the home of this elderly woman, they showed great concern for her, sparing her, as much as possible, any extra work and expense. You could see all four of them getting washed around the well in the morning, in their shirt-sleeves, on the cold, damp, snowy days, splashing water onto their pale, pink skin typical of all the men from the North, while La Mère Sauvage bustled about, preparing her soup. Then they cleaned the kitchen, scrubbed the floors, chopped the wood, peeled the potatoes, washed the clothes, did all the household chores, like four good sons with their mother.

But the old woman thought about her own son constantly, her tall, thin son with his hooked nose, his brown eyes, the thick moustache that covered his upper lip with a strip of dark hair. Every day, she asked one of the soldiers living with her:

"Do you know where the Twenty-third French Regiment has gone? My son is with them."

"No, not know, not know anything."

And since they understood her pain and anxiety—they too had mothers back home—they were attentive to her in hundreds of little ways. And she liked them very much, her four enemies, because the country folk rarely harbor any patriotic hatred; that is common only among the well-to-do. The lower classes, the ones who pay the most because they are poor and because every new tax is more of a burden to them, the ones who are killed en masse, the ones who are the true cannon fodder because they are the majority of the population, the ones, in the end, who suffer most cruelly the atrocious miseries of war because they are the weakest and can defend themselves the least, these poor people understand little of the thirst for war, the easily aroused sense of honor and the so-called political strategies that wear down two nations in the space of six months, two nations: both the conquered and the conquerors.

Whenever they talked about La Mère Sauvage's Germans, the townspeople always said:

"Those four sure got themselves a good home."

Now, one morning when the old woman was alone in the house, she saw a man in the distance, walking across the plain toward her cottage. She soon recognized him; he was the mailman who delivered the letters on foot. He handed her a folded piece of paper; she took the glasses she used for sewing from their case and began to read:

Madame Sauvage,

I am writing to give you some very bad news. Your son Victor was killed yesterday by a cannonball, which virtually cut his

*body in half. I was close by, as we always walked side by side
in the regiment, and he talked to me about you so I could let
you know right away if anything happened to him.*

*I took the watch out of his pocket to bring back to you
when the war is over.*

> *Yours sincerely,*
> *Césaire Rivot,*
> *Private 2nd class, 23rd Regiment*

The letter was dated three weeks earlier.

She did not cry, not at all. She stood dead still, so overwhelmed,
so stunned that she did not yet feel any pain. "So now Victor is dead,"
she thought. Then tears slowly rose to her eyes, and pain pierced
her heart. Ideas occurred to her, one by one, horrible, agonizing
ideas. She would never hold him in her arms again, never kiss him
again, her child, her boy, never again, never again! The police
had killed her husband, the Prussians had killed her son . . . His
body had virtually been cut in half by a cannonball. And she felt she
could picture what happened, the horrible thing that had happened: his head slumped down, his eyes open as he chewed on the
corner of his long moustache, the way he always used to when he
was angry.

What had they done with his body, afterwards? If only they had
brought her child's body back to her the way they had given her husband's body to her, with the bullet in the middle of his forehead.

She heard voices. It was the Prussians coming back from the village. She quickly hid the letter in her pocket and wiped the tears
from her face; she greeted them calmly, making sure her face gave
nothing away.

All four of them were laughing, delighted because they had
brought back a nice live rabbit, stolen no doubt, and they gestured
to the old woman that they would have something good to eat.

She immediately began preparing lunch; but when it came time
to kill the rabbit, she didn't have the heart to do it, though it would
not have been the first time. One of the soldiers smashed his fist
against the back of its head and killed it.

Now that it was dead, she skinned it, pulling its red body from
under the skin, but as she worked, the sight of the blood that covered her hands, the sensation of the warm blood she could feel cooling and coagulating, made her whole body tremble, and she kept
seeing her son cut in half and covered in blood, just like this animal
whose flesh was still quivering.

She sat down at the table with the Prussians, but she couldn't eat,
couldn't eat a single mouthful. They wolfed down the rabbit without
giving her a thought. She watched them, furtively, without speaking,

forming an idea, and her face was so impassive that they didn't notice a thing.

Suddenly, she said: "I don't even know your names and it's been a month since we've been together." They understood, not without difficulty, what she wanted, and told her their names. But that wasn't enough; she wanted them to write them down on a piece of paper, with the addresses of their families; and placing her glasses on her large nose, she studied their strange handwriting, then folded the paper in half and put it in her pocket, along with the letter telling her that her son was dead.

When the meal was over, she told the men:

"I'm going to do something for you."

And she began carrying hay up into the loft where they slept.

They were surprised to see her do this; she explained they would be warmer and they helped her. They piled the bales of hay right up to the thatched roof; and they made a kind of large bedroom with four walls of fodder, warm and sweet-smelling, where they would get a wonderful night's sleep.

At suppertime, one of them was concerned that La Mère Sauvage was still not eating. She said she had an upset stomach. Then she lit a nice fire to keep warm, and the four Germans climbed up into their room on the ladder they used every night.

As soon as the trap door was shut, the old woman moved the ladder away, then silently opened the front door, went out and came back with enough bales of hay to fill the kitchen. She walked barefoot in the snow, so quietly that not a sound was heard. Every now and then, she listened to the muffled, irregular snoring of the four sleeping soldiers.

When she felt she had prepared everything well enough, she lit one of the bales of hay and threw it into the house; when it spread to the others, she went back outside and watched.

In seconds, a bright flash of light lit up the entire inside of the house, then it became a terrifying inferno, an enormous, blazing furnace whose bright light streamed through the narrow window, casting a reddish glow over the snow.

Then a great cry came from the top of the house, the roar of human voices, heartrending cries of anguish and terror. The trap door crashed down and a swirl of fire rushed through the loft, pierced the thatched roof and rose into the sky like an immense burning torch; the entire cottage was ablaze.

Nothing could be heard inside except for the crackling fire, the creaking walls, the wooden beams crashing down. Suddenly, the roof caved in, and from the glowing shell of the house, a great plume of smoke filled with sparks flew up into the air.

The countryside, white with snow, lit up by the fire, glistened like a silvery cloak tinged blood red.

In the distance, a church bell began to ring.

La Mère Sauvage remained there, standing in front of her house, armed with her rifle, her son's rifle, in case any of the men had managed to escape.

When she saw that it was all over, she threw her gun into the fire. She heard it explode.

People began to arrive, farmers, Prussians.

They found the old woman sitting on a tree stump, calm and contented.

A German officer, who spoke French like a native, asked:

"Where are your soldiers?"

She stretched out her thin arm toward the red rubble of the fire that was starting to die out. "In there!" she replied in a loud voice.

Everyone rushed around her.

"How did it catch fire?" the Prussian asked.

"*I* set it on fire," she replied.

No one believed her, thinking the disaster had suddenly made her go mad. Since everyone was standing around and listening to her, she told her story from start to finish, from the arrival of the letter to the final cries of the men burning inside her house. She left out no detail about what she had felt or what she had done.

When she had finished, she took the two papers from her pocket and adjusted her glasses to see them better in the light of the dying fire, then she held one of them up and said: "This one is about Victor dying." Holding up the other one, she nodded toward the flaming ruins and added: "This one is their names so you can write to their families." She calmly handed the white sheet of paper to the officer who was holding her by the shoulders.

"You'll write and tell them what happened, and you'll tell their parents that I, Victoire Simon,[4] La Mère Sauvage, was the one who did it! Don't forget."

The officer shouted out orders in German. They grabbed her, threw her against her house, against the walls that were still warm. Then twelve men quickly lined up opposite her, about twenty yards away. She stood dead still. She had understood, she was waiting.

An order was shouted out, followed by a long volley of gunfire. One shot rang out alone, after all the others.

The old woman did not fall down. She sank to the ground as if someone had cut off her legs.

---

4. As an authorial comment on her action, her real name is now revealed as *Victoire*—Victory.

The Prussian officer walked over to her. She was almost cut in half, and in her clenched hand, she held her letter, soaked in blood.

"Destroying my château was as an act of reprisal by the Germans," my friend Serval continued.

I thought about the mothers of the four kind young men who had burned to death in that cottage, and I thought of the horrific heroism of that other mother, gunned down against the wall.

And I picked up a small stone that was still charred, black from the fire.

The Prisoners†

Not a sound in the forest apart from the gentle flutter of snow drifting onto the trees. It had been falling since noon, a light, fine snow that covered the branches in an icy, frothy powder, casting a silvery glint over the dead leaves that still clung to the trees. It spread an immense, soft white blanket over the roads and intensified the endless silence of this sea of trees.

In front of the cottage in the forest, a young woman with bare arms was chopping wood over a stone with an ax. She was tall, slim but strong, a young woman of the woods, the daughter and wife of foresters.

"We're alone tonight, Berthine," a voice called from inside the house. "Better come inside, it's gettin' dark and maybe some Prussians and wolves are prowling round."

The woodcutter split a large log with powerful blows that made her chest expand every time she raised her arms.

"I'm done, Ma," she replied. "I'm here, it's okay, don't worry; it's still light out."

Then she piled the logs and kindling beside the fireplace, went outside to close the enormous hard oak shutters and finally came back inside, locking the heavy bolts on the door.

Her mother was spinning wool by the fire; she was an old woman with wrinkles who had grown more fearful with age.

"I don't like when your pa ain't here," she said. "Two women alone ain't strong enough."

"Oh!" the young woman replied, "I'd happily kill a wolf or a Prussian, you know."

And she glanced over at a large revolver hanging above the hearth.

---

† First published in the *Gil Blas* on December 30, 1884 and often reprinted. The text translated here is the revised version included in *Toine* (1886).

Her husband had been taken into the army at the beginning of the Prussian invasion, and the two women had been left alone with her father, Nicolas Pichon, an old keeper nicknamed "Stilts." He had stubbornly refused to leave his house to stay in town.

The closest town was Rethel,[1] an ancient fortified city built high on a rock. Its inhabitants were patriotic and had decided to resist the invaders, to blockade themselves in and fight, following Rethel's tradition. Twice already, under Henri IV and Louis XIV, they had become famous for their heroic defense of the town.[2] And they would do the same this time, you can bet your boots! Or else they'd have to burn them alive within the city walls.

And so they had bought cannons and rifles, equipped a militia, formed battalions and companies, and held drills all day long in the Place d'Armes. Everyone—bakers, grocers, butchers, notaries, lawyers, carpenters, booksellers, even pharmacists—took their turn at military training at precise times of the day, under the command of Monsieur Lavigne, a former Second Lieutenant in the Dragoons, now a notions dealer, since he had married the daughter of Monsieur Ravaudan Senior and inherited his shop.

He had awarded himself the rank of Major, and since all the young men had gone off to the army, he had enlisted all the other men, and they were training to put up a fight. The fat men in town now jogged along the streets to lose weight and improve their stamina while the weaker men carried heavy bundles to build up their muscles.

And so they waited for the Prussians. But the Prussians never came. They weren't far away, though: on two occasions their scouts had already made it deep enough into the woods to reach the house of Nicolas Pinchon, Stilts.

The old keeper, who was as fast as a fox, had gone to warn the town. They had prepared their cannons but no enemy had been seen.

Stilts's house was used as an outpost in the Aveline Forest.[3] Twice a week, he went to town to buy provisions and told the townspeople what was happening in the countryside.

On this particular day, he had gone to tell them that a small detachment of German infantrymen had stopped at his house the day before, then left again almost immediately. The Second Lieutenant in charge could speak French.

1. In the Ardennes, in eastern France, between Rheims and Charleville; in other words, on the route taken by the Prussians after their victory at nearby Sedan.
2. Maupassant has his historical facts a bit muddled here. It was in 1617, under Louis XIII (rather than Henri IV), that Rethel first achieved its reputation for resistance. Later (1650–55), in the reign of Louis XIV, the town was repeatedly besieged, captured, and again liberated.
3. An invented name.

When he went on these trips, he took along his two ferocious dogs—huge hounds with jaws like a lion—and he left the two women on their own with instructions to barricade themselves inside the house as soon as it got dark.

The young woman wasn't afraid of anything, but the old woman was always trembling with fear. "This will end in disaster, it will," she said over and over again. "You'll see, disaster."

That evening, she was even more anxious than usual. "Do you know what time Pa will be getting home?" she asked.

"Not before eleven, for sure. Whenever he has dinner with the Major, he always gets home late."

And the young woman had just hung her cooking pot over the fire to make the soup when she heard a strange noise echoing down the chimney; she stopped stirring.

"There's people walkin' through the woods, seven or eight of 'em at least."

Her mother, terrified, stopping the spinning wheel. "Oh, my God!" she stammered. "And your pa's not here!"

She had barely finished what she was saying when someone started banging angrily at the door, so hard that it shook.

When the women did not reply, a loud, guttural voice shouted: "Open the door!"

Then, after a silence, the same voice continued: "Open now or I vill break down your door!"

Berthine slipped the heavy revolver from over the fireplace into the pocket of her skirt, then put her ear against the door. "Who are you?" she asked.

"I am detachment from the other day," the voice replied.

"What do you want?" the young woman asked.

"I am lost since morning, in dese voods, mit meine men. Open now or I vill break down your door!"

The forester's daughter had no choice; she quickly undid the bolts, then pulling open the heavy door, she saw six men, six Prussian soldiers standing in the snow, outlined in its pale light, the same men who had come the day before.

"What are you doing here at this time of night?" she asked in a firm tone of voice.

"I am lost," the Second Lieutenant said once more, "completely lost und I recognized your house. I have not eaten anysing since dis morning, my men needer."

"But I'm alone here with my mother tonight," Berthine said.

The soldier, who seemed an honest man, replied: "Does not matter. I vill not hurt you but you must to give us somesing to eat. Vee are all dying of hunger und very tired."

Berthine stepped back. "Come inside," she said.

They went in, covered in light snow, and their helmets had a kind of creamy froth on them that made them look, like meringues. And they seemed weary, exhausted.

The young woman pointed to the two wooden benches, one on either side of the long table.

"Sit down," she said. "I'll make you some soup. You really do look worn out."

Then she bolted the door again.

She put more water in her cooking pot, threw in some more butter and potatoes, then took a large slab of bacon that was hanging over the fireplace, cut half of it off and added it to the pot.

The six men watched her every move, a look of intense hunger in their eyes. They had put their rifles and helmets in the corner and were waiting, as well behaved as good little children on their benches at school.

Her mother had started spinning wool again, but constantly glanced over at the invaders in terror. The only sounds were the gentle humming of the spinning wheel, the crackling of the fire and the soup bubbling in the pot.

Then, suddenly, a strange noise made everyone jump, something like the heavy, hoarse breathing of a wild animal at the door.

The German officer had leapt up and was heading toward the rifles. Berthine smiled and gestured for him to stop.

"It's only the wolves," she said. "They're just like you, hungry and prowling around."

He wasn't convinced and wanted to see with his own eyes; as soon as he opened the door, he saw two large, gray animals running away with quick, rapid strides.

"I never vould have believed it," he murmured, sitting down again.

And he waited for his food to be ready.

They wolfed their meal down, their mouths gaping open so they could swallow more, their wide eyes opening and closing in unison with their jaws, and their throats made the same noise as water gurgling down a drainpipe as they swallowed the soup.

The two women stood there, silently watching the rapid movements of their long red beards; the potatoes looked as if they were sinking into undulating sheepskins.

They were thirsty too, so Berthine went down into the cellar to get some cider. She stayed down there for a long time. It was a small vaulted cellar that had been used as both a prison and a hiding place during the Revolution, or so people claimed. You reached it by opening a trap door and going down a narrow, winding staircase at the back of the kitchen.

When Berthine returned, she was laughing, laughing slyly to herself. She gave the Germans the jug of cider.

Then she and her mother had their supper at the other end of the kitchen.

The soldiers had finished eating; all six of them were falling asleep at the table. Every now and again, someone's head dropped down with a thud, then he would quickly wake and sit up straight again.

"Why don't you all go lie down by the fire," Berthine said to the officer. "There's plenty of room for all six of you, you know. I'm going upstairs to my room with my mother."

And the two women went up to the second floor. The soldiers could hear them lock the door and walk about for a while; then they didn't make any more noise.

The Prussians stretched out on the floor, their feet toward the fire, their heads on top of their rolled-up coats, and all of them were soon snoring: a medley of six different snores, from dull to shrill, but all continuous and loud.

They had been sleeping for quite a long time when a gunshot rang out, so loudly that it sounded as if it had been fired right at the wall of the house. The soldiers sprang up. Then they heard two more gunshots, followed by three others.

The door from the second floor opened suddenly and Berthine appeared barefoot, wearing only her nightshirt and skirt. She held a candle in her hand and looked terrified.

"It's the French army," she stammered. "There must be at least two hundred of 'em. If they find you here, they'll burn down our house. Quick, get down into the cellar, and don't make a sound. If you make any noise, we're finished."

"*Ja, ja*, vill go," the terrified officer whispered. "How do vee get down?"

The young woman hurriedly opened the narrow, square trap door and the six men disappeared down the small winding staircase, backwards, one after the other, so they could feel their way down the steps.

As soon as the spike on the last helmet had disappeared, Berthine slammed shut the heavy oak door—as thick as a wall, as strong as steel—complete with hinges and a lock big enough for a dungeon; she turned the key twice and started to laugh, a silent laugh of delight, and she was filled with a mad desire to dance over the heads of her prisoners.

They made no noise, locked down there as if they were in a safe, a safe made of stone with only a small barred vent to let in some air.

Berthine immediately relit the fire, put the cooking pot back over it and made some more soup.

"Pa will be worn out tonight."

Then she sat down and waited. The only sound that broke the silence was the dull, regular *tick-tock* of the clock's pendulum.

Every now and again, the young woman glanced anxiously at the clock, with an expression that seemed to say:

"He's taking his time."

But soon she thought she could hear mumbling beneath her feet. Incomprehensible words spoken in low voices rose up through the brick-work from the cellar. The Prussians were beginning to guess she had tricked them, and before long, the Second Lieutenant went to the top of the little staircase and started pounding on the trap door.

"You vill open it," he shouted.

She stood up, walked closer and, imitating his accent said: "Vat do you vant?"

"You vill open it."

"I von't."

"Open or I vill break down the door!" the man said angrily.

She started to laugh: "Go ahead and try, little man, just you try!"

And he began hitting the solid oak trap door above his head with the butt of his rifle. But the door would have stood firm against a battering ram.

Berthine heard him go back down the stairs. Then the soldiers each came, in turn, to inspect the door and try their strength. Realizing their efforts were pointless, no doubt, they all went back down into the cellar and started talking amongst themselves.

The young woman listened to them, then went to open the front door to see if she could hear anything in the dark.

She heard the sound of barking in the distance. She gave the kind of whistle a hunter would, and almost immediately, two enormous dogs came out of the darkness and playfully leapt around her. She grabbed them by the scruffs of their necks and held them so they wouldn't run away. Then she shouted as loudly as she could: "Hey! Pa?"

A voice replied, still quite far away: "Hey, Berthine."

She waited a few seconds, then said again: "Hey! Pa."

The voice was closer now and replied: "Hey, Berthine."

"Don't go past the cellar window," she continued: "There's Prussians down there."

And suddenly the tall silhouette of the man could be seen to her left, standing still between two tree trunks.

"Prussians down the cellar. What're they doin' there?" he asked, sounding worried.

The young woman started to laugh: "It's the ones what came yesterday. They got lost in the forest. I put them down the cellar to cool 'em off."

And she told him the whole story, how she had frightened them by firing the gun and locked them down the cellar.

The old man looked worried: "What am I supposed to do with 'em at this time of night?"

"Go get Monsieur Lavigne and his men," she replied. "He'll take them prisoner. He'll be real happy, he will."

Old Pichon smiled: "Y'know, he will at that."

"I made some soup," his daughter continued. "Eat it real quick and then get goin'."

The old keeper put two plates of food on the floor for his dogs, sat down at the table and ate his soup.

The Prussians heard people talking and went quiet.

Stilts left fifteen minutes later. And Berthine sat, her hands supporting her head and waited.

The prisoners started getting restless. They were shouting now, calling out, angrily beating the unmovable trap door of the cellar with the butts of their rifles, over and over again.

Then they started firing shots through the cellar window, hoping, no doubt, to be heard by some German detachment that might be passing through the woods.

Berthine sat absolutely still but all the noise was upsetting her, irritating her. A feeling of malicious anger ran through her; she would have gladly killed them all, the villains, just to shut them up.

Then she grew more and more impatient, and started watching the clock and counting the passing minutes.

Her father had left an hour and a half ago. He would have reached the town by now. She pictured what he would do. He would tell his story to Monsieur Lavigne, who would turn pale with emotion and ring for his maid to bring his uniform and his weapons. She felt she could actually hear the drummer rushing through the streets. Terrified faces pressed against windows. The citizens' army would rush out of their homes, out of breath, still buckling their belts, and run toward the Major's house.

Then the troop, with Stilts leading the way, would set out through the night, through the snow, toward the forest.

She looked at the clock. "They could be here in an hour."

She was overwhelmed by anxious impatience. They were taking so long!

The time she had imagined they would arrive came at last.

She opened the door once more to see if she could hear them coming. She caught a glimpse of a shadow walking cautiously toward the house. She let out a cry of fear. It was her father.

"They sent me to see if anything's changed," he said.

"No, nothing."

Then he gave a long, shrill whistle out into the night. Soon, they could see dark shapes emerging slowly from behind the trees: ten men had been sent on ahead of the rest of the soldiers.

"Don't walk by the cellar window," Stilts said over and over again.

So the first men to arrive showed the ones behind them where the dangerous vent was.

Finally, the main body of the troop appeared, two hundred men in all, each carrying two hundred bullets.

Monsieur Lavigne, trembling and very excited, ordered them to surround the house, leaving a wide open space free in front of the little black opening at ground level where air was let into the cellar.

Then he went inside and asked how many enemies there were and their state of mind, for they had gone so silent you might have thought they had disappeared, vanished, flown away through the little window.

Monsieur Lavigne stamped his foot against the trap door. "I wish to speak to the Prussian officer," he said.

The German did not reply.

"I want the Prussian officer," he said again.

In vain. For twenty minutes he demanded that this silent officer surrender, along with all their arms and kit, promising that none of them would be killed and that the officer and his men would be treated with military courtesy. But he received no sign of either agreement or hostility. The situation was becoming difficult.

The citizens' army stamped their feet into the snow and slapped their shoulders with their arms to keep warm, the way coach drivers do, and they watched the little window with an increasing, childish desire to walk in front of it.

One of them, a very supple man named Potdevin, finally took a chance. He gathered speed and leapt in front of the window like a stag. He succeeded. The prisoners seemed to be dead.

"No one's down there," a voice cried.

And another soldier walked across the empty space in front of the dangerous vent. Then it became a game. One after the other, the men jumped past the vent, going from one side to the other, like children having a race, and they ran so fast that each one kicked up snow and sent it flying. To keep warm, they had lit fires made with large pieces of dead wood, and the silhouettes of the running National Guard were lit up as they quickly raced from side to side.

"It's your turn, Maloison!"[4] someone shouted.

Maloison was a chubby baker whose fat stomach was the subject of many jokes among his fellow soldiers.

He hesitated. They teased him. So he made up his mind and started running at an easy, jogging pace; he was breathing heavily, which made his fat belly jiggle.

The entire detachment laughed until they cried.

"Bravo, bravo, Maloison!" they shouted, to encourage him.

He had made it about two thirds of the way across when a long, red flame suddenly shot out of the vent. They heard a gunshot and the huge baker let out a horrible scream and fell flat on his face.

No one rushed over to help him. Then they saw him crawling on all fours through the snow, groaning, and as soon as he was out of danger's way, he fainted.

He had been shot in the upper thigh.

After the initial shock and terror had worn off, they all started laughing again.

But Major Lavigne came out onto the doorstep of the cottage. He had just decided on his plan of attack.

"Planchut the plumber and his workmen, now!" he ordered in a booming voice. Three men came forward.

"Detach the drainpipes from the house."

And fifteen minutes later, twenty yards of drainpipes were brought to the commander.

Then, taking infinite care, he had a little round hole cut into the trap door and built a conduit made from the pipes that went from the water pump down into the hole.

"Now we're going to offer our German[5] friends something to drink!" he announced, sounding delighted.

A frenzied "hurrah!" of admiration was followed by shouts of joy and hysterical laughter. And the commander organized groups of men who would work for five minutes and then hand over to the next group.

"Pump," he ordered.

And after getting the pump handle going, they heard the soft sound of water running down the pipes into the cellar, splashing

---

4. Note the way Maupassant names his characters to comic effect: Monsieur Ravaudan's profession relates to *ravauder*, meaning to repair clothes; Major Lavigne evokes a "vine;" *Potdevin* literally means "jug of wine," but also a "bribe" or "backhander;" *Maloison* means "naughty little goose."

5. "Prussian," as used elsewhere in the text, would have been more usual during the Franco-Prussian War; "German" denoted a linguistic rather than political entity until the proclamation of the German Empire on January 18, 1871. It is not entirely clear exactly when, during the winter of 1870–71, this tale supposedly takes place; or whether this designation of the enemy is anachronistic or prescient.

over each step, like a gurgling waterfall flowing into a pool with goldfish.

They waited.

An hour passed, then two, then three.

The agitated Major paced up and down in the kitchen, stopping every now and again to press his ear against the ground to try and work out what his enemies were doing, wondering if they would soon surrender.

Their enemies were moving around now. They could hear them shifting barrels, talking, splashing about.

Then, around eight o'clock in the morning, a voice rose up from the vent:

"I vant to speak to the French officer."

Lavigne replied from near the window, taking care not to stick his head out too close to it.

"Do you surrender?"

"I surrender."

"Then hand over your rifles."

A weapon immediately appeared through the bars of the vent and fell onto the snow, then two, then three—then all their weapons.

"Vee have no more," said the same voice. "Hurry up! I am drowning."

"Stop pumping," the commander ordered.

They stopped and dropped the pump handle.

Then, having filled the kitchen with all the armed soldiers who had been waiting, he slowly raised the oak trap door.

Four heads first appeared, soaking wet, four blond heads with long, light hair, then one after the other, the six Germans emerged, shivering, soaking wet, and terrified.

They were taken and tied up. Then, fearing some unexpected event, the citizens' army left immediately, in two convoys, one driving off with the prisoners, the other with Maloison carried on a mattress on top of some poles.

They entered triumphantly into Rethel.

Monsieur Lavigne was decorated for having captured a Prussian detachment, and the fat baker received a medal for having been wounded by the enemy.

A Duel[†]

The war was over; the Germans were occupying France;[1] the country was trembling like a beaten warrior beneath the foot of the conqueror.

Paris was starving, panic-stricken, in despair. The first trains left the capital, slowly crossing the countryside and villages, headed toward the newly established borders. The first passengers looked out of the windows at the devastated land and burnt-out hamlets. In front of the few houses that remained standing, Prussian soldiers wearing black helmets topped with brass points sat astride chairs, smoking their pipes. Others were working or chatting as if they were one of the family. When the trains passed through the cities, you could see entire regiments practicing maneuvers in the town squares, and despite the noise from the railway tracks, the sound of raucous orders could still be heard every now and then.

Monsieur Dubuis, who had been in the National Guard in Paris throughout the entire siege,[2] was going to join his wife and daughter in Switzerland;[3] he had sent them abroad before the invasion, just in case.

Neither famine nor exhaustion had managed to diminish his big stomach, for he was a wealthy, peace-loving merchant. He had lived through the horrible events with sad resignation and bitter thoughts on the savagery of man. Now that the war was over and he was headed for the border, it was the first time he actually saw any Prussians, even though he had been on duty on the city's ramparts and stood watch on many a cold night.

He looked with annoyed terror at these armed, bearded men who were occupying France as if they were at home, and in his soul, he felt a kind of fever of powerless patriotism along with a great need to beware, a kind of new instinct for caution that remains with us to this day.

---

† First published in *Le Gaulois* on August 14, 1883 and in the text translated here. It was subsequently reprinted in the *Annales politiques et littéraires*, on September 6, 1885, and in the posthumous collection, *Le Colporteur* (1900).
1. The Armistice of January 28, 1871, designed to last until February 19, had led to a permanent cessation of hostilities; the terms of surrender were ratified by the French on March 1, and immediately followed by the triumphal entry of the occupying forces into Paris. Thirty thousand enemy troops remained on French soil. The Franco-Prussian War was only formally ended by the Treaty of Frankfurt on May 10, 1871. The "newly established borders" in the next paragraph refers to the Treaty's incorporation of the French provinces of Alsace and Lorraine within the German Empire.
2. See Introduction, pp. xxii–xxiii.
3. Switzerland and Belgium were the most common destinations for those fleeing the Prussian invasion, as well as for those subsequently trying to escape the repression following the Commune.

In his compartment, two Englishmen, who had come to witness the events, viewed everything through calm and curious eyes. They were both fat and chatted in their own language, sometimes leafing through their tourist guide, which they read out loud in an effort to recognize the places it described.

Suddenly, the train stopped at the station in a small town and a Prussian officer noisily climbed up the steps of the train, his saber clanging loudly as he entered the compartment. He was big, bursting out of his uniform and had an enormous beard. His red hair seemed to be on fire and his long moustache, a bit paler in color, flew up and cut across both sides of his face.

The Englishmen immediately started staring at him, smiling with satisfied curiosity, while Monsieur Dubuis pretended to be reading a newspaper. He huddled in his corner, like a thief in the presence of a policeman.

The train started to move again. The Englishmen continued talking, trying to locate the precise place where a battle had been fought. Suddenly, when one of them pointed to a specific village on the horizon, the Prussian officer stretched out his long legs, leaned back in his seat and said in French:

"I killed tvelve Frenchmen in this village. I take more than a hundred prisoners."

The Englishmen, totally fascinated, immediately asked in French: "Oh! What's this village called?"

The Prussian replied, "Pharsbourg,"[4] then continued, "I took dese naughty boys und teached dem a lesson."

And he looked at Monsieur Dubuis and arrogantly roared with laughter.

The train kept on moving, passing through the occupied villages.

You could see German soldiers all along the roads, near the fields, standing next to the fences or chatting in cafés. They covered the land like a swarm of African locusts.

The officer stretched out his hands.

"If I vere in charge, I vould have taken Paris und burned everysing und killed everyvun.[5] No more France!"

Not wishing to be impolite, the Englishmen simply replied: "Oh, yes."

"In tventy years," the soldier continued, "all Europe, all ov it, vill belong to us. Prussia stronger dan everyvun."

4. Possibly based on Phalsbourg, a town in Alsace that had put up a spirited resistance to the invaders.
5. Some factions within the victorious Prussians had demanded even harsher terms than those eventually negotiated.

The Englishmen, somewhat anxious, said nothing more. Their faces had become impassive and seemed made of wax between their long sideburns. Then the Prussian officer began to laugh. And still leaning back in his seat, he started making jokes. He made fun of defeated, crushed France, viciously insulted his enemies. He made fun of Austria, which had recently been conquered;[6] he joked about the fierce but powerless defense encountered in the provinces; he insulted the troops and their inferior artillery. He announced that Bismarck[7] was going to build an iron city made from the captured cannons. And suddenly, he pressed his boots against Monsieur Dubuis's thigh, whose face burned red with anger; but he turned away.

The Englishmen seemed to have become indifferent to everything, as if they had suddenly found themselves back on their isolated island, far from the maddening crowd.

The officer took out his pipe and stared at the Frenchman.

"You have some tobacco, yes?"

"No, Monsieur," replied Monsieur Dubuis.

"If you please," the German continued, "you vill go und buy me some at next stop."

And he started laughing once more.

"I vill give you a tip."

The train whistled as it slowed down. They passed the burned-out building of a station and came to a stop.

The German opened the door of the compartment, grabbed Monsieur Dubuis by the arm, saying:

"Go on, go do my errand, *und schnell*—fast!"

A detachment of Prussian troops filled the station. Other soldiers stood watch, positioned all along the wooden fences. The train was already whistling to announce it was about to leave. Monsieur Dubuis suddenly jumped out onto the platform and, ignoring the stationmaster who was waving his arms at him, rushed into the next compartment.

He was alone! His heart was beating so hard that he was panting; he opened his jacket and wiped off his forehead. The train stopped again at a station.

And suddenly the officer appeared at the door and got into his compartment along with the two Englishmen, who followed out of curiosity.

The German sat down, opposite the Frenchman and, still laughing, said:

6. Reference to the Battle of Sadowa, on July 3, 1866, which had confirmed the rise of Prussia at the expense of the Austro-Hungarian Empire.
7. Otto von Bismarck (1815–1898), the power behind the throne of Kaiser William I since 1862, was known as "The Iron Chancellor."

"You did not vant to do my errand."

"No, Monsieur," replied Monsieur Dubuis.

The train had just started to move again.

"Then I vill cut your moustache," the officer said, "und use it to fill my pipe."

And he extended his hand toward Monsieur Dubuis's face.

The Englishmen, ever impassive, couldn't take their eyes off them.

The German had already got hold of a bit of hair and was pulling on it when Monsieur Dubuis slapped his arm away with the back of his hand; and grabbing him by the neck, he threw the officer against his seat. Then, overwhelmed with mad rage, his temples pounding, his eyes blazing, he continued strangling him with one hand while punching him furiously in the face with the other. The Prussian tried to fight back, to get his sword out, to overcome this enemy who was holding him down. But Monsieur Dubuis was crushing him with the enormous weight of his stomach, and he kept hitting and hitting, relentlessly, without stopping to catch his breath, without even knowing where his blows were landing. Blood flowed. The German, choking, gurgling, spluttering, tried—in vain—to push off this fat, frustrated man who was beating his brains out.

The Englishmen inched closer to get a better look. They stood there, full of joy and curiosity, ready to bet for or against each of the rivals.

Then suddenly, exhausted by such a struggle, Monsieur Dubuis got up and sat down without saying a word.

The Prussian was so aghast, so stunned, so astonished and in so much pain that he did not pounce on him. When he had caught his breath, he said:

"If you vill not to have a duel with me because of dis insult, I vill kill you."

"Whenever you like," Monsieur Dubuis replied. "With pleasure."

"Here is Strasbourg,"[8] the German continued. "I vill take two officers as my vitnesses; I have time before the train goes."

Monsieur Dubuis, who was puffing as much as the train, said to the Englishmen:

"Would you like to be my witnesses?"

They both replied at once: "Oh, yes!"

The train stopped.

The Prussian quickly found two friends who carried the pistols and everyone climbed up onto the ramparts.

The Englishmen constantly took out their watches to check the time, hurried everyone along and made them go through the

---

8. City on the Rhine with a particularly painful resonance for French readers, now that it had been ceded to Germany.

formalities very quickly, worried that they might not make it back to the train before it left.

Monsieur Dubuis had never held a pistol in his life. He was placed twenty paces from his enemy.

"Are you ready?" he was asked.

As he was replying, "Yes, Monsieur," he noticed that one of the Englishmen had opened his umbrella to protect himself from the sun.

A voice shouted:

"Fire!"

Without hesitating, Monsieur Dubuis fired blindly and was astonished to see the Prussian opposite him sway, fling his arms in the air and fall facedown onto the ground. He had killed him.

One of the Englishmen, full of joy, satisfied curiosity and cheerful impatience, shouted: "Oh!" The other one, who still had his watch in his hand, grabbed Monsieur Dubuis by the arm and started running, dragging him toward the station.

The first Englishman marked time as he ran, elbows close to his body and fists clenched.

"One, two! One, two!"

And all three of them jogged along, in spite of their fat stomachs, like three caricatures in a satirical magazine.

The train was leaving. They jumped into their compartment.

The Englishmen then took off their hats, waved them in the air and shouted, "Hip, hip, hip, hurrah!" three times in a row.

Then, one after the other, they solemnly shook hands with Monsieur Dubuis and sat back down in their seats.

Tales of the Supernatural

Le Horla[†][1]

May 8

What a wonderful day! I spent the entire morning stretched out on the grass in front of my house, under an enormous plane tree that completely covers it, shades it and hides it from view. I like this region, and I like living here because this is where my roots are, the fine, deep roots that tie a man to the land where his ancestors were born and died, roots that tie him to how he thinks and what he likes to eat, to tradition as well as food, to the local dialect, the unique intonation of the farmers when they speak, the smell of the earth, the villages and even the air itself.

I love the house where I grew up. I can see the Seine from my windows; it flows along the edge of my garden, behind the road, nearly up to my house: the wide, long Seine that stretches from Rouen to Le Havre, full of passing boats.

To the left, in the distance, lies Rouen, that sprawling city of blue slate roofs beneath countless tall Gothic steeples, both delicate and solid, in the shadow of the cathedral's iron spire. These steeples are full of bells that ring out in the clear blue light on beautiful mornings, sending me the soft metallic hum of their distant bronze songs that are swept along by the wind, sometimes louder, sometimes softer, depending on whether the bells are starting to peel or are fading away.

How beautiful it was this morning!

At about eleven o'clock, a long convoy of ships passed by my gates: they were pulled along by a tugboat that was as fat as a fly and groaned with the effort, spewing out thick smoke.

After two English schooners, whose red flags fluttered against the sky, came a superb Brazilian three-master, all white, wonderfully

---

† An early version of *Le Horla* was published in the *Gil Blas* on October 26, 1886. Revised and considerably expanded, it appeared in volume form in 1887. The definitive text is the one translated here.
1. The title has been subject to much speculation; the consensus is that this invented word is phonetically related, in French, to *hors-là*, meaning "something beyond, not of this world."

clean and shiny.[2] This ship filled me with such pleasure that I saluted it, I don't really know why.

May 12

I've had a slight fever for the past few days; I don't feel well, or rather, I feel somewhat sad.

Where do these mysterious influences come from that can transform our happiness into discouragement and our confidence into distress? It's as if the air, the invisible air, is full of unknowable Forces, mysterious Forces that close in around us. I wake up full of cheerfulness, with a song in my heart—Why?—I walk down to the water's edge and suddenly, after a short stroll, I come back home in despair, as if some misfortune lies in wait for me in my house— Why?—Has a chill wind swept over my body, setting my nerves on edge and filling my soul with gloom? Has the shape of the clouds, or the colors of the day, the colors of objects, so changeable, flowed past my eyes and unsettled my mind? How can we know? Everything that surrounds us, everything we look at without really seeing, everything we brush against without knowing what it is, everything we touch without actually feeling it, everything we encounter without recognizing it, do all these things have an inexplicable, surprising, immediate effect on us, on our physical being, and through our bodies, affect our thoughts, even our very hearts?

How profound is this mystery of the Invisible! We can never know its depths with our inadequate senses, our eyes that do not know how to truly perceive what is too small, or too big, or too close, or too distant, or the beings that inhabit the stars or a drop of water . . . with our ears that deceive us, for they carry vibrations through the air as sonorous notes. They are fairies that accomplish the miracle of transforming movement into sound and through this metamorphosis, bring music to life, making the silent turbulence of nature sing out . . . with our sense of smell, weaker than a dog's . . . with our sense of taste that can barely determine the age of a bottle of wine!

Ah! If only we had more organs that could accomplish other miracles for us: then we could discover so many things that are all around us!

May 16

I'm not well; there is no doubt about it! I felt so good last month! I have a fever, a horrible fever, or rather, a feverish nervousness that is making my soul suffer as much as my body! I have a continual,

---

2. During the cholera epidemic of 1884, foreign vessels served the quarantined port of Le Havre.

terrifying sense of impending danger, a feeling of apprehension, as if something terrible is about to happen, or that death is drawing closer, a premonition which is surely an expectation of some evil as yet unknown, taking root in my body and my blood.

May 18

I have just come from seeing my doctor for I couldn't sleep any more. He found my pulse racing, my pupils dilated, my nerves on edge, but with no alarming symptoms. I have to take showers and drink potassium bromide.

May 25

No change at all! My condition is truly strange. As evening approaches, an incomprehensible anxiety rushes through me, as if the night is hiding some terrible danger it has in store for me. I eat dinner quickly, then I try to read; but I don't understand the words; I can barely make out the letters. So I pace back and forth through my living room, oppressed by a vague, compelling fear, the fear of sleep and the fear of my bed.

I go up to my bedroom at around ten o'clock. As soon as I am inside, I double-lock the door and secure the bolts; I am afraid . . . but of what? . . . I was never frightened of anything until now . . . I open my wardrobes, I look under my bed; I listen . . . I listen . . . For what? . . . Is it not strange that a simple feeling of unease, perhaps a minor circulation problem, the irritation of nerve endings, a bit of congestion, a very slight disturbance in the very imperfect and delicate functioning of our living organism can make the most cheerful of men morose and transform the bravest into cowards? Then I get into bed and wait for sleep to come as one waits for the executioner. I wait in terror for it to come; and my heart pounds, and my legs shake; and my entire body is trembling beneath the warm sheets, until the moment when I suddenly fall into a deep sleep, the way a man would fall if he were trying to drown himself in deep, stagnant waters. I cannot feel it coming, as I did in the past, this treacherous sleep that hides close by, lies in wait to grab hold of my head, to close my eyes, to send me into dark oblivion.

I sleep—for a long time—two or three hours—then a dream—no—a nightmare seizes hold of me. I can sense quite well that I am in bed and asleep . . . I can sense it and I know it . . . and I also sense that someone is coming closer, watching me, touching me, getting into my bed, kneeling on my chest, grabbing me by the throat and strangling me . . . strangling me . . . with all his strength.

I struggle, I try to fight, held back by this atrocious powerlessness that paralyzes us in our dreams; I want to cry out—and cannot—I want to move—and cannot; I am panting, in anguish, I try with all my might to turn over, to throw off this being that is crushing me, suffocating me—and I cannot!

And suddenly, I wake up, terror-stricken, covered in sweat. I light a candle. I am alone.

After this attack, which happens again and again, every night, I finally go calmly to sleep and do not wake until dawn.

June 2

My condition is getting worse. What can be wrong with me? The bromide has no effect at all; the showers do nothing to help. This afternoon, to tire my body out—even though it is already so weary—I went for a walk in the Roumare woods.[3] At first I thought that the fresh air, so sweet and calm, full of the scent of grass and leaves, would pour new blood into my veins, new energy into my heart. I crossed a wide hunting ground, then headed toward the little village of La Bouille,[4] taking a narrow path lined by two armies of trees that were unbelievably tall, forming a thick, very dark green roof between myself and the sky.

A shiver suddenly ran through me, not a cold shiver, but a strange shiver of anguish.

I walked more quickly, anxious at being alone in this wood, frightened for no reason, absurdly frightened, by my utter solitude. Suddenly, I felt as if I were being followed, that someone was right behind me, close by, so close that he could touch me.

I turned sharply around. I was alone. All I could see behind me was the wide road, empty, long, frighteningly empty; and on the other side it was just the same: it stretched out and was lost in the distance, terrifying.

I closed my eyes. Why? And I started spinning around on my heel, very quickly, like a top. I nearly fell; I opened my eyes again; the trees were swaying; the ground wobbled; I had to sit down. Then, ah! I no longer knew which way I had come! It was strange! Strange! So strange! I had no idea at all. I headed for the road to my right and was back on the avenue that had led me to the middle of the woods.

June 3

Last night was horrible. I will go away for a few weeks. A little trip will no doubt cure me.

3. Forest near Rouen.
4. Village on the Seine, about eleven miles from Rouen.

July 2

I'm back at home. I am cured. I had a wonderful trip. I visited Mont Saint-Michel,[5] where I'd never been.

What a sight it is when you arrive, as I did, at Avranches, toward the end of the day! The town stands on a hill, and I was taken to the public gardens, at the far end of the city. I cried out in astonishment. An endless bay stretched out before me, as far as the eye could see, set between two remote coasts lost in the distant mist. And in the middle of this golden bay, beneath a clear, shimmering sky, a dark, pointed, strange mount rises up from the sand. The sun had just set, and on the horizon, still ablaze, you could make out the silhouette of this incredible rock that bears an incredible monument at its summit.

As soon as day broke, I headed toward it. The sea was at low tide, as it had been the night before, and as I got closer, I could see the astonishing abbey rising in front of me. After walking for a few hours, I reached the mass of stone that supports the small village dominated by the great church. Having crossed the short, narrow street, I entered the splendid Gothic temple built here on earth to worship God, sprawling like a city, full of low rooms that are dwarfed by the vaults, and high galleries supported by slender columns. I entered this gigantic granite gem of architecture, light as lace, covered with towers and svelte little steeples with spiral staircases, all linked by delicately carved arches, and its strange heads of chimeras, devils, fantastic beasts and enormous flowers rise up toward the blue heavens by day and the black firmament by night.

When I reached the top, I said to the monk who accompanied me: "Father, how happy you must be here!"

"There's a lot of wind here, Monsieur," he replied. Then we started to chat while watching the tide rise; it ran over the sand, enclosing it in steel armor.

And the monk told me stories, all the old stories that happened in this place, and legends, all the legends.

One of them struck me forcibly. The people in this area, the ones who live on the top of the hill, claim that they hear voices at night, coming from the beach, sometimes they hear goats bleating, one with a strong voice, the other making a faint sound. The unbelievers say it is only the sea gulls squawking, which sometimes sounds like bleating and sometimes like someone wailing; but the fishermen who stay out late swear they have met someone wandering around the sand dunes, between high and low tide, around the little village so isolated as it is far from the rest of the world: an old shepherd

---

5. An object of intense public concern at the time because of its gradual erosion by the tides.

whose face is always hidden by his coat and who is followed closely behind by a billy goat with the face of a man and a nanny goat with the face of a woman, both with long white hair and talking continually, arguing in an strange language, then suddenly stopping their shouting in order to bleat with all their might.

"Do you believe this?" I asked the monk.

"I don't know," he murmured.

"If beings other than us existed on this earth," I continued, "why have we not known about them for so long? Why haven't either of us—not you, not I—ever seen them?"

"Do we ever see a hundred thousandth of what actually exists?" he replied. "Take the wind, for example, which is the greatest force of nature: it knocks men over, tears down buildings, uproots trees, lifts the sea to form mountains of water, destroys cliffs and forces ships onto the reefs; the wind kills, it whistles, it groans and howls, but have you ever seen it? Could you ever see it? And yet, it exists."

I said nothing in reply to this simple reasoning. This monk was either a wise man or a fool. I couldn't actually tell; but I kept silent. What he had been saying, I had often thought myself.

July 3

I slept badly; there is surely some contagious fever going around, for my coach driver seems to have the same disease. When I got back home last night, I noticed how terribly pale he looked.

"What's wrong with you, Jean?" I asked.

"I just can't sleep any more, Monsieur; my nights are ruining my days. Ever since Monsieur left, I feel as if I'm under some kind of spell."

The other servants seem fine, though, but I am very frightened that I will become ill again myself.

July 4

It is definitely back. My old nightmares have returned. Last night, I felt someone crouching over me who placed his mouth against mine and was sucking the life out of me. Yes, he was drawing the life from between my lips like some sort of leech. Then he got up, sated, and I . . . I woke up, so battered, broken, overwhelmed, that I couldn't even move. If this continues a few more days, I will certainly go away again.

July 5

Am I going mad? What happened last night, what I saw, is so strange that I feel I'm going mad when I think about it!

I had locked my door, as I do every night now; then, as I was thirsty, I drank half a glass of water; I happened to notice that my decanter was full, right up to the crystal stopper.

I went to bed and fell into one of my terrifying sleeps, and woke up after about two hours with a jolt that was even more frightening.

Imagine a man who is asleep, who is being murdered and who wakes up with a knife in his chest; he is gasping for breath, covered in blood, unable to breathe, about to die and doesn't understand why—that was my dream.

After finally calming myself down, I was thirsty again; I lit a candle and went over to the table where I'd left the decanter of water. I picked it up to pour some into my glass; nothing came out—It was empty! Completely empty! At first, I just couldn't understand; then, suddenly, I had a feeling that was so horrifying that I had to sit down, or rather that I needed to collapse into a chair! I sprang up to look around the room! Then I sat down again and looked at the empty decanter, overwhelmed with astonishment and terror! I stared at it wide-eyed, trying to understand. My hands were shaking! So someone had drunk all the water? But who? Me? It had to be me, didn't it? It could only have been me, couldn't it? So I must be a sleepwalker; without knowing it, I was living this mysterious double life which makes us wonder if there are two people who inhabit us, or if some stranger, unknowable and invisible, is awakened at times, when our soul is deadened, our body captive, obeying this other being the way they usually obey us, even more than they obey us.

Ah! Who could understand my hideous anguish? Who could understand the emotion of a man who is of sound mind, wide-awake, completely rational and who stares in terror at an empty glass decanter from which a bit of water had disappeared while he was asleep! I remained there until daybreak, not daring to go back to bed.

July 6

I am going mad. Someone drank all the water in my decanter again last night—or rather, I drank it!

But was it me? Was it me? Who else could it be? Who? Oh, my God! Am I going mad? Who can save me?

July 10

I have just carried out some unusual experiments.

I am definitely insane! Even so!

On July 6, before going to bed, I put some wine, milk, water, bread and strawberries on my table.

Someone drank—I drank—all the water and a little milk. The wine, bread and strawberries remained untouched.

On July 7, I repeated the experiment; same result.

On July 8, I left no water or milk. Nothing was touched.

Finally, on July 9, I only put the water and milk on the table, taking care to wrap the decanters in white muslin and tie string around the stoppers. Then I put some graphite on my lips, my beard and my hands and I went to bed.

Invincible sleep seized hold of me, followed soon afterwards by my horrifying awakening. I had not stirred; even my sheets had no traces of black. I rushed toward the table. The muslin surrounding the bottles was spotless. I untied the strings, my heart beating hard out of fear. All the water was gone! Someone had drunk all the milk! Ah, my God! . . .

I am leaving for Paris right away.

July 12

Paris, I had really gone mad these past few days! My unsettled imagination must be toying with me, unless I truly am a sleepwalker, or have been subject to one of those influences claimed, though unexplained until now, that are called suggestions. In any case, my panic was bordering on insanity, and twenty-four hours in Paris were enough to recover my equilibrium.

Yesterday, after doing some shopping and visiting friends, who filled my entire being with new vitality, I ended my evening at the Théâtre-Français. They were performing a play by Alexandre Dumas the younger,[6] and this vibrant, powerful spirit managed to cure me. Solitude is surely dangerous to active minds. We must have thinking men and conversation around us. When we are alone for a long time, we fill the void with ghosts.

I walked along the boulevards to go back to my hotel, feeling very cheerful. As I rubbed shoulders with the crowd, I thought, not without some irony, about my terrors, my assumptions of a week ago, how I believed, yes, I actually believed, that an invisible being was living under my roof. How weak our minds are, and how quickly they panic and are led astray the minute one small, incomprehensible fact assails us!

Instead of reaching a conclusion with the simple words: "I don't understand because the reason escapes me," we immediately imagine terrifying mysteries and supernatural forces.

---

6. Alexandre Dumas *fils* (1824–1895) was well known as both a novelist and playwright; his *Denise*, first performed in January 1885, had been staged again at the Comédie-Française in September 1886 during the very time that Maupassant was working on *Le Horla*.

July 14

Bastille Day.[7] I strolled down the streets. The firecrackers and flags amused me as if I were a child. And yet it is quite ridiculous to be happy on a specific date designated by a government law. People are a foolish herd, sometimes stupidly patient, sometimes revolting fiercely. When they are told: "Have a good time," they have a good time. When they are told: "You must go to war with our neighbor," they go to war. When they are told: "Vote for the Emperor," they vote for the Emperor.[8] Then when they are told: "Vote for the Republic," they vote for the Republic.

Their leaders are also fools; but instead of obeying men, they obey principles—principles that can only be inane, fruitless and false precisely because they are principles, that is to say, ideas that are deemed to be unchanging and definitive in this world in which no one is certain of anything, because enlightenment is an illusion, great events are an illusion.

July 16

Yesterday, I saw things that troubled me greatly.

I was having dinner at Mme Sablés house; she is my cousin and her husband is Commander of the 76th Regiment of Chasseurs[9] in Limoges.[1] I found myself in the company of two young women, one of whom is married to a doctor, Dr. Parent, who specializes in nervous conditions and extraordinary symptoms that are currently the subject of experiments with hypnotism and the influence of suggestion.

He recounted at length the extraordinary results obtained by English scientists and some doctors from the medical school in Nancy.[2]

The facts he put forward seemed so strange to me that I immediately said I did not believe them.

"We are on the verge of discovering one of the important secrets of nature," he stated, "I mean one of the most important secrets on

---

7. The original French is "Fète de la République." Bastille Day, or le *Quatorze juillet* (Fourteenth of July), had been a national holiday since 1880.
8. Reference to the plebiscite of December 1851; this referendum gave Louis-Napoleon overwhelming public approval for the *coup d'état* by which he had seized power, thereby retrospectively legitimizing his establishment of the Second Empire (1852–70) and his own self-styling as Napoleon III, Emperor of the French.
9. *Chasseurs-à-pied*: infantrymen; *chasseurs-à-cheval*: light cavalry.
1. Two hundred and thirty-five miles south of Paris.
2. In contemporary debates about hypnotism, the leading English specialist (and who was said to have coined the term) was Dr. James Braid (1796–1860), while the Nancy School, at odds with the theories of hypnotherapy of the Salpêtrière Hospital in Paris, was represented in Maupassant's time by Dr. Hyppolyte Bernheim (1840–1919) and Dr. Ambroise-Auguste Liébeault (1823–1904), both then teaching at the University of Nancy.

this earth; for nature certainly holds other important secrets, beyond
this world, in the firmament. Ever since man was able to speak and
write down his thoughts, he has felt the invisible presence of some
impenetrable mystery that his crude, imperfect senses cannot grasp;
and, through the effort of his intelligence, he has tried to compen-
sate for the powerlessness of his senses. When man's intelligence was
still in a rudimentary state, being haunted by invisible phenomena
took on forms that were frightening in the most ordinary of ways.
These led to the birth of popular belief in the supernatural, legends
of wandering spirits, fairies, gnomes, ghosts, I would even go so far
as to say the legend of God, for our ideas about a master creator,
from whatever religion we are taught them, are truly the most mediocre, the most stupid, the most unacceptable ideas to emerge from
the human mind that is afraid of such creatures. Nothing is truer
than what Voltaire once said: 'God made man in his own image, but
man truly returned the favor.'

"But for more than half a century now, we seem to sense something new. Mesmer[3] and others have taken us down a surprising
path, and we have had truly astonishing results, especially in the
past four or five years."

My cousin, also quite skeptical, smiled. "Shall I try to hypnotize
you, Madame?" Dr. Parent asked.

"Yes, willingly."

She sat down in an armchair and he began staring at her and hyp-
notizing her. Suddenly, I . . . I felt nervous, my heart was pounding
and my throat constricted. I watched as Mme Sablés eyes started
feeling heavy, her mouth become tense, her chest started to heave.

Ten minutes later, she was asleep.

"Go and stand behind her," the doctor told me.

So I sat down behind her. He placed a visitor's card in her hand.
"This is a mirror," he said. "What do you see reflected in it?"

"I see my cousin," she replied.

"What is he doing?"

"He is twisting his moustache."

"And now?"

"He is taking a photograph out of his pocket."

"Whose photograph is it?"

"His."

It was true! And the photograph had just been delivered to me at
my hotel that very evening.

"What does he look like in this picture?"

---

3. Franz Anton Mesmer (1734–1815), German doctor whose theory of "animal magnetism,"
   positing a natural transfer of energy between animate and inanimate objects, formed
   the basis of "mesmerism" (as in the now-familiar term "mesmerize"), a popular practice
   associated with hypnotism.

"He is standing up and holding a hat in his hand."

And so she could see in the card, in this piece of white card, as if she were looking in a mirror.

"Enough! Enough!" the young woman said, terrified. "That's enough!"

But the doctor gave an order: "You will get up tomorrow morning at eight o'clock; then you will go to see your cousin at his hotel and you will beg him to lend you five thousand francs that your husband has asked you to give him when he leaves on his next trip."

Then he woke her up.

On the way back to my hotel, I thought about this strange séance and was overwhelmed with doubt, not about the absolute good faith of my cousin—that was above suspicion, as I had known her since we were children and she was like a sister to me—but about the possible hoax perpetrated by the doctor.

Perhaps he was hiding a mirror in his hand that he showed to the hypnotized young woman at the same time as his calling card? Professional magicians do other such extraordinary things.

I went home to bed.

The next morning, around eight-thirty, I was awakened by my valet.

"Mme Sablé is here," he said, "and she is asking to see you right away, Monsieur."

I dressed quickly and went out to greet her.

She was sitting down and looked very upset indeed; her eyes were lowered, and without raising her veil, she said:

"My dear cousin, I have a great favor to ask of you."

"What favor is that, my dear?"

"It troubles me greatly to ask you and yet I must. I need, I am in dire need, of five thousand francs."

"Is that so? You really are?"

"Yes, yes, or rather, my husband is, and he has asked me to find the money."

I was so astonished that I muttered my reply. I wondered if she had actually not plotted with Dr. Parent to trick me, if it were nothing more than an elaborate joke prepared in advance and well played out.

But when I looked at her closely, all my doubts disappeared. Making this request was so painful to her that she was trembling with anguish, and I realized she was trying to hide her sobs.

I knew she was extremely wealthy so I continued:

"What! Your husband doesn't have five thousand francs of his own! Come now, just think about it. Are you sure that he sent you to ask me for the money?"

She hesitated for a moment as if she were making a great effort to remember something.

"Yes . . . yes . . ." she replied. "I'm quite sure."

"Did he write to you?"

She hesitated again and thought about it. I could guess how difficult it was for her to think it through. She didn't know. All she knew was that she was supposed to borrow five thousand francs from me for her husband. And so she actually lied.

"Yes, he wrote to me."

"When was that? You didn't mention anything about it at all last night."

"I got his letter this morning."

"Can you show it to me?"

"No . . . no . . . no . . . It contains personal things . . . it's too personal . . . I've . . . I've burnt it."

"So has your husband been running up debts?"

She hesitated once more, then murmured:

"I don't know."

"It's just that I don't have five thousand francs to lend you at this time, my dear cousin," I said quickly.

She let out a cry of anguish.

"Oh! Oh! I beg of you, find the money for me, I'm begging you . . ."

She was getting very upset, clasping her hands together as if she were praying to me! I could hear the tone of her voice change; she was crying and stammering, obsessed, overwhelmed by the irresistible order she had received.

"Oh! Oh! I'm begging you . . . if you only knew how much I'm suffering . . . I must have the money today."

I took pity on her.

"You will have it this afternoon, I promise."

"Oh! Thank you! Thank you! You are so kind."

"Do you remember what happened last night?" I asked.

"Yes."

"Do you remember that Dr. Parent hypnotized you?"

"Yes."

"Well! He ordered you to come and borrow five thousand francs from me this morning, and you are obeying his command."

She thought for a few seconds.

"But it's my husband who is asking me for the money," she replied.

I tried to convince her for an hour, but without success.

When she left, I hurried to the doctor's house. He was about to go out; he listened to what I had to say and smiled.

"Do you believe in it now?" he asked.

"Yes, I have to."

"Let's go and see your cousin."

She was already half-asleep on a chaise longue, overcome with exhaustion.

The doctor took her pulse, looked at her for a time with one hand raised toward her eyes; she gradually closed them, unable to fight his spellbinding force.

"Your husband no longer needs the five thousand francs," he said, once she was asleep. "You will forget that you asked your cousin to borrow the money, and if he mentions it to you, you won't understand what he is talking about."

Then he woke her up. I took my wallet out of my pocket.

"Here you are, my dear cousin, here is the money you asked for this morning."

She was so surprised that I didn't dare insist. Instead, I tried to help her to remember, but she hotly denied it, thought I was teasing her and, in the end, nearly got angry.

And there you have it! I just got home and this experience upset me so much that I couldn't eat my breakfast.

July 19

Many people I told this story to made fun of me. I no longer know what to think. The wise man says: Perhaps?

July 21

I went to Bougival for dinner, then spent the evening at the dance the boatmen held. Undoubtedly, everything depends on where you are, and the atmosphere. Believing in the supernatural on Ile de la Grenouillière[4] would be the height of folly . . . but at the top of Mont Saint-Michel? . . . or in the Indies? We are intensely influenced by everything that surrounds us. I will go home next week.

July 30

I've been home since yesterday. Everything is fine.

August 2

Nothing new; the weather is sublime. I spend my days watching the Seine flow by.

August 4

The servants are quarreling. They claim that glasses in the cupboards are being broken during the night. The valet accuses the cook, the cook accuses the laundress, who in turn accuses the other two. Who is responsible? Who on earth can tell?

---

4. Known for its bathing, drinking, and general merrymaking, captured for posterity in Renoir's *La Grenouillère* (1869).

August 6

This time, I am not mad. I saw it . . . I saw it . . . I saw it! I can no longer have any doubts. I saw it! I am still frozen to the bone . . . frightened to my very core . . . I saw it with my own eyes!

I was walking through my rose garden, at two o'clock, in bright sunlight . . . in the path where the first roses of autumn are beginning to blossom.

When I stopped to look at a *géant des batailles*[5] that had three magnificent flowers, I saw, I distinctly saw, right next to me, the stem of one these roses bend and then break off—as if some invisible hand had twisted it and picked it from the bush! Then the flower rose in the air, making an arch, as if an arm had raised it to its mouth, and it remained suspended in the clear air, all alone, motionless, a terrifying red patch close to my eyes.

Frantic, I lunged forward to grab it! There was nothing there; it had disappeared. Then I was stricken by fierce anger toward myself, for it is not acceptable for a logical, serious man to have such hallucinations.

But was it really a hallucination? I turned around to look for the stem and immediately found it on the rosebush, freshly broken off, between the two other roses that remained on the branch.

So I went back home, my soul in turmoil. For now, I am certain, as certain as day follows night, that an invisible being is living at my side, a being that drinks milk and water, who can touch things, pick them up and move them, is endowed with physical characteristics that we are quite incapable of seeing, and who lives, as I do, under my roof . . .

August 7

I slept peacefully. He drank some water from my decanter but did not wake me.

I wonder if I am mad. While I was walking along the riverbank in the sunshine today, I began to have doubts about my sanity, not vague doubts like the ones I've had up until now, but precise, absolute doubts. I have known madmen; some of them remained intelligent, lucid, even perceptive about everything in life, except in one way. They talked about everything with clarity, finesse, insight, and suddenly their thoughts would hurtle against the stumbling block of their madness, break up into little pieces, scattering and foundering in a terrifying, raging ocean, full of soaring waves, layers of fog and squalls—the ocean that is called "insanity."

5. A type of rosebush.

Of course, I would believe myself to be mad, absolutely mad, except for the fact that I was perfectly aware, conscious of my condition, for I probed it and analyzed it with complete lucidity. In short, I was, therefore, simply a logical man who was suffering, from hallucinations. Some unknown disorder must have taken hold of my brain, one of those disorders that the physiologists of today attempt to record and define; and this disorder must have left a great crevice in my mind, in the logic and order of my thoughts. Similar phenomena take place in dreams, providing us with the most unbelievably bizarre scenarios, without being in the least surprised, because the mechanism that verifies and controls us is asleep, while our imagination is awake and at work. Perhaps one of the imperceptible ivories on my brain's keyboard no longer works? After an accident, some men cannot remember people's names or certain verbs or figures or simply dates. The location of all the areas of thought has been defined in our time. So why should it be surprising that my ability to control certain unreal hallucinations has gone dead in me at present!

I thought about all these things as I walked along the water's edge. The sun made the river sparkle, the countryside look delightful, filling my eyes with a love of life, for the swallows, whose agility is a joy to behold, a love of the reeds along the riverbank, whose rustling sound brings me happiness.

And yet, little by little, an inexplicable feeling of anxiety ran through me. Some force, or so it seemed, some supernatural force was taking over my body, stopping me, preventing me from going further, forcing me to go back. I felt a painful, oppressive need to go back home, like the feeling you get when you have left a sick person you love in the house and you get a premonition that they are getting worse.

And so, in spite of myself, I went back home, certain that I would find a letter or telegram that contained bad news waiting for me there. There was nothing; and I remained more surprised and more anxious than if I had had some new eerie vision.

August 8

I had a horrible night. He is no longer making his presence known but I can feel him near me, spying on me, watching me, entering my body, taking over; and he is to even more formidable when he hides himself this way than when he makes his constant, invisible presence known through supernatural phenomena.

And yet, I managed to sleep.

August 9

Nothing, but I'm afraid.

August 10

Nothing; but what will happen tomorrow?

August 11

Still nothing; I can no longer stay at home with this fear and these thoughts that have invaded my soul; I am going away.

August 12

Ten o'clock at night—all day I have wanted to leave; but I couldn't. I wanted to accomplish this act of freedom, so easy, so simple—to leave—to get into my carriage and go to Rouen—but I couldn't. Why?

August 13

When suffering from certain illnesses, the inner workings of the physical human body seem to be broken, every type of energy becomes dissipated, all the muscles slack, the bones as soft as flesh and the flesh as liquid as water. I experience this feeling in my soul in a strange, depressing way. I have no more strength, no more courage, no more control over myself, none at all, not even the power to accomplish an act of will. I no longer have a will; someone has taken over my will, and I obey.

August 14

All is lost! someone has possessed me and is controlling me! Someone is commanding my every action, every movement, every thought. I no longer count for anything: I am nothing more than an enslaved spectator, terrified by everything I do. I want to go out. I cannot. He does not want me to, and so I remain overwhelmed, trembling in my armchair where he keeps me seated. I only wish to rise, to stand up, so I can believe I am still my own master. I cannot! I am riveted to my chair; and my chair grips the floor so strongly that no power in this world could release us.

Then, suddenly, I must, I must, I must go to the back of my garden to pick strawberries and eat them. And so I go. I pick strawberries and eat them! Oh my God! My God! Is there a God? If there is, save me, free me! Help me! Forgive me! Take pity on me! Have mercy on me! Save me! Oh! Such suffering! Such torture! Such horror!

August 15

This is surely how my poor cousin was possessed and controlled when she came to borrow five thousand francs from me. She was yielding to some strange will that had entered her, like another soul, like another parasitic, dominating soul. Is the world coming to an end?

But the thing that controls me, what is it, this invisible being? This unknowable creature from a supernatural race who wanders through my soul?

So invisible life forms exist! Well, then, why haven't they shown themselves in such a concrete way since the beginnings of the world, as they have shown themselves to me? I have never read anything that is like what is happening in my home. Oh! If only I could leave, go away, flee and never return. I would be saved then. But I cannot.

August 16

I managed to escape today for two hours, like a prisoner who, by chance, finds the door of his cell unlocked. I felt completely free suddenly and that he was far away. I ordered my carriage to be quickly prepared and I went to Rouen. Oh! What a joy to be able to tell someone: "Drive to Rouen" and have him obey!

I had him stop at a library and asked if I might borrow Dr. Hermann Herestauss's famous treatise on the unknown inhabitants of the ancient and modern world.

Then, just as I got back into my carriage and wanted to say: "Take me to the station!" I shouted—I didn't say it, I actually shouted—in such a loud voice that passersby turned around: "Take me back home." And I fell back against the seat of my carriage, mad and overcome with anguish. He had found me and taken control of me again.

August 17

What a night! What a night! And yet it seems I should be rejoicing. I read until one o'clock in the morning! Hermann Herestauss,[6] Doctor of Philosophy and Theogony,[7] wrote a history of the instances of all the invisible beings who exist alongside man or who are dreamed by us. He describes their origins, their worlds, their powers. But none of them resembles the one who is haunting me. You could say that ever since man was able to think, he could sense and fear some unknown creature, stronger than himself, his successor in this world; and feeling him nearby, yet unable to understand the nature of this master, in his terror he created all the fantastical race of supernatural beings, vague ghosts born of fear.

6. Hermann Herestauss: invented name; one critic has detected within it the German words *Her[r]* (Mr.) and *aus* ("out of" or, in French, *hors*) relating it to the title of *Le Horla*.
7. Study of the genealogy of the deities of heathen mythology.

Having read until one o'clock in the morning, I sat down next to my window to feel the cool, calm wind against my face and refresh my mind in the darkness.

It felt so good; it was warm outside! How I would have enjoyed such a night in the past!

No moon. The stars glistened and shimmered far away in the dark sky. Who inhabits those worlds? What spirits, essences, animals, plants are living there, in the beyond? If there are thinking life forms in these distant universes, how much more do they know than we do? How much more are they capable of than us? What do they see that we have no knowledge of whatsoever? One day, as they are traveling through space, one of them will land on Earth in order to conquer it, just as in the past the Normans crossed the sea to enslave races of men who were weaker than them.

We are all so handicapped, so helpless, so ignorant, so unimportant on this speck of mud that spins around in a drop of water.

I fell asleep in the cool evening air while wondering about such things.

After sleeping for about forty minutes, I opened my eyes without moving a muscle, awakened by some strange, inexplicable, confused feeling. At first I saw nothing, then, suddenly, it seemed that a page of the book I had left open on my table had just turned over by itself. No gust of wind had entered through my window. I was surprised and waited. After about four minutes, I saw, I saw—yes, I saw with my own eyes—another page rise and fall down onto the one before it, as if some hand had been leafing through it. My armchair was empty, at least it looked empty; but I realized that he was there: he was sitting in my chair and reading. I leapt up in a rage, like a wild animal intent on ripping his master to shreds; I crossed my room to grab hold of him, pin him down, and kill him! . . . But before I could get there, my armchair tumbled backwards as if someone was running away from me . . . my table shook, my lamp wobbled and went out, and my window closed as if some evildoer had been discovered and ran off into the night, slamming the door behind him.

So he had run away; he was afraid, afraid of me; *he* was afraid of *me*!

Well, then . . . that means that . . . tomorrow . . . or the day after . . . or some day, I could grab hold of him and crush him into the ground! Don't dogs sometimes bite and kill their masters?

August 18

I thought about it all day long. Oh, yes! I'll obey him, follow his whims, fulfill all his desires, make myself humble, submissive, cowardly. He is the stronger. But the day will come when . . .

August 19

I know . . . I understand . . . I know everything! I have just read this in the *Revue du Monde Scientifique*[8]

> A rather curious piece of news has been brought to our attention from Rio de Janeiro. A form of madness, an epidemic of hysteria comparable to the contagious madness that swept through Europe in the Middle Ages is currently rife in the province of São Paolo. Its terrified inhabitants are leaving their homes, deserting their villages, abandoning their fields, claiming they are being followed, possessed, controlled like human cattle by invisible beings whose presence can be sensed, a kind of race of vampires who feed off their lives while they sleep, and who drink water and milk without appearing to touch any other type of food.
>
> Professor Don Pedro Henriquez, accompanied by several medical scientists, went to the province of São Paolo in order to study the origins and manifestations of this surprising madness on site, and to suggest what measures the Emperor[9] should best take to return his demented people to a rational state of mind.

Ah! Ah! I remember it now: I remember that beautiful Brazilian three-master that passed beneath my windows while gliding up the Seine. It was last May 8. I thought it so superb, so white, so cheerful! The Being was on it, coming from there, from São Paolo where its race was born! And he saw me! He saw my house that was also white; and he jumped off the boat onto the riverbank. Oh, my God!

Now I know, I can sense it. The rule of mankind is over.

He has come. He who is the embodiment of all the primeval terrors of innocent people in this world, He who is exorcised by anxious priests, He who is summoned by witches on dark nights but has not yet appeared, He whom the fleeting masters of this world fear in every monstrous or graceful form: gnomes, spirits, genies, fairies, elves. After the crude ideas of primitive terror, shrewder men have understood Him more clearly. Mesmer had imagined Him, and for the past ten years, doctors have already imagined and detailed the nature of His power even before He used it. They experimented with this new Lord's weapon: the domination of a mysterious will over a human soul that had been enslaved. They called it casting a spell, hypnotism, the power of suggestion . . . what can I know of it? I have watched them amuse themselves with this horrible force like foolish children! How wretched we are! How ill-fated is man!

8. Although this *International Scientific Journal* is invented, the worldwide panic inspired by the cholera epidemic of 1884 was not.
9. Specious reference to Pedro II, who ruled Brazil between 1840 and 1889.

He has come, the . . . the—what does He call Himself?—the . . . I feel as if He is shouting out His name to me and I cannot hear it . . . the . . . yes . . . He is shouting it . . . I am listening but I cannot . . . say it again . . . Le Horla . . . Now I've heard it . . . Le Horla . . . that is who He is . . . Le Horla has come!

Ah! The vulture ate the dove; the wolf devoured the lamb; the lion killed the buffalo with its sharp horns; man killed the lion with his arrow, with his sword, with his gunpowder; but Le Horla will make of man what we have made of horses and cattle: will we belong to Him, become His servant and His food, solely by the power of His will. How wretched we are!

And yet, sometimes an animal revolts and kills whoever has tamed it . . . I too want to . . . I could . . . but first I must know Him, touch him, see Him! Scientists say that an animal's eye is different from ours and see things differently . . . And my own eyes cannot make out this stranger who oppresses me.

Why? Oh! Now I remember the words of the monk at Mont Saint-Michel: "Do we ever see a hundred thousandth of what actually exists? Take the wind, for example, which is the greatest force of nature: it knocks men over, tears down buildings, uproots trees, lifts the sea to form mountains of water, destroys cliffs and forces ships onto the reefs; the wind kills, it whistles, it groans and howls, but have you ever seen it? Could you ever see it? And yet, it exists."

And I went on musing: my eyes are so weak, so imperfect, that when solid objects are as transparent as glass, I cannot even make them out! . . . It's as if a two-way mirror is blocking my path, throwing me around like a bird that gets into the room and crashes into the window, breaking his neck. Do a thousand other things trick him or make him lose his way? So there is nothing surprising about the fact that a bird cannot see a new object when light shines through it.

A new being! Why not? He was bound to come! Why would we be the final race? We cannot make Him out, just like all the others that came before us. It is because His nature is more perfect, His body more delicate and more subtle than ours, because ours is so weak, so awkwardly conceived, burdened with organs that are always tired, always straining as if they were overly complex; we live like plants and animals, existing, with great difficulty, on air, vegetation and meat, a bestial organism prone to illness, deformity, decay; we are short of breath, unstable, naïve and strange, ingeniously but badly designed, with a delicate yet crude construction, a rough sketch of a being with the potential to become intelligent and magnificent.

There are so few of us, so very few species in this world, from the oyster up to man. Why not yet another type of being once the time span has passed that separates the successive evolution of the various species?

Why not one more? Why not other trees and enormous flowers as well, flowers that are dazzling and spread their perfume across entire regions? Why not other elements apart from fire, air, earth and water?—There are only four of them, only four, these elements that nourish our living beings! What a shame! Why not forty, four hundred, four thousand! How feeble, petty and pitiful everything is! Given reluctantly, created quickly, crudely made! Ah! The elephant, the hippopotamus, such grace! The camel, such elegance!

But what about the butterfly, a flower that can fly, you might say. I dream of one that would be as big as a hundred universes, with wings whose shape, beauty, color and movement I cannot even begin to describe. But I can picture it . . . it goes from star to star, cooling them and filling the air with a light, rhythmic breeze as is passes! . . . And the people who live in those distant lands watch it go by, ecstatic with delight.

. . . .

What is wrong with me? It's Him, Him, Le Horla who is haunting me, making me think of such mad things! He is inside me. He is taking over my soul. I will kill Him!

August 19

I will kill him! I have seen him! Yesterday, I sat down at my table and pretended to be writing with great concentration. I knew very well that He would come and hover around me, quite close to me, so close that I might be able to touch Him, grab hold of Him. And then . . . then, I will have the strength of a desperate man: I will use my hands, my knees, my chest, my head, my teeth to strangle Him, crush Him, bite Him, tear Him apart.

And feeling every part of my body ready to pounce, I waited for Him.

I had lit my two lamps and the eight candles on my mantelpiece, as if I might be able to seem Him in the bright light.

Opposite me was my bed, an old oak four-poster bed; to my right was the fireplace; to the left, I had carefully closed my door, after leaving it open for a long time, in order to draw Him in; behind me was a very tall wardrobe with a mirror that I used every day to shave and dress, where it was my habit to gaze at myself, from head to toe, every time I walked by it.

And so, I pretended to be writing, in order to trick Him, for He was also spying on me; and suddenly, I felt, I was certain, that He was reading over my shoulder, that He was there, almost touching my ear.

I sprang up, my fists clenched, and turned around so quickly that I nearly fell over. And then? . . . It was as bright as day inside the room and yet I did not see my reflection in the mirror! . . . It was empty, bright, deep, full of light! But my reflection was not there . . . and I was standing right opposite it!

I could see the clear glass from top to bottom. And I stared at it wild-eyed. I didn't dare take a step forward; I didn't dare make a move, and yet I could sense that He was there—He was there but He would escape my clutches once more, He whose invisible body had devoured my reflection.

I was so very afraid! Then suddenly, I gradually began to see myself in a mist, deep inside the mirror, in a fog as if through a layer of water; and it seemed as if this water glided from side to side, slowly, making my image clearer with every moment that passed. It was like the end of an eclipse. The thing that was hiding me did not appear to have any clearly defined shape, but a sort of opaque transparency that gradually grew more and more visible.

I could finally see myself clearly, just as I did every day when I looked at myself in that mirror.

I had seen Him! I could still feel the terror of that moment that made me continue to tremble.

August 20

How can I kill him? I can't even get hold of him? Poison? But He will see me mix it with the water. And besides, will our poisons have any effect on his invisible body? No . . . no . . . of course they won't . . . So what can I do? What can I do?

August 21

I had an ironsmith come from Rouen and commissioned him to make me some iron shutters, the kind that certain private houses have in Paris, on the ground floor, out of fear they may be robbed. He will also make me a door of the same material. I came across as a coward but I couldn't care less!

September 10

Rouen, Continental Hotel. It's done . . . It's done . . . But is he dead? My mind is in a spin over what I saw.

Yesterday, after the ironsmith had set the shutters and door in place, I left everything open until midnight, even though it was start-ing to get cold.

Suddenly, I sensed that He was there, and a feeling of joy, of mad joy ran through me. I got up slowly and paced back and forth for a long time, so He wouldn't guess anything. Then I casually took off my boots and put on my slippers.

Then I closed the iron shutters and walking calmly toward the door, I double-locked it. I then walked back over to the window, padlocked the shutter and put the key in my pocket.

Suddenly, I realized that He was becoming agitated close by me, that it was His turn to be afraid. He was commanding me to open the door for Him and I nearly gave in. But I didn't give in; leaning against the door, I opened it just a crack, just enough for me—and me alone—to get out. I slowly stepped backwards, and as I am very tall, my head nearly touched the top of the doorway. I was sure that He was unable to escape and I locked Him inside, alone, all alone, completely alone! What joy I felt! I had Him! Then I ran downstairs. I took the two lamps from my sitting room and spilled the oil over the carpet, over the furniture, over everything. Then I set it on fire and ran outside, after having double-locked the large front door.

Then I went and hid at the back of my garden, in a clump of bay trees. How long it took, how very long! Everything was dark, silent, still; not a breath of air, not a single star, mountains of clouds that you couldn't see but that weighed so heavily, so very heavily, on my soul.

I watched my house and waited. How long it took! I thought the fire had already gone out by itself, or that it had been put out by Him, when one of the large windows on the ground floor shattered under the force of the fire, and a flame, a great red and yellow flame, long, languid, climbed straight up the white walls, surrounding them right up to the roof. Light shimmered against the trees, the branches, in the leaves, and a shiver of fear ran through me! Birds woke up; a dog began to howl; it felt as if day were breaking! Two other windows shattered at that very moment and I could see that my entire house had been reduced to a terrifying inferno. But then a woman's cry, a horrible, shrill, heartrending cry was heard through the still night, and two garrets opened! I had forgotten about my servants! I could see their terrified faces as they waved their arms about! . . .

And so, frantic with horror, I started running toward the village shouting: "Help! Help! Fire! Fire!" I came across some people who were already on their way there and I went back with them to see what had happened.

By now, the house was nothing more than a magnificent but horrible funeral pyre, an enormous pyre that was lighting up the earth and burning men to death, the place where He was burning, He as well, my prisoner, the New Being, the new master, Le Horla!

Suddenly, the entire roof collapsed between the walls and a volcano of flames spurted up toward the sky. I could see the fireball through all the open windows of the house and I thought that He was in there, inside that furnace, dead . . .

Dead? Perhaps? . . . But what about His body? His body that light passed through . . . was it not impossible to destroy it in ways that kill our bodies?

What if He weren't dead? . . . Perhaps only time had an effect on this Terrifying, Invisible Being. Why would He have a transparent body, an unknowable body, a body made of pure Essence if He had to fear pain, wounds, illnesses, untimely death just as we did?

Untimely death? All human horror springs from this idea! After man, Le Horla. After we who could die on any day, at any hour, at any moment, through any accident, after us has come the Being who need not die until it is His time, at exactly the right day, hour, minute, because He has reached the end of His existence!

No . . . no . . . there is no doubt, no shadow of a doubt . . . He is not dead . . . And so . . . so . . . it is up to me; I will have to kill myself! . . .

On the Water†

I had rented a little country house last summer on the banks of the Seine,[1] several miles from Paris, where I would go to sleep every evening. After a few days, I made the acquaintance of one of my neighbors, a man of around thirty or forty who really was the oddest character I had ever met. He was an old boating man, mad about boats—always near the water, always on the water, always in the water. He must have been born on a boat and he would surely be carried away on that final journey upriver.

One evening when we were strolling along the riverbank, I asked him to tell me some stories of his life on the river. All of a sudden the good man got so animated that his whole being changed; he was transformed, became eloquent, almost poetic. In his heart he had one great, all-consuming, irresistible passion: the river.

"Ah!" he said, "I have so many memories on this river you see flowing beside us! You city dwellers, you don't really know the river, but listen to a fisherman say that word. To him, it is the most mysterious thing; deep and strange: a fairy-tale world of mirages and spectres, where you see things in the darkness that aren't real, where you hear

† First published, under the title *En canot* and the pseudonym "Guy de Valmont," in the *Bulletin français* of March 10, 1876; it subsequently appeared in *La Maison Tellier* (1881), the version translated here, as well as being reprinted in *L'Intransigeant illustré* of June 26, 1891. Translated by Sandra Smith in collaboration with Eleanor Hill of Sarah Lawrence College.
1. Whether or not the tale is strictly autobiographical, it is based on Maupassant's recollections of his boating expeditions from 1873–75, when he would often rent a riverside room at Argenteuil with his friend Léon Fontaine at the *Petit Matelot* inn.

noises you cannot recognize, where you shake in fear without know-ing why, as if you were walking through a cemetery: in fact, it is the most sinister kind of cemetery: the one with no tombstones.

"Land confines the fisherman, but in the darkness on a moonless night, the river goes on forever. A sailor doesn't feel the same way about the sea. It is often malicious and cruel, that's true, but the great sea cries, it screams, it does not lie: it is trustworthy, whereas the river is silent and treacherous. It does not roar, it flows along without a sound, and it is this eternal movement of the river that is more terrifying to me than any of the highest waves created by the ocean.

"Dreamers claim that the sea hides in its heart immense bluish waters where drowned men float amongst the long fishes, in the midst of strange forests and in crystal caves. The river has nothing but black depths where you rot in the slime. Yet it is beautiful when it sparkles and shines in the light of the rising sun, when it softly laps against its banks covered in rustling reeds.

"The poet speaks of the Ocean:[2]

> *O waves, how many mournful stories you know!*
> *Deep waters, feared by mothers on bended knee,*
> *You tell your stories as you rise with the tides*
> *And they become the despairing voices*
> *We hear at night, as you come toward us*

"Well, I think that the stories whispered by the slender reeds with their soft little voices are far more sinister than any of the tragedies told by the howling waves.

"But since you've asked me for some of my memories, I will tell you of one strange experience that happened to me, here, about ten years ago.

"I was living in the house of Madame Lafon as I am now, with one of my closest friends, Louis Bernet, who had moved into a vil-lage[3] seven miles further down the river. He doesn't go boating any more: he gave up his sloppy clothes along with the glorious pleasures of the river to get into *Conseil d'État*.[4] We had dinner together every day, sometimes at his place, sometimes at mine.

"One evening, I was coming home alone, somewhat tired, in my boat—a twelve-footer that I always took out at night—I stopped for a few seconds to catch my breath beside the reed-covered point as I had been rowing with some difficulty; see, over there, about six

2. Verses (translated by Sandra Smith) from Victor Hugo's *Oceano nox*, in *Les Rayons et les ombres* (1840).
3. The original French reads "village de C . . . ," alluding to either Chatou or Croissy; that it is more likely the former is indicated by the subsequent reference to "the railway bridge" crossing the river between Bezons and Carrières-sur-Seine.
4. See *The Protector*, p. 17, note 2.

hundred feet in front of the railway bridge. It was a beautiful night; the moon shone magnificently, the river shimmered and sparkled in its light, the air was calm and mild. This tranquility appealed to me; I thought it would be pleasant to smoke a pipe there, so I did just that. I took my anchor and cast it into the river.

"The boat floated a little downstream with the current until its chain was taut, then stopped; and I sat in the stern on my sheep-skin, trying to make myself as comfortable as possible. It was silent, absolutely silent: only occasionally I thought I could make out the sound of the water lapping on its banks, although I could barely hear it; and I could just glimpse the strange shapes the group of reeds made on the higher banks; every now and again, they seemed to be flutter.

"The river was perfectly calm, but I found myself moved by the extraordinary silence that surrounded me. All the frogs, the toads, the water creatures that sing in the marshes at night were quiet. Suddenly, a frog croaked to my right. I shuddered: it went quiet; I heard nothing more, and decided to smoke a little to take my mind off it. But although I was well known as a pipe-smoking man, I just couldn't; my stomach turned as soon as I took the second puff and I stopped. I began to sing, but the sound of my voice irritated me, so I lay down in my boat and watched the sky, and after a while, I calmed down. But soon the slight movements of the boat on the water began to worry me; it felt like it was swaying and rocking fiercely against the riverbanks, hitting each of them in turn. I thought that some invisible force or being was slowly dragging my boat to the bottom of the river, then lifting it up just to let it fall back again. I was tossed about as if I were in a storm; I heard sounds all around me; I leapt up; the water was glistening, everything was calm.

"I realized I was a little shaken and decided to leave. I pulled the chain of my anchor and the boat began to move a little, but then, I could feel it was stuck; I pulled harder, but the anchor didn't move; it had caught on something at the bottom of the river and I couldn't pull it free; I tried again, but in vain.

"I used my oars to turn the boat around, hoping that it would change the position of the anchor. But again, it was in vain, it held fast; I flew into a rage and furiously rattled the chain. Nothing moved.

"I sat down utterly discouraged and began to think about my situation. I couldn't even consider breaking the chain or separating it from the boat because it was enormous and attached at the bows to a piece of wood larger and thicker than my arm; but as the weather was so fine, I thought that it surely couldn't be long before some fisherman would come along and help me. My failed attempt had

calmed me; I sat down and could finally smoke my pipe. I also had
a bottle of rum, so I drank a couple of glasses and soon my situation
began to make me laugh. It was very warm, so warm that I could
spend the night quite comfortably sleeping under the stars if I had to.

"All of a sudden, something hit my boat. I jumped; chills ran down
my spine, from the top of my head to the tips of my toes. The sound
had probably been made by some piece of wood that had floated past
with the current, but still, it was enough to fill me once again with
strange, overwhelming anxiety; I tensed my muscle, seized the chain
and pulled desperately. The anchor held firm. I sat down again,
exhausted.

"Meanwhile, the thick white fog was gradually settling low down
onto the river, spreading softly across the water, so that even while
standing I could no longer see the water, or my feet, or my boat. All
I could make out was the tops of the reeds in the distance and the
flat open country, very pale in the moonlight, filled with the long
dark shadows of a cluster of Italian poplars ascending toward the sky.
I felt buried to the waist in a soft cotton cloud of dazzling whiteness,
and I began to imagine all sorts of supernatural things. I imagined
that someone was trying to climb onto the boat—that I could no
longer see—and that the river, hidden in this dense fog, was filled
with strange beings swimming all around me. I felt horribly frightened, my head throbbed and my heart was beating so fast I thought
I would die; panic-stricken, I thought of swimming away, of saving
myself, but even that idea made me shake with terror. I could picture myself lost, drifting through the thick fog, struggling through
the grass and reeds, gasping with fear, unable to escape, unable to
see the riverbanks, unable to find my boat again; and I felt as if I
would be dragged feet-first all the way down to the bottom of this
endless, black water.

"And since I would have had to swim against the current for at
least five hundred yards before finding the gap in the grass and
rushes where I could get a foothold, there was still only a one in ten
chance that I would be able to navigate through this fog and swim
to shore, regardless of how good a swimmer I was.

"I tried to reason with myself. I felt a strong desire not to be afraid,
but something besides this desire burned within me, and this other
thing was afraid. I wondered what it was that I feared; the brave *me*
ridiculed the cowardly *me*, and never so strongly as on this day did
I feel the conflict between these two beings that live within us, one
desiring, the other opposing, and each in turn winning over the
other.

"This ridiculous, inexplicable fear grew and grew until I was completely terrified. I stood absolutely still, eyes wide open, listening

and waiting. For what? I had no idea, but it must surely be something horrible. I believe that if a fish had suddenly jumped out of the water, as often happens, that's all it would have taken to make me drop down, unconscious.

"Still, with extreme effort, I eventually manage to pull myself together. I grabbed my bottle of rum and took a couple of swigs. Then I had an idea, and I began to shout as loudly as possible in every direction. When my throat was absolutely dry, I listened. A dog was howling, far off in the distance.

"I drank some more and stretched out at the bottom of my boat. I stayed like that for an hour or so, perhaps even two, without sleeping, eyes wide open, nightmares swirling around me. I didn't dare get up, although I desperately wanted to; I put it off again and again. I told myself: 'Come on, get up!' but I was too scared to move. I finally stood up very, very cautiously, as if making the slightest noise was a matter of life and death; I looked over the side.

"I was dazzled by the most marvelous, most wondrous display imaginable. It was one of those spectres from a fairy-tale world, one of those visions recounted by voyagers returning from afar that we listen to in disbelief.

"The fog, which two hours earlier had covered the surface of the river, had ebbed away and settled on the riverbanks, leaving the water absolutely clear. It had formed a dense mound on each side, eighteen or twenty feet high, which shone in the moonlight with the dazzling brilliance of snow. You could see nothing but the river gleaming in a fiery light between those two white mountains; and far above my head sailed the great full moon, bright, luminous, amid a milky blue sky.

"All the water creatures were now awake; the frogs croaked loudly, while every now and then, sometimes from the right, sometimes from the left, I could hear the short, sad notes of the toads, their coppery voices echoing up to the stars. The strange thing was, I was no longer afraid; I was in the heart of such an extraordinary landscape that even the most mysterious events would not have surprised me.

"I don't know how long this lasted, for I finally drifted off to sleep, and when I opened my eyes again, the moon was low on the horizon, the sky full of clouds. The water lapped mournfully, the wind sighed, it was cold: darkness reigned.

"I drank what was left of the rum and listened, shivering, to the rustling of the reeds and the sinister sounds of the river. I tried to see, but I couldn't even make out my boat or my hands as I raised them toward my face.

"Little by little, however, the cloud of darkness began to disperse. Suddenly, I thought I could sense a shadow gliding by me; I let out a cry, a voice replied; it was a fisherman. I called out, he came over and I told him about my terrible night. He pulled his boat next to mine and both of us pulled on the anchor. It stood firm. It was dawn, a somber, gray, rainy, icy day, one of those sad, melancholic days. I spotted another boat and we flagged it down. Then the three of us pulled at the chain together and gradually the anchor began to give way. It rose slowly, ever so slowly, loaded down by a considerable weight. Finally, we could make out a black mass, and pulled it on board:

"It was the body of an old woman with a large stone around her neck."

Fear[†]

After dinner, we climbed back up onto the deck. In front of us shone the Mediterranean, not a ripple anywhere; its entire surface mirrored the shimmering, full moon. The vast ship sailed, sending a great serpent of black fumes billowing up toward the sky scattered with stars; and behind us, the water, clear and white, whisked by the rapid passage of the heavy vessel and its propeller, foamed, frothed, seemed to twist and turn, shedding so much light that it seemed as if the moon was bubbling over.

There were six or eight of us, silent, admiring, eyes turned toward distant Africa,[1] where we were headed. The Captain, who had joined us and was smoking a cigar, suddenly continued the conversation we had started at dinner.

"Yes, I was afraid that day. The sea had battered my boat; there was damage from a rock in the hold and we stayed aboard for six hours. But luckily we were picked up by an English coal merchant who'd spotted us."

A big man with a tanned face and a serious expression spoke for the first time. He was one of those men you can tell had traveled to unknown, distant lands and faced constant danger, someone you know had seen strange, mysterious wonders that are carefully kept secret but that you can occasionally glimpse when you look directly into his eyes, one of those men with steely courage.

[†] First published in *Le Gaulois* on October 31, 1882; reprinted in *Contes de la bécasse* (1883), the version translated here. In this collection, it was prefaced by a dedication to J.-K. Huysmans (1848–1907), a gesture toward Maupassant's fellow writer particularly appropriate given the author of *À rebours* and *Là-bas*' own predilection for instances of the bizarre, the fantastic, or the supernatural. Maupassant had recently sympathetically reviewed his friend's *À vau-l'eau*, also in *Le Gaulois*. This story is translated by Sandra Smith in collaboration with Eleanor Hill of Sarah Lawrence College.

1. Maupassant had visited North Africa in 1881. He evokes the sandstorm, in almost exactly the same words, in travel writing collected in *Au Soleil* (1884).

"You say, Captain, that you felt fear that day; I don't believe you. You are not using the right word, and you are mistaken about what you really felt. An active man is never afraid in the face of imminent danger. He is agitated, aroused, anxious; but fear is something else entirely."

The Captain laughed and replied:

"Ha! I swear to you, it was fear."

Then the man with the tanned complexion began speaking, in a slow steady voice:

"Let me explain! Fear is something truly horrifying (and the bravest of men sometimes experience it); it is a terrible feeling, like the rotting of a soul. It stops hearts and thoughts dead, and even thinking about it leaves you shivering in anguish. But when you're brave, you don't feel it when facing an attack, or inevitable death, or even the more common forms of danger; you only feel it in certain, unusual circumstances, under certain mysterious influences and in the face of some vague menace. Real fear is a recollection of fantastical terrors from long ago. A man who believes in ghosts and who thinks he sees one in the dead of night must feel this kind of fear in all its terrifying horror.

"I felt that fear in broad daylight, it must be ten years ago now, and I felt it again this past winter, on a cold December night.

"And yet, I have lived through many dangers, many events that seemed lethal. I have often had to fight for my life. In America, thieves left me for dead; I have been condemned as an insurgent to be hanged; and on the coast of China, I was thrown into the sea from the deck of a ship. Every time I thought I was doomed, I immediately accepted my fate, with no self-pity and even without regrets.

"But true fear is entirely different.

"I felt it in Africa. And yet, fear is the child of the North; the sun banishes it like the morning mist. Think about this, gentlemen. In Eastern countries, life counts for nothing; you are resigned at once; the nights are clear and devoid of legends, and souls are devoid of those dark worries that haunt the mind in colder countries. In the East, they may know panic but they have never experienced fear.

"Well, then, this is what happened to me in Africa:

"I was crossing the great sand dunes to the south of Ouargla,[2] one of the strangest places in the world. You've seen the long, smooth sands of the endless ocean beaches. Well! Imagine the ocean itself turning to sand in the middle of a storm; imagine a silent tempest of unmoving yellow waves of dust as high as mountains, waves as

---

2. A town and oasis in northeast Algeria.

unequal and unique as the waves unleashed in floods, but even higher and striated like watered silk. And the still, silent desert sun pours its remorseless flames straight down onto this furious sea. You have to climb up and down those waves of golden ash, over and over again, without stopping, without resting and without any shade. Horses gasp, sink to their knees and slide down the slopes of those unpredictable hills.

"It was just me and my friend, followed by eight Spahis[3] and four camels with their drivers. We were overwhelmed by the heat: exhausted, dehydrated, totally unable to speak any more. Suddenly one of the men let out a kind of scream; we all stopped dead in our tracks, surprised by an inexplicable phenomenon known to travelers in these lost lands.

"Somewhere near us, though I couldn't tell where, a drum sounded: the mysterious beat of the dunes. It beat distinctively, sometimes loudly, sometimes quietly, then stopped, only to continue its haunting sound again.

"Terrified, the Arabs looked at each other. "Death is with us," one of them said in their language. Suddenly, my companion, my closest friend, whom I thought of as almost my brother, fell straight off his horse, head-first, unconscious with sunstroke.

"For two hours, while I was trying in vain to save him, the strange, sporadic, regular beating of the drums filled my ears; and fear, real fear, monstrous fear, gripped me, right down to my bones as I sat by my best friend's dead body, in that horrible place, scorched by the blazing sun, between four mountains of sand while the mysterious echo of the drum continued to beat furiously, two hundred miles from any French camp, plunging us all deeper into fear.

"That day I understood what it felt like to be afraid, but I felt it even more on another occasion . . ."

The Captain interrupted him:

"Excuse me, Monsieur, but what was the drum?"

The traveler replied:

"I have no idea. Nobody knows. Our officers, who often hear this strange noise, generally believe it is a rising echo, intensified and heightened by the undulation of the dunes, caused by a sandstorm when grains of sand are carried along by the wind and crash into tufts of dry grass; we've noticed that the phenomenon only happens in areas with little plants that are as tough and dry as parchment, completely burnt by the sun.

"This drum is perhaps a kind of sound mirage. Nothing more, nothing less. But I didn't learn that until much later.

3. Locally recruited soldiers in the Cavalry Corps of the French army in North Africa.

"Here is my other story about my experience with fear.

"It was last winter, in a forest in northeastern France. The sky was so gray that it got dark two hours earlier than usual. A local farmer was my guide; he walked beside me on the narrow road under the canopy of fir trees, beneath a sharp, howling wind. In between the tops of the trees, I watched the clouds, frenzied, frantic, as if fleeing from something terrible. Sometimes, under a huge gust of wind, the whole forest groaned in anguish and bowed in the same direction; and the cold rushed through me, despite our quick pace and my heavy coat.

"We were going to get some food and sleep in a cabin belonging to a gamekeeper; it wasn't very far away. I was going there to hunt.

"Every now and then, my guide looked up and murmured: 'God-awful weather!' He then told me about the people we would be staying with at the cabin. The father had killed a poacher two years before and since then he seemed tormented, as if haunted by a memory. His two sons were married and lived with him.

"It was pitch-black; I couldn't see anything in front or around me, and the thick branches of the trees brushed against each other, filling the night with an endless murmur. Finally, I saw a light, and soon my companion knocked on a door. Piercing female shrieks rang out. Then a man's voice, somewhat choked, demanded: 'Who's there?' My guide gave his name. We went inside; the scene we saw was unforgettable.

"Waiting for us in the middle of the kitchen was an old man with white hair, a wild look in his eyes and a loaded shotgun. Two large, burly men, armed with axes, guarded the door, and I could just make out two women kneeling in the dark corners of the room, their faces hidden, pressed against the wall.

"He explained. The old man put his gun back on the wall and gave an order to prepare my room; then, as the women hadn't moved, he suddenly said:

"'The thing is, Monsieur, I killed a man exactly two years ago tonight. Last year, he came back to haunt me. I'm expecting him again tonight.'

"Then, in a tone that made me smile, he added:

"So we're a little nervous."

"I reassured him as best I could, happy to have arrived that evening and to see this spectacle of terrified superstition. I told them stories to pass the time and slowly began to calm everyone's nerves.

"Near the fireplace, an old dog with long whiskers, almost blind—one of those dogs that looks like someone you know—slept with his nose in his paws.

"Outside, the raging storm shook the cabin, and through a small, square pane of glass, a sort of spyhole placed near the door,

I suddenly saw a flash of lightning light up the night sky, revealing a huge mass of trees twisting, turning and thrashing in the wind.

"Despite my efforts, I could clearly see these people were deathly afraid, and every time I stopped speaking, they listened intently for the faintest sound. Weary of being in the presence of such silly superstition, I was about to ask to be shown to my bedroom when suddenly the old gamekeeper leapt off his chair, seized his shotgun and spluttered wildly: 'He's come, he's come! I can hear him!' The two women fell to their knees and hid their faces in the corner; the two sons grabbed their axes again. I was going to try and calm them down again when the sleeping dog suddenly woke up, raised his head, tensed his neck, looked toward the fire with his dull eyes and let out a long, mournful howl, one of those howls that makes travelers shudder at night in vast, shadowy woodlands.

"Everyone turned to stare at him; he didn't move; as still as if haunted by a vision, and then, his fur bristling with fear, he began howling at something invisible, something strange, something truly horrible. The gamekeeper, deathly pale, cried: 'He can sense him! He can sense him! He was there when I killed him!' Both the women, overwhelmed with fear, went mad and began howling along with the dog.

"In spite of myself, an intense shiver ran down my spine. The spectacle of that animal in that place, at that time, with these panic-stricken people, was absolutely terrifying.

"For an entire hour, the dog stood dead still and howled; he howled as if tortured by a dream; and fear, that terrible, horrifying fear, rushed through me. Fear of what, though? How can I explain it? It was quite simply *fear*.

"We stood there, motionless, white as sheets, our ears straining, our hearts pounding every time we heard the slightest sound, waiting for something terrible to happen. Then the dog began to walk around the room, sniffing the walls, whimpering the whole time. This beast was driving us mad! In a fit of furious terror, the man who'd brought me there grabbed the dog, opened the door and flung the animal outside, into a little courtyard.

"He stopped howling at once; and we were plunged into an even more terrifying silence. Suddenly we all jumped; something glided past the outside wall on the forest side; then it came to the door, feeling it tentatively with its hand; for two minutes we didn't hear a sound—it drove us mad; then it came back, scraping against the wall, slowly scratching it like a child would with its nails; then suddenly, a face appeared at the spyhole, a white face with the gleaming eyes of a wild beast. It let out a sound: an agonized, mournful moan.

"A dreadful noise exploded in the kitchen; the old gamekeeper had fired his rifle. The two sons immediately rushed over to the spyhole and covered it up with the large dining table, reinforcing it with the sideboard.

"And I swear to you that at the explosion of that gun, which took me completely by surprise, my heart, my body and my soul filled with such dread that I thought I would collapse, on the point of dying of fright.

"We stayed there until dawn, unable to move or to speak, completely paralyzed by an overwhelming sense of fear.

"We didn't dare take the barricade down until a slim ray of sunlight appeared through a crack in the shutters.

"And at the foot of the wall, against the door, the old dog lay dying, his face ripped apart by a bullet.

"He'd escaped from the courtyard by digging a hole under the fence."

The man with the tanned face fell silent; after a moment, he added:

"Although I wasn't in any danger that night, I would prefer to relive each and every moment of terrible danger I've ever faced than that one minute when the gunshot was fired at the bearded face in the window."

The Apparition[†]

People were talking about a recent trial,[1] a case where someone had been committed to an asylum illegally. It was toward the end of a small gathering of friends one evening on the Rue de Grenelle,[2] in a very old private house, and everyone had a story to tell, a story each person affirmed was true.

Then the elderly Marquis de La Tour-Samuel, who was eighty-two years old, stood up and went to lean against the fireplace. He told his story in a trembling voice:

I also know of something strange, something so strange that it has been the prime obsession of my life. It has been fifty-six years since it happened to me, and not a month goes by without my reliving it again in a dream. From the day that it happened, I was marked,

---

[†] First published in *Le Gaulois* on April 4, 1883; it was included in *Clair de Lune* (1884), the 1888 edition of which is the text translated here.

1. This is a topical allusion to the Monasterio Affair, then the talk of the town: in early 1883 and on the basis of a medical certificate, Fidelia de Monasterio's brother had committed the young woman to a mental asylum. The owner of the house where she had been staying, protesting that she was the victim of a legally sanctioned outrage, brought the matter before the courts at the end of March. Maupassant's was only one of numerous interventions in the press.

2. An upmarket Parisian address, of the kind that Maupassant had only recently begun to frequent.

marked by fear, do you understand what I'm saying? Yes, for ten minutes I was overcome by horrific terror, and it was so strong that ever
since that moment, a kind of endless dread lingers in my soul. Unexpected sounds make me shudder deep inside; objects I can barely
make out in the darkness of evening fill me with a mad desire to
escape. I am actually afraid at night.

Oh! I would never have admitted this until now, having reached
the age I am. Now I can tell you about it. It is acceptable to be fearful when faced with imaginary dangers when you're eighty-two years
old. However, when faced with real danger, Mesdames, I have always
stood my ground.

This event distressed me so deeply, spread such horrific, mysterious and extreme anxiety within me that I have never even told it to
anyone. I kept it hidden in the most private corner of my heart, the
place where we bury our painful secrets, shameful secrets, all the
moments of weakness that have happened to us and that we cannot
bring ourselves to admit.

I am going to tell you what happened without any explanation.
There certainly is an explanation, unless I experienced a moment of
madness. No, I was not mad, and I will prove it to you. Think what
you will. Here are the simple facts.

It happened in July of 1827.[3] I was then stationed in Rouen.

One day, while I was walking along the quayside, I came across a
man whom I thought I recognized, but without being able to place
him. I instinctively hesitated for a moment. The stranger noticed,
looked at me and threw his arms around me.

He was a childhood friend whom I had liked a great deal. In the
five years since I had last seen him, he looked as if he had aged by
half a century. His hair was completely white, and he walked bent
over, as if he were exhausted. He could see my surprise and told me
what had happened. A terrible misfortune had shattered his life.

He had fallen madly in love with a young woman and married her
in a kind of rapture of happiness. After one year of extraordinary
bliss and unabated passion, she had died suddenly of a heart condition, killed by love itself, most likely.

He left his château as soon as the funeral was over and went to live
in his house in Rouen. He lived there alone, in despair, tormented
by grief, so unhappy that all he could think about was suicide.

"Since I've run into you like this," he said, "I'm going to ask you
to do me a great favor, to go to my château and get me some papers
I need urgently; they're in the writing desk in my bedroom, in our

---

3. From the mention of this date, following the narrator's reference to it being fifty-six years
ago, one can calculate that he supposedly tells the story in 1883, giving its readers in *Le
Gaulois* the illusion of immediacy.

bedroom. I can't ask a subordinate or a businessman to take care of this for me for I require the utmost prudence and absolute discretion. As far as I'm concerned, nothing in the world could make me return to that house.

"I'll give you the key to the bedroom that I locked myself when I left, and the key to my desk. And I'll write you a note for you to give to my gardener who will open the château for you.

"But come and have breakfast with me tomorrow, and we can discuss it."

I promised to do this simple favor for him.

Besides, it would just be an outing for me as his estate was located a few miles away, on the outskirts of Rouen. It would only take about an hour on horseback.

I was at his house at ten o'clock the next morning. We had breakfast alone, but he barely spoke. He asked me to forgive him. The thought that I was going to go into his bedroom, where his happiness had died, moved him deeply, he said. He did, in fact, seem unusually upset, preoccupied, as if a mysterious battle were taking place within his soul.

He finally explained exactly what I had to do. It was very simple. I had to take two packets of letters and a bundle of papers locked in the first drawer to the right of his writing desk, to which I had the key.

"I suppose I don't need to ask you not to look at any of them," he added.

I was hurt by his words and told him so, a little angrily.

"Forgive me," he muttered. "I'm in so much pain."

And he began to cry.

I left him about one o'clock to carry out my task.

The weather was beautiful, and I galloped along at a fast pace across the meadows, listening to the singing skylarks and the rhythmic sound of my saber against my boot.

Then I entered the forest and slowed my horse right down. The branches from the trees caressed my face, and every now and again, I would catch a leaf with my teeth and chew on it greedily, experiencing one of those joyous moments in life that, for no particular reason, fills you with intense happiness, an almost fleeting happiness, a kind of surge of power.

As I approached the château, I took the letter I'd been given for the gardener out of my pocket and noticed, with astonishment, that it was sealed. I was so surprised and annoyed that I nearly turned back without carrying out my task. Then I thought that doing so would be to admit I was unnecessarily touchy, which was in bad taste. And besides, my friend must have sealed the note without realizing it, given the emotional state he was in.

The manor house looked as if it had been deserted for twenty years. The gate was open; it was so rotten that it was impossible to tell how it remained standing. The pathways were overrun with grass; you couldn't even see the flowerbeds on the lawns.

I banged my foot against one of the shutters and, hearing the sound, an old man came out of a side door; he was astonished to see me. I leapt off my horse and handed him the letter. He read it, reread it, turned it over, gave me a shifty look and put the paper in his pocket.

"Well! What do you want?" he asked.

"You should know," I replied bluntly, "since you've read your master's orders in that letter. I want to go inside the château."

He seemed appalled. "So, you're going to go into . . . into his bedroom?" he asked.

I was beginning to get annoyed. "Good heavens! Are you really going to just stand there and interrogate me?"

"No . . . Monsieur," he stammered. "It's just that it . . . it hasn't been opened since . . . since the . . . death. If you would wait for me for five minutes, I'll go . . . go and see if . . ."

I cut in. "Really now, do you take me for a fool?" I asked angrily. "You can't go in there because I have the key right here."

He didn't know what to say.

"Well, then, Monsieur, I'll show you the way."

"Just show me the staircase and then go. I'll find it very easily without you."

"But Monsieur . . . all the same . . ."

This time, I got very angry.

"Not another word, now, understand? Or you'll have to answer to me."

I pushed him hard, out of my way, and went inside the house.

I walked through the kitchen, then two smaller rooms where the gardener lived with his wife. Then I crossed a large entrance hall, went up the stairs and found the door my friend had described to me.

I opened it without difficulty and went inside.

The room was so dark that at first, I couldn't make out a thing. I stopped, overwhelmed by that moldy, sickly smell you find in rooms where no one has lived and that have been locked up, funereal rooms. Then, little by little, my eyes adjusted to the darkness and I could clearly see a very large bedroom in total chaos; the bed had no sheets, just a mattress and pillows. One of the pillows had the deep impression of an elbow or a head, as if someone had just lain on it.

The armchairs looked as if they had collapsed. I noticed that one door, from the wardrobe no doubt, had been left ajar.

I went over to the window to let some light in and opened it, but the hinges on the shutter were so rusty that I couldn't get them to budge.

I even tried to break them with my sword, without success. I was getting annoyed by these pointless attempts, and as my eyes had now completely adjusted to the dim light, I gave up hope of seeing any better and walked over to the writing desk.

I sat down in an armchair, raised the flap and opened the appropriate drawer. It was full to bursting. All I needed was three bundles of papers that I knew how to recognize, so I started to look for them.

I opened my eyes wide to see better, and as I was trying to make out the addresses, I thought I heard, or rather felt, something rustling behind me. I didn't think anything was wrong at all: I just thought it was a draft blowing against a piece of fabric. But a minute later, another movement, almost imperceptible, caused an unpleasant shiver to run through my body. It seemed so ridiculous to be afraid, even a little afraid, that I didn't want to turn around, out of a sense of self-respect. I had just found the second bundle of papers I needed, and as soon as I found the third one, a long, painful sigh coming from right behind my shoulder made me start like a madman and jump six feet away. As I leapt, I turned around, my hand on the hilt of my sword, and if I hadn't felt it right by my side, I surely would have fled like a coward.

A tall woman dressed all in white stood watching me, behind the armchair where I had been sitting just a second before.

A shock ran through my arms and legs so powerfully that I nearly fell backwards and collapsed! Oh! No one can understand such terrifying and astounding horrors unless they have experienced them. Your soul fades away, you can't feel your heart beating, any more, your entire body feels as limp as a sponge. It felt like everything inside me was caving in.

I do not believe in ghosts; well, I weakened when faced with the hideous fear of the dead, and I suffered, oh! in those few moments, I suffered more than in all the rest of my life, caught in the spellbinding anguish of supernatural horror.

If she hadn't spoken, I might well have died! But she did speak; she spoke in a soft, mournful voice that made me tremble. I wouldn't go so far as to say that I got control of myself again, or that I was thinking rationally. No. I was so frantic that I didn't know what I was doing any more, but my innate sense of pride as well as a touch of ego that comes from my profession forced me to maintain a semblance of dignity, almost in spite of myself. I stood tall out of self-respect, and for her, of course, for her, whatever she might have been, a real woman or a ghost. I only became aware of all this later on, for I can assure you that the very moment I saw that apparition, my mind was a complete blank. I was quite simply afraid.

"Oh, Monsieur," she said, "I would be so grateful if you could help me!"

I wanted to reply but I couldn't manage to utter a single word. A kind of vague sound came from deep inside my throat.

"Will you?" she continued. "You can save me, make me better. I am suffering so terribly. Suffering . . . oh I am suffering so much!"

She gently sat down in my armchair.

"Will you?" she asked, looking at me.

I nodded, still totally unable to speak.

Then she handed me a tortoiseshell comb.

"Comb my hair, oh! comb my hair," she murmured, "that will make me all better. I need someone to comb my hair. Look at my head . . . I'm suffering so much, and my hair, my hair, it hurts so much!"

Her hair fell loose, and it was very long, very dark, and seemed to hang all the way down the back of the chair and touch the floor.

Why did I do it? Even though I was shaking, why did I let her hand me the comb, and why did I hold her long hair in my hands? It gave me the horrendous feeling I was touching cold snakes. I don't know why.

That feeling is in my fingers still and makes me shudder every time I think of it.

I combed her hair. Somehow, I took her icy mane of hair in my hands. I twisted it, put it up, let it down again, braided it the way you set a horse's mane. She sighed, tilted her head to one side, looked happy.

Suddenly she said, "Thank you!" grabbed the comb from my hand, and ran out through the door I'd noticed was ajar.

For several minutes after I was alone again, I experienced the terror you feel just after you wake up from a nightmare. Then I finally calmed down. I rushed over to the window and angrily broke the shutter open.

A flood of light filled the room. I threw myself against the door where that creature had gone. It was locked and immovable.

Then I was filled with a desperate urge to flee, a panic, the kind of panic you feel in battle. I quickly grabbed the three bundles of letters from the open writing desk, ran through the rooms, leapt down the stairs four at a time, found myself outside, I really don't know how, and spotting my horse a few feet away, I jumped into the saddle in a single bound and galloped away.

I didn't stop until I was in front of my house in Rouen. After throwing the reins to my orderly, I ran to my room and locked myself in so I could think.

For an hour, I anxiously wondered if I hadn't been the victim of a hallucination. I surely must have had one of those incomprehensible nervous attacks, one of those panics in the mind that are the source of miracles, moments that endow the Supernatural with so much power.

And I was about to believe it had all been just a hallucination, a trick of the senses, until I walked over to the window. My eyes happened to wander down to my chest. The jacket of my uniform was covered in long hairs—a woman's long hair—that had got caught in the buttons!

I picked them off one by one, and with trembling hands, I threw them out the window.

Then I called for my orderly. I felt too overwrought, too upset, to go to see my friend the same day. And I also wanted to think about what I should tell him.

I had his letters taken to him and he gave my orderly a receipt. He asked about me in detail. He was told that I wasn't feeling well, that I was suffering from sunstroke, something like that. He had seemed concerned.

I went to see him the next day, just after dawn, determined to tell him the truth. He had gone out the night before and had not returned.

I went back that afternoon but he was still nowhere in sight. I waited a week. He never returned. So I went to the police. They looked everywhere for him but without finding a trace of where he had been or where he was.

A meticulous examination of the deserted château was carried out. Nothing suspicious was found.

There were no indications that a woman had ever been hidden there.

The enquiry revealed nothing; the search was abandoned.

And fifty-six years have passed and I still have learned nothing. I still know nothing more.

The Hand[†]

Everyone gathered around the judge, Monsieur Bermutier, who was giving his opinion about the mysterious case that happened in Saint-Cloud.[1] This inexplicable crime had thrown all of Paris into a panic for the past month. No one understood a thing about it.

[†] First published in *Le Gaulois* on December 3, 1883. The text translated here is the version of the tale collected in *Contes du jour et de la nuit* (1885).
1. Outer Parisian suburb near Versailles.

Monsieur Bermutier stood, leaning against the fireplace as he talked; he brought up evidence and discussed various opinions on the case but came to no conclusion.

Several women got up and went to stand closer to him, concentrating on the judge's clean-shaven face as he spoke in a serious tone of voice. They shuddered and trembled, gripped by fear and curiosity, by a keen, insatiable need to feel terror: it haunted their souls and tormented them like the need for food.

One of the women, paler than the others, broke the silence:

"It's horrible. It's almost 'supernatural.' No one will ever know what really happened."

The judge turned toward her:

"Yes, Madame, it is very likely that we'll never know what happened. But the 'supernatural' as you call it has nothing to do with this case. We are faced with a crime that was very cleverly conceived, very skillfully carried out and so shrouded in mystery that we cannot disentangle it from the enigmatic circumstances surrounding it. However, I did once, long ago, know of a case where something truly inexplicable seemed to be involved. The case had to be dropped, though, as there was simply no explanation for it."

"Oh! Do tell us about it," several ladies urged, all at once.

Monsieur Bermutier smiled, but still looked serious, as was befitting a judge.

"Please do not think, even for a moment, that I assumed something supernatural happened during this case," he continued. "I only believe in natural causes. However, if instead of using the word 'supernatural' to explain things we do not understand, we simply spoke of 'the inexplicable,' that would be more appropriate. In any case, in the story I am about to tell you, it was the external, preliminary circumstances that disturbed me the most. Here are the facts."

"At the time, I was a judge in Ajaccio,[2] a small white city nestled at the edge of a beautiful bay and surrounded on all sides by high mountains.

Most of my cases were to do with murderous vendettas. Some of them were extraordinary, impossibly dramatic, vicious or heroic. Ajaccio is the place where you can find the most amazing motives for revenge you could ever imagine: local feuds that die down for a while but are never forgotten, abominable cunning, assassinations that turn into massacres, acts that could almost be described as noble. For two years, all I heard people talk about was vengeance,

---

2. On the west coast of Corsica. The judge's remark that most of his cases "were to do with vendettas" exploits the island's reputation for these settling of accounts.

the terrible Corsican prejudice that demands revenge for any insult on the offending party, his descendants and his family. I had seen elderly people, children and cousins have their throats slit; my mind was full of such stories.

Now one day, I learned that an Englishman had just taken a long-term lease on a small villa at the end of the bay. He had brought a French servant with him, someone he had found while passing through Marseille.

Everyone was soon talking about this unusual man who lived alone in his house and only went out to go hunting or fishing. He spoke to no one, never went into town, and, every morning, practiced shooting his pistol and rifle for an hour or two.

People started inventing stories about him. Some said he was an important person who had run away from his country for political reasons; others claimed he was in hiding after committing a horrible crime. They even gave particularly gruesome details of the circumstances.

As a judge, I wanted to see if I could get some more information about this man but it proved impossible. He called himself Sir John Rowell.

So all I could do was keep an eye on him from up close, but to tell the truth, there was nothing at all suspicious about him.

Meanwhile, rumors about him continued to spread; they became more and more exaggerated and accepted, so I decided to try to see this foreigner myself, and I started to go hunting regularly in the area near his property.

An opportunity only arose after a long wait. It happened when I shot and killed a partridge right in front of the Englishman. My dog brought it to me; but I immediately took the partridge and went to apologize for my inappropriate behavior and ask Sir John Rowell[3] to accept the dead bird.

He was a big man with red hair and a red beard; he was very tall, very broad, a kind of polite, placid Hercules. He had none of the so-called British reserve and he thanked me warmly for my sensitivity in his broken French, with a thick British accent. By the end of the month, we had chatted together five or six times.

One evening, when I was walking past his house, I saw him in the garden, straddling a chair and smoking his pipe. I greeted him and he invited me to come and have a glass of beer. I accepted at once.

3. The name itself points to a certain "Powell" with whom Charles Swinburne (1837–1909), had been staying at Étretat. Maupassant had gotten to know the English poet there between 1865 and 1868. Among the strange objects collected by Swinburne was a severed hand which later came into Maupassant's possession, inspiring a series of tales starting with *La Main d'écorché* in 1875.

He received me with all the scrupulous courtesy of the English, and spoke in glowing terms of France and Corsica, saying how much he loved this "countryscape" and this "riveredge."

Then, taking the utmost care and under the pretext of being terribly interested, I asked him a few questions about his life and plans. He replied openly, told me he had traveled a lot, in Africa, India and America.

"Oh! Yes, I've had many adventures!" he added, laughing.

Then I started talking about hunting again and he told me the strangest details of the way he had hunted hippopotamus, tigers, elephants and even gorillas.

"All those animals are dangerous," I said.

He smiled: "Oh, no! The worst is man."

Then he started to laugh, the hearty laugh of a big, contented Englishman:

"I also hunted men a lot too, I did."

Then he began to talk about weapons, and invited me to come inside to show me all his different rifles.

His drawing room had black drapes, black silk drapes embroidered with gold. Large yellow flowers ran across the dark material, as brilliant as fire.

"It's Japanese fabric,"[4] he said.

But in the middle of the widest panel, something strange drew my attention. A black object stood out on a square of red velvet. I walked over to it: it was a hand, a man's hand. It wasn't the clean, white hand from a skeleton, but a shriveled-up black hand with long yellow nails, its muscles exposed and traces of old, dried-up blood on the bones, the kind of blood you find on some piece of debris. And the bones looked as if they had been cleanly cut off by an ax, just in the middle of the forearm.

Around the wrist, an enormous iron chain was riveted and soldered to this filthy hand, pinning it to the wall by a ring that was strong enough to keep an elephant in check.

"What is that?" I asked.

"That was my best enemy," the Englishman replied calmly. "It came from America. It has been cut off with a sword and the skin peeled off with a stone, then dried in the sun for a week. Oh . . . very good for me, this."

I touched the human remains that must have belonged to a giant. The fingers were unbelievably long and attached by enormous tendons that still had some shredded skin attached in places. The hand was horrible to look at, flayed the way it was, and naturally made you think of some kind of vicious vengeance.

4. Reference to the contemporary vogue for *japonisme*, all things Japanese.

"The man must have been very strong," I said.

"Ah, yes, but I be stronger than him. I put him on that chain to hold him," the Englishman replied quietly.

I thought he was making a joke.

"That chain is quite pointless now," I said; "the hand isn't going to run away."

"It always tries to escape," Sir John Rowell replied in all serious- ness, "that chain necessary."

I glanced quickly over at him to look at his face. "Is he mad?" I wondered, "or just making it up?"

But it was impossible to read his expression; he remained calm and kindly. I changed the subject, admiring his rifles.

I did, however, notice that there were three loaded revolvers sit- ting on several pieces of furniture, as if he lived in constant fear of being attacked.

I went back to his house several times. Then I stopped going. People had got used to him; no one cared about him any more.

A year passed. Then one morning, toward the end of November, my valet woke me up and told me that Sir John Rowell had been mur- dered during the night.

Half an hour later, I went into the Englishman's house with the chief of police and the Captain. Sir John's valet, distraught and in despair, was crying in front of the house. At first I suspected him, but he was innocent.

The person responsible was never found.

As soon as I walked into the reception room, I saw Sir John's body. He was stretched out on his back, in the middle of the room.

His vest was torn and one of the sleeves of his jacket ripped off; everything indicated there had been a terrible struggle.

The Englishman had been strangled! His dark, swollen face was horrible, and his contorted features meant he had seen something utterly terrifying. His neck was covered in blood and had five punc- ture marks that looked as if they'd been made with iron spikes. There was something between his clenched teeth.

A doctor came in.

He examined the finger marks on the neck for a long time and then said something truly strange:

"You'd think he'd been strangled by a skeleton."

A shudder ran down my spine, and I glanced over at the wall, at the spot where I had seen the horrible flayed hand. It was gone. Its chain hung there, broken.

I leaned over the dead man and saw one of the fingers of the miss- ing hand in his closed mouth. It had been cut, or rather bitten off just above the knuckle.

Then we began investigating. Nothing was found. Not a single door or window had been forced and no furniture had been disturbed. The two watchdogs had not woken up.

Here is a summary of the valet's statement:

"My master had seemed anxious for about a month. He'd received a lot of letters, but he burned them as soon as he'd read them.

"He would often grab a riding crop and in a rage that verged on madness, he would furiously whip the dried-up hand that was chained to the wall. The hand disappeared, no one knows how, on the very night of the crime.

"He went to bed very late and made sure his door was properly locked. He always had a weapon close by. He often talked out loud at night, as if he were having an argument with someone."

That night, strangely enough, he hadn't made any noise, and it was only when the valet came into the room to open the windows that he found Sir John had been murdered. He didn't suspect anyone.

I told the judges and public officials everything I knew about the dead man, and they carried out a thorough investigation throughout the island. Nothing was discovered.

Then, one night about three months after the crime, I had a terrible nightmare. I could see the hand, that horrible hand, scurrying down my curtains and over my walls, like a spider or scorpion. Three times I woke up, three times I went back to sleep, three times I saw the hideous hand hurtling around my bedroom, using its fingers as legs.

The next day, the hand was brought to me; it had been found on Sir John Rowell's grave, in the local cemetery where he had been buried, as we could not trace any of his family. The index finger on the hand was missing.

And there you have my story, Mesdames. I know nothing more.

The women were all pale, trembling, distraught. One of them cried out:

"But that story doesn't have an ending, or an explanation! We're not going to be able to sleep if you don't tell us what you think really happened."

The judge smiled harshly.

"Oh, well, ladies, I am certainly going to ruin your bad dreams. Quite simply, I think that the real owner of the hand was not actually dead, and that he returned with the hand he had left to reclaim it. But I have no idea how he did it, you know. It was a kind of vendetta."

"No, it couldn't be that," one of the women whispered.

But the judge kept on smiling.

"I did warn you that you wouldn't like my explanation."

Lost at Sea[†]

I

Everyone in Fécamp[1] knew the story of poor Madame Patin. She certainly had not been happy with her husband, this Madame Patin: before he died, he used to beat her the way people thresh wheat in their barns.

He was the owner of a fishing boat and had married her, long ago, because she was kind, even though she was poor.

Patin, who was a good sailor, but violent, was a regular customer at Auban's inn, where he normally drank four or five glasses of Marc[2] a day, eight or ten or even more when he'd had a good day at sea, according to his whim, or so he said.

Auban's daughter served the Marc; she was a pretty brunette who attracted people to the inn because of her good looks, for no one ever implied there was any other reason.

Whenever Patin went to the inn, he would simply look at her, at first, and speak politely and calmly to her, like a decent man. After drinking the first glass of Marc, he found he liked her even more. After the second glass, he winked at her. After the third, he said: "If you would like to, Mam'zelle Désirée . . ." without ever finishing his sentence. After the fourth glass, he tried to grab her skirt so he could kiss her, and, when he'd had ten glasses, it was her father who served him the rest.

The old innkeeper, who knew all the tricks of the trade, made Désirée walk around the tables to make people order more drinks; and Désirée, who was not Auban's' daughter for nothing, strolled amongst the drinkers, joked with them, a smile on her lips and a gleam in her eye.

Because he drank all those glasses of Marc, Patin got so used to seeing Désirée's face that he would picture it even when at sea, or when he threw his nets into the water, on the high seas, on windy nights or calm nights, on moonlit nights or in the darkness. He thought about her face when at the helm, or in the back of the boat, while his other four companions were dozing, their heads resting on their hands. He always pictured her smiling at him, pouring the golden Marc with a slight movement of her shoulder, then asking, "There. Satisfied now?" as she walked away.

And because he couldn't stop picturing her and thinking about her, he was overcome by such a desire to marry her that he couldn't hold out any longer and finally asked for her hand.

[†] First published in *Le Gaulois* on August 16, 1888; reprinted in *L'Inutile Beauté* (1890), which is the version translated here. The French title, *Le Noyé*, could also be rendered as "The Drowned Man."

1. Then a fishing port, on the Normandy coast.

2. A very strong liqueur similar to brandy.

He was rich. He owned a boat, his own fishing nets and a house at the foot of the hill on the Retenue;[3] her father had nothing. His proposal was thus eagerly accepted, and the wedding took place as quickly as possible, as both parties were anxious to conclude the business, though for different reasons.

Three days after the wedding, however, Patin just couldn't understand how he might have believed that Désirée was different from any other woman. Had he truly been so stupid as to burden himself with a penniless woman who had seduced him with her Marc? For she had surely put some nasty drug in his drink.

And he swore the whole time he was out at sea, broke his pipe with his teeth, was violent to his crew, and after cursing out loud, using all the vulgar swear words possible against everyone and everything he knew, he vented the rest of his anger on the fish and lobsters caught in one of his nets, throwing them into his large wicker baskets while cursing in filthy language.

Then, once back home, where Auban's daughter, his wife, was in close range of both his foul mouth and his hands, he never failed to treat her like the lowest of the low. But as she listened to him, resigned, accustomed to her father's outbursts, he became frustrated at seeing her so calm, so one evening, he gave her a beating. And life at home then became truly terrible.

For ten years, all anyone ever talked about on the Retenue was the thrashings that Patin subjected his wife to and the way he cursed, about everything, whenever he spoke to her. He swore in a particular way, in fact, with a richness of vocabulary and a thundering voice that no other man in Fécamp could match. As soon as his boat entered the port, after his fishing trips, everyone waited for the first volley of abuse hurled from the jetty to the dock the moment he spotted his wife's white bonnet.

Standing at the back, he would steer his boat, watching the stern and the sail when the sea was rough, and in spite of having to guide the boat through a narrow, difficult passage, in spite of waves that swelled as high as mountains, he would peer through the foamy surf to find his own wife amongst the women waiting for their sailors, his wife, Auban's daughter, the wretched woman!

In spite of the noise of the wind and the waves, as soon as he spotted her, he would start bellowing at her in such a booming voice that everyone would start laughing, even though they felt very sorry for her. Then, as soon as the boat had docked at the quay, he had a way of throwing overboard any ballast of good manners, as he called

---

3. A *retenue* (from *retenir*, "to hold back") is a sink or other structure that prevents water from draining away; here it is the basin in the port where boats can dock and float irrespective of the tide. It is now near the appropriately named Quai Guy-de-Maupassant.

it, while unloading his fish, which attracted all the vagabonds and layabouts from the port around his moorings.

The words flew out of his mouth, sometimes short and horrible, like cannonballs, sometimes like thunder that lasted for five full minutes, such a hurricane of curses that he seemed to have within his lungs all the fieriness of the God of the Old Testament.

Then, after getting off his boat and standing face to face with her amid the fishwives and other curious onlookers, he would fish around his hold for an entire new cargo of insults and harsh words, and they would go back home together, she in front, he behind, she crying, him shouting.

Once he was alone with her behind closed doors, he would hit her for the slightest reason. Any excuse to raise his hand, and once he'd started, he didn't stop, spitting the true reasons for his hatred in her face. With every slap, every punch, he would shout, "Ah, you penniless creature, ah, you tramp, ah! you miserable wretch, I really did myself a favor the day I drank your father's rotgut, that crook!"

The poor woman now lived in constant terror, an endless, gripping fear that ran through her body and soul, in a hopeless state of waiting—waiting for his insults and her beatings.

And this life lasted ten years. She was so fearful that she grew pale whenever she spoke to anyone, and all she could think about were the beatings she was threatened with, so she became thinner, dryer and more yellow than a smoked fish.

II

One night, while her husband was out at sea, she was awakened by the beastly howling the wind makes when it swoops in like a wild dog! She was frightened and sat down on her bed; when she heard nothing more, she climbed back in, but almost immediately, a roar came down the chimney that shook the entire house, then spread across the sky, like a herd of furious snorting, bellowing beasts, stampeding through the night.

She got out of bed and ran down to the port. Women carrying lanterns arrived from all directions. Men rushed over as well, and everyone watched the frothy crests of the waves light up in the darkness above the sea.

The storm lasted fifteen hours. Eleven sailors never returned, and Patin was among them.

The remains of his boat, the *Jeune-Amélie*, were found near Dieppe. His dead crew was discovered near Saint-Valérie,[4] but Patin's body was never found. Since the hull of his boat had been cut in

4. Saint-Valérie-en-Caux is about twelve miles west of Dieppe.

two, his wife expected, and feared, his return, because if there had been a collision, it was possible that the other boat might have picked him up, just him, and taken him far away.

Then, little by little, she got used to the idea that she was a widow, though she would shudder every time a neighbor, a beggar or a traveling salesman unexpectedly came to her house.

One afternoon, about four years after her husband had disappeared, she was walking down the Rue aux Juifs when she stopped in front of the house of an old sea captain who had recently died and whose furniture was being sold.

At that very moment, they were auctioning off a parrot, a green parrot with a blue head, who was watching everyone with an anxious, mean look in his eyes.

"Three francs!" cried the auctioneer. "Here's a bird that can talk like a lawyer, three francs!"

One of Désirée's friends nudged her.

"You should buy it, you've got the money," she said. "It'll keep you company. That bird there's worth more than thirty francs. You can always resell it for twenty or twenty-five francs, you know!"

"Four francs! Ladies, four francs!" the man said again. "He sings Vespers and preaches like the parish priest. He's extraordinary . . . miraculous!"

Madame Patin bid fifty centimes more; the creature with the hooked nose was given to her in a little cage, and she took him away.

Then she got him settled at home; when she was opening the wire door of the cage to give him something to drink, he bit her finger so hard that it cut her skin and made her bleed.

"Ah!" she said. "He's very malicious."

Nevertheless, she gave him some hempseed and corn, then let him preen his feathers while staring at his new house and new mistress, a shifty look in his eyes.

The next morning, just as day was breaking, Madame Patin heard a voice, a loud, deep, booming voice, her husband's voice—there was no mistaking it—shouting:

"Well, are you going to get up, you bitch!"

She was so utterly terrified that she hid her head under the covers, for every morning in the past, as soon as he opened his eyes, her dead husband had screamed those words in her ear, those very words, words she knew only too well.

Trembling, curled up in a ball, her back tensed in anticipation of the beating she expected to get, her face hidden in the bedcovers, she whispered:

"Good God, he's here! Good God, he's here! He's come back. Good God!"

The minutes passed; not a sound broke the silence of her room. Then she lifted her head from under the covers, shaking, sure that he was there, laying in wait, ready to beat her.

She saw nothing, nothing but a ray of sunshine coming in through the window and she thought:

"He's hiding, for sure."

She waited for a long time, then, feeling somewhat calmer, she thought:

"I must've dreamt it, since he ain't here."

She closed her eyes again, feeling less worried, when a furious voice, the thunderous voice of the drowned man, shouted out, quite close by:

"Hell, hell, hell, hell! When the hell are you getting up, b . . . !"

She leapt out of bed, roused by a sense of obedience, the passive obedience of a woman who has been beaten black and blue, a woman who still remembers that particular voice, even after four years have passed, and who will always obey it!

"I'm here, Patin," she said. "What do you want?"

But Patin did not reply.

Terrified, she looked all around her, then checked everywhere—in the wardrobes, in the fireplace, under the bed—finding no one, then collapsed into a chair almost mad with fear, convinced that Patin's soul was there, right next to her, just his spirit, and that it had come back to torment her.

Suddenly, she remembered the attic, and that you could get into it by climbing up a ladder on the outside of the house. He surely must have hidden there to catch her unawares. He must have been held captive by savages on some faraway shore, unable to escape until now, and he had come back, more evil than ever. She had no doubts at all, not after hearing his voice.

"That you up there, Patin?" she asked, looking up toward the roof.

Patin did not reply.

So she went outside, with such fear in her heart that she was shaking, and climbed up the ladder, opened the window, peered in, saw nothing, went inside, looked some more and still found nothing.

She sat down on a bale of hay and started to cry, but while she was sobbing, overwhelmed by some heartbreaking, horrific supernatural fear, she heard Patin's voice saying things, from below, from inside her bedroom. He sounded less angry, calmer as he spoke:

"Filthy weather!—Such strong winds!—Filthy weather!—I ain't eaten, damn it!"

She shouted down through the ceiling:

"I'm here, Patin; I'll make you some soup. Don't get mad. I'm comin'."

And she ran downstairs.

There was no one in her room.

She felt as if she might faint, as if Death itself had touched her, and she was about to run away and get help from her neighbors when the voice shouted into her ear:

"I ain't eaten, damn it!"

And the parrot stared at her from his cage with a wide-eyed, sly, evil expression.

And she looked back at him, terrified.

"Ah!" she whispered. "It's you!"

The parrot shook his head and kept talking:

"Just you wait, wait, wait . . . I'll teach you to be a layabout!"

What went through her mind? She felt, she understood, that it really was him, the dead man, who had come back, hidden in the feathers of this beast in order to continue torturing her; he was going to swear at her all day long, just as he had in the past, and bite her, and, shout out curses to bring the neighbors rushing in, to make them laugh. So she lunged toward the cage, opened it and grabbed the bird; it fought back, tearing at her skin with its beak and claws. But she held onto it with both hands, using all her strength, and throwing herself down on the ground, she rolled on top of it with the fury of a woman possessed, crushed it, turned it into a limp little green lump that didn't move or speak again: it just lay there. Then she wrapped it up, using a dishtowel as a shroud, and went out, barefoot, in her nightgown. She walked across the quayside, washed over by the sea's low waves, and shaking open the cloth, she threw the tiny dead thing in the water; it looked like a little tuft of grass. Then she went home, fell onto her knees in front of the empty cage, and sobbing, distraught at what she had done, begged God's forgiveness, as if she had just committed some terrible crime.

Who Can Know?[†]

I

My God! My God! So I am finally going to write down what has happened to me! But can I? Dare I? It is so strange, so inexplicable, so incomprehensible, so unbelievable!

If I weren't sure of what I had seen, sure there has been no fault in my reasoning, no errors in my findings, no loopholes in all my disciplined observations, I would think I was nothing more than a simple lunatic, at the mercy of bizarre hallucinations. After all, who can know?

† First published in *L'Écho de Paris* on April 6, 1890; reprinted in *L'Inutile Beauté* (1890), which is the version translated here.

Now I am in a mental institution; but I came here of my own free will, out of prudence, out of fear! Only one person knows what happened to me: the doctor here. I am going to write it down. Do I even really know why? To be rid of it, for I feel it within me like an unbearable nightmare.

Here is my story:

I have always been a solitary soul, a dreamer, a kind of lone philosopher, well meaning, needing little to be happy, bearing no bitterness toward men and no grudge against Heaven. I have always lived alone, continually alone, due to a kind of irritation aroused in me by the presence of other people. How can this be explained? I don't know. I don't refuse to socialize, to chat, to have dinner with friends, but as soon as I feel I have been around them for any length of time, even my closest friends begin to bore me, tire me, annoy me, and I experience an ever-increasing, insistent desire to have them go away, or for me to leave, to be alone.

This desire is more than a need, it is an overwhelming necessity. And if I continued to find myself in the company of those people, if I were forced not just to keep hearing their conversations but listen to them as well, something terrible would surely happen to me. What exactly? Ah! Who can know? Perhaps I would simply just faint? Yes, probably!

I like being alone so much that I can't even stand having anyone else sleeping under my roof; I cannot live in Paris because when there, I constantly feel as if I'm about to die. I feel I am dying morally, and my body and nervous system suffer because of the immense crowds swarming everywhere, living all around me, even when they are asleep. When other people are asleep it pains me even more than when they speak. And I can never get any rest when I know, when I can sense, other people behind the wall whose lives are just as broken off, suspended by these regular lapses of reason.

Why am I like this? Who can know? The reason is perhaps quite simple: I grow very tired of anything that doesn't happen within me. And there are many others like me.

There are two categories of people on this earth: those who need others, are entertained, kept busy, calmed down by others, and who are exhausted, worn out, destroyed by solitude, feeling the way they would if they had to climb a mighty glacier or walk across a desert, and those who, on the contrary, are worn out, bored, irritated and pained by other people, while solitude calms them, bathes them in peace through the freedom and imagination of their minds.

All in all, this is a normal psychological phenomenon. The first type of person is made to be extroverted, the others to be introverted. My own attention span for anything outside myself is short and quickly exhausted, and as soon as I can stand no more, an intolerable sense of uneasiness runs through my whole body and mind.

The result of this has been that I become attached, became greatly attached, to inanimate objects, objects that take on the same importance as people to me, and so my house became, had become, a world in which I lived an active but solitary life, surrounded by objects, furniture, curios, that were as familiar and pleasing to my eye as people's faces. I had furnished my home gradually, decorated it, and it was where I felt content, satisfied, as happy as if I were in the arms of a loving woman whose familiar caresses had become the calm, sweet thing I needed.

I had the house built in a beautiful garden that cut it off from the roads, and near the edge of a city where I could have, when necessary, the possibility of mingling with other people, since I did feel that need every now and then. All my servants slept in quarters quite a distance away, at the back of the vegetable garden, surrounded by a high wall. And the darkness of night over the silence of my isolated, hidden home, completely enclosed by the leaves of the tall trees, was so peaceful, so good, that every night I would put off going to bed for hours in order to savor it for longer.

That day, there had been a performance of *Sigura*[1] in the town theater. It was the first time I had seen this wonderful, magical story and heard its music; it gave me much pleasure.

I was walking home, feeling lighthearted, my head full of melodic music and beautiful visions. It was dark, very dark, so dark that I could barely make out the wide road in front of me and I nearly stumbled into a ditch on several occasions. It was about a half a mile from the city limits to my home, maybe a little more, perhaps a twenty-minute walk if you don't hurry. It was one o'clock in the morning, either one o'clock or one-thirty. The sky brightened up a little in front of me and I could see the crescent moon, the sad final stage of the crescent moon. The first crescent moon, the one that appears at four or five o'clock in the evening, is bright, cheerful, tinged with silver, but the one you see after midnight is reddish, somber, troublesome, the true crescent of the Witches' Sabbath[2]. Anyone who is awake late at night must have noticed this. The first quarter, even if it is as slim as can be, casts a joyful little light that delights the heart and casts clear shadows on the ground. The final crescent barely gives off a dying light, so lifeless that it hardly highlights any shadows at all.

1. Opera by Reyer, the adopted name of Ernest Rey (1823–1909), a perennial hit since its inaugural performance in Paris in 1885. Its "magical story," in Wagnerian mode (*Siegfried*, 1876), is that of Norse mythology.
2. The supposed medieval ritual of those practicing witchcraft, meeting between midnight and dawn to preempt the Mass on the Christian Sabbath.

I could make out the dark shape of my garden in the distance, and I don't know why, but I felt somewhat uncomfortable at the idea of going through it. I walked more slowly. It was very mild out. The high cluster of trees made me think of a tomb in which my house was buried.

I opened my gate and went down the long path lined with sycamore trees that led to the house. They formed a high archway like a tall tunnel, through impenetrable clumps of trees and winding around the lawns full of flowerbeds, oval forms with indistinct shapes beneath the fading shadows.

As I approached the house, a strange feeling of uneasiness spread through me. I stopped. There was not a single sound. Not the slightest wind through the leaves. "What's wrong with me?" I thought. I've been coming home like this for ten years without feeling the least bit anxious. I wasn't afraid. I'm never afraid at night. Seeing a man, some prowler or thief, would have filled me with rage, and I would have attacked him without a second thought. I did have a weapon, though. I had my revolver. But I wouldn't touch it, for I wanted to overcome this feeling of dread growing within me.

What was it? A premonition? The mysterious premonition that takes over your senses when you are on the brink of experiencing the inexplicable? Perhaps . . . Who can know?

The closer I got, the more I felt myself shuddering, and when I was in front of the wall, near the closed shutters, I knew I would have to wait a few moments before opening the door and going inside my spacious house. So I sat down on a bench under my living room windows, I stayed there, feeling rather shaken, my head leaning against the wall, staring into the leafy darkness. For the first few moments, I noticed nothing out of the ordinary around me. My ears were humming, but that often happens. Sometimes I think I can hear trains passing, bells ringing, a crowd of people walking by.

The humming soon became more distinct, more precise, more recognizable. I had made a mistake. I was not hearing the usual humming of blood rushing through my veins but a unique yet very vague sound that was definitely coming from inside my house.

I could hear it through the wall, a continuous sound, more like something moving than a noise, the muted movement of a great many things, as if someone had lifted up all my furniture, put it down and slowly dragged it along.

Oh! For a long time after, I still doubted what I was hearing. But I pressed my ear against the shutter to better hear this strange commotion in my house, and I remained convinced, certain, that something abnormal and incomprehensible was happening inside. I was not afraid, but I was—how can I express it?—I was so surprised that

I was scared to death. I didn't load my revolver—I could tell there was no need at all to do that. I waited.

I waited for a long time, unable to make a decision of any kind; my mind was clear but I was incredibly nervous. I stood there, waiting, continually listening to the sound that grew louder and every now and again became powerfully intense, as if it were groaning with impatience, with anger, in mysterious turmoil.

Then, suddenly, ashamed of my cowardice, I grabbed my bunch of keys, chose the one I needed, forced it into the lock, turned it twice, and pushing open the door with all my might, I slammed it against the wall inside.

It sounded as if a rifle had been fired, and then, from the top to the bottom of my house, this explosion was followed by a thunderous uproar. It was so unexpected, so horrible, so deafening that I took a few steps back and pulled my revolver out of its holster, even though I could sense it was pointless.

I waited some more, but not for long. I could now make out the extraordinary sound of footsteps on my staircase, on the parquet floors, over the rugs, footsteps not made by shoes, by people's shoes, but by crutches, wooden crutches and metal crutches that vibrate like cymbals. Then, suddenly, I saw an armchair, the large armchair from my study, shuffling out onto the doorstep. It went out into the garden. Others followed: chairs from my living room, then small sofas dragged along like crocodiles on their short legs, then all of my chairs, leaping about like goats, and little footstools scurrying along like rabbits.

Oh, I was so afraid! I slipped into a clump of trees where I remained, crouching down, staring at this endless parade of my furniture—for everything rushed past, one after the other, quickly or slowly, depending on its size and weight. My piano, my grand piano, flew by with the speed of a galloping horse with the echo of music in its flanks; the smallest objects slid across the sandy ground like ants—brushes, fine glassware, cups—and the moonlight cast a phosphorescent glow on them, so they looked like glowworms. Fabrics crept along, spreading out like the tentacles on an octopus. My desk appeared, a precious antique from the previous century that contained all the letters I had received, my entire romantic past, a former love affair which had caused me so much suffering! And there were photographs inside as well.

Suddenly, I was no longer afraid. I leapt at the desk and grabbed it as you would a thief, the way you might catch hold of a woman who was trying to run away, but it was moving so fast that it simply couldn't be stopped, and despite my efforts, despite my anger, I could not even slow it down. As I desperately fought this horrifying force,

I was thrown to the ground in my struggle. Then it rolled me around, dragged me along the sandy ground, and the furniture that followed was starting to walk over me, trampling my legs and bruising them. Then, after I let go, the rest of the furniture charged over my body like cavalry attacking a fallen soldier.

Mad with terror, I finally managed to pull myself away from the wide pathway and hide in the trees again. I watched everything disappear, the tiniest things, the smallest objects, the least valuable, things I didn't even remember had belonged to me.

Then, in the distance, I heard an incredibly loud banging of doors slamming shut in my house that now echoed as if it were empty. Doors banged from the top to bottom of the building, even the front door that I had foolishly opened myself in order to leave slammed shut, the last to close.

I fled, running toward the village, and only calmed down when I met some people in the street who were out late. I went and rang the bell at a hotel where the people knew me. I had brushed the dust off my clothing and explained how I had lost all my keys, including the key to the kitchen garden where all my servants slept in an isolated house, inside the outer wall that protected my fruit and vegetables from thieves.

I covered myself up to the neck in the bed I was given. But I couldn't sleep, so I listened to my pounding heart and waited for dawn. I had asked that my servants be told where I was as soon as it was light, and my valet knocked at my door at seven o'clock in the morning.

He looked completely distressed.

"Something terrible happened last night, Monsieur," he said.

"What was it?"

"All your furniture was stolen, Monsieur, everything, everything, right down to the smallest items."

This piece of news pleased me. Why? Who can know? I was in complete control of myself, certain I could hide my true feelings, never saying a word to anyone about what I had seen, keep it hidden, bury it in my mind like some terrible secret.

"Well, the same people must have stolen my keys," I replied. "You must go and tell the police at once. I'll get up and meet you there shortly."

The investigation lasted five months. Nothing was ever found, not the smallest stolen item, not the slightest trace of the thieves. Heavens! Imagine if I had said something about what I knew . . . If I had told them . . . they would have locked me up, me, not the thieves but the man who had witnessed such a thing.

Oh! I knew how to keep silent. But I didn't refurnish my house. It was quite pointless. It would have happened again. I didn't ever want to go back there. I never saw it again.

I came to Paris, to a hotel, and I consulted doctors about my nervous condition, as it worried me a great deal ever since that hideous
night.

They suggested that I travel. I took their advice.

II

I began with a trip to Italy.[3] The sun did me good. For six months, I
wandered from Genoa to Venice, from Venice to Florence, from
Florence to Rome, from Rome to Naples. Then I explored Sicily, a
wonderful place thanks to its landscape and monuments, relics left
by the Greeks and Normans. I went to Africa, peacefully crossing
the calm, golden desert where camels, gazelles and nomadic Arabs
wander past, where, under the clear, light sky no haunting thoughts
float around you, not in the daytime, not at night.

I returned to France through Marseille, and despite the city's live-
liness, the light in Provence was less brilliant, which saddened
me. When I got back to this continent, I had the strange feeling I
was a sick man who thinks he is cured but who still experiences
some slight pain, a warning that the source of his illness has not
disappeared.

Then I returned to Paris. By the end of the month, I was bored.
It was autumn, and I wanted to take a short trip to Normandy before
winter, as I'd never been there.

I started in Rouen, of course, and for a week, I wandered through
this medieval city feeling entertained, delighted, enthusiastic in this
surprising museum of extraordinary Gothic monuments.

One afternoon, around four o'clock, as I was following an amazing street along a river as black as ink called the "Eau de Robec,"[4]
giving all my attention to the unusual ancient architecture of the
houses, I was suddenly distracted by the sight of a series of second-
hand shops set all in a row.

Ah! They had chosen this spot well, these sordid dealers of things
from the past, in this eerie alleyway, along this sinister flowing water,
beneath the pointed slate and tile roofs where old weathervanes still
creak!

Deep inside these dark shops, you could see piles of carved
chests, earthenware from Rouen, Nevers, Moustiers, statues, some
in oak, others painted, figures of Christ, the Virgin Mary and the
saints, church ornaments, liturgical vestments, even sacred vessels
and ah old tabernacle in gilded wood from which the Sacred Host
had been removed. Oh! The strange cellars in these tall houses, in

---

3. The itinerary was also Maupassant's, travels detailed in *La Vie errante* (1890).
4. Stream (now largely culverted) running along, and giving its name to, one of the very
   oldest streets in Rouen, lined by Renaissance houses.

these large houses, completely full, from top to bottom, full of objects of all kinds that seemed to no longer exist, objects that had outlived their original owners, their centuries, their eras, their styles, in order to be bought, as curiosities, by successive generations.

My fondness for curios was reawakened in this neighborhood of antique sellers. I went from shop to shop, taking two great strides to leap across the bridges made of four planks of rotting wood placed over the nauseating flow of water from the Eau de Robec.

Mercy, what a shock! I could see one of my most beautiful wardrobes at the side of an archway stuffed full of various objects; it looked like the entrance to the catacombs of a cemetery of antique furniture. I walked closer to it, trembling from head to foot, trembling so much that I didn't dare touch it. I stretched out my hand, then hesitated. It really was mine, though: a unique Louis XIII[5] wardrobe, recognizable by anyone who had ever seen it even once. Quickly glancing a little further away, toward the back of the room, which was even darker, I spotted three of my armchairs upholstered in petit point tapestry, then, even further away, my two Henri II[6] tables, so rare that people used to come from Paris just to see them.

Imagine, just imagine my state of mind!

And I walked closer, suffering, paralyzed with emotion, but I walked closer, for I am brave, I moved closer like a Knight of the Dark Ages entering a witches' den. With every step I took, I saw everything that had once belonged to me, my chandeliers, my books, my paintings, my clothing, my weapons, everything, everything except my desk full of letters; that was nowhere to be seen.

I walked through the shop, going downstairs to dark rooms only to go back upstairs again. I was alone. I called out; no one answered. I was alone; there was no one else in this enormous house with as many twists and turns as a labyrinth.

Night fell, and I had to sit down on one of my chairs, for I did not want to leave. Every now and again, I shouted, "Hello, hello! Anybody there?"

I had surely been there for more than an hour when I heard footsteps, soft, slow footsteps, coming from somewhere, I couldn't tell where. I nearly ran off, but I drew myself up to my full height and called out once more, then I saw a light in the next room.

"Who's there?" said a voice.

"A buyer," I replied.

"It's very late to be coming to antique shops," he said.

"I've been waiting for you for more than an hour," I replied.

"You can come back tomorrow."

5. On the French throne, 1610–43.
6. On the French throne, 1547–59.

"I will have left Rouen by tomorrow."

I didn't dare go any closer, and he wasn't coming to me. I could see his light shining on a tapestry with two angels flying above the dead on a battlefield. It, too, belonged to me.

"Well!" I said. "Are you coming?"

"You come to me," he replied.

I stood up and walked toward him.

In the middle of the large room was a very small man, very small and very fat, as fat as a freak, a hideous freak.

He had a short beard, dotted with sparse, yellowish hairs, and not a hair on his head! Not a single hair? He held his candle up to see me, and his skull looked like a small moon in this vast room stuffed with old furniture. His face was wrinkled and puffed up, his eyes barely visible.

I bargained with him to buy three chairs that were mine, and paid a great deal of money for them. I paid for them right then and there, giving him only my room number at the hotel. They were to be delivered the next morning before nine o'clock.

Then I left. He walked me to the door and was very polite.

I headed straight for the police headquarters and told the Captain about the theft of my furniture and what I had just discovered.

He immediately sent a telegram for information to the Public Prosecutor's Office that had dealt with the matter and asked me if I would wait for their reply. An hour later, he got his answer, which completely vindicated me.

"I'm going to arrest that man and question him immediately," he said, "for he might have become suspicious and gotten rid of your belongings. If you go and have supper and come back in two hours, I'll have him here and will question him again in front of you."

"Very gladly, Monsieur. I thank you with all my heart."

I went and dined at my hotel, with a much better appetite than I thought I would have. I felt rather satisfied. They would get him.

Two hours later, I went back to the police station where the Captain was waiting for me.

"Well, Monsieur," he said as soon as he saw me, "we haven't been able to locate your man. My detectives couldn't arrest him."

Ah! I felt myself weakening.

"But . . . you found his house all right?" I asked.

"Absolutely. It has been put under surveillance and will be watched until he returns. As for him, though, he's disappeared."

"Disappeared?"

"Disappeared. He normally spends every evening at his neighbor's place; she's an antiques dealer too, an odd old witch, the widow Bidoin. She didn't see him tonight and couldn't give us any information. We'll have to wait until tomorrow."

I left. Ah! How sinister, troubling and haunted the streets of Rouen seemed!

I slept very badly and had nightmares every time I fell asleep.

The next day, not wishing to appear too anxious, I waited until ten o'clock before going to the police station.

The merchant had not come back. His shop remained closed.

"I've taken care of all the necessary formalities," the Captain said. "The Public Prosecutor's Office is aware of what's happened; we will go to the shop together and open it up, and you can point out all the things that are yours."

We were driven there. Some policemen stood in front of the shop with a locksmith; it had been opened.

When I went inside, I saw none of the furniture, nothing that had been in my house, nothing at all, not my wardrobe, not my armchairs, not my tables, while the day before, I hadn't been able to turn around without seeing something of mine.

The Captain, surprised, looked at me suspiciously at first.

"My God, Monsieur," I said, "the disappearance of my furniture coincides strangely with the disappearance of the merchant."

He smiled. "How true! You shouldn't have bought and paid for your things yesterday. That must have aroused his suspicions."

"But what is completely incomprehensible," I continued, "is that all the space taken up by my things is now filled with other furniture."

"Oh!" the Captain replied, "he had all night, and accomplices, no doubt. This house must adjoin the neighbors' place. Don't worry about anything, Monsieur, I'm going to stay on top of this case. This crook won't evade us for long since we're watching his hideaway."

. . . .

Ah! My heart, my heart, my poor heart, how fast and hard I felt it beat!

. . . .

I stayed in Rouen for two weeks: The man never returned. Good heavens! Good heavens! Who could possibly stop that man or catch him off guard?

On the morning of the following day, I received a strange letter from my gardener, who had been looking after my empty, pillaged house. This is what it said:

> *Dear Monsieur,*
>
> *I am pleased to inform you that last night something hap-*
> *pened that no one can understand, not us and not even the*

police. All the furniture was back, all of it, without excep-
tion, right down to the smallest items. The house is now
exactly as it was just before everything was stolen. It's enough
to drive anyone out of his mind! It happened between Friday
night and Saturday morning. The paths are ripped apart as if
everything had been dragged from the gate to the house. It
was the same the day it all disappeared.
   We await Monsieur's arrival.

                Your very humble servant,
                Philippe Raudin

Ah! No! No! No! I will not go back there!

I took the letter to the Captain of Police in Rouen.

"It's a very clever move, taking back all your things," he said. "We'll lie low. We'll get him, one of these days."

. . . .

But they didn't get him. No. They didn't get him, and I'm afraid of him now, as if he were a ferocious beast let loose to attack me.

Impossible to find! He is impossible to find, that monster with the moon-shaped head! They'll never catch him. He'll never go back to his place. What does he care? I'm the only one who might run into him, and I don't want to.

I don't want to! I don't want to! I don't want to!

And what if he does come back, what if he goes back to his shop? Who could prove that my furniture was ever there? It's my word against his; and I can tell my story is already starting to look suspicious.

Ah, no! I couldn't live like this any more. And I couldn't keep what I saw a secret. I couldn't continue living like everyone else with the fear that something similar might happen again.

I came to see the doctor who runs this hospital and I told him everything.

After questioning me for a long time, he asked:

"Would you agree to stay here for a while, Monsieur?"

"Very gladly."

"Are you wealthy?"

"Yes, Monsieur."

"Would you prefer to stay in private quarters, isolated?"

"Yes, Monsieur."

"Would you like to have your friends visit?"

"No, Monsieur, no, no one. That man from Rouen might dare to follow me here, to take revenge."

And so for three months I have been alone, alone, all alone. I feel calm, more or less. I have only one fear . . . What if that antiques dealer went mad . . . what if they brought him to this mental hospital . . . Even prisons are not always safe.

A Nightmare[†]

I love the night passionately. I love it the way you love your country or your mistress, with an invincible, deep, instinctive kind of love. I love it with all my senses, my eyes that can see it, my sense of smell that breathes it in, my ears that can hear its silence, with my whole body caressed by its shadows. The larks sing in the sunshine, in the blue sky, the warm air, the gentle breeze of bright mornings. The owl flies at night, a dark shape crossing the dark skies, and, rejoicing, intoxicated by the infinite blackness, he lets out his resonant, sinister cry.

Daytime bores and tires me. It is harsh and noisy. I get up with difficulty, dress wearily, go out reluctantly, and every step, movement, gesture, word, thought exhausts me as if I were trying to free myself from some crushing burden.

But when the sun sets, my body is filled with overwhelming joy. I awaken, become alert. The darker it gets, the more I feel myself becoming someone else, someone younger, stronger, more attentive, happier. I watch the great, soft shadows grow darker as they descend from the sky: they drown the city, like an intangible and impenetrable wave, hiding, obliterating, destroying colors and shapes; they surround houses and people and monuments with their feathery-light touch.

Then I feel the desire to cry out with pleasure like the owls, to run over the rooftops like the cats; and an impetuous, invincible desire sends fire rushing through my veins.

I go out, I walk, sometimes in the somber outskirts of the town, sometimes in the woods just outside Paris, where I can hear my sisters, the animals, and my brothers, the poachers, rushing about.

Whatever you love passionately ends up killing you. How can I explain what is happening to me? How can I even make you understand that I might be able to explain it? I don't know, I don't know any more, I just know what happened. Here it is.

So yesterday—was it really yesterday?—yes, of course, unless it was before then, a different day, a different month, a different year—I don't know. Yet it must have been yesterday, since it is not

---

[†] First published in the *Gil Blas* on June 14, 1887; reprinted in *Clair de Lune* (1888), which is the version translated here. The original French title is *La Nuit; Cauchemar* (A Nightmare) which is Maupassant's own subtitle.

yet daylight, since the sun has not yet risen. But how long does night last? How long? Who can say? Who could ever know?

Yesterday, I went out after dinner, as I do every evening. The weather was very lovely, very mild, very warm. As I walked down toward the boulevards, I looked above my head at the dark river full of stars that served as a backdrop to the rooftops on the winding street, making this moving stream of stars undulate as if it were a real river.

Everything was bright in the light air, from the planets to the lampposts. So many fires burned high above and in the city that even the shadows looked lit up. Luminous evenings are more joyful than bright sunny days.

On the wide avenue, the cafés were brightly lit and people were laughing, walking by, drinking. I went into the theater for a few minutes. Which theater? I don't recall. It was so light inside that I was saddened, and I went outside again feeling my heart heavier because of the shock of that brutal light on the gilt balcony, the artificial sparkling of the enormous crystal chandelier, the blazing footlights, the melancholy of this unnatural, raw brightness. I walked along the Champs-Élysées where the *cafés-concerts*[1] looked like houses on fire amid the trees. The chestnut trees swathed in a yellowish light seemed covered in phosphorescent paint. And the electric globes—pale, dazzling moons, lunar eggs fallen from the sky, monstrous, pulsating pearls—made the strings of colored lights and the fine streams of filthy, vile gas grow pale beneath their regal, mysterious, pearly light.

I stopped under the Arc de Triomphe to gaze down the wide boulevard, the long, attractive avenue all ablaze that led to Paris in between two rows of fire. And the stars!

The stars above, the mysterious stars randomly scattered into infinity where they form strange shapes that make us wish and dream so very much.

I went into the Bois de Boulogne and stayed there a long, long time. A peculiar shiver had rushed through me, a surprising, powerful emotion, an intense euphoria that bordered on madness.

I walked for a very long time. Then I turned back.

What time was it when I walked back under the Arc de Triomphe? I don't know. The city was asleep, and the clouds—great dark clouds—were spreading slowly across the sky.

---

1. Centers of summer-evening entertainment; these large outdoor cafés, often opening out onto city squares or gardens, had a stage where singers entertained huge crowds of patrons who would come and go at their leisure. They are often depicted in contemporary painting, notably by Edgar Degas. The most famous, on the Champs Élysées, were the Alcazar-d'Été and the Café des Ambassadeurs, both of which were established in the 1870s.

For the first time, I felt that something new, something strange was about to happen. It seemed as if it had suddenly turned cold, as if the air was denser, as if the night, my beloved night, weighed heavily on my heart. The wide avenue was deserted. Only two police-men were walking around where the horse-drawn carriages[2] were lined up, and, on the street, barely lit by the gaslights that seemed to be dying out, a row of carts full of vegetables headed toward Les Halles.[3] They drove slowly, laden with carrots, turnips and cab-bages. The drivers dozed, invisible, while the horses fell into step, following the carriage in front, making no noise on the cobblestones. As they passed in front of each streetlight, the carrots lit up bright red, the turnips gleamed white, the cabbages glowed green, and the carriages passed by, one after the other, red carriages, fiery red, car-riages as white as silver, as green as emeralds. I followed them, then turned down the Rue Royale and went back along the wide boule-vards. No one in sight, no more bright cafés, just a few people out very late hurried past. I had never seen Paris so dead, so deserted. I looked at my watch. It was two o'clock.

Something forced me to keep going, a need to keep walking. So I walked as far as the Place de la Bastille. Once there, I realized I had never seen such a dark night, for I couldn't even make out the Col-onne de Juillet;[4] even its golden statue was invisible in the impene-trable darkness. A canopy of clouds, as thick as infinity, had engulfed the stars and seemed to weigh down on the earth, as if to blot it out.

I headed back. There was not a soul in sight. At the Place du Château-d'Eau,[5] however, a drunkard nearly bumped into me, then disappeared. For some time, I could hear his uneven, echoing footsteps.

I kept walking. At top of the Faubourg Montmartre, a horse-drawn carriage passed by, heading down toward the Seine. I called out. The driver didn't reply. A woman was wandering around near the Rue Drouot: "Monsieur, listen, please." I rushed ahead to avoid her out-stretched hand. Then nothing more. In front of Le Vaudeville,[6] a

---

2. The French term *fiacres* refers to horse-drawn taxis.
3. The central markets in Paris (moved to the outskirts in 1971), to which fresh produce was hauled in throughout the night from the surrounding countryside
4. Monument, decreed in 1831 to commemorate the Revolution of July (*Juillet*) 1830, bringing an end to the reign of Charles X and marking the beginning of the "July Mon-archy" of Louis-Philippe. It stands at the center of the Place de la Bastille, named after the fortress of the Bastille demolished in 1789. The bronze column consists of twenty-one cylindrical drums, through the centre of which rises a spiral stair. On its top is the "Genius of Liberty" sculpted by Augustin-Alexandre Dumont, while spaces within the base (straddling the vaulted tunnel of the Saint-Martin canal) accommodate the remains of more than 500 victims of the 1830 Revolution.
5. The present-day Place de la République.
6. The Théâtre du Vaudeville, located at the corner of the Rue de la Chaussée d'Antin and the Boulevard des Capucines, specialized in light comedy known, precisely, as *vaude-ville*. It closed down in 1925.

ragman was rummaging in the gutter. His little lantern flickered at the water's edge. "You there, what time is it?" I asked him.

"You think I know!" he grumbled. "I ain't got a watch."

I suddenly noticed that the gaslights had gone out. I know they are turned off early, before daybreak at this time of year, to save money; but it was a long time until dawn, a very long time!

"Let's go to Les Halles," I thought. "There should be people around there at least."

I set off, but it was so dark I couldn't even see where I was going. I walked slowly, the way you do in the woods, counting the streets I passed to recognize them.

In front of the Crédit Lyonnais bank,[7] a dog growled. I turned down the Rue de Grammont and got lost; I wandered around, then recognized La Bourse[8] and the iron gates that surround it. All of Paris was asleep, in a deep sleep, terrifying. Yet in the distance I heard a carriage, just one carriage, perhaps the one that had gone by me a little while ago. I tried to find it, heading toward the sound of its wheels through the dark, empty streets, so very dark, as dark as death.

I got lost again. Where was I? What madness to turn off the gaslights so early! Not a single passerby, not one person out late, no one wandering around, not even the meowing of a cat on the prowl. Nothing.

Where were the policemen? "I'll call out," I said to myself, "and they'll come." I cried out. No one replied.

I shouted louder. My voice faded away, weak, without an echo, stifled, obliterated by the night, by this impenetrable night.

I screamed: "Help! Help! Help me!"

My despairing cry went unanswered. What time was it now? I took out my watch but I had no matches. I listened to the watch's faint *tick-tock* with a strange, unfamiliar feeling of joy. It seemed to be alive. I felt less alone. It was so mysterious! I started walking again, like a blind man, feeling my way along the walls with my cane, and constantly looking upward toward the sky, hoping that day would finally break; but the sky was black, utterly black, even darker than the city.

What time could it be? I felt as if I had been walking forever, for my legs were giving way beneath me, I was panting and starving half to death.

I decided to ring the first door I came to. I pressed the brass doorbell and I could hear it reverberate through the house; it echoed strangely, as if this quivering sound was the only thing in the house.

7. Its main offices were situated at no. 19, Boulevard des Italiens, between the Rue de la Michodière and the Rue de Grammont.
8. The Paris Stock Market, in the 2nd *arrondissement* (an administrative district of the city).

I waited, no one replied, no one opened the door. I rang the bell again; I waited some more—nothing!

I was afraid! I ran to the next house, and twenty times in a row, I rang the doorbell in the dark entrance where the concierge must be sleeping in his room. But he didn't wake up, so I went further down the street, knocking with the brass rings and pressing the bells with all my strength, banging at the doors with my feet, my cane and my fists, but they remained obstinately closed.

And suddenly, I realized I had reached Les Halles. It was deserted, not a sound, not a carriage, not a soul, no vegetables, not a bunch of flowers.

The entire place was empty, still, abandoned, dead!

Terror ran through me—horrifying. What was happening? Oh, my God! What was happening?

I walked away. What time was it? What time? Who could tell me the time? Not a single sound from the clocktowers or the monuments. "I'll open the glass cover of my watch," I thought, "and feel for the hands with my fingers." I took out my watch . . . it wasn't working . . . it had stopped . . . There was nothing now, nothing, not the slightest movement in the whole city, not a sliver of light, not the faintest echo of a sound through the air. Nothing! Nothing! Not even the distant sound of the carriage—simply nothing!

I was by the quayside, and an icy chill rose from the river.

Was the Seine still flowing?

I wanted to know, I found the steps and went down . . . I couldn't hear the water bubbling beneath the arches of the bridge . . . More steps . . . then sand . . . sludge . . . the water . . . I put my arm in . . . the river was still flowing . . . flowing . . . cold . . . cold . . . cold . . . almost freezing . . . almost dried up . . . almost dead.

And I truly felt that I would never have the strength to pull myself away again . . . and that I would die right there . . . I too would die, of hunger—of exhaustion—of the cold.

CONTEXTS

The Craft of Fiction

Preface to *Pierre et Jean*[†]

The Novel

* * *

To contest an author's right to create a poetic or realistic work is to want to force him to change who he is by temperament, to deny his originality, to refuse to allow him to use the eyesight and brain nature has given him.

To reproach him for seeing things as beautiful or ugly, minor or epic, attractive or sinister, is to blame him for being at odds with convention in some way and for not seeing the world as we do.

Let him remain free to understand, observe and conceive the world as he thinks fit, as long as he does so as an artist. To judge an idealist, we should rise to poetic heights if only to show him that his dream is unexceptional and banal, insufficiently fantastic or magnificent. But if we are judging a naturalist writer, let us point out the ways in which the truth of real life differs from that in his book.

It is self-evident that literary schools so different from each other have had to use radically contrasting methods of composition.

The novelist who transforms the unchanging, stark and unpleasant truth, extracting from it an exceptional and compelling story, must, without being overly concerned with its plausibility, have the freedom to manipulate events, preparing and organizing them for the reader's benefit, getting him involved or moving him to tears. The organization of his novel is merely a sequence of ingenious

---

† From the Preface to Maupassant's *Pierre et Jean*, translated for this edition by Robert Lethbridge. The original French text is to be found in every edition of the novel since it was first published in 1888. While Maupassant devoted several, mainly biographical, essays to contemporary writers, this is the only extended statement of his own aesthetic principles. Its relationship to the novel it prefaces is tangential (appearing in the *Figaro*'s literary supplement of January 7, 1888, a couple of days before it was printed alongside *Pierre et Jean* in response to Maupassant's publisher's need to fill out what would have been too slim a volume); and although entitled "Le Roman" (The Novel), it is not limited in scope to that particular genre.

devices leading skilfully to the denouement. Incidents are positioned
so as to culminate in the effect produced by the ending of the story,
in the shape of a really decisive event providing a satisfying answer
to the questions posed at its beginning, putting an end to that initial interest and closing off the narrative so completely that the
reader has no desire to know what happens next, even in the case of
the most appealing characters.

On the other hand, the novelist who claims to provide us with an
accurate picture of life must carefully avoid linking events in ways
which would seem out of the ordinary. His aim is not to tell us a
story, to entertain or move us, but rather to force us to reflect and
understand the profound and hidden meaning of events. Through
his observation and powers of thought, he looks at the universe,
things, facts and mankind from a perspective which is his own and
which is the result of his insights. It is this personal vision of the
world which he is trying to communicate to us by reproducing it in
a book. In order to make us feel what he has himself experienced,
he must reproduce for us with unerring exactitude the spectacle of
life as he has seen it. So he must put his work together with such
skill and in such an artless way that it is impossible for us to detect
its techniques of composition or its authorial intentions.

Instead of a contrived plot unfolding to capture our attention right
up until the end of the story, he will focus on his characters at a
certain moment in their lives and lead them, through various natural stages, to the next. In this way, he will show how people change,
either through the influence of circumstance or how feelings and
passions develop: how people love or hate; how they adapt to their
social environments; how they are caught in conflicts of bourgeois,
financial, family or political forces.

The skill involved in this kind of composition has nothing to do
with intensity of feeling, whether in a beguiling opening or sensational catastrophe, but rather in an ingenious and insistent group-
ing of little factual details from which the real meaning of the work
will become apparent. If, in the space of three hundred pages, the
writer has to condense ten years of a life in order to demonstrate its
particular and characteristic significance, he has to be able to eliminate from the innumerable events of daily existence everything
superfluous to his purpose, thereby throwing into sharper relief
all those which might have remained unnoticed by the casual
observer and thus endowing his book with implications for its
value as whole.

It is obvious that such a method of composition, so different from
former techniques visible to every reader, often leaves the critics
confused, for they fail to detect those slender and virtually invisible

threads woven by modern artists instead of the single piece of string called the Plot.

In a word, if the Novelist of yesteryear selected and narrated the crises of existence and the paroxysms of soul and heart, the Novelist of today writes the story of heart, soul and mind in their normal state. In order to produce the desired effect, namely the sense of the reality from which he can extract an artistic truth and reveal how he views contemporary men and women, he must limit himself to facts irrefutably and invariably true.

But while adopting the perspective of these realist artists, it remains necessary to discuss and challenge a theory which seems to be encapsulated in these words. 'The whole truth and nothing but the truth'.

Their intention being to discover the ideas underlying certain unchanging and common facts, they will often have to modify events for the sake of plausibility and to the detriment of truth, for: *'the true can sometimes lack verisimilitude'*.[1]

The realist, if he is an artist, will provide us not with a photographic slice of ordinary life but rather with a more complete, striking and penetrating vision than reality itself.

To recount it all would be impossible, as it would require at least a volume per day to accommodate the innumerable insignificant incidents which fill our lives.

So a choice has to be made—and that's the first problem with the theory of the absolute truth.

Besides, life is made up of many different things, some unforeseen, contradictory and incoherent; it is brutal, arbitrary, disconnected, full of inexplicable disasters and illogical incidents without rhyme or reason which can only be classified under the heading of *faits divers*.[2]

That is why the artist, having selected his theme, will take from a life cluttered with trivialities and the consequences of chance only those characteristic details which serve his purpose, leaving on one side all the rest.

One example out of a thousand:

A huge number of people, as a result of accidents, die every single day. But does that mean the writer should have a roof tile drop on the head of a major character, or throw him under the wheels of a carriage, simply in order to give accidents their due?

---

1. Cited from Nicolas Boileau's *Art poétique* (1674), III, v. 48, famous poetic statement of the criteria governing each literary genre in the period of French Classicism.
2. Section of miscellaneous news items in French newspapers.

What is more, life does not distinguish between foreground and background, hurries on events or drags them out indefinitely. Art, by contrast, depends on forethought and preparatory moves, and on subtly managing indiscernible transitions, illuminating essential events through skilful compositional devices, and setting them off against others according to their significance in order to create a sense of the special truth the writer wants to reveal.

To convey reality, therefore, requires producing an illusion of reality consistent with the logic of the commonplace rather than transcribing such events in the haphazard order in which they occur.

From which I conclude that talented Realists should instead be called Illusionists.

In any case, how infantile it is to believe in a single reality, when each of us, in mind and body, has our own. Our eyes, ears, sense of smell and taste create as many truths as there are men on earth. And our brains, receiving instructions from bodily organs themselves subject to various influences, understand, analyse and judge as though each one of us belonged to a different race.

Each one of us simply creates for himself an illusion of the world which may be poetic, sentimental, joyful or melancholy, sordid or lugubrious depending on our nature. And the writer's only mission is to faithfully reproduce that illusion with all the artistic techniques he has learnt and has at his disposal.

Illusion of beauty—a human convention! Illusion of ugliness—a matter of opinion! Illusion of truth—it changes from one day to the next! Illusion of the vile—so attractive to so many! Great artists are those who impose their particular illusion on humanity.

So we should not take exception to any theory, because each and every one is simply the generalized expression of a temperament analysing itself.

There are two theories, in particular, which have often been discussed in terms of opposition rather than allowing for the validity of both: that of the pure psychological novel and that of the objective novel. The proponents of the former require the writer to concentrate on the slightest movements of the human mind and the most secret determinants of our actions, relegating an actual event to the margins. That event is where it all leads, just a marker, a pretext for the novel. According to them, such works, both precise and visionary, in which imagination is indistinguishable from observation, have to be written in the manner of a philosopher putting together a psychological treatise, tracing causes back to their most distant origins, explaining the impetus of desires and discerning every reaction of a personality subject to self-interest, passion or instinct.

On the other hand, the proponents of objectivity (what a horrible term!) claim to represent exactly what happens in life, carefully avoiding complicated explanations or discourses on motivation, restricting themselves to showing us directly characters and events.

For them, psychology should be as concealed in a book as it is in the facts and events of existence.

The novel conceived in this manner thereby gains in intensity, in the pace of its narrative, and in its color and dynamism.

Therefore instead of explaining at great length a character's state of mind, objective writers track the actions or gestures which are inevitable in the case of such an individual in a given situation. And they make him behave accordingly, from beginning to end, with all his acts and movements, and trains of thought and desires or hesitations, reflecting his inner self. Thus they hide the character's psychology rather than displaying it, making it the underlying anatomy of the work, just as the invisible skeleton is the framework of the human body. The painter who paints our portrait does not show our skeleton.

It also seems to me that the novel executed in this way gains in authenticity. Firstly, it is more credible, for those we see around us do not tell us what makes them act as they do.

And, following on from this, we should bear in mind that even if our observation of human beings allows us to determine their natures accurately enough to be able to conclude with some certainty: 'Such a man, with such a temperament, in such a case, will do this', it does not mean that we can assess, one by one, each and every hidden stage of a thought process which is not our own, or those mysterious instinctual drives which are not like ours, all those complex promptings of his nature, the bodily organs, nerves, blood and flesh which are different from our own.

However brilliant a man he may be, the feeble and gentle individual with no experience of passion, whose life is devoted exclusively to study and work, will never be able to get sufficiently inside the mind and body of some exuberant, violent and sensual fellow, driven by every imaginable desire, or even vice, to be able to understand and point out the most intimate compulsions and sensations of someone so different from himself, however successfully he can both predict and record what he actually does.

In fact, the writer engaged in pure psychology can only substitute himself for all his characters in the various situations in which he places them, for it is impossible for him to change his own organs, which are the only intermediaries between the outer world and ourselves, which impose on us their impressions, determine our sensibility and create in us an inner self differentiated from those around us. We cannot help transferring to the characters, whose inner lives we claim to reveal, our own vision and knowledge of the world acquired through our senses and ideas about existence. So it is always ourselves we display, whether incarnated in a king, a murderer, a thief or an honest man, a courtesan, a nun, a young girl or a fishwife, because we are forced to put the problem to ourselves in this way: 'If I myself were a king, murderer, thief, courtesan, nun, young girl or fishwife, what would *I* do, what would *I* think, how would *I* act?' And so the only way we vary our characters is by changing their age, sex, social rank and all the circumstances of *our own* self which nature has surrounded with an impenetrable barrier of bodily organs.

The skill lies in not letting the reader identify that self beneath all the masks we use to hide it.

But if pure psychological analysis is questionable in terms of complete accuracy, it can nevertheless offer us works of art as perfect as those created by other methods.

Today, for instance, we have the Symbolists.[3] And why not? Their artistic vision is worthy of respect; and what is particularly interesting about them is that they are aware of, and proclaim, the extreme difficulty of art.

You have got to be completely insane, very daring, very presumptuous or extremely stupid to be engaged in writing at all in this day and age! After so many writers of every kind, geniuses each in their own way, what remains there to be done that has not already been done, or what is left to say that has not already been said? Which of us can boast that he has written a page, or even a sentence, which is not to be found elsewhere, more or less? So saturated are we in French writing, our very bodies seeming like a paste made of words, that when we ourselves read something, do we ever come across a line or an idea that is not familiar to us or, at least, that we have not had already somewhere in our minds?

The writer who seeks only to entertain his readers through the use of well-tried techniques can confidently produce, with all the innocence inseparable from mediocrity, works intended for the ignorant masses in search of distraction. But those weighed down by the literary legacy of centuries past, whom nothing will satisfy, to whom everything is distasteful compared to their dream of something

---

3. Writers such as Stéphane Mallarmé (1842–1898), Jules Laforgue (1860–1886), Villiers de L'Isle-Adam (1838–1889), and Jean Moréas (1856–1910), whose Symbolist manifesto had been published in *Le Figaro* on September 18, 1886. This may also be a more topical reference to *Les Demoiselles Goubert* (1887) by Moréas and Paul Adam (1862–1920), transferring to fiction aesthetic priorities usually associated with Symbolist poetry.

better, for whom everything seems to have been deflowered and
who feel their own work is useless and commonplace, come to consider literature as an intangible and mysterious phenomenon, of
which only a few pages of the greatest masters of the art give us a
fleeting glimpse.

Twenty lines of verse, or twenty sentences suddenly discovered
pierce us to the core like an astonishing revelation; but the following lines are like any other, and the prose that flows on afterwards
has nothing remarkable about it.

Men of genius doubtless have no such anguish and torment
because they have within them an irresistible creative energy. They
do not subject themselves to self-criticism. Others of us, who are
merely conscientious and tireless workers, can only struggle vainly
against discouragement by unrelenting effort.

Two men, by their simple and illuminating teachings, have given me
this strength to go on trying: Louis Bouilhet and Gustave Flaubert.[4]

If I now speak of them and myself, it is because their advice, which
can be summed up in a few words, might be of use to some young
men with less confidence in themselves than one normally has when
starting to write.

Bouilhet, whom I grew close to first, about two years before gaining Flaubert's friendship, by reiterating that a hundred lines, or perhaps fewer, are enough to establish a reputation, provided that they
are faultless and contain the essence of the talent and originality of
even a second-rate artist, made me understand the following: that
continual work and a thorough understanding of the writer's craft
can, on a day of lucidity, power and inspiration happily coinciding
with a subject perfectly attuned to the tendencies of the writer's
mind, bring into the world a short, unique work as perfect as we can
produce.

I subsequently understood that the best-known writers have seldom left more than a single volume and that, above all, we need the
good fortune to recognize, amid the multitude of subjects from
which we can choose, the one which will absorb all our creative faculties, everything that is of value to us and all our artistic power.

Later on, Flaubert, whom I used to see occasionally, took a liking
to me. I dared to submit a few of my efforts for his scrutiny. He was
good enough to read them and said: 'I don't know whether you'll have
the talent. What you've given to me to look at is evidence that you're

4. Bouilhet (1822–1869) had been a friend of Maupassant since his schooldays in Rouen;
he was a fine dramatist and poet in his own right, much admired by Flaubert. On Maupassant and Flaubert, see Introduction, pp. xiii–xv.

intelligent, but never forget this, young man, that talent—to cite Chateaubriand[5]—is simply endless patience. Get to work'.

I did work, and often went to see him again, realizing that it gave him pleasure, for he had begun to call me, in jest, his disciple.

For seven years I wrote poetry, tales and short stories, and even an appalling play. None of this has survived. The master read it all and then, the following Sunday over lunch, he would elaborate his criticisms and gradually drummed into me two or three principles which are the essence of his long and patient instruction: 'If you have originality', he would say, 'you must give it free rein; if you don't, then it has to be acquired'.

Talent is endless patience. It involves looking long and closely enough at something you want to express to discern in it an aspect which nobody else has ever seen or noted. There is an unexplored element in everything around us because we habitually use our eyes only while remembering what others before us have thought about what we are looking at. The most insignificant thing has something unknown about it. We must find it. To describe a burning fire or a tree on a plain, we need to stand in front of that fire and that tree until for us they no longer look like any other tree or fire.

That is how one becomes original.

Moreover, having propounded this truth that nowhere in the world are there two grains of sand, two flies, two hands or two noses exactly alike, he forced me to express, in a few sentences, a being or an object so as to define its particularity, distinguishing it from every other being or object of the same race or kind.

'When', he said, 'you go past a shopkeeper sitting on his doorstep, or a concierge smoking his pipe, or a cab-rank, show me everything about that shopkeeper or concierge, their stance, their physical appearance also revealing, thanks to the acuteness of the image, their whole character; and do so in such a way that I could not confuse them with any other shopkeeper or concierge, and allow me to see, by your use of a single word, how one cab-horse is distinct from the fifty others in front of, and behind, it'.

I have set out elsewhere his ideas on style.[6] They are closely related to the theory of observation I have just set out.

Whatever we want to convey, there is only one word to express it, one verb to bring it alive and one adjective to qualify it. We must go on looking for that word, verb and adjective until we find them, and

5. The reference to René de Chateaubriand (1768–1848) was in fact a misquotation; the aphorism is ascribed to Georges-Louis Leclerc, Comte de Buffon (1707–1788), as Maupassant's readers were quick to point out, leading him to ask the editor of *Le Gaulois* to publish a correction on his behalf.
6. Notably in the preface Maupassant wrote about an 1884 edition of Flaubert's letters to George Sand (1804–1876).

never be satisfied with approximations, never have recourse to sleights of hand, even inspired ones, or the antics of language to get around a difficulty.

The subtlest things can be conveyed and registered by applying this line by Boileau: '*the power of a word lies in its positioning*'.[7]

There is no need for a bizarre lexicon of outlandish complexity, such as is being forced on us today under the banner of *l'écriture artiste*,[8] in order to capture every nuance of thought; but one must distinguish, with the utmost clarity, the changes of meaning ascribed to a word depending on its positioning. Let us have fewer nouns, verbs and adjectives with almost incomprehensible values, but instead a wider range of sentences, variously constructed, ingeniously sectioned, and full of sonorous effects and subtle rhythms. Let us strive to be excellent stylists rather than collectors of rare words.

It is in fact more difficult to shape a sentence as desired, to make it say everything, including what it fails to spell out, and fill it with suggestions, secret and unformulated intentions, than to invent new expressions or dig out of ancient, unknown tomes, all those no longer used or understood, and which are for us so much dead verbiage.

It must also be said that the French language is like pure water that mannered writers have never succeeded in muddying and never will. Each century has thrown into this limpid stream its fashions, its pretentious archaisms and its affectations, but none of these useless attempts and impotent efforts have risen to the surface. The very nature of this language is to be clear, logical and delicate. It will not allow itself to be weakened, obscured or corrupted.

Those who nowadays create images without being careful about abstract terms, who hurl hail or rain on the *cleanliness* of window-panes, are also adept at throwing stones at the simplicity of their fellow writers! While they may hit writers who have a body, they will never strike the simplicity which does not.

---

7. Another citation from Boileau's *Art poétique*, I, v. 133 (cf. note 1, above).
8. While this can be translated as "artistic style," *l'écriture artiste* in the original French, immediately designated a style associated with Edmond de Goncourt (1822–1896), characterized by verbal dexterity to the point of virtuoso literary effects.

Politics

Letter to Gustave Flaubert[†]

10 December 1877

I've been meaning for a long time to write to you, my beloved Master, but *politics*!!! have prevented me from doing so. The current political situation[1] is stopping me from working, going out, thinking or writing. I'm like one of those normally indifferent people who become as passionately engaged as pacifists turned war-mongers. Paris is living through a dreadful contagious fever which has gripped me too, with everything in limbo in anticipation of an impending earthquake. No longer laughing, I'm now really angry. The irritation caused by the shameless maneuvering of those wretches is so intense, continuous and getting under one's skin that it becomes an obsession day and night, as unrelenting as a mosquito-bite, eating away like a canker even when you're lying on top of a woman. Your patience snaps, faced with the criminal imbecility of that cretin. This general[2] beggars belief: having long ago won a battle thanks to his personal inanity and the vicissitudes of fate, he has since lost two others of historic importance by trying to repeat precisely the strategy which luck had helped him realize the first time; who deserves the pretentious titles of Grand-Duke of Reichschoffen and Archduke of Sedan, as well as that of Duke of Magenta; who, on the pretext of the risk of the stupid being governed by the more intelligent, has made the poor even more destitute (it's always the poor) and put a stop to the whole country's intellectual activity, exasperating the peaceful-minded and provoking civil war, like those miserable creatures driven mad in the bullrings of Spain.

---

† From *Correspondance*, vol. I, ed. Jacques Suffel (Evreux: Le Cercle du Bibliophile, 1973), pp. 139–41. Translated by Robert Lethbridge for this Norton Critical Edition.
1. A succession of ineffectual governments had fallen during 1877; it was only three days after this letter that the National Assembly finally reasserted itself against the increasingly unconstrained presidential power of General MacMahon (1808–1893).
2. General MacMahon had been president of France since 1873. He had achieved military fame in the French victory of the Battle of Magenta in 1859. Subsequent ironic references at his expense are to his failures in the Franco-Prussian War, notably his army's crushing defeat at Reichschoffen on August 6, 1870.

I seem sententious—too bad. I demand the suppression of the rul-
ing classes: that jumble of ridiculous gentlemen frolicking about
under the skirts of that old trollop of a *dévote*[3] called respectable
society. They're sticking a finger up her aged cunt[4] while whispering that society is in danger and that they're threatened by freedom
of expression!

Ah well—I now think that 93[5] was mild; that the Septembrists
were merciful; that Marat was a lamb, Danton a white rabbit and
Robespierre a turtledove. As today's governing classes are as stupid
and incompetent as their predecessors, as vile, cheating, and obstruc-
tive, we've got to suppress them too, drowning those cretinous
handsome gents along with their beautiful wenches. Oh! you Radi-
cals, although you often have red wine where your brains should be,
deliver us from saviours and military men who have in their skulls
only patriotic refrains and holy water. * * *

Article in *Le Gaulois*, September 8, 1881[†]

[Politicians and Principles]

* * * What a miserable career, that of a politician! I'm obviously not
talking about the clowns who only perform on the electoral trapeze.
Whatever happens, those who make up the parliamentary majority
don't deserve our sympathy. Thanks to an easy job, these hacks without a shred of talent, penniless lawyers with neither property nor
widows to represent, doctors without dying patients, all make a living of a kind such professional impotence would never provide. It's
a convenient process. As soon as they become aware of their failure
in normal bourgeois life, they start shouting at the top of their voices:
"Long Live the Proletariat!" That's all there is to it. Asked about their
political credo and program, a loud "Long Live the Proletariat!"
In Parliament, in every debate, they resort to "Long Live the

---

3. To call a woman a *dévote* is to point to someone characterized by obsessive religious
devotion.
4. The original French is "qui batifolent dans les jupes de cette vieille traînée dévote et
bête qu'on appelle la bonne société. Ils fourrent le doigt dans son vieux cul." The correspondence between Maupassant and Flaubert (and, indeed, other male friends) is
notorious for its occasional obscenity.
5. In others words, the phase of the French Revolution known as The Terror. The *Septem-
bristes* were those responsible for the wholesale massacre of political prisoners between
September 2 and 6, 1792; the leading radical inspiring this atrocity was Jean Marat
(1743–1793); Georges-Jacques Danton (1759–1794) and Maximilien de Robespierre
(1758–1794) were the other two equally fearsome revolutionaries, both ultimately guil-
lotined in the cycle of violence they could no longer control.
† From *Chroniques*, vol. I, ed. Gérard Delaisement (Paris: Rive Droite, 2003), pp. 303–
308. Translated by Robert Lethbridge for this Norton Critical Edition. The article's
original title is *Va t'asseoir!* (Take your Seat), i.e., in the Chamber of Deputies.

Proletariat!" decorated with some hot air. If they're threatened, they take to the street, screaming "Long Live the Proletariat!" And the canny working class says to itself: "As long as they're always doing that, that's fine."

But they get older. With their wizened voice-boxes, they start to screech; and they breathlessly groan, like perennial drunks: "Long . . . Proletariat!"

And the working class finds it hilarious. It recognizes the tone and murmurs: "That chap is solidly behind us; let's vote for him." And that's what happens.

And so, from cradle to the grave, you see the same jaws endlessly droning on, gradually losing their hair on the back of their seats in the debating chamber. They become bearded old men, as immortal as the principles of 1789.[1] * * *

Let's undermine immortal principles.

Monarchies have passed away, their time has gone. A new and bold generation has done away with the balancing principle of divine right by arguing that, underpinning good government, is the assumption that every individual has as much intelligence, native wit, knowledge, and as much, and as varied, talent, etc. as any other.

These revolutionaries were right; they've triumphed. But they have replaced the discarded principle by others, judged to be immortal, which are as fantastic and as false as the former. Let's undermine those too. Today's government is founded on the idea that every citizen should have an equal role in the running of the country; and that the voice of the most remarkable of men is of no greater value than that of the stupidest.

That's called equality! What a joke!

As human beings are equal neither in their lives nor in their standing, why should they compete on an equal footing in the functioning of society or the State? * * *

Article in *Gil Blas*, April 7, 1885[†]

[Elected Representatives]

* * * Across the length and breadth of France * * * encroaching even on the opinion of the working class, there is today an increasingly critical attitude, a growing scepticism and contempt for the country's representatives.

1. Those of *Liberté, Égalité*, and *Fraternité*, promulgated by the French Revolution of 1789.
† From *Chroniques*, vol. II, ed. Gérard Delaisement (Paris: Rive Droite, 2003), pp. 965–69. Translated by Robert Lethbridge for this Norton Critical Edition. The article's original title is *Philosophie-Politique*; it is a savage critique of the colonial policy of the government of Jules Ferry (1832–1893).

Go into any small restaurant in Paris where working men go to eat: people chatting to each other mock their elected representatives, speaking of them as they would of ridiculous old fools.

Cab-drivers, waiting at their stops, next to the policeman checking their registration, laugh at the expense of those elected by the people.

In reception rooms, when you see somebody come in and be totally ignored by everyone present, and the question arises: "Who's that?" at the response: "It's a Deputy," you're overcome with a vague pity.

The Chamber provokes such mirth and derision, offers us so many reasons to blame, mock, and scorn it, with its incompetence so blatant and its outbursts so grotesque, that the profession of Deputy has become that of a comic clown inspiring the gentle disdain even of children.

And yet one meets among the country's elected representatives many distinguished men, both educated and intelligent; but they have no collective vision because it requires much political experience for an assembly to become intelligent as a whole.

All the qualities enjoyed by the rare exceptional individual, such as intellectual initiative, independence of mind, and wise and penetrating reflection, generally disappear once he is indistinguishable within a crowd. * * *

Article in *Le Gaulois*, December 23, 1889[†]

[Republicanism]

* * * Indifferent to politics as we are, * * * artists, scientists and generally all those who live the life of the mind, contemplate the machinations of our ephemeral governments with a mixture of tranquillity and gentle disdain, but free of hatred. Hesitating between, on the one hand, old theories about monarchy which often served France well and, on the other, young republican ones which seem difficult to implement in practice, a huge number of independently minded and disinterested people would simply like the current authorities to display some evidence of thought, authentic power, perspective, and competence, so as to be able—without the pretext of stooping to the repugnant brutality of the mass electorate—to give their attention to the workings of society and adopt an overview of

† From *Chroniques*, vol. II, ed. Gérard Delaisement (Paris: Rive Droite, 2003), pp. 1249–52. Translated by Robert Lethbridge for this Norton Critical Edition. The article's original title is *Danger public* (The State in Danger), a highly ironic commentary on the banning of a play by François Coppée (1842–1908), in which the evocation of the internecine strife of the 1871 revolution of the Commune was judged by the authorities to be too explicit to be staged.

innate or acquired rights, value, activity, intelligence, education, wealth, and so on.

It's not actually very difficult to win over and satisfy these independently minded and disinterested people, of whom there are many and within every social class, and whose revulsion can suddenly destabilize public opinion, as it has so strangely threatened to do so this very year.

At this moment, especially, tolerance is the order of the day. Whatever and whoever are acceptable as long as they give every semblance of being something or someone. We've just seen this. It takes very little indeed to satisfy us; our indulgence is pathetic, because we're so exhausted, but to the point where from such exhaustion will come anger. * * *

We'll be happy when we have the slightest guarantee of competence, security, and honesty. We're waiting to cheer the first republican, or republicans in the plural, who give us the impression of a government as enlightened as it's strong, giving us confidence in its independence and impartiality.

Men are judged by their actions: by the splendid panic of deputies and senators alike, who have fearfully turned on an all too-timid aspirant and put him to flight like a terrified dog facing its herd. But what we are witnessing today is an entirely different kind of mindlessness, so wretched, miserable, and astonishing that one is stupefied by the imbecility or the cowardice of those in power.

It's not some ambitious general, it's Monsieur François Coppée, of the Académie Française, who is now threatening the Republic. * * *

War

Letter to Gustave Flaubert[†]

5 January 1880

* * * In producing [*Les Soirées de Médan*], we weren't motivated by anti-patriotism or, indeed, anything else; we simply wanted to give, in each of our stories, an accurate reflection of what war is really like, to strip them of a chauvinism *à la Déroulède*[1] and that false enthusiasm hitherto seen as necessary in any narrative where there are red trousers and a rifle. Rather than being fonts of mathematical precision bubbling with noble and altruistic feelings, generals are as mediocre as anybody else, but wearing gold-braided peaked caps and organizing the killing of men, through sheer stupidity rather than malice. This integrity in relation to military matters, on our part, gives to the volume as a whole one hell of a flavor; and our wilful disinterestedness in this respect, but to which each of us subconsciously brings our feelings, will annoy the bourgeois reader more than a frontal attack. It will not be anti-patriotic, but simply true: and what I say about the inhabitants of Rouen is still pretty mild compared to the reality. * * *

Article in *Le Gaulois*, April 10, 1881[‡]

War

When I hear the word, War, I'm as alarmed as if one was speaking of witchcraft or the Inquisition, something over and done with, in the past, barbaric, monstrous and against nature.

[†] From *Correspondance*, vol. I, ed. Jacques Suffel (Evreux: Le Cercle du Bibliophile, 1973), pp. 252–54. Translated by Robert Lethbridge for this Norton Critical Edition. On the publication of *Boule de suif* within *Les Soirées de Médan*, see Introduction, pp. xxi–xxii.

1. Paul Déroulède (1846–1914) was a politician and poet, whose emblematic *Chants du soldats* made his name synonymous with uncritical patriotism and militaristic chauvinism.

[‡] From *Chroniques*, vol. I, ed. Gérard Delaisement (Paris: Rive Droite, 2003), pp. 187–91. Translated by Robert Lethbridge for this Norton Critical Edition. Maupassant reused this text, only slightly modified, in the *Gil Blas* of December 11, 1883, under the pseudonym "Maufrigneuse," and yet again, in 1889, as the preface to Vsevolod Garchine's novel, *La Guerre*. Although originally occasioned by topical reports of the overseas campaigns being fought by France, notably in Tunisia, this text thus gives expression to Maupassant's consistent anti-militarism from the Franco-Prussian War onward.

War! . . . Fighting! . . . Killing! . . . Massacring human beings! . . . And today, in our own times, with our civilization and the reaches of science and philosophy achieved by the genius of mankind, we have academies where one is taught to kill simultaneously, from a great distance and with precision, a huge number of people, poor innocent wretches with families to support and without a criminal record! And what is astonishing is that society as a whole finds this entirely natural! Had it not been Victor Hugo, one would have shouted down anyone who dared cry, as he did: "Nowadays, force is synonymous with violence and is being judged as such; war is in the dock; civilization, pleading on behalf of mankind, is organizing the prosecution and establishing the criminal file on conquerors and generals. The peoples of the world are beginning to understand that the price is not worth it; that, if killing is a crime, then mass killing does not make it less so; that if theft is shameful, invasion is not glorious. Ah! Let us proclaim these absolute truths . . . Let us strip War of honor!"[1]

One of the supreme practitioners of the art, a killer of the highest order, Monsieur de Moltke,[2] recently responded to the delegates of the Movement for Peace in the following bizarre fashion: "War is sacrosanct, divine in its origins; it is one of the sacred laws of the world; it inspires in men all the most noble feelings, honor, selflessness, virtue and courage, and prevents them from being subject to the most hideous materialism" (it's surprising that he didn't say Naturalism).

Thus, to herd two hundred thousand men, marching day and night without a break, unthinking, and studying, learning and reading nothing, rotting in filth, sleeping in the mire, living like automata, pillaging towns, and burning villages, ruining their inhabitants, then coming across yet another pile of human carnage, pouncing on it, creating pools of blood, losing their legs and arms, having their brains splattered and putrefying in some corner of a field while wives and children die of starvation, that's what's called not being subject to the most hideous materialism (or Naturalism).

Everything would be just about alright if only we had the pragmatism of savages, using all that flesh for food; if war was a means for impoverished nations to stock up; if you could export marinated soldiers as the Americans do with beef and pork. Wives would sometimes have to make a meal of their roasted husbands. That would be part of the struggle for life, that same right to kill in order to eat which we exert in the case of animals. But that's not it. We kill for pleasure and honor, leaving all those corpses by the wayside; they

---

1. Victor Hugo (1802–1885) had long been a critic of militarism; this is an approximate quotation from his oration on Voltaire, delivered in 1878 on the hundredth anniversary of his death.
2. General von Moltke (1800–1891), famous for his military victories, not least over the French in the Franco-Prussian War.

just give us plague and cholera. Take note: the real savage is the so-called civilized human being. He's a monster. Cannibalism, by contrast, is logical; I've no quarrel with it, as it's consistent with Nature, left untouched by civilization.

But just go and ask a gold-braided general what he thinks of the Kanaks[3] who feast on human flesh. * * * Governments wage war as you bet your fortune on "double or quits." It's only a small stake this time round. But, never mind. It's got the potential for glory, prestige and panache. War is an abyss which makes commanders giddy, irresistibly drawn toward it.

But I'll never forget an old peasant woman I saw one morning by the side of the road, with her huge basket and immense umbrella, watching infantry maneuvers in a field. As I passed her, she turned to me and said, in a heartbroken and indignant lament: "That's all they're taught! It's shameful! They're taken from us for five years to do that,[4] and when they return they're no good for anything useful. As if there weren't already enough misery and suffering and all the rest; so we send them off to kill a few more people!"

The little soldiers marched back and forth, first one leg then the other, eyes to the right, tramping along like idiots with their fixed stares. The voice of their instructor boomed across the morning sky; and a lieutenant walked around mournfully, with his hands behind his back.

As a poor stone-breaker on the road continued his monotonous and meaningless labors, I replied to the old woman: "Yes, but they're learning how to defend the country." To which she responded: "As I see it, sir, we're worse than animals." * * *

3. Indigenous population of New Caledonia, in French Polynesia, reputedly engaging in cannibalism.
4. France had been the first modern state to introduce universal military conscription as a condition of citizenship. Under the Third Republic, the French Army became the "school of the nation," utilizing general military service following the Prussian model. In 1863, the length of military service had been seven years, but this was progressively reduced until its abandonment in 2006. What Maupassant implicitly alludes to here is the fact that the peasantry and workers bore an unequal burden in this respect, the professional middle class finding ways to be exempted.

Social Types

Article in *Le Gaulois*, June 9, 1881[†]

The Social Hierarchy

It seems that certain professions are marked by dignity of a particular kind, imposing special obligations and exceptionally rigid codes of behavior. Isn't a notary, for example, forced to assume a white-tied seriousness? Isn't it true that he must dance only with propriety, or abstain from dancing altogether? His work condemns him to an unmitigated severity of mien. A will-o'-the-wisp, witty and bantering notary would seem like a monstrous contradiction in terms. But why should a notary be obliged to be more serious than an infantry captain? Don't ask me, I've got no idea; but that's how it is.

It also appears that there is a ranking of importance and respect accorded to common professions; and that an acute observer must instantly sense the degree of social esteem to be granted to a lawyer, accountant, office-manager, deputy public prosecutor, auctioneer, stockbroker, or inspector of something or other, etc.

If you give some architect the impression that he merits the same degree of respect as a pharmacist, he will doubtless hold it against you until his dying day; but if your tailor suspected that you didn't think of him as infinitely superior to your bootmaker, he would never forgive you.

Isn't it also a fact that officials and those with titles are one step ahead of others simply working in the liberal professions? Take a good look, when you're in a *salon*, at one of those womanizing individuals temporarily filling some ministerial brief standing opposite some brilliant artist: the artist will always remain in the background, overshadowed by His Degenerate Excellency leaving trails of esteem in his wake.

A man who has been decorated (with a medal for long-serving bureaucrats) seems superior to someone without an award. Even foreign ones afford a gloss of respect. State employees consider

---

[†] From *Chroniques*, vol. I, ed. Gérard Delaisement (Paris: Rive Droite, 2003), pp. 214–18. Translated by Robert Lethbridge for this Norton Critical Edition.

themselves to be above those in trade; shopkeepers despise stall-holders. There's an entire complicated hierarchy, as confusing as it's surprising. If you do this, you're approved of; if you do that, you're not. This is nobler than that. * * *

Article in *Le Gaulois*, January 4, 1882[†]

[Government Employees]

* * * Let's talk about their lives.

On the front door of any Ministry should be engraved in black lettering Dante's famous phrase: "Abandon all hope, ye who enter here."

You go through it at about twenty-two and stay there until you're sixty. And during all those years, nothing happens. The whole of existence leaks away in a dark office, unchanging and with its walls lined with green file-boxes. You enter when you're young, when hopes are high. You leave elderly, ready to die. Every chance encounter in a life of freedom, every unexpected event, sweet or tragic love-affair or adventurous voyage, the entire harvest of the past remembered is not available to these convicts.

Every day, week, month, season, and year is the same. You get to work at the same time; you have lunch at the same time; you leave at the same time; and that's your life from age twenty-two to sixty. There are just four things that happen to you that are worthy of note: marriage, the birth of a first child, the death of your father, and then of your mother. Nothing else; oh! sorry, I forgot: there's also promotions. You remain ignorant of normal life, or even of Paris. You have no idea what it's like to stroll down a street on a sunny day, or wander across the fields: because you're never released before the regulatory hour. You're taken into custody at ten o'clock in the morning; the jail opens its doors at five, just as night is falling. But, by way of compensation, you have a fortnight by right—a right much debated, haggled over and disapproved of—to stay shut up at home. For where can you go without any money?

The carpenter climbs into the sky, the cab-driver makes his way round the streets, the engine driver takes his train across forests, plains and mountains, constantly breaking out of the city walls towards the wide blue horizons of the ocean. The civil servant clerk

---

† From *Chroniques*, vol. I, ed. Gérard Delaisement (Paris: Rive Droite, 2003), pp. 413–16. Translated by Robert Lethbridge for this Norton Critical Edition. The original French title is *Les Employés*.

never leaves his office, the tomb of the living; and in the same small mirror in which he saw himself as a young man, with his blond moustache, on the day he started work, he sees an image of himself, on the day he retires, balding and with a white beard. And that's the end of it: life is over, the future closed. How has that point already been reached? How has one grown old without ever having accomplished or experienced anything? But that's what it's like. Make way for the new young employees!

So off you go, more miserable than ever, with a tiny pension. You retire to some dump of a village on the outskirts of Paris, and you die almost immediately from the sudden break from this long and relentless habit of going to the office, and doing exactly the same mindless thing there, at exactly the same time every single day of your working life. * * *

Essay in *Les Types de Paris* (1889)[†]

[The Laboring Classes]

The bright warm Spring sunshine bathes the great fields of Normandy. The soil oozes with new growth, as if covered by a green froth. The trees cover themselves with leaves and the plain is hidden from view beneath the thick shining grass; and between the hedges you see the farm-girls with their short skirts pulling toward the pastures the heavy cows with their udders swinging between their thighs. There they go, the girl in front and the animal behind, dragging and dragged, the one hurried, the other slowly, with only the reflection of the green grass and trees in their eyes. What are they thinking about? What's the poor girl dreaming of, earning twelve francs a month, sleeping on straw in an attic, dressed in rags and never having washed her wiry body, as strong as a man's, in the cold water of a stream or in a steaming bath? Would she perhaps like to clothe it with some finery to attract the ploughman working over there on the edge of the plain, behind his narrow plough drawn by two russet horses? In her fleeting and animalized daydream, there arrives the salesman, with his ribbons, bonnets and scarves, tempting peasant women as he travels the roads. They hear the bell of a donkey, the yapping of a dog, the cry of the man announcing his wares; and a need shadows her wretched heart, the need to be finely

† From the collective volume, *Les Types de Paris* (Paris: Plon, 1889), reprinted in *Chroniques*, vol. II, ed. Gérard Delaisement (Paris: Rive Droite, 2003), pp. 1194–97. Translated by Robert Lethbridge for this Norton Critical Edition.

dressed, on a beautiful Sunday morning, as she goes into the church, watched by all the young men.

The bright warm Spring sunshine bathes the trees along the Champs-Élysées. * * * The wet-nurses * * * in pairs, with a child on their arm and the slow step of animals bursting with milk, cradle newly born human beings on the fleshy pillow of their huge soft mammary glands. From time to time, they chat to each other, with the accent and slang of the distant countryside bringing to mind the heavy brown cows lying in the long grass.

These women full of milk come and go, rocking babies back and forth, remembering the fields, thinking of nothing other than the countryside left behind and almost indifferent to the big and long red, blue or pink silk ribbons trailing down their backs from head to toe; and to their beautiful bonnets, as light as cream; and to the elegant outfits in which the mothers have dressed them, those pale and emaciated mothers living in the rich mansions the length of the Avenue.

Every now and again they sit down, reach into their dresses and pour into the greedy mouths of famished little things the white stream swelling their bosom; and the passer-by, out for a walk, seems to detect in the breeze the strange smell of animals, a human stable and fermented milk. * * *

[Housemaids]

* * * The housemaid trots along the Rue Notre-Dame-de-Lorette. She's got to do everything and does everything in the home; she scrubs, cooks, remakes the beds, polishes shoes, brushes trousers and repairs skirts, washes the children, swears when the door-bell rings and knows a thing or two about the morals of the master of the house. The housemaid does everything, she certainly does. She trots around in worn slippers, with dubious-looking stockings, but with an ample bosom wrapped tightly enough to attract the attention of the passer-by, the young man leaving his office, the cab-driver making some ribald remark, the omnibus driver, following on foot behind the yellow box full of passengers, who gives a French military salute as the housemaid passes by. The grocer calls her "Mademoiselle," the butcher "Mam'zelle," while the milk-lady adds her first name and the costermonger, less formally, "My Dear."

She's in such a daze from morning to night, ordered to do this and that, with so many things to do, her head back to front and her hand out of control, rushing everywhere, that she feels she's living in a whirlwind reducing her brain to mush.

What is she thinking about? Four *sous*[1] worth of milk . . . six of cheese . . . two of parsley . . . ten of oil . . . I'm three *sous* short! I'm missing three *sous*! What did I spend them on? . . . Honestly, sir, it's indecent . . . If the grocer kisses me one more time, I'm going to tell his wife. I don't want that sort of tittle-tattle in the neighborhood . . . He's alright, Monsieur Dubuisson's driver . . . I'm still three *sous* short . . . Oh! dear! Am I never going to get any peace of mind? What was I told to get for dinner? What kind of soup was it, cabbage or sorrel? I've got no idea any more, and I'm going to cop it from Madame. What kind of life is this? . . . I'm going to have to make it five *sous'* worth of milk, eight of cheese, three of parsley and twelve of oil, which is going to leave me with three *sous*, on top of the three I've made up.

"Good morning, Madame Dubuisson."

"Good morning, dear."

Madame Dubuisson is in fact Monsieur Dubuisson's cook, and the legal wife of that driver who's alright. In due course, the housemaid will aspire to herself become a Madame Dubuisson, majestically carrying a basket full of very expensive items as she parades her huge stomach through the streets.

Could she do that? To get there, you need to be smart, well behaved, organized and canny, as well as knowing how to cook.

They know each other well, these two commanders of the stove, and exchange greetings worthy of princesses.

They're presumably aware of what they each earn in wages and on the side. They talk loudly, treat the shopkeepers imperiously, block the sidewalk in front of the shops with their bulk, forcing the crowd of pedestrians to make their way around them. Slow-moving, determined and careful, and however hurried and unconcerned about her purchases the housemaid might be, they have a nose for good fish, testing the weight of the fruit, scrutinizing fowl and game with suspicion, relentlessly driving a bargain without saving a penny for their employers.

They have one, secret, vice: the bottle or love. Sometimes the grocer blushes when they come in, or the wine-merchant slips a liter of rum into their baskets without adding it to the bill.

But they're respected and handled with consideration, because they are powers in the land. They're fought over, captured from rivals, served before anybody else. And they have the look and disdainful tone of sovereigns as they respond to the greetings of humble housemaids, those slatterns treated like garbage by the masters of the house. * * *

---

1. A *sou* was worth 5 centimes.

Article in *Le Gaulois*, March 16, 1883[†]

[Good Citizens of France]

* * * If you need examples of quiet and peaceful-minded human beings, think of the following: wretched employees of the State; customs officials; clerks in the *préfecture*[1] or tasked with keeping records; forest wardens; and others who are also sober, well behaved, economical in their spending and habits, and for whom the slightest deviation from the straight and narrow would be fatal; they're the most honest, hard-working, and deserving people in France, with wives and children and earning between six and twelve hundred francs a year.

You're the good souls who should be in a state of revolt! And as nobody listens to your mild complaints, you should take your bosses by the throat and strangle them, so that they finally pay you some attention.

Stand up, you civil servants working in Ministries and *préfectures*, and grab your pens and paperknives and surround ministers and prefects in their offices. It would be so easy for you to hold a minister captive for four or five days. But you're quiet and peaceful-minded bourgeois and you will starve to death in silence, while the loud-mouthed hordes, who earn in a couple of months what you do in a year, go on the rampage, pillaging the bakeries.

What fun it would be to hear one evening that all the ministries have taken their minister prisoner, only willing to give them back to France after a general increase in salaries.

As for next Sunday's rioters, there's a very simple and fair way to deal with them.

They should be rounded up and their pockets gone through. Anybody with more than a hundred *sous*, demanding bread, should be fed by the State for six months in the shade of a prison; and their hundred *sous* should be distributed among the soldiers forced to deal with these jokers. * * *

[†] From *Chroniques*, vol. I, ed. Gérard Delaisement (Paris: Rive Droite, 2003), pp. 636–40. Translated by Robert Lethbridge for this Norton Critical Edition. Originally entitled *Le haut et le bas* (referring to the *upper* and *lower* classes), this article is a scathing denunciation of the sporadic strikes and street riots in Paris during the winter of 1883.

1. France is administratively organized in *préfectures*, each headed by a *Préfet*.

Article in *Le Gaulois*, January 3, 1883[†]

[The Parisian Provincial]

What a strange spectacle they are, a crowd on a national holiday, awkward and ill at ease, dressed in their Sunday best, incapable of getting anywhere or out of the way, blocking up the sidewalks, a sort of swarming *pâté*, a plate of human macaroni to untangle.

And just look at their heads! Those of smalltown folk, with badly cut hair, looking grotesque. Passing before us are the provincial inhabitants of Paris.

They know and suspect nothing about the frenzied, intense, nerve-racking, and accelerated life of the great city in which they live. In Paris, it's as if they were in Clermont-Ferrand,[1] and that's simply because they are provincial through and through, only fit to live in a small town. Their minds are closed.

Their horizons are defined by household chores and their social situation; their ideas don't extend beyond a certain number of principles handed down through the family and a few political notions; their interests are devoid of scope. Many of them, however, were born in Paris, of Parisian parents; and they're the most provincial of all. Their world is bounded by their own street, their own neighborhood, and a few acquaintances.

At the bottom end of the scale, they're shopkeepers soldered to their counters; the tobacconist who, for the last twelve years, has taken a walk no further than the *boulevards* on her days off.

At the other end of the social hierarchy, there are the officials and bureaucrats dozing in their regular habits, sometimes inviting you for dinner *en famille* to relive memories of two decades ago in the paternal home. They dish up *vol-au-vent* and little cakes reminding you of those you ate when you were young, and fruit preserves in a bell-shaped glass jar.

And absolutely nothing can rouse them from their torpor. They're a race apart, the race of provincials. It's in their nature, their constitution and their veins. It's often thought that this provincialism is a function of their humble jobs. Not so. A civil servant earning merely two thousand francs a year, enclosed in some dark office, is perfectly able to head off into the city to enjoy the theaters and the *salons*; he's a Parisian in his bones, sensitive to every imperceptible,

---

[†] From *Chroniques*, vol. I, ed. Gérard Delaisement (Paris: Rive Droite, 2003), pp. 599–604. Translated by Robert Lethbridge for this Norton Critical Edition. The original French title of the article is *Pot-pourri* (Hotchpotch).

[1]. Often designated as the town at the geographical center of France, located 205 miles south of Paris.

bizarre, contradictory, and varied nuance which constitute the essence of life in the city.

There is nothing sadder than the spectacle offered by the *boulevards* on a national holiday.

It's often said that Parisians are the only ones who know nothing about Paris. In fact, they know just what they need to: they breathe in its atmosphere. The provincial inhabitant will visit all the tourist sites, but will vigorously protest that the air in Paris is similar to that in Lyons or Rouen, only worse for your health. The Parisian provincial inhales on the Champs-Élysées or the *boulevard* the same air found in Lyons or Rouen, and there's really no difference. It would be useless to try to explain the subtleties to him, as he wouldn't understand.

As for the Parisian, it has to be admitted that he's as enclosed in his own habits and hardly sees anything around him. You could point out to him, on any day of the week, some of the seething and mysterious city's amazing and comical sights; and he would raise his arms in astonishment. * * *

Women, Love, and Marriage

Article in *Le Gaulois*, December 30, 1880[†]

[Schopenhauer's View of Women][1]

* * * In spite of my profound admiration for Schopenhauer, up to now I've always considered that his view of women was, if not exaggerated, at least inconclusive. Here's a summary:

Their appearance alone reveals that they are capable of neither intellectual greatness nor material work; what makes women particularly suitable to care for us during our childhood is the fact that they themselves remain childlike, useless, and narrow-minded; and they spend their whole lives as adolescents, half-way between a child and a grown-up human being.

Men only reach their rational and mental maturity at about twenty. Women, on the other hand, reach it at eighteen. Thus their capacity for rational thought has had only eighteen years to develop. They only see what's in front of them, live for the present, take appearances at face value and prefer silly things to important ones. As a result of their feeble powers of reasoning, they're so in thrall to the visible and immediate that they ascribe no value to abstract ideas, established maxims, forceful resolutions, an awareness of the past and future, or the absent and present. Unfairness is therefore the primary defect of women. That's a result of their lack of common sense and, as already mentioned, their inability to think; and what makes it worse is that, lacking physical strength, they have been endowed by nature with cunning; as a result of which they instinctively cheat and have an unremitting tendency to lie.

---

† From *Chroniques*, vol. I, ed. Gérard Delaisement (Paris: Rive Droite, 2003), pp. 126–30. Translated by Robert Lethbridge for this Norton Critical Edition. The original French title of the article is *La Lysistrata moderne*, alluding to the play by Aristophanes whose heroine's forcefulness is exemplified by her persuading the women of Atticus to refuse their husbands their conjugal rights until peace had been negotiated with Sparta.

1. The German philosopher, Arthur Schopenhauer (1788–1860), enjoyed a huge vogue in certain circles in France at this time. Writers like Maupassant, predisposed to pessimistic ideas, found in Schopenhauer's writings, translated into French from 1880 onward, compelling arguments to justify their views.

Thanks to the supremely absurd way in which society is organized, which allows them to share the status and position of men, they relentlessly fire up the latter's most ignoble ambitions, etc. One should take as a rule the pronouncement made by Napoléon I: "Women have no rank." Women are the *sexus sequior*, the second sex in every respect, to be kept on the sidelines and in the background.

In any case, as some stupid laws have given women the same rights as men, they should also have been given a virile mind, etc.

It would take a whole volume to cite all the philosophers who have thought and said the same thing. Since the contempt voiced by Socrates and the Greeks, who confined women to the home to provide the republic with children, people the world over have been agreed that superficiality and fickleness are the basic characteristics of women. * * *

Was Schopenhauer wrong? As women are demanding rights equal to those enjoyed by men, let's consider their representatives, those female citizens speaking in their name, the modern Lysistrata. * * *

Please forgive me if this article offends in any way; I am on my knees, lovingly brushing the tips of your pink fingers with a kiss, in homage to all you women who merely seek to seduce and please us, whose hand squeezed in ours sets our heart aflutter and whose glance sets us dreaming, those of you who are the source of all our happiness and pleasure, all our hopes and consolation.

Letter to Gisèle d'Estoc[†]

January 1881

* * * I'm the most disillusioning and disillusioned of men; the least poetic and sentimental.

I think of love as a religion, and religion as one of the stupidest of all human beliefs.

Are you shocked, Madame?

I'm a passionate admirer of Schopenhauer, whose theory of love seems to me the only one to which we should subscribe. Nature, which requires procreation, has decorated the trap of reproduction with the bait of feeling. * * *

Whenever I meet two lovers, I'm irritated by their stupidity. "I love you, I adore you, with all my heart and soul, you're my whole life,

---

[†] From *Correspondance*, vol. II, ed. Jacques Suffel (Evreux: Le Cercle du Bibliophile, 1973), pp. 5–6. Translated by Robert Lethbridge for this Norton Critical Edition. Widowed since 1875, Paule Parent-Desbarres (*née* Courbe, in 1845), was a sculptress intermittently working under the name "Gisèle d'Estoc." She was one of numerous women who sent Maupassant anonymous letters and engaged in a flirtatious correspondence with him before becoming his mistress, in this case at the end of March 1881.

etc." Just because they're of a different sex. Wouldn't it be simpler to say: "I've got all the instincts of my gender, nature and maleness. So I desire women, as my body dictates, as does the law determining the behavior of animals: but I'm superior to those animals and, instead of simply doing what they do, I seek, imagine and perfect every sensual refinement possible."

* * * Feelings are the imaginings inspired by the reality of sensation.

You say that I'm inspired by nature? That's because, I think, I'm something of a fawn. Yes, I'm a fawn from head to toe. I spend months in the countryside, often out on the water alone for the whole night or, during the day, alone in the woods and vineyards, under the beating sun, all alone.

I'm never saddened by the melancholy of the soil: I'm a sort of instrument of sensation resonating with the dawn, the noonday sun, sunset, the night and much else. I live alone for weeks at a time, and am quite content to do so, without any need of human affection. But I love the bodies of women in the same way as I love the grass, the rivers, and the sea.

Article in *Gil Blas*, October 29, 1881[†]

[The "Parisienne"]

* * * What is a *Parisienne*? She's not beautiful, she's hardly pretty. Far from her body being like that of a Greek sculpture, it's often small and skinny though industrially enhanced, a woman who's a fake. But everything about her has more effect on a refined man than perfect beauty. Her eyes speak of what her mouth doesn't say. Her gestures and smile, the flash of her teeth, the movement of her tiny hand, a slight ripple of her dress as she stands up or sits down, what she implies, her charming, malicious, and perfidious babbling, her intoxicating and artificial charm, everything she can be thanks to her sensitive intelligence, all of that envelops you in a seductive aura, an atmosphere of delicious, adorable, penetrating, and irresistible femininity. If you try to detail it, it's nothing or almost nothing: charm is something to savor. Her real beauty is almost invisible, but she fills you with a more troubling feeling than any perfect living statue. * * *

---

† From *Chroniques*, vol. I, ed. Gérard Delaisement (Paris: Rive Droite, 2003), pp. 350–53. Translated by Robert Lethbridge for this Norton Critical Edition. The original French title of the article, published under the pseudonym "Maufrigneuse," is *Les Femmes* (Women).

The special quality unique to women is their ability to behave as they should in any social circle in which they find themselves. With their gift for tact and subtlety, their instinctive and acute understanding, their impressionability and willingness to be influenced by others, their surprising talent for guesswork, domination, maneuvering, deception, and seduction, women assume the characteristics of the age in which they live. They are nowadays, however, a bit disorientated in social circles of men with roughly the same upbringing, smelling of tobacco and withdrawing to the smoking-room after dinner, and then going on to their clubs, spending time at the Stock Exchange rather than in the *salons*, reading nothing about what makes life agreeable, ignorant of the art of paying compliments and kissing a hand, sometimes preferring a mistress rather than a maid, enjoying a men-only supper and paying for love.

There are no longer ladies, it is said. Let's acknowledge instead that "there are no longer men for whom women want to be seductive."

But all those latent qualities which—and the fault is ours—are no longer cultivated in the *salons* of high society, exist nonetheless, more discreet and hidden at a deeper level, like buds ready to open as soon as a little sunshine warms this woman of France, the only one in which can be found the genius of the race; others know how to love and attract love; only the Frenchwoman knows how to be exquisite.

They're no longer, in our country, triumphant queens reigning over society. That, I admit! But are you sure they're not still invisibly mastering events? Who could vouch that their delicate little hands are not still driving the huge political wagon? They have, I know, a great rival in the shape of money. In the olden days, poets sung their praises. Today, they do so at so much a line! But these women are still, and always will be, powerful.

Pay them a visit. There are in Paris discreet little *salons*, to be found in the fourth *arrondissement*,[1] where every thread leads. There you can meet apparently unremarkable women who, with three words and a signature, can end the career of a prefect, have a general moved, and stir up a hornet's nest in a large Ministry full of civil servants.

Others, whatever may be said, are even more brilliant, and still incarnate the legendary seduction of the woman of France.

1. Paris has twenty *arrondissements*, or zones; the fourth lies to the east of the National Assembly and the fashionable Faubourg St. Honoré, Maupassant thereby suggesting that such political influence is now exerted far from the traditional centers of power.

Article in *Le Gaulois*, November 22, 1881[†]

[Marriage and Adultery]

* * * The majority of young women, in our society, are brought up far from pleasure, strictly and chastely. * * * In general, they're handed over to their fortunate husbands in an immaculate state. * * *

For them, marriage is a liberation. * * * She goes into circulation, as it's said in the business world, and the expression seems to me exactly right in every respect. Before her marriage, she never went out to a ball or to the theater, never danced or enjoyed the compliments or admiration of a man. In other words, she led the life of a recluse. Flirtation was forbidden. But now she's married, that's to say, launched into the world of the *salons*. And now, according to our laws, habits and rules, she can flirt, be elegant and surrounded by men, be the object of adulation and adoration. She is a high-society lady. She is a *Parisienne*. That's to say that she has to be seductive, charming, and the breaker of hearts: that her only role and ambition is to *please*, to look beautiful and adorable, to be the envy of women and idolized by every single man!

Is that really true? Isn't it the duty of women to trouble us? Do we not consider legitimate all her wiles and ruses, the artifice of her makeup and the skill involved in wearing fashionable clothes? What would we say of a *Parisienne* who made no effort to be the most beautiful and adored? Aren't we proud of her even though we're not their husband? We boast about how beautiful they have made themselves, celebrate their graciousness, and praise their seductiveness!

And you stupid moralists claim that all that expense is a waste of money. You would want these women to devote themselves, body and soul, to the art of pleasure, for no reason at all? You want them to drive us mad with desire without ever getting involved, never surrendering to our obsessive pursuit, never falling into our desperate arms? You really are devoid of feeling, you advocates of marital fidelity. That would require doing away with the world of the *Parisienne* which civilization has created, allowing women to be only in the home, always struggling with housework or washing children or counting the laundry, and dressed as simply as a goose.

It wouldn't be much fun to live in a society in which there were only such women!

[†] From *Chroniques*, vol. I, ed. Gérard Delaisement (Paris: Rive Droite, 2003), pp. 374–77. Translated by Robert Lethbridge for this Norton Critical Edition. The original French title of the article is *Un Dilemme* (A Dilemma).

Let's leave behind this dilemma: has the woman of high society, as we conceive her role, a mission to please men? If so, you cannot claim that she will never get burnt by the fire she constantly lights in us. * * *

And there's one more thing I want to say. Once the honeymoon is over, it's impossible to sustain love within a marriage, isn't it? Anyway, it's mighty rare. But love outside marriage is a crime, according to the law. So we have to either renounce the love often ordained by nature or commit a fault condemned by human morality. What's to be done? Disobey the law or nature? Not get married at all, you might suggest? . . . That's all very well for a man; but a woman would find herself at odds with convention, put on the Index of Society.[1]

There's just one remaining solution. That of hypocrisy, keeping up appearances. That's not the one that would satisfy me, and I would like to have, on the subject, the views of a woman, one both sincere and without too many prejudices.

Preface to René Maizeroi's *Celles qui osent* (1883)[†]

* * * We men love *Womankind*, and when we select one for a while, we're paying homage to her entire race. You can adore brunettes because of their brown hair, blondes for theirs, one woman for her eyes that pierce your heart, another because her voice excites you, this one for her red lips, that one for her curves. But because we can't, alas, pick all these flowers at the same time, nature has created love, infatuation, a passing fancy, which allows us to desire them one after another, increasing the value of each in succeeding moments of passion.

That passion, it seems to me, should be limited to the period of anticipation. Once desire has been satisfied and the unknown explored, love loses its principal value.

Every conquest proves to us, yet again, that every woman in our arms is more or less the same. Aren't even idealists, always in search of illusory dreams, brought to earth after possessing a woman? Should the rest of us, who ask less of love, have the right to be grateful for what it offers intelligent and demanding men?

---

1. Wordplay on the "Papal Index" of proscribed books.
† Reprinted in *Chroniques*, vol. I, ed. Gérard Delaisement (Paris: Rive Droite, 2003), pp. 714–18. Translated by Robert Lethbridge for this Norton Critical Edition. The original French title is *Celles qui osent!* (Those who dare!), which is also that of the first of the twenty texts published in volume form in October 1883 by Maupassant's friend René Maizeroi (1856–1918), the adopted name of Baron René-Jean Toussaint.

Constancy leads either to marriage or the ball and chain. Nothing in life seems to me sadder and more painful than those long-lasting relationships.

Marriage, if you take it seriously, suddenly suppresses the possibility of new desires, future tenderness, tomorrow's fantasy, and the charm of amorous meetings. In addition it has the inconvenience of condemning the married couple to a deplorable banality. For what husband would feel able to take with his wife the delicious liberties lovers immediately engage in.

And that, let's admit it, is what makes love worthwhile, that freedom to try everything. In love, you have to dare, again and again. We would have very few mistresses if we weren't more daring than husbands in our caressing, if we were satisfied with the boring, monotonous, and basic habits of conjugal nights.

A woman is always daydreaming: of what she doesn't know, but guesses and suspects. After the startling newness of her wedding night, she starts daydreaming again. She's read things, and she goes on reading At every moment, obscure expressions, barely audible jokes and unknown words heard by accident reveal to her the existence of things she knows nothing about. If, by chance, she hesitatingly asks her husband a question, he immediately adopts a severe tone and replies: "Those things are none of your business." But she reckons that those things are as much her business as any other woman's. What things? Do they exist? Mysterious, shameful, and good things, as they're whispered about with such relish. Prostitutes apparently keep hold of their lovers by engaging in obscene and irresistible practices.

As for the husband, who knows about such things all too well, he dares not reveal them to his wife during their nights together, because a wife, for goodness sake, is different from a mistress! And because a man must respect his WIFE who is, or will be, the mother of his CHILDREN. So in order not to give up those things which he daren't do within a legally sanctioned marriage, he finds some whore and gets on with it.

But the wife begins to rationalize her situation in clear and simple terms. You only live once. Life is short. A woman married at twenty is at her prime at thirty and past it at forty. And if you do nothing, remain ignorant, and enjoy nothing before then, it will be over and done with, for ever.

Conjugal love has lost its attractions. She's fed up with it and nauseated by it.

So how about taking a lover? Why not? All those things, which you might dare do *in adultery*, are perhaps wonderful!

Once the thought and the desire are in her head, giving in to them is not far off.

She does dare, but quietly and bit by bit. She holds back: there are limits: that, yes; but that, no. These distinctions, once the first step has been taken, are surprising and grotesque, but very common. You would think that, from the moment a woman decides to try out the kind of love which is proscribed, refined, and inventive, she would always be wanting to go further, to explore different and more intense forms of caress. Well, in fact, that's not the case. Morality, however strange and misplaced, still has a hold on her. * * *

Preface to Paul Ginisty's *L'Amour à Trois* (1884)[†]

* * * A woman is brought up to please, taught (by society, that is) that love is her specialist domain and her only source of happiness; that she's been created by nature to be weak, inconstant, capricious, and amenable; and, by both society and nature, that she's flighty, destined to live much of the time alone while her husband enjoys doing what he wants. A woman thus lets herself be captivated by a man who devotes all his skill, experience, passion, and power to over-come her resistance! He's just playing his role as a man of the world, the seducer! She falls into his arms, giving in to irresistible love; and she thereby commits a blameworthy act, in the eyes of the law, but a human and fated one, so fated that it has never been overcome by the religious and civil rules of morality struggling against it. And the woman is treated as a wretch, a wench, a whore. * * *

Article in *Le Gaulois*, June 25, 1882[‡]

Elderly Women

Is there anything more adorable than an elderly woman? Who once upon a time was beautiful, coquettish, seductive, loved, and who still knows how to act as woman, but one from the past, still coquettish, but of an ancestral kind.

If a young woman is charming, isn't an older one exquisite? And don't you feel, standing next to her, something indefinable, like a sort

---

[†] Reprinted in *Chroniques*, vol. I, ed. Gérard Delaisement (Paris: Rive Droite, 2003), pp. 824–28. Translated by Robert Lethbridge for this Norton Critical Edition. It was originally published in the *Gil Blas* on March 4, 1884, under the title of this novel (with connotations of "A Threesome" as well as a "Love Triangle") by Paul Ginisty (1855–1932), who would later return the favor in an admiring review of Maupassant's 1889 novel, *Fort comme la mort*.

[‡] From *Chroniques*, vol. I, ed. Gérard Delaisement (Paris: Rive Droite, 2003), pp. 529–31. Translated by Robert Lethbridge for this Norton Critical Edition. The French title is *Les Vieilles*.

of love not for what she is but for what she was? A delicate tenderness, full of regret, gallant and reverential, refined and slightly pity-
ing, for that woman who survives in another, forgotten, dead, and
destroyed; loved by men, her lips crushed by their embrace, dreamed
of, and fought over, the woman of feverish nights, suffering, and pal-
pating hearts.

Those who really love women, who love everything about them,
from head to toe, simply because they're women, are those who can't
help trembling at the sight of curls on a nape, or down on an upper
lip, or the small wrinkle in the corner of a smile, or the overwhelming
power of her gaze; those who want to love all women—not just one,
but all of them, with their contrasting seductiveness, their different kinds of elegance, and varied charm—must, without exception,
adore the older woman.

She's no longer a woman as such, but seems to incarnate a longer
history of women; she becomes for us something like those beautiful antique objects that remind us of an entire epoch. Liberated by
her white hair shaking off its dusting, she dares speak about everything: all those mysterious and treasured things that remain a secret
between us and a young woman, whoever we are and whoever she
is, everything left unspoken but unmistakeably eloquent in a look,
a smile, or an attitude when we find ourselves face to face with Her.

In the street, on a staircase, in a *salon*, in the fields or on an omnibus, wherever it might be, when two young people exchange a glance,
there is a sudden blossoming of gallantry as eyes fill with a strange
desire, and it seems as if there is an invisible thread along which a
current of love binds them together.

But that's something unspoken, or hardly ever spoken about. The
elderly woman dares to say it all. She can do so without the immod-
esty or impropriety characteristic of the young, and it's a singular
pleasure to talk to a real woman at length, quietly and somewhat
obliquely, but freely, about the intoxication of the senses and the
heart.

And that's what they do, these elderly women, with a contented
disinterestedness; but still salivating, as if they had picked up the
aroma of a favorite meal of which they can no longer partake. They
talk of love in maternal and benevolent tones; sometimes they'll
throw in a crude term, a striking image, a risqué thought or slightly
salacious joke: and, in their mouths, that takes on the antique charm
of an earlier century; rather like a daring pirouette allowing just a
glimpse of thigh.

And when they're coquettish—and a woman always should be—
they give off a wonderful scent, that of yesteryear, as if all the per-
fumes applied to her skin had left behind a subtle waft of evaporated
essences: the delicious and discreet scent of iris and Florentine rice

powder. You sometimes feel you want to take her soft white hand in yours, overcome by these fragrances of love-affairs long past, and to place on it an everlasting kiss in homage to the tender moments of the life we have lived.

But that's not true of every elderly woman.

There are some who are truly awful who, instead of becoming more kindly and loveable, and less constrained in their language and moral views, have become embittered. And they're nearly always women who have hardly ever, if at all, experienced love, having lived a strictly unimpeachable life. They become grumpy and stuck-up old women, aggressively reproachful, female eunuchs, the guardians of everybody else's private life, always doing others down and in whom there seethes the rage of pensioned-off policemen.

The Supernatural

Article in *Le Gaulois*, November 8, 1881[†]

[Mystery and Myth]

* * * Goodbye to all that nonsense: the mysteries of olden times, the superstitions of our fathers, the legends of childhood, the old background of a world long gone.

With a smile of pride, we can consider in tranquility the ancient lightning of the gods, that of Jupiter and Jehovah now bottled for consumption!

Oh! yes, long live science and the genius of the human race! All hail the labors of that little thinking animal gradually unveiling the mysteries of the universe!

We're no longer astonished by the starry sky. We know the life-cycle and movement of the planets, and how long it takes for their light to reach us.

We're no longer terrified of the dark, now rid of its ghosts and evil spirits. Every phenomenon can now be explained by a natural law. I no longer believe in the tall stories of our ancestors. Those who claim to have witnessed a miracle are victims of hysteria. I reason, research and am liberated from superstition.

Well, in spite of myself, my willpower and the benefits of such a liberation, I'm still saddened by the unveiling of these mysteries. It seems to me that the world has been impoverished. The Invisible has been suppressed. And everything appears silent, empty, and abandoned!

When I go out at night, how I would like to shiver with the fear which inspires old women to make the sign of the cross as they proceed along the walls of a cemetery, and to sustain the last of the superstitious faced with the strange emanations of a marsh and the will-o'-the-wisp of the fantastic. How I would still like to believe in something vague and terrifying I imagined I saw in the gloom! How

† From *Chroniques*, vol. I, ed. Gérard Delaisement (Paris: Rive Droite, 2003), pp. 358–61. Translated by Robert Lethbridge for this Norton Critical Edition. The French title of this article is *Adieu Mystères* (Goodbye to Mysteries).

much darker the shadows of evening used to be when they were crawling with all those fabulous creatures! And here we are now, unable to marvel at the thunder and lightning because we've seen them close-up, resigned to their having lost their power.

Article in *Le Gaulois*, October 7, 1883[†]

The Fantastic

Very gradually, over the last twenty years, we have extracted the supernatural. It has evaporated like the scent of an uncorked bottle. Putting its opening to our nostrils and inhaling long and deeply, we can barely detect it. It's over.

Our grandchildren will be astonished by their fathers' gullibility about such ridiculous and incredible things. They will never know what was once, in the night, a fear of the mysterious and the supernatural. Only a few hundred people still cling to the idea of visiting souls, the influence of certain beings and things, lucid sleepwalking, and phoney ghosts. It's over.

Our poor anxious minds, limited in their capacity to understand anything without an apparent reason, terrified by the endless spectacle of an incomprehensible world, have for centuries been subject to strange and childish beliefs with which to explain the unknown. Now, aware of how mistaken we were, we still seek to understand, without knowing for sure. But the first great step has been taken. We have rejected the idea of the mysterious, which is now simply what remains to be explored.

In twenty years' time, not even the peasantry will retain a fear of the irrational. It's as if Creation is now viewed from another perspective, assuming an appearance and significance altogether different from that it had in the past. And that will certainly result in the end of the literature of the fantastic. That tradition has had various periods and forms, from the novels of chivalry, *The Thousand and One Nights*[1] and heroic poetry, all the way to fairy tales and the troubling works of [E.T.A.] Hoffmann and Edgar Allan Poe.[2]

When human beings were unquestioning in their beliefs, writers of the fantastic didn't make much effort as they spun their surprising tales. From their beginning, they plunged us into the impossible

---

[†] From *Chroniques*, vol. I, ed. Gérard Delaisement (Paris: Rive Droite, 2003), pp. 719–22. Translated by Robert Lethbridge for this Norton Critical Edition. The French title is *Le Fantastique*.

1. Persian tales translated into French in 1874.

2. Hoffmann (1776–1822) and Poe (1809–1849) were the most famous and influential examples of the nineteenth-century genre known as *le conte fantastique*.

and remained there, in an infinite variety of unlikely plots, apparitions and terrifying strategies in order to scare us out of our wits.

But when scepticism had finally overcome superstition, art became more subtle. The writer played with ambivalence, touching on the supernatural rather than being immersed in it. He created terrifying effects while still remaining within the realm of the plausible, leaving the reader hesitant and fearful. That reader, left unsure what to believe, lost his footing as in water where you can't see the bottom, clinging on desperately to reality only to immediately fall back even deeper, once again struggling in a confusion as awful and as frightening as a nightmare.

The extraordinary terrifying power of the writing of Hoffmann and Poe comes from such a skill, this particular and disturbing way of bringing us into contact with the fantastic, evoking a world of fact where there remains, nevertheless, something unexplained and nearly impossible. * * *

Pessimism, Illness, and Despair

Letter to Caroline Commanville[†]

24 May 1880

Dear Madame

Your letter did me good, because I'm in a dreadful state. The further away we get from Flaubert's death, the more I am haunted by my memories of him and the more I suffer, broken-hearted and bereft. His image is ever-present, as I see him standing before me in his huge brown dressing-gown which got bigger each time he raised his arms and spoke. All his gestures and intonations come back to me, as do the sentences in my ear as if he was still muttering them. It's the first of brutal separations, this disintegration of our lives, as one after the other of our nearest and dearest disappear, those who were part of our memories and with whom one had the closest conversations.

These blows leave their mark on our souls and a never-ending pain in our minds. * * *

At the moment, I acutely feel the pointlessness of existence, the sterility of any effort, the hideous monotony of events and things, and the moral isolation at the core of our lives, but which were made bearable when I could talk to him; because he had, unlike anybody else, that all-embracing cast of mind which allowed us to contemplate from a great height the whole of humanity and from which it was possible to better understand "the eternal sadness of everything." * * *

† From *Correspondance*, vol. II, ed. Jacques Suffel (Evreux: Le Cercle du Bibliophile, 1973), pp. 281–82. Translated by Robert Lethbridge for this Norton Critical Edition. Caroline Commanville (*née* Hamard, married to Ernest Commanville) was the niece of Gustave Flaubert who had very recently died (May 8, 1880). On Maupassant's seminal relationship with Flaubert, see Introduction, pp. xiii–xv.

Article in *Le Gaulois*, February 25, 1884[†]

[The Ravages of Age]

* * * At twenty, you're happy. Because physical strength, the passion in your blood, and the vague hope of delicious things to come which almost seem within your grasp, all suffice to infuse you with the vibrant sense of being alive. But then there's later, when you see, know and understand! How do you retain your faith in a little happiness when your hair starts to turn white and every day, once you've turned thirty, you lose something of your vigor, confidence, and health?

Like an old house from which fall, year in and year out, the odd tile and stone, and which has cracks lining its frontage and moss long ago making it look the worse for wear, so death, in all its inevitability, stalks and degrades us. From month to month, it takes from us once and for all the freshness of our skin, the teeth which will not be replaced, the hair which will not grow back; it disfigures us, making of us, in the space of a decade, such an entirely different person that we can longer recognize ourselves; and the further we proceed, the further it pushes us along, weakening us, wearing us down and ravaging us.

From one moment to the next, we crumble under its pressure. Every day, hour, and minute, once that destruction has begun, we die a little. Breathing, sleeping, drinking and eating, walking, going about one's business, everything we do, ultimately living is dying! But fortunately we hardly ever think about it! We still have hopes for a happiness just round the corner, and we dance at the carnival. Poor souls that we are!

And what kind of happiness do we dreamers dream of? What are we waiting for other than death approaching us at speed? What illusory hopes do we nurture? For humanity always hopes for something good, however imprecise.

For many, it's love! A few caresses, a few intense evenings, long looks lovingly exchanged, then tears, unforgiving misery and forgetting, that's all! And then death.

For others, it's making money, the luxuries of life, the delicacies of existence, fine meals which give you gout, parties which sap a man over just a few years, rich furnishings and the kow-towing of

---

[†] From *Chroniques*, vol. I, ed. Gérard Delaisement (Paris: Rive Droite, 2003), pp. 820–24. Translated by Robert Lethbridge for this Norton Critical Edition. The original French title of this article is *Causerie triste*, which translates roughly as "Melancholy Musings."

servants; that's simply to run towards death in a carriage rather than on foot.

For others still, is it power, the pride of authority, the right to sign papers which transform the lives of human beings? * * * For others, it's the simple life, led with honesty, without accident or disruption, in the midst of one's children; a life as flat as the open road, as devoid of features as the ocean and as monotonous as the desert. Is it possible for anyone with a spark of life *not* to hope for, and dream of and desire, the unexpected, the extraordinary and the surprising? The fear of death and the unknown lying in wait drives others to a penitent, cloistered existence. They renounce everything that life, however wretched, offers us by way of pleasure, motivated by the terror of a mysterious punishment from on high and the hope of an everlasting reward. What do these fearful egoists gain from that?

Whatever our hopes, we're always disappointed. Death is the only certainty! I believe in that irresistibly powerful fatality!

But people still dance at the carnival! * * *

Article in *Gil Blas*, June 10, 1884[†]

[Blessed Are the Content]

Blessed are they who are satisfied with life, who enjoy it to their heart's content.

There are some people who like everything, enchanted by it all. They love the sun and the rain, the snow and the fog, going out and staying in, everything that they do, say, and hear.

Some of these people lead a pleasant, quiet, and satisfying life, surrounded by their children. Others lead a life of frenetic pleasure and distractions. Neither group are bored. Life for them is a sort of amusing play in which they themselves have a part, a good and varied existence which, without surprising them too much, makes them very happy.

But there are yet other human beings, swiftly casting their minds across the narrow scope of possible sources of contentment, who remain crushed by the meaninglessness of happiness and the monotony and sterility of earthly joy. For them, once they're past thirty, it's all over. What are they hoping for? Nothing distracts them any more; they've exhausted the round of meager pleasures available to us.

† From *Chroniques*, vol. I, ed. Gérard Delaisement (Paris: Rive Droite, 2003), pp. 856–62. Translated by Robert Lethbridge for this Norton Critical Edition. The original title of this article is *Par-delà* (Over and Beyond), serving as a review of *A Rebours* (Against Nature), the 1884 novel by J.-K. Huysmans (1848–1907), whose protagonist displays precisely the world-weariness to which Maupassant subscribes.

Blessed are they who are ignorant of the abominable revulsion pro-voked by the same things repeated again and again; blessed are they who have the strength, each day, to start again on the same tasks, with the same movements, in the same setting, with the same hori-zons and sky, who are able to set off down the same street where they'll meet the same faces and the same animals. Blessed are they who don't notice with disgust that nothing changes, nothing hap-pens, and that everything wears away. What a slow, closed, and undemanding attitude we need to have to be content with what there is. How is it that the audience of society has not yet shouted: "Cur-tains!" insisting that there be another performance with actors other than human beings, with other kinds of celebration, plants, stars, inventions, and adventures. Because nobody has yet felt a hatred for an unchanging human face, or for a dog wandering along the road, or more especially a horse, that horrible animal on four pegs whose feet look like mushrooms.

It's in the eyes that you have to look at a creature to judge its aesthetic qualities. Look at a horse, with its monstrous and mis-shapen head planted on its bony, knotted, and grotesque legs! And when those appalling beasts are pulling along a yellow carriage, they become something out of a nightmare. Where can you escape in order no longer to see these living or inanimate things, not to have to begin all over again everything we do, not to have to talk or think?

Truly, we're content with very little. Can it really be that we're sated with the happiness we glean? Don't we always feel ravaged and tortured by the desire for something new and unknown?

What do we in fact do? What are the limits of our satisfaction? Just look at women. Their greatest mental exertion is to combine col-ors and materials to hide their bodies and make them more attrac-tive. How pathetic!

They dream of love. Whispering that same word, time and time again, when looking deep into the eyes of a man. How pathetic!

And what about us? What gives we men pleasure?

Is it, as so I'm told, the deliciousness of holding yourself upright on the back of a galloping horse and making it go over jumps, know-ing how to make it move in one direction or another simply through the pressure of a knee?

Or is it the deliciousness of wandering across the woods and fields with gun in hand, killing animals fleeing in your path, or partridges falling from the sky in a shower of blood, or deer with eyes sobbing like a child, so gentle that you would like to stroke them? Or is it the deliciousness of winning or losing money in the process of exchang-ing with someone else, according to a set of accepted rules, little colored cards? You can apparently spend whole nights playing these games, adoring them beyond measure!

Is it delicious to jump around in time and rhythmically turn, with a woman in your arms? It's certainly delicious, if you like her, to place your mouth on her hair or even on the edges of her clothes.

And that's all our great pleasures consist of! How pathetic!

Other men love the arts and Thinking! Do you imagine that thinking ever changes? * * *

For human thought is unchanging. Its precise and unalterable limits, once reached, it goes in circles like a horse in a circus-ring, or a fly in sealed bottle, fluttering back and forth as it repeatedly hits the glass. We too are imprisoned within ourselves, unable to extract ourselves, condemned to drag behind us the ten-ton weight of our earth-bound dreams.

The progress of all our cerebral efforts amounts to no more than recording insignificant facts with the ridiculously imperfect instrument supplementing the incapacity of our bodily organs. Every twenty years, some poor scientist sacrificing his life to his research discovers that air contains some as yet unknown gas, or that an inexplicable and unquantifiable energy is generated by rubbing a sheet with wax, or that amongst the innumerable unknown stars there is one, near another which we have spotted and to which we have given a name long ago, which has not yet been identified. So what?

Our illnesses come from microbes? Very well. But where do microbes come from? And what about the illnesses afflicting these invisible bacteria? And the planets, where do they come from?

We know nothing, we can see nothing, we can't do anything, we can guess nothing, we can imagine nothing; we're locked in, imprisoned within ourselves. And to think that people marvel at the genius of the human race!

Our memories cannot retain one in ten thousand of the confused and insignificant observations recorded by scientists and published in books. We're not even aware of our weakness and incapacity; for, in measuring one human being against another, we fail to measure a general and definitive impotence.

There's no solution. Some people travel. They'll see nothing but other human beings, plants, and animals. It's when wanting to go far away that one understands that everything is near, brief, and empty. It's in seeking the unknown that one notices that everything is mediocre and ephemeral. It's in circling the globe that one becomes aware of how small it is and always the same.

Blessed are they whose appetites perfectly accord with their means, who are content with their ignorance and their pleasures; those not subject to an impetuous and vain striving for what lies beyond their lives, for other things, for the mysterious immensity of the Unknown. Blessed are they who are still committed to living, who can appreciate it and bear it. * * *

Letter to Jean Bourdeau[†]

October 1889

My dear friend

I'm still in Florence where I received your letter. I have been very ill here and the doctors would be glad to see the back of me, but I myself know that it's nothing serious and that everything will soon be alright. I have had violent bleeding of the intestines, though these have now healed, leaving visible lumps. It's been another trick played on me by my nervous system and that hateful regulator of physical functioning stupidly called *Le grand sympathique*.[1] My own, when a climate doesn't suit, tries to kill me by shutting down one of these networks, thus paralyzing a vital organ. It's done that to my heart, my legs, my stomach, and skin, which left me bald a week ago. It's now playing the same trick on my gut, without giving me any warning. I woke up in the night bleeding like a woman in labor. I feel myself all over. It hurts! I call my doctor who finds inflammation and tearing devoid of the usual symptoms in the case of such medical problems. * * *

Letter to Dr. Grancher[‡]

1891

My dear friend

An injection of morphine has left me in such a state that never have I suffered as much. My eyes, which had been feeling much better, are haggard and so contracted that I can't use them at all, and once again I can neither read nor write. I have spent the whole winter being unable to work. This latest setback has been terrible for me. As for sleep, I've just spent the night getting up and then going back to bed, as if I'd had a cocaine injection, haunted by nightmares, visions and noises.

Please could I come and see you as soon as possible. I spent the whole of yesterday in bed.

[†] From *Correspondance*, vol. III, ed. Jacques Suffel (Evreux: Le Cercle du Bibliophile, 1973), pp. 108–10. Translated by Robert Lethbridge for this Norton Critical Edition. Maupassant had met Jean Bourdeau (1848–1928) only that year, in 1889, but had long been acquainted with his French translation of Schopenhauer (see p. 273). After returning from Tunisia in September, Maupassant spent much of the next month in Italy, in Livorno, Pisa, and Florence.
1. French expression for the central nervous system.
[‡] From *Correspondance*, vol. III, ed. Jacques Suffel (Evreux: Le Cercle du Bibliophile, 1973), p. 193. Translated by Robert Lethbridge for this Norton Critical Edition. Dr. Joseph Grancher (1843–1907), a pediatric specialist, was a collaborator of Louis Pasteur in his work on rabies, but (as Pasteur was not qualified to do so) had been the first doctor to experiment with injections, in 1885. He became a friend of Maupassant as well as his most trusted personal physician.

Telegram to Henry Cazalis[†]

January 1891

* * * I can assure you that I'm losing my mind. I'm going insane. I spent yesterday evening at Princesse Mathilde's,[1] stumbling for words, no longer able to speak or remember anything. I came home to bed, but my distress kept me awake. I took a sleeping draught; nothing worked. I paced up and down in my room. Do come and see me. The reason for all this simply has to be found.

Letter to Henry Cazalis[‡]

January 1891

* * * I am seriously ill. I can no longer see anything. I can't write because I can no longer control my words. My pen writes others.

I saw Robin[1] the other day; he's prescribed a mass of drugs. I think he hasn't understood my condition and that his treatment is itself making me ill. I have always reacted badly to these kinds of complicated internal medication.

I'm not going out during this bitter cold spell. If you have a minute, please come and see me. I would be very grateful.

Letter to Henry Cazalis[*]

[end of August or beginning of September] 1891

* * * I can't sleep or eat, dragging my migraines along the roads, painfully slowly as we're in the mountains, which I've never been able to get near. It's all related to my tooth. * * * When I arrived here, I could eat for ten; now I'm back to nibbling, as repulsed by food as before, unable to walk as my stomach hurts so much, with neither

---

† From *Correspondance*, vol. III, ed. Jacques Suffel (Evreux: Le Cercle du Bibliophile, 1973), p. 195. Translated by Robert Lethbridge for this Norton Critical Edition. Henry Cazalis (1840–1909) was one of Maupassant's doctors, as well as a literary colleague writing under the name of Jean Lahor.
1. The niece (1820–1904) of Napoleon Bonaparte; she was at the very center of French high society and her *salon* was the most glamorous of those frequented by Maupassant. It was through the good offices of Flaubert that he had got to know her in the late 1870s.
‡ From *Correspondance*, vol. III, ed. Jacques Suffel (Evreux: Le Cercle du Bibliophile, 1973), pp. 195–96. Translated by Robert Lethbridge for this Norton Critical Edition.
1. Dr. Albert Robin (1847–1928), who had a list of very distinguished patients, was one of the many physicians consulted by Maupassant during this period.
* From *Correspondance*, vol. III, ed. Jacques Suffel (Evreux: Le Cercle du Bibliophile, 1973), pp. 232–34. Translated by Robert Lethbridge for this Norton Critical Edition. Maupassant is writing from the "Chalet du Mont-Blanc" in Divonne-les-Bains, the French spa in the foothills of the Jura, just over the border with Switzerland.

willpower nor energy, more discouraged than ever. I need warmth and exercise, but I can't take any, so crushed do I feel by the depression weighing me down. And what sort of exercise, anyway? Walking? To go where? I've seen everything there is to see. I'm not going to start all over again. My immobility makes even taking a shower painful, almost useless. The body is strong, the mind more diseased than ever. There are days when I want to put a f . . . bullet in my brain. I can't read; every letter I write gives me a terrible stomachache, making me swell up so much that I have to unbutton all my clothes. * * *

CRITICISM

Early Criticism

HENRY JAMES

[Maupassant and the Senses]†

* * *

* * * As regards the other sense, the sense *par excellence*, the sense which we scarcely mention in English fiction, and which I am not very sure I shall be allowed to mention in an English periodical, M. de Maupassant speaks for that, and of it, with extraordinary distinctness and authority. To say that it occupies the first place in his picture is to say too little; it covers in truth the whole canvas, and his work is little else but a report of its innumerable manifestations. These manifestations are not, for him, so many incidents of life; they are life itself, they represent the standing answer to any question that we may ask about it. He describes them in detail, with a familiarity and a frankness which leave nothing to be added; I should say with singular truth, if I did not consider that in regard to this article he may be taxed with a certain exaggeration. M. de Maupassant would doubtless affirm that where the empire of the sexual sense is concerned, no exaggeration is possible: nevertheless it may be said that whatever depths may be discovered by those who dig for them, the impression of the human spectacle for him who takes it as it comes has less analogy with that of the monkeys' cage than this admirable writer's account of it. I speak of the human spectacle as we Anglo-Saxons see it—as we Anglo-Saxons pretend we see it, M. de Maupassant would possibly say.

* * *

† From "Guy de Maupassant," *Partial Portraits* (Westport, Conn: Greenwood Press, 1970), pp. 253–54, 264–66. Originally published by Macmillan in 1888. In an 1889 essay in the same vein, Henry James (1843–1916) wrote of Maupassant, whom he knew personally, that "what is clearest to him is the immitigability of our mortal predicament with its occasional beguilments and innumerable woes," lamenting the lack of moral complexity and that "his strong, hard, cynical, slightly cruel humor can scarcely be called a theory" ("Introduction," *The Odd Number. Thirteen Tales by Guy de Maupassant*, trans. Jonathan Sturges [London: McIlvaine, 1891], p. xiii). Aimed at an Anglo-Saxon public, James's writing on Maupassant is informed by his embarrassment at the writer's emphasis on physiology at the expense of psychological analysis.

297

He has produced a hundred short tales and only four regular novels; but if the tales deserve the first place in any candid appreciation of his talent it is not simply because they are so much the more numerous: they are also more characteristic; they represent him best in his originality, and their brevity, extreme in some cases, does not prevent them from being a collection of masterpieces. (They are very unequal, and I speak of the best.) The little story is but scantily relished in England, where readers take their fiction rather by the volume than by the page, and the novelist's idea is apt to resemble one of those old-fashioned carriages which require a wide court to turn round. In America, where it is associated pre-eminently with Hawthorne's name, with Edgar Poe's, and with that of Mr. Bret Harte, the short tale has had a better fortune. France, however, has been the land of its great prosperity, and M. de Maupassant had from the first the advantage of addressing a public accustomed to catch on, as the modern phrase is, quickly. In some respects, it may be said, he encountered prejudices too friendly, for he found a tradition of indecency ready made to his hand. I say indecency with plainness, though my indication would perhaps please better with another word, for we suffer in English from a lack of roundabout names for the *conte leste*[1]—that element for which the French, with their *grivois*, their *gaillard*, their *égrillard*, their *gaudriole*, have so many convenient synonyms. * * *

For the last ten years our author has brought forth with regularity these condensed compositions, of which, probably, to an English reader, at a first glance, the most universal sign will be their licentiousness. They really partake of this quality, however, in a very differing degree, and a second glance shows that they may be divided into numerous groups. It is not fair, I think, even to say that what they have most in common is their being extremely *lestes*. What they have most in common is their being extremely strong, and after that their being extremely brutal. A story may be obscene without being brutal, and *vice versa*, and M. de Maupassant's contempt for those interdictions which are supposed to be made in the interest of good morals is but an incident—a very large one indeed—of his general contempt. A pessimism so great that its alliance with the love of good work, or even with the calculation of the sort of work that pays best in a country of style, is, as I have intimated, the most puzzling of anomalies (for it would seem in the light of such sentiments that nothing is worth anything), this cynical strain is the sign of such gems of narration as *La Maison Tellier, L'Histoire d'une Fille de Ferme, L'Ane, Le Chien, Mademoiselle Fifi, Monsieur Parent, L'Héritage, En*

---

1. A *conte leste* is a risqué or smutty story; *grivois, gaillard, égrillard,* and *gaudriole* are synonyms of bawdy or lewd.

Famille, Le Baptême, Le Père Amable. The author fixes a hard eye on some small spot of human life, usually some ugly, dreary, shabby, sordid one, takes up the particle, and squeezes it either till it grimaces or till it bleeds. Sometimes the grimace is very droll, sometimes the wound is very horrible; but in either case the whole thing is real, observed, noted, and represented, not an invention or a castle in the air. M. de Maupassant sees human life as a terribly ugly business relieved by the comical, but even the comedy is for the most part the comedy of misery, of avidity, of ignorance, helplessness, and grossness. * * *

* * *

JULES LEMAÎTRE

[Maupassant's Misanthropy]†

* * *

* * * [I]n spite of his natural gaiety, M. de Maupassant, like many writers of his generation, affects a moroseness, a misanthropy that gives an excessively bitter flavour to several of his narratives. It is evident that he likes and searches for the most violent manifestations of love reduced to desire, of egoism, of brutality, of simple ferocity. To speak only of his peasants, some of them eat black-puddings over their grandfather's corpse which they have stuffed into the trough so that they may be able to sleep in their only bed. Another, an innkeeper, who has an interest in the death of an old woman, rids himself of her gaily by killing her with brandy in every way he could. Another, a worthy fellow, rapes his servant, then, having married her, beats her to a jelly because she does not give him children. Others, these latter outside the law, poachers and loafers of the Seine, amuse themselves royally by shooting an old donkey with a gun loaded with salt; and I also commend to you the amusements of Saint Antony with his Prussian.

M. de Maupassant searches out with no less predilection the most ironical conjunctions of ideas or of facts, the most unexpected and most shocking combinations of feelings, those most likely to wound in us some illusion or some moral delicacy. The comic and the sensual mingling in these almost sacrilegious combinations, not precisely to

† From "Guy de Maupassant," *Literary Impressions*, trans. A. W. Evans (London: Daniel O'Connor, 1921), pp. 154–86. Jules Lemaître (1853–1914) was one of the leading critics of his generation, publishing his seven-volume *Les Contemporains* between 1886 and 1899, from which this excerpt has been translated. He consistently decried the kind of realist writing exemplified by Maupassant and Émile Zola.

purify them, but to prevent them from being painful. While others depict for us war and its effects on the fields of battle or in families, M. de Maupassant, hewing out for himself from this common material a portion that is indeed his own, shows us the effects of the invasion in a special world and even in houses which we usually designate by euphemisms. You remember Boule-de-Suif's astonishing sacrifice, and the unheard-of conduct of those whom she obliged, and, in *Mademoiselle Fifi*, Rachel's revolt, the stab, the girl in the steeple who is afterwards brought back and embraced by the parish priest and at last married by a patriot who has no prejudices. Remark that Rachel and Boule-de-Suif are certainly, along with Miss Harriet, little Simon, and the parish priest in *Un Baptême* (I think that is all), the most sympathetic characters in the tales. Look also at the Tellier household taken by 'Madame' to her niece's first Communion, and the ineffable contrasts that result from it; and Captain Sommerive's dodge to make little André disgusted with his mamma's bed, and the peculiar impression that comes from that tale (*Le Mal d'André*), of which one asks oneself whether it has a right to be comical, though it is 'terribly' so.

There is in these stories and in some others a triumphant brutality, a determination to regard men as sad or comical animals, a large contempt for humanity, which becomes indulgent, it is true, immediately when there comes into play *divûmque hominumque voluptas, alma Venus*: all this saved in most cases by the rapidity and frankness of the narrative, by the out-and-out gaiety, by the perfect naturalness, and also (I scarcely dare say it, but it will explain itself) by the very depth of the artist's sensuality, which at least always spares us mere smuttiness.

*   *   *

Thus we see how many new elements are added to the old and eternal foundation of smuttiness—observation of reality, and more readily of dull or violent reality; instead of the old wantonness, a profound sensuality enlarged by the feeling of nature and often blended with sadness and poetry. All these things are not encountered at the same time in all M. de Maupassant's tales. I give the impression left by them taken as a whole. Amidst his robust jollities, he has sometimes, whether natural or acquired, a vision similar to that of Flaubert or of M. Zola, he also is attacked by the most recent malady of writers, I mean pessimism and the strange mania for making out the world to be very ugly and very brutal, for showing it governed by blind instincts, for thus almost eliminating psychology, the good old 'study of the human heart,' and for endeavouring at the same time to represent in detail and with a relief that has not yet been attained this world which is of so little interest in itself and only of interest

as material for art; so that the pleasure of the writer and of those
who enjoy him and enter fully into his thought consists only of irony,
pride, and selfish pleasure. No concern about what used to be be
called the ideal, no preoccupation with morality, no sympathy for
men, but perhaps a contemptuous pity for absurd and miserable
humanity; on the other hand, a subtle skill in enjoying the world in
so far as it falls within the senses and is of a nature to gratify them;
the interest that is refused to things themselves fully granted to the
art of reproducing them in as plastic a form as possible; on the whole,
the attitude of a misanthropical, scoffing, and lascivious god. * * *

                              *   *   *

He is one by his form. He joins to a vision of the world, to feelings and preferences of which the classics would not have approved,
all the external qualities of classic art. Moreover, this has been also
one of Flaubert's originalities; but it seems to be more constant and
less laborious in M. de Maupassant.

'Classical qualities, classical form,' are easy words to say. What
exactly do they mean? They imply an idea of excellence; they imply
also clearness, sobriety, the art of composition; they mean, finally,
that reason, rather than imagination and sensibility, presides over the
execution of the work, and that the writer dominates his material.

M. de Maupassant dominates his material marvellously, and it is
through this that he is a master. From the first he has conquered us
by qualities which we enjoyed all the more as they are regarded as
characteristics of our natural genius, as we found them where we
had not dreamed of expecting them, and as, besides, they gave us a
rest from the tiring affectations of other writers. In three or four
years he became famous, and it is a long time since a literary reputation has been established so suddenly. * * *

                              *   *   *

ARTHUR SYMONS

[Maupassant's Cynicism]†

                              *   *   *

Every artist has his own vision of the world. Maupassant's vision
was of solid superficies, of texture which his hands could touch, of

† From "Introduction," Guy de Maupassant, *Eight Short Stories*, trans. George Burnham
  Ives, ed. Arthur Symons (London: Heinemann: 1899), pp. x–xv. Arthur Symons (1865–
  1945) was a British poet, critic, and magazine editor who worked tirelessly to bring major
  nineteenth-century French writers to the attention of an English-speaking readership.

action which his mind could comprehend from the mere sight of its incidents. He saw the world as the Dutch painters saw it, and he was as great a master of form, of rich and sober colour, of the imitation of the outward gestures of life, and of the fashion of external things. He had the same view of humanity, and shows us, with the same indifference, the same violent ferment of life—the life of full-blooded people who have to elbow their way through the world. His sense of desire, of greed, of all the baser passions, was profound: he had the terrible logic of animalism. Love-making, drunkenness, cheating, quarrelling, the mere idleness of sitting drowsily in a chair, the gross life of the farm-yard and the fields, civic dissensions, the sordid provincial dance of the seven deadly sins, he saw in the same direct, unilluminating way as the Dutch painters; finding, indeed, no beauty in any of these things, but getting his beauty in the deft arrangement of them, in the mere act of placing them in a picture. The world existed for him as something formless which could be cut up into little pictures. He saw no farther than the lines of his frame. The interest of the thing began inside that frame, and what remained outside was merely material.

A story of Maupassant, more than almost anything in the world, gives you the impression of manual dexterity. It is adequately thought out, but it does not impress you by its thought; it is clearly seen, but it does not impress you specially by the fidelity of its detail; it has just enough of ordinary human feeling for the limits it has imposed on itself. What impresses you is the extreme ingenuity of its handling; the way in which this juggler keeps his billiard-balls harmoniously rising and falling in the air. Often, indeed, you cannot help noticing the conscious smile which precedes the trick, and the confident bow which concludes it. He does not let you into the secret of the trick, but he prevents you from ignoring that it is after all only a trick which you have been watching.

There is a philosophy of one kind or another behind the work of every artist. Maupassant's was a simple one, sufficient for his needs as he understood them, though perhaps really consequent upon his artistic methods, rather than at the root of them. It was the philosophy of cynicism: the most effectual means of limiting one's outlook, of concentrating all one's energies on the task in hand. Maupassant wrote for men of the world, and men of the world are content with the wisdom of their counting-houses. The man of the world is perfectly willing to admit that he is no better than you, because he takes it for granted that you will admit yourself to be no better than he. It is a way of avoiding comparison. To Maupassant this cynical point of view was invaluable for his purpose. He wanted to tell stories just for the pleasure of telling them; he wanted to concern himself with his story simply as a story; incidents interested him, not ideas, nor even characters, and he wanted every incident to be immediately effective. Now cynicism, in France, supplies a sufficient basis for all these requirements; it is the equivalent, for popular purposes, of that appeal, to the average which in England is sentimentality. Compare, for instance, the admirable story[1] which is here translated, perhaps the best story which Maupassant ever wrote, with a story of somewhat similar motive—Bret Harte's "Outcasts of Poker Flat." Both stories are pathetic; but the pathos of the American (who had formed himself upon Dickens, and in the English tradition) becomes sentimental, and gets its success by being sentimental; while the pathos of the Frenchman (who has formed himself on Flaubert, and on French lines) gets its success precisely by being cynical.

And then the particular variety of Maupassant's cynicism was just that variation of the artistic idea upon the temperament which puts the best finish upon work necessarily so limited, obliged to be so clenching, as the short story. Flaubert's gigantic dissatisfaction with life, his really philosophic sense of its vanity, would have overweighted a writer so thoroughly equipped for his work as the writer of "Boule de Suif" and "La Maîson Tellier." Maupassant had no time, he allowed himself no space, to reason about life; the need was upon him to tell story after story, each with its crisis, its thrill, its summing up of a single existence or a single action. The sharp, telling thrust that his conception of art demanded could be given only by a very specious, not very profound, very forthright, kind of cynicism, like the half kindly half contemptuous laugh of the man who tells a good story at the club. For him it was the point of the epigram.

Maupassant was the man of his period, and his period was that of Naturalism. In "Les Soirées de Médan," the volume in which "Boule de Suif" appeared, there is another story called "Sac au Dos," in which another novelist made his appearance among the five who "publicly affirmed their literary tendencies" about the central figure of Zola. J. K. Huysmans, then but at the outset of his slow and painful course through schools and experiments, was in time to sum up the new tendencies of a new period, as significantly as Maupassant summed up in his short and brilliant and almost undeviating career the tendencies of that period in which Taine[2] and science seemed to have at last found out the physical basis of life. Now it is a new realism which appeals to us: it is the turn of the soul. The battle which the "Soirées de Médan" helped to win has been won; having gained our right to deal with humble and unpleasant and sordidly

1. The reference is to "The Adventure of Walter Schnaffs," compared in tone to Bret Harte's "The Outcasts of Poker Flat" (1869).
2. Hippolyte Taine (1828–1893) was the most influential philosopher of the period, associated with Positivism—based on the premise that human behavior could be analyzed in terms of the determinants of history, social context, and race.

tragic things in fiction, we are free to concern ourselves with other things. But though the period has passed, and will not return, the masterpieces of the period remain. Among these masterpieces, not the least among them, is "Boule de Suif."

JOSEPH CONRAD

[The Austerity of Maupassant's Talent]†

To introduce Maupassant to English readers with apologetic explanations as though his art were recondite and the tendency of his work immoral would be a gratuitous impertinence.

Maupassant's conception of his art is such as one would expect from a practical and resolute mind; but in the consummate simplicity of his technique it ceases to be perceptible. This is one of its greatest qualities, and like all the great virtues it is based primarily on self-denial.

To pronounce a judgment upon the general tendency of an author is a difficult task. One could not depend upon reason alone, nor yet trust solely to one's emotions. Used together, they would in many cases traverse each other, because emotions have their own unanswerable logic. Our capacity for emotion is limited, and the field of our intelligence is restricted. Responsiveness to every feeling, combined with the penetration of every intellectual subterfuge, would end, not in judgment, but in universal absolution. *Tout comprendre c'est tout pardonner.* And in this benevolent neutrality towards the warring errors of human nature all light would go out from art and from life.

We are at liberty then to quarrel with Maupassant's attitude towards our world in which, like the rest of us, he has that share which his senses are able to give him. But we need not quarrel with him violently. If our feelings (which are tender) happen to be hurt because his talent is not exercised for the praise and consolation of mankind, our intelligence (which is great) should let us see that he is a very splendid sinner, like all those who in this valley of compromises err by over-devotion to the truth that is in them. His determinism, barren of praise, blame, and consolation, has all the merit

† From Guy de Maupassant, *Yvette and Other Stories,* trans. A. G., with a preface by Joseph Conrad (London: Duckworth, 1904), pp. v–xvi. Conrad (1857–1924), the renowned novelist, played an influential role in trying to overcome Victorian susceptibilities toward Maupassant. He chose the stories for this collection. The anonymized translator of them, "A. G.," was his friend Ada Galsworthy, the future wife of John Galsworthy (1867–1933), English novelist and playwright. Conrad's 1904 Preface is a response to the rather critical one Ford Madox Ford had provided for a Duckworth edition of nine of Maupassant's tales the year before.

of his conscientious art. The worth of every conviction consists precisely in the steadfastness with which it is held.

Except for his philosophy, which in the case of so consummate an artist does not matter (unless to the solemn and naïve mind), Maupassant of all writers of fiction demands least forgiveness from his readers. He does not require forgiveness because he is never dull.

The interest of a reader in a work of imagination is either ethical or that of simple curiosity. Both are perfectly legitimate, since there is both a moral and excitement to be found in a faithful rendering of life. And in Maupassant's work there is the interest of curiosity and the moral of a point of view consistently preserved and never obtruded for the end of personal gratification. The spectacle of this immense talent served by exceptional faculties triumphing over the most thankless subjects by an unswerving singleness of purpose is in itself an admirable lesson in the power of artistic honesty, one may say of artistic virtue. The inherent greatness of the man consists in this, that he will let none of the fascinations that beset a writer working in loneliness turn him away from the straight path, from the vouchsafed vision of excellence. He will not be led into perdition by the seductions of sentiment, of eloquence, of humour, of pathos; of all that splendid pageant of faults that pass between the writer and his probity on the blank sheet of paper, like the glittering cortège of deadly sins before the austere anchorite in the desert air of Thebaïde. This is not to say that Maupassant's austerity has never faltered; but the fact remains that no tempting demon has ever succeeded in hurling him down from his high, if narrow, pedestal.

It is the austerity of his talent, of course, that is in question. Let the discriminating reader, who at times may well spare a moment or two to the consideration and enjoyment of artistic excellence, be asked to reflect a little upon the texture of two stories included in this volume: "A Piece of String," and "A Sale." How many openings the last offers for the gratuitous display of the author's wit or clever buffoonery, the first for an unmeasured display of sentiment. And both sentiment and buffoonery could have been made very good too, in a way accessible to the meanest intelligence, at the cost of truth and honesty. Here it is where Maupassant's austerity comes in. He refrains from setting his cleverness against the eloquence of the facts. There is humour and pathos in these stories; but such is the greatness of his talent, the refinement of his artistic conscience, that all his high qualities appear inherent in the very things of which he speaks, as if they had been altogether independent of his presentation. Facts, and again facts are his unique concern. That is why he is not always properly understood. His facts are so perfectly rendered that, like the actualities of life itself, they demand from the reader that faculty of observation which is rare, the power of appreciation which is generally wanting in most of us who are guided mainly by empty phrases requiring no effort, demanding from us no qualities except a vague susceptibility to emotion. Nobody had ever gained the vast applause of a crowd by the simple and clear exposition of vital facts. Words alone strung upon a convention have fascinated us as worthless glass beads strung on a thread have charmed at all times our brothers the unsophisticated savages of the islands. Now, Maupassant, of whom it has been said that he is the master of the *mot juste* has never been a dealer in words. His wares have been, not glass beads, but polished gems: not the most rare and precious, perhaps, but of the very first water after their kind.

That he took trouble with his gems, taking them up in the rough and polishing each facet patiently the publication of the two post-humous volumes of short stories proves abundantly. I think it proves also the assertion made here that he was by no means a dealer in words. On looking at the first feeble drafts from which so many perfect stories have been fashioned, one discovers that what has been matured, improved, brought to perfection by unwearied endeavour is not the diction of the tale, but the vision of its true shape and detail. Those first attempts are not faltering or uncertain in expression. It is the conception which is at fault. The subjects have not yet been adequately seen. His proceeding was not to group expressive words that mean nothing around misty and mysterious shapes dear to muddled intellects, belonging neither to earth nor to heaven. His vision by a more scrupulous, prolonged and devoted attention to the aspects of the visible world discovered at last the right words as if miraculously impressed for him upon the face of things and events. This was the particular shape taken by his inspiration; it came to him directly, honestly in the light of his day, instead of on the tortuous, dark roads of meditation. His realities came to him from a genuine source, from this universe of vain appearances wherein we men have found everything to make us proud, sorry, exalted, and humble.

Maupassant's renown is universal, but his popularity is restricted. It is not difficult to perceive why. Maupassant is an intensely national writer. He is so intensely national in his logic, in his clearness, in his aesthetic and moral conceptions that he has been accepted by his countrymen without having had to pay the tribute of flattery either to the nation as a whole, or to any class, sphere or division of the nation. The truth of his art tells with an irresistible force; and he stands excused from the duty of patriotic posturing. He is a French-man of Frenchmen beyond question or cavil, and with that he is simple enough to be universally comprehensible. What is wanting to his universal success is the mediocrity of an obvious and appealing tenderness. He neglects to qualify his truth with the drop of facile sweetness; he forgets to strew paper roses over the tombs. The disregard of these common decencies lays him open to the charges of cruelty, cynicism, hardness. And yet it can be safely affirmed that this man wrote from the fulness of a compassionate heart. He is merciless and yet gentle with his mankind; he does not rail at their prudent fears and their small artifices; he does not despise their labours. It seems to me that he looks with an eye of profound pity upon their troubles, deceptions, and misery. But he looks at them all. He sees—and does not turn away his head. As a matter of fact he is courageous.

Courage and justice are not popular virtues. The practice of strict justice is shocking to the multitude who always (perhaps from an obscure sense of guilt) attach to it the meaning of mercy. In the majority of us, who want to be left alone with our illusions, courage inspires a vague alarm. This is what is felt about Maupassant. His qualities, to use the charming and popular phrase, are not lovable. Courage being a force will not masquerade in the robes of affected delicacy and restraint. But if his courage is not of a chivalrous stamp, it cannot be denied that it is never brutal for the sake of effect. The writer of these few reflections, inspired by a long and intimate acquaintance with the work of the man, has been struck by the appreciation of Maupassant manifested by many women gifted with tenderness and intelligence. Their more delicate and audacious souls are good judges of courage. Their finer penetration has discovered his genuine masculinity without display, his virility without a pose. They have discerned in his faithful dealings with the world that enterprising and fearless temperament, poor in ideas, but rich in power, which appeals most to the feminine mind.

It cannot be denied that he thinks very little. In him extreme energy of perception achieves great results, as in men of action the energy of force and desire. His view of intellectual problems is perhaps more simple than their nature warrants; still a man who has written "Yvette" cannot be accused of want of subtlety. But one cannot insist enough upon this, that his subtlety, his humour, his grimness, though no doubt they are his own, are never presented otherwise but as belonging to our life, as found in nature whose beauties and cruelties alike breathe the spirit of serene unconsciousness.

Maupassant's philosophy of life is more temperamental than rational. He expects nothing either from gods or men. He trusts his senses for information and his instinct for deductions. It may seem that he has made but little use of his mind. But let me be clearly understood. His sensibility is really very great; and it is impossible to be sensible, unless one thinks vividly, unless one thinks correctly, starting from intelligible premises to an unsophisticated conclusion.

This is literary honesty. It may be remarked that it does not differ very greatly from the ideal honesty of the respectable majority, from the honesty of law-givers, of warriors, of kings, of bricklayers, of all those who express their fundamental sentiment in the ordinary course of their activities, by the work of their hands.

The work of Maupassant's hands is honest. He thinks sufficiently to concrete his fearless conclusions in illuminative instances. He renders them with that exact knowledge of the means and that absolute devotion to the aim of creating a true effect—which is art. He is the most accomplished of narrators.

It is evident that Maupassant looked upon his mankind in another spirit than those writers who make haste to submerge the difficulties of our holding place in the universe under a flood of false and sentimental assumptions. Maupassant was a true and dutiful lover of our earth. He says himself in one of his descriptive passages: "*Nous autres que séduit la terre. . . .*" It was true. The earth had for him a compelling charm. He looks upon her august and furrowed face with the fierce insight of real passion. His is the power of detecting the one immutable quality that matters in the changing aspects of nature and under the ever-shifting surface of life. To say that he could not embrace in his glance all its magnificence and all its misery is only to say that he was human. He lays claim to nothing that his matchless vision has not made his own. This creative artist has the true imagination; he never condescends to invent anything; he sets up no empty pretences. And he stoops to no littleness in his art—least of all to the miserable vanity of a catching phrase.

AARON SCHAFFER

[Maupassant's Technique and His Philosophy of Life][†]

*   *   *

One additional word as to Maupassant's technique as writer of novels and short-stories; his handful of plays, his travel-sketches and his essays in literary criticism call for no further comment, as they add but little to his literary stature. It must be admitted that there has been in recent years a definite attempt to whittle down this stature. Two objections are leveled against his fiction; the first is that his short-stories are too mechanical, written in accordance with a ritual worked out in the course of his career, including such elements as the surprise-ending, so dear to the heart of our own O.

---

† From "Introduction," Guy de Maupassant, *Pierre et Jean* (New York: Charles Scribner, 1936), pp. xxv–xxix. Professor Schaffer (1894–1957) was a distinguished literary critic, teaching at the University of Texas at Austin between 1920 and his death.

Henry, the recounting of incidents as remembered anecdotes by one person to a group seated in a drawing-room, a train-compartment, and so on; the second is that his fiction, both novel and short-story, is too unrelievedly gloomy, harsh, morbid, immoral. With reference to the first objection, we may admit occasional artificiality, chiefly in the stories written under high pressure; for Maupassant became at times a sort of fictional machine, grinding out weekly *feuilletons* for the newspapers and issuing volume upon volume each year to enable him to live in the style to which he had accustomed himself. He was, we are told, a very methodical craftsman, spending the hours from seven to twelve every morning at his desk and producing a daily average of six pages, and one need not hesitate to admit that his work was by no means uniformly good and that many of his stories are, indeed, of inferior quality. But the tales of the genuinely fecund years, from 1880 to 1885, are, for the most part, straightforward narratives which have the double merit of being both fascinatingly interesting, from the point of view of plot-construction, and magnificent sociological documents on those strata of French life of which Maupassant had first-hand knowledge. In fact, to the more mature reader, the actual plots of these stories, bitterly true or grimly amusing though they may be, fade into insignificance before the searing veracity of their social content. For stylistic vividness, for simplicity of diction which does not disdain, where necessary, to employ the humblest or the most plain-spoken expressions, for economy of both language and theme, Maupassant equaled, where he did not surpass, such of his predecessors in his own country as Mérimée and Flaubert, and he has rarely been matched since. The man who could write "Boule de Suif," "La Maison Tellier," "Toine" and "L'Infirme," whatever be one's opinion of the themes of these stories, the man whose pages fairly teem with life and with living human beings, would seem undeniably to belong, together with Boccaccio and La Fontaine, among the world's great *raconteurs*.

The second objection involves a consideration of Maupassant's philosophy of life. We may dispose at once, however, of the common notion that his writings are immoral, by making the inevitable distinction between immorality and pornography. Maupassant's serious work (and this includes everything he wrote with the exception of a few trifling and totally insignificant poems) is motivated by the frank attempt to look the facts of life squarely in the face; these facts and what he honestly believes to be hidden behind appearances, Maupassant sets down in a clean-cut and, above all, artistic manner. Questions of good and bad, of right and wrong, rarely concern him; he is interested in what is, not in what ought to be. He has no moral or sociological doctrines to preach; he is, insofar as it is possible for any writer to suppress his own individuality, objective and dispassionate. With this in mind, we may then freely admit that Maupassant's work is pervaded by a definite philosophy of life. This philosophy is thoroughly materialistic and pessimistic. Maupassant had no illusions about existence and human nature; like Zola and his other fellow-Naturalists, he considered all men fundamentally alike, beasts at bottom ruled by bestial instincts; unlike Zola, he saw no reason to suppose that men would ever cease to be beasts, so that there is in him not the slightest trace of the reformer. Zola's notion that man is essentially an animal but that he may hope to become an angel must have struck Maupassant as a ludicrous contradiction. As for death, Maupassant deemed it the end of everything: "le suprême Oubli," "la fin sans recommencement, le départ sans retour, l'adieu éternel à la terre, à la vie." Other tenets in his creed may be briefly stated: that individual and social conduct are universally governed by stupidity and self-interest and that no man can really know any one of his fellow men; that what we call Reality as well as all abstract concepts such as Beauty and Truth are but vain illusions (though, as a writer, he seems to have cherished such illusions); that Nature, lovely as she is in many of her manifestations, is indifferent, when not actually cruel; that God does not exist and that, consequently, there is no place for religions and theologies. In a word, as has been pointed out by the author of a brief study called *le Pessimisme de Maupassant*, the novelist arrived at a philosophy of absolute determinism which led ineluctably to nihilism, both moral and intellectual. It might be shown without difficulty that Maupassant does not apply this philosophy with anything like rigorous consistency to his own conduct and attitudes; and, as Anatole France has said of Leconte de Lisle, if he did not believe in his own reality, he probably believed firmly in that of his artistic creations. Be that as it may, and whatever may have been the physical factors underlying his outlook on life, Maupassant's work is basically sad, lacking in both faith and hope; nevertheless, one comes away from a perusal of his pages with the stimulating feeling that one has been face to face with a man of penetrating vision and powerful intellect.

What items, then, belong on the credit side of Maupassant's ledger? He was master of the art of story-telling, whether in short-story or in novel, to such an extent that writers ever since have been going to his work to learn the tricks of the trade. He peopled his stories with flesh-and-blood persons who represent a broad cross-section of the France of the eighteen-eighties. He sketched in his physical setting with an unfailing eye for significant detail and, in so doing, achieved many bits of effective description, especially of the landscapes of his native Normandy. He possessed a graphic, incisive style which makes many of his stories real gems of simple yet vigorous prose; his language, in the words of Anatole France, who could imagine no finer compliment to bestow upon it, is "du vrai français." His themes, though worked out in their application to individuals of all classes—peasant, soldier, government-clerk, merchant, noble, priest, tradesman and professional—concern themselves with universals and cover a wide range of human emotions. And, finally, he was not afraid to grapple with the problems that have exercised thinking men since the dawn of recorded history, and to offer his own answers to these problems. In the words of a student of French literature since 1875: "He kept a resolute eye on the truth as he saw it, and painted what he saw with a master's hand. It would be worse than idle to reproach him for not seeing more or seeing it differently. We should rather admire the patient courage with which he perfected his powers as an imaginative writer, and accomplished a mass of artistic work, which, in spite of its limitations, will always be a source of pleasure to the ordinary reader and of appreciative amazement to those who study the secrets of his craftsmanship." * * *

Modern Criticism

DAVID COWARD

[Maupassant's Cruelty and Compassion]†

* * *

Sometimes acceptance of the plenitude and beauty of nature blocked [Maupassant's] despair. He was also prepared to concede that the man of independent judgement who keeps an open mind and sees life for what it is may rise above the forces which control his destiny. The philosopher, the scientist, and the artist create truths which defeat time and rob nature of her secrets. Yet he found little to comfort him. Man is not merely the victim of nature but her instrument, for in our misery we make others miserable. Human beings are rapacious, egotistical, demanding, cruel, and unfeeling, and Maupassant saw in them neither good nor the potential for good. And if man is spiritually vile, he is also physically repulsive, a temporary agglomeration of meat and juices which will rot and leave nothing behind. We are born in the bloody entrails of our mothers and we end in a mess of putrefaction.

If men are disgusting and women nauseating, society can be nothing but sham, betrayal, and exploitation. Maupassant had an idealistic sense of justice, but he viewed politics with distaste. The introduction of universal male suffrage had given France the corrupt, pompous, and stupid leaders she so richly deserved: 'Once upon a time, a man who could do nothing became a photographer; nowadays he becomes a member of parliament.' The public was a mindless herd which did what it was told, and democracy promised nothing less than the rule of vulgarity. Popular education, for instance, had merely released popular stupidity and enabled even larger numbers of imbeciles to say half-baked things. He regarded

† From Guy de Maupassant, *A Day in the Country and Other Stories*, trans. and ed. David Coward (Oxford: Oxford University Press, 1990), pp. xvi–xix. © David Coward 1990. Reprinted by permission of Oxford University Press.

the Eiffel Tower as an appropriately tasteless monument to 'egali-tarian' cant and nationalistic humbug: patriotism, he said, was 'the egg of war'. Society was run by bombastic and incompetent shams who attempted the ludicrous task of directing the collective destiny and thwarted the men of talent and vision at every turn. Like Vol-taire's, Maupassant's preference was for enlightened despotism and a society of intelligent and civilized men which he called the 'intel-lectual aristocracy'.

Though he felt his disgust with the world deeply, it was a consid-ered attitude which was normally overlaid by simpler, warmer, more spontaneous reactions. He had a highly developed comic apprecia-tion of human conduct and laughed readily, if rather cruelly, at the flies struggling in the unavoidable spider's web. But he also showed fellow-feeling, and sometimes genuine compassion, for those who were the victims of fate, society, or other people: Mademoiselle Pearl or the *curé* of *The Christening* are presented delicately and with genuine sympathy and understanding. And though he put patriotism high on the list of the causes of war, he clearly admired the patriotism of Old Milon and the courage of Irma who accounted for more Prussians than the fine Captain Epivent. He might despise the common herd, but he was not without compassion for the weak, or for women, such as Clochette who sacrifices herself for love, or Rosalie Prudent who kills her babies because she is too poor to keep them. If Maupassant never alienated the large popular audi-ence which he professed to despise, it was because his savage irony reduced readers of all kinds to a sense of helplessness as they pon-der such intensely real glimpses of life's wretchedness.

Yet this gap between the bleak mood of his fatalism and the spon-taneous warmth of many of his reactions reveals a dualism in Mau-passant's character which he forced himself to explore. If most of nature's drives were clear to see, not all were exposed to the light of day, and those which remained hidden filled him not with disgust but with fear and horror. He had a natural fascination with the macabre, as instanced in his reaction to the Swinburne hand, but even in his earliest stories he shows a strange tension between our conscious desires and dark, mysterious, irresistible forces inside us. If the narrator of *Out on the River* overrides his baser self, 'Beau Signoles', who wants to fight his duel in *A Coward*, is prevented from doing so by a power stronger than his will. In *Le Horla* this inner force not only gains the upper hand but emerges as a superior being having a separate existence. The psychological motivation behind such stories (to which *The Little Roque Girl* may be added) belongs less to the field of observation and behaviour than to the explora-tion of those neuroses which nascent psychoanalytical science was beginning to explore. In this sense, *Le Horla* may be set alongside Stevenson's *The Strange Case of Dr Jekyll and Mr Hyde* (1886), its almost exact contemporary, which anticipated the notion of the 'split personality'. But the intensity with which Maupassant handles such ideas separates him from Stevenson and other writers of horror stories who merely seek to thrill with the sensational and the supernatural. Maupassant communicates a sense of danger made more horrible by the fact that the threat comes from the darker side of the character's own personality, so that he feels that in some obscure but increasingly real and terrifying way he is himself what he fears most. When a man ceases to know who he is and loses confidence in his own will, he becomes mad. Maupassant's finest stories do not merely thrill: they disturb. Other short-story writers might control their material better: few convey the sense of menace and horror more completely.

In a sense, Maupassant's general handling of human psychology derives less from observation of habit and gesture and eccentric motivation than from his feeling that all actions are Pavlovian reactions to natural stimuli. He does not explain why Madame Oreille in *The Umbrella* is careful with money; he simply shows us how she acts. But the fact that he usually deals with obsessive characters hoist on their own compulsions does not mean that his understanding of psychology is superficial. On the contrary, the fact that his characters are eternally at the mercy of circumstances or of their own temperaments is precisely what creates the powerful sense of inevitability which hovers over his tales. The form of the short story, with its sudden illuminations and ironic twists, tends to stress the inescapable predicament, and there is little doubt that Maupassant was attracted to it for this reason. His stories vary considerably in length; some are strongly plotted and others, such as *Strolling*, hardly plotted at all; and the mood runs from the brooding of the horror tales to private tragedy or broad farce, as in *Our Spot*, and satire, as in *A Coup d'État*, via comic dramas such as *Family Life* or *Riding Out* which, though they amuse, usually involve a death or a humiliation and regularly leave us feeling not so much entertained as distinctly ill at ease. For even when he is in playful mood, Maupassant seems to relish making us feel uncomfortable. He rarely points up moral lessons but walks away from the end of a story leaving us to decide whether Madame Loisel, in *The Necklace*, is the victim of fate or of her own pride. He treats honesty and courage with sympathy, but always shows honesty abused and courage defeated. Occasionally he allows a happy ending, but not before Simon or Rose, the farm-girl, have suffered long and hard. They are the fortunate ones, for his stories are so many chronicles of missed opportunities

and broken lives engineered by the inhumanity of man and the ruth-
less demands of nature, which, like some poisonous flower, fills
Maupassant's world with treacherous poetry.

His answer to the nastiness of life was thus to show it at work and
reveal its absurdity. But the remedy ran the risk of being no more
comforting than the ill it sought to cure. For Maupassant goes beyond
laughter into acid cynicism and even sadism. When he was a boy he
was known as a practical joker. Even at the height of his fame he was
fond of releasing mice in the presence of ladies, whom he would scare
by describing the swollen corpses of suicides regularly fished out of
the river by the police. In a sense, his aim as a story-teller was to put
spiders down the neck of his reader, to make us jump, to teach us a
lesson, to jolt us out of our complacency. Locked in the grim, bleak,
gloomy world of his pessimism, he sought to spread the truth as he
saw it: life is not just an empty farce but an extremely bad joke. Maupassant's perfect stories are the celebration of a fine contempt.

TREVOR A. LE V. HARRIS

[Maupassant's Journalism]†

* * *

* * * Maupassant the journalist clearly had an extensive influence
on Maupassant the writer of fiction, and it is the mistaken propen-
sity to disregard the relationship between these two aspects of his
work which has encouraged the misleading view of the author as an
instinctive, unreflective producer of entertaining but only semi-
serious fiction.

Among the important conclusions to emerge from a detailed consideration of the *Chroniques*, given the vast spread of subjects which
Maupassant tackles there, is that it is very difficult to persist in seeing him as this gifted but intellectually limited craftsman of letters.
Maupassant was in touch. Art, history, love, marriage, fashion, politics, religion: the list of themes running through his journalism
could be extended almost indefinitely. Even more striking, as the
preceding pages show, is the stability of tone in a body of material
spanning a period of some fifteen years. Nostalgia and elitism are
never out of view.

At the centre of the elitist consideration of contemporary
French political life, of what he sees as the intellectual and artistic
mediocrity which blights the country, is a profound anxiety about

† From *Maupassant in the Hall of Mirrors: Ironies of Repetition in the Work of Guy de Maupassant* (London: Macmillan, 1990), pp. 35–36. © Trevor A. Le V. Harris, 1990.

the function and status of the individual human being. It is not only that fewer great men seem to be coming forward, but also that even those intelligent individuals that do exist are reduced to insignificance by the standardising influence of the amorphous, anonymous mass around them. People, for Maupassant, especially men, are in danger of becoming reduced to a purely group function which robs them of their specificity, their personality. They are cast, as it were, in the same mould and therefore replaceable.

TALES OF FRENCH LIFE

ANN L. MURPHY

Narration, the Maternal, and the Trap in Maupassant's *Mademoiselle Perle*[†]

Recent Maupassant scholarship having a psychocritical orientation has examined the role of the maternal in Maupassant's writings. Naomi Schor's study "*Une Vie* or the Name of the Mother," first published in 1977, is seminal in this regard. For Schor, the importance of the mother and of the maternal in Maupassant's creative imagination is evidenced by the preponderance in his titles and place names of the syllable *or*, a repetition of a vocable in the first name of Maupassant's mother, Laure (49–50). Continuing the study of this "cult of the Mother" from the point of view of Maupassant's penchant for various onomastic practices is Philippe Bonnefis. This critic sees a reinforcement of the "lien matrilinéaire" (99) at the expense of the reproductive father in Maupassant's assigning to his characters first names as last names[1] and, when real last names are used, his using and re-using the same ones from work to work. Schor's commentary also informs that of Danielle Haase-Dubosc

---

[†] From *The French Review* 69.2 (1995): 207–16. Reprinted by permission of the American Association of Teachers of French.

1. The characters whose names exemplify this practice are for the most part illegitimate, though others, most notably M. Chantal, the protagonist of *Mademoiselle Perle*, are not. The participation of this character in the Maupassantian "cult of the mother" is further marked by the fact that he bears a last name which is a female first name. On the other side of the coin, moreover, Bonnefis finds that identification with the mother is equivalent to alignment with "la pulsion d'avoir-un-nom" (106), the mother being nothing other than "le désir insatiable d'un nom" (111). Outlined here is a paradox which is relevant for the purposes of this essay, and which lies in the contradiction between mother as both the desire for selfhood and that which prevents this desire from being absolutely fulfilled.

who, in her search for a feminine "subject of discourse" ("la mise en
discours du féminin-sujet") in Maupassant's fiction, finds a relevant
point of departure in Schor's feminist analysis of the character's
destruction of the mother's love letters. The maternal writer/receiver
of writing would be a feminine "*writing* subject" and the author of
a certain *Ur-text* the pulverization of which would be necessary in
order that the the the son's text be "authorized" (140).

Rather than the pulverization of the maternal, Antonia Fonyi
associates Maupassant's writing activity with its structuring, with
the effort to render legible, that is, to dominate the fear of being
swallowed up or otherwise entrapped by "la mère utérine." Thus, the
story of the trap ("la fable du piège" [74–75]) which Fonyi identifies
as the narrative structure underlying the plot configurations of all
of Maupassant's tales, and which traces efforts on the part of characters to leave permanently an enclosure which imprisons, repeats
from tale to tale unsuccessful attempts to leave the womb, to be born,
to be freed from the grasp of the maternal. Representing negative
maternal elements or forces within the structure of a fictive form,
particularly that of the well-defined short story, and allowing them
even to triumph there, may ensure that such a catastrophe is avoided
in real life, or, as Fonyi states, maintains the subject within the
realm of "pre-psychosis."

While one cannot deny what is found in Maupassant's texts, one
might believe that this type of approach to his work is guided, or at
least facilitated, by what is commonly known about the writer's life.
This is not an irrelevant issue for Naomi Schor who, while stressing from the start that "what is at stake" in aspects of her analysis
"exceeds the particular case of the mother-son relationship of Guy
de Maupassant the man" (50), later asks discretely (in a note): "Can
one do without biographical information when one uses a 'psychocritical approach'? This nagging question returns insistently after
its long repression" (171 n. 23). Haase-Dubosc refrains from overtly
alluding to any aspect of Maupassant's biography, while Fonyi identifies one biographical fact as another "symptom" having the same
psychological source as those found in his texts: "Si [Maupassant]
n'a jamais été amoureux, c'est à cause d'une fixation trop forte à un
stade primitif de l'évolution de la personnalité, fixation que révèle
la présence, déterminante dans son œuvre, de l'image d'une mère
qui n'est qu'un utérus" (95).

The biographical data is, indeed, well known and, although not
sufficient in itself, does support efforts to underscore the importance
of the maternal in Maupassant's writings. One need only consult his
biographers to learn that Laure de Maupassant was "as dominant a
mother as it is possible to imagine" (Steegmuller 30). Of particular
interest for us is the fact that not only was Maupassant's personal

behavior symptomatic of this dominance, as Fonyi implies, but also, and perhaps most interestingly, his choice of profession. In this respect biographers have well documented the extent to which Maupassant's mother directed her son toward a career of art and literature, how she, following her separation from the boy's father, "captured him for art" (Wallace 14). As other biographers would explain, Laure de Maupassant was "convinced that Guy was destined to literary greatness" because of his resemblance to her beloved late brother Alfred Le Poittevin, also childhood friend and idol of Gustave Flaubert, himself to become Maupassant's mentor (Wallace 13; Lerner 70–73). Thus, one aspect of Maupassant's destiny as writer was to realize the childhood ambitions of his mother for herself, for a third (Alfred), and perhaps even a fourth (Flaubert).[2] Finally, there are the words of Laure de Maupassant herself who would state late in life and long after her son's death that while "[her] own genius was latent and scattered . . . it was within [her] that Guy acquired the gift of writing" (Steegmuller 348).

Thus in life as well as in art the Maupassantian maternal is linked with both storytelling and entrapment. Not all tales are informed by the presence of all three elements; however, the hidden richness and complexity of at least one text, *Mademoiselle Perle* (1885), do rest upon this relationship. In fact, the connection between the maternal, storytelling, and entrapment is one of the things revealed in this text about revelation whose settings are two Epiphany celebrations and whose principal leitmotiv is discovery. *Mademoiselle Perle* is one of Maupassant's less-known or at least less-analyzed works probably because it does not, on the surface in any case, exhibit any of the more troubling psychological features of the purely fantastic tales or the more salient aspects of man's inhumanity to his fellow as developed in the works with a rural setting; nor, finally, does its ending have that surprise twist seemingly so essential to the bourgeois domestic tales in which category it may be placed. Yet in it mothers abound; storytelling and allusions to the act of storytelling play a central role; and, finally, the tale is that of the trap and entrapment.

2. Commentary contained in a review by Pierre-Marc de Biasi of *Correspondance Gustave Flaubert/Guy de Maupassant* (Paris: Éditions Flammarion, 1993) reinforces the picture of these relationships that Maupassant's biographers have pieced together. Among other things, as de Biasi uncovers, these letters reveal "le rôle stratégique joué par Laure Le Poittevin, la mère du petit Guy, sur la vocation littéraire de son fils; la ténacilé avec laquelle elle a fabriqué de toutes pièces la filiation intellectuelle entre Gustave Flaubert et le jeune apprenti écrivain; le rôle décisif d'un fantôme qui hante toute cette histoire, celui d'Alfred Le Poittevin, frère adoré de Laure, ardent amour adolescent de Gustave, disparu tout jeune, et dont Guy devient, pour tous deux, une sorte de *réincarnation*; comment le jeune Maupassant finit par figurer, pour Laure, l'enfant qu'elle aurait aimé avoir de son grand frère, et pour Gustave, celui qu'il aurait voulu avoir avec Alfred; la manière dont Flaubert, pour l'amour d'Alfred, entre, consciemment, dans la logique un peu délirante de cette identification . . ." (85).

Viewed from the narratological perspective adopted by Antonia Fonyi, the trap in Maupassant is a "modèle dynamique" in addition to being the "thème principal" and the "structure dominante de l'œuvre de Maupassant," described by Micheline Besnard-Coursodon in her important book on Maupassant (Fonyi 93).[3] Furthermore, as Fonyi explains, Maupassant's conception of the trap differs somewhat from the traditional understanding of this mechanism:

> La logique ordinaire, c'est-à-dire la pratique du piège, veut que celui-ci soit tendu à un certain point de l'espace et que la victime, partie d'un autre point, s'y trouve prise tout à coup. Chez Maupassant, en revanche, on est placé d'avance, on vit, semble-t-il, dans un piège, et c'est lors qu'on croit en sortir qu'il se ferme. (93)

So it is in the beginning of *Mademoiselle Perle*, where the narrator Gaston, annual guest at the Chantal family's Epiphany dinner, includes an allusion to a physical enclosure in his description of the type of existence led by the Chantals:

> [Les Chantal] vivent à Paris comme s'ils habitaient Grasse, Yvetot ou Pont-à-Mousson.
> Ils possèdent auprès de l'Observatoire, une maison dans un petit jardin. Ils sont chez eux, là, comme en province. De Paris, du vrai Paris, ils ne connaissent rien, ils ne soupçonnent rien; ils sont si loin, si loin! (52)

Mademoiselle Perle is the tale of the main character M. Chantal's unconscious efforts to liberate himself, however temporarily, from the closed and monotonous existence suggested by this beginning and developed during the first third of the story as narrated by Gaston. Indeed, the Chantals live virtually under the sign of repetition and the same. Occasionally they do manage to leave their neighborhood and venture across the Seine, but they observe certain rituals when they do so, always organizing major shopping expeditions in the same way, and going out to the theater only when "la pièce est recommandée par le journal que lit M. Chantal" (53). In addition, Epiphany is always celebrated according to the same traditions: Gaston is always the only guest; it is always M. Chantal who finds the porcelain doll in his piece of the *galette*; and he always chooses his wife as queen.

The Chantal family members themselves, as described in Gaston's narrative, all exhibit characteristics governed by monotony and sameness. The two Chantal daughters—whose own connection with "sameness" is reinforced by Gaston's reference to "deux gouttes

---

3. See Micheline Besnard-Coursodon, *Etude thématique et structurale de l'œuvre de Maupassant: le piège*, Paris: Editions A.-G. Nizet, 1973.

d'eau" (56)—are so well-brought up that they are almost invisible; life has not changed them, nothing affects them. We learn that the family's isolation and detachment from life and its experiences are the result of the attitude of M. Chantal himself whose love of peace and quiet, as Gaston describes, "a fortement contribué à momifier sa famille pour vivre à son gré dans une stagnante immobilité" (54). The terms "mummification" and "immobility," in addition to suggesting paralysis and confinement, designate a state suspended between life and death, and may be equated, if not with a physical prison, certainly with a moral or spiritual one.

It is perhaps the features associated with Mme Chantal which most suggestively, for our purposes, evoke the routine and repetition which represent the moral and spiritual prison enclosing the Chantal family. Moreover, as the following description reveals, "sameness" and "monotony" in the maternal are clearly linked to certain speech habits: "Mme Chantal, une grosse dame dont toutes les idées me font l'effet d'être carrées à la façon des pierres de taille, avait coutume d'émettre cette phrase comme conclusion à toute discussion politique: 'Tout cela est de la mauvaise graine pour plus tard'" (55). In a development which Gaston somewhat enigmatically marginalizes, insisting that "ça importe peu," he elaborates on what he might mean by "idées carrées," contrasting these with "idées rondes":

> Pourquoi me suis-je toujours imaginé que les ideés de Mme Chantal sont carrées? Je n'en sais rien; mais tout ce qu'elle dit prend cette forme dans mon esprit; un carré, un gros carré avec quatre angles symétriques. Il y a d'autres personnes dont les idées me semblent toujours rondes et roulantes comme des cerceaux. Dès qu'elles ont commencé une phrase sur quelque chose, ça roule, ça va, ça sort par dix, vingt, cinquante idées rondes, des grandes et des petites que je vois courir l'une derrière l'autre, jusqu'au bout de l'horizon. (55)

The squareness of Mme Chantal's ideas are related to their repetitive, limited, and limiting nature, in contrast to "round ideas" which are communicated in sentences which suggest dynamism, movement, and displacement, which, as one might also deduce, transport the listener away from the familiar and toward other, different perspectives. Indeed, through her discourse, Mme Chantal is the embodiment of intellectual and spiritual confinement.

On the other hand, everything associated with the tale's title character, Mademoiselle Perle, promises, if not always overtly, at least symbolically, difference and otherness. The particular Epiphany celebration during which this story takes place is marked by instances of rupture and discontinuity several of which have Perle at their center, a place the self-effacing woman who seemed only to want to blend into the background with the others obviously did not wish to occupy.[4] That evening, as Gaston recounts, it was he rather than M. Chantal who discovered the tiny porcelain doll in his piece of pastry and, instead of choosing Mme Chantal as queen as M. Chantal had always done, or one of their daughters as he also might have done had he not feared being trapped into marriage, Gaston offers the symbolic doll to Mlle Perle. Another break with routine linked to Mlle Perle is Gaston's contemplation of this character—"Alors *pour la première fois de ma vie,* je regardai Mlle Perle, et je me demandai ce qu'elle était" (56, emphasis added)—the result of which is his realization of her hidden grace, her suppressed beauty, and perhaps most significantly, her superiority to Mme Chantal: "Et brusquement, je la comparai à Mme Chantal! Certes! Mlle Perle était mieux, plus fine, plus noble, plus fière" (58).[5] Perle is otherness and difference hidden but valorized.

Mlle Perle, springboard for the unprecedented and embodiment of difference and otherness is, in the first instance and not surprisingly, the vehicle for M. Chantal's exit from the prison of his monotonous existence, a vehicle that on this level assumes the form of storytelling. Indeed, Mlle Perle is for M. Chantal first and foremost a *story* to be told as is evidenced by his excited reply to Gaston's unexpected question, "Dites donc, Monsieur Chantal, est-ce que Mlle Perle est votre parente?" (58): "'Comment, tu ne sais pas? tu ne connais pas l'histoire de Mlle Perle?' . . . 'Ton père ne te l'a jamais racontée?' . . . 'Tiens, tiens, que c'est drôle! ah! par exemple, que c'est drôle! Oh! mais, c'est toute une aventure!'" (58–59). Seizing the opportunity to recite Perle's story, or, in Fonyi terms, accepting the invitation to leave the enclosure of his existence, M. Chantal proceeds to narrate a detailed and impassioned account of how, during an Epiphany dinner more than forty years before, members of his own family, following a series of extraordinary events, discovered an abandoned infant in a sled attached to an unknown dog in the middle of a snow-covered plain below their home. This story of Perle is the story of her otherness, of her essential unrelatedness to the Chantals; it is also the story of M. Chantal's long-past attraction to, or preference for, difference and otherness: "On se remit à table

4. Perle's self-effacement is intrinsic to her "non-being," a component of what Mary Donaldson-Evans refers to as Maupassant's "reification of women" (45). Mademoiselle Perle's "state of non-being," as this critic reminds us, "is likened to that of an old armchair" (144, n. 5).
5. The extraordinary nature of the events which Gaston recounts in these passages is underscored by his use of the adjective "stupéfait" to describe his reaction to them: first, to his discovery of the porcelain doll in his mouth at dessert—"Aussi fus-je *stupéfait* en sentant dans une bouchée de brioche quelque chose de très dur qui faillit me casser une dent" (55, emphasis added)—and then, to what he was able to uncover from his contemplation of Mlle Perle—"J'étais *stupéfait* de mes observations" (58, emphasis added).

et le gâteau fut partagé. J'étais roi; et je pris pour reine Mlle Perle, comme vous, tout à l'heure" (65).

Yet given the connection that I suggested earlier between story-telling and the trap, it is not surprising that the narrative act in M. Chantal's case is only deceptively liberating. Telling Perle's story might be the means by which he escapes the prison of his everyday routine, but it is also the reason for which when he returns to it he will be more confined than before, as he will know he is trapped. Indeed, it is precisely at the moment of his liberation that M. Chantal is the most vulnerable to the hazards of the trap. For instead of returning immediately to the relative security of the present monotony, M. Chantal moves further out on the limb, as it were, contemplating half-privately, half-aloud additional recollections of his past. Thus, interrupting M. Chantal's exclamatory description of Perle's unique beauty at the age of eighteen is the inevitable question posed by Gaston: "Pourquoi ne s'est-elle pas mariée?" (66) to which M. Chantal responds, "Elle n'a pas voulu! Elle semblait triste à cette époque-là. C'est quand j'épousai ma cousine, la petite Charlotte, ma femme, avec qui j'étais fiancé depuis six ans" (66–67).

At this response, a considerable curiosity overcomes Gaston, accompanied by a flash of insight—an "epiphany" à la James Joyce—which he describes as follows:

> Je regardais M. Chantal et il me semblait que je pénétrais dans son esprit, que je pénétrais tout à coup dans un de ces humbles et cruels drames des cœurs honnêtes, des cœurs droits, des cœurs sans reproches, dans un de ces cœurs inavoués, inexplorés, que personne n'a connu, pas même ceux qui en sont les muettes et résignées victimes. (67)

Gaston's question is the beginning of the "accident" which will forever prevent M. Chantal from returning to his former state of calm routine and self-ignorance. For Gaston formulates his "insight" with the following sentences to each of which M. Chantal reacts with expressions of horror and disbelief: "C'est vous qui auriez dû l'épouser, monsieur Chantal? . . . Parce que vous l'aimiez plus que votre cousine . . . Parbleu, ça se voit . . . et c'est même à cause d'elle que vous avez tardé si longtemps à épouser votre cousine qui vous attendait depuis six ans" (67).

In Maupassant's text, a special image is associated with M. Chantal's reaction to these revelations. Filled with emotion upon encountering a long-repressed or long-ignored truth about himself, about his inner life, M. Chantal sobs uncontrollably into what is referred to as "le linge à craie," a cloth used to erase the points on a chalkboard during games of pool, and which, according to Gaston, was filled with the chalk dust of at least the preceeding two or three years. The action of hiding his face and eyes under white dust is clearly an echo of the snow that obscured the location of the infant Claire/Perle and of the layers of the *galette* which enclose the porcelain doll.[6] This action might be read as the efforts on M. Chantal's part to deny what Gaston has revealed to him, to escape the pain associated with an unrecognized, impossible, and unfulfilled love—in other words, to reject the revelation and to return to his prior state of blindness—these efforts have the opposite effect as well. The more M. Chantal rubs his eyes with the chalk dust-filled cloth in an attempt to keep hidden what he has learned about himself, the more what he wishes to keep "inside" is exposed and flows to the outside—in the form of tearing, spitting, coughing, sneezing, throat-clearing, etc.—forcing him, along with Gaston and the reader, to acknowledge the truth (67).

The double-edged complexity of the image created here represents effectively a dialectic whose terms are liberation/(new) prison. What has freed also imprisons: the knowledge M. Chantal has acquired about himself, about his life, while momentarily liberating him from the self-ignorance that threatened to immobilize him completely, also burdens him with the knowledge of his true unhappiness which, for the sake of decorum and familial harmony, he will be obliged to keep forever to himself.[7] His new prison will indeed be worse than his old one of which he was hardly aware.

Furthermore and profoundly significant, not only is narrative the mechanism of this second entrapment, it is also responsible for the very creation of the trap, and in this, is even more pointedly related to the maternal: contained in the embedded narrative itself, that is, in M. Chantal's account, is his allusion to an earlier telling of Perle's story, this time by his mother, "une femme d'ordre et de hiérarchie."[8] Reference to this original tale of origins appears when M. Chantal alludes to his mother's handling of Claire's presence in the family: while agreeing to treat the girl "comme ses propres fils," she insisted upon maintaining "la distance qui [les] séparait" (65). The mother, then, attempted to structure around Claire a rather paradoxical system whereby the "propre" and the same would be balanced with/against the distant and the different. Most notably, moreover, telling

6. It is in large part upon the oppositions inside/outside and hidden/revealed that Krystyna Falicka bases a structuralist reading of this tale.
7. M. Chantal's intention not to reveal his discovery to the rest of his family is repeated and underscored by the explanation he and Gaston invent for his red and watering eyes, a speck of dust which no one, of course, can find: "chacun voulut chercher le grain de poussière qu'on ne trouva point . . ." (68).
8. The fact that narration, and in particular the narration of Perle's story, is, in this text, a maternal activity, and decidedly not a paternal one, is reinforced by the fact that Gaston's reply to M. Chantal's earlier question, "Ton père ne tu l'a jamais racontée?" is negative. The father's role is, in fact, diminished: although he was a co-discoverer of the baby Claire, M. Chantal's own father is described as "un peu impotent (il traînait une jambe depuis qu'il se l'était cassée en tombant de cheval)" (61).

Claire "her story" is a means for the mother of reinforcing this "order and hierarchy": "Aussi, dès que l'enfant put comprendre, elle *lui fit connaître son histoire* et fit pénétrer tout doucement, même tendrement dans l'esprit de la petite, qu'elle était pour les Chantal une fille adoptive, recueillie, mais en somme une étrangère" (65; emphasis added).

The result of telling Claire's story to her makes explicit the paradox upon which the maternal system is based. Knowing instinctively how to adapt to the situation as defined by the mother, that is, knowing how to be a Chantal daughter without really being one, earns for Claire first the appellation "ma fille" and then the name "Perle":

> Ma mère elle-même fut tellement émue par la reconnaissance passionnée et le dévouement un peu craintif de cette mignonne et tendre créature, qu'elle se mit à l'appeler: "Ma fille." Parfois, quand la petite avait fait quelque chose de bon, de délicat, ma mère relevait ses lunettes sur son front, ce qui indiquait toujours une émotion chez elle et elle répétait: "Mais c'est une perle, une vraie perle, cette enfant!"—ce nom en resta à la petite Claire qui devint et demeura pour nous Mlle Perle. (65–66)

In relating to Claire her story, the mother placed emphasis on the distance/difference term of the opposition defining the child's situation; however, Claire's successful conforming to this earned for her names that are linked to the proper/same term. How this functions in the possessive nomination "ma fille" is evident. However, the more complicated economy of "pearlness" perhaps makes of it a more apt homologue to Perle's position with respect to the Chantal family.

In French as in English, the primary purpose of employing the expression "a pearl" to characterize an individual is, of course, to underscore the person's superlatively positive qualities, attitudes, and behavior, a usage certainly exploited by M. Chantal's mother. For my purposes, however, the more literal referent of the term is richer in significance. The word "pearl" designates the hard, spherical object which is produced when the substance secreted by an oyster (the nacre or more commonly, the "mother-of-pearl") accumulates around a foreign body which has been introduced into it. The pearl, then, both is and is not part of the oyster; the oyster produces it, but only via a stimulus whose own origins are elsewhere and whose presence is finally concealed by the process itself. Changing Claire's name to Perle merely repeats the synonymity of two processes: the "naturalization" of an unknown "enfant naturel" indeed parallels the production of a pearl.

It is this obscuring of Perle's otherness, of her original difference—the ultimate consequence of the mother's narration of Perle's story—that connects the maternal narrative activity with the creation

of a prison. The story of Mademoiselle Perle—which is also that of
M. Chantal—is the story of imprisonment and entrapment in that
it recounts the tragedy of the homogenization of existence, wasted
potential, and the elimination of choice, all of which are the direct
results of the repression of difference as embodied by Perle, first
by M. Chantal's mother and then by the entire Chantal family.
Repression of difference, repression of desire: the young M. Chantal's sublimation of his love for Perle and his eventual marriage to
his first cousin[9] are so many symptoms of his having succumbed
to the tyrany of the same, and merely echo the transformation of
"Claire" into "Perle," a transformation which, indeed, as I have
shown, has its source in maternal storytelling.

It is thus from an absolute repression of desire that M. Chantal
frees himself in telling Perle's story, but which he must also immediately reconstruct; for him, as for all of Maupassant's characters,
there can be no outside. Yet how does storytelling connect with liberation, on the one hand, and entrapment, on the other, in the case
of such a prolific writer as Maupassant? The writing of each new
story might certainly represent for him liberating self-expression and
creative renewal since no two of his tales present the same characters nor repeat the same events. Yet on another level, if, as Fonyi's
title reads, "un écrivain raconte toujours la même histoire," narration as creation would appear to be illusory as well. The narrative
act for Maupassant, then, is both creation and repetition, each effort
to escape repetition succeeding on the one hand, but serving to reinforce it on the other, further ensnaring the writer in the vicious
circle of his own creative energies.

Finally, in *Mademoiselle Perle* it is possible to find a clue as to the
connection between the maternal and Maupassant's imprisoning
compulsion to release these creative energies. Simultaneous with the
discovery of the baby Claire is the uncovering of gold in her swaddling; as M. Chantal recalls: "Et on trouva dans ses langes dix mille
francs en or, oui, dix mille francs! que papa plaça pour lui faire une
dot" (64). This gold being the only thing that accompanies Claire
from the outside, it represents not only her essential otherness with
respect to the Chantals, but also her essential selfhood with respect
to her original being, neither of which, since she never married, are
exchanged, exploited, or developed. Her dowry in gold accumulates,
accrues in value—M. Chantal eventually refers to Perle's "trente
mille francs de dot" (66); however, never spent, it is never enjoyed,

9. Indeed, while marriage between first cousins was common practice during the nineteenth century, the fact that M. Chantal grew up under the same roof with his cousin
underscores the stultifying continuity which characterizes this man's existence, there
being essentially no passage from childhood to adulthood.

in the same way that her selfhood precisely as otherness is never permitted to be expressed.

Indeed, destiny for Maupassant consisted of the impossibility, the sheer inconceivability of "marrying another woman," of detaching himself from maternal dependence and aspirations: the maternal—ever-present and ever-unchanging—accumulates, grows heavy, anchors. Perhaps directing, in part, what Mary Donaldson-Evans has identified as a "nefarious feminine principle" (60), embodied by the figure of the *femme fatale* as well as by the supernatural constructs of Maupassant's later works, and responsible for the "dispossession" (139 and *passim*) of the Maupassantian male, is already a "negative maternal principle," an original *mère fatale*. One does not write oneself out of the womb when writing *is* the womb; like M. Chantal, Maupassant can only reveal the trap.

WORKS CITED

Bonnefis, Philippe. *Comme Maupassant*. Lille: PU de Lille, 1981.

De Baisi, Pierre-Marc. Rev. of *Correspondance Gustave Flaubert/ Guy de Maupassant*. Ed. Yvan Leclerc. *Magazine Littéraire* (Jan. 1994): 85–87.

Donaldson-Evans, Mary. *Woman's Revenge: The Chronology of Dispossession in Maupassant's Fiction*. Lexington, KY: French Forum Publishers, 1986.

Falicka, Krystyna. "Lecture sémiologique d'un texte naturaliste: structures spatio-temporelles dans *Mademoiselle Perle* de Maupassant." *Approches méthodologiques de la recherche littéraire*. Ed. Alexander Ablamowicz. Katowice: Universytet Slaski, 1985. 38–46.

Fonyi, Antonia. "Un Ecrivain raconte toujours la même histoire." *Fiction, narratologie, texte, genre*. Ed. Jean Bessière. New York: Peter Lang, 1989. 89–95.

Haase-Dubosc, Danielle. "La Mise en discours du féminin-sujet." *Maupassant: miroir de la nouvelle*. Eds. Jacques Lecarme et Bruno Vercier. Paris: PU de Vincennes, 1988. 125–44.

Lerner, Michael G. *Maupassant*. London: George Allen and Unwin, Ltd., 1975.

Maupassant, Guy de. *Mademoiselle Perle*. *Vingt-et-un contes*. Eds. Leon P. Irvin and Donald L. King. 3rd ed. New York: Harper & Row, 1965. 52–70.

Schor, Naomi. *Breaking the Chain: Women, Theory, and French Realist Fiction*. New York: Columbia UP, 1985.

Steegmuller, Francis. *Maupassant: A Lion in the Path*. Freeport, NY: Books for Libraries Press, 1972.

Wallace, A. H. *Guy de Maupassant*. New York: Twayne Publishers, 1973.

ANGELA S. MOGER

Narrative Structure in Maupassant:
Frames of Desire[†]

* * *

But there are other effects and economies made possible by the framing of the narrative. Another story may illuminate even further the reasons for Maupassant's frequent reliance on this narrative form. "En voyage," or, rather, the drama at its center recounted by the doctor, is extremely melodramatic and so charged with romantic clichés as to be a caricature. Because of the architecture of the whole, however, its credibility is not seriously questioned. Again it is fruitful to ask how we would judge the story of these two romantically stereotypical creatures—one a beautiful Russian noblewoman stricken with a mortal illness (respiratory, of course) and the other a dashing outlaw—if we were to come up on the story without the ingenious prologue and epilogue affixed to the love story by the doctor's "sponsor." To start with the obvious, the reader of the story of the Countess Marie Baranow and her mysterious admirer would find it quite improbable as it stands: they love each other from afar; she has extracted, in their only meeting, a promise that he will never attempt to speak to her again. That meeting takes place in her private compartment on a train bringing her from Russia to southern France.[1] The door of the compartment is suddenly flung open in the middle of the night, and the countess finds herself confronted by a young man in evening dress, bleeding profusely from a wound in the hand. He begs her to conceal him until they have crossed the border. "Je suis un homme perdu, un homme mort, si vous ne m'aidez à passer la frontière . . . Si vous ne me secourez

---

[†] From *PMLA* 100 (1985): 315–27. Reprinted by permission of the copyright owner, the Modern Language Association of America. With the exception of the one below, notes have been omitted.

1. According to Jean Pierrot, there is a great deal of moving about in public conveyances throughout Maupassant's work, and these "displacements" are significant. One comment seems particularly pertinent to the story at hand:

> Mais surtout, le mouvement, le déplacement paraissent entretenir, dans cette oeuvre, des rapports particulièrement étroits avec la femme et avec la sexualité. Et d'abord parce que, sortant l'individu de son environment habituel, ils offrent l'occasion par excellence de la rencontre amoureuse. On ne cesserait pas d'énumérer les textes de Maupassant dans lesquels une intrigue amoureuse se noue, ou s'esquisse, à la faveur d'un voyage ou d'un déplacement.

> But especially, moving about, traveling appear to be intimately related in this work to woman and sexuality. And first off because, removing the individual from his or her usual environment, they furnish the perfect opportunity for the amorous encounter. It would be difficult to enumerate all the texts of Maupassant in which an amorous intrigue is launched or developed by means of a trip or some other geographical displacement. (186)

point, je suis perdu. Et cependant, Madame, je n'ai ni tué, ni volé, ni rien fait de contraire à l'honneur. Cela je vous le jure. Je ne puis vous en dire davantage" 'I am a lost man, a dead man, if you do not help me cross the border. . . . If you don't help me I am lost. And yet I have neither killed anyone, nor robbed, nor done anything contrary to honor. This I swear to you. I cannot tell you more' (639).

The countess does indeed help him cross the border, passing him off as her servant, and they part—never, indeed, to speak again. Over the next several years, she dies slowly; he stands under her window in the street, hoping to catch a glimpse of her, and follows her when she occasionally goes out. Finally, he takes to visiting the doctor to have news of her condition. On the day she dies, the doctor grants him an audience with the corpse, whose hand he kisses violently before he disappears forever.

Who was this man? Why was he wounded and why was it a matter of life and death to get out of Russia? What was the state of Marie Baranow's marriage? Why did her husband send her away to die? What were her feelings for the singular man whom she liked to see beneath her window but whom she would not allow to speak to her in spite of their mutual desolation? Without the formal cadre affixed to the story, which gives it at least the superficial appearance of fullness and completion, one would need more details and explanations to accept that things could have happened this way; and one would simply want more information about the principals. The author has been relieved of any obligation to develop character gradually and fully or to provide the detailed context of the lives of his protagonists. Because we meet the countess as a figure in another character's story, we accept the selection and compression of the portrait. We accept that the doctor's aim is to impart a certain story and not to describe in detail a certain woman. We would expect something different if our narrator had introduced her. The trompe l'oeil has worked, for in fact he has! By wielding his narrative device to alter our expectations, the author induces our credulity with regard to characterization, the passage of time, the outcome of events. We forget to be suspicious of the partial information or the caricatures because what we read is not the "main story"; it is only a sort of digression or intermission. It acts on us, nonetheless, with all the power of a main story. There is a double standard here—the framed narrative has only limited accountability and the privilege of totally exploiting the resources of (unframed) narrative.

In point of fact, however, the paucity of information promotes an understanding that the dual level of narration is itself more central as a subject matter than the characters presumably under scrutiny. In the absence of any detailed explanation concerning them, our consciousness as readers shifts to the potential significance of having a character tell the story; indeed, this delegation of the telling to a secondary narrator may afford us a first insight into the real focus of the story. That is, we experience the refraction as gratuitous; we are vaguely aware that the narrator persona might more naturally have been the conventional invisible narrator, encountered only in his voice in the first line of the story. The awareness is distracting, and the distraction is then enhanced by the curious attitude of this arbitrary figure toward what he recounts.

At the end of "En voyage," as at the conclusion of "La rempailleuse," there is an equivocal comment on the whole by the internal narrator himself, followed again by a reaction from a female listener who is extremely moved. And there is the same short circuit in communication between the teller and the listener that obtained in the other story. The narrator persona, in contributing this story, has merely been observing the established theme set out in the beginning of the whole tale: passionate crimes and adventures befalling travelers in the course of their journeys. Thus the doctor observes only, "Voilà, certes, la plus singulière aventure de chemin de fer que je connaisse. Il faut dire aussi que les hommes sont des drôles de toqués" 'There you have, certainly, the strangest railroad adventure I know of. It must also be said that men are queer lunatics' (643). His detachment seems rather exaggerated, considering the tragic death and separation he has recounted. Is he teasing his listeners or is he genuinely unmoved by the situation he has described and presumably witnessed? Similarly, when the doctor-narrator in "La rempailleuse" says, "Voilà le seul amour profond que j'aie rencontré dans ma vie," the reader is uncertain whether this is a sincere, carefully deliberated opinion or a bitterly ironic barb directed at all those around him who would think they alone had experienced "l'amour profond." As we have seen, the marquise ignores his comment and makes of the story what she chooses. Although it is less clear what the woman at the end of "En voyage" has concluded, the description of her reaction is similarly calculated to draw the reader into speculation and involvement: "Une femme murmura à mi-voix: 'Ces deux êtres-là ont été moins fous que vous ne croyez. . . . Ils étaient . . . ils étaient. . . .' Mais elle ne pouvait plus parler, tant elle pleurait. Comme on changea de conversation pour la calmer, on ne sut pas ce qu'elle voulait dire" 'A woman murmured softly: "Those two people were less crazy than you think. . . . They were . . . they were. . . ." But she was crying so hard that she could no longer speak. As the subject was changed to calm her, no one ever knew what she meant' (643). By now the reader's attention has turned from the lovers and their plight to wondering what, indeed, "elle voulait dire" and what would have been the end of her sentence, had she voiced it. More important, why is the story orchestrated so as to end with this ambiguity?

Does the author just want to break the spell harshly, to bring us back to reality with a jolt, or does he want the reader to reflect, rather, on the relationship between the listener and the story? By leaving us to finish her sentence, he draws us into identifying with the listener. We cannot remain in the passive role of mere audience to his story—we are compelled to review the story in order to guess what she was on the verge of saying. We do not know what the relation between the containing narrative and the one contained is supposed to be.

When, on rereading the story, we perceive that the structure of the relationship between the two lovers is analogous to the structure of the story, we begin to sense that the relationship between the two stories, not a specific aspect of plot, is meant to be the focus of our attention. A particular passage of "En voyage" is worth scrutinizing for its metaphoric value; the doctor is describing the distance that the two lovers reverently preserved:

> Alors, j'assistai à une chose surprenante et douloureuse, à l'amour muet de ces deux êtres qui ne se connaissaient point.
>
> Il l'aimait, lui, avec le dévouement d'une bête sauvée, reconnaissante et dévouée à la mort. Il venait chaque jour me dire: "Comment va-t-elle?" comprenant que je l'avais deviné. Et il pleurait affreusement quand il l'avait vue passer plus faible et plus pâle chaque jour.
>
> Elle me disait:
>
> "Je ne lui ai parlé qu'une fois à ce singulier homme, et il me semble que je le connais depuis vingt ans."
>
> Et quand ils se rencontraient, elle lui rendait son salut avec un sourire grave et charmant. Je la sentais heureuse, elle si abandonnée et qui se savait perdue, je la sentais heureuse d'être aimée ainsi, avec ce respect et cette constance, avec cette poésie exagérée, avec ce dévouement prêt à tout. Et pourtant, fidèle à son obstination d'exaltée, elle refusait désespérément de le recevoir, de connaître son nom, de lui parler. Elle disait: "Non, non, cela me gâterait cette étrange amitié. Il faut que nous demeurions étrangers l'un à l'autre."
>
> Quant à lui, il était certes également une sorte de Don Quichotte, car il ne fit rien pour se rapprocher d'elle. Il voulait tenir jusqu'au bout l'absurde promesse de ne lui jamais parler qu'il avait faite dans le wagon.

> Then I witnessed a sad and surprising thing, the mute love of these two beings who were not acquainted with each other.
>
> He loved her with the devotion of a rescued animal, grateful and devoted to the death. He came every day to ask me, "How is she?" understanding that I had guessed his feelings. And he wept frightfully when he had seen her going by, weaker and paler every day.

> She said to me:
>
> "I have only spoken once to that singular man, and yet it seems as if I have known him for twenty years."
>
> And when they met she returned his bow with a serious and charming smile. I felt that she was happy, that although she was given up and knew herself lost she was happy to be loved in this manner, with this respect and constancy, with this exaggerated poetry, with this devotion, ready for anything.
>
> Nevertheless, faithful to her fanatical obstinacy, she absolutely refused to receive him, to learn his name, to speak to him. She said: "No, no, that would spoil this strange friendship for me. We must remain strangers to each other."
>
> As for him, he was certainly a kind of Don Quixote too, for he did nothing to get closer to her. He wanted to keep to the end the absurd promise never to speak to her that he had made in the car.						(642)

The particular aspects of the "love affair" that the doctor underlines in his summary of the relationship bear examination.

This love—as the doctor says in the first paragraph above—is "l'amour muet" between persons "qui ne se connaissaient point." They are separated as if by an invisible barrier, but they are also together. In the second and third paragraphs, each lover speaks of the other to the doctor, who plays the classic role of confidant in this drama. In the following paragraph the doctor assures his audience that the countess enjoyed being loved in this fashion, "avec cette poésie exagérée," and did not want any direct contact with the man who loved her so desperately: "'Non, non, cela me gâterait cette étrange amitlé. Il faut que nous demeurions étrangers l'un à l'autre.'" "Gâter" and "il faut" amount to strong language; indeed, the expression of the thought is so emphatic that it arrests our attention on the principle being articulated. What is that principle? Distance—removal from the desired object—is proposed as a value. And the particular form of distance that is most important is silence. The countess is willing to look at her lover and even to smile at him in the street, but she will have nothing of him that words might convey. The text insists on this verbal distance from the outset. In the space of three pages there are so many explicit references to the absence of verbal communication between the lovers that the absence becomes a presence, an object of scrutiny to the readerly consciousness. In their first meeting, we are not surprised, given the circumstances, that "Elle ne répondit rien" or that, a few sentences later, "Elle ne disait toujours rien" (639). Nor are we particularly distracted, on the same page, by the outlaw's returning her purse to her "sans ajouter un mot" 'without adding a word' (639) and by her remaining "immobile et muette" (640) in the face of apparent danger. But, something else begins to happen, although we may not perceive it consciously at that precise juncture; the silence begins to be loud when, on the next page, we find the somewhat redundant cluster of the following scene: "'Je ne mets qu'une condition à ce que je fais: c'est que vous ne me parlerez jamais, que vous ne me direz pas un mot, ni pour me remercier, ni pour quoi que ce soit.' L'inconnu s'inclina sans prononcer une parole" "'I make only one condition to what I am doing: that is that you never speak to me, that you shall not say a word to me, either to thank me or for anything whatsoever.' The stranger bowed without uttering a word' (640). A few sentences later, there is the (superfluous?) additional detail: "Pendant toute la nuit ils restèrent en tête-à-tête, muets tous deux" 'During the night they sat opposite each other, both mute' (641).

Part 2 of the story opens, moreover, with the sentence "Le docteur se tut une seconde, puis reprit" 'The doctor fell silent for a second, then began again' (641). Finally, when the countess confides to the doctor that this man whom she does not know follows her everywhere—"Je le rencontre chaque fois que je sors; il me regarde d'une étrange façon, mais il ne m'a jamais parlé 'I meet him every time I go out. He looks at me in a strange way, but he has never spoken to me' (641)—the reader realizes what trouble she and the story have taken to make that statement possible. It has become clear that the absence of speech to which the countess refers is a positive value before the reader ever reaches Marie Baranow's ultimate revelation: "Non, non, cela me gâterait cette étrange amitié. Il faut que nous demeurions etrangers l'un à l'autre." The verbal removal preserves an apparently precious distance. The love duet has an intermediary, and we sense that this refraction somehow makes the duet more satisfying.

Should we regard this curious love affair as a kind of cryptogram, decipherable for an understanding of the story we are reading? "En voyage" presents the frame and the framed, a pair, joined together but also separated "as if by an invisible barrier." The two interact only because of a third party, the reader, who receives the statements of both and performs an interpretive act of combination, conferring meaningful integration on the disparate elements. Furthermore, the very gratuitousness of the structure of the story suggests that something important is invested in the distance created by the frame. What would be "spoiled" by direct contact with the main story? What is preserved by the story's inaccessibility?

Like "La rempailleuse," "En voyage" contains another story, a self-sufficient unit that, in its proportions, dominates the story in which it has been inserted. Since the tale imparted by the doctor could easily be made complete in itself, why has the author not given it to us directly? Why is the reader forced to perceive it only at some distance, through the refractions of another tale? What has been

accomplished by using the travelers-telling-each-other-stories topos
to motivate the story of the countess and her admirer? Maupassant
apparently saw some advantage in casting their situation as a tab-
leau mounted in a frame and therefore not immediately available to
the beholder. (For the purposes of my argument, I provisionally
invoke the spatial model.) Indeed the onlooker is conditioned to a
particular interpretation by the angle of vision he or she is forced to
adopt. The words of the countess come back: "cela me gâterait. . . ."
She obviously wants this relationship to remain unrealized, to preserve
the inaccessible, untouchable quality of the ideal. She wants none of
the dynamism of process here—they are not going "to love"—she
wants, instead, the stasis of the object: there is to be the substance,
"their love," an entity, not an activity. Their love is essentially a story
she tells: it seems to come into being as a result of the presence of the
audience, the doctor. Where the Countess Baranow is concerned, the
fixity inherent in definition as story not only gives permanency to their
love: narrative removal permits the preservation of the ideal. In the
story of their love, nothing has been metamorphosed into something
(for nothing indeed has ever transpired between them after their first,
brief meeting); the love is frozen at the moment of virtuality, which
preserves it uncompromised and ensures its immortality. It seems
that desire thrives on distance; the object of desire does not suffer
the degradation provoked by familiarity, since its mundanity and its
flaws are not perceptible from afar. Marie Baranow's love, then, is
given permanency at the cost of dynamism; it is converted into a fictional object of art to ensure its duration and "integrity." To be con-
stituted as story, however, it must have an addressee who, in receiving
its details, confirms and perpetuates it as a love story. And this is the
doctor. The way he characterizes the relationship between Marie
Baranow and her admirer suggests the relationship's impulse to story
status. When the doctor says things like "Je la sentais heureuse d'être
aimée ainsi, . . . avec cette poésie exagérée" and "il était certes égale-
ment une sorte de Don Quichotte," his self-consciously literary diction invites us to make an analogy between their love and our story.
If it seems that the story of a love is more satisfying than the love
itself, we can infer that the story of a particular story might have
some advantages not enjoyed by the original, unframed narrative.
  We cannot know much more of the story we are eager to possess
than the young man can know of the woman whom he yearns to possess. As we have seen, there are many details missing—we would
like to have had direct contact with the doctor instead of receiving
his remarks through the narrator. But the story would seem less
exciting, less irritating, and, therefore, less desirable if it were not
mounted, like a jewel, in its setting. The *enchâssement* of the lovers'
story has, perhaps, enhanced their sparkle for us, creating a kind of

halo of otherworldliness about them, projecting them as platonized lovers, as archetypes, rather than as flesh-and-blood creatures with limitations. (We might have learned from interrogating the doctor that she coughed and spat constantly and that her lover had fled Russia in fear of a jealous husband's threats.)

We contemplate the story of the lovers from a point of removal that guarantees their perfection but, more important, allows blanks in their story, for (the reader's) pleasure proceeds from what is suppressed rather than from what is given. Let us explore in what sense this is true. The frame story lends the symmetry and weight that, through a kind of trompe l'oeil, make the central story seem properly proportioned, formally complete. In fact, a story about Marie Baranow and the outlaw, told head-on (third-person narration), would demand greater detail and a more rounded treatment than we expect in a vignette of the sort tossed out by the doctor to his fellow travelers. But there is something quite provocative in the very partiality of their story; it is sustained at the delicious moment of incipience, when all pleasure lies ahead and much is yet to be known. There is intense excitement as a storyteller begins a tale, giving a few inviting details about whom and what will be described; and there is keen disappointment as we realize from the musical overvoice or from the paucity of pages beneath our thumbs that a compelling movie or novel is coming to a close. If we can know the whole story, eliminate all the mysteries present at the outset, we replace a presence with an absence; gratification of a desire, after all, cancels the desire. There is, finally, something more satisfying than satisfaction. Desire is made up of two conflicting impulses: the longing to overcome the distance between oneself and the object of desire, to "coincide," so to speak, with that object, and the impossibility of closing that gap if desire is to survive. In order to preserve her love the countess takes care to remain on its threshold. The story embedded in "En voyage" is in a similar state of virtuality—a condition, indeed, made possible by its being a story within a story. The presence of the frame legitimizes the internal narrative; it is that outer casing which makes the encased material appear to conform to the aesthetic and logical demands of the mechanism known as story. Thus the principal narrative can remain in the sketchy state that most stimulates a reader's fantasies, its desirability perpetuated by its inaccessibility. We have the illusion of possession without the deprivation engendered by possession. We enjoy simultaneous satisfaction of our desire for closure and for ever-renewed mystery.

As we see in "En voyage," a framed story can simulate a purposeful progression while actually remaining permanently in a provocative phase of anticipation and speculation. One wonders, indeed, if the unfinished sentence of the lady at the end of "En voyage" is to be read as an emblem of the principle incarnate in the story: the promise of something is more beautiful than the fulfillment, the suggestion more seductive than the definition. Her comment certainly draws us in all over again, sending us right back to dream anew over the story she has just heard.

In other words, the framed story can "have the cake and eat it"— and in more ways than one. For the frame both gives immediate structural support to the internal narrative and allows the author preemptively to undercut that story. He not only gets to tell a rankly sentimental tale, he blocks our opportunity to find it so by making fun of it himself. In the frame his narrator figure deflates its pathos, and the listener figure is often mocked for having taken it seriously or misunderstood it. The author, then, can present these two mutually exclusive points of view because the reader is propelled into acting as mediator. Just as the countess, by using the doctor as intermediary, can have her love and yet not have to have it, the author can have it both ways because a link, a dialogue, is created between the members of this narrative pair by the reader, whose very act of reading holds the two together.

What has been said, however, would not account for one particular problem: the doctor-narrator is consistently undermined by the syntax of the narrative, if only by a few words of rejection (or simply by rejection of the narrator's own reaction to the story he tells, as in "En voyage") or by misinterpretation of his story. This recurrent pattern explicitly dramatizes the essential dilemma of the storyteller: he has no control over what is heard. Although he creates the message, he cannot control how it is read. The friction between the narrator and his audience establishes as a basic proposition that stories are not understood; they are transformed by their addressees, who respond to different texts from the ones that were dispatched. If Maupassant does indeed subscribe to this equivocal view of the efficacy of storytelling, a message his stories might work at transmitting, in their very articulation, is that stories do not signify of themselves and are "created" as much by their audience as by their originator. But the reader senses more in this unwillingness to suppress the other point of view (whether "romantic" reading or simply uncomprehending rejection), this dramatization of the story's failure to transmit any message other than that failure. At the level of the text is the implicit suggestion that stories may not be understood, because someone will insist on approaching them from the standpoint of a truth-lie polarity when it is the fact of electing that polarity as an approach to fiction that is an issue under discussion. Thus, when the narratees in these stories evaluate what they have heard in terms of whether it corresponds to their experience—is it true or false of life?—the larger narrative problematizes that criterion. When the marquise finds that, ah yes, "only women . . . know how to love" and when the listener in "En voyage" assesses the reasonableness of the lovers' attitudes and ignores all other aspects of what she has been told (who is doing the telling? to what end? with what kind of connection to the "travel adventures" theme?), the text undermines the "content" their readings infer, shifting emphasis instead to the questioning of all such referentially oriented interpretations. The compulsive cancellation of a story's intentions, in the reactions of its audience, may point to an underlying conviction that stories read as imitations of life are always lies, deserving of the rejection inherent in lack of comprehension. If, then, as we have said, the story is presented as a solid, circumscribed artifact surrounded by a frame, perhaps that frame is to be read as a parenthesis indicating that what is contained is unreal. Thus the frame would italicize the framed, implying that the story's mimetic status is a self-deception on the part of the reader, whose earnest attitude is implicitly derided. By the same token, then, the frame may be a means of discussing the limitations of stories—perhaps they are not meant to exalt any more than to reproduce reality—as much as the erroneous expectations of addressees. Consequently, the mechanization of life (analogous to the automatism of jokes), conveyed by the rhythm and caricaturing inherent in the framed structure, may exist as an equivocation concerning the true function of the enterprise rather than simply as the manifestation of a particular worldview.

Furthermore, the professional identity of the narrator warrants consideration if we are to understand some other implications of these stories. Why does the author so frequently—in these and many other tales—assign the narrator role to a physician? It seems he does so not only because doctors are ubiquitous and powerful figures in the moments of highest drama in human life, becoming repositories of everyone's significant "stories," but also because their involvement differs from the involvement of others. They deal unemotionally with things that are greatly charged for the layperson. Maupassant creates a world devoid of governing principle; because he does not subscribe to any particular code, his logical choice of narrator is someone who accepts everything and does not make moral judgments (moral judgment is here replaced, in fact, by the doctor's apparent detachment). As a reporter of events, the physician can be assumed to have no moral or political or social bias and, moreover, as a scientist can be relied on for accuracy and careful observation. The doctor is called on as "arbitre" (to use Maupassant's own term) in matters hotly contested and is considered all-knowing about human events. Consequently, the deployment of the doctor-narrator enhances the credibility of the narrative and at least initially gains the confidence of the reader. If readers have begun to question the authority and reliability of writers of fiction, the refraction effected by the framing of the story permits the author to suggest to the mind's eye that the narrative is not the creation of a litterateur but the firsthand report of a scientist.

That is our initial experience of the doctor-narrator. But Maupassant has not really left matters there. We have a delayed reaction, as well, and find that the text propels us into a more problematic sense of the doctor. The fabled detachment appears to have further ramifications. At second glance, we appreciate that the choice of the physician as narrator permits Maupassant to suggest not only "scientific" objectivity but also the price paid for that objectivity. The doctor's neutrality and prestige may induce our credulity on a certain level, but they do not prevent our being startled by that very detachment in his reactions and attitudes. Can we ultimately lend credence to the appraisal of someone so remote, so indifferent to chicanery and suffering?

In *Sur l'eau* Maupassant speaks of "cette seconde vue qui est en même temps la force et toute la misère des écrivains" 'that second sight which is at once the gift and the curse of writers' (*Œuvres* 80), describing the condition of the writer in the following terms:

> il vit condamné à être toujours, en toute occasion, . . . un reflet des autres, condamné à se regarder sentir, agir, penser, aimer, souffrir et à ne jamais souffrir, penser, aimer, sentir comme tout le monde, bonnement, franchement, simplement, sans s'analyser soi-même après chaque joie et chaque sanglot.

> he lives condemned to be always, on every occasion, . . . a reflection of others, condemned to watch himself feel, act, think, love, suffer, and never to suffer, think, love, feel as everyone else does, plainly, frankly, simply, without analyzing himself after each joy and each sob.
> (82)

These remarks imply that only distance gives perspective and that vision is a kind of voyeurism indicative of estrangement from others and from the self. And when the author here suggests that if artists do indeed see well, it is because they do not live as others do, his comment provokes an analogy to the "unwholesome" condition of the physician as we encounter him in Maupassant's stories. That is, since the doctor, as dispenser of the narrative, is unquestionably a persona of the author and since his essence seems to be his cool removal from the passions he observes, it is interesting to reflect on his function in the light of Maupassant's description of the writer. Perhaps the doctor-narrator is itself a metaphor for nonintegration in the life process.

The doctor, it seems, "knows," "understands" in just such measure as he has become separate, distant, alienated. Thus the recurring motif of the doctor as agent of narration operates on two levels simultaneously; it is both a trick played and the exposure of the trick, the calling of the question, through that author persona, of what fiction is and at what cost it is created. The doctor-narrator functions to make an equivocal statement about the story and the optic that produces it, and these matters finally displace, as the focus of the story, the little melodramas reported by the doctor.

Indeed, the tendency to frame stories betrays an awareness of a shift in what stories may validly take as their subject. That is, they must address the "predicament" of stories, a subject matter dramatized in the tension between teller and listener. The special structure of these narratives is emblematic of this new consciousness in the author. Putting himself at a distance from his own material (the narrator persona tells the story), raising questions about the function and meaning of that material (the theme of the story is the telling of a story—a story, moreover, that doesn't "work"), leaving those questions dangling (the reader is exposed to divergent points of view)—all these gestures indicate the neutralization of traditional content. The alienation implicit in the material is virtually organic. The French expression for a parenthetical unit that bisects a sentence, *une incision*, suggests, with its nuance of a threat to the organic integrity of the whole, the syntax particular to the framed tale. (Here is another reason for the choice of physician as narrator; the doctor is one who operates in the presence of pathology. Moreover, while an incision violates the body, it also ultimately restores it.) The narrative form, then, signifies the basic cleft in the artistic imagination whereby the author both performs the conventional telling and judges it, trying to reconcile conflicting impulses (through irony, if that is the only mode of reconciliation). It permits the author to express structurally the dilemma of the creative mind caught between the desire for the fully formed artifact, an entity that betokens certitude, and the awareness of the prevarication inherent in any such creation. Each story "means" to inquire into the way stories are made, "means" to confront the dubious relationship between certitude and wisdom.

The framing of a tale permits Maupassant to elucidate rhetorically the properties and potential effects of stories. At the same time, it affords the reader a dynamic function in the making of the story, a story kept interesting and vital because inaccessible to direct contact. But the framing device has further implications. In creating the reader who misreads in these stories, the narratee, Maupassant sets up a particularly disorienting paradox. Although the author himself shows that stories involve subterfuge, failed communication, and closure, he demonstrates those points by means of a frame that, revealing all this to the reader, simultaneously reopens the artificially closed narrative. A dynamism is thus reintroduced into the stasis that is a (contained) story. Therefore, in one sense the containing narrative cancels out the contained one, since this tendency to unravel what had been so neatly woven exposes the artifices and illusions that constitute a story for the teller and the listener. But it goes beyond disclosure.

This gesture of rhetorically uncovering the sleight of hand and the power dynamics intrinsic to stories creates the potential for the rectification of any such flaws. Given the importance, to the "successful" story, of blanks and unanswered questions, it should be clear that any dynamism in a given story results from an element of virtuality in the story's composition. At the same moment that Maupassant's frame points up (by implied contrast) the static reification of one contained narrative and supports the precarious but more vital partiality of another, it corrects both problems by compelling readers, almost in spite of themselves, to perform an integrative operation that releases meaning. The detraction implicit in the "undoing" performed by the frame automatically allows the frame to be read as a complement to the framed material instead of as a parenthesis or set of quotation marks stressing the unreality of the material set off. The frame and the framed can be integrated along a paradigmatic axis such that the dynamism results from the combinatory effort required of the reader and not from the mere "unsealing" of the tale by the frame of the stories we have considered. Thus meaning is not encoded into specific components of the story, awaiting discovery, but is created as a by-product of a process the reader undergoes in the very attempt to make sense of the seemingly arbitrary juxtaposition of frame and framed. Meaning is a do-it-yourself project that incidentally and paradoxically removes the story from any condition of stasis.

We see, finally, that the cleft that the reader encounters in the syntax of the narratives—containing story and contained—and the compulsion to build in a dual perspective on the contained narrative—doctor and listener—may be the "reflection" of the conflict between the exigencies of truth and the exigencies of stories. That is, the creation may present itself as two unintegrated pieces because that form best expresses the conflicting desires we feel on writing and reading stories. Consequently, the self-analysis and dismemberment thematically and structurally manifest in these stories may constitute an awareness that the stories' only power lies in the preemptive assertion of impotence. The stories' exposition of their failure is, indeed, their success, given the author's ultimate preoccupations.

Maupassant's stories, in being framed, unravel themselves and, giving up their rights, sacrifice themselves to something that surpasses certitude and closure. The story is there but, mounted in the frame, raises questions about itself, that carry it beyond mere answers to knowledge, if knowledge of ignorance. A story that takes a frame can mythologize: it can use the failure it articulates to intimate things larger than life, greater than its own capacities. In removing to the plane of relation rather than of representation, in focusing on a dynamism that reflects on, and thereby transcends, mimesis, the framed narrative transmits a knowledge it does not master; it enacts the movement, not the fulfillment, of desire and hence affords us that fragile but lasting pleasure which is, perhaps, the essence of the literary.

WORKS CITED

Barthes, Roland. *S/Z*. Paris: Seuil, 1970.

Chklovski, Victor. "La construction de la nouvelle et du roman." *Théorie de la littérature*. Ed. T. Todorov. Paris: Seuil, 1965. 170–96.

Crouzet, Michel. "Une rhétorique de Maupassant?" *Revue d'histoire littéraire de la France* 80 (1980): 233–61.

Fish, Stanley. *Self-Consuming Artifacts: The Experience of Seventeenth-Century Literature*. Berkeley: U of California P, 1972.

Genette, Gérard. *Figures III*. Paris: Seuil, 1972.

Goffman, Erving. *Frame Analysis: An Essay on the Organization of Experience*. Cambridge: Harvard UP, 1974.

Greimas, A. J. *Maupassant: La sémiotique du texte: Exercices pratiques*. Paris: Seuil, 1976.

Iser, Wolfgang. *The Implied Reader*. Baltimore: Johns Hopkins UP, 1974.

Lubbock, Percy. *The Craft of Fiction*. 1921. Rpt. New York: Scribner's, 1955.

Maupassant, Guy de. *Contes et nouvelles*. Ed. Albert-Marie Schmidt. Paris: Albin Michel, 1973.

———. *Œuvres complétes*. Paris: Louis Conard, 1947.

Moger, Angela S. "That Obscure Object of Narrative." *Yale French Studies* 63 (1982): 129–38.

Pierrot, Jean. "Espace et mouvement dans les récits de Maupassant." *Flaubert et Maupassant: Ecrivains normands*. Ed. Joseph-Marc Bailbé. Paris: PUF, 1981. 167–96.

Prince, Gerald. "Introduction a l'étude du narrataire." *Poétique* 14 (1973): 178–96.

———. "Nom et destin dans 'La parure.'" *French Review* 56 (1982): 267–71.

Smith, Barbara Herrnstein. *Poetic Closure: A Study of How Poems End*. Chicago: U of Chicago P, 1968.

Spoerri, Theophil. "Mérimée and the Short Story." *Yale French Studies* 2.2 (1949): 3–11.

Todorov, Tzvetan. *Poétique de la prose*. Paris: Seuil, 1971.

Tolstoy, Leo. *Guy de Maupassant*. Trans. U. Tcherkoff. 1898. London: Haskell, 1974.

TALES OF WAR

MARY DONALDSON-EVANS

The Decline and Fall of Elisabeth Rousset: Text
and Context in Maupassant's *Boule de suif*†

It has been more than one hundred years since the appearance, in
1880, of *Les Soirées de Médan*. Intended as a display of unity and
adherence to Zola's naturalistic principles, this collection comprises
six stories which were authored by Zola and five of his then disci-
ples and rather loosely connected by the theme of the Franco-
Prussian War. For Maupassant, the publication of this slim volume
had special significance, for it signalled his entry into the sacred
society of letters. Critics were unanimous, then as now, in acclaim-
ing the superiority of Maupassant's contribution, "Boule de suif".
Flaubert's judgment ("'Boule de suif' [. . .] est un *chef d'œuvre*; je
maintiens le mot, un chef d'œuvre de composition, de comique et
d'observation")[1] was typical of the untempered enthusiasm which
greeted the publication of this story. It is thus somewhat surprising
to note that, despite a large and growing body of scholarly works
devoted to Maupassant's fiction, critics have barely begun to scratch
the surface of the rich mine of themes and symbols contained in
"Boule de suif".[2] The present study represents a step towards rem-
edying this situation.

At the risk of being dismissed as a subscriber to what in recent
criticism has been called the "referential illusion", I should like to
suggest that a full appreciation of "Boule de suif" is possible only if
one takes into account the "hors-texte" of the Franco-Prussian War
of 1870–71, for it provides both background to the story and a vital
part of its symbolism. Historians have suggested that this tragic year,
with its three-part catastrophe (the battles of the Empire against
Prussia, the Republic against Prussia, and Versailles against the
Commune) marked the end of the French self-image of grandeur,

† From *Australian Journal of French Studies* 18 (1981): 16–34. Reprinted by permission of
Liverpool University Press.
1. Quoted in Maupassant, *Contes et Nouvelles*, ed. Louis Forestier, Pléiade, Paris, Gallimard, 1974, I, p. 1296. Subsequent references to the story and to Forestier's commentary, given in the text, will be from this edition.
2. The most noteworthy attempt to do so in recent years is Alain Boureau's "Maupassant
et le cannibalisme social", *Stanford French Review*, II, 1978, pp. 351–62. Boureau sees
the story as an allegorized version of the birth of the Third Republic, the prostitute's
victimization equivalent to the suppression of the Commune by the combined forces of
Bismarck and the Versailles regime.

that after the devastating defeats suffered at the hands of the enemy and the fratricidal bloodbath which followed, France was no longer able to look upon herself as "la Grande Nation".[3] Maupassant, a young idealist at the time of the war, had enlisted a year before he was obliged to, so eager was he to participate in a French victory which he felt to be imminent.[4] For him too, the disastrous outcome was a turning point, an end to his youthful optimism and naïveté. He was to spend the next several years meditating upon the causes of "l'Année Terrible", a meditation which would bear fruit in the writing of "Boule de suif".

Although the basic plot of "Boule de suif" is probably well-enough known, it is important to recapitulate the main events of the story in order to bring certain details into sharper focus. The tale begins with a description of the battered and undisciplined French army retreating through Rouen in striking contrast to the orderly arrival of the Prussians the next day. The Rouen bourgeois, "émasculés par le commerce", (p. 84) await the Enemy with fear and trembling. Once the occupation is peacefully accomplished, however, they turn their thoughts once again to their all-consuming passion, making money. So it is that early one cold winter's morning, several of Rouen's citizens find themselves huddled together in the courtyard of the Hôtel de Normandie, all having obtained permission to travel to Le Havre. Their destination, occupied by French troops, must be read not only referentially but taking account of the meaning of its signifier: *le havre* is indeed a haven for all, and despite their ostensible reasons for wishing to leave Rouen, they are in fact following the movement of the French troops, fleeing the Prussians. There are, in all, ten people embarking upon the voyage: the Count and Countess Bréville, Monsieur and Madame Carré-Lamadon (owners of cotton mills), Monsieur and Madame Loiseau (wholesale wine merchants), two nuns, the Republican Cornudet, and Elisabeth Rousset, a fleshy young prostitute known to everyone as Boule de suif. Expecting to arrive in Tôtes by midday, the group is dismayed by a late departure and heavy snows which slow their carriage. Their hunger grows; roadside taverns are boarded up, and suspicious farmers refuse to feed them, clearly identifying them with the pillaging French soldiers who had passed only a short time before. Finally Boule de suif, the only one who has thought to bring provisions, pulls a basket from beneath her seat—enough food to have lasted her for the duration of the three-day journey but which she humbly offers to her ravenous travelling companions. The basket is emptied

---

3. See for example Koenraad Swart, *The Sense of Decadence in Nineteenth Century France*, The Hague, Martinus Nijhoff, 1964, p. 138.
4. Michael Lerner, *Maupassant*, New York, George Braziller, 1975.

in short order and the initial repugnance which the travellers had felt upon recognizing the prostitute is dissipated "dans la communauté de la mangeaille".[5] As if the one function of the mouth generated the other, they begin to converse, and Boule de suif reveals that she is in fact escaping Rouen where she had been in hiding since attempting to strangle the Prussian assigned to her home. Her political sympathies lie with the Empire; she reacts violently when Cornudet "le démoc" insults Napoléon III. Despite their political differences, however, Cornudet cannot help approve of this prostitute's courage, and the other travellers, especially Mesdames Carré-Lamadon and Bréville, are drawn to this strumpet "pleine de dignité, dont les sentiments ressemblaient si fort aux leurs" (p. 97).

In Tôtes, what was to be a one-night stay stretches into five when the Prussian officer stationed at the hotel takes a fancy to Boule de suif and decides to detain all of the travellers until she has agreed to gratify his lust. Her indignant refusal is first met with sympathy by her travelling companions, but as the days drag on, their impatience to reach Le Havre finally draws them together in a plot to overcome the harlot's resistance. It is the vulgar Madame Loiseau who first expresses what each had been secretly harbouring: "Puisque c'est son métier, à cette gueuse, de faire ça avec tous les hommes, je trouve qu'elle n'a pas le droit de refuser l'un plutôt que l'autre." (p. 110) The plan of attack is decided while Boule de suif attends a baptism; upon her return she finds herself privy to a conversation mysteriously focused upon devotion and sacrifice. Unwavering, the prostitute refuses the Prussian's request a third time and the coalition begins to weaken until the casuistic reasoning of the elder nun is brought to bear on the question: "rien, à son avis, ne pouvait déplaire au Seigneur quand l'intention était louable" (p. 113). Representative, through her chastity, of Boule de suif's diametric opposite on the "moral" scale, this "saintly" nun is solely responsible for reviving the forces of collaboration, weakening at last the courtesan's resistance: "chaque parole de la sainte fille en cornette faisait brèche dans la résistance indigrée de la courtisane" (p. 113). The following day, the count, who stands at the opposite extremity of the *social* scale, delivers the "coup de grâce" (or, in this case, *disgrâce*): through flattery and subtle reasoning he finally succeeds in shattering the resistance first cracked by the nun. At dinner-time, Boule de suif sends word that she is "indisposée" and her sacrificial act is performed while the travellers take part in a celebration dinner, complete with champagne furnished by Loiseau.

---

5. Marie-Claire Bancquart, *Boule de suif et autres contes normands*, Paris, Garnier, 1971, p. xxxiv.

The journey continues the next morning. Boule de suif, no longer of any use to her companions, has been reduced to her original value, and is treated with the same scorn which was her lot at the outset of the trip. This time it is she who has neglected to bring supplies; yet the others have no intention of sharing their collations with her, and the plump prostitute watches them eat, "exaspérée, suffoquant de rage" (p. 119). Her anger soon gives way to despair, and she begins to cry silently. Cornudet, to irritate the others, begins to hum the Marseillaise (not yet a national anthem and associated at the time with the Republican movement) and the story ends to the tune of this revolutionary hymn, punctuated by the mumbling of the nuns in prayer and an occasional sob from the harlot.

As can be discerned from this outline, "Boule de suif" is constructed upon the interplay of three thematic "sub-codes"—the nutritional, the politico-economic and the military—with the main code which is sexual. To understand the way in which these codes function, it is necessary to consider the text in both its diachronic and synchronic dimensions. It is also useful, although not essential, to place "Boule de suif" in the context of Maupassant's war stories, on the one hand, and his "whore" stories, on the other. It is not by chance that the two themes frequently collide, and that his most unforgettable prostitutes are war heroes as well.

Let us begin, then, with the sexual code. As a prostitute, Boule de suif is the incarnation of sexuality. She is a "marchande d'amour", her *marchandise* being her body. Aggression is the *sine qua non* of her trade. In the eyes of society, she is immoral, ignoble; yet, as Forestier has pointed out, Boule de suif, like many of Maupassant's prostitutes, has managed to retain her self-respect by transferring her moral sensibility to a domain other than the sexual (p. 1299). She thus possesses a sense of dignity despite public opinion, and when the whispered insults reach her ears at the outset of the journey, she is not intimidated; rather, she looks directly at her insulters with "un regard tellement provocant et hardi qu'un grand silence aussitôt régna" (p. 91). That they let themselves be silenced by her is not an indication of respect, however, and the epithets used to describe the prostitute as seen through their eyes ("honte publique", "vendue sans vergogne") make it quite obvious that at this point in the story she is held in low esteem indeed. In fact, a study of the terms used for the prostitute throughout the story reveals that they follow a curve, corresponding closely to the rise and fall of her "value" in their eyes. Her proper name, Elisabeth Rousset, is used only four times, in each case by the innkeeper Follenvie in transmitting the Prussian's message. To the others, and to the narrator, she is Boule de suif, an *objet de consommation* in the eyes of all.[6] Moreover, as Sullivan has suggested, the evocation of the bourgeois origins of the French military officers, "ex-marchands de suif ou de savon" (p. 83) is not gratuitous;[7] rather, it establishes a symbolic link between these ill-qualified leaders "nommés officiers pour leurs écus ou la longueur de leurs moustaches" (p. 83) and the travelling bourgeois who use Boule de suif as their merchandise, who reify her and look upon her as a means to their dual end, escape from the Prussians (hence freedom) and financial gain.

If the women are, or pretend to be, shocked by the presence of a harlot in the carriage, the men are clearly aroused. The vulgar Loiseau is the only one not to lower his eyes under the prostitute's provocative gaze; rather, he continues to look at her "d'un air émoustillé" (p. 91). Cornudet, the only male traveller unaccompanied by a woman, can afford to be bolder. The first night in Tôtes, he openly propositions her in the hotel corridor and only reluctantly returns to his own room after her adamant refusal, somewhat impressed despite himself by "cette pudeur patriotique de catin qui ne se laissait point caresser près de l'ennemi" (p. 103). Maupassant cleverly presents us this scene through the eyes of Loiseau who, peeking through the keyhole from his hotel room, is sufficiently titillated to return to his bed and the "dure carcasse de sa compagne" (p. 103) to whom he transfers his sexual interests (one is reminded here of the French adage, "Faute de mieux on couche avec sa femme"). The other two male characters, prevented by their class consciousness from any overt reaction to the prostitute's sexuality, effect a similar transfer the last night when, during the "celebration" dinner, they engage in a seemingly innocent flirtation with one another's partners: "Le comte parut s'apercevoir que Madame Carré-Lamadon était charmante, le manufacturier fit des compliments à la comtesse." (p. 115) The evening, filled with laughter and bawdy jokes made at the prostitute's expense, is not without orgiastic overtones. Loiseau's tasteless and vulgar farces shock no one "car l'indignation dépend des milieux comme le reste" (p. 116) and even the women and the count make a few discreet allusions to what is taking place upstairs. Only Cornudet does not participate, and his departing words ("Je vous dis à tous que vous venez de faire une infamie [. . .] une infamie!"—p. 116) threaten to end the evening on a sour note until Loiseau, doubling over with laughter, reveals to the others "les mystères du corridor" (p. 117). Indeed, it must be said

---

6. The view of the prostitute as consumer product is further supported by the fact that her nickname evokes a fat which, along with butter, was in extremely short supply during the war. See Edmond de Goncourt, *Journal*, Vol. V: *Année 1870*, entries for 8 December and 7 January, Flammarion, 1956.

7. E. D. Sullivan, *Maupassant: The Short Stories*, Barron's Educational Series, 1962.

that Cornudet *is* somewhat tainted by his attempted seduction of the prostitute, and his refusal to collaborate with the others cannot be unequivocally attributed to purely Republican patriotic sentiments. Moreover, he is himself identified with the Prussian, not only by his relationship to the prostitute, but also by his pipe and his favorite beverage, beer. The first two syllables of his name clearly suggest his role at the sexual level of the text: he is indeed the cuckold, betrayed by Boule de suif herself and above all by the others who have served as *proxénètes*, forcing her into the arms of the Prussian officer for their own monetary benefit (for they have "de gros intérêts engagés an Havre"—p. 86).

The sexual activity of the first night in the hotel had been limited to Cornudet's fruitless attempt to overcome the resistance of Boule de suif and Loiseau's supposed seduction of his wife. The only sound disturbing the silence of the night had been Follenvie's heavy breathing, "un ronflement puissant, monotone, régulier, un bruit sourd et prolongé avec des tremblements de chaudière sous pression" (p. 103) In contrast, the last night in the hotel is a restless one:

> Et toute la nuit, dans l'obscurité du corridor coururent comme des frémissements, des bruits légers, à peine sensibles, pareils à des souffles, des effleurements de pieds nus, d'imperceptibles craquements. Et l'on ne dormit que très tard, assurément, car des filets de lumière glissèrent longtemps sous les portes. Le champagne a de ces effets-là, il trouble, dit-on, le sommeil. (p. 117)

Follenvie exits from the story once his role as go-between has ended, but the emotion evoked by his patronym has remained and once again it is *folle-envie* which troubles the stillness of the night. Whether the sexual activity of the last night is legitimate is not made explicit by the text, but the fact remains that the travellers' prurient appetites have been aroused—and satisfied—by the presence of Boule de suif.

Nor do the other women play a completely passive role. Even the nuns, whose position places them beyond sexuality, are involved. Maupassant's ingenuity in using a nun to weaken the prostitute's resistance must not be forgotten, and the elder nun's *emportement* is not unlike Boule de suif's own. In fact, a study of Maupassant's lexicon reveals the presence of a contiguous relationship between Boule de suif and the nuns. For example, the prostitute's chubby fingers, "pareils à des chapelets de courtes saucisses" (p. 91) evoke both the literal *chapelets* of the two nuns and the *saucisson* upon which they lunch during the final stage of the journey. Moreover, the nuns are characterized as "de saintes filles habituées à toutes les soumissions" (p. 98), and are the first to obey the Prussian officer when he asks the voyagers to exit from the carriage upon their arrival in Tôtes. Only the epithet "saintes" apparently subverts the equation nuns = prostitutes, and one senses that, in the case of the elder nun at least, it is merely an accident of nature (the disfiguring smallpox) which made of her a "sainte fille en cornette" rather than a "fille" *tout court*. Her virtue is only habit-deep and when she surprises everyone by her unhoped-for complicity in the plot, Maupassant cleverly shifts from indirect dialogue to direct, thereby enabling his countess to address the nun as "ma sœur". More than a mere formula, these words strongly suggest that the nun has been accepted into the sisterhood of all women. Seen in this light, the "forbidden pleasure" represented by the nuns' first-ever taste of champagne during the celebration dinner must be accorded its full symbolic value.

Among the other women, it is clearly Madame Carré-Lamadon who bears the closest resemblance to Boule de suif, despite physical dissimilarities mirrored in the geometric connotations of the names by which they are most often known in the text (*Boule* de suif and *Carré*-Lamadon). Pretty and delicate, Madame Carré-Lamadon is much younger than her husband; the statement that she was "la consolation des officiers de bonne famille envoyés à Rouen en garnison" (p. 89) is deliberately suggestive, and the frequent references to her sexual fascination with the Prussian officer are not gratuitous.[8] Once again, it is the jealous termagant Madame Loiseau to whom is given the role of making specific what is merely suggested elsewhere in the text. Speaking of "cette chipie" (p. 117), Madame Carré-Lamadon, she laments to her husband, "Tu sais, les femmes, quand ça en tient pour l'uniforme, qu'il soit Français ou bien Prussien, ça leur est, ma foi, bien égal. Si ce n'est pas une pitié, Seigneur Dieu!" (p. 117). In fact, even Madame Loiseau is not beyond imagining herself in the prostitute's place, and her statement that the Prussian officer would doubtless have preferred one of the three married women can only be regarded as wishful thinking.

The countess' virtue is equally questionable. She is not of noble birth and it is above all her sexuality ("elle [. . .] passait même pour avoir été aimée d'un des fils de Louis-Philippe"—p. 90) which has won for her the respect of her adoptive class. Her duplicity is underlined often and her own role in the seduction of the prostitute is a major one, since it is she who brings the elder nun into the plot.

---

8. "Madame Carré-Lamadon, qui avait connu beaucoup d'officiers et qui les jugeait en connaisseur, trouvait celui-là pas mal du tout; elle regrettait même qu'il ne fût pas Français" (p. 109); "Les yeux de la jolie Madame Carré-Lamadon brillaient, et elle était un peu pâle, comme si elle se sentait déjà prise de force par l'officier." (p. 110); and "La gentille Madame Carré-Lamadon semblait même penser qu à sa place elle refuserait celui-là moins qu'un autre." (p. 111).

Only the younger nun does not participate actively in the alliance against Boule de suif, although her silence must be understood as compliance with the efforts of the other women. Among the male travellers, the prostitute's ostracization on sexual grounds is mirrored by Cornudet's politico-economic isolation, as Sullivan has suggested (p. 38). Just as the women are sisters in their supposed "virtue", the men draw together against Cornudet, "frères par l'argent" (p. 92). In actual fact, however, the distance which separates the moneyed males from Cornudet is travelled as quickly as that separating the "virtuous" women from the prostitute. Cornudet has inherited a large sum of money from his bourgeois father. Unlike the other bourgeois, however, he was not imbued with the bourgeois ethic. Rather than invest his money to increase his wealth, he had spent it; rather than work, he had played. Now a "have not", he is associated with the prostitute who is by definition *déclassée*.[9] Unlike her, however, he is untrue to himself, and his passive role in the collaboration (he does nothing to alert Boule de suif to the plot and only expresses his dismay after it has succeeded) makes a mockery of the ideals embodied in his loudly proclaimed Republicanism. In his case, too, liberty, equality and fraternity have sold out to egotism. As eager as the others to reach Le Havre, he has sacrificed Boule de suif just as surely as they have. For him, too, the prostitute has a *valeur marchande*. That her value in his eyes is sexual rather than material is of little importance, for the result is the same: not only does he fail to defend her against the collaborators, but he shows no pity for her when the voyage resumes, his sense of fraternity for this unfortunate war victim being too weak to persuade him to share his lunch with her. Equally absent from Cornudet's moral makeup are sentiments of equality. The social superiority displayed by the Carré-Lamadons and the Brévilles is matched by Cornudet's intellectually superior attitude. Apart from singing the Marseillaise, smoking his pipe and drinking beer, his activity in the story is very nearly confined to approving or disapproving the opinions of others. Furthermore, although his flight from Rouen, like Boule de suif's, can be justified (having had trees felled, traps set, holes dug around Rouen in order to retard the Enemy's invasion of that city, he is now going to organize similar defensive activities around Le Havre), Cornudet is above all characterized by his refusal to confront the Enemy. When the news of the Prussians' approach reached Rouen, "il s'était vivement replié vers la ville" (p. 91); when the other male travellers ask him to accompany them to the Prussian's chambers where they hope to learn the cause of their detention (hardly a compromising mission), he refuses, proudly declaring that "il entendait

9. For a different perspective on Cornudet's role, see Bourneau, p. 353.

n'avoir jamais aucun rapport avec les Allemands" (p. 105). This fear
of confrontation masquerading as pride is in stark opposition to
Boule de suif's humility and courage. Cornudet, with his knowing
smiles and political aphorisms, is a man of words, not of action, and
his Republican reputation has been established largely in cafés.[1] It
is hardly surprising, then, that his pipe enjoys among his followers
"d'une considération presque égale à la sienne" (p. 105) or that he
himself has difficulty in distinguishing between his two passions,
"le Pale-Ale et la Révolution" (p. 100).

The thinly veiled sensuality with which Cornudet contemplates
his beer, his extreme physical enjoyment of his pipe which is
"admirablement culottée [. . .] parfumée, recourbée, luisante,
familière à sa main" (p. 105) are but variants upon what one might
refer to as the nutritional code, a lexical and metaphoric network
which threads its way into every corner of the text and which, as
Boureau has pointed out (p. 355), is closely affiliated with the
sexual.

The nutritional code is present at all levels of the text. The
alimentary uses of animal fat are well-known, and Boule de suif
is the first to be assimilated to the nutritive, both literally and
metaphorically:

> Petite, ronde de partout, *grasse à lard*, avec des doigts bouffis,
> étranglés aux phalanges, pareils à des chapelets de courtes *sau-
> cisses* [. . .] elle restait cependant *appétissante* et courue, tant
> sa *fraîcheur* faisait plaisir à voir. [. . .] Sa figure était *une
> pomme rouge* [. . .] (p. 91; italics mine)

If the metaphorical alliance of the sexual and culinary can be considered a literary commonplace, as James Brown has shown,[2] Maupassant's exploitation of the theme is far from hackneyed, thanks to
the constant *va-et-vient* between the literal and the figurative. As a
prostitute Boule de suif is to be bought and consumed, much as one
would buy a cutlet from a butcher shop. Moreover, it is clear that
her bourgeois travelling companions are voracious consumers, and
Maupassant's description of the contagious yawning which is trans-
mitted from one to another places the emphasis, not upon the various "styles" of yawns dictated by etiquette and social class, but rather
upon the common "trou béant d'où sortait une vapeur" (p. 93). The

1. Goncourt's journal entry for 4 September 1870, suggests that this rather unflattering
   portrait of the Republican was not totally unfounded. Describing the crowds celebrating the declaration of the Republic which followed the defeat of MacMahon and the
   Emperor's captivity, Goncourt writes, "il ne me paraît pas retrouver dans cette plèbe
   braillarde les premiers bonshommes de l'ancienne Marseillaise: ça me semble simplement des voyous d'âge [. . .] des voyous sceptiques, faisant de la casse politique, et
   n'ayant rien, sous la mamelle gauche, pour les grands sacrifices à la patrie."
2. "On the Semiogenesis of Fictional Meals", *Romanic Review*, LXIX, 1978, pp. 322–35.

intensity of their hunger darkening their moods, the travellers react
with shock when Loiseau jestingly proposes to do as the popular
song says and to eat "le plus gras des voyageurs" (p. 93). The allusion to Boule de suif is direct and is followed almost immediately in
the text by the harlot's sudden resolution to take out her basket of
provisions. That it had been hidden under the bench, "sous ses
jupons" (p. 93) establishes a blatant link with the sexual and Loiseau's earlier stares at the prostitute are matched now by his lascivious ogling of the chicken. The first to accept Boule de suif's offer
of food, he is followed by the two nuns, then by Cornudet, finally
by the more "distinguished" company, but only after Madame
Carré-Lamadon has fainted from hunger. The rapidity with which
the travellers empty the strumpet's basket, and the savagery of their
appetites are suggestive of a cannibalistic carnage, the victim of
which is Boule de suif herself: "Les bouches s'ouvraient et se fer-
maient sans cesse, avalaient, mastiquaient, engloutissaient féroce-
ment." (p. 94) While part of the savagery of this scene may be
explained by Maupassant's desire to remain faithful to the tenets of
Naturalism, we can also see in it a scarcely veiled Darwinism which
is verbalized later in the tale by the count himself: "Il ne faut jamais
résister aux gens qui sont les plus forts." (p. 100) Indeed, the sacrificial nature of Boule de suif's generosity and the humility with
which she offers to share her food are thrown into relief by the
hubristic condescension of the others whose reluctance to sully
themselves by accepting the harlot's food is finally overcome by the
anguish of their hunger.

   In Tôtes (which suggests "tôt" and "toast", both derivatives of the
Latin *tostus* meaning "grilled" or "cooked") the metaphorical union
of the sexual with the nutritional is again underlined by the fact that
each of the Prussian officer's three "invitations" to the prostitute is
extended, through the intermediary of the aptly named Follenvie,
at dinnertime. The fifth dinner, which we have characterized as a
celebration dinner, is, as we have seen, consumed in the absence of
Boule de suif who is otherwise engaged upstairs, this time quite literally sacrificing herself for the good of her compatriots. But unlike
the previous nutritional sacrifice, this giving of herself had not been
spontaneous; rather it had been wrenched from her through a carefully planned and skilfully executed verbal aggression. The scenario
of the conspiracy had been sketched the previous day while Boule
de suif attended a baptism. Thus, while the prostitute, ostensibly the
symbol of vice, prayed, the married couples, apparent bastions of
all that is proper and "moral", plotted against her, the women in
particular deriving vicarious pleasure from their planning. Maupassant's choice of a culinary metaphor to describe their activity is not
unexpected:

> Un étranger n'aurait rien compris tant les précautions du lan-
> gage étaient observées. Mais la légère tranche de pudeur dont
> est bardée toute femme du monde ne recouvrant que la sur-
> face, elles s'épanouissaient dans cette aventure polissonne,
> s'amusaient follement au fond, se sentant dans leur élément,
> tripotant de l'amour avec la sensualité d'un cuisinier gour-
> mand qui prépare le souper d'un autre. (p. 111)

Assimilated at once to the food itself and to the gluttonous cook, it
is these women who, beneath their veneer of sophistication and
righteousness, are the true *marchandes d'amour*.

The attack is mounted at lunchtime and, given renewed vigour
by the nun's timely intervention, the attempts at persuasion continue through the evening meal as well. Here too, the concomi-
tance of these two activities is quite deliberate, and such temporal
indications' as "Aussitôt à table, on commença les approches"
(p. 112) or "Aussitôt le repas terminé on remonta bien vite dans les
chambres [. . .]" (p. 114) are more than merely referential. The
warmth, the sense of community and *bien-être* afforded by a meal
are guarantors of vulnerability as well as being evocative, throughout Maupassant's work, of that other physical pleasure which is
the prostitute's special fare. Boule de suif's hypocritical travelling
companions choose their moments as carefully as they choose their
words.

The final betrayal of Boule de suif, the arrogance which the bourgeois display as they continue their journey, and their insensitivity
and egoism in eating in her presence and without offering her even
their leftovers (the nuns wrap up their remaining sausage after having eaten their fill) once again evoke the culinary. The fact that the
prostitute is identified with animal fat by her nickname, and that
all but one of the travellers lunch on meats (suggestive of Boule de
suif's role by the nouns used to characterize them: *morceau, gibier,*
etc.) reinforces the notion of self-sacrifice. Cornudet, whose meat-
less repast consists of eggs and bread, is the only one who has not
enjoyed a "forbidden pleasure" at Boule de suif's expense.

This discussion of the nutritional code would be incomplete
were we to fail to evoke the most arresting metaphor of all, that of
the pigeons pecking at the horses' steaming excrement in the final
scene at Tôtes. The passage deserves to be quoted in its entirety:

> La diligence, attelée enfin, attendait devant la porte, tandis
> qu'une armée de pigeons blancs, rengorgés dans leurs plumes
> épaisses, avec un œil rose, taché, au milieu, d'un point noir, se
> promenaient gravement entre les jambes des six chevaux, et
> cherchaient leur vie dans le crottin fumant qu'ils éparpillaient.
> (p. 117)

The solemnity and decorum with which the coprophagic pigeons
feed upon the horses' dung is clearly symbolic of the arrogance and
outward "dignity" with which the travellers had committed the most
shameful and undignified of betrayals. The double evocation of the
digestive in this passage (the pigeons ingesting what is in fact the
residue—one is tempted to say "end-product"—of the alimentary
process) in addition to suggesting the repulsive nature of the bourgeois' treason and collaboration with the Enemy, mirrors the circular movement of the narrative itself and subverts the notion of a plot
built upon the horizontal line of a journey. Many critics have
remarked upon the symmetry of the last carriage scene and the first:
it does indeed close the circle, and such oxymoronic expressions
as "voyageurs immobiles", "gredins honnêtes" suggest the paradox
implicit in the text itself. Despite the geographic distance covered,
these bourgeois have not budged from their stance of hypocritical
complacency. With the exception of their physical mobility (which
had been effected by the horses and, not coincidentally, by Boule
de suif who might be likened to the "pauvre cheval qui ne venait pas
volontiers"—p. 88), the only movement they had ever known had
been the vertical movement of their climb through society. It is not
by chance that this movement, too, had been made possible by the
sacrifice of the humble.

Finally, the almost obsessive identification, in Maupassant's work,
of the sexual with the excretory,[3] finds its echo in this passage, and
the repulsion which the travellers display towards Boule de suif on
the last lap of the journey indicates clearly that they no longer see
in her a saviour, a *mère nourricière*, but rather a whore who, like the
horses' excretions, represents "[un] contact impur" (p. 118) from
which they must keep their distance, "comme si elle eût apporté une
infection dans ses jupes" (p. 118).

In addition to its frequent intersections with the sexual, the nutritional code is closely associated with the military. The first and most
obvious meeting takes place at the semantic level of the plot. The
Rouen bourgeois lodge and nourish the occupying army, affecting
alienation and animosity in the street while displaying an obliging
hospitality and even a certain affection for the soldiers in the pri-
vacy of their own homes:

> On se disait enfin, raison suprême tirée de l'urbanité française,
> qu'il demeurait bien permis d'être poli dans son intérieur

---

3. Cf. "L'Inutile Beauté": "Qu'y a-t-il, en effet, de plus ignoble, de plus répugnant que cet
acte ordurier et ridicule de la reproduction des êtres [. . .]? Puisque tous les organes
inventés par ce créateur économe et malveillant servent à deux fins, pourquoi n'en a-t-il
pas choisi d'autres qui ne fussent point malpropres et souillés, pour leur confier cette
mission sacrée [. . .]?", Maupassant, *Contes et Nouvelles*, ed. Louis Forestier, Pléiade,
Paris, Gallimard, 1979, II, p. 1216.

pourvu qu'on ne se montrât pas familier en public, avec le sol-
dat étranger, (p. 85)

The bourgeois' hypocrisy (represented by the interior-exterior opposition) stems both from their materialism (they would perhaps be
given fewer soldiers to feed if they caused no trouble) and from their
cowardice ("pourquoi blesser quelqu'un dont on dépendait tout à
fait?"—p. 85). Such egotistical logic brought to the defence of what
is in fact collaboration with the Enemy stands in direct contrast to
the passionate patriotism of the lower classes, farmers, prostitutes,
petites gens of all sorts whose silent nocturnal murders of Prussian
soldiers endanger their lives without bringing them fame or glory:
"Car la haine de l'Etranger arme toujours quelques Intrépides prêts
à mourir pour une Idée." (p. 86) It is not these fearless idealists, true
heroes of the war, who are responsible for France's defeat, but rather
the bourgeois whose economic clout has placed them in positions
of military as well as social leadership. And what about this formidable enemy, the Prussian? The modest citizens of Tôtes, who,
unlike the wealthy *Rouennais*, are not versed in the art of hypocrisy,
make no secret of their relationship with the Enemy, and the latter
can be seen scrubbing floors, peeling potatoes, caring for babies,
splitting wood:

> [...] et les grosses paysannes dont les hommes étaient à
> "l'armée de la guerre", indiquaient par signes à leurs *vainqueurs
> obéissants* [italics mine] le travail qu'il fallait entreprendre [...]
> un d'eux même lavait le linge de son hôtesse, une aïeule toute
> impotente. (p. 103)

That these plump provincial women have succeeded in domesticat-
ing the occupying soldiers can only be seen as a further indictment
of the "bourgeois émasculé". Throughout Maupassant's war stories,
Prussian officers are portrayed as barbaric, destructive, insensitive
and sadistic ("Mademoiselle Fifi", "Deux Amis", "Un Duel") but the
foot soldiers are more often than not described as merely naïve, even
stupid, *l'air bon enfant* ("Saint Antoine", "L'Aventure de Walter
Schnaffs", "La mère Sauvage"). France's ignominious defeat by these
unworthy opponents becomes thus all the more difficult to accept
and, notwithstanding the truism advanced by the old sexton of
"Boule de suif" ("c'est les grands qui font la guerre"—p. 104), the
outcome of this war was made possible by complicity at all levels.
The exemplary value of Boule de suif's resistance is lost upon her
bourgeois travelling companions who are incapable of any action
which would jeopardize their own material welfare. In their betrayal
of the prostitute, they are comparable to the bourgeois who quietly
nourish the occupying soldiers: indeed, they "feed" Boule de suif to

the Prussian in exchange for their own freedom. With their help, he realizes a sexual invasion of the unwilling prostitute which is but a metaphor for his army's military invasion of France. Little wonder, then, that the vocabulary of their conspiracy is borrowed from the arsenal of military terminology:

> On prépara longuement le blocus, comme pour une forteresse investie. Chacun convint du rôle qu'il jouerait, des arguments dont il s'appuierait, des manœuvres qu'il devrait exécuter. On régla le plan des attaques, les ruses à employer, et les surprises de l'assaut, pour forcer cette citadelle vivante à recevoir l'ennemi dans la place. (p. 111)

Seen as a mirror-perfect image of France herself, *la belle, la douce France,* humiliated and betrayed by her very own people, those whom she had succoured and nourished, Boule de suif acquires a tragic grandeur. In the story's final scene, it is not a mere prostitute who sobs; rather, in the words of Armand Lanoux, "c'est la France qui est humiliée, qui pleure et se révolte"[4]. In the wake of the Franco-Prussian war, Frenchmen could find no justification for their ignominious losses. It was France itself which had so confidently declared war, convinced of the invincibility of its army, the French bourgeois who had made the occupation so effortless for the Enemy, the French Republicans who had needlessly prolonged the war after the defeat of the Empire, when Prussia's final victory seemed to all but a reckless few a foregone conclusion, the French who, in the end, turned against their own compatriots in one of the bloodiest civil wars in French history, the war against the Paris Communards. The disarray and unpreparedness of the French army is attested to by historians[5] as is the disgraceful ease of the invasion and occupation of Rouen. Maupassant's version of the retreat is further corroborated by an eye witness account of the events which took place in Rouen on 4 and 5 December 1870, as described in a letter written by a well-known Rouen citizen, Dr Hellish.[6] Besides confirming the precision of detail which characterizes Maupassant's narrative, Hellis' letter sheds a new light on the story as political allegory in its revelation of the occurrences which preceded the army's retreat:

> Dimanche 4 décembre MM. de la Rouge firent une démonstration contre l'hôtel de ville; tout étant en désarroi, ils trouvèrent des armes et saccagèrent l'intérieur. Ils se promirent [. . .] de proclamer la république rouge avec l'établissement de la commune comme à Lyon. [. . .] Le lendemain, les frères et amis

---

4. *Maupassant le Bel-Ami*, Paris, Fayard, 1967, p. 119.
5. Michael Howard, *The Franco-Prussian War*, New York, Macmillan, 1962.
6. First brought to the attention of the critics by Marie-Claire Bancquart, the letter is quoted in Forestier's notes to "Boule de suif" (pp. 1298–9).

> se rendent à la place Saint-Ouen pour achever leur ouvrage
> quand tout à coup la panique s'empare de tous. Les Prussiens,
> les Prussiens! A ce mot nos braves s'enfuient jusqu'au dernier
> et la place fut entiérement vide. J'étais là [. . .] j'ai vu arriver
> nos vainqueurs. Sans tambours ni musique, au pas, graves,
> silencieux, comme stupéfaits d'un succés aussi inespéré [. . .]
> (p. 1298).

Hellis' legitimistic prejudices are obvious here; they even lead him,
later in the letter, to write almost affectionately of the Prussians
whom he credits with having saved Rouen from the revolutionaries!
One would be hard put to find a more apt illustration of the bourgeois attitude which Maupassant so mercilessly ridiculed in "Boule
de suif". But the real interest of this letter lies in the documentary
proof which it offers of the Revolutionaries' attempted takeover of
Rouen prior to the Enemy's invasion. Seen in the perspective of these
occurrences, Cornudet's attempted seduction of Boule de suif
acquires symbolic value, clearly evocative of the Revolutionaries'
interrupted looting of the town hall. For Cornudet, Boule de suif
was *la gueuse Marianne*, and his desire for her was as great as his
desire for the establishment of the Republic, identified in his mind
(and in the minds of all of Gambetta's followers) with a French victory over the Prussians. The Prussian officer's triumph over Boule
de suif thus comes to symbolize the humiliating Prussian victory
over France. It should be remembered too that Boule de suif, as a
bonapartiste, represents the Empire; by not allowing Cornudet to
possess her, she was resisting the Republic. As for the other characters, all had prospered under the reign of Napoleon III, and the Second Empire saw, for a time at least, the alliance of two conservative
forces, the bourgeoisie and the Church.[7] Seen in this light, the nun's
collaboration is not unexpected. It is, finally, with a stroke of malicious irony that Maupassant paints even his supposed aristocrats the
same colour as the bourgeois, not only because of their mercenary
attitudes, but also by specifying that their nobility had been pur-
chased. The historical *justesse* of this phenomenon is well-known,
but Maupassant cannot resist adding a sexual dimension to his
account of the Brévilles' aristocratic origins. The count Bréville has
Henri IV to thank for conferring upon his ancestors their nobility:
"Henri IV [. . .] suivant une légende glorieuse pour la famille,
avait rendu grosse une dame de Bréville, dont le mari, pour ce fait,
était devenu comte et gouverneur de province." (p. 90) The count's
nobility thus results directly from a royal indemnity to a cuckold!
To further mock this ignoble pair, Maupassant asserts that the

---

7. See John B. Wolf, *France: 1815 to the Present*, New York, Prentice Hall, 1940,
pp. 267–8.

countess' "nobility" is acquired at least partly through her sexual activities.

As morally dissolute as the more distinguished company, but without their overlay of elegance, Loiseau and his wife become the *porte-parole* of the group, verbalizing what the others dare not express. The wine merchant who, not surprisingly, lives on the Rue du *Pont*, is thus the first to bridge the social gap and to open the dialogue with the prostitute, and the first to accept her offering of food. It is he, moreover, who makes it possible for the others to accept her food without suffering a loss of dignity in the process. ("Et, parbleu, dans des cas pareils tout le monde est frère et doit s'aider. Allons, mesdames, pas de cérémonie: acceptez, que diable!"—p. 95) The count, finally, is persuaded to speak for the foursome (the Brévilles and the Carré-Lamadons) and his acceptance, executed with a curious mixture of condescension and genteel humility, unseals the mouths of his starving companions. The historical event to which Maupassant alludes in describing the difficulty and sudden resolve of the count's decision to accept is highly significant: "Le premier pas seul coûtait. Une fois le Rubicon passé on s'en donna carrément." (p. 95) Our appreciation of Maupassant's punning ("carrément") should not blind us to the *sérieux* of the classical allusion. Caesar's crossing from ancient Gaul back into Rome despite the order of the Roman Senate carried with it the notion of betrayal. In a similar way, this sharing of Boule de suif's abundant provisions is the first step in the bourgeois' betrayal of the prostitute and, by metaphorical extension, of France.

This evocation of the Roman Empire is not isolated in the text. The examples upon which the bourgeois, "millionaires ignorants" (p. 112) base their persuasion of Boule de suif are largely drawn from the events of Roman history—or rather, Roman history as confused and distorted by them. Judith, Lucretia, Cleopatra—all are mentioned, and others as well: "On cita toutes les femmes qui ont arrêté des conquérants, fait de leur corps un champ de bataille, un moyen de dominer, une arme." (p. 112) As one might expect, Boule de suif is unconvinced by these analogies, false to the core, which liken her situation to the heroic self-abasement of Roman women "qui ont vaincu par leurs caresses héroïques des êtres hideux ou détestés, et sacrifié leur chasteté à la vengeance et au dévouement" (p. 112). *Vaincu*? *Chasteté*? *Vengeance*? The absurdity of these words in the context of their request brings into even sharper relief the heroism of Boule de suif's resistance. Through her *refusal* to acquiesce, she is indeed making of her body "un champ de bataille, un moyen de dominer, une arme"; hence, giving in to the Prussian represents not victory, but capitulation, not domination, but submission, surrender. The irony is bitter, and the egotism, the twisted logic and bad faith

of the bourgeois are all the more despicable when regarded as
symbolic of their nefarious role in the Franco-Prussian War. Moreover, their suggestion that Boule de suif should "do as the Romans
do" could very well have been interpreted by Maupassant's late
nineteenth-century readers as a sign of the times, an ominous *rap-
prochement* of decadent France with the deteriorating Roman
Empire during the period of the decline. This comparison was not
unheard of at the time, and many historians, subscribing to the cycli-
cal notion of Eternal Return, saw in the Second Empire's hedonis-
tic materialism a sign of France's impending destruction. Taine and
Gobineau, among others, had drawn gloomy parallels between the
two cultures. Seen from another point of view, the identification of
the French prostitute with figures from Roman history may be considered a call to treason since, like the Prussians, the Romans once
invaded Rouen (the site of a Celtic settlement in ancient times). The
allusion to an Englishwoman "de grande famille" (p. 112) who had
once had herself vaccinated with a syphilis virus, intending to pass
the dreaded disease on to Napoleon, "sauvé miraculeusement, par
une faiblesse subite, à l'heure du rendez-vous fatal" (p. 112) is equally
ludicrous, firstly because England's inglorious role in Rouen's history makes this suggestion as improper as the other, secondly
because Boule de suif herself is a *bonapartiste* and could hardly be
expected to find inspiration in the figure of a woman who had
attempted to kill Bonaparte, finally in the allusion to the Emperor's
impuissance. The obvious model of patriotism and courage for a
Rouennaise, Joan of Arc, is not mentioned, for the act to which the
prostitute is being summoned is base, a travesty of honour, tantamount to betraying her country rather than saving it.[8] Moreover,
the self-serving bourgeois who persuade her to capitulate are as
self-destructive as the Garde Nationale which, "fusillant parfois ses
propres sentinelles" (p. 84), is characterized above all by its cowardice. The bourgeois themselves are not known for their bravery, "la
témérité [n'étant] plus un défaut des bourgeois de Rouen, comme
au temps des défenses héroïques où s'illustra leur cité" (p. 85).
Maupassant's use of litotes is painfully ironic, and the meaning of the
nominative *défaut* is immediately subverted by the epithet *héroïques*
and the verb *s'illustrer*. Things are not the way they used to be, and
the ignominious present bears no resemblance to the illustrious
past. Thus, the absence of Joan of Arc in the text is not oversight.
For the Rouen citizens of "Boule de suif", the prostitute represents
not a national victory but personal freedom. The bitter irony evoked

---

8. The fearless harlot Irma of "Le lit 29", on the other hand, who contracts venereal disease, then deliberately communicates it to as many Prussian soldiers as she can, is not
   so subtly likened to the heroine of the Hundred Years War: she lives on the rue Jeanne
   d'Arc.

by the lyrics of the hated Marseillaise in the story's final scene derives from the mental image which they inevitably bring to mind, that of the figure of "La Liberté", a woman dressed in Roman garb which was popularized by nineteenth-century artists (Delacroix and Bartholdi being the best known).[9] "La France agonisante" which the bourgeois military leaders claimed to support "sur leurs épaules de fanfarons" (p. 83) is indeed a woman, a whore who has been exploited and enjoyed and vilified, then abruptly abandoned when she has passed, through the fault of her own people, into the hands of the Enemy.

Unlike the pure young woman of "Le mariage du Lieutenant Laré', (a story published two years previously) who had been quite literally carried through the snowy French countryside by a troop of exhausted French soldiers, and who was responsible for renewing their strength and faltering courage and leading them to the completion of a successful campaign against the Prussians, Boule de suif fails to overcome the egotism of her compatriots, inspires no one to patriotism. And yet she is, in a peculiar way, an *inspiratrice*. Among the many symbolic roles played by the fat prostitute, her extratextual role is no doubt the most important, for she is at once fictional creation and creator's muse, source of creation. The real-life harlot after whom Boule de suif is modeled, Adrienne Legay, is merely the first in a long series of women who awakened Maupassant's authorial being, provided it with the nourishment upon which it was to feed for ten years. Maupassant's unsuspected talent, revealed *du jour au lendemain* with the publication of "Boule de suif", may have caused some *mauvaises langues* to wag about collaboration with Flaubert (a rumour belied by the correspondence between the two men);[1] a retrospective look reveals that Maupassant's true "collaborator", in this as in countless later stories and the novels as well, is *la Femme*, Woman, who becomes the inspiration and the meeting place for metaphors as widely divergent as those evoked here. Whether viewed as a nourishing mother, a symbol of the Empire, the desired Republic or a humiliated France, Boule de suif and her avatars throughout Maupassant's gynocentric fictional universe remain intimately linked to their creator's literary triumph.

9. The notion of prostitute as *Liberté* is explicit in "La Maison Tellier": one of the harlots, nicknamed Cocotte, always dresses "en *Liberté* avec une ceinture tricolore" (I, 259).
1. Forestier's quotations from the men's letters (p. 1296) convincingly refute this unjust accusation.

RICHARD BOLSTER

Mademoiselle Fifi: An Unexpected Literary Source[†]

* * *

In fact the study of the whole of Maupassant's war stories leads one
to the conclusion that he had a marked preference for plots which
almost proclaim their fictionality. The caricatural nature of the characters in *Un duel* is even stated explicitly: we are told they are like
comic figures in a satirical newspaper. Similarly, the story *Deux amis*
is reminiscent of children's tales in which there is an ogre who eats
human flesh. The Prussian officer in this tale is described as a hairy
giant. The killing of the two child-like Frenchmen is expressed in a
metaphor of eating which is used by one of the victims when he says
that if they are captured by the Prussians they will give them fish to
fry. The fish who will be fried will be themselves, and the elimination of the Frenchmen in *Deux amis* is a mirror image of the killing
and eating of the Prussians by the Turcos in *Tombouctou*. Maupassant's war stories are a mixture of two conflicting elements, one ludic
and ironic, the other serious and patriotic. At times the mixture
appears unstable, and one also observes a tension between his occasional denunciation of war in general, including reminders that the
Prussians too had suffered losses, and an imperfectly repressed ger-
manophobia which reasserts itself in revenge themes.

It is precisely this uneasy conjunction of conflicting messages
which, in my opinion, makes many of his war stories inferior to those
of Daudet. The latter possess greater thematic coherence and avoid
the cliché of the odious Prussian, that quickly stereotyped fictional
figure which appeared on the French literary scene in 1870–75. An
example of this mediocre patriotic literature is provided by P. Joliot's
novel *Les Trois Hulans* (1872), in which the action concludes with
the cliché of a plucky French girl defending her honour by killing a
lecherous Prussian, just as Maupassant's Rachel will kill Fifi. It must
be admitted that, with the exception of *Boule de suif* and *Mademoiselle Fifi*, Maupassant's war stories are not his best productions.
Despite this, they have struck the popular imagination in a way that
the more refined, moderate and subtle war stories of Daudet have
not achieved. It is certain that the popular success of the war stories of Maupassant can be explained by their dramatic and patriotic
tendencies.

The discovery of a literary source for *Mademoiselle Fifi* enables us
to study Maupassant's creative method. It also raises the question

† From *Maupassant Conteur et Romancier*, ed. Christopher Lloyd and Robert Lethbridge
(Durham: DMLS, Durham University Press, 1994), pp. 36–39. Reprinted by permission
of the author.

of originality. This was a matter on which he had expressed himself explicitly in his article 'Le Roman' (*R.*712): 'Qui peut se vanter, parmi nous, d'avoir écrit une page, une phrase qui ne se trouve déjà, à peu près pareille, quelque part'. His reply to this question was an assertion of the possibility of originality for the modern writer, despite the great monument of past literature. Originality was 'une manière spéciale de penser, de voir, de comprendre et de juger'. *Mademoiselle Fifi* takes the essential facts of the Judith story and modifies them in significant ways. One change made by Maupassant is stylistic, as he creates a sophisticated network of metaphors related to cutting, mutilation, invasion and violation. Another modification is the downgrading of the character of the invader into a figure who is a combination of cruelty and effeminacy. Whereas Holophernes is manly, Fifi is small, blond, and coquettish in dress. In his requests to his superior officer he has 'des grâces de chatte, des cajoleries de femme, des douceurs de voix d'une maîtresse affolée par une envie' (I, 390). An important change made by Maupassant's tale is therefore the transformation of a warrior into a woman, in a reversal of the earlier transformation of woman into warrior which is a striking feature of the biblical story. But whereas the virtuous Judith kills Holophernes treacherously in his bed while he sleeps, Maupassant's frank and reckless prostitute kills Fifi in frontal attack, like a man. Where Judith is calculating and cool, the patriotic act of Rachel is impulsive and accidental. Another difference in the treatment of the theme by Maupassant can be seen in the tone of the narrative. That of the biblical account is serious and moralistic, and there is textual evidence that it was probably written by a source close to the high priest Joachim, who receives flattering mention. By contrast, Maupassant's version contains elements of comedy and irony. The portrayal of the Prussians by Maupassant tends towards caricature, whereas the Book of Judith does not describe the Assyrians as sadistic, wanton or odious. In short, the biblical story has the serenity of an account of a distant past in which history has been softened and turned into patriotic legend. It is conceived as an uplifting and morally useful fable, whereas Maupassant's story expresses anger, the memory of recent suffering, the desire for revenge, and the provocative theme of the accidentally heroic prostitute and delinquent.

Maupassant knew that the history of literature was full of accounts of war, some openly fictional, some attempting to be factual, some a mixture of the two. There were ancient and prestigious examples like the works of Homer and Virgil, and more recent ones like those of Stendhal and Tolstoy. The theme of war, so frequently treated over the centuries, has not produced a proportionate amount of great literature. But the unknown author of the Book of Judith knew how

362 RACHEL KILLICK

to narrate a tale. His account has the timeless elements of sex, violence, patriotism and revenge. Whether or not the Israelites did
really win a war by the method related in the Bible, we can understand why Maupassant felt that the story of Judith deserved to be
resurrected discreetly and applied to the events of his own time. He
believed that this horrific tale of the temptress and decapitator contained an old and essential truth about human nature. It expressed
dramatically the idea that life is made of conflict, of sexual impulse,
of war between nations and between the sexes. For Maupassant, the
essential theme in *Mademoiselle Fifi* was probably the war between
the sexes. His story is based on the principle that modern literature
may owe much to the observation of contemporary reality. The modern world provides a store of verifiable events. But it is also a source
which is encumbered by chance events and unnecessary detail. He
therefore believed that a writer should be capable of looking beyond
realism and the observation of contemporary reality. This is why he
returned to ancient literature and to myth, adapting its structures
and repeating some of its portrayal of a human nature which he saw
as unchanging, disturbing and incorrigible.

Maupassant's adaptation of the Judith story is in several ways
parodic. Whereas the Bible narrates the killing of the commander
of a great army, and the defeat of an empire, he reduces it to a minor
event in a French village. The transformation of the pious biblical
heroine into a prostitute is part of the parodic adaptation. Yet the
patriotic theme remains a central part of the plot, for Maupassant's
intention was not solely parodic. There remains the question of literary quality already mentioned: did he successfully combine the
serious nature of the Bible story with the ironic elements added
by himself? Not all readers will feel that Maupassant did this in a
wholly satisfactory manner. Yet the added parodic element was the
original contribution of a writer hungry for new themes, and who
must have enjoyed the joke of taking a good story furtively from the
Bible, leaving just one small clue in the tale of his Jewish Rachel.

RACHEL KILLICK

Mock Heroics? Narrative Strategy in a Maupassant War Story[†]

Discussion of authorial and narratorial perspective in Maupassant's
tales, first explored by J.-P. Sartre in *Qu'est-ce que la littérature?*
(1948), has recently acquired new impetus with the appearance of a

[†] From *Modern Language Review* 82 (1987): 313–26. Reprinted by permission of the author.

number of articles dealing with Maupassant's manipulation of narrative stance and frame narration. Some of these, seeing in the subject-matter merely a metaphor for narrative process, endeavour, somewhat unconvincingly, to transform Maupassant into a crypto-structuralist.[1] Others, accepting the intrinsic interest of the author's chosen material, point helpfully to the often considerable narrational ambiguities of the superficially innocent Maupassant text and the tensions of attitude and philosophy which are thereby revealed.[2] Where the Franco-Prussian War is concerned, it seems clear that Maupassant is treating a subject important to him on its own merits and that any interpretation failing to take this into account could be only a perverse one. However, it is also true that his handling of the theme shows an acute awareness of the different impact of various narrative strategies and that these are skilfully exploited to allow both for the prejudices of a varied public and for his own ambiguities of attitude. A particularly clear demonstration of the use of a range of different narrational possibilities is given by the three successive versions of his tale *Le Mariage du lieutenant Laré* (1878), reworked in *Souvenir* (1882) and in *Les Idées du Colonel* (1884).[3]

J. Thoraval, in *L'Art de Maupassant d'après ses variantes* (Paris, 1950), extensively considered the first and last of these versions as one of the main illustrations of his general thesis of a move in Maupassant's technique towards greater realism and greater coherence and precision. However, his comparison of *Le Mariage du lieutenant Laré* and *Les Idées du Colonel* is carried out piecemeal over a number of chapters dealing separately with plot, characterization, description, and so on, and there is no unified discussion of the two versions as individual units, each with its own narrational technique and shape. Furthermore, he appears unaware of the second version of the story, *Souvenir*, which forms an important intermediate stage in the evolution of the text. In contrast, this article proposes an examination of all three versions, considering each in its entirety in order to show how changes in narrative stance and frame technique modify the reader's perception of the text and make increasingly evident the ambiguous attitude of the author towards those displays of daring, valour, chivalry, and national feeling which combine to form a stereotype of heroic behaviour.

---

1. For example, Angela S. Moger, 'That Obscure Object of Narrative', *Yale French Studies*, 63 (1982–83), 129–38, and 'Narrative Structure in Maupassant: Frames of Desire', *PMLA*, 100 (May 1985), 315–27.
2. For example, Gerald Prince, 'Nom et destin dans *La Parure*, *French Review*, 55 (1982), 267–71.
3. Maupassant, *Contes et nonvelles*, 2 vols, edited by Louis Forestier (Paris, 1974, 1979), I, 65–69; I, 362–66; II, 162–67. Further references are by volume number and page number to this edition.

   The original story, *Le Mariage du lieutenant Laré* is one of Maupassant's earliest tales and the first concerned with the Franco-
Prussian War, antedating by two years the publication of *Boule de
suif* in the *Soirées de Médan* (Paris, 1880). It recounts how a young
lieutenant leads his men to relieve a beleaguered general, rescuing
on the way a young girl and her father, who are fleeing from the
Prussians, and killing a dozen uhlans whom they encounter en route.
Narration is in the third person, a mode suggestive of neutral 'fac-
tuality' to the casual or naive reader. The reality is, however, that
preconceptions and assumptions may often be volunteered as 'truth'
by the third-person mode, the absence of any obvious proponent
conferring on them a spurious universal validity. In fact, the story
here is a highly programmed one. It relies on an implicit consensus
between narrator and reader as to what a hero is and the rewards
he should receive and constructs the hero-figure in terms of a number of easily recognizable *topoi*. The traditional centring of the
narrative on a single individual (the 'hero' in the literary sense)
constitutes an initial stage, creating that assumption of individual
value and individual effectiveness upon which the notion of heroism depends. From the very first sentence the story concentrates on
the young officer Laré and his outstanding military prowess. Developing this perspective, the three opening paragraphs form an exposition that successively proposes three different aspects of Laré's
military achievement and simultaneously acts as a 'mise en abyme'
for the forthcoming action, setting out in advance a model of heroic
action and reward (paragraph 1) and explicitly foreshadowing the
saving of the general and the killing of the uhlans (paragraphs 2
and 3).
   The first paragraph, isolating a single daring exploit, establishes
Laré as a man of action, moving swiftly to take the initiative. The
grammatical subject of the first sentence, he directs its activity, setting up an atmosphere of decision and control operative throughout
the story: 'Dès le début de la campagne, le lieutenant Laré prit aux
Prussiens deux canons.' In a pattern that is paradigmatic for the
story as a whole, public recognition of his daring ('Son général lui
dit: "Merci, lieutenant", et lui donna la croix d'honneur') follows
instantly in the second sentence, the immediate juxtaposition of
thanks and reward to action in adjacent but uncoordinated main
clauses suggesting an inevitable and self-evident pattern of cause
and effect which a linking conjunction could only have weakened.
   The figure of Laré, man of action, is followed in the second paragraph by that of Laré, leader of men. The single act of daring of the
first paragraph is now expanded into a general assessment of his
qualities. Following the *topos* of a fairy-tale ('as good as she was
beautiful, as handsome as he was brave') these are now enlarged to

encompass the complementary virtue of prudence, a trait explaining his outstanding success not merely as the exponent of individual acts of bravery but also as a responsible leader of others, capable of raising his men to a heroic level comparable to his own.

The third paragraph adds a further dimension to the stereotype of the young officer-hero, developing his role as the miraculous saviour of his country. From the beginning of the exposition the unpalatable fact of invasion and defeat is carefully neutralized, the first paragraph showing Laré taking the initiative against the Prussians, the final clauses of the second paragraph ('et il organisa un service d'éclaireurs qui, dans les retraites, sauva plusieurs fois l'armée') enveloping the phrase 'dans les retraites' in an account of his dynamic organizing and the successes of his scouts. Now the saviour motif comes to the fore, the invasion, presented as elsewhere in Maupassant in terms of an overwhelming natural cataclysm, being juxtaposed with the quasi-miraculous ubiquity and skill of the lieutenant who constantly gets the better of an enemy that far outnumbers him while managing against all the odds to keep his brigade virtually intact.

The account of the rescue mission and the killing of the uhlans in the story proper allows a more detailed display of these exceptional talents and is presented in terms which emphasize the formidable, not to say superhuman, endurance of Laré and his men. The logistics and problems of the operation are clearly set out: the number of men involved, the distance to be marched, the tightness of the time factor, the threat of enemy encounter en route, the hostile weather. Laré and his men, however, seem impervious to the difficulties. They advance in good military order and the men left as markers, 'fantôme(s) blanc(s) debout dans la neige', remain unaffected by the cold, standing as 'échelons *vivants*' (my italics) for the main force that is to follow. Laré himself plays a leading role throughout, heading the march with a small advance platoon of men and reconnoitring the wood and the château with them. He is manifestly in control of the situation, knowing the exact whereabouts of his party, and, in a development of the *topos* of the military man as a man of few but telling words initiated in the general's thanks of paragraph I, handling the interrogation of the old man with terse efficiency. The portrayal of his military skills reaches a climax first in the incident with the uhlans, then in the successful repulse of the Prussians at Blainville. The uhlan patrol is depicted as totally overwhelmed by Laré's force, which in one united burst of gunfire dispatches at a single stroke all twelve horses and riders. Similarly, in the larger encounter with the Prussians at the end of the story, Laré and his men display almost unbelievable efficiency and energy; arriving in the camp in a winter's dawn, they are fighting by nine o'clock and by twelve o'clock have forced the Prussians to withdraw, a retreat given misleading conclusiveness by careful choice of tenses: 'A neuf heures les Prussiens *attaquaient*. Ils *battaient* en retraite à midi' (my italics). Following the pattern established in the first paragraph, public recognition of Laré's services is immediate ('Le soir . . . le général le prit par la main . . . "voici un de mes meilleurs officiers . . . le meilleur"'), and the last paragraph of the story, echoing the insistence of the first on Laré's military rank, confirms his military success as it notes the 'fait accompli', one year later, of his promotion to captain.

The story does not confine itself, however, to stereotypes of military daring and valour in the field. Instead, in an overdetermination of the heroic figure, it develops in parallel with the figure of the dashing young officer saving his country that of the knight of romance, assisting the weak and defenceless and rescuing the damsel in distress. Here again Laré displays his characteristic efficiency and decisiveness; the order for the building of the litter to transport the girl when she is incapable of walking further is presented in the pluperfect tense ('L'officier avait donné un ordre'), the narrator thus suggesting the amazing ease with which Laré resolves an unforeseen and difficult situation. But the main function of the encounter, which in this first version is of capital importance for Laré's designation as hero, is less to provide supplementary reinforcement to the portrayal of the military superman than to enable a reference to a complementary code of chivalrous gallantry. The imagery used to describe the girl situates her clearly within the stereotype of the heroine of romance. On the one hand, the well-worn simile of dawn, superficially motivated by the day-break entry into camp, suggests an idealization of her youth, beauty, freshness, and purity. On the other, the comparison to the oriental queen borne along by her slaves links the elevation of the girl on her makeshift litter with the associated trend to idolization, characteristic of the conventions of courtly love. Laré's response to the plight of the girl and her father is in the best tradition of the genre. He triumphantly survives the 'test' imposed on him by their humble disguise, treating them with courtesy and consideration; he slays the 'monster' threatening them (in this case the uhlan patrol, which appears in the distance 'comme un monstre fantastique, qui s'allongeait ainsi qu'un serpent'); finally he is duly recompensed by the hand of the young girl who turns out to be not only beautiful but aristocratic and rich. This marriage into the aristocracy acts as a kind of consecration of Laré as true knight and hero. Heroism, so the incident suggests, is the apanage in the first instance of an aristocratic élite. The old Count, whose nobility of mind transcends his physical frailty, is the model here and it is he who provides the explicit formulation ('"Mon lieutenant", dit-il en sanglotant, "nous gènerions trop votre marche. La France avant tout. Laissez-nous"') of the ethos of forgetfulness of self and commitment to country assumed throughout by the third-person narrator.

Presentation of Laré as a hero also depends, of course, on the reader's perception of his enemies. It is clear that the third-person narrator, far from being impartial, sees Frenchness as an automatic positive value. This view is explicitly formulated in the remark of the Count cited above and in the loving reference by the narrator to the inspirational effect of woman on 'le vieux sang français'. But it is implicit throughout in the contrast between the French soldiers who can do no wrong and the Prussian soldiers who can do no right. The latter, shown initially as a sort of destructive force of nature which a tiny band of daring Frenchmen has to overcome against all the odds, are presented subsequently, in the account of the old man, as individually brutal—in total contrast to the perfect conduct of the chivalrous lieutenant and his men.[4] Their killing of innocent civilians (the Count's servants) makes their own demise a just retribution, thus eliminating any suggestion of brutality on the part of the French. Furthermore, the whole scene of the ambush takes place in an unreal and fantastic atmosphere which leaves no room for meditation on the human suffering involved in war. Glimpsed far out on the plain, first as 'une grande ombre noire qui courait' then as 'un monstre fantastique' and 'un serpent', the uhlans are perceived by the reader not as individual human beings suddenly and dreadfully done to death but as a fearful and treacherous monster, a target clearly ripe for the attentions of those giant-slayers, Laré and his men.

The various *topoi* used by Maupassant are clear, the story apparently resting on the assumption that narrator and reader have the same view as to their value. What is not entirely clear, however, is the extent to which the author can be identified with the view of the narrator. Is Maupassant the exploiter or the victim of the clichés which he utilizes here? The most likely possibility would seem to be the most obvious one: namely, that the story is a naive piece of youthful wishful thinking, both on the course of the Franco-Prussian War and on the more general questions of heroism and patriotism.[5] However, two alternative readings cannot be totally excluded, though the early date of the story and the subsequent modifications to it make them arguably less probable. The first would see the story as an opportunistic piece, a comforting fairy tale deliberately aimed at

4. Huysmans, Sac au dos, and Hennique, L'Affaire du grand 7, in the Soirées de Médan, provide a powerful corrective to this idealized view of the French soldier.
5. Maupassant's persistent emotional attachment to a patriotism that he intellectually rejects is indicated in conversations recorded by Zola, quoted in André Vial, Guy de Maupassant el l'art du roman (Paris, 1954), p. 166, and by Maupassant's valet, François Tassart, Souvenirs (Paris, 1911), pp. 298–99.

a simple or revanchist public still smarting from defeat, and hence as an early example of that preoccupation with his potential audience that informs Maupassant's later career as a professional writer. The second, more subtly, remembering Maupassant's reputation as a joker and the fact that by 1878 he was already in contact with Zola and the future participants in the *Soirées de Médan*, would favour the idea of a tongue-in-the-cheek exercise exploiting two levels of reading to satisfy simultaneously three groups of readers: those who would like to rewrite the scenario of the Franco-Prussian War; those who would like to debunk the heroic mythology of war altogether; and those, perhaps including the author himself, who cannot make up their minds between these alternatives.

The one certain aspect is the very different attitude emerging clearly in *Boule de suif*, two years later, and the very different slants given to the two subsequent versions of our particular story by a change in both to first-person narration and the introduction in both of a frame story. Louis Forestier assimilates the first-person narrator of *Souvenir* to the third-person narrator of *Le Mariage du lieutenant Laré*, seeing them as similarly anonymous and exterior to the action they recount, but this is a reading that overlooks the crucial significance of the move to a participant narrator (Maupassant, II, 1364–65). It is true that the narrator's identity is never clearly established; he is absorbed from the beginning into the communal pronouns 'on' and 'nous'; only in the postscript does he emerge as an independent 'je', and even then he remains anonymous in the shadow of the transcriber of the anecdote, Maupassant's *alter ego*, Maufrigneuse. But the important thing is that he offers an inside view of war as experienced by the nameless mass of the soldiers, a view based not on heroic deeds of individual derring-do but on shared physical hardship and suffering. The exposition of *Le Mariage du lieutenant Laré*, with its heroic *topoi*, is abolished in favour of direct entry into the realities of the situation, the story opening, like many others in which Maupassant deals with the experiences of 1870, on the theme of hunger, followed by references to cold, weariness, and general demoralization. This time there is no legerdemain on the part of the narrator to transform the Prussian invasion into an occasion for miraculous feats of daring and valour. Instead, the French are shown at bay, reduced in a month from 800 to 200 men, the account of their retreat no longer neutralized in the midst of a sentence recording their successes but emphasized by a descending threefold repetition of despairing participles—'Nous battions en retraite, entourés d'ennemis, cernés, perdus'. Their march through the snow is undertaken not to relieve their fellow soldiers but as a desperate attempt to reach the safety of their own lines. In accordance with this portrayal,

there is no victorious repulse of the Prussians at the end of the
story, merely an account of the safe entry of the soldiers into the
Blainville camp, and the details of the march that takes them there
are now orientated to emphasize the difficulties of the undertaking:
'douze lieues', not eight, separate them from Blainville; time is very
short, perhaps has already run out—'Si nous ne parvenions dans la
nuit à faire les douze lieues qui nous séparaient de la ville; ou bien si
la division était éloignée, plus d'espoir!'. The reason for marching at
night (to avoid the ubiquitous Prussians) is now spelled out in a separate single-sentence paragraph. Above all, the snow, only summar-
ily described in *Le Mariage du lieutenant Laré*, where it functions
as a means of revealing the hero's imperturbability, takes on an
active impeding role. The narrator lingers on the description of the
relentlessly falling flakes, associating them with images of collapse
and death ('Les muets flocons tombaient, tombaient, ensevelis-
saient tout dans ce grand drap gelé'). The snow-covered soldiers do
not appear as picturesque 'fantômes blancs' as they wait 'échelons
vivants', for the main force that is to follow but, in line with the general atmosphere and following through the logic of the image, they
are perceived by the narrator (who is one of them) as 'des fantômes,
comme les spectres de soldats *morts*' (my italics). Weariness and dis-
organization are total, the main body of the march no longer the two
disciplined columns of *Le Mariage du lieutenant Laré* but a confused tangle of weary men advancing 'en bloc, pêle-mêle, au hasard
des fatigues et de la longueur des pas' stopping to rest at random
before dragging themselves on again 'd'une allure exténuée'.

   This demythologizing first-hand presentation of the miseries of
war by an unnamed soldier-narrator also carries with it a comment
on the ability of individuals to control the course of events. The ill-
defined status of the narrator, allowing him a position that is simultaneously inside and outside the action, is crucial here. On the one
hand, he is a participant, realistically describing the plight in which
he and the other soldiers find themselves. On the other, he appears
to take little active part in the encounters he records and assumes
no responsibility for attempting to resolve either the military situation
or the problem created by the advent of the girl and her subsequent
exhaustion. His military rank is never stated. We do not know
whether he is an officer or an ordinary soldier, but from the beginning
his account makes it clear that the hierarchical distinction between
officers and men is an illusory one that has collapsed under pressure
of levelling external phenomena: hunger, cold, fear, despair.[6] His

---

6. 'Depuis la veille, on n'avait rien mangé. Tout le jour, nous restâmes cachés dans une
grange, serrés les uns contre les autres pour avoir moins froid, les officiers mêlés aux
soldats, et tous abrutis de fatigue' (I, 362).

passivity is part of an overall lack of determination and initiative which shows itself in a general fragmentation of figures of authority. There is no longer, as there was in *Le Mariage du lieutenant Laré* an outstanding officer and leader on whose bravery and decisiveness everyone and everything depends. Instead, the focus of attention, whether for passive experiencing or for decision-making, is the amorphous 'on' ('Depuis la veille on n'avait rien mangé . . . on changeait [les sentinelles] d'heure en heure') or, less frequently, reflecting the limited degree of the narrator's personal involvement, 'nous'. In contrast to *Le Mariage du lieutenant Laré*, leadership of the column and responsibility for handling the encounters, first with the civilians, then with the uhlans, devolve on two separate individuals: first, an unidentified lieutenant, mentioned only once as the leader of the initial platoon and more remote and unimportant than the anonymous narrator; then the captain, also anonymous, who deals with father and girl and with the uhlans. Handling of the captain-character, initially at least, again suggests low profile and indecision. There is no mention of him till after the girl and the old man are apprehended and his reaction subsequently to the problem they pose is one of indecision mingled with exasperated sympathy. It is true that his directing role in the uhlan incident, more realistically described in this soldier's-view version, is more clearly indicated than was Laré's, but the story peters out with the safe arrival of the soldiers in camp and, unlike Laré, the captain has no opportunity for further demonstrations of valiant leadership in beating back the Prussians.

This is not to say that all traces of heroism have vanished from the story. Qualities of compassion and courage are obviously still present, but what seems significant now is that as well as using his participant narrator to demythologize the conditions of war, Maupassant has been able, by removing the emphasis on the individual protagonist, to subvert the cliché of the gallant officer and transfer qualities of initiative, altruism, and bravery to the mass of the men. Reversing the pattern of *Le Mariage du lieutenant Laré*, it is now they who inspire the captain and find a solution to the problem posed by the girl, a change reflecting a general tendency in Maupassant's war stories, from *Boule de suif* onwards, to take people from the most ordinary and sometimes most despised sections of society as exponents of heroic behaviour.

The result of this displacement, however, here as elsewhere, is twofold. On one level it enables Maupassant to undermine the traditional view of bravery and self-sacrifice as qualities particularly associated with an upper-class élite. In line with this, *Souvenir* sees the disappearance of the knightly stereotype central to the action of *Le Mariage du lieutenant Laré*. Captain and girl no longer participate in a special relationship in which the rest merely play a (literarily!) supporting role and there is no concluding fairy-tale marriage to confirm the officer's status as hero. At the same time, the Count is presented in a more realistic and less sentimental light and his grandiloquent heroics are suppressed. The girl, losing the idealizing and idolizing images that characterized her in *Le Mariage du lieutenant Laré*, is assimilated first to average womanhood ('Tout à coup un cri aigu, un cri de femme, cette déchirante et vibrante note qu'*elles* jettent dans leurs épouvantes, traversa la nuit épaissie par la neige' (my italics)), then, in a complete departure from the courtly convention and reflecting now the political adherence of the ordinary soldiery, to the idea of the Republic.

On another level, however, this modification of the stereotype produces more ambiguous results. The portrayal of the men seems favourable both in the incident with the girl and in their reaction to the killing of the uhlans, where their comments may be construed as showing more sense of the horror of war and more human awareness than the captain's heartless totting up of the number of his victims does. On the other hand it could be argued that they are also depicted as naive and unduly influenced by the clichés with which their society is permeated. The notion of the inspirational effect of Woman upon the chivalrous French, propounded as an incontrovertible truth by the third-person narrator of *Le Mariage du lieutenant Laré*, reappears in *Souvenir* as part of the mental furniture of the first-person narrator who, replacing the image of the Queen and her slaves with that of the 'coup de vin', formulates it, without the rhetoric of the original version, in terms appropriate to his own situation.[7] However, despite the more down-to-earth quality of his style as compared with that of the third-person narration of *Le Mariage du lieutenant Laré*, the narrator seems content at this point to echo a prevailing social view and shows no tendency to question its validity or implications. It could perhaps be seen as significant, though, that later on, in contrast to his fellow soldiers, he apparently plays no part in actively helping the girl. If the narrator's position remains uncertain, the author does set out the problem rather more clearly by introducing into the text a replay of the cliché, where the neutrally literate style of the narrator is replaced by the

<hr>

7. Thus 'comme une reine d'Orient portée par ses esclaves, [la jeune fille] fut placée au milieu du détachement, qui reprit sa marche plus fort, plus courageux, plus allègre, réchauffé par la présence d'une femme, cette souveraine inspiratrice qui a fait accomplir tant de prodiges au vieux sang français' (*Le Mariage du lieutenant Laré*) becomes 'la jeune fille . . . se trouva soulevée par six bras robustes qui l'emportèrent. On repartit comme si on eût bu un coup de vin, plus gaillardement, plus joyeusement. Des plaisanteries couraient même, et cette gaieté s'éveillant que la présence d'une femme redonne toujours au sang français' (*Souvenir* I, 67–68, 364).

crude and uneducated speech of the old 'franc-tireur': 'Je n'suis plus jeune, moi, et bien, cré coquin, l'sexe, y a tout d'même que ça pour vous flanquer du cœur au ventre.' The effect of this addition to the text is not to resolve the ambivalence vaguely exemplified in the narrator but rather to highlight it in a way capable of satisfying two diametrically opposed publics: on the one hand, it could be argued that Maupassant is bringing extra stress to the presentation of the simple heroic chivalry of the ordinary man; on the other, that the linguistic shortcomings of the addition provide a critical gloss on the dubious nature of the cliché. If the narrator's position on the generally held view of Woman is ambiguous, his reticence with regard to the political views of his fellow soldiers is relatively obvious. He does not appear to share in their transformation of the girl into an image of the Republic and identifies their shout of 'Vive la République!' with a sort of mass hysteria, using vocabulary which suggests his distaste for the unreflective flag-waving mentality it reveals: 'Et un *enthousiaste*, pour exprimer sa joie, ayant *vociféré* "Vive la République!" toute la troupe, *comme prise de folie, beugla frénétiquemnet*: "Vive la République!"' (my italics).

The common soldier, then, seems to be presented as a hero in so far as he is called upon to suffer hardship and danger, but he is an unsatisfactory hero in so far as his attitudes are formed unreflectively and are bound up in his general acceptance of the stereotyped patterns of behaviour foisted upon him by his society.

On the French side, the *topos* of heroism has been shifted from officers to men and has been further shaken by the implication of a certain naivety at its roots. Furthermore, the sense of the heroism of the French is modified by a nuancing in the presentation of the Prussians. The initial effect here of the change to first-person narration is a greater awareness of Prussian mastery, now experienced directly and not dissembled as in Le Mariage du lieutenant Laré, behind a consoling façade of French heroics. Subsequent reference to the individual brutality of the Prussians (the killings at the château) remains the same. However, in contrast to the earlier version, the first-hand account of the participant narrator of Souvenir also allows, in counterpoint to Prussian violence, a more realistic account of the ambush of the uhlans by the French, the horrific detail of war now replacing the 'twelve at one blow' fairy-tale tidiness of Le Mariage du lieutenant Laré.[8]

8. 'Cinquante coups de fusil crevèrent le silence gelé des champs; quatre ou cinq détonations attardées partirent encore, puis une autre, toute seule la dernière; et quand l'aveuglement de la poudre enflammée fut dissipé, on vit que les douze hommes, avec neuf chevaux, étaient tombés. Trois bêtes s'enfuyaient d'un galop forcené, et l'une traînait derrière elle, pendu par le pied à l'étrier, et bondissant, le cadavre de son cavalier' (I, 365).

The theme of the fragility and vulnerability of the human being is further supported by the comments of two anonymous soldiers underlining the human costs of the incident: 'Voilà des veuves!' and 'Faut pas grand temps tout d'même pour faire le saut'. This new emphasis on the human suffering involved in war diminishes the sense of the Prussians as alien creatures with whom the French can have nothing in common and throws into doubt the 'heroism' of the French attack, setting it more in parallel with the earlier brutalities of the Prussians at the château.

Overall in *Souvenir*, then, use of a first-person narrator, who stands within the mass of the men, produces an emphasis on the day-to-day reality of war, absent in *Le Mariage du lieutenant Laré*. This emphasis implies a judgement, destroying any sense of the glories of war. The introduction of a frame story fulfils an analogous function. Here the frame is a minimal one, superimposed on the central story only at the end in the form of a postscript which locates the event related twelve years earlier and explains the title, *Souvenir*. An initial reading thus leaves all the stress on the events of the 1870–71 winter's night and the casual reader might well see the postscript as a dispensable extra of no particular value or interest. On closer analysis, however, the four short closing paragraphs can be seen as having an effect quite disproportionate to their length, playing an important part in determining the reader's evaluation of the heroic significance of the central story. Replacing the French 'victory' and the marriage of the lieutenant of the first version, they close the text on a series of non-conclusions, allowing a clear realization of the negligible long-term results of the double incident of the rescue of the girl and the killing of the uhlans. There is no comment on the outcome of the war generally, the reader's perception of it, in the context of the story, remaining within the atmosphere of invasion and retreat, and there is no reference to the subsequent fate of the captain or that of his men. Where the narrator is concerned, his random remembrance of the incident, despite his emphasis on the clarity of the memory, testifies to its lack of moment in his experience. As for the girl, her life appears to have continued on its set course with a marriage within her own aristocratic circle, an ironic contrast to the soldiers' temporary association of her with the idea of the Republic. Furthermore, the value of the soldiers' actions in themselves, as examples of altruism and bravery providing a degree of moral compensation for the general brutality of war, is radically undermined by the sudden contextualization of the story in a forgotten past. Reduced to a mere anecdote, arising quite fortuitously from the chance glimpse of a long-forgotten protagonist, the events related become remarkable chiefly for their lack of permanent worth, the frame thus serving to destroy the very concept on which the heroic ethos is based.

Le Mariage du lieutenant Laré, as I have shown, could lend itself to a number of different readings, but it is difficult to assess whether any but the most obvious is intended by the author. In *Souvenir*, on the other hand, Maupassant clearly offers his varied readership a text susceptible of a range of interpretations. Either it can be seen as a tribute to the ordinary soldier who is forced to suffer the hardships of war and who is yet on occasion capable of generous and courageous conduct or, more subtly, in view of the indeterminate status of the narrator and the perspective given by the frame, it may be considered a critique of the motivations and ultimate relevance of so-called 'heroic' behaviour. Lastly, an ambiguous reading is possible, one combining the two elements, admitting the genuineness of human bravery and generosity of spirit, but questioning the limitations of human intellect which allow those qualities to be manipulated in the service of war.

In the third version of the story, *Les Idées du Colonel*, both narrative stance and frame technique undergo further modification and development. First-person narration is retained but the narrator moves from being an anonymous figure occupying an ambivalent position, half inside and half outside the mass of the soldiers, to becoming the commanding officer himself, the protagonist of the story he recounts. On one level there seems to be a return to the character-centred presentation of *Le Mariage du lieutenant Laré*, the reader once more being offered the traditional hero-figure of the brave officer successfully struggling against the odds to lead his men to safety. In the 1884 version, moreover, it could be argued that the heroism of the protagonist emerges more convincingly because of the more realistic presentation of the circumstances with which he is called upon to deal. Whereas the third-person narrator of *Le Mariage du lieutenant Laré* builds up the exceptional nature of Laré and his achievements by an initial list of his qualities and exploits which has to be taken on trust, the picture of physical exhaustion and general demoralization in *Les Idées du Colonel*, given first-hand by a soldier-narrator, underlines the extent of the qualities of leadership and courage demanded by the situation. The effect is increased by the soldierly vigour of the captain's language as compared with the neutral and anonymous style of the unidentified narrator of *Souvenir*.[9] Furthermore, the presentation is sharpened by the fact that the narrator is no longer an anonymous soldier, passively

---

9. 'Nous étions cernés, pourchassés, éreintés, abrutis, mourant d'épuisement et de faim. Or, il nous fallait avant le lendemain gagner Bar-sur-Tain, sans quoi nous étions flambés, coupés et massacrés' (II, 163).

contemplating a 'débâcle' which is beyond his authority or will to control, but the commanding officer, who has the responsibility of dealing with the situation and whose awareness of the gravity of his problem is all the more acute for that responsibility.[1] Against this background the captain, showing qualities of authority and toughness to ensure the obedience and hence the safety of his men, displays a heroism consonant with the extreme circumstances in which he and his men are placed.[2]

However, though the captain could thus be perceived by the reader as a hero-figure, it would also be possible to argue that he does not fulfil all the requirements for such a designation. Though he is clearly a more forceful leader than the two officers of Souvenir, he equally clearly lacks Laré's quality of imaginative initiative and is at a loss when he has to deal with a situation unforeseen by the military rule-book. Thus, in the incident with the girl, as in Souvenir, it is once again the men, led here by an individual significantly nick-named 'Pratique', who take over his leadership function. Les Idées du Colonel continues, though to a less-marked degree, the displace-ment of heroic qualities away from the officer-figure towards the ordinary soldier. However, this displacement, already ambivalent in Souvenir, now reflects its ambivalence back upon the officer/narra-tor in a new development, suggesting a further restriction on his des-ignation as a heroic figure. Where the narrator of Souvenir appears to maintain a certain detachment from the attitudes of his fellow soldiers, the captain, though distinguished by his rank from the mass of the men, nevertheless clearly identifies closely with them.[3] Unlike the vocabulary of the narrator of Souvenir, who expresses himself in a way that is linguistically distinct from the rest of the soldiery, the speech habits of the captain, though somewhat less 'populaires' than those of his men, are not markedly dissimilar in choice of words and in general tone,[4] suggesting a mode of thought which, like theirs,

1. Hence, in part at least, his reiterated insistence on the direness of the predicament: 'Nous avions donc douze lieues à faire pendant la nuit, douze lieues sous la neige, le ventre vide. Moi, je pensais: "C'est fini, jamais mes pauvres diables d'hommes n'arriveront"' (II, 163). 'La neige semblait nous ensevelir tout vivants; elle poudrait les képis et les capotes sans fondre dessus, faisait de nous des fantômes, des espèces de spectres de soldats morts, bien fatigués. Je me disais: "Jamais nous ne sortirons de là à moins d'un miracle"' (II, 164). The other and no doubt dominant factor is the colonel's desire to prove his point concerning the galvanizing effect of Woman on the French sol-dier (see my subsequent discussion of the story).
2. Their demoralized lack of reaction when ordered to march out is overcome by a show of force, Laporte threatening to shoot those who fail to comply and placing 'les plus sol-ides par-derrière avec ordre d'accélérer les traînards à coup de baïonnette . . . dans le dos' (II, 163, 164).
3. The terms 'les enfants' (Laporte to his men) and 'frérots' (Pratique to his fellow soldiers) underline the quasi-familial relationships.
4. As the exchange between Laporte and Pratique well suggests: 'Pratique prononça: "Allons, les camaraux, faut porter cette demoiselle-là, ou bien nous n' sommes pu Fran-çais, nom d'un chien!" Je crois, ma foi, que je jurai de plaisir. "Nom d'un nom, c'est gen-til, ça, les enfants"' (II, 165).

is essentially that of a man of action, not of reflection. As they march into the camp with the girl to the shout of 'Vive la France!' the captain's reaction is as emotional and as unanalytical as that of his men ('Et, *je ne sais pourquoi*, je me sentis tout remué' (my italics)), and he fails totally to appreciate the gap between his idealizing perception of the girl as France and madonna combined and her lightweight self-interested reality, as it emerges in the exchange following the Prussian deaths: 'Elle murmura: "Pauvres gens!" *Mais* comme elle avait froid, elle redisparut sous les capotes' (my italics).

Through his choice and handling of a first-person protagonist/narrator, Maupassant is thus able to suggest the possibilities and limitations of the traditional soldier-hero in the real conditions of war. A final element in this portrayal is provided by the presentation of the uhlan incident. As in *Souvenir* the realistic first-hand account has a significant role in undermining the mythology of the heroic glory of military slaughter. However, in *Les Idées du Colonel* the plot is also modified to make the point yet more obvious. In contrast to the other two versions, the girl and her father flee their home, not because the Prussians have actually killed anyone but because they are drunk. It also seems doubtful that the uhlan patrol encountered by the captain and his men is the same as that occupying the house of the old man and his daughter. The 'douze uhlans perdus dans la nuit', shadowy figures dimly apprehended in the gloom, of *Le Mariage du lieutenant Laré* and *Souvenir*, now become 'douze uhlans perdus qui cherchaient leur route', a change that not only suggests a different group of uhlans but also stresses their isolation and vulnerability. The French assault upon the Prussians can thus no longer be perceived either as the heroic slaying of a dangerous monster (*Le Mariage du lieutenant Laré*) or as a justifiable act of revenge (*Souvenir*). Instead, the incident reinforces a view of war not as heroic activity but as a slaughter of lost and helpless innocents.

The central story already displays a certain ambiguity regarding the heroic status of Laporte, but it is an ambiguity which the reader, on the basis of the central story alone, might infer or not, as he or she chooses. The author, however, through his use of a frame structure, developing the key factor of the character of his protagonist/narrator, does in fact impose a definite perspective on the story, decisively indicating an appropriate interpretation of it. The frame element of *Souvenir* was concentrated as a postscript at the end of the text, thus leaving to the central story the possibility of an initial undirected reading. The major section of the frame element of *Les Idées du Colonel* is placed at the beginning and thus controls the reader's perception of the entire text. Laporte's introduction of himself and his views forms a short exposition, analogous to that of

Le Mariage du lieutenant Laré that establishes the value system upon
which the central story is based. However, in contrast to the original version, where the third-person narrative, citing Laré's exploits
and qualities, offers them as examples of a code of heroic behaviour
unquestioningly accepted by narrator and reader alike, the presentation here of the code of chivalry through the mouth of the individual Laporte situates it, in line with the title, as an *idea*, a personal
construct bearing more relationship to the character and beliefs of
its proponent than to an absolute system of moral values. The initial atmosphere, moreover, is one of dissent, the colonel apparently
advancing his story in response to an objection raised in an ongoing
conversation. The end of the text reiterates this impression, the colonel concluding his tale with a defiant repetition of his opening
remarks.

The reader is thus invited from the outset to make a critical assessment of the colonel's value system, taking into account his nature
and personality as revealed in his conversation. Laporte is clearly a
dyed-in-the-wool traditionalist, hankering after the soldier's erst-
while vocation as God's crusader and seeing his present role still
very much in terms of the chivalry of the knight-errant, which he
identifies in particular with the chivalry of the French towards a
pretty woman. Tradition is for him a value in itself and, significantly,
after initially presenting his own longevity in a negative context of
physical immobilization ('je suis vieux, j'ai la goutte, les jambes
raides, comme des poteaux de barrière') he almost immediately proceeds to valorize age by reference to the good old codes of behaviour of his youth ('je suis un vieux galantin, moi, un vieux de la
vieille école').

Though Laporte makes a positive correlation between the age and
value of tradition, age, as represented by the colonel himself in the
manner of his argument, emerges in a much more negative light,
throwing into question the ideas supposedly sanctified by it. For the
colonel lacks not only physical agility but mental agility. The physical petrification of his limbs has as a counterpart the linguistic petrification apparent in his habit of incessant repetition, particularly
of the already repetitious phrase 'une femme, une jolie femme'. Awk-
wardness of physical movement is matched by the clumsy incompetence of his intellectual processes. He argues dogmatically from his
particular experience to the general, reiterating the pattern in order
to reinforce his point. At the same time he is quite unanalytical
about the nature of his responses: 'Moi, devant les yeux d'une femme,
d'une jolie femme, je me sens capable de tout . . . j'ai envie de *je ne
sais quoi*, de me battre, de lutter, de casser les meubles, de montrer
que je suis le plus fort, le plus brave, le plus hardi et le plus dévoué des
hommes' (my italics). The phraseology, anticipating that of the

central story, underlines the colonel's incapacity to see the long-standing social manipulation exemplified in his own and the soldiers' reactions to the girl. His view of woman is simple and quite unreal. Following the courtly tradition he idolizes her, failing to realize the enormous power which this gives her and which may well become the subject of abuse.[5] The opening image of jumping to her tune ('si une femme, une jolie femme, m'ordonnait de passer par le trou d'une aiguille, je crois que j'y sauterai comme un clown dans un cerceau') is thus a revealing one, whose significance the colonel himself fails to appreciate. Similarly, at the end of the text, the colonel's idea of a young girl as a kind of mascot for each regiment and his characterization of such a girl as a madonna ('Nom d'un nom, comme ça donnerait du vif au troupier, d'avoir une madone comme ça, une madone vivante, à côté du colonel') is patently ridiculous in any real-life military situation. Such females as might provide genuine military inspiration by their own military prowess are, on the other hand, assimilated willy-nilly to the bland madonna stereotype. Thus Joan of Arc is pressed into the service of the colonel's thesis on the inspirational effect of womankind apparently on the basis of her femininity rather than of her military skill (the latter representing a takeover of function from the traditionally male military hero which the colonel is apparently unable to acknowledge even in the sacrosanct person of France's national heroine).

Thus the obvious function of the frame narrative here is to undermine the heroic status of the protagonist by revealing his naivety of mind and his unquestioning acceptance of received ideas. It is, however, a procedure that Maupassant handles with subtlety and nuance. One might, for example, see the dependent status of the central story on the frame narrative ('Je me rappelle justement une petite anecdote de la guerre qui prouve bien que nous sommes capables

---

In 'La Lysistra moderne' Maupassant identifies the courtly view of Woman with a generalized female conspiracy: 'Grâce au christianisme, la femme au Moyen Age est devenue une espèce de fleur mystique, d'abstraction, de nuage à poésies. Elle a été une religion. Et sa puissance a commencé! / Que dis-je sa puissance? Son règne omnipotent! C'est alors seulement qu'elle a compris sa vraie force, exercé ses véritables facultés, cultivé son vrai domaine, l'Amour! L'homme avait l'intelligence et la vigueur brutale; elle a fait de l'homme son esclave, sa chose, son jouet. Elle s'est faite l'inspiratrice de ses actions, l'espoir de son cœur, l'idéal toujours présent de son rêve. / L'amour, cette fonction bestiale de la bête, ce piège de la nature, est devenu entre ses mains une arme de domination terrible: tout son génie particulier s'est exercé à faire de ce que les anciens considéraient comme une chose insignifiante la plus belle, la plus noble, la plus désirable récompense accordée à l'effort de l'homme. Et nous l'apercevons chez tous les peuples. Reine des rois et des conquérants, elle a fait commettre tous les crimes, fait massacrer des nations, affolé des papes . . .' (*Le Gaulois*, 30 December 1880, collected in Maupassant, *Chroniques*, edited by Hubert Juin, 3 vols (Paris, 1980), I, 130–31). In 'Zut', however (*Le Gaulois*, 5 July 1880, *Chroniques* 1, 262–67), it is journalists and politicians who are blamed for using the stereotype of the medieval knight, defender of the honour of his country, to arouse the patriotic fervour of the public.

de tout devant une femme') as symptomatic of the narrator's loss of personal independence *vis-à-vis* the clichés of his society. The central story, as related by the colonel, is no longer a tale involving individual decision or concerned with individual destiny. The later fortunes of the girl are irrelevant, as is the effect of the incidents related on Laporte's subsequent career. In contrast to *Le Mariage du lieutenant Laré*, the text makes no link between his current status as colonel and his previous rank as captain. Though Laporte is the ostensible protagonist, in reality the 'protagonist' is the corpus of 'ideas' which directs all his conduct. Heroism, the supposed purview of free, independent spirits, has been reduced to mere conformism.

Yet, even here, Maupassant leaves the door open for a more favourable estimation of the hero-figure, for another way of seeing the relationship between the frame and the central story would be to stress rather the gap between the two elements. In this context the argument might be that the split between the discursiveness of the frame and the activity of the central story is the formal exteriorization of the inner split between the colonel's capacities as a man of action and his ineptitude as a reflective and critical observer of the assumptions of his society. Within the context of the relationship of frame narrative to central story, as within that of the central story alone, the reader might thus feel able to compartmentalize the positive and negative aspects of the character and hence to make a qualified affirmative judgement on Laporte's status as hero.

Maupassant's reutilization of his fictional and journalistic material is sometimes adduced in support of a view that sees him as nothing more than a literary capitalist, interested only in securing the largest possible financial returns from his writing. However, as Thoraval points out, in the fiction at least, reutilization does not imply artistic laziness or dishonesty, since invariably significant rethinking and reworking of the text is involved. In the story considered here, the reworkings demonstrate clearly the increasing effort and skill of Maupassant as a narrative strategist, able to appeal to a wide range of audience opinion and simultaneously able to preserve the integrity of his evolving personal vision. In line with remarks in his various contemporary 'chroniques', he moves towards an increasingly pointed criticism of the heroic mythology of war, using the permutations of a first-person narrator and of frame technique to query, first discreetly (*Souvenir*) then more radically (*Les Idées du colonel*, the assumptions taken as read by the third-person narration of *Le Mariage du lieutenant Laré*. Yet, at the same time, the credibility of the heroic ethos is not entirely destroyed, for the same narrative devices are also used to suggest a distinction between the positive qualities of physical endurance and human compassion displayed by the protagonists and the clichéd rhetoric that exploits such qualities to promote and glorify the brutality of war. Reworking has thus produced two texts whose narrational subtleties, allowing a variety of interpretations and emphases, reveal Maupassant's growing maturity and skill as a writer and the use of that skill to propose and invite an essentially critical but nevertheless nuanced approach towards the stereotype of the traditional military hero.

TALES OF THE SUPERNATURAL

ROGER L. WILLIAMS

[Maupassant's Pathological Themes]†

* * * Many forms of fear appeared in Maupassant's work, but they were always morbid fears, never physiological. We understand that fear is a normal instinct which contributes to the preservation of the individual. Morbid, abnormal, or pathological fears are not associated with self-preservation, but, on the contrary, contribute to self-injury or self-destruction. Normal fear is not a phobia, but phobia is a morbid fear. The fears, or phobias, which Maupassant understood so astutely, derived from abnormal circumstances or mysterious influences which he found inexplicable or irrational, but which he never ascribed to the supernatural. Nor were his victims of phobias or obsessions portrayed as having lost their minds. Their ability to reason was unaffected, and they were fully conscious of the inexplicable horror that had entered their lives: lucid, not mad. People with phobias are particularly susceptible to hallucinations, just as there is an association between phobias and obsessions. But their hallucinations must be distinguished from those suffered by the mad. That is, they are autoscopic phenomena.

Two extreme interpretations of Maupassant's treatment of pathological themes can be found in the medical literature on him. Aided by the knowledge that Maupassant would end his days in an asylum, one group looked to his literary works for evidence of the disease that killed him. Assuming that his tales were the product of

† From "Guy de Maupassant," *The Horror of Life* (London: Weidenfeld and Nicolson, 1980), pp. 238–40. Reprinted by permission of the University of Chicago Press, the Orion Publishing Group, and the author.

precise self-observation, these observers not only detected the signs of approaching madness, but some suspected that Maupassant had suffered from moments of temporary madness long before he was shipped into seclusion: that he had experienced a progressive, systematized delirium with all the characteristics of paranoia, which led in the end to general paralysis. It must be emphasized that members of this group studied Maupassant's case before the connection between general paralysis and the tertiary stage of syphilis had been established.

The second extreme position took into account, quite correctly, that the period in which Maupassant wrote his stories of the terrifying irrational was a time when there was considerable research on psychic behavior, and when public attention was much occupied with such mysterious powers as somnambulism, magnetism, and hypnotism. Since Maupassant was far from indifferent to earning money, as it guaranteed him emancipation from the hated ministry, it was argued that he had catered to current public taste and interest by writing of the mysterious and the irrational. On sending his story *The Horla* to the publisher, Maupassant is said to have predicted that the newspapers would soon report him to be insane; but he insisted that he was quite sane and that the story had been deliberately designed to make the reader shudder.

Maupassant was indeed fortunate in the timeliness of his subject matter, but that does not account for his remarkable insight into the realm of phobias, obsessions, and hallucinations. It bears repeating that Maupassant could not have suffered himself from all the psychopathic maladies he so skillfully described. On the other hand, one can detect several thematic phobias and obsessions in Maupassant's literature, which, because of their repetition, may be considered his own. They gave him insight into related phenomena. It can be shown, moreover, that the various themes in Maupassant's dismal stories of human suffering were united by several common threads drawn from his personal experience. While he might say that a particular story had been deliberately designed to make the reader shudder, he also said that his larger purpose was not to amuse or to appeal to our feelings, but to compel us to reflect on the deeper meaning of events and to understand the occult. In particular, he endeavored to transmit his personal view of life and the world.

*   *   *

382

ALLAN H. PASCO

The Evolution of Maupassant's Supernatural Stories[†]

"Folie,"[1] "Les Chemins de la Démence,"[2] "Un témoignage
semi-autobiographique, où sont transposées des alarmes encore
confuses"[3]—despite the objections of a more perceptive minority of
writers who have treated Maupassant's supernatural stories as literature,[4] such one-sided conclusions reflecting biographical and
psychological bias have been detrimental to a critical appreciation
of these stories. The efforts Maupassant made to resolve the difficulties which differentiate this type of fiction from the rest of his
work indicate that he considered it a worthy endeavor.

He described these problems in an 1883 article, "Le Fantastique":

> Quand l'homme croyait sans hésitation, les écrivains fantas-
> tiques ne prenaient point de précautions pour dérouler leurs
> surprenantes histoires [. . .]
> Mais, quand le doute eut pénétré enfin dans les esprits, l'art
> est devenu plus subtil. L'écrivain a cherché les nuances, rôdé
> autour du surnaturel plutôt que d'y pénétrer. Il a trouvé des
> effets terribles en demeurant sur la limite du possible, en jetant
> les âmes dans l'hésitation, dans l'effarement. Le lecteur indé-
> cis ne savait plus, perdait pied comme en une eau dont le fond
> manque à tout instant, se raccrochait brusquement au réel pour
> s'enfoncer encore tout aussitôt, et se débattre de nouveau dans
> une confusion pénible et enfiévrante comme un cauchemar.

† From *Symposium* 23.2 (1969): 150–53, 156–59. Reprinted by permission of the publisher,
Taylor & Francis, Ltd.
1. Zacharie Lacassagne, *La Folie de Maupassant* (Toulouse, 1907), pp. 36–48.
2. Group title for the section which includes many of the stories which will be considered
in the next few pages, *in*: Albert-Marie Schmidt (ed.), *Guy de Maupassant: Contes et
nouvelles*, II (Paris, 1957), 1178–85. All the references to Maupassant's stories are
taken from this two-volume edition and will be identified solely by Roman numerals for
the volume and Arabic numerals for pagination. The supernatural stories in order of
publication are: "La Main d'écorché," "Sur l'Eau," "Magnétisme," "Fou?," "Conte de
Noël," "Apparition," "Lui?," "La Main," "La Chevelure," "Un Fou?," "Lettre d'un fou,"
"La Petite Roque," "Le Horla" (1st version), "Le Horla" (1887, definitive version), "La
Mort," "Qui sait?" Other stories of interest in this study: "Rêves," "La Peur," "Le Loup,"
"La Folle," "Auprès d'un Mort," "Suicides," "La Peur," "L'Horrible," "Le Tic," "Un Fou,"
"Le Diable," "Un Cas de Divorce," "L'Auberge," "Madame Hermet," "La Nuit,"
"Moiron," "Allouma," "L'Endormeuse," "L'Homme de Mars."
3. Pierre-Georges Castex, *Le Conte fantastique en France de Nodier à Maupassant* (Paris,
1951), p. 377.
4. See, e.g., Ferdinand Brunetière, "Les Nouvelles de Maupassant," *Revue des Deux
Mondes*, LXXXIX (1 octobre 1888), 704; Alphonse Daudet quoted by Saint-Réal, *Le
Gaulois*, 8 janvier 1892; Leo Tolstoy, *Zola, Dumas, Guy de Maupassant*, trans. E.
Halpérine-Kaminsky (Paris, 1896), pp. 145–68; René Dumesnil, *Le Réalisme* (Paris,
1936), pp. 420–21; André Vial, *Guy de Maupassant et l'Art du Roman* (Paris, 1954),
p. 242; Jean Thoraval, *L'Art de Maupassant d'après ses Variantes* (Paris, 1950), pp. 48–53,
66–74; Edward D. Sullivan, *Maupassant: The Short Stories* (London, 1962), pp. 23–35.

L'extraordinaire puissance terrifiante d'Hoffmann et d'Edgar Poe vient de cette habileté savante, de cette façon particulière de coudoyer le fantastique et de troubler, avec des faits naturels où reste pourtant quelque chose d'inexpliqué et de presque impossible.[5]

When studied in order of publication, the supernatural tales show that Maupassant continued to experiment with them until the period of "Le Horla," in the attempt to find the most efficacious technical combination for producing the desired state of *ébranlement* in the reader. As the passage from "Le Fantastique" indicates, his techniques were always those of a realist, depending on concrete detail to impart credibility to events that are far more "exceptional" than, for example, a tile falling on the head of a fictitious character.[6] Nevertheless, to say that Maupassant's devices were "realistic" gives no indication of how they were consciously built into the stories, in order to create the proper environment for the reaction he wished to elicit. Neither does it indicate which techniques he employed, which ones he later abandoned. Nor does it provide possible reasons for such change from 1875 to 1890.

"La Main d'Écorché," first published in 1875, exhibits many of the characteristics which became familiar through the whole of Maupassant's work. The story is anchored in a framework, for example— "Il y a huit mois environ, un de mes amis, Louis R . . . , avait réuni, un soir, quelques camarades de collège; nous buvions du punch" (II, 758)—which identifies the narrator and sets the scene. Narrated in the past tense of the impersonal first person (the narrator is not the protagonist), the story is full of specific concrete detail, even to the point of including two fictional newspaper clippings. Maupassant also uses the antiquated technique of suggesting a character is real by identifying him with an initial and ellipses. This latter device must have seemed ineffective to the author, for it does not appear in his late stories.

The detail and the calm, dispassionate narration—"En effet mon pauvre ami était fou" (II, 762)—were expected to render the tale realistic and believable, but Maupassant relied on the shock of violent contrast to create an effect on the reader. The laughter, the puns, the schoolboy jokes of the first few pages are laid against the announcement of a violent death; the beautiful day and the narrator eating a mulberry are opposed to the gravediggers preparing his friend's grave; the laughter of the laborers to the "main d'écorché."

---

5. "Le Fantastique," *Le Gaulois*, 7 octobre 1883; reprinted *in* Gérard Delaisement (ed.), *Maupassant: Journaliste et Chroniqueur* (Paris, 1956), pp. 236–37. See Maupassant's similar discussion in "La Peur" (II, 958–60).
6. "Le Roman," *Pierre et Jean*, ed. A. Schaffer (New York, 1936), pp. xxxix–xl.

Such contrast may shock the reader, of course, but it will not instill belief. Maupassant had not yet learned to lead his reader slowly and subtly into the realm of the supernatural. Neither had he learned to suggest or show rather than tell, to "[faire] passer des frissons dans les veines [. . .] sans mots à effet, sans expressions à surprise,"[7] since examples of the type: "Il avait un aspect effrayant" (II, 760), "Il eut peur" (II, 761), "Je me promenais tristement" (II, 762) abound.

In "Sur l'Eau," first published in 1876 under the title "En Canot," Maupassant used the personal first person (the narrator is also the protagonist). The story is written in the past tense and laid in a framework similar to that of "La Main d'Écorché." It is handled far more expertly than Maupassant's first attempt in this genre, for he has learned to build the feeling of fear by using the protagonist's uneasy, physical reactions, e.g., "Dès la seconde bouffée, le cœur me tourna et je cessai. Je me mis à chantonner; le son de ma voix m'était pénible" (II, 771). In addition, the author employs the low night noises on the river and their impression on the protagonist, e.g., "Soudain, un petit coup sonna contre mon bordage. Je fis un soubresaut" (II, 772).

In the recurring attacks of fear throughout the story, Maupassant used extensive repetition of short- to medium-length clauses beginning with "Je," as when the narrator says, "Je n'osais pas me lever et pourtant je le désirais violemment; je remettais de minute en minute. Je me disais" (II, 774) to simulate the staccato, panting thoughts of a frightened man.

The most important aspect of the story, from the point of view of Maupassant's evolution in the genre, is the appearance of a reasoning protagonist fighting against and succumbing to unreasoning fear. Although the hero is uneasy, he attempts to rationalize his fright away: "Ce bruit venait sans doute de quelque bout de bois entraîné par le courant" (II, 772); "J'essayai de me raisonner [. . .]. Je me demandai ce que je pouvais redouter" (II, 773). Maupassant had recognized the importance of reader identification for producing a shiver of vicarious fear. Since he knew his middle-class readers were proud of their unshakable grasp on reality, he presented them with a sensible protagonist who knew the river, who would not be afraid of trifles, but whose reason and logic failed to explain the inexplicable: who became afraid. If the reader begins to experience empathically with the hero, the fear may be communicated. This character serves as the model for the subsequent narrator-protagonists who guarantee the truth of the story by their skepticism, their probity, and their social status. They may or may not have attested to it, as the doctor in "Conte de Noël" had; they may or may

7. "Le Fantastique," pp. 237–38.

not specifically say, "Je vous jure qu'elle [l'histoire] est vraie d'un bout
à l'autre" (II, 1246), as the Marquis d'Arville does in "Le Loup"; but
merely by their presence they serve to give the impression of veracity. It is with them that the reader is asked to identify.

For a time, Maupassant continued to employ the third person
past and the familiar framework which united narrator and audience. "Magnétisme," for example, shows a skeptic mocking his companions' belief in the popular "science." He takes the floor to tell
two stories which supposedly exemplify magnetism. The first is an
example of telepathic communication which he successfully discredits. Then, from his own experience, he relates the story of a woman's
strange influence over him. The latter tale has the unexpected result
of convincing his audience that such unnatural events are possible
(II, 780). In this story the reader is still a part of the audience, and
Maupassant apparently hoped to evoke the same reaction from him
as he drew from his fictional assembly.

Skeptical narration of the inexplicable is done best in "La Main,"
the second version of "La Main d'Écorché." M. Bermutier, an examining magistrate, tells how an Englishman, John Rowell, was strangled. Without attempting to hypothesize, the magistrate presents the
background and facts about the crime in a clear, unemotional, and
objective fashion. M. Bermutier's audience, convinced that Rowell
was strangled by a severed hand, presses him to explain the strange
events.

> Le magistrat sourit avec sévérité:
> "Oh! moi, Mesdames, je vais gâter, certes, vos rêves terribles.
> Je pense tout simplement que le légitime propriétaire de la main
> n'était pas mort, qu'il est venu la chercher avec celle qui lui
> restait [. . .]. C'est là une sorte de vendetta."
> Une des femmes murmura:
> "Non, ça ne doit pas être ainsi." (II, 894)

With these words the reader is left to decide; Maupassant, however, has hinted broadly at the conclusion he wished the reader to
reach.

In 1882, several months after the appearance of "Magnétisme,"
Maupassant published "Fou?," a tale that is only a short step away
from Robinson Jeffers' "Roan Stallion": the protagonist becomes
insanely jealous of his wife's horse, finally kills it and his wife. His
crime, contrary to what one would expect, does not free him of either
his wife or his compulsive love for her. For the purposes of this study,
its interest lies primarily in the use of the present tense of the personal first person, in the fact that it is not in any fictional after-dinner
or railway carriage gathering, a framework which rarely appears in
the supernatural stories after the publication of "La Main" a little

over a year later, and in the presence of more or less well employed morphological and syntactical techniques which will be perfected in succeeding tales. * * *

* * * Later, in the hallucinatory tale "Un Fou," Maupassant uses logic to catch the reader's attention and then to lead him into horror. However, it is in "Le Horla" that this latter device is combined with the others already discussed and used with what is perhaps the most telling effect. Following the pattern which Maupassant has been developing, the story is told in the first person diary form by a wealthy and educated man living near Rouen. As Maupassant first demonstrated in "Un Fou," the fictional diary allows the author to display the innermost thoughts of the protagonist and provides the work with considerable verisimilitude. It does, however, make some of Maupassant's more effective techniques for showing fear and mental confusion seem strange. Not many people, for example, would write in their diary: "Je sais . . . je sais . . . je sais tout!" (II, 1172). Maupassant must have considered such disadvantages far outweighed by the advantages of a realistic framework.

As usual, Maupassant employed extensive concrete detail to make even the most strained moments seem credible, e.g., "En face de moi, mon lit, un vieux lit de chêne à colonnes; à droite, ma cheminée; à gauche" (II, 1120); he mentions events of the time, like the play by Dumas *fils* (II, 1105); he cites recent medical discoveries, fictitious historians, and quotes from the *Revue du Monde scientifique* (II, 1117)—the title appears to be an invention of Maupassant's. In addition, the narrator always finds a logical explanation that the reader will accept: "J'avais donc perdu la tête les jours derniers! J'ai dû être le jouet de mon imagination énervée, à moins que je ne sois vraiment somnambule, ou que j'aie subi une de ces influences constatées, mais inexplicables jusqu'ici qu'on appelle suggestions" (II, 1105). Then, as suggested in the last sentence of this passage, Maupassant filled his story with such well attested but inexplicable phenomena as the experimental data of Mesmer and Charcot, and with acceptable hypotheses which rise from what the protagonist knows to be true: air is present, but we do not see it—what else is on earth which we cannot perceive? All of these serve to give the story a realistic framework.

Slowly, hesitantly, Maupassant introduces the reader to the world of the story: a beautiful day, exuberant love of nature, country, and home, and a lovely picture of ships on the Seine. Among the boats is a superb Brazilian three-master. A little fever begins to bother the protagonist, then inexplicable uneasiness, then nightmares, then the feeling that someone is watching him. The narrator finally decides that a little trip might help him, and he leaves home. A month later, he returns and is cured. Soon, though, the fever recurs and the tension increases. Short clauses, repetition, exclamations, interrogatives and apostrophes serve to dramatize his malaise: "Je deviens fou. On a encore bu toute ma carafe cette nuit;—ou plutôt, je l'ai bue! Mais, est-ce moi? Est-ce moi? Qui? Oh! Mon Dieu! je deviens fou! Qui me sauvera?" (II, 1104). Tranquillity returns when he once again departs. Counting the introduction and the illusory escape to Rouen, there are four periods of calm in the story. During each of them the reader is obliquely offered material that will make him more prone to identify with the hero. After each sucessive interval of relief, the tension is more prolonged. Finally, when the protagonist comes back from Rouen, the pressure builds to an almost unbearable pitch and is maintained to the end.

Perhaps more important is the play between the past and the present verb tenses, resembling that of "Fou?," which has the specific goal of giving immediacy to the progressive power and domination of the "Horla" over the protagonist. The past tenses recount the events, since the past tenses with their feeling of the historical, recorded fact are more capable of gaining the reader's acceptance of improbable occurrences. It is always the immediate past, though, and often there is a direct shift to the present tense, the present being used to express such eternal truths as: "Le peuple est un troupeau imbécile" (II, 1106), to relate his hypothesizing as when he asks, "Qui habite ces mondes?" (II, 1106), on one occasion to highlight a long, uneasy night: "Puis, je me couche, et j'attends le sommeil" (II, 1099), and throughout the story to intensify his sensations of desperation: e.g., "Qu'ai-je done? C'est lui, lui, le Horla, qui me hante, qui me fait penser ces folies! Il est en moi, il devient mon âme" (II, 1120). The power of the story comes from the immediacy which arises in great measure from the use of the present tense. The past tenses serve as a foil for the present; once their function is fulfilled, they step aside for the present tense, a shift which accentuates the continuing influence of the "Horla": "J'ai vu . . . j'ai vu . . . j'ai vu! . . . Je ne puis plus douter . . . j'ai vu! . . . J'ai encore froid jusque dans les ongles . . ." (II, 1111); "Je rentrai chez moi l'âme bouleversée, car je suis certain maintenant, certain [. . .] qu'il existe près de moi un être invisible" (II, 1112).

The present tense, or an occasional future, is once again used to relate the results of his reasoning. The narrator compares his cousin's situation under the influence of Dr. Parent to his own and establishes the similarity. He is convinced that he also is under the power of an alien influence, since something unseen has drunk his water and upset his household, "donc les Invisibles existent" (II, 1115). He has noticed that animals sometimes revolt and kill the person who has tamed them; because the "Horla" has fled him, he concludes "Je pourrai donc le tenir sous mes poings et l'écraser contre le

ALLAN H. PASCO

sol!" (II, 1117). Carried away by his logic, he burns both his beloved
house and his forgotten servants. The deed done, he is once again
the prey of his reason which leads him with seeming inevitability to
the end: "Après l'homme, le Horla.—Après celui qui peut mourir
tous les jours, à toutes les heures [. . .] est venu celui qui ne doit
pas mourir qu'à son jour [. . .], parce qu'il a touché la limite de son
existence! Non . . . non . . . sans aucun doute, sans aucun doute . . .
il n'est pas mort . . . Alors . . . alors . . . il va donc falloir que je me
tue, moi!" (II, 1123) Thus the real, the reasonable, the logical serve to
set off and, at the same time, to palliate the illogical and the unreal
or supernatural.

Because of its nearly perfect construction, and its exact correlation between the internal syntax and morphology and the impression
and tone desired, "Le Horla" is certainly one of Maupassant's masterpieces. After this story the frequency of the supernatural tale
decreases. Between 1875, the date of the publication of "La Main
d'Écorché," and 1887, that of the second version of "Le Horla," some
thirteen supernatural stories came from Maupassant's pen. After
"Le Horla" there was "La Morte," scarcely more than a grotesque
joke, "La Nuit," which is essentially a study of solitude, and "Qui
sait?," an inferior tale which follows the general pattern of "Le
Horla," that is, it has a realistic framework with abundant concrete
detail, and personal first person present-past written narration. Like
"Le Horla," "Qui sait?" depends on contrasting periods of calm and
tension, on reasoned conclusions, and on the syntactical techniques
of "Fou?" for immediacy. "Qui sait?" is, however, marred by a too
frequent and thus ineffectual use of repetition, apostrophes, and an
inability to find the emotionally evocative expression.

"Qui sait?" then, is the only true supernatural tale after "Le Horla,"
and it does not show the technical experimentation and innovation
which is apparent in almost every prior tale. Lacking Maupassant's
attestation, one should not assume that he felt he had achieved his
goals for the supernatural story with "Le Horla," and subsequently
lost interest in the genre. One may, however, conclude that he considered the supernatural tale a valid artistic endeavor that justified
critical comment and years of experimentation, in an attempt to find
the most effective means of achieving reader identification and the
subsequent fear and horror. The supernatural story differs from the
rest of Maupassant's work in that the objectivity, elsewhere so
marked, continues in these tales only as the essential but docile
adjunct of subjectivity which is almost absent from the major portion of his fiction. The supernatural stories show extensive use of
objective-realistic techniques ranging from the omniscient narrator
to concrete detail, but such devices only prepare the way for the sub-
jective and the surreal.

Steegmuller has suggested that Maupassant continues to be what Henry James called "A lion in the path," that is, the strongest exponent of the objective story.[8] Perhaps Maupassant's very real achievements in this field, plus the susceptibility of the supernatural tales to a strictly biographical interpretation, have for too long veiled his accomplishments in another direction. For it is the supernatural genre, coupled with the hallucinatory stories, that takes Maupassant beyond the past, beyond the position at the end of a long evolution, and makes him, although not the initiator of a new trend, at least a man of his time searching to express and communicate the inner self faced by the unknown, the inexplicable.

RUTH A. HOTTELL

The Delusory Dénouement and Other Narrative Strategies in Maupassant's Fantastic Tales[†]

Tzvetan Todorov's seminal work, *Introduction à la littérature fantastique*, establishes the fantastic as a genre, defining it as a hesitation between the supernatural and the uncanny. The supernatural, like fantasy, deals with an "unreal" world, a world not defined in terms of the laws we know. In the world of the supernatural, frogs can turn into princes at the touch of the beautiful princess, and princesses can be awakened by the kiss of a heroic prince. The domain of the supernatural, then, is the realm of the fairy tale, of fantasy literature, in which the author's creative imagination knows no ground rules, no restraints in spinning the tale for the reader's delectation.[1]

On the other hand, the uncanny abides by the rules and laws of the order we know. It is firmly rooted in phenomena which could actually occur, representing an event which is strange, yet plausible. The word Todorov uses for the uncanny is *l'étrange*, which is literally translated as strange. The uncanny is just that, strange yet plausible. It could occur although it is a phenomenon which should not normally be brought into the open light of public attention.

The fantastic is the bridge between the supernatural and the uncanny—it is the moment of hesitation the reader undergoes before classifying the text's events as belonging to the realm of the supernatural or the uncanny. Charles Grivel comments on the nature of

---

8. Francis Steegmuller, *Maupassant: A Lion in the Path* (New York, 1949), pp. 324–25.
† From *The Romanic Review* 85.4 (1994): 573–76, 580–86. Copyright by the Trustees of Columbia University in the City of New York. Reprinted by permission of the author.
1. Considerations of a possible relation between superstition and literature and a certain interference between Romanticism and fantastic literature are found in Tobin Siebers, *The Romantic Fantastic* (Ithaca: Cornell University Press, 1984) and Tobin Siebers, *The Mirror of Medusa* (Berkeley: University of California Press, 1983).

this hesitation, the paradox inherent in the fantastic, and the close ties between the genre and narrative logic:

> Le fantastique désigne une feinte de la raison narrative: quelque chose est posé qui m'en est donné. Tout tient, dans le fantastique, à ce paradoxe dubitatif, a ce trouble éphémère, à cette hésitation localisée: une impossible cause a été invoquée, et ce qu'on m'en dit conforte son apparition. Cette indétermination où je suis, ce suspens d'un ordre évident nié par tout aussi évident que lui rattache à son existence et m'en détache aussi. (27)[2]

The questions which concern us in this study are: How do texts create the atmosphere of the fantastic? How do they represent the rupture into the well-ordered universe? How is traditional narrative logic subverted to encourage the presence, albeit ephemeral, of another kind of logic?[3]

The process of identification plays a central role in producing the fantastic. The reasons for this importance are rather self-evident: the reader actively participates in the work, continually interpreting actions, trying to classify them (i.e., Do they respect the laws of reality, or are they governed by another order, one with which we are unfamiliar?). Involving the readers emotionally in the narrative allows the author to catch them off-guard. That is, one is caught up in the action and is surprised along with the characters by the sudden eruption of an inexplicable occurrence. Consequently, the moment of shock, of hesitation, caused by this abrupt action is felt by the reader along with the characters in the text. (S)he is participating in the action with the characters, forming images with them and, as such, experiencing shock along with them. Therefore, identification is a crucial criterion for producing the fantastic. To successfully evoke the fantastic, all the components of the text must work together to elicit identification and participation.

Authors working in the fantastic often choose the short story in order to overcome the problems of retaining identification and suspense posed by longer works. In the short story, the task of sustaining the readers' attention and of building suspense is facilitated—when assured that curiosity regarding the denouement will be satisfied within a short period of time, we are less likely to read ahead or to lose interest.

---

2. Awareness of the intellectual component integral to the fantastic in French literature is ever-present and implicit throughout Grivel's study. His work therefore is particularly useful to scholars working in comparative studies seeking to delineate the differences between French fantastic literature and that of other national traditions in literature and film.

3. General discussions of the fantastic can be found in Eric Rabkin, *The Fantastic in Literature* (Princeton: Princeton University Press, 1976). For an introduction to the social history of the fantastic, see José B. Monleón, *A Specter Is Haunting Europe. A Sociohistorical Approach to the Fantastic* (Princeton: Princeton University Press, 1990).

In discussing fantastic production, Todorov singles out Maupassant's texts as the last aesthetically satisfying examples of the fantastic (174–75). Although the veracity of the adjective *last* is debatable, Maupassant's fantastic work is undeniably aesthetically pleasing, and a study of it would help to understand the art of the fantastic tale.[4] Roger Bozzetto gives an eloquent description of the diversity of Maupassant's work:

> Il tente de cerner la diversité de la réalité sociale par la multiplicité des sujets traités et des formes pour l'aborder. Ses nouvelles fantastiques: *La Peur, Sur l'eau, La Chevelure, Le Horla, Lettre d'un fou* ou *Qui sait?* présenteront la même diversité formelle que celle de ses nouvelles "réalistes": journal intime, lettre, récits enchâssés, ou cas singulier . . . Elles renverront à des thèmes que l'écrivain aborde de biais dans ses textes réalistes: l'obsession, l'angoisse, la folie, la peur ou le double. . . . Tout l'impact de la rencontre avec "l'impossible et pourtant là" passe par la construction de la nouvelle, trajet chaque fois original, qui rend compte d'un regard affolé plus que d'événements extraordinaires. (81–82)

Maupassant transforms daily preoccupations and objects into a web encasing the characters and the readers in a feeling of disquieting strangeness. In this study, we will examine the method surrounding those objects—the process through which Maupassant transforms the familiar into the strange. In discussing his technique, the same questions should be kept in mind as for the fantastic in general: How does Maupassant create the atmosphere of the fantastic? How does he represent the rupture into the well-defined universe? How does he create and maintain tension and identification? Finally, what techniques are used to prolong the eerie feeling for the reader after the dénouement?[5]

In fact, a kind of delusory dénouement, a conclusion which is not one, is set up in order to avoid a return to the fantastic/marvelous or fantastic/uncanny after the end.[6] In discussing examples of what he calls the pure fantastic proper, Carroll emphasizes the need to

---

4. For discussions of Maupassant's fantastic tales, see the chapter entitled "GUY DE MAUPASSANT *ou le fantastique à durée limitée*," in Francis Lacassin, *Mythologie du fantastique. Les rivages de la nuit* (Monaco: Editions du Rocher, 1991), 221–234; and Marie-Claire Bancquart, *Maupassant conteur fantastique*. (Paris: Lettres Modernes Minard, 1976).

5. See Allan Pasco, "The Evolution of Maupassant's Supernatural Tales," *Symposium*, 21 (1969), 150–59.

6. For further study of these terms and their specificity to a delineation of the "pure fantastic proper," see Todorov, *Introduction à la littérature fantastique* (Paris: Seuil, 1970), and Carroll, "The Fantastic," a section inside the chapter "Plotting Horror," in *The Philosophy of Horror* (New York: Routledge, 1990), 144–57. In the latter, Carroll shows the relevance of Todorov's theories to scholarship in the 1990s and adroitly describes manifestations of the pure fantastic proper in film and literature.

leave the reader wavering between interpretations. In reference to *The Turn of the Screw* by Henry James, he explains:

> . . . the book supports two alternative readings: a supernatural one and a naturalistic one—the latter explaining the anomalous events in the story psychologically; the former accepting those events as real. The astute reader realizes that neither of these interpretations is conclusive, and, therefore, vacillates or hesitates between them. For Todorov, this vacillation or hesitation between supernatural and naturalistic explanations is the hallmark of the fantastic. (145)

Maupassant creates texts which vacillate between the domains of the supernatural (the *merveilleux* or the marvelous) and the naturalistic (the *étrange* or the uncanny). His fantastic short stories can function as case studies of how to create and prolong the fantastic throughout the reading and how to end the tale in the realm of the fantastic, never giving full reliance on an "explanation" of narrative events.

In general, Maupassant's fantastic short stories are exactly that—short. He does not spend paragraphs or pages giving descriptions which are not directly relevant to his narrative. The stories, then, are short enough to be finished in a brief period of time. The reader is not tempted to put down the text; the emotional experience is completed in one sitting. In most cases, Maupassant provides a frame which firmly implants the narrative in reality. For example, in "Magnétisme" (1882) and "Rêves" (1882), friends unite for dinner, then tell stories to each other, stories which they declare to be true. In "Magnétisme" (97–101), the stories return to the frame at the end, with the narrators explaining the strange occurrences as coincidences. In "Rêves" (103–07), the friends recount strange dreams which are attributed to the use of ether.

Discussions between two people are also used to base the tale in reality. In "Sur l'Eau" (1876), the narrator describes a night spent alone on a boat as a result of his anchor having lodged itself under a heavy object. All his efforts to free himself proving fruitless, he is forced to await aid from a passerby. During the night, he witnesses strange noises and experiences the odd sensation of no longer being alone in his boat. With the morning sun, he finds that, in fact, he is alone, yet an eerie feeling lingers. With the help of two passing fishermen, he manages to liberate the anchor. When it surfaces, they spy a black mass—undoubtedly the same mass which has blocked the anchor throughout the night. The mass reveals itself as the cadaver of an old woman with a huge stone around her neck. This revelation, "C'était le cadavre d'une vieille femme qui avait une grosse pierre au cou," stands alone as a paragraph and the last sentence of the tale. Since the tale is narrated in chronological order, the reader has no prior clue of the outcome. Instead, he lives the story along with the narrator, as a witness to his increasingly uneasy sensations. With the arrival of the corpse, the reader retrospectively considers the emotions of the narrator and, having no further explanation, is left with a feeling of unease himself. In this instance, then, Maupassant's refusal to return to the frame, to the discussion between the narrator and the narratee, lends added eeriness to his tale. * * *

* * *

In many of Maupassant's short stories, [the] explanation comes from a qualified interpreter of psychoses, a doctor in a mental clinic. Such is the case in the first version of "Le Horla," one of his best known fantastic tales. Two versions of the story exist—the first published on October 26, 1886, and the second in 1887. In the first version, the narrator relates strange occurrences which happened to him. He recounts the visit of a being he refers to as the Horla, a sort of invisible vampire which nourishes itself from the breath of its victims while they sleep, and which only drinks water and sometimes milk. The story is told to a group of eight specialists:

> Le Docteur Marrande, le plus illustré et le plus éminent des aliénistes, avait prié trois de ses confrères et quatre savants, s'occupant de sciences naturelles, de venir passer une heure chez lui, dans la maison de santé qu'il dirigeait, pour leur montrer un de leurs malades. (271)

The patient tells his tale to the specialists, adding details and proof of its reality. He reads an excerpt from a newspaper from Rio de Janeiro:

> Les habitants de plusieurs villages se sont sauvés abandonnant leurs terres et leurs maisons et se prétendant poursuivis et mangés par des vampires invisibles qui se nourrissent de leur souffle pendant leur sommeil et qui ne boiraient, en outre, que de l'eau, et quelquefois du lait! (279–80)

Thus, the existence of these strange beings is documented in newspapers as a phenomenon which has reproduced itself in other parts of the world. This fact adds another dimension to the tale and roots it in reality. That is, the narrator has not been alone in his suffering; the existence of others in a similar predicament adds more possibility of truth rather than insanity.

The narrator also calls on doctor Marrande to testify to the veracity of his story:

> Trois de mes voisins, à présent, sont atteints comme je l'étais.
> Est-ce vrai?
> Le médecin répondit: "C'est vrai!"
> Vous leur avez conseillé de laisser de l'eau et du lait chaque nuit
> dans leur chambre pour voir si ces liquides disparaissaient. Ils
> l'ont fait. Ces liquides ont-il disparu comme chez moi?
> Le médecin répondit avec une gravité solennelle: "ils ont
> disparu."
> (278)

The unfortunate man, with proof from newspapers and the testimony of the doctor, establishes himself not as a paranoid schizophrenic but as a harbinger of the arrival of new life: "Donc, messieurs, un Être, un Être nouveau, qui sans doute se multipliera bientôt comme nous nous sommes multipliés, vient d'apparaître sur la terre" (278).

The narrator concludes that the mysterious Being must have arrived on a Brazilian ship which he had seen pass near his house a few days before his woes began. He ends with: "Je n'ai plus rien à ajouter, Messieurs" (280).

Doctor Marrande finishes the story with a final remark which serves as narrative closure and as a final note of credibility:

> Le Docteur Marrande se leva et murmura: "Moi non plus. Je ne
> sais pas si cet homme est fou ou si nous le sommes tous les
> deux . . . ou si . . . si notre successeur est réellement arrivé."
> (280)

The tale, thus, ends as it began—with remarks by Doctor Marrande to his colleagues. This frame serves to root the narrative in reality particularly because the Doctor, whom we presume to be sane and rational, implicates himself in the story. He admits that he doesn't know whether the man is insane or if they both are, for he has seen the proof that others have experienced the same misfortunes as the patient. The patient, through his calm way of recounting the circumstances, also helps to root the story in reality for, other than experiencing these strange happenings, he has not acted in an irrational manner. After witnessing proof of the existence of the creature, he closes himself up in a clinic, presumably to escape the Being.

The documented proof adds yet another note of the fantastic since proving the Being's existence also implies acceptance of a reality governed by rules other than the ones to which we are accustomed. The world, thus defined, would belong to the supernatural or science fiction. The reader once again hesitates, then, between the supernatural and the uncanny.

In the second version of "Le Horla," however, the victim does not remain rational—he even sets fire to his house in order to kill his tormentor. He acts so quickly that he forgets his servants, sending them to a fiery death along with Le Horla. Unlike the first version, no frame exists—instead, we are presented with a journal. Since the victim is either dead or past the point of reasonable explanations, he cannot tell his own story retrospectively. We must, therefore, begin where his experience begins in order to appreciate his growing panic and torture. The last lines of the text are: "Non . . . non . . . sans aucun doute, sans aucun doute . . . il n'est pas mort . . . Alors . . . alors . . . il va donc falloir que je me tue, moi! . . ." (308). We do not know, then, if the narrator has committed suicide; we do not know how or where his journal was procured; we do not receive a learned interpretation from a doctor. No other narratee is placed between the narrator and the reader. The journal begins on May 8, a day described in the following way: "Quelle journée admirable! J'ai passé toute la matinée étendu sur l'herbe, devant ma maison, sous l'énorme platane qui la couvre, l'abrite et l'ombrage tout entière" (281). Unlike the narrator in the first version, who begins his story afterwards in a mental clinic, this narrative starts at the beginning. The scene is a calm one; the narrator, tranquil and happy with his life.

At the onset of the strange occurrences, however, the pace of the text changes. We find question marks and dashes setting off the recurrent question:—Pourquoi—? The victim's surprise at his condition is registered through short exclamations and hesitations:

> Je suis malade, décidément! Je me portais si bien le mois dernier! . . . Aucun changement! (283)
>
> A peine entré, je donne deux tours de clef, et je pousse les verrous; j'ai peur . . . de quoi? . . . Je ne redoutais rien jusqu'ici . . . j'ouvre mes armoires, je regarde sous mon lit; j'écoute . . . j'écoute . . . Est-ce étrange qu'un simple malaise . . . (283)

The suspension points are in the text, serving to show the narrator's growing panic. In the passage, an emphasis is placed on serenity prior to the arrival of L'Être. Last month, he was doing well; he was afraid of nothing. Now, he checks in his closets and under his bed; he listens anxiously.

At first, the cause of his anxiety is rather nebulous—he feels ill and sad. This change in his mood is prefigured in an indirect way, a way which only becomes obvious after further developments and manifestations of the Being. On May 8, the day of the first entry in the journal, the narrator spent his time watching boats on the Seine. The last paragraph of the entry is: "Après deux goélettes anglaises, dont le pavillon rouge ondoyait sur le ciel, venait un superbe trois-mats brésilien tout blanc, admirablement propre et luisant. Je le

saluai, je ne sais pourquoi, tant ce navire me fit plaisir à voir" (282).
This involuntary wave is the first sign of control from an exterior
force, but we realize the significance of the sign much later, along
with the narrator. Three months after this first entry—three months
during which the narrator's mental state becomes gradually more
agitated—he reads of a strange epidemic of insanity in Rio de
Janeiro: "Une folie, une épidémie de folie, comparable aux démences
contagieuses qui atteignirent les peuples d'Europe au moyen âge,
sévit en ce moment dans la province de San-Paolo" (302).

In the first version, credibility had already been added in this way.
The narrator, however, had simply shown the doctor a fragment from
a newspaper, without naming it. In the second version, the veracity
of the phenomenon is further reinforced by naming the paper, the
Revue du Monde Scientifique. Consequently, it is no longer a question of just any newspaper, of an article which could still be refuted
due to its ambiguity and anonymity. Now we are dealing with a
respected, serious, scientific journal. The mere fact that such a journal has run the story discredits any claims of journalistic sensa-
tionalism, for science deals only with data that can be gathered, not
simply with human-interest stories. If this journal cites the phenomenon, it must exist. The interpretation of the occurrence, however,
has been left to the narrator and the reader. Perhaps the reader has
forgotten the arrival of the Brazilian ships; if so, the narrator reminds
him:

> Ah! Ah! je me rappelle, je me rappelle le beau trois-mats brésil-
> ien qui passa sous mes fenêtres en remontant la Seine, le 8 mai
> dernier! Je le trouvai si joli, si blanc, si gai! L'Être était dessus,
> venant de là-bas, où sa race était née! Et il m'a vu! Il a vu ma
> demeure blanche aussi; et il a sauté du navire sur la rive. Oh!
> mon Dieu! (302)

Thus we see, along with the narrator, the origin of the strange
creature as well as the moment of the rupture of the inexplicable
into the well-ordered world. That is, the narrator experiences strange
sensations almost immediately upon seeing the ship. On May 12,
he writes:

> —J'ai un peu de fièvre depuis quelques jours; je me sens souf-
> frant, ou plutôt je me sens triste.
> D'où viennent ces influences mystérieuses qui changent en
> découragement notre bonheur et notre confiance en détresse?
> (282)

The calm of the narrator's world has been disrupted, and along
with it, ours. The tale began with a journal entry, giving the impression of a sort of voyeurism, letting us peer into someone else's world.

This someone else sets himself up as a normal, happy, calm person, but suddenly his mood changes. The reader can understand and identify with the mood change, since everyone experiences periods of anxiety and sadness. This identification cannot be escaped because the narrator addresses us directly in this version, rather than passing through a doctor as intermediary, and asks us the origin of these mysterious influences which change happiness and confidence into despondency and distress.

The narrative strategy for introducing and maintaining the atmosphere of the fantastic in the second version of "Le Horla" is similar, then, to that of "L'Auberge" because, although "L'Auberge" is written in third-person narration, the reader does acquire information along with the young guide, Ulrich. Ulrich's emotions are described to the reader in such a way as to evoke identification. Ulrich begins to experience adverse reactions almost immediately after the onset of his forced solitude; the narrator in "Le Horla" begins to feel anxious and ill almost immediately after sighting a Brazilian three-master on the river near his house. We have seen Ulrich's mounting anxiety and tension, shown through a series of interrogatory and exclamatory phrases. A look at the last two passages discussed will show us how a similar technique is used in "Le Horla." As he starts to feel ill, the narrator begins to ask questions of the reader: "D'où viennent ces influences mystérieuses . . . ?" As the anxiety rises, so does the tension in the text; the sentences become shorter and express more emotion.

We find exclamations of one or two words which begin and end the paragraph in the second passage. ("Ah! Ah! . . . Oh! mon Dieu!") Within the quotation, we find that eight of the nine sentences are exclamatory, with four of them consisting of one or two words. The short, exclamatory sentences heighten the tension and the emotion conveyed in the text.

Twenty days elapse between the last two entries in the journal (August 21 and September 10). Separating these two entries is a series of periods like the one dividing "L'Auberge." After the division, the narrator becomes calmer as he relates the steps taken to kill the Being. His calmness dissipates quickly however as he realizes that he has also imprisoned his servants in the inferno: "Mais un cri, dans la nuit, et deux mansardes s'ouvrirent! J'avais oublié mes domestiques! Je vis leurs faces affolées, et leurs bras qui s'agitaient!" (308). The calm after the division in "Le Horla" is like the eye of the storm; it is a brief respite prior to the crashing violence of the end. Not only has the victim killed all his servants, he is no longer certain he has freed himself from the obsession: "Mort? Peut-être . . . son corps? son corps que le jour traversait n'était-il pas indestructible par les moyens qui tuent les nôtres?" (308).

The journal ends with the narrator's final realization and resignation that the only path to freedom is to end his own life: "Non . . .
non . . . sans aucun doute, sans aucun doute . . . il n'est pas mort . . .
Alors . . . alors . . . il va donc falloir que je me tue, moi! . . ." (308).
The narrator has, thus, entered the world of the supernatural, for
he totally believes in the existence of the invisible vampire. The
reader, on the other hand, is left wondering, wandering in indecision. That is, the twentieth-century reader may not believe in vam-
pires or possession, but space travel has forced him to accept the
possibility of life from other planets travelling to Earth. Possible
veracity is further reinforced by the article in the *Revue du Monde
Scientifique*. The reader, then, must recognize a certain degree of
reality in the narrator's tale, but it still eludes hard and fast catego-
rization. Should the tale be interpreted as uncanny, as obeying the
rules of the world as we know it? That is, should we classify the narrator as a paranoid schizophrenic, and call the other manifestations
coincidences (as in "Magnétisme" and "Rêves")? Or, does the tale
belong to the realm of the supernatural; is it governed by a different
set of rules, unknown to us? After all, admitting the existence of
creatures superior to human beings is tantamount to admitting
another system of hierarchies, or rules of reality. These are the questions which remain with the readers of any century. These are the
hesitations which lead us back to THE hesitation which defines the
fantastic. The dénouement does not fit the classical definition of
the term, for we find no solution to the problems set forth by the narrative, no untying of the knots wound by the text. In the place of the
traditional resolution, the reader is faced with a delusory dénouement, one which leaves her/him mulling over the interpretations left
open. Herein lies another key to the aesthetic genius displayed in
these texts—the lack of closure which elicits reader response and
encourages participation in the creative process.

WORKS CITED

Bancquart, Marie-Claire. *Maupassant conteur fantastique*. Paris:
    Lettres Modernes, Minard, 1976.
Bozzutto, Roger. *L'Obscur objet d'un savoir. Fantastique et science-
    fiction: deux littératures de l'imaginaire*. Aix en Provence: Publica-
    tions de l'Université de Provence, 1992.
Carroll, Noël. *The Philosophy of Horror*. Routledge, 1990.
Donaldson-Evans, Mary. *A Woman's Revenge. The Chronology of
    Dispossession in Maupassant's Fiction*. Lexington, KY: French
    Forum, 1986.
Gordon, Rae Beth. *Ornament, Fantasy, and Desire in Nineteenth-
    Century French Literature*. Princeton: Princeton University Press,
    1992.

Grivel, Charles. *Fantastique-fiction*. Paris: Presses Universitaires de France, 1992.

Lacassin, Francis. *Mythologie du fantastique. Les rivages de la nuit*. Monaco: Editions du Rocher, 1991.

Maupassant, Guy de. *Contes fantastiques complets*. Verviers: Bibliothèque Marabout, 1983.

Monleón, José B. *A Specter Is Haunting Europe. A Sociohistorical Approach to the Fantastic*. Princeton: Princeton University Press, 1990.

Pasco, Allan. "The Evolution of Maupassant's Supernatural Tales." *Symposium*, 21 (1969) 150–59.

Rabkin, Eric S. *The Fantastic in Literature*. Princeton: Princeton University Press, 1976.

Siebers, Tobin. *The Mirror of Medusa*. Berkeley: University of California Press, 1983.

———. *The Romantic Fantastic*. Ithaca: Cornell University Press, 1984.

Todorov, Tzvetan. *Introduction à la littérature fantastique*. Paris: Seuil, 1970.

KATHERINE C. KURK

Maupassant and the Divided Self: *Qui Sait?*[†]

In 1890, Guy de Maupassant wrote a brief, first-person narration, "Qui sait?" (first published on April 6 in the *Echo de Paris*), which was subsequently incorporated into the collection of short stories, *L'Inutile Beauté*. It has been labeled by Albert H. Wallace to be "the last of the stories that seems clearly tied to Maupassant's rapidly deteriorating mental health,"[1] and it is the culmination of Maupassant's tales grouped together by Albert-Marie Schmidt as "Les Chemins de la démence."[2] On the other hand, Paul Voivenel and Louis Lagriffe describe the *conte* as "un véritable rêve, pour ne pas dire un véritable délire, simplement exposé, sans explication aucune,"[3] while Angel Flores maintains that "the imaginative 'Who Knows?' . . . is a felicitous blend of humor and fantasy, not at all typical of his [Maupassant's] usual slick style."[4] To be sure, all of these

---

† From *Nineteenth-Century French Studies* 14 (1986): 284–94. Copyright 1986. Reprinted by permission of the University of Nebraska Press.

1. *Guy de Maupassant* (Boston: Twayne, 1973) 144.
2. Guy de Maupassant, *Contes et Nouvelles*, ed. Albert-Marie Schmidt (Paris: Albin Michel, 1957) 2: 1186–1199. Subsequent references are to this edition and are incorporated in the text.
3. *Sous le signe de la P.G.* [*Paralysie Générale*]: *La Folie de Guy de Maupassant* (Paris: La Renaissance du Livre, 1929) 207–208.
4. *Nineteenth Century French Tales* (New York: Ungar, 1960) 352.

elements—*dementia praecox* (the early title for schizophrenia), humor, hallucination, and fantasy—are present. And there is no doubt but that the narrator of "Qui sait?" undergoes a serious emotional crisis and that his prognosis is not good. Yet the condition of Maupassant, the person, is not so clearly demonstrated as is the vision of Maupassant, the creator, who precurses R. D. Laing's therapist, a doctor who "loves" his patient, who recognizes his difference and despair, and who transposes himself into an alien world in order to communicate with and understand "the divided self."[5] Maupassant gives a lucid and accurate portrayal of schizophrenia which rivals the discoveries of his famous contemporary, Jean-Martin Charcot, on hysteria[6] and which finds significant modern parallels in the analyses of Laing and Silvano Arieti.

These resonances are implicit in the very text. The narrator of "Qui sait?" has voluntarily entered a sanatorium and decides to reveal the reason for his flight from the world. He has always been a loner and a dreamer, has always lived apart, in the country, surrounded by cherished furniture and ornaments, in a large house with surrounding garden. One evening, after a trip to the local theater to see the play *Sigurd,* he walks home in the light of the last quarter crescent moon. He feels curiously uneasy and decides to rest on a bench before opening his door. Suddenly he hears noises, the tramping of wooden and iron stumps, and much to his amazement, his armchair—unaided by human accomplice—struts down the front steps. In a 19th-century Fantasia, the sofa, chairs, footstools, piano, cut glass, and goblets follow suit while carpets and wall hangings eerily ooze their way through the procession. The "running" tapestries, I would suggest, recall the melting clocks of Salvador Dali. Arieti believes that psychiatry owes a tremendous debt to Dali, who makes madness "available" in his pictorial medium wherein the paranoiac world testifies to the universality of the primary process while Dali retains complete control and contact with the secondary process, "an overall pattern of exactitude superimposed on the absurd content."[7] Mesmerized by such literal *mobilier,* the narrator watches his desk walk out, and this is too much for him! He grapples with the priceless *bureau* only to be thrown to the ground

5. *The Divided Self: A Study of Sanity and Madness* (London: Tavistock Publications, 1960) 35.
6. That Maupassant and Charcot knew much about each other's work has been well documented. For example, see: Roger L. Williams, *The Horror of Life* (Chicago: Univ. Press of Chicago, 1980) 217–72. In fact, some critics suggest that Maupassant deliberately wrote on such topics as the irrational, psychic behavior, and somnambulism in order to attract the public (Williams, 239). Also see: Francis Steegmuller, *Maupassant: A Lion in the Path* (New York: Grosset and Dunlap, 1949) 253–254.
7. *Interpretation of Schizophrenia*, 2nd ed. (New York: Basic Books, 1974) 367–368.

and trampled into the dust by a herd of recalcitrant furniture thundering down the garden path. They all disappear and the doors in the house close one by one. Dusty and shaken, the narrator retreats to town and takes a room in a hotel. The next morning, a servant reveals that he has been robbed. The police search for the thief for five months—the narrator does not tell his story—but no furniture can be found. With the confession that his nerves have been bothering him, the narrator then consults doctors who urge him to travel. He takes their advice, yet after a while, he returns to Paris and decides to tour Normandy, beginning with Rouen. There, late on a dark afternoon, he discovers an antique store which houses his belongings. He confronts the shopkeeper, whose face appears as a miniature moon, and makes arrangements to buy back his furniture. However, the merchant disappears and the narrator's possessions along with him. He then receives a letter from his servant caretaker that the furniture has all returned home and that the paths are in a bizarre state, "comme si on avait traîné tout de la barrière à la porte" (1198). The police cannot catch the antique dealer, who never returns to his shop, and the narrator dares not go home. He tells his story to a doctor who invites him to stay in the hospital "quelque temps" (1199) where he now lives in a private room, avoiding company, and fearful that the man with the lunar visage will, too, be sent there to haunt him.

"Qui sait?" is one of the last texts that Maupassant completed before undertaking a series of increasingly frenetic travels including trips to Cannes, Divonne-les-Bains, Nice, St.-Tropez, Lyon, and Marseille. By 1890, writing was becoming more and more difficult for him. He renounced the short story genre, started and abandoned his novel, *L'Ame étrangère*, then began in 1891 his last great literary project, *L'Angélus*, a manuscript unfinished at the time of his death. In January 1892, Maupassant unsuccessfully attempted suicide by slitting his throat and was hospitalized at the *maison de santé* of Passy until he died at the age of forty-two on July 6, 1893. Although there is consensus that Maupassant was mad, considerable controversy exists over the exact nature of the illness—syphilis (for he was a chronic womanizer), congenital eye disease, exophthalmic goiter, migraine—which led to his eventual demise.[8] His younger brother, Hervé de Maupassant, had already died in 1889 after a two-year

8. The number of books, articles, and notes on the "accurate" Maupassantian diagnosis is surprising. See: Paul Ignotus, *The Paradox of Maupassant* (New York: Funk & Wagnalls, 1966) 228–229; Charles Ladame, "La Vraie Maladie de Guy de Maupassant (Un point de vue nouveau)," *Zeitschrift für Kinderpsychiatrie* 14 (1947): 64–68. Williams' *The Horror of Life* contains an extensive bibliography on this subject as well as an insightful account of Maupassant's physical and emotional symptoms.

internment, in severe mental and physical distress generally attributed to venereal disease.[9] As early as 1880, Maupassant suffered from partial blindness, loss of vision in the right eye. Even before that, he gave evidence of hypochondria with complaints of nicotine poisoning, herpes, rheumatism, poor circulation, colic, intestinal bleeding, and high fever. The conflicting diagnoses of physicians often left him emotionally paralysed. In the midst of one of his numerous sea voyages in June, 1889, he debarked at La Spezzia, Italy, only to find that a case of scarlatina was reported in the area. He ignored the lunch waiting for him at the hotel and went back to the boat. In addition, the fear of illness, both real and imagined, led Maupassant to a dalliance with hashish, morphine, and opium, and to an excessive usage of his favorite anesthesia, ether. Under the influence of this drug, he imagined various voices and sounds, little red men in armchairs, and a splitting of the soul from the body.[1] At one point of an ether-induced euphoria, Maupassant remarked to his confidant, Paul Bourget: "Une fois sur deux, en rentrant chez moi, je vois mon double. J'ouvre ma porte et je me vois assis sur mon fauteuil. Je sais que c'est une hallucination au moment même où je l'ai. Est-ce curieux? et, si on n'avait pas un peu de jugeote, aurait-on peur."[2]

William B. Ober, in his amusing and perceptive collection, *Boswell's Clap and Other Essays*, counsels that when the physician/reader is

> confronted by a novel written during its author's last illness, [he] should be alert for the effects of disease upon literary production. Almost all prose fiction contains a clue to biography, however deeply hidden or remote. Implicit in the concept of psychosomatic medicine ... is the idea that a patient's symptoms, or literary productions, if he is a writer, will reflect something of his intrapsychic conflicts. Such revelations ... are more likely to be enhanced by a chronic, disabling, even life-threatening illness.[3]

This has unquestionably been the approach most favored by critics of Maupassant's "Qui sait?." Wallace links the narrator and his beloved belongings to the author with his yacht, the *Bel-Ami*, and

9. If there is one area of investigation not completely explored by Maupassant's biohistorians, perhaps it is the relationship of Guy and Hervé, their similar illnesses, and the psychogenetic factors and results of the complex family climate which they both shared. There is an uncanny correspondence between the Maupassant brothers and the siblings "Peter" (the elder, a severely neurotic patient with schizoid traits) and "Gabriel" (the younger, total schizophrenic) discussed by Arieti, 133–145.
1. See Albert-Marie Schmidt, *Maupassant*, Ecrivains de Toujours, 61 (Paris: Seuil, 1962) 131–140.
2. Quoted in Pierre Borel, *Le Destin tragique de Guy de Maupassant* (Paris: Editions de France, 1927) 31–32.
3. "Lady Chatterley's What?" in *Boswell's Clap and Other Essays* (Carbondale: Southern Illinois Univ. Press, 1979) 89.

his hermitage, *La Guillette*. Furthermore, he maintains that the narrator's fatigue with the dinners and gossip of society mirrors Maupassant's own sentiments in later life.[4] It is indeed evident that Maupassant, the person, demonstrated classic symptoms of schizophrenia. Yet the "clues" to biography in "Qui sait?" have consistently been misread.

The life deliberately chosen for and by the obsessed narrator in no way reflects Maupassant's own prepsychotic stage with its gregarious, even exhibitionist tendencies. While Laing does not distinguish between early patient types in the "false self" system, Arieti divides the prepsychotic phase of the schizophrenic into schizoid and stormy personalities. Maupassant's life, replete with practical jokes, drinking parties, indiscriminate sexual alliances, and a basic need for self-confirmation via others, is a model of the stormy, and not the schizoid, self. Stormy personalities live in an atmosphere of continual crisis and are progressively weakened by drugs and inappropriate actions until they reach the stage of injury to self. The narrator of "Qui sait?" is more accurately described as the schizoid personality. He is detached, peculiar, and suspicious, and preserves his self by avoiding contact with others:[5]

> J'ai vécu seul, sans cesse, par suite d'une sorte de gêne qu'insinue en moi la présence des autres. . . . lorsque je les sens depuis longtemps près de moi, même les plus familiers, ils me lassent, me fatiguent, m'énervent, et j'éprouve une envie grandissante, harcelante, de les voir partir ou de m'en aller, d'être seul. Cette envie est plus qu'un besoin, c'est une nécessité irrésistible. . . . J'aime tant être seul que je ne puis même supporter le voisinage d'autres êtres dormant sous mon toit; je ne puis habiter Paris parce que j'y agonise indéfiniment. Je meurs moralement, et je suis aussi supplicié dans mon corps et dans mes nerfs par cette immense foule. . . . (1186–1187)

Maupassant, like Arieti, recognizes that both personalities are essentially anxious and that both suffer from a lack of communication:

> Nous sommes deux races sur la terre. Ceux qui ont besoin des autres, que les autres distraient, occupent, reposent, et que la solitude harasse, épuise, anéantit . . . et ceux que les autres, au contraire lassent, ennuient, gênent, courbaturent, tandis que l'isolement les calme, les baigne de repos dans l'indépendance et la fantaisie de leur pensée. (1187)

---

4. Wallace, p. 145. Also see: Robert J. Niess, "Autobiographical Symbolism in Maupassant's Last Works," *Symposium* 14 (1960): 213–220, and Steegmuller, 318–319.
5. Arieti, 103–115.

In essence, this is an announcement that he, Maupassant, is the former, a "stormy" personality, apparently outgoing while inwardly tormented, but that his creation, the narrator, is the latter type, equally alone, equally maladapted, who retreats into himself as a psychological armor to ward off the "distressing other."[6] Maupassant and the narrator "know" each other well, and may be destined for the same psychotic end, but they are *not* the same.

More important, to read "Qui sait?" as the product of a certain "creative malady,"[7] to trace the indices of syphilis in his entire body of work in search of the quintessential Maupassantian diagnosis, to debate whether or not it is the madness of the man which creates the text is to fall into a trap which blinds the reader to Maupassant's insight. For it is, instead, the text which reveals a madness of mankind, and "Qui sait?" is a supremely conceived and carefully executed exposé of the very bases of schizophrenia which are only today beginning to be understood. Maupassant enters his own work, not as the subject, but as the therapist who has, in Laing's terms, "the plasticity to transpose himself into another strange and even alien view of the world. In this act, he draws on his own psychotic possibilities, *without forgoing his sanity* . . . thus . . . he can arrive at an understanding of the patient's [the narrator's] existential position" (emphasis mine).[8] In "Qui sait?" Maupassant, like Dali, retains complete control.[9]

Within the narrative structure of a framework—a madman in an asylum revealing why he is there—Maupassant demonstrates that he, the therapist author, is close to the narrator by using a first-person character. The reader, however, is doubly removed (i.e., choice of persona and the limit of the frame) from the narrator's emotional and psychological state. Thus the reader is allowed to decipher the narrator's condition. Maupassant repeatedly poses the question "Qui sait?" (in the title and 1186, 1187, 1189, 1192) along with: "Comment expliquer cela? . . . Je vais l'écrire. Je ne sais trop pourquoi"; "Pourquoi suis-je ainsi?" and "Pourquoi?" (1186, 1187,

6. Arieti, 103.
7. I use the term coined by Sir George Pickering in his book by the same name, *Creative Malady* (New York: Oxford Univ. Press, 1974). Persuasive as Pickering's arguments are (cf. Ober and Arno Karlen, *Napoleon's Glands and Other Ventures in Biohistory* [Boston: Little, Brown, and Co., 1984]), one should also consider the "mystique" which the 20th century accords mental illness: "Insanity is the current vehicle of our secular myth of self-transcendence. The romantic view is that illness exacerbates consciousness. . . . it is insanity that is thought to bring consciousness to a state of paroxysmic enlightenment." Susan Sontag, *Illness as Metaphor* (New York: Farrar, Straus and Giroux, 1977–78) 36.
8. Laing, 35.
9. For a general assessment of Maupassant as interpreter, rather than subject, of psychological phenomena, see: Francine Morin-Gauthier, *La Psychiatrie dans l'œuvre littéraire de Guy de Maupassant* (Paris: Jouve, 1944).

1192), in order to elicit a response from the reader, to engage him in understanding the patient.[1] Maupassant quite obviously portrays the narrator as a divided self, one who sees himself as an actor in the past, and also as the object of the action, which accounts for his present condition in the sanatorium.

As if the framework itself were not a sufficient clue to the dual construct of the protagonist's mind, Maupassant deliberately divides "Qui sait?" into two segments of equal length, announced by Roman numerals. The first section contains the narrator's provocative questions, while the second, in a reversal, indicates that the same persona possesses a secret knowledge: "Il n'y a que moi qui peux le [the moon man] rencontrer, et je ne veux pas" (1198) and the imperative: "Songez! songez à l'état de mon âme!" (1194). Arieti has noted that often the schizoid acquires insight into his personality. Strange events appear to him to have been purposefully arranged and this "psychotic insight" is a signal that the paranoid pattern is established. Arieti further states that the layman is capable of recognizing the supposedly clear and "reasoned" mad logic of the schizophrenic.[2] Maupassant, as therapist *and* medium, likewise gives the reader all the signals necessary to identify the narrator's psychosis.

At the beginning of "Qui sait?" the patient admits he is an introvert and he transferred his love and attention from people to inanimate objects, his furniture. Laing observes that "the schizoid individual fears a real live dialectical relationship with real live people. He can relate himself only to depersonalized persons, to phantoms of his own phantasies (imagos), perhaps to things, perhaps to animals."[3] The narrator reveals that in the midst of his ornaments, which he considers to be friends, he feels as happy as if "entre les bras d'une femme aimable dont la caresse accoutumée est devenue un calme et doux besoin" (1188). No mention has been made of his mother or of a lover, but the absence of such a figure, coupled with the desired vision, the unfulfilled wish for regular physical contact, and the implied statement that such a relationship is a necessity, is clear.[4]

It is entirely possible for the prepsychotic schizoid to exist indefinitely in this state of social drama—alienation from others—without

---

1. Voivenel and Lagriffe also note the role of these signals: "Ce sont des répétitions, des interrogations, des points de suspension, qui, véritables points d'angoisse, à tout instant, coupent le récit" (208).
2. Arieti, 393.
3. Laing, 80.
4. Arieti discusses the "state of communion" in which "the child or the youngster does not have the experience of being invaded and possessed by the glance of others, for instance, of the good mother or of the good friend. On the contrary, the glance of mother is an act of love, is reassuring, and has the flavor of a caress, an embrace" (104).

the internalization of his symptoms. The narrator constructs his own house with a separate out-building for the servants, becomes increasingly fascinated by night and darkness, less and less related to others. In this stage he is vulnerable to an event which can induce or unchain his schizophrenia, a precipitating crisis.[5] In "Qui sait?" the event which unleashes the psychotic stage is the narrator's attendance at the play, *Sigurd*. The *Nibelungen* tradition, of German and Scandinavian origin, is a legend of mistaken identity, love abandoned and betrayed, conflicting familial ties, and death of the protagonist (Sigurd/Siegfried). Not unimportantly, the hero is endowed with special powers which let him understand the speech of birds and which give unusual significance to objects around him. Siegfried also performs great feats of heroism with the aid of an "invisible cap."[6]

On the way home, the narrator relives the play, "la tête pleine de phrases sonores, et le regard hanté par de jolies visions" (1188), and as Arieti notes, "in spite of his detachment [the patient] harbors secret desires of experiencing feelings again and of making excursions into life."[7] A precipitating event has the power to recall a traumatic incident of early existence,[8] and the narrator has already implied the loss of a feminine contact. Like Siegfried, he now feels that he can "read" nature: the sycamores bend over him; the crescent moon looks ominous; he hears a buzzing, a warning in his ears. Instinctively he knows that his revolver will not help him. And then the very things which he has cherished turn against him—his furniture walks out. On one level, this episode denotes the final break with the "distressing other." The one piece that more than any other becomes his enemy is the desk, container of "toutes les lettres que j'ai reçues, toute l'histoire de mon cœur, une vieille histoire dont j'ai tant souffert! Et dedans étaient aussi des photographies" (1191). He struggles with it "comme on saisit une femme qui fuit" (1191). The desk symbolizes the failure of his symbiotic relationships and it also is his own identity, the fragile truce that he has effected with his life, which flees.

While the police search for the felon who stole his possessions, the narrator keeps his secret about the fateful night. The ability to lie is a good prognostic sign but evasion of the situation is less hopeful. The patient does not deny his illusions.[9] In addition, his

5. Arieti, 130.
6. See: Winder McConnell, *The Nibelungenlied* (Boston: Twayne, 1984), and Hugo Bekker, *The Nibelungenlied: A Literary Analysis* (Toronto: Univ. of Toronto Press, 1971) 101–117.
7. Arieti, 130.
8. Arieti, 131.
9. Arieti, 66.

psychotic insight appears: "Mais je ne remeublai pas ma maison. C'était bien inutile. Cela aurait recommencé toujours" (1192). The narrator's problem is in the house, one which he built and ordered himself, and which is a metaphor of his mind.[1]

Almost a year passes before the narrator discovers the antique shop in Rouen. This, too, is an unusual structure "vaste et tortueuse comme un labyrinthe" (1194) that he penetrates. He descends the dark corridors, climbs to the upper stories, and everywhere he goes, he is alone. When he calls out, there is no answer. The narrator has once more confronted his own self, and is cut off from others, alienated. When he does finally see a light in another room, "human" contact is made with him only by voice from a creature who refuses to come close to him. Maupassant gives the reader an obvious symbol of the psychological drama that will be unveiled: "Je voyais toujours la lueur de sa lumière éclairant une tapisserie où deux anges volaient au-dessus des morts d'un champ de bataille. Elle m'appartenait aussi" (1195).

The encounter with the antique dealer is the critical scene of "Qui sait?" for it reveals the psychological "truth" behind the story of the ambulatory furniture and definitively moves the psychosis of the narrator from intrapsychic dynamics to an external projection of the self. The shopkeeper whom the narrator describes is very short and very fat, hideous, with a sparse, unkempt, yellow beard, "et pas un cheveu sur la tête! Pas un cheveu! Comme il tenait sa bougie élevée à bout de bras pour m'apercevoir, son crâne m'apparut comme une petite lune. . . . La figure était ridée et bouffie, les yeux imperceptibles" (1195). He is, in fact, the narrator himself. The candle functions as a signal of this synodic relation by recalling the definition of "moon" as a satellite which only shines as a result of the sun, and which revolves around the earth, inseparable from it. The narrator has previously identified himself with the sun ("Le soleil me fit du bien," 1193) and states that without solar warmth, he cannot be cured: "la lumière diminuée du ciel m'attrista" (1193). This meeting with his "other self" takes place at night, and the folds and bulges of its non-human countenance, proven by the lack of eyes, is none other than a moonscape with obscured mountains and craters.

Nowhere is there more evidence of Maupassant's comprehension and control than in the textual structure. The narrative once more underscores the identification of the divided self. Before the direct encounter, there is dialogue between the protagonist and the moon man, but they are presented only as voices, shouting across the

---

1. Cf. "Examinée dans les horizons théoriques les plus divers, il semble que l'image de la maison devienne la topographie de notre être intime." Gaston Bachelard, *La Poétique de l'espace* (Paris: Presses Universitaires de France, 1957) 18.

haunted house/mind. The shopkeeper's final words, "Je vous attends" (1195), juxtapose the two halves in a natural syntactic tandem. After the protagonist "sees" the merchant, there is no more direct discourse, merely narration of what allegedly took place. At no time is there a conversation between the "two" personae when they are supposedly in "face-to-face" confrontation and, in the *intrigue* itself, the narrator and the shopkeeper are never seen together by a third party.

Upon the subsequent vanishing of the dealer and the purloined items, the protagonist exclaims: "Mon Dieu, Monsieur . . . la disparition de ces meubles coïncide étrangement avec celle du marchand!"—and implicitly with his own presence. He is unduly agitated when the police swear to catch the *lunatic*: "Ah! mon cœur, mon cœur, mon pauvre cœur, comme il battait" (1197) and confidently incredulous that the thief can ever be discovered: "Parbleu! parbleu! Cette homme-là qui est-ce qui aurait pu l'embarrasser ou le surprendre?" (1197). His "psychotic certainty" has dramatically increased for he believes that he alone holds the key to the robber's whereabouts: "Introuvable! il est introuvable, ce monstre à crâne de lune! On ne le prendra jamais. Il ne reviendra point chez lui. Que lui importe à lui. Il n'y a que moi qui peux le rencontrer, et je ne veux pas. Je ne veux pas! je ne veux pas! je ne veux pas!" (1198). Only the narrator can find the dealer, an extension of himself.

When read in the light of schizophrenic symptomatology, the earlier episode of the furniture becomes decipherable not as sheer fantasy but as the initial manifestation of the narrator's psychosis. Prophetically it takes place in the feeble, fitful light ("rougeâtre, morne, inquiétant," 1188) of a crescent moon (the sign of the divided self), not the later full moon which reveals a total vision of the psyche's "other," but a first-quarter sliver which affords a disguise, a partial recognition. Laing has noted that "the hysteric often begins by pretending he is not in his actions while really actualizing himself through them."[2] Coming home after the power and activity of *Sigurd*, the narrator rejects his own sterile and passive existence but cannot openly face his self-accusation and denial. The buzzing in his head, the eerie sounds he hears, are his own self-recriminating voices. It is commonplace for the schizophrenic to act out the commands or ideas suggested by his hallucinations and Arieti has noted the large number of patients whose violence is directed toward furniture and home-related objects.[3] The narrator, like Siegfried, dons a "cap of invisibility" (which explains why he cannot "see" a perpetrator) and, through active concretization, symbolically battles

2. Laing, 103.
3. Arieti, 307–309.

himself and the insufficient substitutes he has chosen for human contact.

It is important to note that all temporal and spatial clues in the text point to the possible existence and activity of an "other self." After the furniture "runs away," the protagonist says that he goes to town, leaves instructions for his servants to be notified at dawn, and settles down in bed. Yet he confesses: "Mais je ne pus dormir, et j'attendis le jour en écoutant bondir mon cœur" (1192). It is conceivable that he was not able to rest because his alter-ego was hiding the traces of his life, an occupation which also would make the heart race. Furthermore, when the servant tells him he has been robbed, the narrator paradoxically responds: "Cette nouvelle me fit plaisir" (1192). The police search for the missing objects for five months and the narrator purportedly travels for an additional six. Not only does this give him time to arrange another "identity," and to cache successfully his belongings, but it also is a credible time span for the deterioration of his emotional condition. For the half year in which the narrator travels—from Genoa to Venice to Florence to Rome to Naples to Sicily to Africa—seems almost an illusion. There is no description of events, persons, or places save a eulogy of the sun and "ce grand désert jaune et calme" (1193), antithesis of the moon-shaped vision, and the whole journey is recounted in one short paragraph. Finally, more than two weeks elapse from the time the furniture disappears from the antique shop until the narrator "hears" that it has resurfaced at his old home. Anyone who lives in the servants' quarters "dans un grand bâtiment éloigné, au fond du potager, qu'entourait un grand mur" (1188) could not witness how this took place.[4]

At the end of the story, the narrator has accepted that he is ill: "Je ne pouvais pas continuer à vivre comme tout le monde avec la crainte que des choses pareilles recommençassent" (1199) and has found shelter in a mental hospital. Yet this is not hope for recovery. Rather, the prognosis is poor for he has reached the second, or advanced, stage of schizophrenia. The symptoms seem crystallized and the anxiety, decreased: "Et je suis seul, tout seul, depuis trois mois. Je suis tranquille à peu près" (1199). While the patient ostensibly wishes to retain contact with fleeting reality, a slight disturbance can trigger extreme distress. The narrator lives in fear that the "antiquaire" (1199) will also go mad and be put in the same sanatorium: "Les prisons elles-mêmes ne sont pas sûres" (1199). Arieti

4. It is curious, too, that the only person who seems to know the antique dealer in Rouen is an old neighbor woman, an elusive widow, with whom he usually spends his evenings, while the protagonist's past life also contains a mystery woman and the vestiges of a ruined love.

has noted that second-stage schizophrenics have the habit of writing letters which delineate their role as victim of planned persecution.[5] The narrator, too, writes what has happened to him and calls out to his reader "Qui sait?"—a euphemistic *cri de cœur* for interpretation and compassion.

Maupassant has clearly heard the plea. For "Qui sait?" is not mere biographical revelation tied to the idiosyncracies of a famous writer going mad. There is nothing disordered in his sensitive portrayal whose very structure, with frame, division, signposts of chronology and spatial orientation, reveals the fragmentation of a life in symbolic disarray. Instead, when read in its full psychological potential, "Qui sait?" is an intricate and accurate portrayal of the enigma of schizophrenic complicity, created by a sympathetic clinician one hundred years before his time. Thus Maupassant, the misunderstood, helps us all to understand.

5. Arieti, 398–399.

Guy de Maupassant: A Chronology

1850	August 5: birth of Henri René Albert Guy de Maupassant, the first child of Gustave de Maupassant and Laure Le Poittevin.
1851–54	The Maupassants live in a number of places in Normandy before moving into the Château de Grainville-Ymauville near Le Havre. This remains Guy's home for the first ten years of his life.
1856	Birth of Guy's brother, Hervé.
1861	Guy's parents experience marital problems. His father remains in Paris. Laure and her two sons move to Étretat.
1862	Legal separation of Guy's parents, although divorce was not legalized until 1884.
1863–68	Guy is expelled from a Catholic school in Yvetot for his disrespectful attitude toward religion, then sent as a boarder to the Lycée Impérial in Rouen. He gets to know Louis Bouilhet, the writer, city librarian, and close friend of Gustave Flaubert. Both men encourage and advise him in his writing, initially of poetry.
1869	The death of Louis Bouilhet leaves Flaubert as Maupassant's mentor. Enrolls as a law student in Paris.
1870	July 15: France declares war on Germany, the start of the Franco-Prussian War. Maupassant is drafted and works in the military administration in Rouen. September: the French are defeated at Sedan. Maupassant joins the army's retreat to Le Havre.
1871	January 28: Armistice signed. A few months later, Guy leaves the army to continue his law studies.
1872	Applies unsuccessfully to join the Ministry for the Navy as a civil servant, but is offered an unpaid position pending a vacancy. He becomes a frequent weekend visitor to Argenteuil, on the Seine, enjoying boating and entertaining women.
1873	Finally appointed to a position at the Ministry.

1875   February: Maupassant's first short story, *La Main d'écorché. (The Flayed Hand)*, is published under the pseudonym Joseph Prunier, and some poetry under another pseudonym: Guy de Valmont.

1876   Maupassant becomes increasingly involved in Parisian literary life with Flaubert, Mallarmé, Zola, Daudet, Huysmans, Edmond de Goncourt, Turgenev, and others. His first critical article on Flaubert is published.

1877   Maupassant becomes aware of having contracted syphilis (probably in 1875) and suffers from hair loss, headaches, eye problems, and stomach pains.

1880   Publication of the collection *Les Soirées de Médan*, including *Boule de suif.*
         May 8: Flaubert dies suddenly.

1881   Publication of *La Maison Tellier (The House of Tellier)*, the first of Maupassant's many collections of short stories.

1883   *Une Vie* published; Maupassant also produces some sixty short stories.

1884   Starts work on *Bel-Ami*, his second novel, while another fifty short stories are published this year.

1885   *Bel-Ami* published. For the first time, critics recognize Maupassant as a major writer.

1886   Maupassant works on the definitive version of *Le Horla*.

1887   *Mont-Oriol* published. He spends the summer working on *Pierre et Jean*. Goes to Antibes in September, much concerned by signs of his brother's mental illness. At the end of the year, Guy takes Hervé to spend a month in an asylum near Paris.

1888   Publication of *Pierre et Jean*, his fourth novel, and *Sur l'eau (On the Water)*, his second travel book.

1889   Publication of *Fort comme la mort (Strong as Death)*, his fifth novel.
         August: he arranges for his brother to be committed to an asylum near Lyons.
         November 13: death of Hervé, Maupassant at his bedside.

1890   Publication of *La Vie errante (The Life of a Wanderer)*, his third travel book. His final completed novel, *Notre cœur (Our Heart)*, is published.
         Maupassant's long-standing health problems have now become increasingly acute.

1891   Contemporaries note the writer's obvious physical and mental disintegration, while he desperately ranges through a succession of doctors, thermal spas, and medical treatments.

1892   After visiting his mother on New Year's Day, Maupas-
              sant returns to his home in Cannes and slits his throat,
              either intentionally or in a state of delirium. A week
              later, he is taken (straitjacketed) to Paris and interned
              in Dr. Blanche's clinic. He has clearly gone insane. Mod-
              ern medical opinion leaves little doubt that the symp-
              toms of the diagnosed "general paralysis" are those of
              the tertiary stage of syphilis.

1893   July 6: death of Maupassant, at age forty-two.

Selected Bibliography

• indicates works included or excerpted in this Norton Critical Edition.

I. COLLECTED PRIMARY WORKS IN FRENCH

Maupassant, Guy de. *Correspondance.* 3 vols. Ed. Jacques Suffel. Evreux: Le Cercle du Bibliophile, 1973; accessible at http://maupassant.free.fr/correspl .html
———. *Contes et Nouvelles.* 2 vols. Ed. Louis Forestier. Paris: Gallimard (Bibliothèque de la Pléiade), 1974–79.
———. *Romans.* Ed. Louis Forestier. Paris: Gallimard (Bibliothèque de la Pléiade), 1987.
———. *Chroniques.* 2 vols. Ed. Gérard Delaisement. Paris: Rive Droite, 2003.

II. SECONDARY WORKS IN ENGLISH

1. General

Bryant, David. *The Rhetoric of Pessimism and Strategies of Containment in the Short Stories of Guy de Maupassant.* Lampeter: Edwin Mellen Press, 1993.
Cogman, Peter. *Narration in Nineteenth-Century French Short Fiction.* Durham: Durham University Press, 2002.
• Conrad, Joseph. "Preface." Guy de Maupassant, *Yvette and Other Stories.* Trans. A[da] G[alsworthy]. London: Duckworth, 1904.
• Coward, David. "Introduction." Guy de Maupassant, *A Day in the Country and Other Stories.* Trans. and ed. David Coward. Oxford: Oxford University Press, 1990.
Donaldson-Evans, Mary. *A Woman's Revenge. The Chronology of Dispossession in Maupassant's Fiction.* Lexington, KY: French Forum, 1986.
Dugan, John Raymond. *Illusion and Reality. A Study of Descriptive Techniques in the Works of Guy de Maupassant.* The Hague: Mouton, 1973.
Fusco, Richard. *Maupassant and the American Short Story.* University Park: Pennsylvania State University Press, 1994.
Gregorio, Laurence A. *Maupassant's Fiction and the Darwinian View of Life.* New York: Peter Lang, 2005.
• Harris, T. A. Le V. *Maupassant in the Hall of Mirrors. Ironies of Repetition in the Work of Guy de Maupassant.* London: Macmillan, 1990.
———. *Maupassant. Quinze contes.* London: Grant & Cutler, 2005.
Ignotus, Paul. *The Paradox of Maupassant.* London: University of London Press, 1967.
• James, Henry. "Guy de Maupassant." *Partial Portraits* [1888]. Westport, Conn.: Greenwood Press, 1970. 241–87.
• Lemaître, Jules. "Guy de Maupassant." *Literary Impressions.* Trans. A. W. Evans. London: Daniel O'Connor, 1921. 154–86.
Lerner, Michael G. *Maupassant.* London: Allen & Unwin, 1975.

MacNamara, Matthew. *Style and Vision in Maupassant's 'Nouvelles'.* Berne: Peter Lang, 1986.

Poteau-Tralie, Mary. *Voices of Authority, Criminal Obsession in Guy de Maupassant's Short Works.* New York: Peter Lang, 1994.

• Schaffer, Aaron. "Introduction." *Pierre et Jean.* New York: Charles Scribner, 1936.

Steegmuller, Francis. *Maupassant: A Lion in the Path.* London: Macmillan, 1972.

Stivale, Charles J. *The Art of Rupture: Narrative Desire and Duplicity in the Tales of Guy de Maupassant.* Ann Arbor: University of Michigan Press, 1994.

Sullivan, Edward D. *Maupassant: The Short Stories.* London: Arnold, 1962.

• Symons, Arthur. "Introduction." Guy de Maupassant, *Eight Short Stories.* Trans. George Burnham Ives. London: Heinemann, 1899.

2. Tales of French Life

Lethbridge, Robert. "Transpositions: Renoir, Zola, Maupassant" [on *Une Partie de Campagne*]. *Text(e)/Image.* Ed. M.-A. Hutton. Durham: Durham University Press, 1999: 126–42.

• Moger, Angela S. "Narrative Structures in Maupassant: Frames of Desire." *PMLA* 100 (1985): 315–27.

Mortimer, Armine Kotin. "Secrets of literature, resistance to meaning" [on *En Voyage*]. In *Confrontations: Politics and Aesthetics in Nineteenth-Century France.* Ed. K. Grossman. Amsterdam: Rodopi, 2001: 55–66.

• Murphy, Ann L. "Narration, the Maternal, and the Trap in Maupassant's *Mademoiselle Perle*." *French Review* 69.2 (1995): 207–16.

Scott, C. "Divergent Paths of Pastoralism: Parallels and Contrasts in Maupassant's *Une Partie de Campagne* and *La Femme de Paul*." *Forum for Modern Language Studies* 16 (1980): 270–80.

York, R. A. "*Le Baptême*: A Reading," *Journal of the Modern Language Association of Northern Ireland* 13 (1984): 13–19.

3. Tales of War

• Bolster, Richard. "*Mademoiselle Fifi*: An Unexpected Literary Source." In *Maupassant Conteur et Romancier.* Ed. Christopher Lloyd and Robert Lethbridge. Durham: Durham University Press, 1994: 29–39.

———. "The Patriotic Prostitutes of Maupassant: Fact or Fantasy?" *French Studies Bulletin* 51 (1994): 16–17.

Chaplin, Peggy. *Guy de Maupassant: 'Boule de Suif.'* Glasgow: University of Glasgow French and German Publications, 1988.

• Donaldson-Evans, Mary. "The Decline and Fall of Elizabeth Rousset: Text and Context in Maupassant's *Boule de suif*." *Australian Journal of French Studies* 18 (1981): 16–34.

• Killick, Rachel. "Mock Heroics? Narrative Strategy in a Maupassant War Story" [on *Lieutenant Laré's Marriage*]. *Modern Language Review* 82 (1987): 313–26.

Moreau, John. "Maupassant's Empty Frame: A New Look at *Boule de suif*." *French Forum* 34.2 (Spring 2009): 1–16.

Weatherilt, Michael. *Maupassant's 'Boule de suif' and the Tales of the Franco-Prussian War.* Wrexham: Bridge Books, 2001.

4. Tales of the Supernatural

Abecassis, Jack. "On Reading Maupassant's *Le Horla* Problematically." *Revue internationale de philosophie* 61 (2007): 391–413.

Fitz, Brewster E. "The Use of Mirrors and Mirror Analogues in Maupassant's *Le Horla*." *The French Review* 45.5 (1972): 954–63.

Fortin, Jutta. "The diary as transitional object in Maupassant's *Le Horla* (1886)." *Australian Journal of French Studies* 41 (2004): 39–47.

Godfrey, Sima. "Lending a Hand: Nerval, Gautier, Maupassant and the Fantastic." *Romanic Review* 78 (1987): 74–83.

Hadlock, Philip C. "Telling Madness and Masculinity in Maupassant's *Le Horla*." *L'Esprit créateur* 43.3 (2003): 47–56.

Hampton, Morris D. "Variations on a Theme: Five Tales of Horror by Maupassant." *Studies in Short Fiction*. 17.4 (1980): 475–81.

• Hottell, Ruth A. "The Delusory Dénouement and Other Narrative Strategies in Maupassant's Fantastic Tales." *Romanic Review* 85.4 (1994): 573–86.

• Kurk, Katherine C. "Maupassant and the Divided Self: *Qui Sait?*" *Nineteenth-Century French Studies* 14 (1986): 284–94.

• Pasco, Allan H. "The Evolution of Maupassant's Supernatural Stories." *Symposium* 23.2 (1969): 150–59.

Scott, Hannah. "Le Blanc et le Noir: The Spectre behind the Spectrum in Maupassant's Short Stories." *Nottingham French Studies* 52.3 (2013). 268–80.

Villarreal, Lisa Ann. "'L'à-bas, où sa race est née': Colonial Anxieties and the Fantasy of the Native Body in Maupassant's *Le Horla*." *Nineteenth-Century French Studies* 42 (2013–14): 74–84.

• Williams, Roger L. "Guy de Maupassant." *The Horror of Life*. London: Weidenfeld & Nicolson; Chicago: University of Chicago Press, 1980. 217–72.